A mot...
can trus...
her husband's best friend...
Passion and adventure run as high
as the Rockies in

ROCKY
MOUNTAIN
MEN

Relive the romance...

Three complete novels by some of
your favorite authors!

LINDA RANDALL WISDOM

has worked in personnel, marketing and public relations, all of which gave her a wealth of experience on which to draw when creating characters. Linda knew she was destined to write romances when her first sale came on her wedding anniversary. She lives in Southern California with her husband and a houseful of pets.

LYNN ERICKSON

is the pen name of the prolific writing team of Molly Swanton and Carla Peltonen. Since they began working together in 1980 they have crafted almost forty books, and to date they're still going strong. They especially enjoyed writing *Silver Lady* because they both live in Aspen and "it was lots of fun describing all our favorite restaurants."

DEBBI BEDFORD

has written award-winning novels that have appeared in fifteen different countries in over twenty different languages. She and her husband, Jack—a true Rocky Mountain Man—live with their two children and numerous animals in a gingerbread house in Jackson Hole, Wyoming.

ROCKY MOUNTAIN MEN

Linda Randall Wisdom
Lynn Erickson
Debbi Bedford

Harlequin Books

TORONTO • NEW YORK • LONDON
AMSTERDAM • PARIS • SYDNEY • HAMBURG
STOCKHOLM • ATHENS • TOKYO • MILAN
MADRID • WARSAW • BUDAPEST • AUCKLAND

HARLEQUIN BOOKS

by Request—ROCKY MOUNTAIN MEN

Copyright © 1997 by Harlequin Books S.A.

ISBN 0-373-20138-9

The publisher acknowledges the copyright holders of the individual works as follows:
CODE OF SILENCE
Copyright © 1989 by Linda Randall Wisdom
SILVER LADY
Copyright © 1992 by Carla Peltonen and Molly Swanton
TOUCH THE SKY
Copyright © 1985 by Deborah Pigg Bedford

Printed in U.S.A.

CONTENTS

Anne Sinclair thought she and her daughter would be beyond the arm of the law, safe in remote Dunson, Montana. But she was wrong. Dunson's sheriff, Travis Hunter, and his own young daughter posed the double threat of love and the law.

CODE OF SILENCE

Linda Randall Wisdom

Prologue

So much blood. She looked down at her trembling hands, not even noticing when her numb fingers released the gun. Dazed, she watched it drop to the carpet. She couldn't stop staring at the man lying on the floor before her, a large spot of red flowering obscenely on his white shirt. *So much blood.* He couldn't still be alive with such a horrible wound in his chest, but she was afraid to go closer and make sure. Her face still burned where he had struck her; she hadn't been about to give him a chance to go after her again. She clenched her hands in front of her, finding them slippery with sweat. Fear coursed through her veins. Thunder rumbled outside, and lightning shot white-hot through the darkened room.

"Mommy! Daddy!"

The tiny voice was enough to pull her back to the present. She turned and stared at the little girl standing in the doorway, her heart-shaped face puffy from the bruises marring the pink skin that was shiny with tears.

"Mommy," she whimpered, holding up her arms for comfort.

"Everything's fine, honey." She ran over and picked her up, holding her tightly. She cradled the child's face against her breast to hide the horrifying sight behind her and swallowed the hysterics that threatened to burst forth at any moment, as the enormity of what she had just done hit home. It hadn't been so much that he had struck her in a drunken rage, which was nothing new; it was that he had attacked their little girl, and she had honestly feared he would kill the child. She was only grateful that she'd been able to stop him before their daughter was badly hurt. She wasn't going to allow her to suffer the way she herself had all these years.

What was she going to do now? She should call the police, tell them she had just shot her ex-husband. But that would bring in the entire Sinclair family, and she wouldn't have a chance of revealing the truth then; as if anyone would believe her. Joshua Sinclair hadn't liked her from the beginning. Shooting his only son would surely give him cause to have her shut away for the rest of her life. A terrified cry bubbled up her throat. For a moment she visualized police cars surrounding the house, then remembered the nearest neighbor was a mile and a half away and that the thunderstorm overhead had probably made it impossible to hear the shot.

She concentrated on remaining calm in what appeared to be an insane situation. Maybe he wasn't dead, she told herself. In that instant she made her decision, aware that if she was successful, there would be no turning back. Carrying her daughter, who had wrapped her legs around her waist, she raced down the hall and entered the first room on the right. She set the girl on the bed, but the child promptly began crying again and held up her arms.

"Shh, it's all right." She laid a finger across her lips, then spoke urgently. "Honey, I want you to take off your nightgown and put on some play clothes."

"Are we going somewhere?"

She threw open the closet door and pulled out clothing. "Yes, we are."

"Is Daddy going with us?" Her daughter's voice was muffled by the nightgown she was pulling over her head.

The mother saw the red haze descend over her eyes again. "No."

She quickly pulled open dresser drawers, tossing clothing onto the bed next to a tote bag she had found in the bottom of the closet.

"Honey, you need to get dressed as quickly as possible." Her tone was urgent, yet without the panic she felt deep inside. "Can you do that for me?" She paused, looking around at the frilly room decorated in yellow and white, filled with more toys than one child could play with in a lifetime. Was she right in taking her away from all this luxury when she had no idea what her own future held? Not to mention if she herself were caught? No, she couldn't allow herself to think that way. She had to succeed, for her daughter's sake, more than her own. She took several deep breaths to calm the hysteria that still threatened to burst out. She had to keep her wits about her. Time was of the essence. She would break down later.

I have to keep thinking that I can do this. I have to find the courage, she ordered herself, zipping up the bag after filling it with clothing and a few toys. *Contrary to what you've been led to believe, you are a strong person. Do this for Nicola. Don't let her down. She needs you.* She used the back of her hand to wipe the tears from her cheeks.

"Mommy, where are we going?" the little girl whispered as her mother pulled her outside through the sliding glass door in the master bedroom. Lightning flashed again across the sky. Anne breathed deeply. She wanted nothing more than to collapse and allow someone else to sort out this mess, but she couldn't do that because without proper representation, she would be found guilty and be locked up.

"We're going away, honey. Far away." How was she able to keep her tone so collected, considering the raw state of her nerves? She put her daughter into the car and returned to the house to make a quick phone call to the police. Saying she had heard a gunshot, she gave the address and hung up, before they could question her further.

When she returned to the car, Anne looked down at the delicate features of her daughter, marred now by an ugly bruise on one cheek. She blinked back the tears. How could someone so young be forced to suffer because a man felt he had the right to punish, no matter how petty the grievance or how small the victim? The sight of the bruise that he had inflicted on Nicola earlier strengthened her resolve to get them far away, where she would never be hurt again.

Her brain was already clicking away, deciding what steps had to be taken. Once she left the house, there was no turning back; her life would never be the same again. She was grateful that she had picked up her dry cleaning on her way to see Nicola, so she had some clothing to take with her without stopping at her apartment first. Now she would only stop at the automated banking teller to withdraw cash. No charge cards for this trip. "We're on our own now."

THE LARGE NEWSSTAND was known for carrying major newspapers from all over the country. The blond woman wearing oversize sunglasses scanned the papers until she spotted the one she wanted. She found it difficult to appear matter-of-fact when she visualized a policeman around every corner, waiting to arrest her. She hurriedly paid and returned to the small motel down the street, where a tired little girl was still sleeping. She let herself in and headed for a table next to the grimy window. She quickly leafed through the newspaper until she found what she had been looking for.

Lloyd Sinclair, heir to Sinclair Manufacturing, is listed in stable condition after a shooting incident in his home eight days ago. Anne Sinclair, his ex-wife, is being sought for attempted murder and the kidnapping of their four-year-old daughter, who was the object of a bitter custody battle. Any information as to their whereabouts should be reported to the local authorities.

She laid the newspaper on the table and moved away to stare at herself in the mirror. The dark blond hair rinse did nothing for her coloring, but it did change her looks. Now she should do something about the color of her eyes. She'd seen an ad in the paper for colored contact lenses. She had some jewelry with her, and could sell it a piece at a time when she needed to. Anne thought of the driver's license and social security card in her wallet and wondered what to do about them. Something else to consider as she descended into an uncertain future.

She looked back at Nicola, who had put so much trust in her during these last bewildering days. Little did she know that her mother was wondering if she could take care of herself, let alone a child. But her decision had been made more than a week ago, and she couldn't back down now. The girl turned over, rubbing her eyes with bunched fists.

"Mommy," she whimpered. "Are we going home today?"

"I'm afraid not," Anne murmured. "From now on, our home will be wherever we are."

Chapter One

"Dad, it's not fair. Tell her, okay?"

Travis looked up from the newspaper he was trying so hard to read and smiled at the pleading expression on his daughter's face. "What's not fair? And who am I supposed to tell that to? Honey, did you take shorthand in your speech class? Because it would be nice if you spoke in complete sentences, then I wouldn't have to ask so many questions."

"Nikki Davis. Her mom won't let her come to my birthday party." The child bounced on the chair, her two braids dancing around her shoulders. "Talk to her mom, *please*. Nikki has to come."

Travis sighed and put away his newspaper. It was obvious he wasn't going to be allowed to read it this morning.

"Susie, did you ever stop to think her mother might have a very good reason for saying no?"

She grimaced at his logic. "Not Nikki's mom. She never lets her do anything fun. After school she has to go straight home, and she can't go anywhere on the weekends."

He looked skeptical, by now used to his daughter's elaborate explanations. "Honey, aren't you exaggerating just a bit?"

"No, I'm not!" Her hazel eyes sparkled with youthful indignation. "Her mom practically keeps her a prisoner."

He sighed. "Okay, who exactly is this monster of a mother?"

"Mrs. Davis works at Lorna's as a waitress," Susie replied. "And they moved here just after Christmas, so Nikki doesn't know all that many kids, and I figured my party would give her a chance to know them better."

Travis couldn't help smiling. If nothing else, his daughter was generous to a fault. As far as she was concerned, the entire world should be friends, and she worked hard at doing her share.

"So will you talk to her? Please?" she pleaded, looking at him with what he privately called her "waif" look. He knew he could never turn her down when she looked at him like that.

"All right, I'll talk to Mrs. Davis." He held up his hand to halt her squeals of excitement. "But if she says no, that's it, Susie. There will be more than enough guests to make your seventh birthday memorable, and I'm sure this Nikki will soon make plenty of friends on her own." He stood up and dropped a kiss onto the top of her head before striding out of the kitchen. In the hallway he stood in front of the large wall mirror, adjusting the gold sheriff's badge on his shirt, then set his tan Stetson on his head.

"I gather Susie was adding a few more gray hairs to your collection," a woman's voice broke in.

"Hey, I'm still the best-looking guy in Dunson, lady," he said with a grin, sketching a salute at the reflection of the tall woman standing behind him. "And this badge just adds to the appeal. Women just fall at my feet. They see me as a western Superman fighting for truth, justice and the American way. But I'm still an all-around humble kind of guy."

She gave a most unladylike snort; but then Maude Hunter never had considered herself a lady.

"If the badge adds to the appeal, it's because you never bothered to get that broken nose of yours fixed, which only makes you look like a good-looking thug."

Travis shook his head. "I got this distinctive nose running for a very important touchdown during the homecoming game," he recalled fondly. "And later on I got Karen Peterson in the back seat of my '58 Chevy."

Maude sighed. Her son's exploits as high school football star and sex symbol were legendary. "And now you're the sheriff of a small town, whose most exciting moment was when Sy Williams dropped his pants in front of the Thursday Afternoon Ladies Club. I'm sorry to tell you this, but your only appeal is in the fact you're single."

His lips twitched in an answering grin. He knew she was kidding, but it was a game they enjoyed playing. "From what I heard, that was the liveliest meeting they'd had in more than thirty years." He glanced down at his watch. "Susie, if you want a ride to school, you better be outside in thirty seconds!" he bellowed.

"Coming," she sang out.

Five minutes later Travis ushered his daughter into the dark blue

Cherokee parked in front of the large ranch house. After dropping her off at the school, he headed for the sheriff's office located next to the city hall.

Cal, Travis's deputy, sat at the front desk, engrossed in keeping the contents of a jelly doughnut from sliding onto his lap.

"Hi ya, Travis." His words were muffled as he talked around the doughnut. "It's been quiet."

"What else is new?" Travis said dryly, picking up the weekend report. "Cal, I thought you were giving those up."

The young heavyset deputy looked sheepish as he finished the last bite of the sugar-dusted confection.

"Yeah, well, I stopped by to say hi to Mary Ellen, and she had just finished filling these with raspberry jam." He looked as if his explanation said it all.

Travis picked up a large earthenware mug decorated with the words Number One Dad in red, filled it with coffee and carried it into the tiny cubicle he called his office. His favorite joke was that if he turned around, he'd bump into himself.

He sat at his desk looking over the weekend report, which was pretty much like the previous ones over the past few months. No criminal activity, nothing.

"So why am I here?" he muttered. He knew why. His sheriff's salary was being put away to pay for a new bull his ranch badly needed. That was the only reason he had taken the job in the first place. The previous sheriff had died and the town council had asked him to take over, since Travis was one of the few people with any kind of criminal justice experience, thanks to a stint in the navy's military police. As he read the report, he was vaguely aware of the phone ringing and Cal's low rumble.

"Travis." The younger man appeared in the doorway. "Wilma just called. Zeke's at it again."

He groaned. "Damn, you'd think he would have learned by now. Well, you better get out there before Wilma carries through her long-term threat and shoots him in the family jewels. As if Zeke would even think of fathering a child this late in life."

Cal nodded. This was nothing new to them. Zeke Carlson had a bad habit of sneaking off and visiting the widow Lassiter. His wife had tartly informed him that an eighty-four-year-old man had no business sniffing around other women. His reply was always the same; he was old, not dead.

"And if Wilma has that scattergun of hers out, take it away and bring it in," Travis ordered. "I don't want her to go ahead and use that sawed-off shotgun on him. Oh, Cal." He held up a hand to halt the other man's exit. "Do you know a Mrs. Davis working over at Lorna's?"

Cal frowned. "Mrs. Davis doesn't ring a bell, but Lorna did hire a new waitress named Lee, who works there during the day. Why?"

"No special reason. Her daughter's in Susie's class."

"I don't know that much about her," Cal admitted. "You want me to find out?"

"No, I think I'll just head on over there myself," Travis decided. "You go on out and talk to Wilma."

Cal puffed up with pride at the thought of being given an important assignment. "I'll do you proud."

"Just bring back the gun."

Travis spent the rest of the morning doing the paperwork that never seemed to end, and talked to the deputy who patrolled the town streets. Cal returned later with an old-fashioned scattergun cradled in one arm, and the news that Wilma was now threatening to either divorce her wandering husband or castrate him.

"Sure hope it's the former." Travis stood up and slapped his hat onto his head. "I think I'll head on out to lunch."

The restaurant was a short distance from the office, and apart from one of the taverns that only served dinner, was the only eating place in town. Lorna, a heavyset woman of indeterminate age with brassy blond hair and faded blue eyes, kept the interior homey looking with red gingham curtains and matching tablecloths. Travis walked in, greeting friends, and immediately headed for the end of the counter, sitting down on one of the stools and setting his hat on the empty one next to him.

"Travis, you sly one." A woman's hand, its nails polished a lethal-looking red, covered his shoulder. "Come on over here to one of my tables. I'll see you get extraspecial service."

"Sally, if you weren't happily married to a man who's four inches taller and definitely outweighs me, I'd sure be tempted." He grinned rakishly.

The blond waitress chuckled. "Will doesn't mind my flirting, as long as I don't touch." Looking up when someone called out her name, she wrinkled her nose at Travis and sauntered away, swinging her hips in a sultry motion.

Travis looked down toward the other end of the counter, where a petite woman stood taking an order from the town's only plumber.

She looked to be in her late twenties. Her tiny figure was clothed in a red knit pullover top and jeans, the usual uniform for Lorna's waitresses, and her shoulder-length brown hair was brushed back from her face and tied with a red ribbon. Her features were expressionless and her voice was low.

"Mornin', Travis." A dark-haired man in dusty denim overalls stopped for a moment before leaving.

He looked up, smiling a greeting at the man and at the same time seeing the waitress turn in his direction. For the briefest moment her eyes widened, then a polite mask seemed to slide over her face as she walked toward him.

"Sheriff." Her low voice, with the barest hint of a Southern accent, didn't reveal any of her initial trepidation. "What would you like?"

"Oh, a cheeseburger with the works, fries and coffee. I'll wait until my meal for my coffee." He smiled up at her. "You're Mrs. Davis, right?"

She nodded stiffly, then fear clearly took over again. "Is it my daughter? Has something happened to her?" She held her order book in front of her, her pen clutched between her fingers.

"No, nothing's happened to Nikki," he hastened to assure her. "Although I am here because of her. Actually, it's on behalf of my daughter, Susie."

"Susie Hunter," she murmured. "Yes, Nikki's mentioned her. I believe they're in the same class."

"Well, I'm afraid Susie's convinced her life will be over if Nikki can't come to her birthday party next Saturday," he explained, with an easy grin and the tone of a parent well used to a child's exaggeration.

She shook her head, offering a slight smile. "I'm sorry, but we have plans for that day."

"Are they something you might be able to change? It's all fairly normal. We have a barbecue at the ranch and a general all-around brawl, but a well-supervised one." He kept smiling.

She realized he wasn't going to allow her to get away with a vague excuse. "Well, let me think about it. I'll put your order in," she murmured, moving away.

When Lee slapped the order onto the counter in front of Lorna, the older woman grinned broadly.

"I see you met our sheriff," she commented.

"He's here because he would like my daughter to attend Susie's birthday party," Lee mumbled, picking up an order and wondering why she even bothered to explain.

"Well, isn't that nice he came by to deliver the invitation personally.'' Lorna used the metal spatula to turn over a sizzling hamburger patty on the grill. She slapped one finished patty onto a bun and added the usual fixings.

Lee wasn't about to agree. As far as she was concerned, men were a species she could do without.

A few minutes later she set the food and coffee in front of Travis. "Would you like anything else, Sheriff?"

He opened a bottle of catsup and tapped a portion next to his French fries. "Just your consent that Nikki can come to Susie's party. You're also invited. The parents are always more than welcome," he added when he noticed her hesitation. "Look, if she's grounded for some reason you don't want to talk about, I won't press the issue. After all, Susie's been punished more than a few times in her short life."

"No, that's not it." She told herself it wasn't his charming smile that was making her change her mind. It was more the memory of Nikki's tear-filled eyes.

"She'll be able to run and scream to her heart's content," he cajoled her. "I guarantee you'll get a very tired kid in return. And how many times does that happen?"

"I..." What could she use for an excuse? "Next Saturday?"

"Yes."

She nodded before she lost her nerve. "What time should she be there?"

"One o'clock. If you'd like, I can pick her up."

"No," Lee said hastily. "I'll drive her out."

Travis sensed this wasn't a time to push. "Fine, we'll see you then."

She nodded stiffly and moved away.

He watched Lee out of the corner of his eye as he ate his hamburger and drank his coffee. Sally halted long enough to refill his cup and ask about Maude and Susie.

Travis drew a rough map on a napkin and gave it to Lee when he paid his bill.

"Please plan on staying, too," he urged her. "I think you'd enjoy yourself. You'd also get to meet a lot of the parents of kids from Nikki's class."

A thin smile was her only answer as she accepted the napkin.

Lee watched him leave the restaurant and couldn't help but fear what would happen next. From the moment she'd seen the khaki uniform and gold badge, she'd felt as if her body was held in a gigantic vise that was squeezing the life out of her.

She ordered herself to calm down before her anguish was revealed on her face. After all, he was the law and might wonder why she was afraid of him. She had to be careful. She turned away, picking up a damp rag to wipe down the counter. She figured if she kept busy, she'd forget how much her feet ached. She had worked as a waitress on and off for the past three years, but she had never got used to it. Still, she was usually lucky enough to find a position that let her work her own hours, so she could be home with Nikki in the late afternoon.

Lee already regretted saying Nikki could go to the party. She hated herself for denying her daughter those all-important friendships during the time when a girl needed so badly to belong to a group. And she hated herself for not being able to tell Nikki the truth behind her admonitions. All the girl knew was that because of their gypsy lifestyle, making friends was painful. It appeared that Susie Hunter was proving to be an exception.

Lee spent the rest of her shift serving customers, wiping off tables and taking inventory in the storeroom until it was time to leave. Since the small house she rented was only a few blocks away, she walked whenever she could to save gas, and in a town this size it was easy to do.

Lee enjoyed the crisp, early-spring day as she walked down the sidewalk. She recalled the morning she and Nikki had arrived in Dunson, Montana a couple of months ago. She had only meant to stop for gas and some breakfast, but after driving through the small town with its friendly populace she'd felt as if she had come home. She had meant to travel another couple of hundred miles before looking for another place to settle in, but Lorna's need for a waitress had prompted her to stay. While rentals certainly weren't the norm in such a small community, she found an available house, when a retired couple wanted to move south but didn't want to sell their home. It was as if fate had meant Lee to stay there.

"Three years," she whispered, unlocking her front door and entering the tiny living room. As always, her eyes swept through the room to see if anything looked out of order. Nothing appeared unusual, not the oatmeal fabric-covered couch, the two dark gold easy chairs or the lamps. There were no personal mementos scattered around. The house might look more sterile that way, but it was easier if they had to leave in the dead of night. "Please, God, don't let this town be my downfall. Don't let him find me."

Glancing at the clock and realizing Nikki would be home from school soon, she hurried into her bedroom and exchanged her top for a dark blue sweatshirt with three ducks dancing on the front; it had been a Christmas gift from Nikki the previous year. She brushed out her hair, pinning it up in a loose knot.

"Mom?" a young voice piped up, just as the screen door slammed.

"No, the Easter bunny," she teased, walking into the kitchen just as her daughter opened the refrigerator door and withdrew a milk carton. "How was school?"

Nikki wrinkled her nose. "Mrs. Lansing wants us to make up posters about the four basic food groups for Parents' Night. Can you believe it?"

"Sounds healthy."

"But that kind of thing is for little kids," she informed her mother with all the maturity of a seven-year-old, sometimes going on thirty, as Lee would say teasingly. "We should do something more serious. Mom, she is so boring."

"Something more serious? What do you have in mind, *War and Peace*?"

Nikki rolled her eyes but said nothing.

"Susie's father came to see me today," Lee remarked casually.

The girl's eyes widened. "Because of the party? Are we going to have to leave here?"

Lee wanted to cry at her daughter's saddened tone. How many times had they crept out of a town in the middle of the night because someone had shown even a trace of interest in either mother or daughter? While Nikki might not know the reason behind their constant moves, she'd grown to accept them.

While Lee had thought large cities were safe, she quickly discovered they weren't. There'd been Kansas City, where a nosy neighbor had read about Anne Sinclair in the paper and begun to take too close an interest in Nikki and herself. So she'd decided a small town would be better—until Homer's Run, Nebraska, where the school had wanted more information on Nikki's past than Lee was willing to give. She had gone as far west as Flagstaff, Arizona, only to leave late one night because of a renewed television story about Lloyd Sinclair's shooting that was accompanied by an appeal for Anne Sinclair's apprehension, and as far east as a small Vermont town, where a detective had shown up, looking for her. And with each move, Lee had felt her stomach tear into tiny pieces.

She couldn't remember the last time she'd had a peaceful night's sleep. She was so afraid of the moment when Nikki would be old enough to ask for the truth. What would happen then? Would her daughter turn against her for what she had done? Or would she be able to search her memory, recall the truth and understand why Lee had done what she did?

"Sheriff Hunter came to convince me to allow you to go to his daughter's birthday party," she said quietly.

Nikki's mouth opened and closed, but nothing came out. She obviously feared the worst.

Lee smiled. "I said you could go."

She ran over, hugging her mother so tightly that Lee laughingly complained her ribs would surely crack.

"I love you, Mom." Nikki's words were muffled against her mother's shirtfront.

Lee grasped her shoulders and drew her back, so that she could gaze down into the tiny, heart-shaped face so like her own.

"And I love you so very, very much." Her voice broke. "And I'll always be here for you."

Nikki squealed. "I'm gonna call Susie." She raced out of the kitchen.

Lee chuckled as she picked up the discarded milk glass and rinsed it out.

"If the daughter is anything like the father, no wonder Nikki wants her as a friend," she murmured, thinking of the sheriff who had watched her so closely. Even as emotionally scarred as she was where men were concerned, she had to admit he was a nice-looking guy. Determined to put Travis Hunter out of her mind, she left the kitchen to finish her housekeeping chores.

"NOTHIN' ever happens around here," Cal groused, standing in the doorway of Travis's cubicle.

Travis cocked an eyebrow. "What about this morning with Wild-eyed Wilma, or are you looking for a major crime wave?" He was aware that Cal sometimes had enough trouble with hotheaded Wilma, and doubted he could handle a real criminal. Travis wondered if even *he* could; it had been many years since those busy days in the military police.

The younger man reddened. "Hell, you know what I mean. All we ever get around here are the Saturday night drunks. It's nothin' that would put this place on the six o'clock news."

Travis nodded, understanding Cal's frustration. "Television makes our job look glamorous and dangerous all at the same time. Instead, we have kids cutting school or skinny-dipping in old man Wilson's pond, not to mention breaking up the teenage lovers parked out on back roads. Yeah, it isn't anything we'd get medals for, but if trouble ever did show up, we'd be here to protect the townspeople. That's what counts. If you want the big action, you're going to have to go to the city, and to be honest, I don't think you'd be happy there.''

Cal nodded. ''Yeah, you're right, but it can't stop a guy from hoping that something exciting might happen around here.''

Travis chuckled as he stood up. ''Tell you what. If any big-time cattle rustlers come around, I'll let you handle the case.''

''You can joke about it, but you never can tell.''

''That's true, but I've lived here all my life, and hardened criminals don't usually show up in Dunson.'' He patted Cal's shoulder as he passed by. He nodded at the other deputy as he entered the office. ''Hi, Marv, all's quiet.''

Marv grinned. ''Tell me something new.''

As Travis drove home, he wondered if he wasn't living in one of the most boring towns in the country. After his travels in the navy he had wondered if he wouldn't return home and feel dissatisfied with the ranch. Surprisingly, he hadn't. He liked living in a small town. And with all the gossip and crazy intrigue that went on, he really couldn't call it dull. He sped down the side road leading to the house and parked in the rear.

''You're late.'' His mother stood in the open doorway.

''Cal was talking about his dream of solving the crime of the century.'' He climbed out of his truck and slammed the door.

Maude shook her head. ''That boy shouldn't watch *Miami Vice*. He has enough ideas as it is.''

''Dad!'' a high-pitched voice squealed, just before a small body propelled itself at him. ''Thank you, oh, thank you! You're the best dad in the world!''

He started laughing as he lifted Susie into his arms. ''I am, huh? I think I want to preserve this moment for the next time you tell me how horrible I am when I order you to clean up your room.''

Susie grimaced at his teasing as she was lowered to her feet. ''You know what I mean. You made Mrs. Davis let Nikki come to my party.''

He shook his head. ''Whoa there, kiddo. I didn't *make* her do anything. I merely talked to Mrs. Davis, assuring her the party will be properly supervised and she would have nothing to worry about. The end decision was still hers.''

''But you don't understand. She never lets Nikki go anywhere. It's as if she's afraid something would happen to her if she didn't go home straight from school.''

Travis's mind backtracked again to Lee Davis's first reaction to him. "She's a single parent. You may not realize it, but I worry about you, too. The only difference is, I know your grandmother is here when I'm not. So why don't you lighten up a bit, okay?"

"And wash your hands for dinner," Maude interjected.

"I don't care how you did it. I'm just glad she's coming." Susie loped out of the room.

Travis turned to his mother. "What is so special about this Nikki?"

Maude shrugged. "You know Susie, she takes everyone under her wing. Nikki Davis is her latest project, although I feel it's more than that, this time around. Susie seems to feel she doesn't have any fun, so she's determined to liven up her life."

"Some would say Susie has a very generous streak in her. I'd call it pushy." Travis hung up his hat.

"She obviously felt it was for a good reason." Maude began setting covered dishes on the table. "So what is Nikki's mother like?"

"Someone easy to forget. Nice looking, but nothing to write home about."

"That's not saying very much. You still haven't told me *about* her."

Travis shrugged. "Brown hair, brown eyes, a little over five feet tall, very thin, that's it. As I said, nothing memorable." Except the most delicate features he had ever seen on a woman. Almost as if an old-fashioned cameo had come to life. He hoped she would also come to the party, because he was curious to learn why she'd first acted as if she were afraid of him.

Maude watched her son across the room, a slight smile crossing her face. Travis might say the woman was easily forgettable, but she had an idea he wasn't listening to himself. Her son had been restless lately. Maybe a new woman in town was just what he needed.

"I'll be very interested in meeting the mysterious Mrs. Davis," she commented, all too casually.

Travis shot her a sharp look. "You're never interested in meeting anyone new."

"True, but I'm also allowed to change my mind. Now go wash your hands for dinner. It's my poker night, and I don't intend to be late."

AFTER NIKKI WENT to bed, Lee turned on the small television set to an old movie and sat curled up on the couch with yarn she was crocheting into an afghan, but her mind wasn't on either the film or her task.

When Nikki had asked her if they were going to have to leave town, she'd almost said yes—all because Nikki's new friend was the town sheriff's daughter.

The town sheriff. She leaned back her head, her eyes closed in a weariness that was more emotional than physical—a tiredness that came from keeping secrets that grew heavier and more dangerous with each passing day—secrets that left her suspicious of everyone she came into contact with, especially the sheriff, no matter how kind his eyes were.

"A nice-looking man who could easily sign my death warrant," she murmured to herself.

Chapter Two

"See, I told you everyone would wear jeans to the party, Mom," Nikki wailed, looking out the car window as they approached the Hunter ranch. "Susie said we'll be able to ride horses. You have to wear jeans when you ride a horse." She spoke as if it was a hard-and-fast rule.

Lee sighed. "Whatever happened to frilly dresses and Pin the Tail on the Donkey?"

"Nobody wears frilly dresses in Montana," she informed her mother as if she had lived there all her life.

"I'm discovering that," she said dryly.

"Are you going to stay? Susie said some of the parents do," Nikki continued.

"I don't know yet." Just looking at the cars parked on the hard-packed dirt in front of the house made her body tense. Not to mention the idea of spending a few hours in the sheriff's house. Why couldn't he have been a dentist or plumber? Then she wouldn't feel as if the dark cloud continually following her was now threatening to descend and smother her.

Lee parked the car, barely stopping before Nikki was out and running. Lee followed her daughter's trail, intent on telling her she would return for her later.

"Lee, glad to see you decided to stay," Travis said genially, holding out his hand in greeting. "The adults are keeping a safe distance from the kids. It saves wear and tear on the sanity. Come on over and meet the others."

She held back. "No, really, I wasn't—"

If he heard her weak attempt at turning him down, he ignored it as he cupped her elbow with his palm and guided her toward the rear of the house. She looked up at him with huge eyes when he touched her, but he had no idea how much self-control she had to exert not to pull away from him. "Everyone, this is Lee Davis. Carol Talbot, John and Rita Carter," he went on, introducing her to the other parents, who were sitting on the deck overlooking a large barn and several corrals.

"I was just going to explain that I'd be back later for Nikki," Lee managed to say with a weak smile.

"Nonsense." A tall, gray-haired woman stepped out onto the deck. "I'm Maude Hunter, this ruffian's mother. And I would guess the pixie out there is yours." A smile softened her normally stern features. "Susie performed a rapid-fire introduction. Your daughter has beautiful manners. She actually called me ma'am."

"I try." Lee felt tongue-tied, facing this dominant personality. Now she knew where Travis had inherited his own forceful appeal.

Maude nodded. "We'll talk later." It sounded more like an order than a mere polite phrase.

"Her bark is much worse than her bite," Travis murmured, sensing Lee's unease. He gestured toward a large coffee maker that stood on a table near the door, along with a platter piled high with pastries. "Help yourself. We're all very casual around here."

Seeing she wasn't to be given a chance to leave, Lee poured herself a cup of coffee but resisted food. She knew her churning stomach wouldn't accept anything solid. She perched on the edge of a chair, listening to the conversation flowing around her, but soon learned she wasn't to be just an observer, as she had hoped.

"Travis, I heard Zeke was out cattin' around again." Dave, the father of a freckle-faced Stuart, grinned. "I'm surprised Wilma hasn't given him a butt full of buckshot yet."

"She would have this last time, but I had her shotgun taken away," Travis told him, then went on to explain to Lee the story of the eternally unfaithful Zeke.

She smiled, but it didn't quite reach her eyes. "It appears he has a habit that's difficult to break."

"You haven't been here very long, have you?" Carol questioned Lee.

She smiled briefly. "A few months."

"More people move out of Dunson than move in," Jim commented. "We don't have all that much to offer new residents."

"Small towns are nicer," Lee said tersely. She could have said she felt safer there rather than in the city, even though she could lose herself more easily in the latter. But in this small town she also felt more vulnerable. "At least here I wouldn't have to worry about Nikki joining a street gang."

"That's true," Rita agreed. "We've never had that problem here. Of course, Travis probably has something to do with that!" She laughed. "But we want to hear about you."

Lee fought down the panic that had begun to claw its way up her throat. She kept telling herself that everyone was merely being friendly, but they were so damn curious about her!

Rita smiled. "Where did you live before you arrived here?"

"Kansas City," she replied, lying without hesitation.

"How long have you been divorced?" Carol asked.

"Four years." At least that was the truth.

"Does your ex-husband ever see Nikki?"

"He died not long ago." A lie she wished was true. She could feel the acid burning her stomach. It took every ounce of courage she had to sit there and politely answer their questions. "He had a heart attack."

"You poor thing. You've really had it rough, haven't you?" Carol commiserated. "Don't you have any family at all?"

She willed herself to remain calm, but it wasn't easy. What would they think if she told them about her mother and father, the two people who put up such a pious front in public, and who were so emotionally abusive behind closed doors? "No, no family," she replied quietly.

One of the other women spoke up next. "At least you have Nikki," she said. "Children are such a comfort, aren't they?"

Lee's smile felt stiffer by the moment. "Yes, they are." She forced herself to relax the hands that lay clenched in her lap.

"Didn't your husband have any family?" someone else asked.

"Where are you from originally?"

"How do you like Dunson?"

Lee felt as though the questions were rolling around in her head like so many marbles. It might have been simple curiosity on their part, but it was pure agony to her. She'd always been able to deal with nosy people, but how could she be rude to ones who were so sincere? Still, she couldn't stem the panic in her body. In the end, it was easier to smile and excuse herself, saying she wanted to go to the corral to watch the children.

It hadn't taken her long to realize that this group of people was close-knit, but willing to allow in newcomers. And while they asked questions like a district attorney, they were equally willing to talk about themselves.

"I say the guy doesn't have a chance." Jim was arguing amiably with Travis about a court case that was making headlines all over the country.

"Why not? He's in the right. Everyone knows that," Travis argued back.

"So he's in the right. The other guy has the clout and the expensive lawyers. Who do you think will win? The one with the power. Come on, you've been around long enough to know better. Get your head out of the clouds."

Travis grinned. "I still like to think that the law will back the right person, okay?"

He perched his hip on the deck railing, his position enabling him to watch Lee at the corral without her being aware of it. Today her hair was left loose, its ends curling under, just above her shoulders. He noticed she wore little makeup except for a pale peach lipstick. Her tan slacks and off-white polo sweater were nothing special, almost as if she preferred to blend into her surroundings. His instincts told him that she sat there looking cool and composed, but wasn't that way inside. Every now and then he'd swear a flash of fear darkened her eyes. He just wished he knew why. There was definitely more to this woman than met the eye. Her skittish reaction to him prompted him to wonder if she hadn't had a good marriage; that would have been an excellent reason for a divorce. His attention shifted when he noticed his mother's sharp gaze was fixed on him. He smiled blandly, but knew she had caught him staring at Lee and would be sure to question him later. Slowly he straightened and walked down to the corral to stand behind Lee. Before he could say a word, she tensed, clearly sensing his arrival, and moved away as if she were merely shifting her weight.

"Don't mind them," Travis said softly. "A town this small doesn't get new residents very often, so they'll pounce on anyone new, first chance they get."

"I guess I'm not used to it," she murmured, her head bowed.

Travis caught the faintest hint of a light, spicy floral scent in the air. For the longest time after his wife died, he had been convinced he wouldn't be attracted to another woman. Although "intrigued" would be the proper word where Lee was concerned.

Maude spoke up. "Travis, don't you think we should start the barbecue now?"

"Sounds about right." He moved back to the deck, somewhat reluctantly.

"That is one frightened woman."

Travis turned his head at his mother's pronouncement. "Who's the cop here?"

"Reading someone's actions has nothing to do with police work," Maude scoffed. "She answers questions, but says little or nothing. She remains separate, even as she sits in the middle of a group. I also noticed her daughter says little, which you have to admit is unusual for a child that age."

He stared at his mother. "You interrogated her?"

Maude showed no remorse. "Of course not. I merely wanted to get to know my granddaughter's new friend."

"Yeah, sure." He accepted the platter of hamburger patties she held out.

"It's a sad day when a man won't believe his own mother," she muttered, returning to the kitchen.

Left alone, Travis once again looked down at Lee in the corral. As if sensing she was being watched, she turned her head, looking toward the house. For a brief moment their eyes rested on each other, then Lee slowly turned away.

Dangerous, her brain warned her as the group was led to lunch by a band of shouting, hungry children. Several tables had been set up, with one off to one side for the adults.

"These hamburgers aren't from one of your cows, are they?" Jim joked. "This isn't Ivy, is it? She used to follow everyone around, remember?"

"Oh, Dad, that's gross!" moaned his daughter Stephanie.

"James, you've never lost that sick sense of humor, have you?" Maude said, filling the children's glasses with lemonade. "Of course, I can't think of any other four-year-old who would walk into church wearing only his underwear, because he claimed it was too hot for clothes. I will admit you did it with flair."

All eyes turned on the man who shifted uncomfortably in his seat.

"Maude, don't you ever forget anything?" he muttered.

"No. Why do you think so many people are afraid of me?"

"Mom thinks she's the perfect example of the crotchety old lady everyone is intimidated by," Travis confided to Lee.

"We'll dispense with the 'old,' thank you very much," Maude said tartly.

Travis saw the barest hint of a smile touch Lee's lips, then just as swiftly disappear. He wondered what it would take for her to display a real smile that would light up her face and eyes. He watched her glance at him again, then her gaze skittered away when she found him looking at her again.

Lee's appetite was gone, but she forced herself to finish her food, to converse naturally, to do anything to give an appearance of normalcy. She knew it should be second nature to her by now, because lies had become so much a part of her life over the past few years. She looked at Nikki sitting at the other table, laughing and talking with the other children, and felt pleased that she looked so happy.

"Come on," Susie called to her playmates, jumping up from the table and running off.

Nikki immediately followed her friend, but stumbled and would have fallen if Travis hadn't caught her. His teasing words about not being so much in a hurry froze on his lips when he noticed how she abruptly backed away from his helping hand, looking just a bit fearful, her eyes wide.

"Are you all right?" he asked gently, thinking her fright came from almost falling.

She nodded, the motion jerky as she backed away, not allowing her gaze to leave him until she was several feet distant.

After that little incident, Travis wasn't surprised when Lee and Nikki were the first to leave the party.

"Thank you for having me," Nikki whispered, refusing to look at Travis as he walked them out to the car.

"I'm glad you could come." He smiled at Lee in a reassuring manner. "You see, we're not so bad. Well, not as bad as we could be."

Without saying another word, Nikki scrambled into the car.

"She—ah, she has trouble making friends," Lee said, thinking she should explain her daughter's obviously rude behavior. "Susie has been great in trying to get her out of her shell."

"What about her mother? Does she have the same problem?"

"Her mother has enough going on between her job and being a mother." Lee smiled coolly. "Thank you for having us."

"I'm glad you came. And I'm sure we'll be seeing each other again. In a town this size it can't be helped," he said with a chuckle.

As Lee drove off, she could see Travis in the rearview mirror standing in the driveway.

"Did you have fun?"

"Yes." Nikki paused. "Susie's dad is real big."

Lee now understood her reserve. One thing she had been grateful for was that Nikki had been too young to appear to remember her father's violent nature, though she couldn't ignore the fact that the child suffered from nightmares. "He just seems that way to you, honey, because he's a tall man and you're still a little girl."

Nikki's lower lip trembled. "He's not tall, Mom, he's big."

Once they arrived home, Lee told Nikki to take a bath before getting ready for bed. An hour later she showered quickly and retired with a book, but soon fell asleep.

Her sleep was restless, though. Lee was Anne again and back in Texas. In the house where she had spent so much time keeping up appearances.

LLOYD, IMPECCABLY dressed as usual, was pacing the length of the living room, his classically handsome face marred by the fury etched on his features.

"Did I say you could give her a party?" he demanded in the voice that could ooze honey or spit acid. "She's too young to appreciate one."

She stood before him, feeling like an errant child with her hands clasped in front of her. "I didn't realize I had to ask your permission, Lloyd." She kept her voice bland, because she knew better than to further antagonize him when he was in this mood.

He spun around, spearing her with icy eyes. "Dammit, Anne, it's my money you're wasting here," he snarled.

"It's her third birthday—the first one she'll really remember. She should have something special."

"Give her another teddy bear and she'll be happy."

"Lloyd, we're not talking about a tremendous cost here. Just a cake, ice cream, some games and a few friends over," she pointed out, still keeping her voice soft so as not to agitate him. "They'll be gone and any mess cleaned up before you get home from your golf game. It will be as if they weren't here."

"You got the last part right, because they won't be here. You want the party so badly, you get off your butt and earn the money for it. Otherwise you cancel it," he ordered in the tone that brooked no disobedience.

Anne took a deep breath. "It's too late. The invitations have already gone out and the cake has been ordered. I honestly didn't think it would upset you this much."

When he stared at her, she felt the waves of anger rolling across the room and choking her. "Upset me? You do nothing but aggravate and embarrass me. What do I have to do to get you to listen to me?" He advanced on her. "I don't care if that party is in five minutes. I want it cancelled, do you hear me? For once in your life, do what I say!"

She heard him and knew what was coming next, but had no way of stopping it. Curses, shouting and then the pain. Bruises she would have to hide from the outside world.

"No," LEE MOANED, thrashing around in bed. *"No!"* she screamed, jerking upright.

Her eyes flew open and she breathed deeply to still the stampede in her stomach. She could feel the sweat trickling down her back and between her breasts, and the pounding in her head from the trauma her nightmare had caused.

"Mom?" Nikki stood in the doorway, wide-eyed and very frightened. "You screamed."

"Everything's fine." Lee held out her arms, and the girl sprang onto the bed and into them.

"It was one of your bad dreams again, wasn't it?" Nikki asked, snuggling as close to her mother as possible.

"I'm afraid so. Probably from mixing the chocolate cake with the hamburger." Lee felt the fear slowly drain from her body as her daughter's body heat warmed her.

They huddled together for the rest of the night, Nikki subconsciously protecting her mother from the past, Lee hoping to keep the nightmares at bay. But she knew they'd return again, no matter how far or for how long she and Nikki ran from the past.

"WHAT ARE YOU GOING to do about it?"

Travis looked up from the cigarette he had been contemplating. "I know, I said I'd quit, but I'm weak. What can I say?"

Maude shot him a look of frustration as she sat in the chair next to him. "You know very well what I mean."

"She's an interesting woman," he admitted.

"This from the man who stated he would remain a single parent, because he didn't care to get involved again." She sipped from the glass of whiskey she held in one hand.

He drew on his cigarette. "She seems to be a classy lady, and I think she needs a friend." Travis looked out over the darkness, hearing the sounds of horses nickering among themselves.

"Maybe she does, but are you sure that's what you're looking for?" Maude inquired bluntly. With that she rose slowly to her feet and walked into the house. "You're not getting any younger, you know."

"Interfering old woman," he muttered, a slight grin on his face. "I told you to knock off calling me old!"

WHEN LUNCHTIME rolled around, Lee wasn't surprised to see Travis walk in and seat himself at the counter.

"Mornin'," he greeted her with a broad smile as he set his hat on the empty stool next to him.

"Sheriff," she replied, unable to resist returning his smile as she filled his glass with water. Why did one of the nicest men she had ever met have to turn out to be a lawman?

"Travis," he corrected her. "I only expect to be called Sheriff when I'm on official business. Right now, I'm just a guy who's hungry for some of Lorna's beef stew and dumplings."

She nodded and moved away.

Travis turned to speak to several of the other men present, then gave Lee a thank-you smile as she placed a cup of coffee in front of him.

"I know you didn't ask for any, but I've heard that sheriffs only drink coffee," she explained shyly.

He lifted the cup to his lips, pleased she had made the special effort, even though she still showed a wariness around him. "You're right. I probably drink too much of it, but I wouldn't know how to begin the day without a cup, even when it's as lousy as Cal's. Thank you."

A moment later Lee returned with Travis's bowl of stew, topped with fluffy dumplings.

"You going to Parents' Night on Thursday?" He threw out the question just as she prepared to leave him. He really wished he knew what to talk about with someone as skittish as Lee, because he wanted to receive a real smile from her. He didn't know what he'd have to do, but he'd find out.

She shrugged. "I hadn't thought about it one way or another."

"You should. It's one of the town's big nights. I'm talking wild here. The teachers tell us how great our kids are and how they're positive they'll be our future leaders," Travis intoned. "See what fun you can have there?"

She nodded. "Oh yes, it sounds like a barrel of laughs."

"So I'll see you there?" he asked.

Lee braced her hip against the counter, looking as if she was prepared to stay for more than thirty seconds, which was what Travis had hoped for. "I admit Nikki has talked about her art project, so I'm certain she'll want me to go and see it."

He smiled. "Then I'll see you there."

Lee stared into Travis's warm brown eyes, unconsciously noting the gold flecks sparkling in the dark depths. She wasn't sure how he had so neatly trapped her into a decision, but with his friendly manner he had done it. Because of one man she found it difficult to trust any other, although she worked hard not to instill that distrust in her daughter. She turned to pick up the coffeepot and refilled Travis's cup.

"Yes, I'll be there. You better eat your food before it gets cold," she said huskily before moving down the counter to greet a new customer, aware that Travis's eyes were on her every step of the way. What she didn't know was that her lips were curved in a faint smile, and that he was the cause.

"Tell Lorna she's outdone herself, as usual," Travis told her, leaving a tip by his plate. He paused, looking at Lee with a searching gaze. His mouth opened, wanting to tell her that she should wear her hair a bit fluffier, rather than skinned back in that ponytail. Instead he merely smiled again and stood up. She dropped her tip into her apron pocket and smiled at him. He again noticed that her smile still failed to reach her eyes.

"Don't let Lorna overwork you," he advised lightly as he placed his hat on his head and left the restaurant, lighting a cigarette as soon as he was outside.

Travis's afternoon was uneventful as Cal recounted the gory news of a killing spree in Chicago he'd read about in the newspaper, and of the later high-speed chase that had eventually caught the killers.

"You wouldn't be happy there," Travis told him. "They'd make you go on a diet."

"No Mary Ellen Coffman," he muttered.

"And no Mary Ellen," Travis agreed. "But don't let that stop you from dreaming. None of us would get very far without our dreams."

"Such as you, hoping you'll have enough saved up for a new bull before the next election rolls around," Cal guessed.

Travis nodded. "You got it. Come election year, I'm hoping to gracefully step down and allow someone else to pin on this badge."

"Since I prefer to remain the ever-faithful deputy, I don't know who they're going to find to replace you."

"Stan Richards would jump at the chance."

Cal grimaced. "He'd declare martial law within a month."

"And the streets will be safe to walk again," Travis laughingly intoned. "Yep, Stan would be just what this town needs."

The deputy eyed him slyly. "Rumor has it you're stopping by Lorna's for lunch because of the new waitress."

"The new waitress's daughter goes to school with Susie," Travis pointed out. "The lady's also new to the town, and doesn't seem the type to make friends easily."

"And you're a friendly guy."

Travis leaned back in his chair, his hands clasped behind his head. "Sure am. Hell, I'm Mr. Personality."

"Well then, one thing I know, Lorna's lunchtime business is gonna increase, 'cause everyone's interested in a possible new romance." Cal rubbed his hands in anticipation. "Yes sir, the bets are going to be flying high."

"Cal, gambling's illegal."

"Then it's a good thing I'm a member of the law. That way, if I get caught, I can just go ahead and arrest myself."

Chapter Three

"Mom, you can't wear that!" Nikki wailed, flopping onto Lee's bed.

"Honey, you're going to wrinkle your clothes, lying like that. And what is wrong with this? It's a perfectly good dress." She indicated the navy dress with a red leather belt.

"It's bo-ring." Nikki slid off the bed. "Why don't you wear that yellowish dress?" She disappeared into the depths of Lee's closet until she found a dull gold soft wool dress. "This one."

Lee's fingers flexed as she resisted the urge to touch the soft wool. She had forgotten all about it, although she had carried it with her all this time. It had once been her favorite dress. She started to shake her head, then caught the pleading look in Nikki's eyes.

"Well, if you want me ready in time, you'd better let me get dressed." She pulled the dress off the hanger, keeping her face averted to hide her smile. She knew exactly what her daughter was doing. From the beginning Nikki had been extremely vocal in expressing her opinion of Lee's new hair color, saying it made her look too drab.

Twenty minutes later, Lee was dressed and following an excited Nikki out the door. She found herself experiencing a few butterflies of her own at the idea of moving among so many people.

"YOU LOOK PRETTY," Nikki whispered as they entered the brightly lighted school building.

"You're only saying that because you chose the dress," Lee said lightly. "Now, where to first?"

"The assembly hall." Nikki's head bobbed right and left as she greeted other children.

"Nikki!"

They both turned to see Susie charging down the hall, dragging her father with her, while Maude sauntered slowly after them.

"Tommy Myers said hi to me!" Susie whispered, grabbing Nikki's arm.

Nikki's eyes widened. "He did?"

Travis grimaced over the girls' heads. "I'd had no idea they started talking boys so young. All I cared about at that age was horses and baseball."

"With me it was dolls," Lee confided.

Travis's eyes swept over her dress, noticing how the dull gold color of the sheath complemented her skin tones, and how the dark brown leather belt accented a tiny waist. He was no judge of women's clothing, but the dress and belt appeared to be of excellent quality and not something a waitress making minimum wage could afford.

"Then you two haven't lived until you've heard all about Tommy's good points," Maude interjected. "It appears he's a seven-year-old hunk."

Travis nodded. "That explains everything then. I just wish Susie would wait a few years before she decides boys are better than her horse—say twenty or thirty." He stood in the crowded hall looking relaxed in jeans, an earth-tone plaid shirt and rust-colored V-neck sweater. Tonight he didn't look at all like the town sheriff, but Lee still didn't feel calm.

"Where do I find your classroom?" inquired Lee, tugging at her daughter's hand.

"First is the principal's speech of welcome to the parents." Travis lightly tapped Susie on top of her head. "C'mon, kiddo, let's see if the esteemed principal has finally come up with a new speech this year, or if he'll again talk of children being our greatest assets in life."

"That speech is older than I am," Maude said dryly. "Morton probably learned it from his father." She turned to Lee. "His father was principal here and his grandfather before him."

Lee opened her mouth to protest being swept along in their company, then just as quickly closed it. She was astute enough to know that an argument on her part would only arouse suspicion. She nodded and walked down the hall with Travis walking beside her, the two girls and Maude ahead of them.

Lee was aware of every step they took and every stare directed their way, not to mention whispers of speculation. For a long time she had worked hard to remain in the background, but with Travis she had been set at center stage. She felt even more uncomfortable as they entered the large assembly hall and took seats near the front.

Lee looked around at the off-white painted walls, the stage with its deep red velvet draperies, the old wooden theater seats. She leaned toward Travis.

"I have an idea that no matter what town a person is in, I bet all school assembly halls look the same," she murmured. "If I didn't know better, I'd swear this was the same hall from my old school, even down to the gold tasseled tiebacks on the drapes, and seats needing new padding."

"Maybe it's part of the blueprint for every school," he replied with a grin. "In fact, it looks the way it did when I attended here and that was more years than I'd care to count."

"I'm certainly glad someone else is admitting their age." Maude gave her son a telling look.

The principal, Morton Ellis, stepped up to the podium.

"Good evening." His greeting hummed over the microphone. "And welcome to Parents' Night." He went on in a drone, his speech obviously one he had given many times. As he went on about the children being assets, Lee ducked her head to hide her smile.

Travis leaned over to murmur in her ear. "He'll also talk about our need to nurture them."

The principal spoke slowly. "And we must nurture them, so that they'll grow tall and strong."

Lee coughed to cover the laughter bubbling up her throat.

Travis cleared his own throat, pleased he'd given her a reason to laugh, because the sound was music to his ears. He wanted to hear it more often.

"I told you, it never changes," he muttered.

Mercifully the speech was kept short, and the members of the audience were invited to visit their children's classrooms and meet the teachers.

"Mrs. Lansing is nice, but boring," Nikki told Lee as they walked down the hall, the girl pulling on her mother's hand so that they were ahead of the Hunter family. "At least Mrs. Spenser lets us do what we want. I like her."

The classroom was set up with the children's names on each desk. Mrs. Lansing stood at the front of the room, talking to the parents. Lee went forward, introducing herself to the woman. It didn't take her long to realize Nikki was right—she doubted the teacher had ever had an original idea in her life. Lee thought of her years in college and the dream of becoming a teacher; until a dark prince had swept into her life and carried her off.

"Do they ever work on one large project together?" Lee asked the woman, remembering her stint as a student teacher. "Or even work individually on something that could later be put together? I know of one class that decided to build a model of their state capitol. It was also a wonderful way for them to study history."

Mrs. Lansing smiled thinly. "The way you talk, someone would think you were a teacher at one time. Besides, you have to remember the children are only in the first grade, Mrs. Davis. They certainly can't take on something so ambitious."

"I'm a parent concerned that her daughter receives the best education possible. Besides, age has nothing to do with what's inside a child's imagination when it's given full rein," Lee argued.

Travis stood off to one side, his arms folded across his chest as he listened to Lee's discussion with Mrs. Lansing. He liked her idea of working more closely with a child. While it was well-known Mrs. Lansing was an excellent teacher in the basics, she wasn't long on imagination. The class projects were the same every year and showed little individuality, because the children's input wasn't encouraged.

Lee's gaze wandered for a second and caught Travis listening to her with intense concentration. Horrified at the idea that she had brought such attention to herself, she mumbled an excuse and searched out Nikki, suggesting they look in at her art classroom. There, Lee was pleased to meet a teacher who encouraged her students to be creative and innovative.

"Nikki shows a flair for the unusual," Janice Spenser told Lee, her slender hands moving restlessly as she talked. "She especially enjoys creating collages." She gestured toward one on the wall, which was a large piece of colorful poster board, covered with bits of fabric, lace and trims. "She calls it New Wave Fashion." She smiled, turning her head when someone called her name. "Excuse me. If you have any questions, please feel free to ask."

"Think they're allowed to express their individuality in here?" a low voice asked from behind, once Lee was alone.

She didn't turn around. "Judging from some of these portraits of life on other worlds, I'd say they're more than allowed." She gestured toward one drawing, depicting a plaid planet with its inhabitants color-coordinated. "Sometimes I wonder where they get their ideas."

Travis grimaced at the neon colors used in one picture. "Judging from this, I'd say late-night television."

Carol approached them. "Lee, how nice to see you again. Hello,

Travis. Did you two come together?'' Her bright eyes darted from one to the other.

"No, I'm afraid this strange man keeps insisting on following me around,'' she confided, showing more animation than she ever had before, as Travis was quick to note. "And if he doesn't stop doing it, I'm going to be forced to call the sheriff.''

"You'd have better luck calling his mother,'' Maude observed from behind them with a chuckle.

Carol giggled. "Dial 911,'' she advised, then walked away.

"Well, well, the lady has a sense of humor.'' Travis cocked his head to one side, pleased to see Lee's cheeks turn pink. "I have to say you're full of surprises. I wonder how many more there are. I think it's going to be interesting to find out.'' He reached out and lightly grasped her arm.

Lee ducked her head, trying unobtrusively to move away from his touch. "Sometimes I just forget myself.''

"Please, do it more,'' he encouraged.

Nikki and Susie stood across the room, watching their parents. When they joined the girls, Nikki looked pensive.

"Can we go home now?'' she asked in a stiff voice. Her tiny face looked pale and pinched with tension as she stared up at her mother.

Lee looked surprised at her request, since Nikki had been the one so eager to come in the first place, but she couldn't miss the pleading look in her eyes, and guessed that the reason for it had something to do with the way her daughter had kept demanding her attention all evening.

"I thought we could stop by the drive-in for a soda,'' Travis suggested, sensing the silent communication between mother and daughter, but not the reason behind it.

"Yes!'' Susie squealed, pleased with the idea of staying up past her bedtime. "Come on, Nikki, it'll be fun. I hardly ever get to stay up this late.'' She looked up at her father under coyly lowered lashes.

"No.'' Nikki kept her eyes on Lee's face. "I just want to go home, Mom. Please.''

"All right,'' she murmured, turning from her daughter to Travis. "Thank you for the invitation, but I think Nikki has discovered she's more tired than she thought she was. So we'll just say good-night here.'' She looked at him sharply as he followed them out of the room.

"As the law in this town, the least I can do is see you to your car,'' he explained smoothly.

"From what I've heard, the crime rate here is extremely low,'' she said dryly, walking swiftly down the hall, but Travis easily kept up with her as they exited the building.

"Smart move," he complimented, noticing she had parked under one of the lights in the parking lot.

"A woman alone learns very quickly how to protect herself," Lee replied, unlocking the car door and ushering Nikki inside.

Travis placed one hand on the car roof and the other on top of the door, stopping Lee from getting inside.

"For some reason, Nikki doesn't want to go with us," he said softly, his expression solemn. "Now I can't imagine it has anything to do with Susie or my mother, so it must be me. I've never thought of myself as a monster."

Lee took a deep breath. "As I said before, I think she's just tired. Good night, Sheriff."

"I told you, the name's Travis. And what about the mother? Does she see me as a bad guy, too?" he asked quietly, moving just a shade closer.

Lee looked down at the ground, but all she saw was his highly shined boots. She discovered a light woodsy scent in her nostrils—something sharp and tangy, not cloying like the expensive cologne Lloyd always wore. "No," she whispered, slowly lifting her head to look into the dark eyes that were warm with kindness. "Travis."

He stepped back, as if satisfied just to hear his name on her lips. "Good night. Drive safely."

Lee drove off, one eye on her daughter, who sat as close to her as was possible with her seat belt on. Their lives were taking some very abrupt turns and right now, she wasn't sure what to do. Her first instinct was to run, but something was stopping her. Perhaps because no matter what, she still felt safe in Dunson. But she reminded herself that it wasn't a good idea to fall into complacency, because the vultures were still out there, ready to pick her bones clean.

"Is that coffee still good?" Maude asked, entering the kitchen that was lighted only by the light burning over the stove.

Travis shrugged as he sipped the hot liquid. "Must be. This is my third cup."

"That's only because it's the only thing that gets you going in the morning. Did you eat anything?" she asked, opening a cabinet door and pulling out a frying pan.

"Not yet. I was hoping you'd wake up and take pity on me."

"I'm your mother, Travis, not your wife."

"I know, but only mothers take pity on a starving man." He watched her pluck eggs and bacon out of the refrigerator. "Especially when the starving person is their favorite son."

"You're my only son," she reminded him, then added casually, "Susie told me she wouldn't mind having Nikki for a sister."

Travis choked on his coffee and began coughing, until Maude administered a firm slap between the shoulder blades.

"Damn!" he gasped. "Kill me, why don't you!"

"This is purely Susie's idea."

He picked up a napkin and wiped his mouth. "And not a new one, either. As for the lady in question, I'd say she has a few secrets. No one like her chooses to settle in Dunson. She's much too intelligent to work at a low-paying job, unless she prefers to keep a low profile. Besides, I'm perfectly happy playing the role of a swinging bachelor."

Maude raised an imperious eyebrow. "Swinging bachelor? I can't remember the last time you went out on a date, not to mention indulging in an affair."

Travis looked wild-eyed at the latter suggestion. "Mom, you're supposed to protect your darling boy from such things. Besides, I told you Lee Davis isn't my type, and you agreed." For a brief moment the image of her glowing in the gold dress flashed before his eyes. He caught his mother's suspicious gaze and relented. "Okay, she might be my type, but I don't think she's in the market for a new husband. And I'm no expert on women's clothing, but that dress didn't look like something off a discount rack. She's a woman of many contradictions."

"The belt was real lizard skin, which is not cheap, and you're right about the dress. Now she could have bought it at one of those stores that feature designer clothing at a reduced price, but for some reason I don't think so. I've done enough sewing to recognize quality fabric, and that dress was top of the line."

A smile touched his lips. "You sound the way Cal does, when he's dreaming of a major crime wave hitting town and he gets a chance to solve it."

Maude dished bacon and eggs onto a plate and set it on the table.

"Speaking as a woman who notices things, I'd still say she's running from something," she pronounced, pouring a cup of coffee for herself.

"And being a nosy old broad, you'd love to know her so-called secret."

"Don't call me old." She looked at him with what he laughingly called her Queen Elizabeth manner.

"Then don't play detective." He waved his fork in her direction. "If the lady turns out to be a new Bonnie Parker, I'll take care of it, okay?"

Maude drew herself up to her full height. "I am not speaking of Lee in the negative sense, Travis. She seems like a very nice person, but not the kind to put down roots in Dunson, as I told you before." Her dark eyes, so much like her son's, were serious. "There's something about her that reminds me of a lost kitten thrown out in the rain. She'll just head on, looking for a dry place."

Travis rose to his feet, carried his dishes to the sink and rinsed them off. On his way out he paused long enough to drop a kiss onto the top of her head.

"You know, Mom, you're a regular old softie," he murmured. "What you'd really like to do is take Lee and Nikki under your wing and protect them from all the imagined horrors in the world. But don't worry, I won't give your secret away." He strode outside.

Maude watched him leave. "Deep down in these old bones I feel their horrors just might be more real than we can imagine. And if so, they won't be ending anytime soon." She looked out the window. "A storm is coming, Travis. And I don't mean just the weather."

TRAVIS SIGHED as he gazed into the occupied cell.

"Dan, when are you going to give up these nights of drunken debauchery?"

The man seated on the cot looked up at Travis with bloodshot eyes.

"Hell, Travis, if it wasn't for my fines, you wouldn't have these luxurious surroundings for your guests," he drawled. "Not to mention you have excellent room service."

Travis shook his head at the man whom he had grown up with and who owned the ranch next to his.

"All this gets you is an evening of brawling, a night in jail and a lousy hangover in the morning. Is it really worth it?"

"Sure."

Travis shook his head again. "You're killing yourself by degrees, old buddy. I don't want to see you in here for a long time." He walked away.

"You say that every month," Dan called after him. "Do me a favor, when you come by next time, think up something new."

Cal was waiting for Travis in his office.

"Marv said Dan dropped the fine off when he first came to town," Cal told him. "He told Marv he thought he'd pay in advance for once, so he'd save time."

Travis raked his fingers through his hair. "All because he fell in love with the wrong woman. Funny, I never thought he'd take the easy way out. Of course, I guess we should be glad he only gets drunk once a month, when he sends out the alimony check." He picked up the report lying on his desk and scanned it quickly. "You feeling all right, Cal?"

He frowned at the sudden question. "Yeah, why?"

Travis lifted an eyebrow. "I didn't see any doughnuts on your desk."

Cal flushed. "Mary Ellen told me if I didn't lose a few pounds she wouldn't see me anymore. She said it was for my own good. And all because she started reading those fitness magazines. Hell, Travis, I'm no Arnold Schwarzenegger and I don't want to be."

No matter how much he tried to visualize it, Travis couldn't see Cal as another Conan, either.

"She just wants you healthy, that's all." Travis smiled at the younger man. He knew a lot of law officers wouldn't want Cal as their deputy. But he knew for a fact that Cal was methodical with the paperwork and was excellent when dealing with children. Cal was also one of the finest trackers Travis had ever known, and he couldn't imagine having anyone else by his side during a crisis.

"Let him stew in there a couple more hours before you let him out," Travis told him. "Also tell him the fine will be stiffer next time, and his incarceration will be extended for an additional twenty-four hours every time he's arrested for drunk and disorderly conduct."

"I'll tell him," Cal replied.

After that Travis spent the morning visiting the local businesses, a practice he had begun when he first took over the position of sheriff. At each store he asked about any security problems they might be having.

"If I could get the kids to buy the magazines instead of standing around and reading them, I'd be a happier man," Lonnie Stevens, pharmacist and owner of the town's only drugstore, declared. A man in his seventies, he had a smile for everyone and was known to open his store in the middle of the night for an emergency.

"Well, Lonnie, I'm afraid that other than setting the magazines behind the counter, you don't have much chance," Travis told him. "After all, I used to be one of those kids you yelled at."

The older man chortled. "You never read them, you only looked at the centerfolds."

Travis shrugged. "Yeah, I was into art then." He finished the cup of coffee the druggist had poured him a few minutes before.

"How's Susie doing? Maude hasn't been in for any more earache medication, so I figured she was over it." Lonnie slipped his hands into the pockets of the white smock he wore.

"So far, so good." Travis put his notebook into his jacket pocket. "At least she isn't getting us up at 2:00 a.m. I'm grateful for that."

"Say, I heard you've been hanging around Lorna's new waitress," the older man said slyly. "That you even were together at the school's open house."

Travis rolled his eyes. "Her daughter is good friends with Susie. As for me, between Susie and my mother I have more than enough female influence in my life."

"It's not the same, boy. After all, your mother's influence didn't stop you from looking at those centerfolds, did it?"

He grinned. "Mom's favorite saying was 'Always look and don't touch.' So I looked a lot."

Chapter Four

"Mrs. Davis, I'm afraid Nikki had an accident on the playground and injured her arm. Now, please don't worry, nothing was broken, but we did want the doctor to look her over." The principal's voice was sincerely apologetic. "Our nurse took her to the clinic, where she's being treated."

From the moment Lee heard those words, panic overtook all other feeling. A hurried drive to the small medical clinic assured her there was no serious injury, although Nikki would have to be kept in bed for a few days. She called Lorna to explain the problem, and the older woman gave her the time off. She drove Nikki home and settled her in, staying with her until she fell asleep. Then Lee wandered into the kitchen with the intention of making herself a snack, and finally settled on a glass of milk and a couple of graham crackers. How long she sat there, thinking of everything that could have happened to Nikki, she had no idea.

"Mom?"

Lee looked up to see her daughter standing in the doorway, staring at the box of graham crackers with a hungry look.

"I suppose you want peanut butter on your graham crackers?" she asked with a smile.

Nikki nodded as she walked over to the table and hoisted herself onto the chair. Her eyes were slightly puffy from crying and from the pain medication she had been given earlier.

"I didn't get any lunch." Her lower lip pushed out a bit.

"How does your arm feel?" Lee spread the chunky peanut butter on two graham crackers.

She wrinkled her nose. "It hurts. I wish I could have had a cast. Then everyone could have signed it. When Kirk broke his leg, all the kids got to sign his cast, and Mrs. Spenser drew a picture of a horse on it.''

Lee smiled wryly, relieved there hadn't been a cast.

"I don't suppose you'll be all that unhappy that you'll have to stay home for a couple of days,'' she told her daughter.

Nikki's eyes lighted up. "That means I get out of my math test.''

"I'm sure your teacher will give you a makeup test.'' She smiled at her daughter's downcast expression. "And of course, just because you have to stay at home, it doesn't mean you can't keep up with your homework and studying.''

"Oh, Mom!''

"Oh, Mom!'' Lee mimicked her wail, as she poured a glass of milk and set it in front of her. She looked up when the doorbell rang. "I wonder who that can be,'' she muttered, wiping her hands on the front of her jeans as she walked to the front door.

"Hi,'' Travis greeted her, standing behind Susie, who held a large stuffed animal in her arms. "I hope you don't mind that we stopped by to see how Nikki was doing.''

"Oh, no.'' Lee stood back. "In fact she just woke up.'' She led them back to the kitchen, where Nikki was still munching on her crackers, her bare feet swinging back and forth. "Honey, you have visitors.''

"Susie!'' Her face broke into a broad smile when she saw her friend—the smile dimmed when she saw who stood behind her.

"Nikki, what do you say?'' Lee prompted.

"Hello, Mr. Hunter,'' she muttered in a low voice.

"Nikki.'' He smiled warmly as if nothing had happened.

"This is for you.'' Susie held out the large toy pelican with a fish in its mouth. "I hope you feel better soon.'' She appeared to be reciting a rehearsed speech.

Nikki squealed with delight and hugged the toy against her chest. "Mom, can we go in my room?'' she appealed, staring at Travis with wary eyes.

Lee nodded. "Just be careful with your arm. And put some slippers on your feet.'' After the girls ran out of the kitchen, she turned to Travis. "Ah, won't you sit down?'' She gestured to the table. "I'm afraid we're not exactly equipped for company. Would you like some coffee or milk?'' She flashed a weak smile.

Travis's smile was a great deal brighter, in an attempt to put her at ease. "No, thanks. I've had so much coffee today that I'm practically walking on the ceiling, and I gave up milk on my tenth birthday, when I informed my mother I was old enough to drink something a bit stronger.''

"What did she say?" she asked curiously, already drawn into the story.

He chuckled. "She handed me a cup of coffee that was so strong it could suck the fillings out of your teeth. I immediately switched to juice. My fledgling male ego wouldn't allow me to go back to milk."

Lee sat at the table, clasping her hands in her lap. "It's—ah—it's very nice of you to bring Susie over here and to bring Nikki a gift."

He took off his hat and set it on the adjoining chair before sitting down. "No problem. Susie was pretty worried about Nikki getting hurt and wanted to see for herself that she was all right." He eyed her critically. "Although you look a little the worse for wear."

Lee shrugged. "Receiving a call from the school that your daughter has injured herself from a fall on the jungle gym can turn any red-blooded mother's bones to jelly. I'm feeling a lot more stable now."

He nodded. "I remember when Susie decided to take a dive off the top of the slide about two years ago. I probably aged fifteen years before the doctor said she was all right."

Lee smiled, this time more warmly than ever before. "You're a very caring father," she said softly.

"I'm a father panicking at the idea of his daughter turning into a teenager, who goes out with boys driving fast cars and eventually decides some pimply-faced guy with a squeaky voice is better than her old man," he confessed ruefully. "Crazy, huh?"

She shook her head. "Not really. Fathers aren't the only ones to have those fears. Nikki already prefers devouring old issues of *Glamour* and *Cosmopolitan*, asking what they mean about the rights of women and one-night stands. I feel as if she isn't going to have a real childhood." A strange dark light entered her eyes for just a moment, then disappeared, but not before Travis noticed it. She stared down at the table. "I don't want her to miss out on that," she whispered, then shook herself, returning to the present. "Well, how did we get off the subject so quickly?"

"We didn't. We were just picturing ourselves as grandparents." Travis attempted to keep his voice light.

"Mrs. Davis." Susie stood in the doorway. "Nikki wants to know if she can have some juice."

Lee turned and smiled at the girl. "Would you like to have some, too?"

Susie looked at her father, who gave a slight nod. "Yes."

"Yes, please."

She grinned at her father. "If I'm getting the juice instead of you, how come you're saying please?"

"Smart-mouthed kid," he muttered, not looking angry at all. "You take after your grandmother."

"She says I take after you."

Lee poured juice into two paper cups and handed them to Susie.

"Your mother appears to be a strong-willed person," she commented, returning to the table.

"Substitute 'stubborn as a mule,' and I'll agree with you whole-heartedly," he said. "My dad died when I was eight, and Mom was left with a ranch to run and a wild kid to herd. I'd say she's done great on both counts. I'd say you had a similar problem, although Nikki's a lot tamer than I was."

Lee's face turned a delicate shade of pink. "I haven't done anything special."

"I'd say you've done a heck of a lot more than you give yourself credit for." Travis pushed back his chair and stood up. "Consider it a trained observation from the local law," he joked, turning away to pick up his hat and missing the way her face whitened. He walked out of the room, setting his hat on his head as he spoke again, louder this time. "Come on, Susie. We've got to get going. If we're late for dinner, your grandmother will nail both our hides to the barn door."

"It was very nice of you to stop by," Lee said politely, following him to the door.

"No problem," he assured her with a smile, glancing to the side when Susie ran out, with Nikki following at a slower pace.

"Mom, could Susie spend the night sometime?" Nikki begged, sidling up to Lee and hanging on to her waist. "Please?"

Lee looked helplessly from the two expectant children to Travis, who was grinning. "Nikki, it isn't polite to ask like that," she scolded. "You're putting Sheriff Hunter on the spot, just as badly as you're putting me."

"Why don't we adults discuss it sometime when the two pair of big ears aren't around?" he suggested, ruffling his daughter's hair with his large hand.

"Thank you for my pelican, Susie," Nikki said after a subtle prodding from Lee.

Her friend beamed. "You're welcome. I hope you get to come

back to school soon. I'll call you tomorrow and tell you what happened.''

After the front door closed, Nikki hung tightly on to her mother's waist with her good arm. "Mommy," she mumbled. "I like having a friend."

"I know you do, honey." Lee hugged her back. "Now, why don't you sit on the couch with a blanket and pillow and watch TV, while I fix us some dinner?"

She brightened instantly. "Yeah! I'll bring Elmer with me."

"Elmer?"

"My pelican. We decided he looked like an Elmer." With that, Nikki ran toward her bedroom.

"Don't run!" Lee warned. "I don't want you to bang your arm against anything so I have to take you back to the clinic." She laughed softly and shook her head. "I should know well enough by now not to bother, because she'll do exactly what she wants."

"DAD, NIKKI'S LIKE ME, isn't she?" Susie suddenly declared during the drive to the ranch.

Travis glanced at her, puzzled by her question. "If you're asking if she's a girl, yes, she certainly is."

She put on a long-suffering look. "No, what I mean is, she doesn't have a dad while I don't have a mom, so she's a half orphan, too."

He wondered where her line of thought was taking her. "Yes, I guess so."

Susie nibbled on the tip of one finger. "She doesn't even have a picture of her dad, like I have one of Mom in my room. I asked her if she remembered him, and she looked kinda scared."

Travis shrugged, used to his daughter delving into subjects others might prefer to leave alone. "She might not remember him and that bothers her. Perhaps that's a subject better left unspoken," he advised.

"She doesn't have very many toys, because they move around a lot," Susie went on. "And Nikki is afraid of making friends, because she never knows when they'll move again. That's why she wasn't very friendly with me when she started school."

He sighed. "Susan Elizabeth Hunter, we have to discuss your nosy manner."

"Grandma says you never learn anything unless you ask," she protested.

"There's a difference in asking polite questions and asking im-

polite ones. We'll discuss the difference tonight right after dinner.''
He turned off the main road onto the paved one leading to the ranch.

"After dinner? What about TV?"

"Trust me, it will still be there tomorrow night. Tonight, we're going to do something entirely different. We're going to talk."

"HOW'S YOUR LITTLE girl doing?" Lorna asked, watching Lee wipe off one of the tables that had just been vacated.

She smiled. "At least she's back in school now, and I'm grateful for that. She enjoyed lying around watching TV for the first day, and after that she found the enforced inactivity boring and was more than ready to return to school today. Susie Hunter promised to look after her and make sure she didn't try anything too difficult."

Lorna chuckled. "That Susie is something. She's just like her mother, always willing to help out someone."

Lee drew the damp rag over the table again, although it was already clean. "What was her mother like?" She deliberately kept her voice casual.

The older woman looked at her for a moment, but only saw a bowed head. "Julie was one of the kindest and warmest people around. She always said that she had so much that she just had to share it with others. Travis used to tease her, saying if a needy person wanted the ranch, she would have given it to them. That girl had a heart of gold and there wasn't a mean bone in her body. Why, she didn't even like to gossip. Said all it did was hurt others. It near killed Travis when she died."

"How did she die?" Her question was a low-voiced murmur.

Lorna sighed. "One of those senseless car accidents. She'd driven into Helena to do some shopping, and some kid who was high on drugs ran into her. Wouldn't you know he didn't have a scratch on him? Such a shame someone so full of life had to go so young." She shook her head, recalling the tragedy that had struck the tiny town. "How did your husband die?"

Lee's eyes were unseeing. "An accident," she whispered, still pushing the rag over the table, as if she were trying to rub the surface free of some unseen stain.

"Too much of that happening nowadays," Lorna commented, taking several blueberry pies out of the oven. "It's a shame the good people have to go so young, isn't it?"

"It's not only the good," Lee murmured under her breath, straightening up from her task. She kept her face averted from Lorna, fearing her tortured thoughts might be mirrored in her eyes. She looked up, relieved, when a customer entered the restaurant, calling out a greeting to the other diners and seating himself at the counter.

"Hi, darlin'," he drawled, flashing a gap-toothed grin at Lee. "Give me a steak that's still mooin', a bunch of hard-fried eggs and plenty of coffee."

"You got it." She smiled in return, happy that life was now back to normal.

"Look, Wilma, no matter how mad you get at Zeke, you just can't go after him with a shotgun," Travis said, feeling all his patience leave his body as he faced the stern-looking woman.

She crossed her arms in front of her, her stiff demeanor indicating she would do as she pleased. "Travis, I have known you since you were toddling around in a droopy diaper," she stated in her no-nonsense fashion. "If you think just because you're wearing that tin badge you can dictate to me, you've got another think coming. I just want Zeke to know he can't continue cattin' around at his age. And if he keeps on tryin', he's just going to miss some important parts of his anatomy."

Travis smothered his groan of frustration. "Wilma, you're talking about doing something illegal. And as an officer of the law I would have to lock you up if you did it. Now why can't you and Zeke just settle this between yourselves in a less forceful manner?"

She pounded the top of the kitchen table with the flat of her hand. "Because that old coot won't listen to anything less forceful! Now why don't you worry about real criminals instead of Zeke's and my little upsets?"

Travis munched on another peanut butter cookie that Wilma had brought out when he stopped by. "Because right now, you and Zeke are the only criminals I have," he explained mildly.

"Pish tosh!" She waved a hand dismissively. "We're no more criminals than you are. This is just called one of those marital disputes."

"We're not talking one of your soap operas here." Travis felt as if he were beating his head against a brick wall. "Wilma, all I'm asking is that you quit chasing Zeke around town waving that gun."

She eyed him slyly. "If I agree to lock the gun up in the cabinet, will you quit harpin' on it?"

He sensed a trap here and knew he would have to choose his words carefully. He reminded himself that they didn't own another gun and felt safe enough to say, "You'll lock the gun away?"

She nodded.

"Then I'll quit harping on it," he promised.

Wilma looked extremely pleased as she bustled around the kitchen, pulling a brown paper bag out of a drawer and filling it with cookies. "Here, you take some of these home. Maude never did learn how to make good peanut butter cookies. Hers were always too crunchy. Proper ones should be chewy with crushed peanuts on top."

Travis accepted the bag and prepared to leave the house, Wilma standing on the front porch.

"I don't want to see that gun out of the cabinet again," he reminded her.

She smiled warmly. "It won't be, Travis. 'Course, I didn't promise that if Zeke goes sniffin' around that woman again, I won't dig out my granddaddy's buffalo-skinnin' knife." She turned away and walked into the house.

Travis's eyes bulged. "Wilma!" He ran back up the steps.

The older woman peeked around the screen door. "Just funnin', Travis," she assured him, her faded eyes twinkling. "I swear, your face turns a strange shade of purple when you get upset. You should watch that. It might have something to do with your blood pressure. That's not something to fool around with."

"If I have problems with my blood pressure, it's because of you and Zeke making me crazy," he muttered, unsure whether to put his fist through the wall or heave a sigh of relief. In the end he thought about the bottle of whiskey he kept in the bottom drawer of his desk for emergencies. Right about now, that idea sounded a great deal more palatable. He walked down the cracked and broken sidewalk, determined to get to the sheriff's station as soon as possible; then he glanced across the street and noticed a familiar small figure loaded down with grocery bags.

"What are you trying to do?" he demanded, walking up to her.

"Augh!" a voice yelped in frightened surprise as its owner bent to keep hold of a bag that was threatening to slip out of her arms. Travis grabbed hold of it.

"Don't you think you've taken on more than you can handle?" he asked.

"I was doing all right." Her face reddened at her lie as another bag tilted badly to one side; Travis grabbed hold of that one also.

"Sure you were," he teased gently. "I can't believe you're doing all this for the exercise."

Lee grimaced. "The car wouldn't start this morning, and the cupboards were bare."

"You should have just done enough shopping to get you by until you had your car looked at," Travis scolded. "Come on, the station isn't very far from here. I'll drive you home."

"Oh, no, I couldn't have you doing that," she protested. "I can handle everything, if you'll just be kind enough to stack those bags on top of these."

He took her arm, not missing her subtle attempt to move away from him. "Kindness is driving you home, so don't argue with the law."

Since Travis had already turned away, he didn't see her eyes widen with fear as she stared at the neatly pressed khaki pants and the shirt bearing the metallic star. For a moment she had forgotten the meaning of his uniform.

"Of course," she murmured, rearranging the other two bags before one of them spilled its contents onto the sidewalk. "The law rules."

Travis looked down, puzzled by her cryptic remark.

"How's Nikki doing?" He shortened his steps to accommodate her slower pace.

A faint smile warmed her face. "Just fine. The swelling has gone down, but she's still following the doctor's orders by being careful," Lee explained.

When they arrived at the station, Travis suggested they go inside first, so he could check on messages before he drove her home.

"I can make it fine from here," Lee protested, a hint of panic in her voice.

"It will only take a minute," he promised, steering her inside.

From the moment Lee stepped inside she began counting in her head. None of it calmed the fear that was racing through her body. Her eyes swept the large room, dissected by a long counter and several desks, and landed on the row of Wanted posters stapled against a wall. A brown-haired woman kindly offered her some coffee, but she could only mutely shake her head.

"Why don't you put those heavy bags down and take a seat?" the woman suggested. "The sheriff shouldn't be long."

Lee gingerly lowered her body to a stiff-backed chair, one of the bags slipping to the floor next to her. She wanted nothing more than to run out of the building. Only the knowledge that Travis would run after her and demand an explanation kept her glued to the uncomfortable chair. She swallowed, but the lump in her throat refused to be dislodged. The longer she sat there, the more nervous she felt.

She was convinced that the walls were slowly closing around her until there would be no escape.

"Ready?"

Lee yelped, her body jerking like a puppet. She looked up, her dark eyes huge in her face.

Travis hunkered down next to her, one of his large hands covering her fingers. He was stunned to find them ice-cold to the touch. "Hey, are you okay?"

She nodded mutely. "I—I guess I was off somewhere and didn't hear you coming. I was startled, that's all."

His brow furrowed with concern. He sensed it was much more than that, but knew this wasn't the time to pursue it.

"Okay," he said finally, straightening up. "Let's get you home." He led her outside to the parking lot, where his Cherokee was parked. Within minutes her shopping bags were set in the rear and Lee was ensconced in the passenger seat.

Once Travis was sitting behind the wheel he took a long and hard look at the tiny woman huddled next to him. The jacket she wore looked more suited to cool late-summer evenings than the chilly days that heralded spring in this part of the country.

"You should have worn something warmer," he chided, switching on the engine. "You could have easily turned into an icicle by the time you made it home."

"It isn't that cold," Lee argued.

"Maybe the air isn't, but the wind chill factor can get you every time." Travis turned on the heater and adjusted the vents until they blew directly onto her. "All right?"

"I was all right before."

He smiled. "You're a stubborn little thing."

Her eyes flashed danger signals. "Don't make me sound like somebody's puppy or kitten."

Travis continued grinning, enjoying her show of defiance, pleased that her previous wariness had disappeared.

"Okay, I get the hint. No more teasing you about your height."

All the same, Lee was relieved the moment they reached her house. She informed him she could handle the bags, but he made a point of carrying them into the kitchen and setting them on the counter.

"You should be flattered. I don't do this for just anyone," he told her. "Even my mother doesn't get this kind of special treatment."

"I don't want to take you away from your work," she persisted, standing by helplessly as he deftly emptied the contents of each bag onto the counter. She stood to one side, her hands clenched tightly at her sides. "Please, I can do that."

Travis stopped, hearing something akin to alarm in her voice. He turned around, looking at her stiff posture.

"You're right, I do have some things to do," he said quietly, pushing himself away from the counter.

Lee followed him to the door a bit too quickly. "Thank you for your help," she intoned.

Travis opened the door and turned his head. "If you need anything, give a call, okay? As for your car, Jim Scott's a good mechanic, and his prices are more than fair."

Lee nodded. "I will." *Please, just leave,* she whispered in her head.

She stood in the open doorway, watching Travis walk to his truck and drive away with a casual wave of his hand. The minute he was out of sight, she made a dash to the bathroom, where she was violently ill.

Chapter Five

"Mary Ellen can't break up with me! We've been going together since the third grade," Cal moaned, collapsing into his chair, which uttered a squeaky groan of protest.

Travis traded looks with Myrna, the office clerk. They'd been through this before, and were certain it wouldn't be the last time.

"You mean the two of you have gone together and broken up on a regular basis since the third grade," he corrected.

"I wouldn't worry, Cal," Myrna consoled the younger man. "You two will be back together in no time."

He shook his head, looking like a mournful sheepdog. "She's met someone new. Well, not new. Brad Jackson came back to see his folks, and they ran into each other at the drugstore and he asked her out."

"Brad Jackson, the heartthrob of the class of '78?" Myrna asked. "My, my, he is a hunk, isn't he?"

Cal now looked like a wounded puppy.

"Cal, it isn't as if the two of you have a commitment," Travis said carefully. In all the times his deputy had gone through separations from the girl he loved, he had never looked this pitiful.

"But it was always understood," Cal argued.

"Honey, nothing is understood unless it's put down in writing or said out loud," Myrna pointed out, putting an arm around his shoulders. "Now you just go out and find someone else who will appreciate you, instead of keeping you on a string the way Mary Ellen does. She doesn't deserve someone as good as you. There's plenty of girls out there who would jump at the chance of going out with you."

He looked up, his hazel eyes showing hope. "You think so?"

"I know so. Now buck up. Show Mary Ellen that she doesn't mean that—" she snapped her fingers "—to you."

He sat up and straightened his shoulders. "You're right." He stood up and adjusted his belt over his bulging belly. "I'll take the morning patrol, boss." He walked out of the station, looking like a new man.

"Talk about a transformation. I'm impressed." Travis saluted Myrna.

"After raising three sons who went through problems with girls from day one, I can handle this kind of thing in my sleep," she replied, stacking the reports that needed to be typed. "That Mrs. Davis is a mousy bit of a thing, isn't she?"

Travis cocked his head to one side, surprised by the abrupt change of subject. "I wouldn't exactly call her mousy," he mused, recalling the swift flash of temper she had displayed toward him.

"Well, she's got a pretty enough face, but she doesn't do anything to set it off," Myrna went on. "You'd think she didn't want anyone to notice her."

"Maybe she doesn't." Travis wondered where the conversation was leading and feared he knew. "She likes to keep to herself."

"She shouldn't," Myrna pronounced stoutly. "She has a child to look after and needs a man around to help."

He leaned across the counter and tapped the tip of her nose with his pencil. "Sorry, Myrna, this is the eighties, where a woman doesn't need a man to survive."

"Maybe so, but she needs someone to look after her, no matter what manner she puts on for the public. Your mother would agree with me on that."

"Since she never thought of remarrying all these years, she might not," he said lightly.

Myrna was undaunted. "Still, she'll agree some women need a good man." She eyed him keenly.

Travis groaned, now seeing where the conversation was leading. "Oh, no, leave me out of this." He held up his hands in protest. "Just because a single woman comes to town doesn't mean that we'll end up as the ideal couple. I'm perfectly happy as I am."

Myrna fixed him with the snapping dark eyes that saw more than most people did. "Then why did you drive her home that day?"

"Her car was on the fritz, and she had more groceries than any one person should have to handle!"

"Then I'm surprised you haven't followed her the last two times to the store to drive her home." Myrna smiled smugly.

His brows drew together. "What do you mean, the last two times?

She didn't say all that much about her car, but I doubt the problem could have been that extensive for her to be without it all this time."

Myrna raised her eyes heavenward. "Did you ever stop to think that she might not have been able to afford the repairs? Travis, Lorna pays decent wages, but that doesn't mean they cover unexpected car repairs. I've seen that girl walking home from the store twice more since the day you drove her home. I stopped and offered her a lift, and she refused both times, polite as you please."

Travis let out a rough gust of air. "I should blast you and my mother for your snoopy natures, but after all this time I don't think it would do any good."

"We've always helped out others in this town. I don't think this is the time to stop that practice." Having said her piece, Myrna returned to her work.

"And they wonder why I won't remarry," he muttered, hiding in his office.

"MOM, ARE YOU awake?" Nikki's loud whisper penetrated the gray fog surrounding Lee.

She opened one eye, seeing her daughter's face close to hers. "I am now." She turned her head and stared at the clock on the small table next to her bed. "May I ask why you are waking me up at six-thirty on a Saturday morning, when I can sleep late?"

"Someone is trying to steal our car," Nikki explained, pulling at her mother's covers.

Lee laughed. "Honey, it doesn't run, so if they want to steal it, they're more than welcome to it." Then she realized exactly what Nikki was saying and that the car, even immobile, represented a modest level of security. She pushed aside the covers and shrugged on her robe.

"I used a chair and turned on the heat before I came in here," Nikki informed her with the pride of a seven-year-old.

Lee checked the thermostat and quickly adjusted it from 85° to 68°. She curled her toes against the cold floor, and decided to return to her bedroom for her slippers before confronting the car thief.

"Honey, you're not just saying this to get me up, are you?" she asked her daughter. "You did see someone around our car?"

She nodded. "A man. A tall one. He's looking into the car's insides, so I couldn't see his face."

Lee's mouth turned dry. Could someone have found her? Fearing the worst, she hurried into the living room, her slippers now forgotten, and peered out between the drawn curtains. All she could see was a denim-covered rear end. Faint sounds of metal striking metal could be heard. Taking her courage in both hands, she opened the front door and ran outside.

"What is going on here?" she cried out, stopping at the front of the car. "What are you doing?"

The body straightened up and dark brown eyes peered down at her shocked features.

"Just making sure everything is all right," Travis replied, looking unperturbed, as if he made it a practice to study her car's engine. "Hi, Nikki. Sorry I didn't bring Susie with me, but knowing her lazy weekend habits, she's still in bed." He looked down at Lee's feet. "You should get something warm on your feet. Your toes are beginning to turn a becoming shade of blue."

Lee blushed, realizing she was standing in the middle of her driveway, wearing nothing more than a robe. And knowing how nosy some of her neighbors were, they were already probably wondering what was going on between the town's newest inhabitant and the sheriff at such an early hour. "You still haven't told me what you're doing here."

Travis straightened up, wiping his hands on a greasy rag. "That's easy. I'm here because your car is out of commission, and you can't make a practice of walking to the grocery store in this cold weather. They may call this spring, but that doesn't mean we're having warm weather yet."

Lee felt her life going out of control with this man. "I'll take it to the mechanic on Monday, I promise," she said desperately.

He nodded, his expression grave. "Lee, do you have any idea what's wrong with it?"

She shook her head.

"For one thing, your battery is shot. That's why it won't start. And your brakes are nonexistent," he added.

Lee blanched. While she knew little about a car's inner workings, she knew what Travis spoke of amounted to very expensive repairs. Repairs she couldn't afford, unless she sold the last of her jewelry; pieces she had kept for an extreme emergency. Yet this was an emergency.

Travis hid the sympathy he felt, because he knew that was the last thing Lee wanted. He knew he had already taken a chance by looking at her car without her permission, but he had an idea that was the only way someone as prickly as she was would accept any kind of help.

"Thank you for the diagnosis," she said stiffly. "I'll be sure to tell the mechanic what you said."

He stood up, shaking his head. "Lee, your nose is growing longer with every word you say," he said gently. "You don't have the money for the repairs, do you?"

She stood up as tall as she could, looking regal even in a robe with her nose and lips turning as blue as her toes. "You have no need to worry about me, Sheriff. I've taken care of myself for many years and survived. I'm sure I can handle this problem."

Travis made the mistake of grinning broadly. "You sure have a passel of pride for someone so small."

Lee breathed deeply, unable to believe one person could goad her so easily. She wrapped her arms around her body and stared down at her bare feet, which were rapidly turning into ice cubes.

"Come on, let's get some coffee." Travis placed a hand on her shoulder.

Shrugging away his touch, she marched back into the house.

"I don't have any coffee made," she informed him haughtily.

"Then would you like me to make the coffee, while you either put on some slippers or warmer clothes?" Without waiting for an answer, he strode into the kitchen. "Nikki, do you mind helping me?"

The little girl looked at her mother with a startled expression. "I have to get dressed," she mumbled, running into her room.

Travis couldn't miss the look on her face, but he merely smiled and shooed Lee out of the room.

"Don't worry. I can find everything myself," he assured her.

Lee escaped to her bedroom and changed into jeans and a sweater in record time. After pulling on two pairs of heavy socks and running a brush through her hair, she returned to the kitchen, inhaling the aroma of perking coffee.

"Just in time," Travis announced, setting out two mugs. He took one of the kitchen chairs, turned it around and sat down, bracing his arms on the back. "Now we can talk."

She was instantly wary. "Talk about what?"

"Your car." Travis watched her pour cereal into a bowl and add a little milk before carrying it and a glass of juice into the living room, where Nikki was watching cartoons. From where he sat, he could see the little girl look up at her mother and seem to be reassured by Lee's smile.

When she returned to the kitchen, she took the chair directly across from his.

"The repairs sound extensive, but they aren't," he went on. "In fact, I've done stuff a lot more complicated than that. All you need to provide is the parts, and I'll provide the labor."

Lee shook her head vehemently. "I can't let you do that."

"I can be just as stubborn as you. If I had an extra car to loan you, until yours could be fixed, I would." He sipped his coffee and found it rich and strong, just the way he liked it. "Lee, out here neighbors help one another in times of trouble. Now I have a hunch that you're not used to our ways, and you're trying to use your pride as an argument. It won't work. Look, let me figure out the parts you need and get them. And if you're trying to come up with another argument, let me remind you about your daughter. What if there was an emergency in the middle of the night? We only have the one ambulance, and if it's already out on a call, you might not have a way to take her to the clinic."

Lee bowed her head, silently admitting defeat. Travis was right about her pride; she didn't want anyone's help. She couldn't allow herself to get close to anyone. But if something did happen to Nikki, and she couldn't get hold of anyone else, she would blame herself for the consequences. She reminded herself that she had no choice but to accept his help. She needed the work done; she couldn't deny that.

"All right," she agreed in a low voice, aware she didn't sound grateful, but had trouble doing so after being bullied in such a subtle manner. Her head snapped up, and she looked him squarely in the eye. "But I will pay for the parts, and I want to repay you for your time."

Travis nodded. He glanced down at his watch. "Fair enough. We don't have a parts store here in town, but the next town over does. I'll head over there when it opens. Until then I'll go back out to my place." He looked at Nikki, who was pushing the bowl and juice glass onto the counter. "Would you like to go back with me and see Susie?"

She spun around. For a brief second, happiness flared in her eyes, only to be instantly dimmed as she realized what his question implied. "No."

"No, thank you," Lee prompted gently.

Nikki hunched her shoulders. "No, thank you," she whispered, slipping away.

Travis looked startled by the little girl's abrupt refusal. "Funny, most kids think I'm a real pushover," he mused, smiling at Lee.

"She's very shy around adults," she explained. "And she hasn't been around men all that much."

Travis thought about the girl running with the other children at the party, and couldn't equate the laughing, happy girl with the fawnlike one in this house.

"Maybe if you came along, she might be more amenable to the suggestion," he recommended.

"I have a lot of work to do around here, and it's actually my only free day."

Travis shot her a dry look. "I can't believe I'm talking to a woman who would prefer to do housework."

"As I said, it's my only real free day," Lee insisted.

"My mother doesn't bite, she just barks a lot," he assured her. "In fact, most people get along with her. Ah, I saw it! A real smile! Not one just on the lips, but one that almost reached the eyes." He looked triumphant, as if he had just been awarded a medal.

Lee shook her head in exasperation. "You don't give up, do you?"

He shrugged. "I'm as stubborn as they come." He finished his coffee, stood up and walked over to the counter. After rinsing out the cup, he placed it in the sink and grabbed his hat on the way out.

"Since Nikki doesn't want to come with me, I'll head on out now. I'll be back later with the parts."

Lee hurried after him. She had worked so hard to put her life back into order, yet she felt helpless next to this human roller coaster.

"Wait!" She grasped the doorknob, watching him stride down the walkway.

"Too late, Lee," he called over his shoulder with a wave of the hand. "Since the day is so cold, you wouldn't mind making me a hot lunch, would you?"

She stood by the half-open door, Nikki peering around her as the Jeep took off.

"The man doesn't listen," Lee murmured, closing the door, shivering at the lingering cold air.

"He's big," Nikki whispered, clutching the hem of Lee's sweater. "Mom, he's not coming back, is he?"

"I'm afraid so, baby." She wrapped a hand around her daughter's cheek, feeling her shiver under her touch and knowing the action had nothing to do with the cold. She crouched, framing her face with both hands. "Nikki, Sheriff Hunter is not a bad man," she assured her. "He wants to help us, okay? He won't hurt you."

Her lips barely moved. "He's still big and dark."

Lee sighed. So many times she had wished she could break through

Nikki's self-imposed reserve, but that had always proved fruitless. In the end, Lee had decided to allow nature to take its course.

"Why don't you get dressed? If you'd like, I could call Susie's grandmother and ask if she could come back here to play," Lee offered. "Would you like that?"

Nikki's eyes lighted up. "She can stay all afternoon?"

She nodded. "If it's all right with her grandmother and her father."

The child chewed her lower lip. "Do you think her dad will let her come?"

Lee nodded again. "I have an idea he won't mind at all."

Nikki smiled and ran off to her room, promising to dress in record time.

Lee straightened up, feeling very old. She remembered the many times her little girl had wanted to have a friend from her preschool over—and the many times Lloyd had loudly rejected it, saying he had enough noise at work. In the end, Nikki had played alone in her room or quietly in the backyard. That was why, no matter how much Lee feared getting close to people, she knew she would do anything for her daughter's happiness.

"Having the sheriff around is playing with fire," she scolded herself. "You never do anything by halves, do you?"

"YOU DON'T have enough work around here that you have to go looking for some?" Maude demanded, as Travis explained his day's activities to her.

"What was I supposed to do? Let her go without transportation?" He poured himself a cup of coffee and helped himself to several pieces of bacon that lay on a paper towel on the counter. "Could I have a couple eggs?"

She braced her hands on her hips. "You're not answering my question."

"You're right."

"What happened to the polite child I raised?" She sighed theatrically.

"I grew up to be just like my dear old mom." Travis kissed her on the cheek, dancing away when she swatted at him like a pesky fly.

"Flattery will not get you breakfast," she informed him tartly as she opened the refrigerator door and withdrew several eggs.

"Her car has broken down, and she doesn't have the money to

pay a mechanic to fix it,'' Travis explained, sipping the scalding brew. "Simple as that."

Maude looked at him sharply. "Is it? Travis, you were never a Boy Scout, and working on a car always leaves you frustrated. Something tells me you aren't doing it just to impress her. So give me a good reason why you are helping her out." She cracked each egg, dropping them into the skillet.

He thought it over. "Because she reminds me of a little lost kitten who's never had anyone look out for her."

Maude fixed him with a look of disbelief. "You hate cats."

"Correction, I'm allergic to cats."

Deftly she flipped the eggs over and used the spatula to place them on a plate, along with three slices of buttered toast. "Call it a mother butting in where she's not wanted, but I'm going to say my piece, anyway."

"What else is new?" he muttered, smiling.

Maude tapped him on the head. "Travis, she doesn't belong to this town. She's basically a drifter. One day she'll suddenly pick up and leave. I won't see you hurt."

He sighed wearily. "Mom, I don't intend to marry the woman. I'm going to just fix her car. As a civil servant I'm supposed to help out the residents. That's all I'm doing," he informed her. "By the way, is Susie up yet? I thought she might like to go back with me and play with Nikki. Just call it another good deed on my part." He smiled winningly.

Maude looked at him, unconvinced. She knew that Travis believed what he was saying, and if she didn't know her son as well as she did, she wouldn't have bothered speaking her mind, even though she knew he would refuse to listen to her.

"Maybe that's all you think you're doing, but you're going to be in for a big surprise before you know it."

Chapter Six

Lee threw herself into her housework with fervor, but that didn't stop her from peeking out through the curtains every so often to watch Travis leaning over the fender of her car and hear the sound of metal striking metal punctuated with muttered curses. Taking her courage in hand, she filled a mug with coffee and walked outside.

"Would this help?" she asked shyly, standing to one side.

He looked up. "Is there any whiskey in it?"

She shook her head.

"Don't take it away. Anything good and hot is more than welcome." He wiped his hands on a rag before accepting the mug and drinking deeply.

"You don't like to work on cars, do you?" Lee asked, holding out her hand for the mug when he finished.

"Nope," Travis said cheerfully.

"Yet you're working on mine."

"Yep." He picked up a wrench and surveyed the size.

"Why?"

He shrugged. "Because your car needs fixing, and while I'm not an expert, I can put a battery in where it belongs and hook it up correctly."

Lee still couldn't comprehend someone doing a favor without expecting some type of payment. Her father and Lloyd had drummed that philosophy into her head long ago.

"You are a very kind man, Travis Hunter," she whispered, hurrying back into the house before she said too much and caused questions she couldn't answer.

Lee checked on the two girls, who were playing together in Nikki's room, planning an elaborate wedding for their Barbie and Ken dolls.

"Your dress is so pretty," Susie cooed, fingering the white gown Lee had slaved over one year for Nikki's Christmas gift.

"Mom made it," Nikki said proudly. "She made all the clothes." She looked up, beaming at her mother.

"And when I finished the last outfit, I vowed to never do it again," she replied dryly. "How do you two feel about some lunch?"

"Could we eat it in here?" Nikki pleaded. "We'll be real careful, I promise."

"All right. In fact, we'll set it up like a picnic," she suggested. "Who wants to help me fix the sandwiches?"

"Me!" the girls said in unison.

Lee's task took longer with two seven-year-olds helping, but she wouldn't have traded their assistance for all the experienced cooks in the world. She soon had them settled on a blanket that she placed on the bedroom floor, lunching on peanut butter and jelly sandwiches and milk, with the promise of angel food cake for dessert.

"Where are the girls?" Travis asked, when Lee called him in for his lunch.

"Having a picnic." She dished a hearty beef noodle soup into a large bowl and set it on the table.

He looked at her, then out the window, where rain clouds threatened ominously. "You're kidding."

Lee shook her head. "They have everything they need for the picnic except ants, and for all I know, they're pretending they have those. They're in Nikki's bedroom, pretending it's the Fourth of July."

A smile split his face. "Brave soul."

"They promised to clean up, and I intend to hold them to that." Lee poured him a cup of coffee.

Travis sat down at the table and watched her bustle nervously around the room. "Will you give us both a break and sit down?" His lips twisted when she perched on the edge of a chair. "Aren't you eating anything?"

"Not right now." Not when her stomach was rolling a mile a minute. Nikki was right; he was tall and dark and his strength was frightening. Yet he had never raised his voice to either of them or to his own daughter, so why couldn't she feel more comfortable around him?

Travis took a tentative sip of the hot soup. "This is very good."

Lee shrugged. "Part can, part spices. I'm afraid I have a habit of throwing spices and herbs into everything, whether it needs it or not."

"My mother does the same thing," he replied, picking up a warm muffin and slathering margarine onto it. "She doesn't feel anyone can spice up food the way she can, and she doesn't care who knows it. Did you learn about cooking from your mother?"

Her lashes swept downward, hiding the expression in her eyes. "No, I read a lot of cookbooks." She jumped up, hurriedly refilling his cup.

Travis watched her nervous movements, once again wondering why she acted so warily around him. He tried to tell himself it might be men in general. After all, she was a widow; he doubted that she dated very much. At least, that was what his intuition told him.

"I wish you would eat something," he urged. "I bet you've been on the go since you got up this morning, and probably didn't eat any breakfast, did you?"

Her reply was an undignified rumble in the depths of her stomach. She blushed. "I usually only drink coffee in the mornings."

"Not a very good example, when you're trying to tell your kid she should eat something from the four basic food groups."

"Nikki's idea of the four basic groups is anything chocolate, Cheetos, blueberry pie and root beer."

Travis made a face. "Talk about a royal upset stomach. Sounds like Susie's favorites. That's probably why they get along so well."

Lee jumped when the phone rang. She reached for the receiver and lifted it gingerly. "Hello?"

"Lee? This is Maude Hunter. Is my son still there?"

"Yes, he is. I'll get him for you."

"No, it's you I want to talk to." She chuckled. "Actually, I called to see if you would like to come to dinner tomorrow."

Lee felt tongue-tied. "Well—"

"No refusals, now," Maude went on. "We usually eat around two. If you'd like to come over earlier, that's fine also. We get home from church between twelve-thirty and one."

Lee gripped the receiver, staring at Travis with pleading eyes. He got up and took the phone out of her hands.

"Mom?" He rolled his eyes as he listened to her rambling. "Yes, I'm almost finished here. Yes, I'll pass on the message. Yes, you are overdoing it." He hung up and turned to Lee. "Trust me, you're better off accepting the dinner invitation. When my mother gets something into her head, she keeps on until she gets her way."

"You don't understand," she said, feeling more helpless than she had in a long time.

"Then why don't you tell me?" he suggested gently.

Lee snapped her mouth shut, afraid she'd say too much. "It's just that Nikki and I don't make friends easily."

"Are we going away again?" Nikki stood in the doorway, looking appalled at the idea. Susie stood behind her, looking just as upset. "Mom, you promised we could stay here. You said everything would be all right. I have a friend now!" She spun around and ran off.

"Susie, go with her," Travis said quietly, noticing Lee's white features. "Look, I'm almost done outside. I'll finish in record time and get out of your hair. And don't worry about tomorrow. I'll get you off the hook." He walked out the back door.

Lee collapsed into a chair, feeling as if her world could soon collapse around her.

"If I hadn't gone over there that night," she muttered. "If I had only fought back more when it counted. If only..." She blew out a gust of air and straightened. She grabbed the phone book, found the number she was looking for and dialed, before she lost her courage. "Mrs. Hunter? This is Lee Davis. Yes, tomorrow would be fine," she said swiftly. "Is there anything I can bring? No? All right, we'll be there before two, and thank you for asking us." She hung up and leaned against the counter, feeling as if she had just run the Boston Marathon. She couldn't help but wonder if she hadn't just lost what little sanity she still had left.

"WHY DIDN'T YOU tell me yesterday she was coming, instead of listening to me give you all those plausible excuses as to why she couldn't?" Travis demanded, watching his mother take a roast out of the oven and baste it.

"Because it was infinitely more interesting, listening to you give all those ridiculous reasons," she said serenely, pushing the pan back into the oven. "Now why don't you change out of your suit before you get something on it? I already told Susie to change her clothes and make sure her room was picked up."

"Mom, I am not ten years old," he insisted between clenched teeth.

"Maybe not, but you certainly act it sometimes." Maude brought out a mixing bowl and ingredients for frosting.

He loosened the tie that seemed to be constricting his breathing. "You only asked her over to find out about her."

"Is that so wrong? You seem interested in her, so I would like to know more about her." She measured powdered sugar and poured it into the bowl along with softened margarine and milk. "It's a mother's prerogative."

Travis released the strangling collar button. "I am not interested in the woman. And she's definitely not interested in me, so let it rest, all right?"

"Let me be the judge of that. Now will you please change your clothes?"

"Why should I be interested in a woman?" he grumbled, stalking out of the kitchen. "I have more than enough women around here to boss me around."

"Put on that dark green shirt. It does nice things for your eyes," Maude called out.

ANY MISGIVINGS Lee had about having dinner at the Hunter household were dispelled by Nikki's excitement at the prospect of spending more time with her friend. For once Lee didn't have to order the girl to make her bed or put her dirty clothes into the hamper before they left.

Maude's casual greeting also helped relax Lee as she ushered them inside and suggested Susie take Nikki to her room.

"Can we go out and look at the kittens?" Susie pleaded.

Maude shook her head. "You wouldn't have time to thoroughly clean up before dinner." She turned to Lee. "Travis is allergic to cats, but they keep the barn rodent-free, so he takes medication when he has to work in there. Why don't you come along to the kitchen while I put the finishing touches on dinner? Would you like some coffee or iced tea? I know this weather isn't exactly normal for cold drinks, but sometimes I get so tired of hot drinks just because it's chilly outside."

"Iced tea sounds fine," Lee replied, following her into the large kitchen, which was clearly one of the most used rooms in the house. "I agree with you. One time there was a blizzard outside, and I was inside making lemonade, just because it sounded good."

Before she knew it, she was sitting at the butcher-block table with a glass of iced tea before her and a bowl of beans to be snapped. Maude thought nothing of roping company into helping with dinner preparations.

"How do you like it in Dunson?" Maude asked as she frosted a white cake and sprinkled coconut on top.

"It's very nice, and I'm not saying it for lack of anything else to say."

The older woman nodded. "We like it. Of course, I grew up here and the population wasn't exactly booming then, but with all the surrounding towns and their slow but steady growth, most of us don't mind the solitude. We all pretty much stick together, probably because we're all we have."

"I think you can get used to anything, if you put your mind to it." Lee finished the beans and put the bowl to one side. "Now, what else would you like me to do?"

Maude chuckled. "Since you're such a willing helper, how about rinsing off the salad makings?" She opened the refrigerator door and withdrew the proper ingredients.

"All right." Lee pushed up her sweater sleeves past her elbows and turned on the faucet as she grasped a head of lettuce.

Maude glanced over, then looked again as something caught her attention. Feeling her gaze on her, Lee looked up, then lowered her eyes to the several small round puckered scars that marred the soft skin on the inside of her elbow.

"An odd place for a burn," Maude commented.

"Not if you're a smoker," Lee said, sounding too casual.

"I didn't realize you were a smoker."

"That's why I quit." Lee kept her head down as she rinsed the fresh vegetables.

Maude said nothing, but studied the small scars on Lee's arm a moment longer, before returning to her own task.

Lee quickly finished the vegetables and pushed down her sweater sleeves; without saying a word, she hunted through the drawers until she found a knife and began cutting them up and layering them in a glass bowl with deft efficiency.

"I should have you over more often," Maude complimented her, looking at the colorful salad. "Mine don't come out half as nice."

Lee blushed. "I've always liked working around the kitchen," she said enthusiastically, "but Nikki isn't eager to try anything that doesn't resemble hamburgers, hot dogs or spaghetti."

"That sounds just like Susie. I made teriyaki chicken one night, and my granddaughter acted as if I was trying to poison her," Maude said. "It seems I only get to try out any new recipes on the ladies' club."

Lee's gaze swept over the shelves filled with various cookbooks and was frankly envious.

"Go ahead and browse through them," Maude invited. "I can handle everything from here."

Lee needed no further urging, and ran her finger along the book spines until she came to one that looked interesting. She sat down at the table to leaf through its many pages.

"The way you're devouring that book, I'd say you must have a large collection yourself," Maude commented.

She thought of the library of cookbooks she had been forced to leave behind. "Not anymore," she murmured. "It's difficult to keep track of things when you move around a lot." Lee froze, hoping her slip of the tongue wasn't noticed.

If Maude heard her, she gave no indication. "Then please feel welcome to borrow any of them. I can only use one at a time, and the rest tend to gather dust."

"I'd like that, thank you," Lee said quietly, accepting the silent offer of friendship that she sensed went along with the offer. She laughed softly. "Perhaps I can find something that will tempt Nikki's taste buds."

Maude walked over to one of the shelves and selected a book, handing it to her. "This one should work."

Lee read the title and laughed. "Oh yes, I'm sure *365 Ways to Cook Hamburger* would be entirely to her liking. But I'm also tempted to study one of the county fair cookbooks."

"Oh yes, they are just wonderful. I have friends living around the country I trade books with. They send me theirs, and I send them the one from our fair. I think you'd enjoy this one." Maude handed her another book.

"What's this, you two swapping recipes already?" Travis teased, walking into the kitchen, bringing the crisp outdoors coupled with the earthy scent from the barn with him.

"No, I'm telling her what a horrible child you were. And after dinner I intend to bring out the photo album and show her all your baby pictures," Maude said serenely. "Especially the ones of you reclining on the bearskin rug."

Travis rolled his eyes. "I guess I'd better head for the family room and hide those albums, although why you would want to ruin her dinner with pictures of a bare-bottomed baby, I don't know."

Lee smiled. "I think it would be fascinating to see pictures of the sheriff in a less than professional setting."

"There's no problem there," Maude said with a laugh. "Now, Travis, you go in and get washed up, because dinner will be ready soon. And tell the girls to wash their hands, and to use soap this time."

Lee was grateful that Nikki ate her roast and mashed potatoes without any fuss. She decided that the fact that Susie ate heartily had something to do with it. As she ate, she watched the way grandmother and father listened to the two girls' chatter with amused smiles. No matter how outlandish Nikki's and Susie's comments were, they were never made to feel silly. It was such an enjoyable change from her other life. For one very brief, improbable moment, Lee wondered what it would be like if they were a real family.

The dishes may have been blue- and pink-flowered white stoneware instead of fine china, but it didn't detract from the good taste of the food. Neither did it matter that their napkins were paper instead of linen, nor that the tablecloth, an old, but she felt a treasured one, was on the kitchen table instead of on a formal dining table, in a room furnished with all the trappings of the wealth she had once been smothered by.

Lee knew of another very important difference: the company. She wasn't listening to her husband complain that she hadn't cooked the meat properly. Nor did she hear her father make a negative comment about the vegetables. And her mother wasn't there to look around the room with that narrow-eyed glance of hers, trying to find fault with something or other. Lee had never enjoyed any of those dinners; in fact, she'd usually left the table feeling a terrible burning in her stomach. It wasn't until just before the divorce that she'd discovered she was suffering from an ulcer.

"You look as if you're off in another world," Travis commented, noticing first her smile, then how a bleakness shadowed her eyes.

She shot him an apologetic glance. "I was so busy enjoying this food, I forgot about anything else."

"Then I hope you aren't going to mind if I recruit you to help with the dishes," Maude warned.

"After this meal, the exercise of washing dishes will be appreciated."

"What prompted you to choose Dunson to live in?" Maude asked, flashing a pointed look at the cauliflower on Susie's plate. The girl wrinkled her nose and picked up her fork, beginning on what was obviously her least favorite part of the meal.

For once, Lee decided to tell the complete truth. "Actually, I was only passing through, but the Help Wanted sign in Lorna's restaurant and her agreeing to hire me, then finding the house seemed to be a sign," she replied. "I can't really express it. There was just something about this town that said 'Stay.'"

Maude nodded. "I surely can understand that."

Lee applied herself to the meat, cutting it into tiny pieces. "The people are real here," she murmured.

Travis frowned, sensing more than had been said. But with two children with extremely big ears sitting at the table, he felt he couldn't pursue the subject.

"We get dessert, don't we?" he asked, deciding it was time to change the course of the conversation.

"When you clean your plate." Maude silently directed the girls to carry their dishes to the kitchen counter.

Travis grinned at Lee. "As you can see, my mother doesn't care how old you are. You still have to eat your vegetables if you want dessert."

"You won't be giving this woman any bad habits, if I have any say in it," Maude said tartly.

Nikki's head turned from one adult to the other, her tiny face reflecting her worry at what appeared to her to be the beginning of a quarrel.

"I ate all mine," she said in a quavery voice, gazing up at Maude with wide eyes.

Maude looked down at her and immediately realized the cause of her distress. "You certainly did, pet, and you shall have the first slice of cake," she promised with a broad smile. "In fact, would you like to help me serve it?"

Nikki looked at Lee, who smiled and nodded.

"Yes, please," she whispered, sliding off her chair.

Under Maude's direction, Nikki proudly carried slices of the white cake and portions of chocolate ice cream to each person. She kept a close eye on Travis as she slid his plate in front of him, then scurried off, not hearing his quiet thanks.

When they finished, Maude suggested that the girls watch a Disney videotape and that Travis join them while she and Lee did the dishes.

"I know I'm considered a tyrant," Maude told Lee as they rinsed off plates and loaded the dishwasher. "But I have to be, so no one ever finds out what a softie I really am."

"Meaning you're all bark and no bite."

"Oh, I'd bite if necessary. Especially where my family is concerned." With everything done, she dried her hands and squirted on a dollop of cream, rubbing them briskly. She turned to Lee, her dark eyes piercing as she asked in a matter-of-fact voice, "Why is your daughter so afraid of adults?"

Chapter Seven

Lee's mind raced madly for an answer that wouldn't prompt further questions. She knew she couldn't offer a flip answer because Maude was too astute to be put off.

She spoke slowly, her words chosen very carefully in an artful mixture of truth and lies. "Her grandparents were very stern people," she explained. "They were of the school that believed children must display proper table manners, no matter how young they are, and they were never to speak unless spoken to. And heaven help a child who spilled anything on their clothing or the tablecloth."

Maude looked shocked. "Even as a toddler?"

Lee nodded. "That was the way they believed a child should be raised, whether one of theirs or someone else's."

"What about your views and your husband's? Surely he didn't agree with them?"

She didn't want to tell the older woman that Lloyd had always agreed with her parents.

"My—husband had trouble relating to a little girl. Many men do," she said defensively, inwardly wincing as she recalled the loving and easy relationship Travis enjoyed with his daughter. "I just wanted Nikki to have a normal childhood, but it wasn't always easy to do."

"Some parents are too hard on their children," Maude acknowledged after a moment. "I think the best thing for Nikki is to discover that all adults aren't like that. I want you to know that she's welcome here anytime."

Lee licked her lips, trying to figure out what to say without giving anything away. "That's very kind of you."

She chuckled. "Kindness has nothing to do with it. It's much easier to have two children underfoot than one. Besides, I'm sure there are times you wouldn't mind having an afternoon to yourself.''

Lee smiled. ''I have to admit the idea is tempting, but I couldn't allow you to do that.''

''Of course you can. Besides, if I want an afternoon to myself, I'll just let you take Susie,'' Maude said shamelessly. ''Believe me, there're times she's a real handful. She takes after her father more than her mother.''

''What was her mother like?'' Lee asked curiously, wondering what Maude thought of the woman Travis had married.

The older woman smiled. ''Julie was one of the dearest and kindest women you would ever know. She never had an unkind word for anyone and always had a ready smile.'' Her own smile disappeared. ''Sometimes I think she was too good for this world. It was a shame they never had more children.''

Lee felt a lump in her throat as she listened to the description of what sounded like a perfect marriage. She felt she would never be allowed to experience something that special, and after what she had gone through in the past, wasn't sure she could ever trust a man enough to find out. Yet there was something about Travis that fascinated her.

''I just wish he would find someone before he turns old and cranky,'' Maude went on. ''But I doubt he will.''

''Because of love for his wife?'' Lee probed, then fell silent, realizing she had no right to be so curious.

''More like because he doesn't want to take the time to court a woman,'' Maude rumbled. ''Well, should we see what the trio is up to?''

They entered the den, finding Susie snuggled up next to her father on the couch, while Nikki lay sprawled on the carpet as they watched *Cinderella*. By the time the animated feature was over, both girls' eyes were drooping from fatigue.

''Time for someone to be in bed,'' Lee spoke up, kneeling beside Nikki. ''Come on, honey, time for us to be going home.''

''I'm not tired,'' she protested even as she yawned widely, lifting her arms to her mother.

''You want me to take her?'' Travis offered. ''She's too heavy for you.''

Nikki's eyes flew open. ''I can walk,'' she said swiftly, scrambling to her feet.

''The independence of a seven-year-old,'' Lee told Travis in an effort to soften Nikki's rejection. ''Sometimes she acts like my baby, and other times I wonder if she isn't rapidly approaching her thirtieth birthday. This was a very nice day. Thank you for inviting us.''

Travis walked them out to the car, where Nikki quickly climbed inside. ''And to think you weren't too sure you wanted to come,'' he teased softly.

Lee shrugged. ''People can be wrong, as you delight in pointing out.''

Travis smiled down at her. ''Perhaps next time my mother will be kind enough to allow me to sit in on some of the discussion.''

''Perhaps,'' Maude interjected as she bore down on them, carrying what appeared to be several books. She pressed them into Lee's hands. ''But I sincerely doubt it.''

Lee looked down, discovering several cookbooks. ''Thank you,'' she said softly.

The older woman's normally stern features softened. ''No matter how independent some of us try to be, there might be a time we could use a fairy godmother.''

''YOU'RE GOING to the carnival, aren't you, Lee?'' Jake Hale, one of the neighboring ranchers, asked her as he dug into his apple pie à la mode. ''You sure can't miss one of our biggest social events of the year.'' He grinned. ''Hell, excuse my language, it's our only social event!'' he guffawed.

''The way Nikki has been talking about it, I don't think I'll have any say in the matter,'' she replied, refilling his coffee cup. ''It appears they even close the schools for two days.''

''It's the first big event we have, once spring starts showing its head around here, so we don't like the kids to miss out on it,'' he explained. ''Although I think the adults have more fun than the children.'' He winked at her.

''Hey, Jake, does your wife know you're flirting with beautiful women?'' Travis slid onto the stool next to him.

''She doesn't mind as long as I don't touch,'' Jake replied with a grin. ''How ya doin', Travis?''

''Fair enough.'' He smiled at Lee. ''How about a bowl of Lorna's heartburn chili and a large glass of water to wash it down with?''

''I'll bring the antacid tablets with your meal,'' Lee said pertly, writing out his order and moving away.

''She's sure not the same woman who first came to work here,'' Jake commented when Lee was out of earshot. ''She smiles a lot more and even jokes with us now.''

"She's probably realized it's the only way to survive in this crazy place." Travis watched Lee's slim figure move behind the counter, stopping to inquire if the other customers needed something and taking away dirty dishes or refilling coffee cups. He couldn't keep his eyes off her rear end, encased in snug jeans.

A few moments later Lee set a steaming bowl in front of him. "Lorna said to tell you she added extrastrength chili powder, just for you."

Travis took a cautious bite and gasped, reaching for his glass of water. "No kidding," he wheezed. "Lorna, murdering an officer of the law is a felony," he called out.

"This from the man who's always sworn he has a cast-iron stomach," she responded with a laugh. "Don't worry. Lee can just leave a pitcher of water with you."

When Travis later paid his bill, he held on to his money as he offered it to Lee.

"You going to the dance?"

She stared down at his hands, a funny feeling curling deep in her stomach. "I don't think so. I'm sure by then Nikki will be tired from the carnival, and she isn't old enough to appreciate a dance."

"Then why don't you let her spend the night with Susie and you could come with me?" he suggested matter-of-factly.

Lee's face snapped upward. "Are—" she swallowed "—are you asking me to go to the dance with you?"

He smiled. "I thought I was. Of course, I am out of practice, so I may not have done it right. Should I try again?"

Lee laughed nervously. She felt flattered that he'd asked her. "I haven't danced in a long time," she said, thinking to warn him.

Travis's smile broadened. He was glad she hadn't given him an outright rejection. "Then we'll be perfect together, because I have two left feet," he told her in a low, confiding tone. "We don't even have to stay the entire evening, if you don't want to. Still, I think you'd have a lot of fun. All right?" He looked hopeful.

She nodded, summoning a faint smile. "All right."

"Fine, we can work out the details later. Look at it this way. You sure couldn't be with anyone safer than the town's sheriff."

Lee looked out the plate glass window, watching him stride down the sidewalk.

"You're right, I couldn't be safer," she murmured with a wry smile on her lips.

"MOM, LOOK!" Nikki's head swiveled first one way, then another so quickly that Lee was certain it would snap off at any moment. She pulled on her mother's hand, obviously hoping to make her walk faster.

"Honey, calm down, we're going to be here all day," Lee said and laughed.

"But I don't want to miss anything," the child almost wailed, looking up at her mother with a pleading expression.

"I promise you we won't miss anything," she vowed. She understood the girl's excitement. After all, this was her first carnival. And now she herself felt more comfortable moving among the public. Thanks to working in Lorna's restaurant, she had already met most of the town's residents, and while she was extremely careful not to relax her guard, she wasn't about to deny her child a day of fun.

"Hi Lee," Jake greeted her, his footsteps dogged by his wife and five children. "I see Lorna let you have the day off."

"She told me it was for Nikki's sake," she explained. "And Sally said she could handle it on her own. She preferred letting her husband bring their kids here." Lee looked around the large lot dotted with colorful striped tents and the typical carnival rides. The air was permeated with the smells of popcorn, cotton candy and every other kind of junk food imaginable. "I can see why she didn't mind my coming."

"This is my first carnival," Nikki spoke up proudly.

Jake hunkered down until he was at eye level with the girl. Nikki tightened her hold on her mother's hand, but didn't back away from him. Obviously the kind-looking older man didn't frighten her, Lee thought. "Then, honey, it will be the most special carnival you will ever know," he informed her with a smile. He straightened up, groaning as all the children began talking at once, each having their own idea about what to do first. "Okay, I get the hint." He grinned at Lee. "Have fun."

"What first?" Lee asked when they were left alone. Feeling the morning chill, she zipped up her cream-colored heavy fleece jacket and tucked her hands into the deep kangaroo pockets.

Nikki screwed up her face, looking around. "I don't know," she admitted with a mournful sigh.

"Then let me make a suggestion. Try the clown faces," a jovial male voice intruded.

They both turned, to see Travis walking toward them with a giggling Susie tucked under his arm.

"It's easier to keep track of her this way," he told Lee, letting Susie down.

"What's a clown face?" Nikki was clearly screwing up her courage to ask him, although she still refused to look directly at him, even when Lee nudged her for her rudeness.

"People paint clown faces on us," Susie said excitedly.

"For once the kids have paint that washes off easily all over their faces," Travis assured Lee.

Nikki's mouth opened wide. "Can I have a clown face, Mommy, can I?" she pleaded, tugging on her hand. "Please?"

"May I."

"That's what I said!"

Lee hesitated. It appeared that this might be the beginning of the two families spending the day together. She could feel her muscles tighten and stomach burn at the idea. Yet she had already agreed to attend the dance with him, so why was she bothered about their being together today? Why should she worry, when there were all these people milling around? And deep down inside, she did want to spend the day with him. She tried telling herself it was because of Nikki that she wanted to do this; to give her a chance to learn that not all men were cruel. But she knew better.

She smiled down at her daughter. She would do anything to keep that expression of happiness on her face. "It appears you're going to end up with a funnier face than the one you normally wear."

Travis lowered his head and murmured into Lee's ear, "If it will make you feel better, you can have a clown face, too."

She shot him a wry look. "I think that's one treat I can live without."

Lee and Travis stood back, watching two gaily dressed young women apply a white base to the two girls' faces and then add bright orange circles on the cheeks and bright red lips. When finished, Susie had a blue tear under one eye and Nikki boasted a gold-painted star on her cheek.

"Think we can handle squiring around such colorful kids?" Travis asked Lee as they walked along.

"At least they'll be easy to find."

He stopped her with a hand on her shoulder and pointed with the other. "Think so?"

Everywhere they looked were children of various ages, boasting brightly painted clown faces.

"Then I'm glad I dressed Nikki in a bright color." Lee indicated the heavy cobalt-blue pullover sweater the girl wore with her jeans.

"That way I'll have a bit of an edge." She glanced at his uniform shirt and faded jeans. "I gather you're here in an official capacity." She hoped the tension she felt wasn't reflected in her voice or body language.

"I'm combining business with pleasure," he explained. "This way someone's on duty here, although Cal will be over later in the day, along with someone else this evening, since the teenagers will be running all over by then. We don't allow beer on the grounds, but they tend to sneak it in, unless we keep a close eye on them. There will be more than one set of parents gotten out of bed tonight to pick up their kids at the station."

Her head was downcast. "You really care about the people around here, don't you?"

He nodded. "Yeah, I do. In fact, we all care about one another." He looked at her. "Obviously you're not used to that."

"No, I'm not. There's a lot of towns where the residents don't believe in that philosophy," she said softly.

"Maybe so, but here we all work together when need be, and we celebrate together."

"'One for all, all for one,'" Lee murmured.

"Is that so bad?" Travis asked.

"No, in fact it's a very nice feeling." Lee turned her head when Nikki tugged on her hand.

"Mom, look!" She pointed at a large merry-go-round in the center of the rides. "Can I go on it, please?"

"Pick out which horse you want to ride."

Nikki and Susie ran toward the carousel and after careful deliberation chose their mounts; Nikki, a white steed with silvery-blue reins and saddle and Susie, a prancing black horse with a bright red saddle. Lee and Travis stood behind the gate with the other parents as the merry-go-round began moving in time to the calliope music.

When finished there they walked over to another ride, where the girls rode bright black-and-yellow bumblebees in a circle around a hive.

"You know, this is the most uninhibited I've ever seen Nikki," Travis remarked.

Lee looked away. "I told you before, she's very shy around people she doesn't know."

"At least you don't try to keep her that way." He went on to explain. "I noticed how you'd give her a nudge anytime she didn't answer one of my questions. I don't want her to feel forced into something she doesn't want to do."

"She's always been very shy around adults, and I don't want her to continue seeing them as something frightening," she replied quietly, flexing her stiff fingers in her pockets.

They stood behind a split rail fence, watching the two girls bounce around inside a large enclosed tent filled with multicolored Ping-Pong balls.

While the girls enjoyed themselves, Travis was able to study Lee's face in great detail; he noticed the graceful sweep of her cheekbones, the curve of her lips touched with coral lipstick, the eyes highlighted with a taupe shadow and deep green eye pencil. The faint scent of a spicy floral fragrance drifted upward. Even with her mousy hair she had a delicacy about her that had caught more than one man's attention today. She was dressed in faded jeans and a heavy sweater, but still radiated a light that fascinated him. But he also saw even more in her. He kept asking himself what a classy lady like Lee was doing in his town, but couldn't come up with an answer. Then he worried that she might decide Dunson wasn't for her and leave before he could learn all about her. He took an extra step to the side until he stood right next to her.

After a messy lunch of hot dogs and French fries they wandered through the many craft booths featuring quilts, knitted goods and carved wooden toys.

"It's more like a fair," Lee told Travis after they stopped by a booth filled with homemade jams and jellies.

"Yeah, I guess it is." He smiled and nodded at a couple walking past them. He touched her shoulder and turned her slightly. "Look over there. That's our infamous Zeke and Wilma."

Lee looked in the direction he indicated and saw a tall, gangly bald man wearing patched jeans, a heavy plaid jacket and a Stetson. The woman walking with him was rawboned and stern looking. She bit her lower lip to keep from laughing.

"That's the Casanova of Dunson?"

He nodded. "That's him, all right. The last time he went roaming, she threatened him with her granddaddy's buffalo-skinning knife. He's lucky he's all in one piece."

A giggle escaped her lips. "Travis, he's so old."

"Well, the way Zeke puts it, being old doesn't mean nothing works," he observed with a chuckle. "To be honest, I think it's a game between Zeke and Wilma. She goes after him with that scattergun of hers, but she hasn't shot him yet. Of course, there is always the first time, so I don't like to get too comfortable where they're concerned."

Lee hurriedly stuck her hands into her pockets to hide their trembling. She looked away, fearing what might be on her face.

"Hey, Sheriff!" Cal walked up with a young blond woman hanging on to his arm. "This is even better than last year."

"I think we say that every year," he replied. "Hi, Mary Ellen. I guess you two have made up."

"Not exactly," she replied pertly. "But I'm considering giving Cal a second chance. Don't worry, I'll make sure he does his duty while he's here."

After the couple walked away, Lee looked down at Nikki, who was leaning against her mother.

"I think someone's had enough of the carnival," she commented, taking hold of her hand. "Time for us to be heading home."

"It's about time for us to think about leaving. We'll walk back with you," Travis suggested.

"Aren't we going to stay?" Susie begged. "Please Dad, I'm not tired at all."

"No." His voice was gentle but firm. "We've seen pretty much everything, and if you'd like we can come back for a little while tomorrow, but there's things to be done at home."

When they reached Lee's car, Travis placed his hand on the hood. "How's it doing? Running all right?"

She nodded. "You may claim you don't know a lot about cars, but I haven't had any trouble with it." She unlocked the passenger door and opened it to allow Nikki to get inside. "Thank you for sharing your day with us," she said softly.

He smiled. "I think it's me who should be thanking you. Susie's already getting to the age where she doesn't like going out with her dad as much as she used to. I'll see you tomorrow night for the dance." He didn't notice Nikki's look of horror.

When they drove away Nikki turned to Lee. "Mom, are you going somewhere with Sheriff Hunter?"

"Yes, he's taking me to a dance," she explained. "And you get to spend the night with Susie. Doesn't that sound like fun?"

She frowned. "Why would you want to go with him?"

"Because he asked me and he's a nice man."

"Aren't you afraid of him?"

Lee sighed. She often wondered if she shouldn't have scraped up the money to take Nikki somewhere for professional counseling, to find out just how much she remembered of their past life. It was at times like this that she feared it was much more than Nikki let on.

"Nikki, Sheriff Hunter has never done anything to frighten me or to hurt you," she pointed out. "Has he?"

"No." The admission was reluctant.

"Has he ever shouted at you?"

"No."

"Or called you bad names?"

"No," Nikki muttered.

"Then there's no reason to be afraid of him, is there?" She wondered how many times she would have to remind her that not all men were bad.

"Will he be there when I'm at Susie's house?" Nikki asked after a long silence.

"I'm sure he will, since he lives there," Lee said reasonably. "But then, we're going out. Besides, you'll be able to play with the kittens in the barn, and Susie's grandmother is going to let you two make fudge tomorrow night. Now doesn't that sound like a lot of fun?" She groaned inwardly at the thought of the massive task ahead of the older woman and silently applauded her patience.

Nikki brightened at the thought. "And we get to stay up late?"

"That will be up to Mrs. Hunter."

She chewed her lower lip. "Well, maybe it won't be so bad."

Lee hid her smile. "Maybe it won't."

Chapter Eight

"As I live and breathe, the man has gotten a haircut, shaved and—" Maude moved closer to take a sniff "—put on cologne. You haven't looked and smelled this good since your senior prom."

Travis shot her a telling look. "All right, you looked almost as good at your wedding—at least, you would have, if you hadn't been so hung over from your bachelor party." She smiled serenely.

"Give me a break, Mom. I'm an adult, the law in this town and you still treat me as if I was still a kid with skinned knees and a black eye."

"That's because I'll always remember you that way." She smiled again, smoothing down his shirt collar over his jacket.

"Where are the girls?" Travis looked around. Maude had driven into town earlier to pick up some groceries and had offered to collect Nikki at the same time.

"In Susie's room, changing into their pajamas before we get down to the serious business of having dinner and making fudge. You just go on and have a nice time," she admonished her son, still smiling.

Travis stopped by the bedroom to say goodbye to Nikki and Susie and left the house, not wanting to be late in picking up Lee. While it might have been a long time since he had gone out on a date, he still remembered that a gentleman didn't keep a lady waiting.

The lump in Lee's throat grew to gigantic proportions when she heard the knock. She smoothed down the front of her lace-tiered skirt and walked slowly to the door. Her hand hovered over the knob before she finally grasped the cool metal and slowly turned it.

"Hello." She offered him a weak smile. "Ah, would you like to come in?" She stepped back.

Travis's eyes widened in amazement. Lee wore an off-white, Vic-

torian-styled blouse with a band of lace for a collar and a peach and
blue floral calf-length skirt with matching lace along the ruffled tiers.
With her hair pinned on top of her head in a variation of a Gibson
hairstyle, she looked as if she had stepped out of a cameo.

"You look lovely," he said huskily, suddenly wanting to take her
into his arms, yet afraid of making any move that would send her
into retreat.

She laughed nervously, just as strongly aware of him as he was of
her. "Thank you. I'll be honest. I've been going crazy all afternoon,
trying to figure out what to wear. I finally called Sally, and she told
me pretty much anything went and not to worry." She looked at his
white shirt and tan Western-cut jacket and slacks and was glad she
had decided to give in to her feminine side.

Clearing her throat, Lee went to the hall closet. Stepping behind
her, Travis took the coat from her and held it out, dropping it slightly
so that she could slip her arms through the sleeves. He looked down
at her nape, softly shadowed by wisps of curls, and inhaled the fragrance of her perfume. He swallowed, wondering if counting to ten
would help him overcome those male urges again. He decided that
even counting to a million wouldn't.

Once her coat was on, Lee stepped away. "Thank you," she whispered, feeling very shy.

"We're lucky tonight isn't too cold," he told her as they walked
outside to his car, a well-cared-for Buick that had to be ten years old.

Lee looked at their mode of transportation. "This doesn't look like
your Jeep."

"That's more my official vehicle and for work around the ranch.
Not the kind of transportation for taking a lady to a dance." He
opened the door with a theatrical flourish.

Lee slid inside and waited until Travis got in. "You don't sound
like a rancher."

He looked amused. "Oh, what is a rancher supposed to sound
like?"

She blushed, realizing her comment could be taken as an insult.
"To be honest, I don't know. I guess someone who worries more
about their cows and hay and whatever else they have on their
ranches than what goes on in the outside world."

"Whereas I sound like someone who's had more than a grade
school education." He still seemed to be more amused than affronted.

Lee looked down at the hands that lay clenched in her lap. "I
made that sound very bad, didn't I? I'm sorry."

"Hey, no apology. It's understandable you would think that we're all country bumpkins. Admittedly, a good many of us come across that way. Actually I graduated from the University of Montana with a business degree to make my mother happy, but ranching had always been in my blood, so I came back here after my stint in the navy, instead of going to New York to take the town by storm, the way my mother hoped I would.''

"What did you do in the navy?" Lee asked curiously.

"Shore patrol."

Her stomach tightened. "Which is why you're the sheriff."

He turned the car into a large dirt parking lot already almost filled with cars and trucks. "It gave me a bit of an edge, since I had some law enforcement experience." He fitted the car neatly between two pickup trucks and switched off the engine.

"Yes, I guess it would," Lee replied, as they walked toward the large hall, through whose open doors the sounds of music were spilling outside.

They entered the hall, finding it lighted by hundreds of tiny twinkling lights over the dance floor, and smiling and greeting people they knew as they went.

"Lee, you look lovely. And here you were so worried earlier." Sally walked up, dragging her husband behind her. "Hi, Travis. You going to save me a dance later on?"

"If Will won't mind giving you up," he teased the florid-faced blond man with a stocky build who was standing behind Sally.

"Hell, the way she likes to dance, you can have her all evening," Will joked back, earning a good-natured pinch from his wife.

"Just for that, you can start making up for that crack right now." With a jaunty wave of the hand she dragged her husband toward the dance floor.

"Poor Will. He has two left feet and is tone-deaf, while Sally dances like Ginger Rogers and sings in the church choir," Travis explained.

Lee's lips twitched in a smile. "The perfect couple."

He looked toward the two people dancing on the fringe of the crowd. "Yeah, they are." Seeming to shake himself awake, he turned back to Lee. "Ready to take a chance? I promise not to step on your feet too often."

The band may have been distinctly amateur and the music more country and western than waltz, but Lee had little trouble learning the steps, and soon discovered Travis had lied about his dancing ability.

"Two left feet, my eye," she declared as they circled the dance floor. "You're a wonderful dancer."

He looked unrepentant. "I figured if I sounded pathetic enough, you'd feel sorry for me and come to the dance."

Lee looked up into his eyes, feeling herself drawn into the dark brown depths. Wildly she wondered if the room temperature had suddenly risen. With Travis's arms loosely draped around her waist she felt protected. She'd never thought she would feel that way in the presence of a man. As the evening progressed, a few men came by to ask if she'd care to try it with them. She couldn't help but notice that Travis didn't bother dancing with any of the other women, but merely stayed on the sidelines, his eyes never leaving her. Lee was certain that if anything happened, he would immediately be at her side. Now she felt more than protected; she almost felt cherished.

She decided that Travis was the perfect escort. When he thought she was looking a little tired, he made sure she had a glass of punch, and coaxed her to try the sugar cookies that lay prominently on a glass platter on the refreshment table.

"Mrs. Zimmerman makes the best sugar cookies I've ever had," he explained. "They're the soft chewy kind, instead of hard and crunchy. I used to stop by her house once a week for some." He smiled at the silver-haired woman presiding over the refreshments. "And she refuses to divulge her recipe to anyone."

Lee bit into a cookie and discovered it was just as excellent as Travis had assured her. "I don't blame her," she said to Travis. "These are wonderful," she told the woman, who beamed at her compliment. "I wouldn't want to give the recipe away, either."

"Oh, someday I will." Mrs. Zimmerman chuckled. "Actually I'll will it to the most deserving person, but they'll have to promise not to give it out to just anyone."

Lee smiled again as she took another cookie. "I think that sounds like a wonderful idea."

They selected a table off to one side that afforded a bit more privacy than the others, but that didn't stop people from wandering over.

Lee shifted uncomfortably after a few minutes of close scrutiny. After several more people had stopped by, she leaned across the table toward Travis.

"Is there a reason for all this attention?" she asked.

He grinned, looking a little uncomfortable himself. "I don't usually escort anyone to the dances."

Lee now felt even more self-conscious. "Are you telling me you haven't dated since your wife's death, and I'm the first?'' Her voice squeaked on the last word.

Travis's face turned a light shade of red. "Not exactly. I just haven't seen anyone who lives around here.''

She was amused to recognize that he felt as uncomfortable as she did. "Oh, I see.''

"Good, then can we please get off the subject?'' he growled, downing his punch as if it were something stronger.

Lee sipped her own punch to hide her smile.

"You look real pretty tonight, ma'am,'' Cal told her as they danced around the floor, his arm pumping hers up and down as if she were an oil well, and his boots narrowly missing her shoes a few times. "It sure surprised us when we saw Travis walking in with you. With a lady, I mean,'' he corrected himself, stumbling over his words.

"I already gathered he hadn't done this before.'' Lee stepped back quickly before her toes were well and truly smashed.

"No, ma'am, he pretty much stays away from these shindigs,'' Cal explained. "Though Maude never missed one.''

"You let your mother miss tonight just to watch our children,'' she accused Travis when she was gratefully released into his care. "I learned that she's never missed one.''

"She volunteered to look after the girls, so you'll have to take that up with her.'' Travis noticed the dimming of the lights. "Means it's midnight and the last dance. Shall we?''

She smiled back. "Why not?''

They slowly circled the floor to "Good Night Ladies,'' their steps in perfect rhythm.

Lee felt a strange tingling, both along her back where Travis's hand rested and on the hand he held in a warm clasp. She slowly lifted her head and found him gazing down at her with a strange look on his face, as if he had never seen her before. Unable to think of something to say to lighten the moment, she could only look into his eyes and wonder what he was thinking.

She's beautiful, Travis thought, stunned by the abrupt shift in his thinking about Lee. She has beautiful eyes, skin, nice figure, and a wonderful personality. Where has she been all this time? His arm unconsciously tightened around her.

Lee could feel the warmth change to an icy cold, but she refused to give in to old fears now. She found it difficult to breathe, yet inhaled deeply, breathing in the spicy scent of Travis's after-shave. When he held her close against his chest, his body heat chased away the cold. Her breasts swelled, the tips brushing against the soft fabric of her blouse and the hard planes of his chest. She closed her eyes, allowing the various sensations to wash over her as the music retreated into the fog that surrounded her in a world where only she and Travis existed. She couldn't remember the last time she'd felt this way, then realized it was because she never had. She tilted back her head, not caring if her thoughts were evident in her eyes. There was a strange tingling feeling running through her veins, and she felt more alive at that moment than she ever had before. As far as she was concerned, it was a night when fairy tales came true.

Travis easily read the unspoken message in Lee's eyes, certain his own said the same. How long before they could be alone? He knew just holding her wasn't nearly enough.

When the music ended, they drew apart, reluctant to return to the real world. Lee wanted to leave as quickly as possible, but the people stopping to chat made their progress to the door slow. So she forced stiff facial muscles to smile and spoke, although later she had no idea what she'd said.

When they finally reached Travis's car, Lee slid inside, unsure whether to feel relieved that she was out of the hall or worried that her new feelings might be wrong.

"I'm sure most men would suggest going out for a drink or something, but this town and the neighboring ones don't go in much for late-night entertainment," Travis said, shrugging and smiling faintly.

"That's all right. I'm awfully tired, anyway," Lee whispered, turning to look out the window. Why had she allowed her new feelings to flower so dramatically? She, who had always examined things so carefully, had ignored good sense and now didn't know what to do to rectify the situation. She felt a need to be alone so that she could examine her feelings toward Travis at greater length.

He frowned, wondering what had prompted the abrupt change in her manner, then put it down to what she had said. He let the motor run for a few minutes before turning on the heater, adjusting the vents to blow indirectly at Lee.

"Warm enough?" he asked, willing her to look at him.

She nodded without turning around.

Travis jockeyed into the line leaving the parking lot and was soon on the road. "Lee, are you sure you're all right?"

"I guess I'm just more tired than I thought. I'm not used to doing all that dancing," she said huskily.

The silence in the car was deafening during the short ride. Travis pulled into Lee's driveway and got out, but before he could walk around to open her door, she was out of the car and walking toward the house.

"I want to thank you for a lovely evening," she said, speaking rapidly, her words blowing gusts of frost into the air as she unlocked the door.

"Just as long as you enjoyed yourself." Travis was still puzzled by the mixed signals he was receiving, and, for the first time in his usually uncomplicated life, wasn't sure what to do. He finally decided to let nature take its course. He inclined his head, lowering it slowly until his mouth rested lightly against hers in the gentlest of kisses.

Lee's heart almost stopped beating at the delicate touch. Her first thought was to push him away and run into the house, where she would be safe. Her next was to hold on to him as tightly as she could. Before she could give in to either idea, Travis moved back, a tiny smile on his lips.

"Thank you for going with me," he said softly. "You better get inside, before you turn into an icicle."

Her head bobbed jerkily, and she quickly opened the door and stepped inside. She leaned against the wall, listening to the sound of the car's engine accelerate, then fade away. Lee touched her tingling lips, unaware of her sad smile. She knew she couldn't afford to let things go too far. Any man in her life could prove dangerous, especially a lawman.

During his drive home, Travis couldn't stop thinking about Lee, the way she'd felt in his arms and especially the way her lips had felt against his. He knew he was grinning like some sappy school kid, but he didn't care. Not after the evening he'd just spent.

After he parked the car in the garage, he walked through the back door into the kitchen, where he found a covered plate of lopsided fudge squares and a carafe, which he knew would hold coffee. He poured himself a cup and took a piece of fudge, then walked into the den, where he found Maude watching the late show. She looked up and flipped the Mute switch on the television's remote control.

"I didn't expect you to be home so early," she greeted him. "How was your evening?"

"How were the girls?" He flopped into his easy chair, sipping the hot coffee.

"Fine, sound asleep. How was your evening?"

Travis nibbled on a corner of the fudge. "Not bad. Who did most of the beating?"

Maude stared at him long and hard. "They both did. Now if I have to ask you about your evening one more time, I won't be responsible for the consequences."

"She looked beautiful tonight." He had an idea he still had that idiotic smile on his face, but he didn't care. He was only speaking the truth.

"And?"

Travis glared at his mother. "Is there a reason why you need a blow-by-blow description of my date?"

Maude smiled serenely. "Yes, because you came home in a strange mood. And because you've always talked over your dates with me. Well, almost always. You never did tell me about that time you went on the hayride with DeeDee Truman." Her eyes danced when she noticed Travis's red face. "I thought so. She always had a reputation. Now, back to Lee. Did you kiss her?"

He rolled his eyes. "Am I not allowed to have any secrets?"

"No." Maude leaned forward. "Travis, you are my only son. Lee is the first woman you've taken out seriously since Julie's death. And that means a lot. You're a man of strong feelings, and I'd say she has done something to knock you for a loop."

He grimaced. "She did. And if you don't mind, I'd like to sort things out on my own."

"I wouldn't expect anything else. Just as long as you know I'm here for you." She paused, then pushed on. "About Nikki."

Travis looked over. "You mean there was a problem, after all?"

She shook her head. "No, she's an absolute darling. But she says so little of what they've done or where they've been before coming here. It's as if they have no past."

His eyes darkened with anger. "Mom, did you try to pump her? A seven-year-old child?"

"Of course not, but many children do talk about things they've done in the past. She doesn't. Nikki appears skittish about certain things. When they were ready for bed, she came up to me and asked if it would be possible to have a night-light. I would go so far as to say she is genuinely frightened of the dark."

He shrugged. "That's nothing unusual. A lot of kids are convinced there are monsters under their beds or in their closets."

"No, nothing like that. I just wish I could put my finger on it," she said with a sigh.

Travis finished the fudge and coffee and stood up. "I'm going to bed. Four-thirty will be here before I know it. I'm too old to hold down two jobs."

"Then tell them to hold the election for sheriff early," his mother suggested.

"Nope, another six months and I'll have more than enough to get a new bull."

"Then something else will come up. You're torn between helping the town and working for yourself," Maude chided. "You want to help too many people, Travis. Pretty soon there won't be enough of you left for anyone important."

He smiled. "For someone important, I'll make sure there's more than enough of me."

"TRAVIS, someone's here to see you." Cal stood by his Jeep as Travis climbed out. His expression and tone of voice indicated that he wasn't impressed with their visitor. "He insisted on waiting for you in your office." He lifted his shoulders in apology. "I couldn't stop him."

Travis nodded, aware his deputy wasn't as authoritative as he could be. "That's okay, Cal. I'll see what he wants."

He strode into his office where he found a heavyset man sitting in the chair across from his own.

"I'm Sheriff Hunter," he said crisply, hanging his hat and sheepskin-lined jacket on the coatrack. "I understand you wanted to see me."

"Sure did, Sheriff." The man spoke with a heavy Southern drawl. He reached into his coat pocket and drew out a white business card, handing it to Travis.

He glanced down at the black engraved print. "J. D. Porter," he read. "Fine, you're a private investigator. What brings you up here from Houston?"

"Hell, this is just another backwater town for me." He dug into his coat's inner pocket and withdrew an envelope. "I've been trackin' a bloodthirsty broad and her child for nigh on to three years now. Thought you might be able to help me out." His smile could only be described as oily.

Travis never liked people who looked down on the residents of small towns. This man's manner put him right into that category.

"I still don't see any reason why you'd try here. Newcomers in this town are few and far between."

The man smirked. "After seeing what little there is, I can well understand why. Let's just say I'm followin' a hunch." He pulled a photograph out of the envelope. "This is about three years old, but it should give you some kind of idea what they look like. Wonder if you'd seen either one of them?" He handed the photograph to Travis.

He stared down at the picture and felt shock waves rock his body, although he was certain their impact didn't show on his face.

The little girl with the broad grin, bright eyes and dark blond curls was Nikki with her beautiful heart-shaped face. The woman standing beside her sent a giant-sized fist to his gut. The hair color was strawberry blonde instead of brown, but the sorrow in those eyes was recognizable. The man standing behind the woman had an arm around her waist in a possessive gesture. He was tall, blond with movie-star good looks and an arrogant manner. Travis didn't know the man and he already didn't like him. He knew he wasn't going to swear the woman and girl were Lee and Nikki, and he certainly wasn't going to say anything to this bulldog until he knew more about the story.

"Why're you looking for them?" he asked, adding just the right casual touch to his voice.

"Anne Sinclair almost killed her ex-husband and kidnapped their kid three years ago," Porter explained. "She was labeled an unfit mother during the divorce case and lost custody of the kid. Let me tell you, anyone who would shoot a guy for no reason at all and kidnap a kid has to be nuts. The father is worried that his daughter will get hurt. 'Course, for all we know, she could have dumped the kid somewhere and taken off with some guy. Sure wouldn't put it past her. Her reputation down there wasn't the best. Mr. Sinclair is offering a hefty reward for her return, and I'm sure anyone in this town could use the kind of money he's offering," he added craftily. "After all, she broke the law and deserves to be locked up."

And I just bet you'll get even more money for yourself, Travis thought grimly to himself. He leaned back in his chair, lacing his fingers behind his head. "What makes you think she got this far north?"

The man shrugged. "A hunch. My last lead was a motel about two hundred miles south of here, where they stayed last fall. 'Course, who knows what name she's using by now. It seems to change with every city, along with her hair and eye color. That's why it's been so damn hard for me to catch up with her. I figured it wouldn't hurt for me to check out some of these small towns. She might have thought it would be safer. I figured I'd check in here first, since you'd probably know if anyone new showed up within the last six months."

Travis worked hard at keeping his expression bland. His first impulse was to throw the odious man out on his fat butt, but he knew the creep would only kick up a fuss, not to mention do some searching on his own, both of which he didn't need. He didn't want that to happen until he'd heard Lee's side of the story, although how he was going to introduce this subject to her was something he didn't know. He recalled Lee's wariness around him and Nikki's fear. As the town's sheriff he had always worked hard to keep an open mind, and he was more than determined to do just that with this situation. He tossed the photograph onto the desk.

"You're right about us being so isolated out here. I'm usually one of the first to hear about any newcomers in this town. It's not as if we have any kind of industry around here that brings in people. Not to mention I'd hear about a good-looking woman like that." He nodded his head slightly in thought. "Yep, I'd guess you're the first stranger we've had in town in well over a year," he lied without a qualm.

Chapter Nine

Travis leaned back in his chair, still studying the damning photograph lying on his desk. He stared down at the woman and girl, picturing them in different clothing and coloring. His gut tightened at the vision.

"Well, Lee or Anne Sinclair, what have you got yourself into?" he muttered.

"Hey, Travis, what's going on with that guy?" Cal stuck his head around the door.

"Good question," he said grimly. "I want you to spread the word that I don't want anyone talking to that creep. He sees us as a bunch of dumb country hicks, so let him keep on thinking that. For once I'm glad we don't have a motel here. No matter what, he'll have to be gone by nightfall, since the nearest motel is sixty miles away. And if he tries to sleep in his car, I'll arrest him for vagrancy."

Cal looked down at the picture, and shock flashed across his pudgy features. "Say, isn't that—?"

Travis's head snapped up, the expression on his face demanding silence. "Just do as I say, Cal, and don't waste any time. And no personal points of view to anyone. Understand?"

The younger man nodded slowly. "Sure, anything you say." He backed out of the office and headed for the front door, determined to do the job his boss had given him.

Travis leaned forward, bracing his elbows on the desk and covering his face with his hands. He suddenly felt as if he had been thrust into a situation he wasn't sure how to handle, without everything blowing up in his face.

"If she's the one he's looking for, I'm hiding a fugitive from the law, and if she's not, I'm protecting her from scum," he groaned, fighting with his scruples. He shut his eyes, wanting nothing more than to forget the past twenty minutes. Then something occurred to him. He grabbed the phone and punched out a number. It was picked up on the first ring.

"Yeah?"

He breathed a sigh of relief that Lorna was the one to answer the phone. "It's Travis. Is Lee working today?"

She chuckled. "Of course she is. Why?"

He paused, knowing he was taking a step in a direction whence there would be no return. "Get her out of there. I don't care how you do it, just get her out right away. There's a private investigator nosing around town, and he's the kind who would sell his own grandmother if the money was right."

Lorna took no time to ask questions. "I'll send her over to the Hendersons for more eggs, and a few places after that. Don't worry, Travis. No one in this place will say anything about her, if they know what's good for them. Not if they want to eat here again!"

He grinned, relaxing for the first time that morning. "Ah, Lorna, if you weren't already taken, I'd marry you."

"Sure. That's why you're looking out for you know who. Now, let me get off the phone so I can get this taken care of."

Travis continued grinning as he hung up. "With Lorna looking out for Lee, no one will dare say anything about her, unless he wants a shotgun shoved up his nose."

"THAT MUST BE a joker's idea of a private investigator," Jake muttered to Lorna, watching J. D. Porter enter the restaurant. Lorna had already alerted the diners to the man nosing around, and it appeared she had done so just in time.

"Mornin'," the man greeted them with a smile, hefting his bulk onto a stool. "My, that pie sure looks good. Is that peach?"

"Yeah, it is." Lorna was unmoved by his praise.

"I sure would appreciate a piece and a cup of coffee," J.D. continued as he looked around the restaurant. He nodded and smiled at some of the other men sitting nearby. "I guess you all would pretty much know everyone in this sweet little town of yours."

"As I've lived here all my life, I 'spect I would," Jake replied. "Why?"

"Well, I'm looking for somebody." He pulled a photograph out of his jacket pocket, along with two twenty-dollar bills. "This lady tried to kill her husband and took their little girl. A dangerous woman, if I do say so myself. Maybe you've seen her pass through town or somethin'?''

Jake studied the photograph and ignored the money. "Can't say as I have.''

"Take another look," Porter invited him. "That picture's a few years old, so the girl would be about seven now. The child's daddy just wants his baby back. He's real worried something might happen to her. He's offering a big reward.''

"Let me see," Ernie, the town's plumber asked. He looked it over carefully and returned it—with a smudge of grease on one corner. "Nah, we'd sure remember someone like her. We don't have a whole lot of good-lookin' women come through here. 'Course, there was Lew Watson's new wife, but she's from Canada.''

"Mister, you can shove that money under my nose, and I'd be only too happy to take it," declared Thaddeus Stone, owner of the hardware store, "but I still ain't seen the lady.''

LEE BEGAN to wonder over the next few days if she had changed, or if the townspeople had. Everywhere she went, she felt as if people looked at her differently. Yet there was nothing to back up her suspicions. If anything, some folk were friendlier. Still, she was jumpy and wary of everyone, beginning to wonder if it wasn't time to move on once more.

"Young lady, you're in need of some of my spring tonic if you're going to do that to my salads," Lorna told her, staring at the salad covered with catsup instead of French dressing.

Lee looked at the concoction, her face a picture of dismay. "I don't know what happened. I was certain I was putting on dressing.''

The older woman glanced toward Travis, who sat at the counter, waiting for his salad. Nothing in his expression gave his thoughts away.

He was proud of the fact that the townspeople had banded together to protect a woman they'd come so quickly to think of as one of their own, even if they weren't aware of the entire story. He was astute enough to know his own backing up of Lee had helped some, but it was mainly the fact she was a woman, alone, with a child that had brought out their protective instincts. He was relieved that the private investigator hadn't gone into great detail about Anne Sinclair when talking to the others. Evidently the man had preferred bringing up the idea of the reward. Little did he know that all people weren't money hungry.

"That sleaze bag you warned me about came in here just after the lunch crowd," Lorna murmured, leaning on the counter in front of Travis. "He flashed around a woman's picture and some twenty-dollar bills to jog people's memories." A smile flickered across her face. "Thaddeus told him he'd be more than happy to take one of the twenties, but he'd never seen the woman. From what I hear, anyone questioned said pretty much the same thing." Her dark eyes reflected worry. "She's sure in a lot of trouble, isn't she? He said she was wanted by the law, but he wouldn't say much else. Told us if we had any information to get in touch with him through his office."

"A lot of people are wanted by the law," Travis said laconically. "Such as Wilma on a regular basis."

"That girl wouldn't harm a fly, so whatever she did can't be as bad as he hinted." She straightened up and smiled as Lee approached them. "I see you found the French dressing."

Lee's face turned a bright red as she set the plate in front of Travis. "I guess my mind was elsewhere." She smiled weakly and hurried away.

Travis looked down at the salad and grimaced. "I didn't have the heart to tell her I ordered blue cheese. I hate French dressing."

When he paid the bill he smiled at Lee. "Mom wants you to come out for dinner again this Saturday," he said. "She has a nasty hen she wants an excuse to roast."

"Oh, no," Lee protested. After the past few days, she knew she couldn't bear the thought of spending any more time in the sheriff's house. "You've had us out there already."

"So? Mom likes to cook, and the more the merrier. The girls can ride in the big corral under adult supervision. You know how much Nikki loves horses."

She did. Nikki had been invited out several times after school, when one of the hands supervised the two girls in taking turns riding a docile mare around the main corral. And each time she returned home, she was even more excited about her newfound riding ability. In fact, as each day passed, Lee saw more and more of the bright-faced little girl she had always hoped Nikki would become.

"You know I can't turn you down," she said with a sigh. "You should be ashamed of yourself, using my child like that."

His grin lighted up his dark eyes. "Hey, whatever works. Why don't you come early? Say about three or four."

Lee couldn't argue, because deep down she looked forward to going out to Travis's ranch. She told herself it was crazy, not to mention dangerous.

"SUSIE'S GRANDMA said I can call her Grandma," Nikki announced out of the blue during the drive to the Hunter ranch.

Lee looked surprised. "Did she?"

Nikki nodded. "And she's gonna let Susie and me make chocolate chip cookies."

"I thought we were going out there so you could ride," she reminded her daughter.

"Oh, we're gonna do that, too," Nikki said blithely, as if time had no meaning.

Lee shook her head, smiling at her daughter's expectation of doing everything at once.

The moment Lee parked along the side of the house, Susie was running toward them, chattering before Nikki had a chance to get out of the car.

"Hey, where's your manners?" Travis shouted, following more slowly.

"Hi, Mrs. Davis," Susie called out, dragging Nikki in the direction of the barn.

He shrugged. "I guess I should be glad she heard me." He closed the car door for Lee and looked her over from head to toe. "Good, you're wearing jeans. Can you ride?"

Lee was surprised by his question. "Some, but it's been a long time."

"It will come back to you." Without touching her, he steered her toward the same barn the girls had run to. "Casey, they all ready?" he asked, looking at a man in his twenties who was leading out two saddled horses.

"Yes sir. I saddled up Starlight for the lady." He nodded toward Lee.

Unthinking, she clutched Travis's sleeve. "I told you I haven't ridden in years," she whispered.

He looked down and smiled. "Starlight's the same as a rocking horse, except she doesn't stay in one place. Don't worry, I'll be right alongside you. You'll do just fine."

With some trepidation she allowed herself to be led to the horse and assisted into the saddle, as Travis gave her a leg up, then handed her the reins. "I'm not so sure this is a good idea." She looked down, discovering the ground was farther away than she'd thought.

"Besides, I came here for dinner. I really should be inside helping Maude." She made a move to dismount, but Travis's hand on her thigh stopped her, his touch burning her through her jeans.

"She knows what we're doing." He moved away and swung into the saddle of a large bay gelding with the ease of a man who spent many hours on a horse. "We decided it was time you saw more than the house and the barn."

Lee swallowed as the horse began to walk slowly, following Travis. Soon enough her body adjusted to the rocking gait, and she began to relax enough to look at her surroundings, not to mention the man riding beside her. Sitting straight and tall in the saddle, Travis looked like an ad for the Old West. Since he was now riding a bit ahead of her, she could look her fill.

The hilly country was still brown from the harsh winter, but she could see tiny shoots of green dotted across the landscape. She sniffed the air and was convinced she could smell spring coming, even though she could feel the chilly air penetrate her heavy jacket. Travis pointed out the grazing cattle, mentioning special points of his plans for them.

She looked over at him, not surprised at his love for his land. She doubted he was the kind of man to do anything halfway and couldn't help but wonder if that extended to his lovemaking. She quickly shook off that thought and forced herself back to reality. "If you're so serious about your ranch, why are you working as sheriff?"

He pulled on the reins and waited until she halted next to him. "Because I need a new bull, and it was a fairly easy way to get the money. Oh, I know it sounds hokey and all that, but I truly believe in the judicial system." For a split second he could have sworn he saw bitterness in Lee's eyes at his words. "If I didn't have the ranch, I probably would have been a lawyer, but I knew I couldn't devote the right kind of time to both, and as far as I'm concerned, the land comes first. Since the town was willing to let me juggle both, and the arrangement isn't permanent, I saw no reason not to take the job on."

Lee wanted to tell him that the system doesn't always work for the right people, but thought better of it. That kind of statement could cause questions she couldn't afford to answer. Instead she chose a safer topic. "You're sheriff because you need a new bull? No offense, but that doesn't make a lot of sense."

Travis pulled his hat down over his eyes, looking out over land that had been in his family for years. "My bull is getting old, and a new one costs money I don't have. When our sheriff died, the town council came to me and asked if I'd be willing to take on his job for the rest of his term. I had experience in the military police, which was why they thought of me. The money was tempting, and I needed it. Admittedly, I had to hire an extra hand to help out at home, but I still have enough left over to put away toward my bull. By the end of the year I should have enough. End of story."

"Do you think you'll run for the position when elections come up?"

He shook his head. "Part of me wants to, but another part reminds me that I should be out here full-time. We have a pretty quiet town except for the occasional drunk. I think it's time to go back to the land." He turned toward her. "What about you? Think you'll stay?" He hoped his question sounded casual, although he waited tensely for her reply.

She forced herself to look him straight in the eye. "Who says what a person will do? Although Nikki's happy here, and that's what counts."

"What about you? Don't you count?" *Trust me,* his mind pleaded with her. *Tell me what that creep was talking about. Tell me why you ran away.*

Lee turned away. "My daughter is all I have, and I'll do anything in my power to keep her safe." Her voice hardened, as memories of the past intruded once again.

Not by a blink of an eye did Travis let his thoughts be shown, but his mind was furiously filing away her statement. Lee had just admitted that Nikki meant everything to her. Was that why she'd shot her ex-husband? Because she lost the custody case?

"Yeah, our kids tend to inspire our protective instincts, don't they?" He decided to subtly press the subject. "Susie got the measles last year, and I suffered through every red spot with her. Mom said she was glad I had gotten them when I was ten, because I'm one of the worst patients around."

Lee's lips curved slightly. "Men usually are."

"Was your husband a lousy patient when he was sick?" He cursed himself when he saw her face freeze.

"He didn't believe in getting sick." Her hands tightened on the reins. "It's getting late, isn't it? Shouldn't we be getting back?"

Knowing he wouldn't get anything else out of her, Travis nodded and guided his horse in the direction they had come from. The ride back to the barn was silent.

When Lee pushed herself out of the saddle, she felt Travis's hands on her waist as he guided her to the ground. She turned around slowly, aware of his hands still resting lightly on her hips. The air fairly vibrated around them as they gazed at each other, each of them trying to read answers to unspoken questions. The warmth of the barn, coupled with the earthy scent of horse and hay mingled in the air, only added to the tension their bodies felt. Lee's mount broke the spell when she turned her head and nudged her in the back. Grateful for the respite, she grasped the reins tightly.

"I'll unsaddle her for you." Travis's voice was rough with emotion, but Lee shook her head.

"I can handle it. As you said, it all comes back to you." She reached under the horse to loosen the cinch and pull off the saddle before leading the mare into the barn. The two of them worked in silent harmony as the horses were brushed down and stabled. When Lee began to leave the barn, Travis walked toward her until she was backed up against a post. She looked up, her eyes wide.

"You have the most expressive eyes, did you know that?" He spoke softly, his tone even. "I would have sworn you thought I was going to hurt you."

"You may be the town's sheriff and a loving father, but that's all I know about you," she whispered, feeling both the unyielding wood behind her and the body heat that was reaching out to her. His hands were braced on the post on either side of her, but he still hadn't touched her in any way. She breathed deeply, but only the scent of horse, leather and man reached her nostrils.

"I'm housebroken, no nasty habits and I'm kind to children and animals."

Lee licked her lips, immediately catching Travis's attention. "Yes, but do you have references?" she murmured, entering into this flirtation game.

"Give me a couple minutes, and I'll write up all the references you'd ever want."

"What are you doing?" Her voice was raw.

Travis's gaze traveled over her, from the dark gold scarf her hair was tied back with to the open throat of the brown and gold plaid wool shirt under her unbuttoned jacket.

"I'm looking at a lovely woman that I wish I knew how to convince I'm not such a bad guy," he murmured, staring at her coral-glossed lips. He slowly lowered his head and lightly brushed his lips across hers. He could feel the tension in her body and sought to banish it.

"Do you know you taste like a rare spice?" he murmured against her tightly closed lips.

"No, I don't," she whispered. "That's the kind of line you read in a book."

"Maybe it is, maybe that's where I got it, but you still taste very special." Travis's tongue darted out to outline her lips, then he concentrated on taking teasing little nips at the corners of her lips and flicking his tongue along her bottom lip. "You know, I think I could stand here all day and just kiss you."

Her breath caught in her throat. "Just kiss me? No man wants just a kiss."

"I'm not just any man." He proved his point by still not trying to touch her anywhere else.

Lee was tempted to believe him, but past lessons had taught her too well. Still, Travis hadn't tried anything else. Not to mention the fact that he made her feel so warm inside. And all this from nothing more than a kiss. Each time his lips touched hers, she relaxed a little more. Very slowly she lifted her hand and rested it on his muscled forearm, feeling the skin tense under her touch. When she tipped her head slightly to one side, he began exploring her ear and along the side of her neck. She shivered at the pleasurable sensations that were skittering across her nerves, inhaling the warm, horsey scent of his skin and thinking it better than any expensive men's cologne.

"Why are you doing this?"

He smiled against her slightly parted lips. "I told you, because you taste like a rare spice."

"Why me?"

"Because you're a little prickly, you don't wear a lot of makeup and you don't chew gum." His tongue found an enticing corner of her lips. "Not to mention you make me crazy, every time I look at you. Is that a good enough reason? If not, I could probably come up with a few more."

"No, I think they're just fine, thank you." Lee's breathing grew labored. She couldn't remember the last time a man had given her so much attention without wanting something in return. In fact, she doubted it had ever happened. Her breathing grew still more labored with each touch, each caress of the lips. Her other hand found his waist, the body hard against her palm. This was the body of a man who worked hard for a living. The muscles were well earned, not the product of a health spa, the hands callused from the same kind of work that kept his body lean. She also didn't miss the fact that he was most definitely aroused, but it didn't frighten her as it would have before, because she instinctively knew he would never do anything to hurt her.

"You know, as much as I would like to stand here and kiss you for the rest of the day, I guess we should get inside before someone walks in here," he said quietly, easing away from her just a bit.

His words were more effective than a cold shower. What if Nikki had walked in and seen them so close together? Would it have brought forth dark memories the little girl had blocked out? She pushed him away and turned around to face the wall, breathing deeply to regain her equilibrium.

"Lee, I won't apologize for what I did." Travis spoke to her back. "In fact, given the chance, I would certainly do it again. I don't know what exactly put you off men, but I don't want to be one of that particular species."

"You're very sure of yourself, aren't you?" Her words were so soft that he barely heard them.

"No, not where you're concerned."

His simple words were enough to make her turn back. Lee stared at him long and hard, but found nothing but sincerity in his gaze. Without saying anything more, she walked out of the barn and up to the house, aware that he followed close behind. Deep in her heart she knew this was a turning point between them. She didn't want to call it a relationship, because it sounded too intimate, not to mention the fact that she couldn't afford to have such a thing happen. She opened the kitchen door and walked in, without bothering to knock, as if she had always done so.

"Dinner will be ready in about fifteen minutes," Maude informed them. "You have just enough time to wash up. Lee, why don't you use the bathroom across the hall from Susie's room? I laid fresh towels out for you."

"I need my purse." She looked around, as if expecting it to materialize in front of her.

"Nikki brought it in for you. I put it in the bathroom."

Lee nodded, her eyes still vaguely unfocused from the events in the barn. She walked out of the room without looking at Travis. Maude grasped his arm as he prepared to leave.

"I may be a woman who's been a widow for a lot of years, but I still know what a well-kissed woman looks like. She's fragile, Travis, handle her with care," she warned.

He smiled. "This from the woman who warned me away from her not all that long ago."

She released his arm. "And I'm still warning you."

Travis nodded, but said nothing more. He, more than anyone, knew one of the reasons why Lee acted skittishly. And he had a strong idea of what made her so wary around men. The idea wasn't a pleasant one, and he knew he was going to have to get her to trust him enough to tell him everything, before he could decide whether to contact the Houston authorities. He knew someone in that area he could talk to, and made a mental note to do just that, first thing Monday. Until then, he would just work on showing Lee that he wasn't like the man who'd so badly frightened her. He had a sick feeling that that person was her ex-husband.

Dinner was punctuated by chatter between Susie and Nikki as they talked about their ride in the main corral. Lee watched her daughter closely, but found nothing to worry about. The little girl talked freely, although she rarely looked at Travis unless he spoke to her directly, and then her answers were mumbled. Lee quietly suggested to her she speak up so she could be heard, but didn't push her in any other way. She knew that Nikki would have to come around on her own.

After dinner, Lee helped Maude with the dishes, while Travis watched a movie with the girls.

"I'd help you ladies, but someone should oversee the children. You know, to make sure they watch the proper programs," he explained, herding Susie and Nikki out of the kitchen.

"You just say that because you don't like to wash dishes and you want to watch the movie with us," Susie accused her father.

He leaned down, tickling her sides until she shrieked with laughter. "Nah, I just like to make little girls laugh themselves silly." He glanced up, noticing Nikki standing to one side, watching them with a solemn look on her face. He could have sworn he also saw longing in her eyes for a brief moment. "Come on, if nothing's good on TV, I'll take you two on in a hot Monopoly game."

"Just don't cheat this time," Susie said haughtily as they walked toward the den.

Lee chuckled. "Are they always like that? Or is it for our benefit?" Her laughter stuck in her throat as she realized what she had just said.

"Usually they're worse," Maude replied, rinsing off the plates and handing them to her. "Sometimes I think I have two children running around here. He can act the father role when need be, but he's also become her friend, and that's very important for a child." She speared Lee with a sharp glance. "It's a shame you weren't allowed that."

Lee grimaced, remembering the few things she had said the last time she and Maude had talked. "I've come to realize that some people aren't meant to be parents. Mine definitely weren't."

She nodded. "An excellent way of looking at it. Just be grateful you didn't turn out like them. So many children turn out to be like their parents, and the end result isn't always a positive one."

Lee knew that fear. She sometimes wondered if she hadn't gone overboard at times to insure she wouldn't become like her mother or father. Every night she prayed it wouldn't happen. So far she considered herself lucky it hadn't.

"Travis is a good man and a good father," Maude went on. "No real bad habits to speak of. At least none I know of. He's tried to quit smoking, but hasn't succeeded yet. He drinks rarely and hasn't gotten drunk since the day he was discharged from the navy. At least, he's always sober around me. He even washes behind his ears."

Lee smiled. She was getting used to Maude's habit of switching subjects in midstream and found it entertaining, because she never knew what the older woman was going to come up with next.

"It sounds as if you're trying to palm him off on some poor, unsuspecting soul." She closed the dishwasher door and leaned against the counter.

"I have an idea a man is the last thing you're looking for," Maude said shrewdly.

Lee busied herself with wiping off the counter with a damp rag. "My marriage wasn't a happy one," she murmured, absently digging at a tiny speck with her fingernail. "I'm not in the market for another one, and to be honest, I don't think Travis is, either."

"Not everyone who's been married before looks actively for a new partner," Maude pointed out. "That doesn't mean they should ignore anyone thrown their way."

Lee carefully rinsed the rag and draped it over the faucet before turning back to Maude. "I admit I don't know you very well, but I would say that you wouldn't see me as a viable partner for Travis."

Chapter Ten

"Mom, are we going away from here?" Nikki asked, watching Lee wipe up the milk she had accidentally spilled as she ate her breakfast.

"What brought that up?" she asked, pouring herself what she knew to be her third cup of coffee.

"Because you always act this way before we move." The young girl drew circles in her cereal with her spoon. "I don't want to leave." She lifted a spoonful of soggy cereal to her lips. "I feel safe here. I even have friends." Her tone was wistful, sending a shaft of pain through Lee's body.

"You've never said anything like this before," Lee said through stiff lips.

"Because you were always worrying and I didn't want you to. I never tell anyone about where we lived before or anything. I just let them talk. But we won't move from here, will we, Mom?" she pleaded. "I can't leave my friends. Plus, I'm working on something important in my art class and I can't leave till it's done." Her large eyes were eloquent with feeling. "And Susie's grandma is teaching me to cook."

Lee sat down in the chair before her legs gave out. She had believed that Nikki had few memories of those early years, because they were never brought up by either one of them. So Nikki's revelation was a big surprise. She had never before told her mother that she felt safe in any of the places where they had previously lived. But then, Lee hadn't felt very secure in them, either. Here she did. Then Travis had offered her friendship. That was what had kept her awake most of the night—fear that he would learn her secret and alert the Texas authorities. After all, he was the town's sheriff and obligated to turn her in. There was no reason for him to believe her side of the story. She looked at the hands lying in her lap, but that didn't stop their violent trembling.

"Sometimes people have to move for reasons beyond their control, Nikki," she said slowly. She leaned forward, her voice low with intensity. "You do realize that what we talk about here in the house cannot be repeated to anyone. Not even to Susie."

The child nodded unhappily, her voice a mere whisper. "I know. I never say anything to anyone, because I want us to live here forever. Can we?"

Lee breathed deeply several times. She hated to act like a heavy-handed mother but she had no choice. "Nikki, you're old enough to know that I can't make any promises."

"Yes, you can!" Nikki burst out. "You've made promises before."

Lee closed her eyes, feeling incredibly weary. "Don't do this. Please try to understand."

The girl's lower lip quivered. "All I want is a friend. Now we'll probably leave in the middle of the night and I'll never see Susie again. It's not fair. I hate you!" She slid off her chair and ran from the room.

"Nikki!" Lee hurried after her and found her sprawled across her bed, crying her eyes out. "Honey." She sat on the edge of the bed and pulled the tiny body into her arms. She felt helpless against a sorrow that had been stored up for so long.

Lee wrapped her arms tightly around her daughter. "Oh, Nikki, you've been robbed of so many things," she whispered. "You deserve so much that I can't give you."

"Don't worry anymore, Mom," she assured her with a wisdom beyond her young years. "We have each other, don't we?"

Lee's laughter was shaky with tears. "Yes, darling, we certainly do. What do you say that we cheer ourselves up with a movie? We could drive over to Cotton Creek for one and a hamburger afterward." She knew she was offering a bribe, but she'd do anything possible to cheer up her daughter.

"And a hot fudge sundae?" Nikki asked hopefully.

Lee burst out laughing. "I think that can be arranged."

For a little while longer the world was right again.

TRAVIS PUSHED HIMSELF through his morning chores like a madman. But no matter how hard he worked, visions of Lee's pale face and haunted eyes swam in front of him. Finally giving up, he swore long and hard before returning to the house. He was barely civil to his mother as he stalked through the kitchen to the small room he used as an office and slammed the door behind him. Rifling through the address book in his desk, he found the Texas number he wanted.

"Travis, old son," Hank Douglas greeted him with the booming voice he well remembered from their years together in the navy. "You finally getting smart and leaving that dead-end town? Or is this an invitation for another one of those infamous fishing trips of yours?"

He chuckled. "No on the former, and I'm not too sure on the latter. We didn't come back with any fish, although we had some pretty powerful hangovers and insect bites. Actually I'm calling for some information, and I figured you might have it, since you have all that fancy computer equipment as a state police officer. You know, we small-town sheriffs are lucky to have an electric typewriter."

The other man laughed. "Give me a break, Hunter. As for the information, it depends on whether it's something I can tell you about," he said cautiously.

"Ever hear of a P.I. named J. D. Porter?"

Hank sighed. "Yeah, I've heard of him, all right. His fees are high, and he's been known to stretch the truth a bit, if it will help him, and he doesn't care who gets hurt in the process. Trust me, Travis, you don't want anything to do with him. He can be a mean bastard when crossed. Tell me, where'd you hear about him?"

He grimaced at the idea of telling the truth, but knew he owed his old friend that much. "He was in my office a little over a week ago, looking for someone."

"Anne Sinclair," Hank said instantly.

Travis's interest was piqued even more. "How did you know?"

"I'd heard the Sinclair family had hired him, along with a few others, but rumor has it Porter's leads are warmer. Still, what was he doing in your neck of the woods? That's pretty far off the beaten track for anyone, even him."

"Looking for Anne Sinclair, what else?" Travis deliberately kept his voice casual.

"And you're calling to find out what the true story is. Well, I can tell you what the Sinclair family says, and what the police think is the truth."

He straightened in his chair. "Shoot."

"I'll try to make it short and sweet. Basically, Anne Sinclair is the daughter of a well-known local banker with a volatile temper." Travis's harsh curse vibrated across the phone lines. "Lloyd Sinclair, heir to a large manufacturing firm, married her but didn't give up his old girlfriends after the wedding. When drunk, he's an extremely abusive man. Anne was in the hospital several times, but that was kept under wraps, due to the Sinclair clout. No one knew exactly why she finally got up the courage to file for divorce and custody of their daughter, but it all hit the fan when she did. Lloyd dragged her name through the mud in order to gain full custody, and Anne was left with nothing.''

"What about her family? Weren't they around to support her through all this?'' Travis demanded, picturing the events in his mind and not liking what he saw.

"Are you kidding? They were both on Lloyd's side. Probably because the Sinclair money resides in the Williams bank,'' Hank said with a snort of disgust. "In my book, she got a lousy deal all the way down the line.''

"So she shot her ex-husband and kidnapped the kid.''

Hank sighed. "Yeah, and what really happened that night, no one knows. At least, not her side of the story. Lloyd claims she came by to ask for a reconciliation, and when he refused she went crazy, found his gun and shot him. He knows what to say to the right people, but I don't really trust the guy. One of his ex-girlfriends claimed he beat her up and had the bruises to prove it. Then when it came time to go to court, she suddenly backed down, saying she had made it all up. She left town soon after. The man is no good.''

Travis groped for a cigarette and lighted it before leaning back in his chair. The harsh tang of nicotine burning his lungs was more than welcome about then.

"You think she had just cause, don't you?'' he rasped.

"This stays between you and me,'' Hank warned. "But you bet I do. I have an idea Lloyd could have easily pushed her into it, maybe even batted her around a bit, before she got hold of the gun and let him have it. He ended up lucky. A few inches lower, and she would have shot him through the heart.''

Travis frowned, not liking the familiar way Hank seemed to talk about Anne. "You seem to know a lot about her.'' He wasn't aware that he sounded more accusatory than casual.

"I should. She was hot news around here for quite a while. You couldn't pick up a newspaper without seeing a news story about her.'' Hank was silent for a moment. "Travis, if you happen to have any information about her...''

"No, I was just curious about Porter and the story he was spreading around. You know me. I don't like anyone I don't know nosing around my town." Travis winced, realizing he came across like television's view of a Western small-town sheriff. "I figured it wouldn't hurt to check up on him."

"Then I'm surprised you didn't do it a week ago," Hank said shrewdly. "As for Anne, I mean it. If you know anything, give me a call. I'm one of the few who's willing to give her a fair shake. She's not helping herself by not coming back and getting this all cleared up. Of course, with the Sinclair family against her, I guess I can't really blame her."

Travis felt sick to his stomach. "I would think after three years a person could be in Mexico or Europe. Look, I'm getting the high sign from my foreman. Why don't I call you in a few weeks and we can talk about another fishing trip?"

"Sounds good to me." Hank appeared to recognize his friend's need for a change of subject. "Give me a call, no matter what. Okay?"

"Yeah."

Travis hung up and sat there staring at the phone for a long time, then slowly rose to his feet. Feeling like a very old man, he walked out to the kitchen, where he found Maude standing at the sink, cutting up vegetables for stew.

"You look as if you just lost your last friend." She watched him pour a cup of coffee and seat himself at the table.

"I only wish it was that easy," he said and sighed.

Maude put down her small knife and rinsed her hands under the faucet, wiping them on her apron. "Does it have something to do with Lee?"

He nodded. "What I'm going to tell you can go no farther than this room. I mean it, Mom."

"Done."

One thing Travis trusted about his mother was her closed mouth. She might like gossip, but she knew when to keep certain subjects to herself. He told her about the private investigator looking for Lee, and his own conversation with Hank.

"Oh, my Lord," Maude breathed, sinking into a chair. "That poor child."

"You're taking her side without even knowing why she did it—if she even is Anne Sinclair."

Maude shot him a sharp look. "Do you believe she is?"

Travis dug into his shirt pocket for the photograph he had kept with him since that day and handed it to her. She studied it carefully for several minutes, and turned it over to read the information written there before handing it back to him.

"The use of some hair color, colored contact lenses, different clothing and she could get away with it," she said. "But the facial features aren't as easily disguised. No wonder she wanted nothing to do with you. She figured you'd put her in jail if you found out who she was. So why didn't you, when you found all this out?"

"Because I have no valid proof she really is Anne Sinclair," he explained. "And if I happened to be wrong, I could be charged with false arrest. Although I'd rather see that happen than find out she really is Anne Sinclair."

Maude's expression said it all. She couldn't remember the last time her son had been wrong where his intuition was concerned. "What are you going to do?"

Travis shook his head, more frustrated with life than he had felt in a long time. "Wish I knew. Somehow I've got to get her to trust me enough to talk about her past. I don't think it's going to be easy."

"Then I suggest you start reading some current magazines," Maude told him. "There've been a lot of articles written about abused women and children."

Travis closed his eyes. Was that why Nikki was so afraid of men? "The thing is, if she really is Anne Sinclair and I have proof, I have to contact the authorities, otherwise I'm in just as much trouble for hiding a fugitive from the law. That's why I need to find out her side of the story before I can do anything. Still, if she had defended herself by shooting him, she should have just told the authorities."

Maude shot him a pitying look. "Travis, you still believe the system works for the wronged party every time. My darling son, it just doesn't. I sure wish you'd get rid of that blind spot of yours before you get badly hurt."

"I'm a lawman and I have to believe it, or I wouldn't be of any use to anyone, would I?"

She nodded, knowing that no matter what, her son would do what was right for the individual, although she feared personal feelings could be involved this time. "You're falling for her, aren't you? You certainly don't believe in doing anything the easy way, do you?"

He slammed his palm on the tabletop so hard that everything bounced, but Maude didn't flicker an eyelid.

"It's a good thing your daughter isn't here to see this horrible display of temper. It might give her ideas she doesn't need. As for Lee, I suggest you start taking her out more, get her to trust you. That's the only way she'll even think about talking about her past.

But don't count on it working right away. By the way, you will be subtle, won't you?''

"Of course I will," he replied crossly.

"Then ask her out to dinner and a movie. You both survived the dance, didn't you?''

"Yes." He gritted his teeth, hating it when his mother treated him as if he were still ten years old, but Maude was blithely talking on.

"Watching two girls is as easy as watching one, so Nikki can stay here. She's a lot more relaxed here than she was the first time. In fact, why not start right now? Give Lee a call. Ask her out for next weekend.''

"Mom, as much as you tend to forget the fact, I am an adult and can make my own dates in my own time," he informed her. Still, he stood up and walked out of the kitchen.

"There's a phone here." Maude gestured to the one near the back door.

"I'm also adult enough to not require my mother's attendance while I call a lady for a date," he frostily informed her.

"Why can't family life be the way it used to be portrayed on TV?" she murmured, returning to her cooking.

"WELL, LOOKIE HERE!" Zeke howled with laughter when Travis entered the restaurant. "Who're the flowers for, Travis? Lorna, the sheriff's come a-courtin'," he shouted toward the rear of the restaurant.

Travis knew his face was bright red as he marched through the dining room with the small bouquet of flowers in his hand. He suddenly wished he had thought of something else, but asking a woman out on a date in front of the gossipy townspeople was new to him.

"Can it, Zeke," he growled. "Or I'll give Wilma back her shotgun.''

"Whoee, who smells so good?" another man chimed in, laughing loudly as he slapped his knee.

Lorna looked up, and a broad smile broke out on her face as she watched Travis seat himself at the counter.

"I guess I can't expect those are for me," Sally teased him as she poured him a cup of coffee.

For a moment Travis panicked. What if Lee wasn't there? He hadn't thought of that.

"Lee will be out in a second to take your order," Sally told him before moving away.

When Lee walked out, she didn't expect to see her newest customer holding a small bouquet of flowers in a delicate vase.

"These are for you," Travis muttered, holding out the vase.

She managed a brief smile as she accepted the offering. "Thank you," she murmured.

Travis grimaced, wishing he had kept trying to get her at home, so he knew he would have to do this while he still had the courage. Or, never hear the end of it from the others.

"I'll just have a burger and fries," he muttered, chickening out again.

She nodded. Lee sensed that he had wanted to say something more, but that something had held him back. "I'll get your burger." With a quizzical expression on her face she walked away to place his order.

"You're batting zero," Fred, a neighboring rancher, teased, as he passed Travis on his way out. "And here we old-timers thought you were one of the smooth ones."

He turned his head and managed to smile. Did everyone but the person involved know what he was clumsily trying to do? "Yeah, well, the movies make it look too easy, Fred."

"If I didn't have to get back home, I'd stay to see how it comes out. Still, I'll know by tonight." The older man clapped him on the shoulder as he left.

Travis took his time eating his hamburger, hoping that everyone would leave, but no luck. Instead, it appeared no one was in any hurry; they all asked for numerous refills on their coffee. By the time Lee left him with his bill, he knew he had to stumble ahead.

"Ah, Lee—" he grimaced "—I was wondering if you'd like to take in a movie this Friday night. My mom said she'd be more than happy to look after Nikki for you."

Lee knew it was dangerous for her to see Travis more than she should, but something deep inside nudged her. She told herself she was only agreeing because she couldn't bear to reject him in front of their avidly listening audience.

"That sounds very nice," she said softly. "I'd like that." Her lips quivered with laughter as she heard the sigh of relief he gave at her reply.

"I guess you could tell I'm out of practice," he whispered as he paid the bill.

"That's all right," she whispered back. "Think of the fodder we've given the town gossips. It will keep them busy for the rest of the afternoon."

LEE SHOULD have known that she couldn't stop with that evening at the dance—not when she was with such a caring man as Travis, who was the perfect escort anywhere they chose to go. After their first public appearance, the town followed the slowly budding romance with watchful eyes.

"Do you realize we've become the talk of the town?" Lee asked Travis one evening, as they walked out of the movie theater in a nearby town.

He grinned. "It's difficult not to."

"But doesn't it bother you?"

Travis shook his head. "Are you kidding? Mom's driving the townspeople crazy by not giving them any good gossip. Right about now I guess we're better than TV." He walked alongside her to his car and unlocked the door. "You want to stop for something to eat before heading back?"

"You certainly can't be hungry after all the popcorn you ate during the movie," she teased.

He smiled, just happy that he made her relax. "Popcorn isn't all that filling. So how about it?"

"Sure, why not?"

Travis found a fast-food restaurant open and they ordered hot dogs and French fries. By unspoken agreement they sat outside in the cool, spring night air.

"It's hard to believe school will be over soon," Lee said with a sigh. "I just wish I knew what I was going to do with Nikki while I work. I asked her if she wanted to take some summer school classes, and she acted as if I had asked her to walk across hot coals."

Travis chuckled. "Susie pretty much got the same suggestion, except it was after I saw her last report card. I admit math has never been my best subject, but I think I did better with the basics than she did."

"I hope Nikki's behaving for Maude." Lee dipped a fry into catsup and nibbled on it.

"The kids worship the ground she walks on, since she promises to allow them to mess up the kitchen, baking all sorts of cakes and cookies. I'm sure they had the time of their lives tonight. In fact, since it's getting so late, why don't you just let her spend the night? Most of the times when we get back, she's already asleep."

"No, I couldn't do that," Lee said swiftly.

"Eat up. You're too skinny." He was used to changing the subject now, in order to keep her from growing too wary of him—just as he kept questions to a minimum and only on a casual basis, in order not to frighten her off. His good-night kisses were kept light and almost impersonal, when all he wanted to do was crush her in his arms and protect her from the world. For his patience he'd gained a woman who smiled more, even when he told her his corniest jokes, and she didn't shy away from his touch when he held her hand in the movies.

"'You can never be too rich nor too thin,'" she quoted.

"Yeah, well, nobody would say that if they saw you. Why do you think Mom cooks all those big meals when you come over for dinner?" Travis swiped one of her fries and dipped it into catsup before offering it to her.

Lee laughed, the sound rich and full before her lips closed on it. When a slight tug from Travis's end caught her attention, she looked up. Her eyes, luminous in the outdoor lighting, caught his and held. For long moments they stared at each other.

Lee knew her body yearned to be closer to Travis, but common sense told her she couldn't take the chance. When a car drove by, stereo sound blasting out through the open windows, the mood was rudely destroyed. Lee's head jerked back, breaking their self-induced trance. She chewed slowly, watching Travis pop the rest of the fry into his own mouth. He acted as if nothing had just happened between them, but from the darkness in his eyes and his flushed features she knew better.

"It's getting late, and we have a long drive back." Lee's voice was raspy with the need she had long denied, but couldn't allow herself to give in to.

Travis gathered up the papers and handed Lee her half-finished cup of soda. She finished it there before tossing it into the trash can. They walked slowly back to the car, both lost in their own thoughts. Travis half turned in the seat, his arm draped across the back.

"If I really kiss you, will you promise not to be frightened of me?" he asked quietly.

Her lips parted slightly, the expression in her eyes giving away her inner feelings.

"I think I gave up feeling frightened of you a long time ago," she whispered, unknowingly admitting she'd once had such a fear. But the doubts reflected in her eyes couldn't be erased as easily.

Travis knew that if he wanted to win her trust, he would have to make each move slowly and carefully and let her set the pace. He brought her palm to his lips.

"Do you know sometimes you watch me as if you're memorizing everything about me?" His breath was warm against her skin. "Although I wouldn't mind if you were watching me because you think I'm the sexiest guy you've ever met.''

"You're the kindest man I've ever met," Lee murmured, not realizing she had moved closer to him.

"I guess that's close to being sexy," he said ruefully.

"Even better.''

Travis lowered his head and brushed his lips softly against hers several times, until he felt them relax under his touch. Even then he waited another minute before he tried to deepen the kiss. When his tongue slid along her lips, they hesitantly parted, just enough to allow him entrance. He felt a rush of heat in his veins, but quickly tamped it down before he moved too fast and frightened her. He continued tantalizing her with light touches.

"Travis," Lee breathed, tentatively sliding her arms around his waist and moving until their upper bodies lightly touched.

"Lee," he whispered, again and again dipping his tongue into the sweet cavern of her mouth.

Her answer was to take one of his hands and place it against her throat with a trust that almost unnerved him. Travis's fingers splayed out, the heel of his palm resting in the valley between her breasts. He could feel her breathing deepen as his fingers moved lightly against the bare skin her open collar revealed. The rust wool sweater carried her body heat and her spicy floral fragrance. When he moved his hand to one side to cover her heaving breast, he felt the tension suddenly enter her body. He did nothing more than keep his hand resting lightly on her breast, making no sudden moves as he compared her to a small wild animal who didn't need taming as much as she needed to know she wouldn't be hurt.

Lee wanted to smile with joy at the idea that such a simple caress could leave her wishing for so much more. She wanted to throw herself into Travis's arms and bury her face against his neck, inhaling the clean fragrance of his skin and absorbing his inner strength. She had been alone with her secrets for so long that the need for someone to share them with grew every time she was with him. She buried her face against his neck, feeling the slightly rough skin against her lips.

"I feel safe with you," she whispered. "You don't know how much that means to me.''

He chuckled. "Maybe about as much as this means to me." When his mouth lowered to hers this time, he didn't hold back. He wanted her to know how much he desired her, and for the moment it was the only way he could tell her.

Lee's hands dug into his scalp, her fingers combing through the thick strands, allowing his hair to curl around them. She tipped her head to one side when his mouth found her ear and sighed when his tongue darted inside the shell-like orifice. When his hand kneaded her breast, plucking at her nipple until it stood up straight, she felt as if she were melting.

"You're making me think of things not suitable for the mother of a seven-year-old child," she whispered on a sigh.

"That's all right. I'm thinking the same thoughts and I'm a father," he murmured, before kissing her harder and even deeper. "Lee, you're going to have to help me here. If we don't stop soon, we may get involved in some heavy-duty necking in the front seat, and that hasn't been my style for about twenty years."

A soft giggle escaped her lips. "It could be embarrassing for us, couldn't it?"

She drew back first, but Travis wasn't about to allow her to withdraw too far. When he slid back behind the steering wheel, he pulled Lee over to sit close beside him.

"Just because I can't kiss you and drive at the same time doesn't mean you can't sit next to me." He switched on the engine and waited a moment before putting it into gear. He turned on the radio and checked the channels until he found one playing golden oldies. To the sounds of the Beach Boys, he gunned the engine and pulled out of the parking lot.

Lee felt freer than she had in a long time as she and Travis talked and laughed during the forty-minute drive back to his ranch. She saw him as more than the town's law officer now; she saw him as a man she was strongly attracted to. She drove all memories of her past out of her mind as she allowed her thoughts to wander to happier ideas— what life with Travis could be like. Again giving in to impulse, she leaned over and planted a kiss on the corner of his mouth.

"What was that for?" he asked, surprised and pleased by her action.

"Just because you're you," she said happily. "And because you make me feel like a new person."

"Be careful, or I'll drive on past my place to yours, where we can discuss this at greater length," he warned playfully.

"Knowing you, there wouldn't be much talking done." Now she even felt free to tease. "So no driving by. Nikki will be expecting me, no matter how late we are." Her attention was diverted when she noticed streaks of white light race across the dark sky. Her body stiffened. Thunder and lightning always reminded her of the night that had changed her life so drastically. She feared for Nikki, who usually suffered from nightmares in weather such as this. She prayed that this time would be different.

"Hmm, looks like we're in for a big storm," Travis commented, unaware of her sudden withdrawal. When the lightning flashed again, Lee jumped. "You okay? It's just lightning. It can't harm you, as long as you don't stand under a tree." He tried to treat the subject lightly, hoping to help her to relax.

"I guess I'm worried about Nikki." She was glad she didn't have to lie about that. "She's never liked thunderstorms."

"Maude's with her," he assured her.

But that didn't comfort Lee at all.

Travis had barely stopped the car in front of the house when Maude, a harried expression on her face, stepped out onto the porch. Lee felt a cold shiver race across her spine as she got out of the car and heard a child's screams echo from the house.

"I don't know what happened." The older woman looked helpless. "She fell asleep on Susie's other bed, then she woke up screaming a little while ago, and won't allow me near her."

Lee barely heard the words. She was racing inside the house and down the hall, where she found her daughter cowering in a corner of the room, while a frightened-looking Susie sat up in bed watching her friend. The little girl looked up when her father and grandmother appeared in the doorway.

"We both woke up because of the thunder," Susie burst out, looking ready to cry, as well. "She wouldn't stop crying, and I didn't know what to do." She looked miserable because she couldn't help her friend.

But Lee knew what to do. Past experience had taught her that. She sat on the floor, holding her daughter in her lap as the little girl clung to her with a death grip, begging her not to leave her.

Chapter Eleven

By the time Lee had Nikki calmed down and back in bed under the warm covers, she felt so exhausted that she could barely walk out to the den. There she found Travis seated in his favorite easy chair, drinking what appeared to be whiskey from a squat, heavy glass. She was stunned when she looked at the clock and saw that more than two hours had passed since she had first entered the house. Maude, seated on the couch where she was mending a pair of Susie's jeans, put her work aside and stood up.

"I put a robe and clean towels in the bathroom. I want you to take a long, hot bath," she ordered, walking over to Lee and putting an arm around her. She held up her hand when Lee opened her mouth. "No arguments. That little girl is exhausted, and so are you. You can sleep in the guest room." She guided Lee out of the room and down the hall. A few moments later Maude returned to the den. "Are you going to wait up for her?"

Travis nodded, still concentrating on his glass.

"Then I'll say good-night," Maude said quietly. "Just remember, it's been as rough a night for her as it was for Nikki."

"I will."

Lee opted for a hot shower instead of a bath, for fear she'd fall asleep if she relaxed in a tub. After pulling on the fleece robe Maude had left out for her, she looked down the hall, noting that the den light was still on. Her first thought was to escape to the guest room, because she didn't know if she could talk to anyone, especially Travis, but something prodded her toward the den. She found him still seated, the one light burning next to his chair. The rest of the room was in darkness, except for periodic flashes of lightning. Lee stiffened at first as memories threatened to overwhelm her. Steeling herself, she walked into the room. Travis looked up.

"Would you like a drink?"

"No, thank you," she murmured, continuing across the room to the large window.

"It happened on a night just like this," she murmured, not even knowing if she was talking to herself or to the man watching her so closely. She rubbed her hands up and down her arms to combat the chill that had stolen into her bones, despite the hot shower. She stood there, staring out the rain-lashed window.

"What did?" His voice was so quiet that it barely reached her ears.

"The night I shot my ex-husband."

Travis sat very still. "You told me you're a widow," he said in a quiet voice.

"No, but I wish I was."

"Well, if you shot him, you must have had a good reason to do it. You don't seem the type to do something just for the hell of it." He kept his voice low, every sense on alert as he sat in the chair watching her. She stood in front of the dark glass, staring at the white-hot flashes of light in the sky as if they had induced a hypnotic trance.

"True, I'm the type to avoid altercations. But I learned that night that when you realize you're going to be killed, you tend to do everything possible to protect yourself," she explained, her voice holding no emotion whatsoever. "After what I had been through, death would have been a blessing, except that there was Nikki. I knew I couldn't let her go through that same kind of hell. Lloyd had hit her. She was so tiny then, so gentle and sweet. She couldn't have survived it. I had to take her away." She reached up, running her hands through the tangled waves of her still-damp hair.

"Did your husband beat you, Lee?"

She laughed, but there was no mirth in the sound. "Let me explain. My real name is Anne Sinclair. My ex-husband is Lloyd Sinclair of Sinclair Manufacturing, Houston, Texas. When I first met him, I was convinced I had met Prince Charming. I received red roses every day, he flew me to New York for dinner and a play one evening. He treated me as if I was someone very special. And when he proposed, I wanted out of my home life so badly that I didn't stop to think. I just said yes and unknowingly went from one living hell to another. You see, my father is a bank president with a very nasty habit. When he had problems at work, he brought them home and took them out on my mother and me with his fists. Not a pretty story, is it? Although nowadays it doesn't seem to be all that uncommon.''

Travis swallowed the nausea rising in his throat. He wanted nothing more than to jump up and hold her in his arms. He wanted to banish all the evil, but he knew he had to sit there until Lee had said all she wanted to say.

''Didn't your mother ever try to fight back or leave him?''

She shook her head, feeling the past begin to smother her, but she fought it. ''No. You see, she felt it was all my fault. She used to enjoy telling me she hadn't wanted children, and if she could have gotten rid of me, she would have. So she didn't care what my father did to me, as long as he left her alone.''

Travis paused to light a cigarette, disconcerted to find his hands shaking as he lifted the lighter. ''Did he ever try anything other than hitting you?''

Lee laughed bitterly. ''No, Clinton Williams just liked to beat his daughter until she cried for mercy. I guess I should be grateful for that.''

He drew the acrid smoke deep into his lungs. ''Did he mind your getting married?''

She continued looking out into the night as if she could find all the answers there. She stood still as a statue, her figure an ethereal reflection in the glass. Her mind was numb, as were her emotions. She knew that if she allowed herself to feel the least bit of emotion, she would break down in a way she had never allowed herself. ''Since the Sinclair fortune was in his bank, he didn't mind one bit. His advice to me was not to screw it up, or he'd make me pay for it.''

''But?''

''But no one told me that Lloyd was an abusive alcoholic,'' she replied softly, her lips twisted. ''Do you understand that term? Of course, you would, wouldn't you? I'm sure most law enforcement officers have dealt with a few in their time.''

''Someone who can't hold their liquor and turns mean when they drink,'' Travis replied woodenly.

She nodded. ''That was Lloyd. I first learned the meaning of the term on my wedding night. Quite an auspicious beginning, wouldn't you say? My new husband had too much champagne during the reception, and by the time we got to our hotel, he was going on about how he was going to show me the kind of wife he wanted.'' She rested her forehead against the cool glass, perversely seeking to chill still more of her already cold body.

Travis's breath hissed between his teeth. He closed his eyes to the visions running through his head. If Lloyd Sinclair had stood there before him, he knew he would have killed the man with his bare hands.

"To his way of thinking, I wasn't the perfect wife," she continued. "I seemed to be always doing something wrong, whether it was dinner being served five minutes late, or his favorite shirt didn't come back from the laundry in time for a certain occasion." Her voice dropped to a pain-filled whisper. "The only time he didn't hit me was when I was pregnant. Probably because his father wanted a grandchild so badly and was the only person Lloyd feared. After all, he could have cared less if he had a family. When I first told him I was pregnant, he told me all he wanted from me was someone to entertain his clients and be in his bed. Nothing else mattered." She held on to one of the draperies as if it were a lifeline, something to keep her in the present, even as the past threatened to drag her back into that black pit. Her hand tightened, then released the heavy fabric.

Travis groped for his pack of cigarettes and lighted another, breathing in deeply. "And then Nikki was born."

Her smile returned to her voice. "Oh yes, my Nikki. Her real name is Nicola Marie Sinclair. She was such a beautiful baby. I'm sure I'm prejudiced, but she was always so happy and never cried. Lloyd liked that, since he didn't like his sleep disturbed." Her voice lost its joy when she mentioned his name again. "Her two grandfathers weren't happy that I didn't give them a grandson. They conveniently forgot that it's the man's genes that provide the sex of the child. In their eyes I could do no right." A tear appeared at the corner of one eye. "Yet that didn't stop them from trying to spoil her. As for Lloyd, I was to hand her over to a nanny and be his hostess again. The only blessing was that he had a mistress, one of many in the course of our marriage, and pretty much left me alone, except for his tries to get me pregnant again. His father still demanded a grandson, to be groomed for the family business, and Lloyd was determined to give him one, no matter how I felt about the subject."

"How did you find out about the other women?" Travis asked, watching her tiny figure standing so straight and tall as she continued with the story that she must have known could send her to prison for many years.

"His current one came to see me. She was convinced if I gave Lloyd a divorce he would marry her. When I told him about her visit, and that if he wanted a divorce, I wouldn't stand in his way, he grew angry, as if it was all my fault. The battle was short and not very sweet, and the girlfriend was never heard of again. A year later I knew I couldn't take any more of his cruelty, so I filed for divorce." She stroked the folds of the drapery absently, apparently using it again as that desperately needed lifeline. "Naturally, Lloyd acted like the wronged husband. He even went so far as to warn me I would lose Nikki, and that my reputation would be shredded beyond repair if I continued with the proceedings."

Travis lighted yet another cigarette, even though he hadn't finished with the one he had. "Why didn't you just get out then?" he asked in a hoarse voice. "You could have filed for your divorce from another state. The law was on your side, Lee, not his."

She shrugged. "When you're convinced you're the wronged party and will see justice served, you're not afraid of anything or anyone. I should have known better, when I had so much trouble finding an attorney who would even consider my case. In the end I had a young man fresh out of an Eastern law school, who had no idea of the Sinclairs' power. Their attorneys chewed him up into little pieces and spat him out. I even told both sets of parents everything Lloyd had done to me over the years, to make them understand why I was divorcing him. My father said that I probably deserved it, that I always was a headstrong child and needed a firm hand." She almost choked on the words. "And Joshua Sinclair said that Lloyd might be a little hotheaded at times, but he knew his son loved me." Now she sounded bitter. "They dared to call the beastly way I was treated love! Well, I learned my lesson quickly. Lloyd fought for custody and won, after he brought in scores of men stating I'd had affairs with them and used drugs. I was branded an unfit mother and he gained full custody. I wasn't even allowed visiting privileges." She held up her head, breathing deeply to calm herself.

"Lee, what about the night you shot him? What happened then?" He forced himself to keep his voice even, because his intuition told him that every word he'd heard so far was the truth. "Can you talk about it?"

She cleared her throat. "Lloyd called me that night. There was a terrible thunderstorm, and Nikki was having trouble going to sleep. He demanded I come over and calm her down. I went, because I hoped to talk to him about working out an alternate custody arrangement. I knew he didn't want her. He just wanted to use her as a tool to hurt me. I found liquor bottles all over the house and a woman in the living room. Nikki was in the bedroom, screaming the way she was tonight. I calmed her down and got her back to sleep, but I also noticed a bruise on her cheek and I knew that he had hit her. I wasn't about to put up with that. The woman was gone when I sought out Lloyd and found him in his study. I tried to talk to him about Nikki, but his answer was always the same. No. Unfortunately I made a big mistake. I lost my temper and told him exactly what I thought of him. He grew even angrier and started hitting me. Nikki woke up and ran into the room, pulling on him and demanding he leave me alone. He hit her again, and I screamed for her to go back to her bedroom. Luckily she obeyed me.'' She closed her eyes, clearly reliving those last few minutes of her old life. Her body tensed, as if those blows were again being directed at her.

''Lee, you don't have to go on with this,'' Travis interjected swiftly. He felt he had to warn her about what she was doing. ''You don't realize—''

She held up her hand. ''Yes, I do.'' Her voice was strong with conviction. ''What I'm telling you will lock me away for the rest of my life and send Nikki back to hell. I always knew I couldn't run forever, and I guess this is as good a place as any to end it. But first I want someone to hear my side of the story, because otherwise it won't have a chance to be told.''

Travis swallowed a lump in his throat. ''What happened next?''

Lee shook her head, for the first time looking bleak. ''I'm not exactly sure what happened. I do remember I was bent backward over his desk with his hands around my throat, choking me. I groped in his top desk drawer, looking for a letter opener, anything to use as a weapon. I only meant to use it to get him away from me. I guess I found the gun and it went off. The next thing I knew, I was standing over him with the weapon in my hand. At first I thought I had killed him, until I saw that he was still breathing. After that I didn't stop to think. I just grabbed Nikki and put her in the car, then called 911, saying I'd heard shots. Although I'm certain if the positions had been reversed, he would have let me die.'' Her body trembled violently.

''Why didn't you wait for the police and tell them what happened? It was a clear-cut case of self-defense,'' Travis pointed out, leaning forward in the chair, his arms resting on his thighs. ''You and Nikki had the bruises to prove he abused you.''

She laughed bitterly. ''Maybe I had that kind of proof, but Joshua Sinclair had the connections, and he never forgave me for daring to divorce his son. He would have made sure I was locked up for the rest of my life, and Nikki would have been poisoned against me, or turned into a battered child without any hope of a normal life. I couldn't allow that to happen. So we've been on the run for more than three years. There're private detectives after us, I'm sure, because the Sinclair family wouldn't allow me to get away with what I did, and because they want Nikki back.'' Slowly she turned, the pain and suffering she had gone through evident in her eyes. "I wouldn't have had a chance, Travis.''

"You don't know that, because you didn't give anyone a chance to help you,'' he argued.

"I know the family. I also know I'll eventually be caught, and then I'll fight for the truth to be known. I'll lose, but I won't go down quietly.'' Slowly she walked toward him, her head still held high. "I'm a fugitive from the law, and as the town sheriff, I understand you will have to lock me up. All I ask is that you do everything possible to help Nikki. She remembers so little from those early years, and it's only been recently that she's begun to be the happy child I want her to be. Please find a way to protect her.''

Travis reached out and pulled her into his lap, wrapping his arms around her.

Lee was so weak from her confession that she didn't bother to struggle. She curled up against his warmth and slipped her arms around his neck, burrowing her face against the slightly rough skin. When warm droplets hit her cheek she tilted back her head. She brushed her fingers across his cheek and turned them around—to find them wet.

"You're crying,'' she murmured.

"Men don't cry,'' he said huskily.

"But you are.'' She stared into his eyes, eyes gleaming with moisture. "You do believe me, don't you?''

"You told me a story that can put you away for many years, but all you care about is the welfare of your child,'' Travis said in a raw voice. "You've been led to believe your very existence is all your fault, yet you turned into one of the warmest, most loving women I have ever met. You're a very special lady.'' He wrapped one hand around her nape and brought her face against his chest.

For the longest time they sat in the chair, forgetting about cramping limbs and the storm overhead. All that mattered was Lee's ability to finally trust someone, and that Travis not only believed her, but called her special.

"Travis?'' Lee's voice sounded sleepy. Her confession had sapped her strength.

"What?'' He knew he should carry her into the guest room and let her sleep in a comfortable bed.

"I don't want you to do anything that will get you into trouble. I understand that I'll have to go to jail now, until you can contact the proper authorities.''

He smiled in spite of himself. ''Are you that determined to be put behind bars?''

''No, but I did shoot him and kidnap Nikki. Those offenses don't exactly merit a slap on the wrist.''

He ran a hand over her hair, tangling his fingers in the silky strands. ''Why don't you just relax and let me handle this, okay? I promise no harm is going to come to you.''

She breathed deeply and exhaled. ''Okay.''

Travis stood up and with her still cradled in his arms, carried her into the guest room and laid her on the bed. After he draped the covers over her, he sat down on the edge of the bed, pulled off his boots and settled down on the other side, drawing Lee back into his arms. As if they had lain together many times, she automatically curled against him, laying her head on his shoulder.

The last words she heard before falling into a deep sleep were, ''Don't worry, Anne, I'm on your side.''

IT WAS THE SMELL of freshly brewed coffee that tempted Lee out of her warm bed and into a quick shower.

''They're right. Confession is good for the soul,'' she murmured as she brushed the tangles from her hair, aware she felt freer than she had in a long time. Yet for just a moment she couldn't help but wonder if she had made a big mistake in confiding in Travis. Her stomach burned with fear and it took her several minutes to calm her racing pulse. Before she dared dwell on it anymore, she quickly left the bathroom.

Maude was sitting at the kitchen table drinking coffee when Lee entered the room. The older woman smiled and gestured toward the coffee maker. ''It's freshly made.'' She rose to her feet. ''How about some breakfast?''

Lee felt the way Alice did when she fell down the hole. ''I—didn't Travis tell you?'' she asked, a note of desperation in her voice.

Maude pulled out two pans and soon had eggs frying in one and sausage in another. ''Yes, he told me everything.''

Lee felt a chill trickle down her spine as she realized that the house sounded suspiciously silent. ''Where's Nikki?'' Her question ended on a frightened squeak. Was she to lose her daughter so quickly?

''She and Susie are out with one of the hands. Don't worry, she's perfectly safe,'' Travis's mother assured her. When the food was ready, Maude set the plate in front of her. "Now I want to see you eat every bite. You're much too thin."

"That's what Travis says," Lee murmured.

Maude sat down again and pulled her coffee cup in front of her. "Lee, or shall I say, Anne, I want you to know that I understand why you did what you did. It shows a great deal of unselfish love that you looked out more for your daughter than yourself. I just hope you're prepared for a battle to keep Nikki and prove you were an innocent victim. I've always believed in being blunt. You're not going to have an easy time ahead of you. My son tends to believe that justice will protect the right and convict the wrong. It's one of his failings, but I have to love him for wanting to see life that way. I only wish it were true. Still, you're going to have to be strong. Are you ready for that?"

"I've always been prepared," Lee said firmly.

Maude eyed her keenly. "Yes, I'm sure you are," she said, then added briskly, "Eat your food, before it gets cold. We have some things to think over. And from now on I'm calling you Anne. It's time you reverted to your real self. What about that hair of yours? Surely that can't be your real color?" She didn't want to tell Anne that she had seen a picture of her, until Travis broke the news about the investigator.

Anne grimaced. "It's a temporary rinse that washes out after so many shampoos."

"And what about your eye color?"

"Extended wear contact lenses."

Maude handed her a napkin. "We may as well begin now."

Anne bent over, using her fingers to stretch her eyes wide open, and brown discs dropped onto the napkin. Maude picked up the paper and tossed it into the trash.

"You won't need those any longer."

"But I have to work in town," Anne protested, seeing her disguise so carelessly discarded. "Everyone will know I'm not who they think I am."

Maude put her fingers under her chin and lifted her face, looking into vibrant green eyes. "My dear, you can't understand everything just now, but you will. Now, eat up, because after you finish your breakfast, we're going to wash that horrible color out of your hair. Let's see if we can find the real you, shall we?"

With Maude's enthusiastic assistance and half a bottle of shampoo, the brown hair color finally trickled down the drain. Anne was ordered to walk down to the barn to see Travis. She felt naked, walking out into the open with her strawberry-blond hair brushed back from her face in a casual style and her eyes their natural color.

When she reached the barn, she stood in the doorway until she heard sounds from the rear. Taking a deep breath to bolster her courage, she stepped carefully through the strewn hay until she found Travis in the rear stall, grooming the bay gelding he usually rode.

"Travis." She bit her lip, unsure how to approach him.

He looked up, smiled, then froze when he saw the woman standing before him. The clothing was the same as that she'd worn last night, but the face appeared different, the skin more translucent. Then he realized she must have worn a darker makeup base to go with the darker hair color. Her eyes were now a gemlike green, her thick hair the color of a rich sunset with red and blond strands blended in profusion. What he had seen in the photograph was a mere shadow compared to the real thing. She had a face he couldn't easily forget.

"I always knew you were pretty, but now you are so beautiful that you make my eyes ache," he said quietly.

She hesitated for a moment before moving closer to him. Travis reached out and drew her into a warm embrace.

"You should hate me," she mumbled against his shirtfront.

"Why?" He kissed the top of her hair.

"Because I'm a liar, a fugitive, so many other things I can't begin to count."

Travis rubbed his cheek against the top of her head. "You can say all you want, and I'll just come up with positive points. Did you eat anything?"

She smiled. "Do you honestly think Maude would allow me to leave the house without eating? She was also the one who made me take out the contact lenses and wash the color out of my hair. I swear my scalp is raw from all the shampooings she made me endure. She's a very strong-minded lady."

He chuckled. "Tell me about it." He nuzzled her ear and murmured, "Hold on to your hat, lady, because I intend to give you a kiss that says a hell of a lot more than good-morning."

Anne lifted her face as Travis sought out her mouth. His tongue darted between her parted lips, showing a passion she hadn't received from him before. Under his touch, she felt freer than she ever had in her life. Her hands roamed up and down his back, feeling the fabric that was damp from his exertions. The warm smells of horse, leather and man filled her nostrils, and she couldn't imagine anything smelling better.

"I don't feel like the same person anymore," she murmured against his mouth.

He grasped her around the waist and pulled her off her feet. "That's because you aren't," he pointed out. "You're no longer the Anne Sinclair from three years ago, nor are you Lee Davis, but you are the best of both women. Anne, I would never hurt you. You know that, don't you?" he insisted.

She smiled. "You've certainly been persistent enough to prove that to me."

Travis released her just a little, so that she slid down his body. "I'm going to do everything I can to help you through this."

"You're trusting me too much," she protested. "You don't know what they're saying about me. How can you believe me so easily?"

"For one very good reason." He brushed a stray lock of hair from her face. "A private investigator was in my office a while back, looking for Anne and Nicola Sinclair, and had a picture."

"You never said anything," she breathed, stunned by his casual announcement.

He rubbed her back between her shoulder blades. "Why should I? There was no guarantee that Lee Davis was Anne Sinclair."

"I'm surprised he didn't talk to anyone else," Anne mused.

"He did."

She was stunned by his revelation. "What?"

He grinned, clearly pleased with himself. "I told the people they weren't to give out any information, and they went along with it. Lorna sent you out on errands, so you weren't in the restaurant, in case he came around, which he did."

"And no one said anything." Anne couldn't believe it. "These people don't even know me."

He smiled. "Yes, they do. They knew enough about you to protect you. I know it sounds corny, but we do protect our own here. And you're one of us, Anne."

She hugged Travis so tightly that she was positive she almost cracked his ribs. "I wish I knew what to say. Nikki once asked me if we could always stay in Dunson, because she felt safe here. Now I truly understand how she felt."

He gently pushed her back a step so he could look down into her face. "You trusted me enough to tell me about your past. Do you trust me enough to help you with your present and future?"

Anne looked into his eyes and saw that Travis really believed that everything would be all right. She sadly wondered how a man so worldly in some ways could be so naive in others.

"Oh, Travis, I only wish it could be that easy," she said with a sigh.

He opened his mouth, prepared to argue with her, but was thwarted before he could say anything.

"Break clean, you two," Maude's voice called out. "The girls are coming in, and I don't want them to get more of an education than they need at this tender age."

Travis cursed under his breath. He held Anne close to him as he worked to regain his equilibrium.

"My mother has an incredible sense of timing." He dug his fingers gently into her scalp and tilted back her head. "Think you're ready to start facing people as yourself?"

"It appears I have no choice."

"I'm not trying to push you into anything you don't want to do," he insisted. "But you can't hide forever, Anne. You'll have to face them sooner or later."

"You may be right, but I also have my daughter to consider. And if it means running again to keep her safe, I will." Her face was stony with resolve, but Travis refused to allow her to even think of such a thing.

His fingertip brushed across her lower lip. "All running away will get you is another searcher, and where they've failed, I won't."

Chapter Twelve

"Mornin' Anne. You're lookin' pretty chipper today," Zeke greeted her as he accepted the cup of coffee she put in front of him.

"The sun's shining, my daughter is getting excellent grades in school, and I found a penny on the sidewalk this morning, so I'm not doing too badly," she replied pertly. "How about you? You behaving yourself?"

"Wilma won't let me do anything else but," he grumbled good-naturedly. "Why don't you give me some of Lorna's beef stew and dumplings?"

Anne nodded. "Right away." As she moved away to drop off the order, she silently marveled at the way the townspeople had so easily accepted the truth about her. From the first day she had walked into the restaurant, everyone had called her by her true name and acted as if she had always been a strawberry blonde! It was as if Lee Davis had never existed. It hadn't been until she sat down and talked with Lorna that she learned just how closemouthed Dunson's residents could be. She was informed that no P.I. was going to get any information out of anyone there. Since then she had lived each day to its fullest, blossoming under Travis's tender regard and the townspeople's easy acceptance of her.

"Hey, Anne." Cal ambled inside and seated himself at the counter.

"Hi, Cal. Where's Mary Ellen? Couldn't she take her lunch hour with you today?" Anne had gotten used to seeing the two come in most days for lunch in the past few weeks.

He flushed and ducked his head. "She's—eating at home today," he muttered.

Her smile dimmed. "Cal, take it from someone who's been there. She isn't worth it. You just go out there and find someone who will really appreciate you, and not only pay attention to you when there isn't anyone else around. Show her she isn't the only girl in town."

He brightened, beginning to look hopeful. "You think so?"

"I know so," Anne said firmly. "You've got a lot going for you." She leaned down to confide, "In fact, didn't I see Carrie Nash looking your way last weekend at the church social? Why, I bet if you asked her out to a movie or something, she'd agree."

Cal considered her words. "I guess I couldn't lose anything by asking."

"And, Cal, if Mary Ellen sees you with other girls and tries to get you back, start thinking about the way she's kept you dangling for so long," Anne advised. "Ask yourself if she's really worth it."

He grinned broadly. "You know, you're right. I've let her lead me around by the nose for quite a while now. In fact, I'm not even going to stop by the bakery tomorrow. And I'll call Carrie when I get back to the station. Thanks."

"No problem. So, what would you like to eat?"

"To be honest, I'd like to see Mary Ellen eat a very large portion of crow."

"I HEARD you're playing Dear Abby now," Travis teased Anne as they relaxed with their after-dinner coffee. Maude had agreed to baby-sit while they went out for dinner at a steak house in a neighboring town.

"So Cal did it," she said happily. "Good for him."

He nodded. "He called Carrie Nash up and talked to her for a solid half hour before asking her out to a movie. I'm sure word will get out pretty fast that this time Cal dropped Mary Ellen, instead of the other way around."

She frowned. "Isn't Cal going a little far?"

"Cal? That was Myrna's idea. She's never been too fond of Mary Ellen. She feels the kid's too full of herself." He chuckled. "I have an idea this is going to get pretty interesting."

"As long as Cal can hold out against Mary Ellen, if she starts coming around again."

"He'll definitely hold out. Everyone knows Carrie's had a crush on him since high school and never thought she'd have a chance. Now that she does, I'm sure she's going to do everything possible to hold on to him," Travis explained.

"Everyone knew about Carrie's crush?" Anne shook her head, laughing softly. "Tell me, are there any secrets in a small town?"

His dark eyes warmed her from across the table. "A few, but usually there aren't any all that well kept."

She knew exactly the few he talked about. When Travis laid a hand on the table, palm up, Anne reached out to cover it with one of her own, feeling his fingers close over hers.

"Tell me about the past three years," Travis said softly, rubbing his fingertips along the back of her hand. He felt safe in discussing it, since the tables around them were empty, and he sensed this might be the time to get her to talk about it more.

Anne trembled, whether from his touch or his question she wasn't sure.

"There's not much to tell," she murmured, feeling the old burning in her stomach that she thought had gone away forever.

He smiled, sensing her distress, but knowing he had to push. He knew he couldn't help unless he had the complete background. "Then the story won't be a long one, will it?"

She sighed. She was more than well aware of how stubborn Travis could be, and this appeared to be a time she couldn't evade the subject. "I won't bother giving you the names of towns we've been in, because I've forgotten most of them. As for jobs, they were basically minimum wage or less, because they were the only ones I could get without references. Most of the time I was a waitress, but I also worked in bakeries and stocked supplies in a hardware store. You name it, I did it. I was fired from my first two jobs as a waitress because I was so incompetent, but I finally got the hang of it and I think I turned out pretty well." She smiled wanly. "At least Lorna thinks so."

But Travis wasn't smiling. He leaned over to tamp out the cigarette he had been smoking, then grasped her hand between both of his. He needed to hold on to her and could only hope she felt the same way. "And that's how the two of you have gotten by all this time?"

She shook her head. "Not entirely. In the beginning, I once hid in a women's shelter for about a week, when one of Lloyd's detectives was too close on my heels. The people there didn't ask any questions, because most of them had been in the same boat. Actually it helped, knowing I wasn't alone. I also learned one very important thing."

"What was that?" He stared at her hair; she had pulled it up into a loose twist on top of her head, with several tendrils hanging down by her ears and caressing her nape. He badly needed to concentrate on something other than the bleakness in her normally bright eyes.

"Because my parents were abusers it didn't mean I had to be one, too," she murmured, lifting her head. "You don't know how frightened I used to be that one day I would lose my temper for no reason at all and strike out at Nikki. I once saw a program that mentioned the high percentage of abused children who turned into abusers themselves. I frightened myself so badly that I almost shipped Nikki back, but a counselor there assured me that didn't mean I would turn into one, especially if I had gone through everything I had without ever physically hurting Nikki.''

"Did you tell her everything about your past?'' He ached from listening to what she'd gone through and wishing he could have been there to help her.

Anne shook her head. "She knew I left my ex-husband and probably suspected I had kidnapped Nikki, but she never questioned me. Do you know there are actually underground railroads for women like me? People who actually help us stay safe. Can you believe it?''

"But you didn't make use of them.'' It was more a statement than a question.

"No, I was given a couple of phone numbers, but I felt the need to do it on my own. Although there were some days when I just wanted to crawl into a corner and hide, because I had no idea what I was going to do.'' Her voice dropped to a bare whisper.

Travis's features tightened at the thought of what she must have gone through. "Just tell me something. How did you get Nikki into school without arousing any suspicion, when she had no papers?''

"I have a fake birth certificate for her. Actually, one of the women in the shelter helped me obtain it. I don't know how she did it and I guess I didn't want to. It cost me my diamond and sapphire ring, but it was worth it, because I wasn't about to let her go without an education because of me. I did worry about what would happen when she reached high school. I guess I hoped and prayed that by then my days of running would be over, and she would be settled somewhere.'' She hated to tell him all this, since so much of it was considered illegal. She also disliked talking about the past, because she sometimes felt as if it held on to her with a grip guaranteed to never release her. There were nights when Anne walked the floors of the silent house, wondering if she wouldn't be better running away, but each time the dark thought came to mind, so did Travis's promise. And she knew he spoke the truth; no matter what happened, he would find her. "As of now I only have a couple of pieces of jewelry left, which I can only use in an extreme emergency.''

Travis couldn't help but notice the tension in her body and traces of fear that still skittered across her eyes. He wanted to see it gone forever and would do anything in his power to do just that. His next words were meant to relax her. "Obviously, your car wasn't an extreme emergency."

Anne grimaced at his gentle teasing. "It was beginning to turn into one, until a certain mechanic turned up."

Travis looked around and realized they were one of the last diners present. He quickly took care of the check and walked Anne outside to his car. They remained quiet during the drive back to her house. When he pulled into her driveway, he cut the engine and turned in the seat to face her.

"Your days of running are over," he insisted harshly. "They're over in more ways than one, if I have anything to say about it. You're not alone any longer."

Hearing the intensity in his voice Anne looked up, finding herself caught in his liquid brown gaze. Very slowly her head tipped to one side and her eyes drooped shut as his mouth brushed across hers, then hardened when he sensed her receptivity. Travis leaned back against the driver's door and pulled her close, his hand cradling her breast in a loving hold as his thumb rubbed the peaking nipple. She moaned softly, a sound more of desire than fear.

"Am I frightening you?" he murmured, trailing nibbling kisses along her jaw.

"No," she breathed, convinced she saw stars behind her closed eyelids.

"I enjoy kissing you because you taste so good." His tongue traced the delicate arch of her eyebrow, then returned to her mouth.

This time she more than welcomed its evocative thrust, as they snuggled together for what seemed like hours, although it could have only been minutes. To Anne, feeling Travis's arms around her and returning his kisses gave her more pleasure than she had ever known before. From the back of her mind came the whisper of a word for the way Travis made her feel, but she ignored it. As she shifted her body, she felt his arousal and shied away.

Travis groaned inwardly, but sensing her withdrawal, gritted his teeth and ordered his body to behave. With great reluctance, he straightened up, keeping her in a loose embrace. He knew the best way to temper the situation, though he couldn't help wondering if this was the proper time to bring up his idea. Then he decided he would just have to take a chance.

"Anne, we have to plan some strategy."

She immediately knew what he meant. Her body tensed in his arms and she began to pull away, but he tightened his embrace so that she couldn't easily escape. But that didn't stop her from turning her face away, while her rigid posture told him she didn't want to listen to anything he had to say.

"Yes, I'm sure the reward money Lloyd is offering for my capture would more than buy that new bull you need so badly, wouldn't it?" She allowed her bitterness full rein. "Better yet, bypass that detective. I can give you Lloyd's number. Just be sure he has the money with him when you turn me in. He likes to play dirty pool."

"What do you think you're saying?" he shouted, grasping her by the arms and shaking her roughly. When he saw her eyes widen, he cursed and pulled her back against him. "Damn, I didn't mean to frighten you," he groaned. "I care for you too much to want to hurt you."

"That's what caring is all about, isn't it?" Tears laced her words. "Hurt and pain. You lost your wife early in your marriage, and I'm certain she wasn't ready to die. I lost my dignity. Is it really worth all that kind of agony?"

"Anne, you're making me crazy." He sighed, refusing to loosen his hold on her, no matter how much she struggled. "No, love doesn't always mean pain. Yes, I loved Julie and yes, it hurt when she died, because her death was a senseless one. But that was a long time ago, and I've gone on with my life. I've had to, because looking back didn't give me anything, and because I knew she would have wanted me to. Just as I would have wanted her to continue, if I had been the first one to go."

"And because of her you haven't remarried."

"That isn't the reason and you know it," he declared.

In the darkness her eyes burned like two glittering gemstones. "I have no future, Travis," she told him in a hard voice, her posture as distant as if she were a thousand miles away. "I shot my ex-husband, kidnapped my child and took her over several state lines. The time will come when I'm caught and it will be all over. No matter how many times I tell myself everything will work out all right, deep down I know differently. And so do you."

"So you get a good lawyer," he persisted, refusing to allow her to think so negatively.

Anne again shook her head, her expression sullen; Travis didn't know the Sinclair family the way she did. "A good lawyer would not take the case because of the power my ex-husband's family has in Texas. Not to mention the fact that I don't have the money to hire a top-notch lawyer."

"I have money put away," Travis insisted. "You'll have your chance."

"No, that's meant for your bull, and I wouldn't take it, even if it wasn't." Her eyes still burned with her resolve. "Travis, please, don't say any more. I'll pick Nikki up tomorrow after breakfast." She twisted away and grasped the door handle, opening it and getting out before Travis could stop her.

"Anne!" He quickly scrambled out of the car to catch up with her, but she had already slipped inside the house. His first instinct was to pound on the door until she let him in. Instead, he knocked and spoke her name softly.

"Please, Travis, no more." She sounded weary. "All we do is argue about this subject."

He closed his eyes and rested his forehead against the cold wood. "What if I told you that the last thing I want to do with you is argue? That I want to make love with you?" But there was only silence on the other side. He waited a few more minutes, sensing Anne was still standing just inside, but when he heard nothing, he finally placed his palms against the door for a moment, then walked away, his head down.

Anne stood by the window, watching Travis leave. For a moment she was tempted to walk outside and stop him, but she couldn't. The past still held on to her with a firm hand.

Travis was in no mood to go home. He drove out of town on back roads until he came to a dead end, stopped and got out. Standing by the open door, he spun around, slamming the top of the car with his fist. While the impact left a burning sensation across his hand, it didn't help.

"What in the hell does it take for her to understand how much she means to me?" he rasped. "Why won't she believe that I only want the best for her? I want a chance to learn if she is the one."

Deep down he felt she was. He stood in the cold night air, reliving every moment they had spent together. The more he stood there and thought about Anne, the more convinced he became that he had to talk to her again. And he wasn't about to wait until morning.

ANNE COULDN'T SLEEP. Every nerve in her body was quivering, and she knew why. All she and Travis had done this evening was skirt the real issue. If they were to see each other any longer, they would have to consider the next step. And by every gesture, every word, she'd basically told him she wasn't ready. Or was she?

"I really haven't given him much of a chance," she told herself, rolling over onto her side and punching her pillow for what was probably the hundredth time. She sighed. "Except I don't want him to be in any trouble because of me." She rolled over onto her back, staring up at the ceiling. She'd begun counting sheep when she heard pebbles being thrown at her window. She slipped out of bed and drew on her robe as she walked over to the window. She wasn't surprised to find Travis on the other side.

"What do you think you're doing?" she whispered furiously, pushing up the window. She wrapped her robe tighter around her to guard against the night's chill.

"I thought this was a romantic way to get your attention." He grasped the windowsill and pulled himself up and inside.

Travis straightened, feeling a nasty strain in his back as he turned around to close the window. "I'm too old for this stuff." He stood still, a few inches from her. "I'll be honest with you, Anne. I didn't come here to talk, so if you want me to leave, say so, and I'll go." He waited for her decision, while his gaze bored into hers with an intensity she hadn't felt before.

Her breath caught in her throat. "You certainly don't beat about the bush, do you?"

He made a face. "I admit I'm not always the most tactful man around, but I can promise you that I will never do anything to harm you."

She smiled. "I know that. But I still ran away from you, because that's all I'm used to doing. I've always run before, because I had no choice. Now I do have an option."

"And?" His voice was harsh with need as he stared at her face, dimly lighted by the street lamp that shone through the curtains.

Anne opened her robe, allowing it to slip off her shoulders and pool around her feet. "I'll be honest with you, Travis. The fear is still there, deep down, because I don't know how to get rid of it by myself. Perhaps that's where I need you."

He froze as he realized the import of her words. "Maybe we need each other." He moved slowly toward her, his hand outstretched until it touched her shoulder, bare except for a narrow ribbon strap. "How do you expect something like this to keep you warm on cold nights?" he muttered, gingerly touching her skin and finding it slightly cool and smooth.

She smiled. "That's why I have an electric blanket."

Travis's heart slammed against his chest at her smile. "Oh, Anne, if you refuse me now, I'll probably go insane."

Slowly she lifted her arms and linked them around his neck. "I don't want you insane. I want you the way you are."

He hesitated no longer. He hauled her into his arms and held on to her tightly before using his finger to lift her face to his for a long and hungry kiss. For a moment Anne froze under the impact of his strength, but Travis's gentle insistence refused to allow her to draw away.

"Let me show you, Anne," he murmured, stroking her upper lip with the tip of his tongue as his hands first framed her face, then slid slowly down her throat and across her shoulders. When they reached her hips, they tightened slightly and moved around to lift her against himself. A tiny sound left her lips as she was swung up into his arms and carried over to the bed. He leaned over her prone figure, digging one knee into the mattress as he looked down at the woman who had occupied his thoughts for so long.

Anne lifted one hand, running it tentatively along his leg. She watched him move away and raise his arms to pull his sweater over his head, then dispense with his slacks. The silvery light slashed across his bare chest, tipping the dark hair moon-white. Leaving on his briefs, he crossed the room to stretch out on the bed next to her, drawing the covers over both of them.

With Travis's arm around her shoulders, Anne slid over and lay down next to him, her head comfortably nestled on his shoulder.

"There's no rush," he murmured. "We're just going to take this slow and easy. I want you to feel entirely comfortable with me before we go any farther. So why don't you just get used to me, the feel of me?" He buried his face in the tangled waves of her hair. "You set the pace, Anne."

Unable to believe he was allowing her so much freedom, she hesitantly touched his shoulder with her fingertips; even though the air was cold, his skin was warm. She traced the muscular structure, memorizing the texture, the path of an angular scar along the back of one shoulder, which she learned had been the result of a fall into barbed wire when he was ten. She immediately kissed it better.

Anne allowed her lips to retrace the scar. "It would be so much easier if our scars were always on the outside," she murmured, returning to her tactile exploration.

She learned that his nipples were as responsive as her own. She circled the brown nub with her nail again and again, fascinated by the way it bloomed under her touch. She raked her fingers through the crisp dark brown hair that arrowed down to his waist. She paused and just looked at Travis. With the way the light streamed across the bed, she felt as if they were in a world of their own making.

Anne slowly pushed down the covers to the end of the bed and looked at the rest of him. She laughed, sounding a little anxious at the sight of his evident arousal and hair-roughened thighs. "You're nothing like Lloyd."

He smiled. "I hope that's good."

"Oh yes," she breathed. "It certainly is," but then she appeared a little nervous.

Travis took her hand, lacing his fingers through hers and placing their entwined hands on his abdomen. "There's nothing to be afraid of," he assured her. "I told you before, you'll set the pace. We won't do anything you don't want to."

She slowly released the three buttons in the front of her nightgown and reached down for the hem, pulling it over her head and tossing it away. She sat there still as a stone as Travis's gaze roamed over her naked form.

"Am I that bad?" She feared the worst as he remained silent.

"No, you're the most beautiful woman I've ever seen," he whispered.

Travis smiled at her formality. His hands warmed her skin as they skimmed over her breasts, finding the swollen nipples that hardened under his touch. Not content just to touch them, he lowered his head and took one nipple into his mouth. He couldn't imagine anything tasting sweeter. His hands moved down to the slender curve of her belly and beyond. She moved restively under his touch, rotating her hips toward him, silently asking for more. But he wasn't finished. He turned her over, dropping a string of kisses across her back and down her spine while his hands molded her slender hips.

Turning her once more onto her back, he began to nibble her lower lip, drawing it into his mouth. "Are you sure?" he murmured.

"Yes!" she gasped, then laughed again, the sound rich with expression and happiness this time. She wrapped her hands around his neck, pulling his face down to hers. Their mouths melded in loving hunger.

"Oh, Anne," he rasped, insinuating one leg between hers. "There have been so many nights I've lain awake, dreaming of you being here like this. So many nights when I've wanted to show you what making love would be like for us." His palm covered her breast in a possessive action. "Can you handle it?"

Her eyes glowed like two gems in the darkness. "Yes."

He groaned deep in his throat, as his mouth trailed moistly across the shadowed valley between her breasts. "Your trust in me means so much. I love you."

She shuddered under his touch, desiring more. Her hands wandered down his back to his flexing buttock muscles, caressing the rounded flesh. She discovered that touching him was something she didn't want to stop doing for a long time.

Anne arched up as Travis caressed her moist flesh with his fingertips, making sure she was prepared for him. It wasn't until then that he moved away to dig something out of his pants pocket. "You are so beautiful," he whispered, moving back over her, joining them together in a smooth, fluid thrust. He remained still for several moments, so that she could adjust to him, even though the tight friction of her body against his own almost drove him out of control. When he felt her relax, he began moving slowly, keeping his hands on her hips to encourage her to equal participation. Silently he urged her to give to him as much as he was giving to her. He gritted his teeth, determined to present Anne with the kind of lovemaking every woman deserved, the kind she'd probably never known.

She kept her eyes wide open, staring at Travis's features because she didn't want to miss one moment of what they were sharing. She had no idea her face was glowing, her mouth stretched in a wide smile. When his movements grew stronger, she rose to meet him, unwilling to be left behind. And when his face tightened, she felt her own release beginning to build. Soft cries escaped her lips, and as the world exploded around her, she could hear Travis say her name in a husky whisper.

Fully spent, Anne lay in his arms, her hand resting on his damp chest, her fingers idly combing the soft hairs. They remained quiet for a long time, reflecting on what had just happened, both unable to believe that their loving could have been so explosive, or that they could still want each other again so soon.

"I wish you had been the first." Her voice was a harsh and abrupt intrusion into their self-made world.

He smiled, understanding what caused her sorrow. "But I was," he corrected. "Because I sincerely doubt you had ever before made love in a man's arms the way you did with me tonight."

"Travis!" Anne hid her head in embarrassment, even though she knew he couldn't see her in the dark.

"Well, did you?" He already knew her answer, but that didn't stop him from asking her.

"You know I didn't." Her voice was muffled against his bare shoulder. "So you don't have to act so pleased about it."

"But I do, because we shared something so special." He sounded pleased with himself. "The only thing I'm going to hate is having to drag myself out of your very lovely bed to sneak back into my house.''

''Um, yes. Maude would have some embarrassing questions for you.'' Anne yawned, feeling more relaxed than she had in a long time. She rolled over onto her side and nestled against him. ''Travis, what will happen to us when the real world intrudes?'' she asked in a low voice.

He knew she meant much more than Maude. ''For now we'll take things day by day. And you're not to worry yourself, because I'm going to be beside you every step. You're not alone anymore, Anne Sinclair.''

She smiled. ''You know, that has a nice ring to it.''

''Anne Sinclair?''

''No, that I'm not alone anymore.''

Chapter Thirteen

"Congratulations! You got in just in time to change your clothes and get out to the south pasture to help the men."

Travis cursed softly as he stumbled over his feet. He straightened and turned around. "Aren't you up a little late?" He tried for a semblance of dignity, but didn't quite make it.

Maude turned on a nearby lamp and faced him with an unreadable expression in her eyes. "As you're a *responsible* adult, I won't ask where you've been until four o'clock in the morning, but as your mother I will speak my piece." When Travis opened his mouth to argue, she held up her hand, indicating she wanted silence. "That woman is very fragile right now. She's held in a very important secret for several years. Don't get into something that can seriously harm everyone concerned, and I'm including two little girls in that group. Now, speaking as a woman and one who's gotten to know Anne fairly well, I can tell you that if she feels emotions she can't afford to handle, she'll run."

"I already told her if she does, I'll find her," he replied in a gritty voice.

Maude's smile was sad. "Oh, my darling, if a person doesn't want to be found badly enough, they won't be."

Feeling the terror he had kept inside for so long, Travis dropped into a chair.

"The lawman in me says she has to go back and get all of this straightened out," he groaned. "The man in me wants to keep her here, where she can have her new life, and where we can learn if it's just more than a strong physical attraction."

"If it was just a physical attraction, you wouldn't have made love to her tonight," Maude stated baldly. "That's just the kind of man you are. Now, think like the lawman and not like a man in love, and do some checking. Find out what you can on Lloyd Sinclair, so you're not just relying on her story. I'm only playing the devil's advocate here because someone has to. Then start making some decisions.''

"I offered her money for an attorney, but she won't take it," Travis replied wearily, half hating his mother for being so logical and loving her for it at the same time.

Maude looked up, beseeching higher powers; how could she have had a son who was so half-witted at times? "Of course she wouldn't! The woman has pride."

"She's going to need an attorney," he insisted.

"And she'll have one. Just go ahead and find one without her knowing it." She walked over and laid a hand on his shoulder. "I have some money put away. Add that to it. If these Sinclairs are half as powerful as she's intimated, we're going to need somebody with guts. Go take a shower while I fix you a large pot of coffee and some breakfast. Things may not look any better, but you won't feel as cranky as you probably do now."

Travis nodded and stood up. Before leaving he hugged his mother tightly. "One thing I hate about you, Mom," he murmured. "You're always so damn right."

"MOM, YOU'RE LATE." Nikki looked up at Anne with accusing eyes as the woman stepped out of the car. "You said you'd pick me up before lunch."

"I'm sorry, honey, I'm afraid I overslept." She smiled and drew her daughter against her for a hug. "Although I doubt you could have missed me all that much."

The little girl still looked suspicious. "You never oversleep."

Anne looked away, afraid the sudden color in her cheeks would give her away. Nikki was right; she was always up before the alarm clock went off. But after Travis had again made beautiful love to her before he had to leave, she'd felt so replete that she could only drift into a deep sleep. When she awoke only a bare hour ago, she'd felt more rested than she had in a long time.

"Even with my being late, were you able to have a good day?" Her voice was husky with the memories of a night filled with whispered endearments and tender caresses.

Nikki pulled away. "Yeah," she replied sullenly.

Lost though she was, Anne didn't miss the tone. "Nikki, sometimes things happen we can't control. Now, let's go inside, shall we?"

"Hello there! We'd 'bout given you up for lost," Maude greeted her. Her sharp eyes didn't miss the betraying flush in Anne's cheeks or the way Nikki hung back. "How about some coffee?"

Anne grasped the lifeline thrown to her with gratitude. "That sounds wonderful. I'm sorry I'm so late."

"No problem. Sometimes it's nice to be able to sleep late. Besides, Nikki here was able to keep Susie out of my hair while I cleaned out the refrigerator." She smiled at the girl. "They just finished their lunch, in fact. Have you eaten? I have plenty of tuna salad left." She nodded at the look on Anne's face as she took matters into her own hands. "Nikki, why don't you find Susie for me while I fix your mother a sandwich?"

Once Anne was seated with her meal and Maude sat across from her, the older woman eyed her keenly.

"You'll have to tell Nikki the whole story."

Anne choked on her sandwich and had to suffer a few hearty claps on the back. "Everything?" she wheezed.

"I'm not talking about last night. I'm talking about why you're running and what can happen. She's not a baby any longer and she's a very intelligent girl. She knows you and Travis have been dating and she doesn't like it, because she fears a man is going to take you away or hurt you again. She remembers more than you think she does, Anne. It's just that she's blocked it off, because she feels safer that way. Tell her," Maude ordered gently.

Anne shut her eyes tightly. "She doesn't remember anything. She was barely a baby then."

"Then why the nightmares? And why does she shy away from Travis?" Maude used each word like a knife, clearly determined to make Anne see the truth.

"She was barely four," she whispered. "And she never spoke of those times, so I thought it better not to bring them up. I'd hoped she had forgotten. But you're right. She just kept it hidden because I had. It was easier to ignore it than to bring it out into the open." She bit her lower lip. "I have to make arrangements to go back."

Maude nodded. "Have you told Travis?"

Anne shook her head. Suddenly her appetite was gone and she pushed her sandwich away. "Besides, you're right. I have to talk to Nikki, and I should do that before I say anything to him. I've kept my head in the sand long enough. Travis basically told me I can't continue running, and he's right, too. I will go to jail." Her voice began to fail her and she rubbed her hands together as if she were suddenly very cold. She coughed, clearing her throat, which was rapidly clogging with tears. "But I won't go without having a chance to air my story, even if no one will believe me." She jumped to her feet and grabbed her purse. "I'm sorry, I..." She shook her head as words failed her. Maude followed more slowly as Anne ran out of the house toward the barn. "Nikki!" she called out. "Come on, we're going."

The girl appeared in the doorway. "Now?"

"Yes, now." Her voice was sharp with agitation.

"I have to get my clothes."

"Then get them."

Nikki wasted no time in grabbing her pink duffel bag and climbing into the car. Without looking to right or left, Anne slid behind the steering wheel and started up the engine, driving away with a squeal of tires.

"Why's Nikki's mom so mad?" Susie came up to stand beside her grandmother.

"She's not, sweetie. She's just got a lot of things on her mind," Maude said softly.

Anne didn't say anything during the drive back to the house. Once Nikki had deposited her duffel bag on her bed, Anne asked her to come into the living room.

"Nikki, I have a lot of things to talk to you about," she said quietly. "Some you may not understand, and if you don't, just say so, and I'll try to explain it better for you. All right?"

Puzzled by her mother's serious tone, the child merely nodded.

Anne took a deep breath, knowing there was no other way than to plunge right in. "We have never talked very much about your father." She noticed the way Nikki stiffened at the word, but forced herself to continue. "Nikki, I had to leave Texas because I shot your father. If I hadn't gone away, I would have been put in jail. I took you with me because I loved you too much to leave you behind."

Nikki jumped up, screaming. "No! You didn't do anything bad, because he was a bad man." She leaned over her stunned mother, her fists clenched at her sides. "And he made you go away. All he did was yell at me and tell me to be quiet and leave me alone at night. And he—he broke the china tea set you gave me for my birthday. I hated him!"

"Oh, my God!" Anne whispered, shocked to the core by what she'd heard. "Nikki, why didn't you ever tell me any of this?" She reached out and grabbed her by the shoulders. "Why?"

Tears shone in her daughter's deep green eyes. "Because he said if I ever told you, a black monster would get me."

Anne breathed deeply through her nose to keep the darkness from overtaking her. She had feared her ex-husband for many years, but now a stronger emotion took over. The hate that was beginning to consume her canceled out the fear.

"No one will take you away from me, honey. No one," she stated emphatically, hauling Nikki into her arms and holding on to her tightly. "I was prepared to go back and take whatever they dished out, but now I'm going back to fight."

Nikki tilted up her head. "Mom, you can't go back there. I understand what you told me. You shot him and took me away. They'll put you in jail for that. And they'll make me stay with him, won't they?"

Anne's face hardened. "They can try, but not without a fight."

"Then we'll leave here, won't we? And I won't see Susie anymore."

Another subject she had to clear up. "Nikki, we also have to talk about the way you act toward Sheriff Hunter."

"I'm polite to him," the girl said stiffly.

"Let me tell you something to think about. Sheriff Hunter learned quite a while ago what I did and that I'm wanted by the police, but he didn't call them. In fact, he wants to help me."

Nikki didn't look convinced. "Are you two going to get married?"

Anne's stomach curled at the idea. While Travis was the kind of man any woman could dream about, she couldn't think about any kind of commitment right now. She had too many other things to worry about.

"No, we aren't."

"But he likes you. He takes you places."

"You and I have our lives to get straightened out before we can think about adding to our family," Anne replied, thrusting Travis from her mind. Right now, she had to concentrate on her daughter. "But I would like you to give him a chance. Think of it this way. If he was a bad man, I don't think Susie would love him so much, would she?"

The girl frowned with thought. "No, I guess not," she said slowly, as she edged out of her mother's lap and sat beside her on the couch.

"Nikki, I tend to forget that you're a big girl now and should be treated as such. I hope I'll do better in the future," Anne told her. "First of all, I think we should talk more about what you remember from years ago."

And for the next two hours, Anne learned that, once released, a little girl's memories were stronger than expected. Afterward, her resolve to go back and fight was even firmer. Deep down, she feared she would lose, but vowed that she would go down fighting.

Travis showed up that evening as Nikki was getting ready for bed.

"Can we talk?" he asked Anne, searching her face for answers to the questions filling his mind.

She nodded, stepping back so he could enter. As he passed her, he could smell the light lemony fragrance of her hair and the scent of her cologne, both of which brought back visions of the night before.

Nikki stood in the hallway, looking a bit uncertain.

"Hello, Sheriff Hunter," she said quietly, raising her head to look at him directly.

He smiled warmly. "Hi, Nikki. I had some of the brownies you and Susie made last night. Don't tell my mother, but they're better than hers," he added in a conspiratorial whisper.

A smile flashed across her lips. "Good night," she murmured, turning around and running back to her room.

Travis looked at Anne, silently asking the reason for the change.

"It's a beginning," she said. "I basically told her that if Susie loved you, you can't be all bad. Would you like some coffee?"

He shook his head. "It has been difficult to wait all day to see you, but after what Mom told me, I knew you'd want some time to yourself."

Anne collapsed into a chair. "Nikki and I had a long talk today. It appears she remembered more about that time than I ever dreamed she did." She quickly filled him in.

When she finished, Travis swore under his breath. "How could a man terrorize his own daughter?"

"If you knew Lloyd, you wouldn't ask that." She sighed. "I have to go back there and demand to be heard. And I am so scared about it that I can't think straight." She looked down at the hands clenched in her lap.

"I want to help."

Anne exhaled deeply and slowly shook her head. "No, Travis, I don't want you involved in this. After all, you are a lawman and should have turned me in the moment you knew the truth. They could charge you with being an accessory."

"Anne, you've been going it alone too long. Let someone help," he insisted, leaning forward, his hands loosely clasped between his knees. "Let me help."

A heartbeat went by before she spoke. "I can't make any promises."

"I'm not asking for any, but it wouldn't hurt for us to take things a day at a time and see what happens, would it?"

She grimaced. "You learned your logic from your mother, didn't you?" She pressed her fingers against her forehead, rotating them slowly. "No matter what I say, you're not going to listen to me, are you?"

"Nope."

"And you're going to stick your nose in where it might not be wanted."

"Yep."

"You're going to be just as stubborn as you were in the beginning."

"Yep."

Anne chuckled at Travis's cheerful tone. "I give up, Sheriff. Besides, it might be a good idea to have your input on how to handle this."

"Even to letting me find a lawyer for you?"

"Do I have any choice?"

"No."

"I thought so." She sighed in capitulation, then whispered, "I can't make love with you again, Travis. I can't afford to think about anything else but what will be coming up."

He stood and walked over to stand in front of her, hunkering down and grasping her hands, gently rubbing them between his own.

"I wasn't looking for a one-night stand, Anne," he said quietly. "I feel we have something, but I also know you have a lot on your mind now. All I ask is that you don't shut me out. That you give me a chance."

She edged her hands away from his and cupped his face, feeling the skin slightly rough from his evening beard. "Oh, Travis, however did you manage to stay single so long?" Her voice trembled with emotion.

He covered one of her hands. "Probably because there wasn't a woman around to catch my interest." He leaned forward and kissed her softly, his lips a breath apart. When her mouth softened under his, he kissed her again, but pulled away before it could deepen too far. "And that's my cue to leave, before I lose all gentlemanly restraint." He squeezed her hands lightly, then got to his feet. "I have some contacts in Texas, so I'm going to make a few calls. I'm not going to use your name," he hastened to assure her when he saw her panic. "But some groundwork has to be laid before you go back."

"I don't know if I'll be able to go in to work tomorrow, acting as if nothing has happened."

He smiled. "Sure you will. You've done well so far. The rest should be a snap." He leaned down and kissed her again.

This time, Anne placed her hands on his shoulders, needing his warmth. A moan bubbled up in her throat to rest on his lips as she pressed herself closer. All the words she had spoken earlier came back to mock her, but she ignored them. As before, Travis drew away first.

"Honey, I can't always be the strong one," he breathed. "Get a good night's sleep. I'll see you tomorrow. Just do me one favor. Have Lorna go easy on the chili powder." He opened the door and left swiftly.

TRAVIS WASTED no time in making his first call. The moment he stepped inside the station, he took care of any minor problems and shut himself up in his office. He sat at his desk for a long time before pulling out his personal address book. He was relieved that his call went through right away, before he lost his nerve.

"Hank Douglas." The drawl boomed in his ear.

"Hank, Travis," he identified himself.

"Is this one business or pleasure?" The man's tone of voice didn't surprise Travis.

"I'll leave that up to you. I want the name of a hard-nosed lawyer in your area who isn't afraid of anyone," Travis said baldly.

Hank swore under his breath. "What's this about?"

Travis leaned back in his chair, propping his booted feet on the desk and lighting a cigarette. "Hey, I'm just asking a favor from a good friend who I know I can count on."

"Does this have anything to do with our previous conversation?" the other man asked tautly, clearly being careful not to mention names over the phone.

"I'm just asking a favor, no more. Everyone needs a lawyer at least once in their lives," Travis said casually.

Hank groaned. "Old buddy, you're asking for something I can't do. I need some answers."

Travis shook another cigarette out of his pack and lighted it, forgetting there was already one burning in the ashtray. "All I'm asking you for is a name."

"Why me?"

"Because you're the only one I can trust," he said crisply.

Hank's sigh was audible over the wires. "All right, I'll get you a name, but you're going to have to be up-front with me when I get back to you. Don't leave me in the dark, for both our sakes."

Travis's voice hardened. "As a lawman my job is to protect the people who need and deserve it."

Hank didn't sound convinced. "How soon do you want a name?"

"Yesterday."

"After I get you somebody, are you planning on coming down here, too?"

"Might be," he drawled, unwilling to give away any more information than he absolutely had to. "It depends on what I find out."

The other man's voice was still taut with tension. "When?"

"When the time is right. Not before."

Hank exhaled, sounding more frustrated by the moment. "All right. I'll get you a name, and you let me know your flight information the minute you have it. Otherwise, old buddy, I won't be able to protect you. I hope you realize what you're doing, because I have a very nasty feeling that no matter how good a lawyer I can get you, this situation is still going to blow up in your face." He hung up without another word.

Travis slowly replaced the receiver. "There's no turning back now," he whispered, already wondering if he had done the right thing—or if he might have signed Anne's death sentence, after all.

"HOW COULD YOU do this to me? Damn you, by playing the role of the all-righteous lawman, you've thrown me to the wolves!" Anne exclaimed, pacing back and forth. Travis had told her at lunch that he'd come by late that evening, because he had something to discuss with her. Unfortunately, she'd had no idea how serious it was until then.

He looked at her pale features and kicked himself again for his impulsive gesture. "Anne, I had to. You had no way to contact anyone without someone leaking the information, and I knew I could trust this man."

"How?"

"He's with the state police."

She threw up her hands. "Oh, with the state police. Wonderful. You're so sure he won't tell a soul? He'll probably just catch the next plane up here and take me back in handcuffs!'' She stared at him, wild-eyed. ''Thank you very much!''

''You know very well we can't put this off,'' he said tersely. ''You talked about going back there, which isn't a good idea until you can have some protection. I'm not letting you set foot inside that state until we have a reputable attorney to represent you. I can get that person for you.''

Her lips twisted. ''You're not? Travis, I know all about extradition. If they find out where I am, they can come up here and just get me if they want to. We both know it.''

He ran his hands through his hair. ''I didn't mention your name, or even why I was asking for a lawyer.''

She walked away, then spun around. Her features were taut with tension. ''Come off it, Travis. The man is not stupid. He probably guessed, the minute you said something. He was the same man you spoke to before, when you asked about me after that private investigator was here. He had to figure it out.''

''So what if he guessed.'' He breathed hard, in an attempt to keep his voice low so they couldn't be overheard. ''Hank is a friend and a good man. He isn't going to say anything. He doesn't feel you got a fair deal before, and I know he'll do what he can for us.''

She too breathed hard and fast, in a vain attempt to calm down. ''Well, I'm glad you feel so confident about that, because it's my life you're playing with. Was it so difficult to wait a few days until we could discuss this? Or is the pull of being a sheriff so strong that you just couldn't resist calling in the big guns?'' she asked in a hard voice.

Anne grew even angrier as Travis's lips started to form a smile. When his shoulders began shaking with restrained laughter, she seriously thought about punching him in the stomach.

''I'm glad you think this is so amusing,'' she said through her teeth, flexing her hands at her sides. ''Because I certainly don't.'' She gasped when he picked her up and spun her around in a circle. ''Travis! What do you think you're doing? Have you lost your mind?''

''You don't see it, do you?'' he asked, slowing down. ''In case you don't realize it, you just lost your temper with me.''

She looked at him as if he didn't make any sense. ''So?''

He shook his head, clucking at her denseness. ''This from the woman who's eluded so many people over the years. You just lost your temper with me—a man,'' he said slowly, enunciating every word.

Anne's eyes widened as his meaning sank in. "I wasn't even thinking about what I was saying," she breathed, then burst out laughing. "I yelled at you. I really yelled at you."

Travis nodded. "You sure did." He hugged her so tightly that she protested about the safety of her ribs. "You yelled at me without even worrying about retaliation. Honey, I'm proud of you."

Anne still couldn't believe what she had done. "I usually gave in because it was easier, if not safer."

He kissed her long and hard. "You know what? I like it when you rip into me," he murmured against her mouth before stealing another kiss.

She buried her face against his shirtfront. "Oh, Travis, what am I going to do with you?" she moaned.

"Mom?"

They turned to find Nikki standing uncertainly in the doorway, her bare feet peeking out from under her nightgown.

"I heard yelling." She looked at Travis with eyes dark with caution and just a touch of fear.

"That you did," Travis said easily, tightening his hold on Anne when she tried to move away from him. "Your mom was letting me have it, for doing some things without asking her permission first."

Nikki tipped her head to one side. "Mom was yelling at *you*?"

He nodded. "Sure was. I'm glad you came out to rescue me."

"And you're not mad at her?"

"No reason for me to be. I did wrong, and she let me know it."

Nikki now looked at them as if they had both lost their minds. "I'm glad you're not fighting." She turned away to return to her room.

"Good night, Nikki," Travis called after her. "Thanks again for the rescue."

"I think some old memories were surfacing for her," Anne murmured.

"Probably, but with some work we can give her some new ones that will make her laugh."

Her lips tilted upward. "Another one of your promises, Sheriff Hunter?"

"The kind you can take to the bank."

Chapter Fourteen

"How do we know he's a good attorney?" Anne demanded, looking at the handwritten slip of paper Travis had given her when he came by the restaurant for lunch. He had deliberately taken an end stool and waited until the area was almost deserted before giving it to her.

"Hank believes in the guy and says nothing fazes him," he replied.

She shot him a knowing look. "How did you feel when you spoke to him?"

Travis looked properly injured. "Hey, I wouldn't do that," he protested.

"Of course not. What did he say?" She smiled. Try as she might, she couldn't get angry with Travis.

He looked chastened. "I just wanted to make sure he was the right person for you."

"Travis, you can be very pushy at times," she said softly, leaning across the counter.

He smiled into her eyes. "It's a crime you ever covered up such beautiful eyes and hair."

"After what I've done, those would only be considered misdemeanors," Anne said wryly.

"You smell good, too."

"You're changing the subject."

"Pushy people tend to do that."

She shot him a telling look that warned he should watch himself. "What did the nice man say?"

He lowered his voice. "He feels you should get back to Texas as soon as possible. Since it involves the Sinclairs, he feels he can get a quick court date for you."

Anne felt the old burning sensation return to her stomach. "It's going to happen, isn't it?"

He nodded. "Are you ready for it?"

"No, but when the time comes, I promise I will be."

TIME FLEW for Anne as she prepared herself for the coming ordeal. Travis had already purchased two plane tickets, reminding her he wasn't about to allow her to go alone. So much of her life had been a dark turmoil until he came along, offering her a peace that couldn't be duplicated.

"Why can't I go with you?" Nikki asked repeatedly. She hung on to Anne more and more since her mother had talked to her about her plans.

Anne sighed inwardly. "We've already discussed this at great length, honey. I want you to stay here with Mrs. Hunter and Susie."

"But Sheriff Hunter is going with you," the child argued.

"There's a reason for that."

Her mouth quivered dangerously. "They're going to put you in jail, aren't they? And if I go with you I'll be put there too, because I told you!"

Anne grabbed hold of her and held on tightly. "No, that isn't why," she soothed. "I just feel you'd be a lot happier here, where you can play with Susie." And be safe, she thought to herself. From the beginning, she had told Travis she wouldn't take Nikki with her, and she was grateful he hadn't argued with that. She wanted her daughter to experience as much happiness and laughter as was possible. Until then, she spent every possible moment with Nikki, since Lorna had given her the time off.

"We'll be praying for you, honey," the older woman had informed her. "Don't you worry at all. You'll be back here in no time." She slipped an envelope into Anne's hand. "Just a little something from everyone around here. And no arguments. We want to help."

When Anne opened the envelope and saw the carefully aligned bills she felt like crying. Instead, she smiled and hugged the woman.

"I never knew what friends really were until I came here," she whispered.

THE NIGHT BEFORE Anne was to leave she was exhausted, but couldn't sleep. She left her bed and crept into Nikki's room, where the girl lay curled in her bed. Anne carefully lifted the covers and crawled in next to her.

"Shh, baby," she whispered when Nikki mumbled. "It's just Mommy." She held her in her arms, holding back the tears as she cradled her daughter against her breast. Anne remained there for the balance of the night, unable to sleep as she imprinted the image of her daughter on her mind. A lone tear appeared at the corner of one eye and trickled down her cheek to lodge at the edge of her lips, but she was determined that any sorrow she had at parting with Nikki would be kept inside when they arrived at Travis's in the morning.

BREAKFAST was a quiet affair at the Hunter household when Anne and Nikki arrived.

"I told Cal if anything comes up he feels he can't handle, to call Ron Johnson over in Cotton Creek," Travis told Maude as he concentrated on his bacon and eggs. "I also have Wilma's promise that she won't go after Zeke while I'm gone. I'd appreciate it if you'd give her a call every so often to keep tabs on her."

"If she knows that's why I'm calling, she'll never forgive any of us," Maude said dryly, eyeing Anne picking at her food. "That's not the way to put meat on your bones, dear."

Anne managed a weak smile. "I'm not a very good flyer, so eating beforehand is never a good idea for me." The fact that her nerves were already frayed was left unspoken but well understood.

"Please try and eat a little," Travis coaxed. "For me."

She nibbled on a strip of bacon, then set it down when Travis's attention was captured by Susie. But Maude noticed and gestured toward the eggs.

All too soon it was time to drive to the small airport nearby for the commuter flight that would connect them to Helena. Standing out on the dusty airfield, Anne hugged Maude and Susie, then embraced Nikki tightly. The little girl never said a word, simply holding on to Anne and kissing her on the cheek. Then Nikki walked slowly over to Travis, who was hunkered down, talking softly to Susie.

Nikki stood very still and stared just over his shoulder, waiting until he turned toward her. "Would you hug me the way you hug Mom and Susie?" Her voice was so low that he had to strain his ears to hear her.

He held out his arms. "If you want me to."

Her steps were tiny and unsure, but soon she stood much closer to him. Still Travis waited for her to make the final decision.

Anne stood back, tears in her eyes as she watched her daughter. Nikki laid a hand on his shoulder, but moved no closer. Travis made no move to enfold her in his arms, but the smile on his face was warm and loving.

"If you ever have to yell at me, it will be because I deserve it, won't it?" Nikki asked softly.

He wasn't going to lie. "Yes."

She chewed on her lower lip. "You'll bring my mom back, won't you?" She took her hand away and stepped back.

He smiled. "You can count on it."

Before long the flight was called and Travis helped Anne board the small plane. They looked out the tiny porthole at figures that steadily grew smaller as the plane took off. She blinked rapidly to hold back the tears and didn't refuse the handkerchief he held in front of her.

"I wasn't kidding," she murmured, wiping her eyes carefully so as not to smudge her makeup. "I'm a very bad flyer."

Travis smiled. "Then I'll keep the airsick bag handy for you."

"Travis." She gripped his hand in a bone-crushing hold. "What if they demand I return Nikki right away? What will I do? I don't want her there during all this turmoil."

He smiled and carefully freed his hand. "Don't worry about it."

"Easy for you to say!"

He kissed the tip of her nose. "It's all taken care of. Just relax."

The rest of the flight was a blur for Anne. Since their plane was late getting into Helena, they had to run to catch their connecting flight to Houston.

By the time the jet landed there, Anne's stomach had grown a million butterflies, and airsickness was only a by-product. She tugged at Travis's hand, silently signaling that she wanted to be the last to depart. He smiled and settled back, waiting for the other passengers to pass by them.

"This is a very bad idea," she whispered, following him down the tunnel at last.

"Don't worry, Hank is meeting us," he assured her. "And we're seeing the attorney in the morning." He scanned the people milling around but didn't see his friend. A strange prickling sensation skittered across the back of his neck, and all defenses immediately shot up. He grabbed her arm in a grip that was tighter than usual. "Anne." He kept his voice low. "Smile. I want you to appear calm, not nervous." Her eyes shot up. "Just do as I say." Keeping smiles plastered on their faces, they walked across the terminal.

"Anne Williams Sinclair?" Two dark-suited men suddenly flanked them. One of them flashed a gold shield and a sheet of paper that

Travis immediately snatched from him. "We have a warrant for your arrest." In a droning voice the stranger began reading her her rights.

"Travis." She looked up at him, shock and fear written on her face, as she was led a few steps away.

"Wait a minute," Travis began angrily, stepping forward, then flinching when flashbulbs seared his eyes. "What the hell is going on here?"

"Mrs. Sinclair is wanted for the kidnapping of her daughter and the shooting of her ex-husband," the other officer explained. "Who are you?"

"Sheriff Travis Hunter, Dunson, Montana."

"Then if you come down to the station tomorrow, we can arrange for you to get the reward money."

"We're to meet a Henry Douglas," he stated, glaring at a photographer who had got in too close. "Get out of my face, unless you want to lose yours," he growled.

"Travis!" Hank ran up, looking confused at the sight of the circus of photographers—and of a stunned Anne, who was being handcuffed. "Wait a minute here." He took one of the officers to one side and began speaking rapidly and gesturing.

"Travis!" Anne was looking more ill with each passing minute.

"Look, she isn't going anywhere," Travis told the man.

"You kidding? She's been on the run for three years. We're not taking any chances."

"Mrs. Sinclair, what have you done during this time?" one reporter shouted.

Anne said nothing, and began crying wildly as she was separated from Travis, who was vainly trying to keep the press away from her.

"Who are you exactly? Are you the latest of Mrs. Sinclair's conquests? Do you have any idea that she almost killed her ex-husband?" one reporter asked, pushing a microphone under Travis's nose.

"Travis!" Anne screamed when the detectives began pulling her away. A furious Hank stood on the sidelines, holding back his friend with a strong grip.

Travis turned on him with murder in his eyes. "You had to call them, didn't you? She was scared enough coming down here, without you turning it into a three-ring circus. I ought to take you apart and really give those news vultures something to film."

"I had nothing to do with this," Hank retorted. "I don't know how they found out, but I intend to."

"Just great. And, while you're doing that, she's turning into a basket case." Travis towered over his onetime friend. "Dammit, she's scared to death and she has good reason to be. I'm surprised they didn't put her in chains!"

Hank dug into his pockets and pulled out some change, heading for a nearby bank of pay phones. "I'm going to call Dave and have him get down there to bail her out."

Travis was on his heels. "Where are they taking her?"

"Oh no, you're not going anywhere near there. One riot is enough. You go down there and you're going to act like the masked avenger, which is the last thing she needs right now. Dave can handle it. I'm getting you to a hotel, where I expect you to stay until this is all straightened out." When his call was connected, he spoke swiftly and concisely. After he hung up, he turned back to Travis. "Dave is leaving now. Come on, let's get a drink and then we'll head for the hotel."

"Make that a double," Travis said grimly, still seeing Anne's tearstained face as she pleaded with him to help her. "Damn, I promised I'd keep her safe. I sure didn't do a very good job of it. She was right. She would have been better off in Dunson."

"No, she wouldn't, because someone would have caught up with her sooner or later." Hank led the way into a dimly lighted bar and found a corner table.

When a waitress approached them, Hank ordered two whiskeys. The two men didn't speak again until their drinks were placed in front of them.

"Am I reading something into it, or do you and Anne have something special between you?" Hank asked, fingering his glass.

"We were just beginning to find out," Travis muttered, tossing back his drink.

Hank's brows arched. "So that's the way it is, is it?"

"Yep," Travis said grimly, gesturing to the waitress for another drink and taking a pack of cigarettes and lighter out of his shirt pocket. "Now why don't you tell me what you know so far?" He made a frustrated gesture. "Damn, how could they just cart her off like an animal?"

"Calm down," his friend ordered in a low voice. "You're not going to be able to accomplish anything if you fly off the handle. And Anne is going to need your strength, if the two of you are as close as you claim you are." He held up his hands in defense. "All right, stupid comment. Just call it a casualty of a crummy day." He slid one of Travis's cigarettes out of the pack and lighted it. "Do you know where the daughter is?"

Travis eyed his friend blandly, now prepared to view him as the enemy until shown otherwise. "Am I supposed to?"

Hank sighed. "Travis, don't make this any harder than it has to be."

Travis's gaze was bone chilling as he leaned back in his chair and stared at the other man. "I'm not the one who allowed storm troopers to spirit away a frightened woman. All I have to say is, your friend better be as good as you claim he is."

"Dave and I had worked together for ten years when he decided to get out of police work and practice law. There's no one else I would trust, and he admitted he would like nothing better than to go up against the Sinclairs. They're not used to losing, and Dave only likes to win, so it should be interesting."

Travis leaned across the table. "Look here. Anne's life is at stake for all we know," he declared. "I'm not going to allow some grandstanding attorney to build up his reputation on her bones."

Hank's gaze hardened. "Don't push it, old buddy. I can understand where you're coming from, so I won't discuss your hiding a fugitive from the law or the consequences if anyone decides to dig into your part." He pulled out his wallet and dropped several bills onto the table before standing up. "Come on, let's get your luggage and get you to the hotel. And I mean it, Travis. You stay put and let Dave and me handle this. Because if you land in jail, I won't bother bailing you out."

Travis fumed as they stood by the luggage carousel, snagging his garment bag and Anne's worn tan leather suitcase.

"This is it?" Hank looked at the two pieces with disbelief.

"Yep," Travis drawled, swinging the garment bag over his shoulder.

Hank swore under his breath as they walked out of the terminal. Soon enough they were at his car and the luggage was stowed in the trunk.

"How long before we get to the hotel?" Travis looked around the booming city with distaste. After his years of living in a small country town he felt more and more like a hick who didn't belong. He wanted to snatch Anne up and go back. As far as he was concerned, it didn't take much to hate the noise, the heavy traffic and people hurrying.

"About an hour." Hank cut across the congested lanes with the ease of one who had done it for a long time. He glanced at his friend who lounged in the passenger seat, his elbow resting on the open window as he stared out. "What has she said about her time with Sinclair?"

His throat muscles convulsed. "Who's asking?"

Hank knew what he meant. "I'm asking as your friend, nothing else."

Travis sighed. "She's told me enough." His expression was filled with bleak pain.

"And the daughter?"

"She's safe," he replied, tight-lipped.

"I didn't hear that," Hank reminded him in a crisp tone. "And to keep her safe, I'm not going to ask any more questions."

The silence between them was heavy during the balance of the drive. When they reached the hotel, the check-in procedure was quickly completed and Hank and Travis rode the elevator up to the assigned room.

"I reserved two adjoining rooms as you requested. And they're both under an assumed name." Hank followed Travis into the room. He paused. "Look, as much as I like seeing you again..."

"You're right. You shouldn't even be seen with us." Travis could taste the bitterness of the past couple of hours. He dropped his bag onto the king-size bed and walked over to unlock the door leading into the next room, so that he could carry Anne's bag in there. He looked around, as if checking to make sure everything was all right, then returned to Hank. "This is very nice. Thank you."

The tension in Hank's features lightened. "I just don't want to screw things up for you. Tell me something. Do you have any idea how tough this is going to be for you, once the press gets wind of who you are? They're going to hound the two of you like crazy."

Travis stood his ground. "That's why I'm here. So Anne won't have to go through this alone."

Hank smiled. "Then old buddy, I have a lot of respect for you, because to be honest, I don't know if I could go through what you have ahead of you." He glanced at his watch. "Sorry I have to run out like this, but I've got some appointments I couldn't cancel. Dave will bring Anne back here. I told the front desk to screen your calls, just in case."

Travis held out his hand. "Thanks."

He took it. "Don't thank me just yet."

The afternoon dragged unmercifully. Travis paced the room until he was positive that the soles of his boots had worn thin. He smoked until his lungs burned, and ordered coffee from room service, drinking it until he felt as if he were floating. He refused to leave the room in case there was a call, and he didn't want to use the phone for the same reason. By the time the phone rang, the room was dark, because he hadn't bothered to turn on any lights. He snatched up the receiver almost before the first ring had finished.

"Yeah?" He spoke abruptly.

"Travis, what is going on down there?" Maude's voice was low-pitched and urgent.

He sighed. "More than you can guess."

"The news showed Anne getting arrested at the airport." Travis closed his eyes and swore pungently under his breath. "I was doing the dishes and had no idea the girls were watching it, until Susie called out to me that Anne was on TV and Nikki was crying. The poor baby was hysterical, and it took me a long time to calm her down and get her to bed."

Travis rubbed his eyes, burning with fatigue, with his fingertips. "Is she all right?"

"Yes, she and Susie are both asleep in my bed," his mother replied. "Was it as bad as it looked?"

"Worse."

"Is Anne all right?"

"I don't know," he burst out, feeling the frustration from the past hours build up. "Hank ordered me not to go to the police station, and the hotshot attorney he recommended is supposed to be bailing her out, but I haven't heard a word from him. If I don't hear anything pretty soon, I'm going to go out there myself."

"No, let a professional handle this," she ordered. "You sound as if you've been living on coffee and cigarettes. And you know what a monster that turns you into. Call down and order up a meal. Give Anne my love." With that she rang off.

Travis ordered a steak dinner but only picked at it, instead drinking even more coffee, which only left his nerves jangling. He lay on the bed, smoking and staring at the ceiling, thinking about Anne's ex-husband.

"Somehow this has to be linked to you, Sinclair," he muttered, drawing on his cigarette. "It just has to be."

The knock sounded loud and foreign in the silent room. Travis climbed off the bed and ran to the door.

Anne stood in front of him with a tall, lanky man in his early to mid-forties.

"Dave Harrison, Sheriff," he introduced himself with a weary smile. "I'm sorry. I had no idea it would take this long."

But Travis's attention was centered on the woman he loved. Her hair, which had been combed into a neat French braid that morning, was now loose and hanging around her face, and her clothes were wrinkled, with smudges of dirt on them. But it was her expression and manner that tore at his soul. She looked as if she had just visited hell.

Chapter Fifteen

Travis stood back and gestured for them to enter, even as he pushed his shirttail back into his pants. He walked around, switching on a couple of lights.

"She's had it pretty bad," Dave murmured, watching Anne walk woodenly across the room and stare out the window.

"What took so long?"

Dave inclined his head toward Anne. "Does she have a separate room?"

Travis nodded. He moved toward Anne, lifting his hands, then froze when she flinched.

"Honey, I put your stuff in your room over there." He pointed toward the open door. "Maybe you'd like to freshen up?"

"Yes." Her voice was devoid of feeling. "I would." She entered the other room and closed the door behind her.

Travis turned on the other man the moment they were alone. "What happened?"

Dave sighed. "It's called musical chairs with a prisoner. They shifted her around, obviously hoping I would get fed up and leave her there. Then I had to get a bail set, which wasn't easy. Let me warn you now, the Sinclairs are going to make it hell for you. Good thing I'm stubborn. Once they realized I wasn't going to give up, things went pretty swiftly. What happened to Anne was basically emotional. I gather they put her into a holding tank with some pretty rough ladies, so if I were you, I'd handle her gently tonight. Now I want to see her tomorrow, so we can get the ball rolling. Say around one?" He handed Travis his business card.

Travis nodded. "I'll have her there."

Dave hesitated. "This fight is going to be dirty. I'll be honest, it doesn't look good for her, so anything she can tell me will be appreciated. I don't like people who feel they can get away with anything, just because of their family name and social position, so I'm more than willing to go through with this. I just want to know, are you? Because once we start, there's no turning back."

There was no hesitation. "Since I intend to marry the lady, I hope we can get this over as soon as possible, but no matter how long it takes, I'll be here."

Dave smiled. "You've got guts, Sheriff. Hank said you did. Good thing, because you're going to need them." After that, he left.

Travis quickly called downstairs, asking for a light meal to be sent up, then walked into the other room. He noticed that the bathroom light was on and the shower running. He paused in the doorway and saw a sight that tore at his insides. Anne stood under the hot spray, crying so hard that her body was convulsed. More than anything Travis wanted to go to her and give her comfort, but sensed this wasn't the time. He quietly backed away and returned to his room to wait for her there.

When Anne finally appeared, she was clad in a robe, with her hair up in a towel, and her eyes were red and swollen.

"I ordered you something to eat." Travis gestured toward the table that had been set up.

She grimaced. "I'm not sure I'm hungry."

"At least try." He noticed that she edged around him as she settled into the chair. "Please."

Anne looked at the fluffy omelet and cut off a small piece with her fork. "I kept washing myself over and over, and I still feel dirty," she said in a small voice that trembled.

Travis reached for her free hand and hung on, even as she tried to pull back. "They're the dirty ones for what they tried to do," he told her.

She nibbled on her food and before she knew it, half the omelet was gone, along with a slice of buttered toast and a large glass of juice.

"I figured I drank enough coffee for the two of us," Travis explained.

She nodded. "Travis, I would rather die than go back there. You're not treated like a person, but some dirty thing that shouldn't be allowed out in public. They even tried to tell me that you only brought me back for the reward, and no one was going to bail me out or help me."

Travis cursed long and hard. "Now you know differently."

Anne glanced at the clock and uttered a sigh of dismay. "I should have called Nikki by now. She must be worried sick."

"I talked to her," he lied. "They're all doing fine. I told her you were with an old friend."

Anne looked at him as if she didn't believe him, but wasn't about to dispute his statement. "I had no idea how long I was there," she murmured. "Time has no meaning." Her lids drooped with exhaustion.

"You need sleep," Travis decided, assisting her out of the chair. "Can you dry your hair by yourself, or do you need help?"

"Myself," she mumbled, heading back to her room. Ten minutes later she appeared again in the open doorway. "I understand the reason for the two rooms, but please don't let me be alone tonight."

Travis pulled back the already rumpled covers on his bed and smashed the pillows a few times before walking over to her. "I don't want to be alone, either."

Anne quickly crossed the room and got under the covers, watching Travis walk around the room, turning off lights and shucking his clothing before he climbed in next to her. With one arm curled around her shoulders he leaned over and switched off the bedside lamp.

"What did you do while you waited for me?" She rolled onto her side to face him.

"Counted the flowers and leaves on the wallpaper, each separately of course, smoked and drank coffee until I was climbing the ceiling, and watched HBO. I think we should invite Sigourney Weaver down. After what she did to those aliens, this would be a snap for her."

Anne showed the first smile of the day. "Sounds fascinating."

"Most of all, I missed you."

"You know how to make a woman feel good." She buried her face in the hollow between his neck and shoulder.

He rubbed his knuckles over her cheek, finding the skin silky-soft to the touch. "At least you got over your airsickness."

She wrinkled her nose. "Not the way you think. I got sick in the car. All over the detective who looked like Sidney Greenstreet."

Travis chuckled. "Serves him right."

"He didn't think so." She rubbed her cheek against the hair tickling her nose and sighed. "Travis, I want you to go back home tomorrow. This is going to turn into a circus, and I don't want you to be a part of it."

"Too late. I'm already in for the duration. Besides, I can't take the chance of you falling for your attorney, can I?" he teased her. "You're supposed to love me, and I don't want you to get confused."

"You don't have to worry. He's not my type." Anne sighed again. "I think Lloyd or his father somehow found out I was on that flight, and alerted the police and probably the media, too. It would be just like them."

His arms tightened around her. As much as he wanted to make love to her, he knew he couldn't after the traumatic day she'd just had.

"Go to sleep," he ordered huskily, fiercely determined to protect her even more after what had happened.

She yawned. "Thank you."

"For what?"

"For being here."

"I'LL BE HONEST with you, Anne, this is going to be a tough fight," Dave said bluntly, as the three sat on a couch in his office. "The Sinclair family wants you behind bars, and they don't care how they do it." There was no apology in his tone for his candid speech. "And after all this time we're going to have trouble proving self-defense. So I'm going to need some information, anything you can remember. Dates you were injured, times you spent in the hospital, names of people who saw you. Anything I can work with."

She nodded. "I understand." Drawing a deep breath, Anne dug deep into her memory and began reciting bits and pieces, as if she were speaking about someone else.

For the next two hours Travis stood at the window, looking out over the skyscrapers, trying not to listen to Anne's softly spoken words but unable to tune them out. When she finished, it took him a few moments to realize there was only silence in the room. He turned and found her gone.

Dave smiled knowingly at Travis's glare. "Don't worry. I haven't spirited her anywhere. She's just down the hall in the ladies' room."

Travis looked at the tape recorder. "What do you think?"

The attorney grimaced. "It's still her word against his, but I'm hoping to find a few more people to back up what she's said."

"Hiring investigators," Travis guessed.

Dave nodded.

"I want to help."

"Not a good idea."

"I know how to take notes and question people without applying thumbscrews," Travis argued.

"But you don't know the area and you don't know the people,"

Dave pointed out. "I know of several reputable investigators who can get the job done. I also want to do some digging into Lloyd Sinclair's background. Judging from what Anne said, it's not exactly spotless, although his father sure worked hard to make it look that way."

"What do you know about them?" Travis leaned against the windowsill, his hands jammed into his pockets.

"Just what the society pages tell us, and more than a few juicy rumors." Dave poured himself another cup of coffee. "The papers make Joshua and Sylvia Sinclair sound like saints. The rumors tell us that the Sinclair fortune was founded by an ordinary horse thief, who shot and killed more than his share of Texas Rangers, then conveniently found a couple of sacks of gold and decided to go legitimate." He glanced through the file folder before him.

"Sounds like the perfect all-American dynasty," Travis commented dryly.

Dave grinned. "Close enough. Joshua Sinclair will do anything for new contracts, and questions were raised when he branched out into the construction business—basically because of his methods of obtaining contracts. But nothing could be proven. Lloyd believes in living hard." He tossed a newspaper photograph of an older man toward Travis. "Some say old Joshua has half the judges in his pocket. I don't think I want to even know about the other half. Most of Lloyd's girlfriends aren't accepted at the family manor, due to their dubious occupations, and the old boy has been harassing his son to get married again and have some more grandchildren. The old man's never forgiven Anne for snatching his only one, even if she was a girl."

"He probably figures Nikki could marry someone worthwhile," Travis growled.

Dave winked. "Bingo."

Travis ground his teeth. "Sounds like something out of a soap opera."

"I agree," Dave said. "I'm going to tell Anne about it, of course, but I've contacted her family."

"I can imagine that went over very well, considering how they feel about her."

"Like a lead balloon," the other man agreed. "The father said as far as he's concerned, his daughter is dead, after disgracing him the way she had, and her mother refused to talk to me or anyone from my office. In fact, I was referred to their attorney. It appears they want a piece of their granddaughter and would be willing to fight the Sinclair family for her. I gather she's safe with your family?''

He smiled coldly. "She's being well taken care of."

"Travis, I'm on your side," Dave reminded him. "It isn't going to take them long to serve Anne with a court order for her to return the child. I'm surprised it hasn't happened yet."

Anne had returned to the office in time to hear his words.

"No," she said coldly. "I will not give her up."

"I told you not to worry about it." Travis reached into his shirt pocket and tossed a long white envelope across the desk. "If they want to make a fuss, you can give them this."

Dave drew out a neatly typed sheet of paper and read it quickly. "Very nice," he complimented. "It's all couched in medical terms. Basically, Nicola Sinclair is under quarantine until further notice. Therefore she cannot be moved."

Travis looked at Anne and saw that she finally realized why he'd never worried about Nikki being easily taken away from her. He flashed her a broad grin. "Exactly."

By THE TIME they left the attorney's office, Anne and Travis were exhausted. Dave had one of his clerks drive them back to the hotel and suggested they get as much rest as possible, because he had an idea things would escalate, once the Sinclairs decided to get the ball rolling.

Little did Anne know how fast things would happen.

When she wasn't having her brain picked about her years with Lloyd, she was trying to rest in anticipation of the upcoming trial and avoid the press. Any calls home were made from pay phones, because Travis refused to trust the hotel. After the press discovered where they were staying, they had no privacy. In the end, Dave offered them the use of a house on the city's outskirts.

"I'll be honest. The two of you cohabiting isn't a good sign," he told them when he drove them out to the house for the first time.

Anne was the one to reply first. "I am no longer a married woman, and I'm certain Lloyd hasn't been celibate during all this time."

"Yes, but you know how it goes. It's always the woman who suffers."

"I'll sleep in a separate bedroom if it will make people feel better, but I won't let Anne stay alone," Travis informed him. "She's been alone for three years because of him. No more."

Dave sighed. "Okay, but be prepared for the mud to be slung. So don't read any newspapers. And I may as well tell you now, the court date has been set for next Monday.''

Anne gasped. ''That soon?''

''I have an idea we got one so quickly because of the Sinclair name. They want this cleared up as soon as possible, while it's fresh in the public mind,'' he replied.

''But you haven't been able to lay all the groundwork you wanted to,'' she protested.

The attorney grinned. ''That's what they're hoping for. Don't worry, I have a few tricks up my sleeve, too.'' He parked in the driveway of a sprawling, one-story house, led them up the walkway and unlocked the front door. ''Rosa does the cooking and cleaning and lives in. She's also very reliable and doesn't gossip. The phone number is unlisted.'' He preceded them into the living room and turned on several lights.

Anne looked around at the Southwestern decor and ran her hand across the back of an apricot-colored sofa. ''This is all very lovely, but I can't understand who you would know who would be willing to loan us this place.''

''My wife. She owned this house when we got married. We usually rent it to business executives who are in the city more than a couple of weeks and want a place a bit more personal. It came available a few days ago, so I decided you two could make better use of it.'' He walked over to the pale blue draperies, drew them open and flipped a light switch.

''Pool and Jacuzzi,'' he explained. ''Great for relieving tension. Rosa's quarters are off the kitchen, so she's available if you need her. This is her night off, but she'll be here to fix breakfast for you in the morning.''

''We might not want to leave after all this,'' Travis commented, looking at the wide-screen stereo television set.

''Trust me. When the time comes, you'll be out of here like a shot.'' Dave tossed him a key ring. ''I'll be off now, but I'll see you tomorrow around eleven.'' He headed for the front door.

Travis followed him. ''Dave, I want to thank you.''

He smiled. ''Wait to thank me after I've nailed them to the wall.'' He waved at Anne and left, after showing Travis how to activate the burglar alarm.

Travis returned to Anne, who was standing at the patio window, looking out at the softly lighted swimming pool.

''Sure a far cry from my place,'' he murmured, sliding his arms around her waist and pulling her toward him.

She tipped her head back and to one side, to allow his lips access to her ear. "Yes, but luxury isn't all it's cracked up to be. I like your place much better. Let's go for a swim," she said suddenly. "Dave said there're extra suits in the bedroom."

She disappeared into the master bedroom and returned in ten minutes, wearing a bright green maillot. She opened the sliding door and pushed it back, along with the screen, then glanced over her shoulder. "Are you coming?"

He grinned, relieved to see her more relaxed than she had been the past few days. "Yes, ma'am."

By the time Travis walked outside, Anne was swimming laps.

He dived into the deep end and swam over to where she was now treading water near the diving board. He grasped the coping as their bodies drifted together, then apart in the warm water.

"Anne, I'm proud of you," he said seriously. "The last few days haven't exactly been easy, and you've handled everything beautifully. Even the reporters."

She smiled. "You frightened most of them away—at least the ones you didn't insult. If your mother heard you, she'd wash your mouth out with soap."

"Nah, she'd be in there slinging mud back with the best of them." He paused. "Anne, I love you."

Her breath caught in her throat. "I'm a woman with a dubious past, who's considered violent."

His lips twitched. "If you're trying to talk me out of it, you're failing miserably."

Anne gripped his shoulders. "Oh, Travis, maybe that's what I've been feeling for you for so long. It's just that I'm afraid. I want to love you. I mean it, but..." Her voice faded. The trial hung over them like a dark cloud.

"Come on," Travis suggested. "I'll race you." When they reached the steps, they settled on the top step, leaning back to look up at the sky. "Remind me to think about building a pool in the backyard," he commented.

"After you buy the bull," she reminded him with a sad smile, as she thought about the money that was being used for her defense.

He grazed her chin with his fingertips. "After I buy the bull." He lay back and looked up at the stars. "They're brighter at home."

"No smog there." She sat up, wringing the water out of her hair.

"You know, you look pretty sexy in that suit," he told her. "Not at all like the mother of a seven-year-old girl," he teased.

Anne looked him over in the navy briefs that showed off his muscled body so well. "You're not so bad yourself. Of course—" she paused, tapping her chin with her forefinger in thought "—you really should watch yourself. After all, you have reached the big four-oh, and if you aren't careful, it could be all downhill from there." She squealed with laughter when he started tickling her. She escaped, only to be playfully tackled on the grass. For the moment the worries of the case were forgotten.

As he lowered his head to catch her lips, he murmured huskily, "Then I guess I'll just have to prove to you this forty-year-old man has plenty of mileage left in him, won't I?"

She looked at him with darkened eyes. "Travis, I..."

He smiled, guessing her unspoken thoughts. "No, sweetheart, I'm just going to kiss us into a frenzy. Anything else can wait until the proper moment."

Anne looped her arms around his neck. "Did I ever tell you how special you are?"

"Yes, but I wouldn't mind hearing it again."

Chapter Sixteen

*The jury has found Mrs. Sinclair guilty of murder. Does the prisoner
have anything to say in her defense?*

This is all wrong! I didn't kill him! You can't do this!

There can only be one suitable punishment....

When Anne woke up that morning with those words ringing in her
ears, she already dreaded the rest of the day. She was grateful for
Travis's calm strength as they entered the courthouse amid a crowd
of reporters and hurried down the hallway to their assigned courtroom.

"I'll be right back," she murmured to Travis and Dave. In the
ladies' room she stared long and hard at her reflection, seeing the
result of sleepless nights. By concentrating hard she was able to
steady her shaking hand just long enough to freshen her lipstick before leaving.

"You look well, Anne, although not your usual stylish self."
Lloyd Sinclair's cold blue eyes flicked over her simple olive skirt
and pale green camp shirt with disdain. "My, my, it must be love
that puts that look in your eyes." His smile was deadly, as was the
expression he flashed toward Travis, who stood with his back to
them, unaware of the confrontation. "Funny, I never would have
figured you for the rough-and-tumble type. You didn't seem to like
it when I wanted a little variety."

Her eyes reflected icy shards. "Probably because you enjoyed
breaking bones too much."

His body stiffened. "So you're into cowboys now. Does he know
all about you?"

She held her head high, determined not to back down.

His gaze hardened. "You're going to lose, Anne, and you're going to jail until you're a very old woman, if I have anything to say about it. I wonder if your cowboy will be around for you then. And I'm going to have Nikki. Just remember that.''

"Anne." Travis's hand rested possessively on her shoulder. "I don't think your lawyer would appreciate you talking to us, Sinclair."

The other man straightened his raw silk jacket. "Funny, I always thought Anne had more taste than to wind up with someone who probably cleans out his own barn. It just goes to show that you never know someone, even if you've been married to them."

"At least I don't go around beating up women."

Lloyd's features tightened. "Be careful, or you'll go down with her." He walked away.

"Don't." Anne held on to Travis's arm, feeling the muscles tense under her touch. "He'd love to provoke you into fighting him, so he can come out looking even better. He's not worth it."

He looked down and smiled at her. "I'm just glad you know that."

They walked back down the crowded hallway, Travis a more than effective shield, keeping all but the most persistent away from Anne.

When Anne saw her parents across the hall, she stiffened but no expression crossed her features. The disgust on their faces was evidence enough that they wanted nothing to do with her, so she was surprised when they walked toward her.

"This ridiculous trick of some small-town doctor, putting Nikki under medical quarantine for an unknown ailment, isn't going to work. You may as well give us her now, Anne," her mother commanded. "Lloyd has promised us custody once she's returned."

Anne turned and stared deep into her father's cold eyes. "And will you hit her if one of your big loans defaults?" she asked with deceptive softness. "Or are you into breaking bones like Lloyd? Frankly, I'll be surprised if he gives Nikki up. She's too big a bargaining tool with his father."

The man's fists clenched at his sides. "You—"

"Don't," Travis advised with a deadly quiet. "Because if you dare to touch her again, I won't be held accountable for my actions."

Her mother shot them both a venomous look, then the couple moved swiftly away.

"I wonder what they promised Lloyd in hopes of getting Nikki," Anne mused, feeling freer than she had in a long time, because she had finally confronted her parents.

"Probably a new toaster and a gold-plated savings book," he muttered, leading her back to Dave, who stood talking to one of his assistants.

"Good news," the attorney greeted them before guiding them into a side room. "And bad news."

Anne sighed. "Give me the bad news first."

"The records for your two hospital stays read that you were in for gynecological problems," he announced.

She closed her eyes. "I cannot believe they've gone so far as to change them. How can they do that?"

"The Sinclairs will do anything to protect themselves," Dave explained.

Anne chewed on her lower lip, unaware that she was nibbling off the lipstick she had just reapplied. "Dave, tell me the truth. Do you believe everything I've told you, even though I don't have a shred of proof to back up my words?"

"Yes," he replied without hesitation.

She had to know more. "Why?"

He grinned. "If you were guilty you would have killed him, left Nikki and taken off for Europe or South America. And only someone incredibly stupid would come back."

Anne heaved a sigh of relief, taking comfort in Travis's fingers, which were laced tightly through hers. "Now what about the good news?"

"I found the nurse who took care of you when you were hospitalized for the broken ribs," he said proudly. "She's willing to testify."

Anne looked more hopeful than she had in days. "That's wonderful! How did this come about?"

Dave shook his head. "She read about it in the papers. And decided to come forward, because she never liked the way you were treated by your husband and family during your hospitalization. She'll be one of our first witnesses."

But Anne was still feeling nervous. "After the prosecution finishes with me, I may not have to worry about anything other than what to wear to my funeral."

"I wouldn't worry," Dave assured her.

But Anne wasn't as confident as she sat next to her lawyer, listening to people talk about her alleged temper tantrums, abrupt changes in mood and the way she refused social invitations; there was even a doctor, testifying she'd been treated for drugs.

Dave was genial as he questioned each witness, sometimes adroitly turning the negative statements in their favor, at other times unable to shake the person's story.

"Mrs. James, did you ever see my client take drugs?" he asked one woman, whom Anne had once thought of as a good friend.

She shrugged. "No, but everyone knew she did."

"I'm not talking about anyone else. I'm asking if *you* did," Dave pressed, still smiling. "Were you present during any of the times my client supposedly took drugs?"

She frowned. "Well, no, but—"

"Thank you. I have no other questions."

"Now, Mr. Carter, you say you and Mrs. Sinclair were lovers for several months." Dave's manner wasn't as friendly with this man, but he still assumed a "good ole boy" attitude.

The man sat back, leering in Anne's direction. "Yeah, we sure were."

"Then you know Mrs. Sinclair very well."

"I'd sure say so." He chuckled, grinning at the laughter running through the courtroom.

Dave nodded "Then you're more than familiar with her birthmark."

He shifted uncomfortably in the chair. "Well, uh—"

Dave leaned on the railing, lowering his voice a fraction. "That cute little star shape on her left hip?"

"What about it?"

He pressed. "You know it?"

"Sure, I do," Carter blustered. "I told you, I know all about her. Couldn't miss something like that, could I?" He winked knowingly at the people in the courtroom.

Dave smiled and stepped back. "Your Honor, I have a doctor's report here that states Mrs. Sinclair has no identifying birthmarks and never has had one. Obviously you didn't know the lady as well as you thought you did. No further questions."

Jed Carter stared at Lloyd, but the other man didn't look up as he walked past.

Lloyd's testimony was still the most damaging. Sitting in the witness stand looking movie-star handsome in a pale blue, Italian-cut suit, he presented the image of a man who had been badly hurt.

"Anne was my life, but when she began to change, I knew our marriage couldn't last. Her many lovers and the way she treated our daughter were just the last straw.

"I had to fight for custody. I didn't want to drag out her dirty linen, but how could I allow her to raise our child?

"That last night I had no idea why she came over. She began screaming obscenities at me, saying if we couldn't be together she'd rather have me dead. I didn't realize she had my gun until it was too late. I'm just glad Nikki was safe in her room. For all I know, she might have tried to hurt her, too. She appeared so unbalanced. I miss my daughter and I want her home with me. Why she refuses to give her up, I don't know, because I doubt she loves her."

A wave of sympathetic murmurs ran through the crowded room.

"If I didn't know better, *I'd* even demand I be lynched," Anne murmured, reaching behind her for Travis's hand.

Dave patted her shoulder and stood up.

"Mr. Sinclair, you say that you asked for the divorce because of your wife's infidelities," he began.

"That's right."

"Then why was Mrs. Sinclair the one to file?"

Lloyd's expression didn't change. "I allowed her to file to save face."

Dave nodded. "Tell me, do you ever lose your temper?"

He shrugged, looking at ease. "Everyone does at one time or another."

"Did you ever lose your temper with your ex-wife to such an extent that you struck her?"

Lloyd's gaze didn't waver. "Never."

"What about the times she was hospitalized for broken bones?"

"The only time she broke a bone was when she broke her wrist falling down the stairs, and she wasn't hospitalized for that," he explained, looking so sincere that Anne felt ill.

"But your house has no stairs," Dave pointed out with maddening logic.

"There are two steps leading to the house and a cement walkway. That's where she fell, because she was drunk when we came home from a party."

Anne moaned softly, scarcely feeling Travis's comforting squeeze of her hand.

Dave nodded. "Do you drink?"

"Socially."

The prosecuting attorney spoke up. "Your Honor, I don't know what Counselor is trying to prove here."

"If you'll give me a moment, it will become clear," Dave responded.

At the judge's nod, Dave continued.

"Ever get drunk?"

Lloyd shrugged, his manner relaxed, his eyes sharp. "As a teenager, like so many did."

"What about as an adult? Ever get drunk enough to hit your wife hard enough to send her to the hospital?"

"Objection!"

"Of course not!"

"Drunk enough almost to kill her, so that she had no choice but to strike out in self-defense and run for fear of her life?"

"Objection! Defense is badgering the witness."

Dave never stopped smiling as he stepped away. "I withdraw the questions."

When Lloyd stepped down, he walked past Anne but gave her a look that could have killed. She just stared at him.

No one was surprised when Travis was called to the stand, since he had already been served with a subpoena. He sat there looking very relaxed and comfortable, fully prepared for anything thrown his way.

"Sheriff Hunter, did you ever meet a J. D. Porter, a private investigator?" the prosecuting attorney asked.

"Yes, I did."

"And did he divulge the reason for his meeting with you?"

"Yes."

"And what was that reason?"

"He was looking for a woman," Travis replied.

"Did he say why he was looking for her?"

"Said she had shot her ex-husband and kidnapped their child."

"Did he show you a picture of the woman and child?"

"Yes."

"Is this the picture?" He held up a photograph.

Travis leaned forward to get a better look at it. "Looks like it, but I couldn't be sure."

"When Mr. Porter explained his business, why didn't you tell him you knew Mrs. Sinclair?" the attorney demanded.

Travis smiled ever so slightly. "Because I didn't know her."

The other man exhaled a frustrated breath. "Are you saying under oath that you didn't know the defendant?"

"No, I'm saying that I didn't know a woman named Anne Sinclair," Travis clarified.

"Then the defendant was using another name?"

"Yes."

"When you discovered who she really was, why didn't you call the proper authorities?"

"I don't believe in jumping the gun until I have all the facts. All

Porter did was ramble on about a bloodthirsty woman and a big reward. That kind of talk doesn't go over very well with me.''

His adversary swaggered. "Is that why the townspeople lied to Mr. Porter, claiming they never saw her, either? You must run a pretty tight town.''

Travis's gaze hardened. "I told you before, we didn't know her by that name.''

The prosecutor consulted his notes. "You accompanied Mrs. Sinclair back to Houston, am I right?''

"Yes.''

"And you are sharing a house with her?''

"Correct.''

"Are you sharing a bed?''

"Objection!''

"Your Honor, I'm trying to prove that this man would lie for a woman he has had intimate relations with,'' the attorney argued, then smilingly backed off. "But if that offends my colleague, I can take a different tack. Are you in love with Mrs. Sinclair?''

Travis didn't hesitate. "As soon as this farce is over, I plan to marry the lady. Is that what you wanted to know?''

"More than enough. Thank you.''

By the time the day was finished, Anne was exhausted. As Dave drove them to the house, she leaned back her head and closed her eyes.

"They made her sound like a cross between Lucrezia Borgia and Mata Hari,'' Travis grumbled from the back seat.

"And I was able to come back at them every time,'' Dave countered. "They're out to prove Anne deliberately shot Lloyd. I intend to show that it was strictly self-defense.''

"It was!'' Anne argued.

"I believe you, but we have to get them to believe us, okay?'' he soothed.

"I should have killed him that night.''

Both men fell still at the low-voiced statement.

"You're talking crazy, Anne,'' Travis said angrily.

"I agree. That's not the kind of thing to say in public,'' Dave added firmly. "Besides, if you had killed him, you wouldn't have a chance in court, and you know it.''

Once they reached the house, Dave reminded them to either let Rosa answer the phone or allow the answering machine to pick up the calls, since he feared the media would soon find them. So far they had been lucky, but they all knew their luck was running out.

After a dinner they hardly touched, Anne and Travis retired to the den to just sit and share each other's closeness.

"It's all starting to close in," she murmured, laying her head on Travis's shoulder. "Lloyd seems to win a little more every day."

"Maybe so, but we're not going to let him win without a fight."

ANNE'S HEADACHE escalated as the day wore on. Dave admitted that his witnesses for the defense were few, since Lloyd's ex-girlfriends refused to testify to his violent nature. The nurse he had located was his first witness, and the woman calmly explained that she had looked after Mrs. Anne Sinclair when she was admitted for a concussion and broken ribs.

"Now Ms. Palmer, how can you be so sure the broken ribs and bruises Mrs. Sinclair sustained were a result of a beating from her husband?" the prosecuting attorney asked with a knowing smirk.

"I never said I was absolutely certain, but she cried all night, begging Lloyd to stop hitting her, and some of the bruises were definitely the shape of a man's fingers," she explained.

"Certainly such behavior could have been a result of painkilling drugs," he pressed. "It's been known to happen."

She shook her head. "She refused all but aspirin, and drugs aren't allowed when a patient has a concussion."

"After all these years, how can you remember one patient so clearly?"

The woman smiled briefly. "It wasn't difficult. We talked about our daughters, who happened to be the same age, and because she once mentioned she prayed to give her daughter a happier childhood than she had."

Dave then called a physician, who attested to Anne's sound mind and declared that he could find no signs of abnormal behavior. Then he called Anne to the stand.

"Mrs. Sinclair, we want to make this as painless as possible for you." He smiled at his client. "But I want the jury to understand a few things. Why did you run away three years ago?"

She spoke in a low but steady voice. "I felt I had no choice."

"Why?"

"Because I knew no one would bother to listen to my side of the story, after what had happened during my divorce." Anne looked up, caught Travis's gaze and gathered strength from it.

"Why did you go to Lloyd Sinclair's house that night?"

She took a deep breath. "He had called me, complaining that Nikki was crying and he couldn't make her stop. He wanted me to come over and calm her down. When I arrived, I found Lloyd and a woman in the living room and could hear my daughter screaming in her bedroom. By the time I finished calming her down, the woman was gone and Lloyd had obviously had a few too many drinks.''

"What makes you think that?"

"The signs. Slurred speech, glassy eyes and the usual hostile manner he got when he drank too much. He also held a large glass of whiskey in his hand.'' She glanced toward the other attorney, seeing he was gearing himself up for an objection. "The smell from the glass was unmistakable, which is why I knew what he was drinking.''

Dave nodded. "Did you leave then?"

She shook her head. "No, I wanted to talk to him about arranging for me to see Nikki more, but he refused to listen. In fact, he said that if I wanted to be with her more, I could do something for him."

"Such as?"

Revulsion showed faintly in her eyes. "Have sex with him."

"Did you agree?"

Her hands twisted in her lap, the only sign of nervousness. "I refused."

"And?"

She shrugged. "I also told Lloyd what I thought of him. That he was a sick, evil man who didn't deserve to consort with decent people. I might have called him some other names, but I don't remember exactly what."

Dave appeared to consult some notes on his table. "And what happened then?"

She licked her lips. As she began to remember the night, her face turned pale, and her eyes grew huge and dark.

"Just take your time," he advised softly, noting her shortness of breath.

She nodded jerkily. "He got angry and threw his glass at me. The next thing I knew, he had hit me in the face a couple of times. Nikki came in and tried to get him to stop, and he struck her across the face. I screamed at her to go back to her room, because I was afraid he'd hurt her badly.'' She paused to take several calming breaths, but her voice still came out unnaturally high-pitched. "I fought back, but he's a great deal larger than I am, so I didn't have much luck. The next thing I knew, he had me bent backward over his desk and his hands were around my throat.'' Anne paused, the glazed expression in her eyes conveying that she was reliving the horror. "And all I knew was that I was going to die unless I could somehow get him off me. I groped around, hoping to find something. One of the top drawers was open, and I guess I grabbed the gun from there. After that I don't remember what exactly happened. I heard a loud noise and when I came to my senses, Lloyd was lying on the floor bleeding, and Nikki was crying in her room. I knew I had only one choice—to get out of there and take my daughter with me. I called 911, told them I heard gun shots and then ran.'' Her voice faded.

Dave's manner was gentle. "Anne, did you shoot your husband deliberately?"

"No, I did not."

He again consulted his notes. "One more thing. Why didn't you go to your own family for help?"

She drew in a deep breath. "Because they wanted nothing to do with me after I divorced Lloyd."

When the prosecuting attorney approached, Anne knew what she was in for, since Dave had prepared her.

"Mrs. Sinclair, you said that your ex-husband struck you that night. Now, couldn't that have been in self-defense?"

"No." *Don't offer anything. Just answer the questions, Anne.*

"You said he had been drinking. A man in Mr. Sinclair's position might drink occasionally, but you're trying to say he's an alcoholic. Aren't you exaggerating just a little?" he insisted.

She looked him squarely in the eye. "No, I am not."

He looked a little frustrated. "What about you? Do you drink?"

Anne held on to the image of Travis in her mind to keep her calm. "Very little."

"What do you consider a little?"

"A glass of wine on special occasions."

He showed disbelief. "No more than that?"

"My system can't tolerate a lot of alcohol. It tends to make me very ill," she explained.

The man nodded, clearly not believing her. "Now, your ex-husband must have been upset that night and might have batted at you if you had lost your temper with him, but nothing that would leave bruises, as you claim he did."

Anne didn't like the man, but she knew she couldn't show her revulsion. "What he did to me was more than batting."

"If Mr. Sinclair was so cruel to you, why did you stay with him? Why didn't you go to his family or your own and tell them what was going on?" he demanded, all pretense of affability now gone.

"I stayed with him because I was stupid enough to think he might change. Also because I had no one else to go to. And when I told his family, his father said that all women needed to be knocked around a bit to keep them in line," Anne said in a hard voice. "And as for my own family, my father had started beating me when I was six and didn't stop until I grew older. I knew I wouldn't get any sympathy from either party. I was told by both sides that I was to bear it silently, that my husband could lose his temper if I served him rice instead of potatoes for dinner, and that I was to look the other way if he wanted to have girlfriends. I soon grew up and realized that I was also a human being, and that there was no reason for me to put up with such humiliation any longer."

The attorney was taken aback, clearly not expecting such a strong reply.

"I move that Mrs. Sinclair's answer be stricken from the record, since most of what she has said is hearsay," he stated, recovering quickly.

By the time Anne left the witness stand, she felt like a strand of overcooked spaghetti. She was relieved when the noon recess was called.

"I blew it," she said with a sigh as they left the courthouse for a nearby restaurant, where they could be assured privacy.

"Don't worry," Dave soothed. "Actually you came across so strong that you did more good than harm."

Anne looked up, her gaze temporarily snared by two pairs of coldly condemning eyes across the room. "I don't think my parents will agree with you."

Travis studied the older couple, who were staring daggers at their table. "How can parents be so cruel?" he murmured.

Dave shrugged. "When you've been involved with divorce and custody cases for as long as I have, you get used to everything."

Travis shook his head. "I couldn't. Give me our little town anytime, where the worst is Wilma going after old Zeke with her shotgun. At least I know I can take it away from her without getting shot up myself."

"Dave, what exactly is going to happen?" Anne asked, knowing that her nerves were rapidly fraying.

"I'm hoping first to show that you had just cause for what you did, then to call for a new custody hearing," he explained. "I may not be able to get all the charges dropped, but I'm going to work for your getting probation." The realization that the verdict might not go that way hung heavily between them.

When they left the restaurant, Anne felt her head practically splitting wide open, even with the extrastrength aspirin she had taken after her meal.

"It's all nerves," she told Travis when he expressed concern.

"How much longer is this going to be?" he demanded of Dave in a low voice, taking the other man aside. "She's tearing herself apart inside."

"It would be a lot easier if we could get some of the old girlfriends to talk," the attorney replied. "But everyone is afraid of the Sinclairs."

"Except me," Anne mused. "I'm the first person to stand up to them, and because of that, they're going to make me pay for it."

Chapter Seventeen

"Hey, sleepyhead, time to get up so we can slay some more dragons."

Anne opened her eyes. When they'd returned to the house the night before, she had taken a long hot bath, eaten lightly, then decided to lie down, hoping to banish her headache. That she had fallen asleep wasn't surprising. That she had slept all night was. She smiled and held out her hand. Travis sat on the edge of the bed and grasped her fingers. She looked up at a man who had asked little but to be with her. He had slept beside her every night, offering quiet-voiced assurances, but nothing else. It was an unspoken agreement that any further development in their relationship was to be put on hold until Anne could call her life her own again. Still, it was as if they both knew that the next step would be permanent.

"What did I ever do to deserve someone as wonderful as you?" she asked softly, lacing her fingers through his.

He smiled, gently squeezing her hand. "It was your lucky day."

"I shouldn't have allowed Nikki to attend Susie's birthday party. Then you would still have your money for your bull, and you'd be living a normal and carefree life, instead of being embroiled in a bitter court case," she murmured.

Travis shook his head. "Wrong. I still would have pursued you because I'm so stubborn. We were meant to be together." He leaned down and brushed his lips across hers. "That's what counts. Now, why don't you put on something a bit more substantial than that skimpy nightgown of yours? Of course, you'd really impress the jury in that little number."

Anne sighed as she sat up. "The way things are going back and forth, I could use it as an edge."

"Nah, wear a short skirt instead, so you can show off those great legs of yours." He pulled her to her feet.

She placed her hands on his shoulders, moving them upward to frame his face. "You've made me whole again, Travis," she said quietly. "Without you, I don't know if I could have gone as far as I have."

"You're wrong, you know. You'd still be in there fighting," he assured her. "Now, get dressed. We're running late today, since I let you sleep a little longer. You needed it badly," he said, showing his concern for her wan features.

"It doesn't seem fair that you know all my secrets and I know so few of yours," Anne grumbled as she put on her makeup.

Travis stood in the doorway watching her. "Ask my mother, and she'll be more than happy to fill you in. Except I don't think I know all of yours." He grinned. "I don't remember ever seeing that star-shaped birthmark Dave was talking about."

"Ah yes, the infamous birthmark," she said dryly as she brushed on mascara. "Amazing I never noticed it, isn't it?" She turned. "Travis, I want you to go back."

His body stiffened. "Not funny, Anne."

"If it goes against me, I don't want you here," she said with a sense of urgency. "And if it comes down to my having to return Nikki to Lloyd, I want you with her. Please understand."

"I do, but she has Maude and Susie to keep her safe. Right now, it's just you and me, kid." He flashed her a loving smile.

"If you weren't so damn stubborn, I could handle this better," she grumbled.

Anne felt as if she was drifting through the days. She missed her daughter, whom she hadn't been able to talk to for the past couple of weeks. She thought longingly of Dunson with its gently rolling hills, of Maude's witty tongue, talking with customers at Lorna's and being with Travis.

"I want life to return to the way it was," she murmured. "All this is a bad dream. Every morning I wake up hoping we'll be back in Dunson."

Travis straightened and walked over to Anne, pulling her into his arms.

"Soon," he soothed, rubbing her back in long, calculated strokes. "We'll even go on a hayride, just the two of us."

She smiled. "Hayrides are meant for more than two people."

"Not the kind I'm planning."

TRAVIS LOOKED over to where Anne sat with one of Dave's associates. While her manner was composed, he knew she was tied up in knots inside.

"You're looking pretty cheerful today," he growled at Dave.

The lawyer smiled. "I have good reason."

Travis's interest sharpened. "Why?"

Dave looked around the courtroom, as if seeking someone in particular. "You'll see soon enough," he murmured.

The minute the court was called to order and Dave stood up, he looked even more self-assured than usual.

"I'd like to call Cynthia Mason to the stand," he announced in a clear voice.

Travis looked at Anne, who paled.

"My God," she whispered. "What is happening?"

"Who is she?" he demanded in a low voice.

She gazed straight ahead. "One of Lloyd's ex-girlfriends." She glanced toward her ex-husband, noticing how his body tensed at the name and seeing the black expression on his face before he turned to speak to his attorney. "Obviously things aren't going the way he thought they would," she murmured.

A brown-haired woman in her early twenties, wearing a simple yellow dress, walked forward to be sworn in. She first faltered when she saw Lloyd's threatening manner, but quickly regained her composure. Dave led her through the first questions, establishing her background and relationship with Lloyd Sinclair.

"Miss Mason, will you please tell the court why you came to me?"

She took a deep breath, keeping her gaze away from Lloyd. "I wanted people to know he isn't as good as he claims he is," she said in a low voice.

"Could you speak up, please?" Dave requested.

Cynthia nodded and managed a weak smile. "Well, when Lloyd—"

"When you say Lloyd, do you mean Mr. Sinclair?" He smiled in an attempt to reassure her. "How long have you known Mr. Sinclair?"

She shrugged. "Maybe six, seven years."

"Now, as to what you know about Mr. Sinclair," he prompted.

"Yes, sir. When Lloyd drank too much, he would talk a lot about how he was fooling his wife, and when he got her back, he was going to teach her a lesson she'd never forget."

"When did he say this?" Dave asked, glancing down at the file folder he held in his hands.

She thought for a moment. "Oh, about a year ago."

"And why should the jury believe you, Miss Mason?" Dave asked.

"Because I have his journal, in which Lloyd commented on how he was going to get back at his wife," she replied.

"How did you happen to have the journal in your possession?" he asked amiably.

Cynthia shook her head. "Lloyd used to keep it in my nightstand drawer and write in it after we made love."

"What was written in it?"

"Stories about what he did to her and what he wanted to do to her. That she'd never see her little girl again, because he'd send her away to some boarding school." She looked apologetically at Anne.

"No!" Anne's mother cried out, standing up. "He would never do that! He loved Nicola!"

"Madam, sit down!" the judge thundered.

Mrs. Williams sat down, digging through her purse for a handkerchief.

Anne could only sit there, feeling the cold seep into her bones. "I had no idea he hated me that much," she breathed.

Dave held up the journal and handed it to the woman on the stand. "Is this the book, Miss Mason?"

She glanced at it. "Yes, sir. It is."

Dave then entered the journal as exhibit A. "I also want to enter in three separate reports from certified graphologists that the handwriting is indeed Mr. Sinclair's."

Anne sneaked a glance at Lloyd. He stared straight ahead, looking at Cynthia Mason as if he wanted to kill her.

"Miss Mason, would you read this particular page in the journal to the court?"

She hesitated as she looked it over. "Anne said she wanted a divorce, which is the last thing I'd do. The old man would kill me. He's on my back more and more for a grandson, but she barely lets me near her. I guess I'm just going to have to force her to get pregnant again. It's pretty much what I had to do before. I'll knock that divorce idea out of her head pretty quickly. It's just a shame she bruises so easily. There's no way she can go to the opera this week. ave to tell the old man she's sick again." She looked up.

d was on his feet by this time, his face flushed. "You bitch!" ed. "I'll kill you! Who do you think you are?" He started toward her with murder in his eyes, but the court bailiff quickly intervened and dragged him away.

Anne slumped into her chair, feeling as if all her bones had turned to water.

After the outburst Dave had no trouble in obtaining a recess. The expression on his face signified that he felt success was definitely on their side.

"I wish it hadn't happened this way," Anne said on the way back to the house.

"Don't be sorry for him, he brought it upon himself," Dave told her. "They already are talking deal, but I'm going to hold out for as much as possible. I'm going to make sure they'll never bother you again," he promised, as he parked in the driveway.

"I can't believe she would come forward to help me," she mused.

"She told me he always promised to marry her, but she finally got smart and knew he only said that to keep her dangling. She's decided to move to another state and make a new life for herself, and doing this was the first step. She didn't want Lloyd to win if the journal could help you," Dave explained. "I wouldn't worry any longer. You won, Anne."

"Think he's right?" Anne asked Travis as they entered the house.

"Lloyd blew it today, so there's a good chance, but then I'm not a lawyer. Dave knows what he's doing." Travis switched on a light. He patted his pockets. "Great, I'm out of cigarettes."

She turned around. "You really should quit."

"Nah, I've got to have one vice." He grimaced. "You going to mind if I drive over to that convenience store?"

"Only if you don't bring me back a Butterfinger," she teased. "In fact, bring me two. I need my vices, too. No wonder you wanted a rental car. You wanted it for last-minute runs to the store for cigarettes."

He kissed her. "I'll bring you a whole box, if it will get you smiling like that. Be back in a few minutes."

Desiring a shower, Anne called out to Rosa, asking if she would make a pot of coffee, and went into the bedroom to change into a robe. When the doorbell rang, she left the room.

"What did you do, forget your keys?" Her teasing smile disappeared when she identified the man standing on the doorstep.

"Sorry, it's not your hayseed lover," Lloyd sneered, pushing his way past her. "But then maybe it's a good thing he's not here, so we can talk in private."

"We have nothing to talk about," she replied grimly, crossing her arms in front of her.

"Oh, we have a lot to discuss. I want you to return Nikki to me tonight and I'll drop all charges. Otherwise, tomorrow we're going to tear your reputation in shreds," he threatened, standing close to her.

Anne's head reeled from the alcohol fumes that emanated from him. "I think the position has been reversed as of today. Your attorney certainly made that clear when he told you to forget about ever getting Nikki back. Or did you choose to forget that part?"

"I fired that jerk. I'll even throw in a hundred thousand dollars for the kid."

"You lost the case, Lloyd. Give it up and get out." Her voice grew hard and cold.

He grabbed her arm in a punishing grip. "Look, Anne, don't make it any harder on yourself."

She snatched her arm away. "Lloyd, you are so low it's pitiful. Get out of here before I call the police."

"Why did you do it?" he demanded. "I gave you everything a woman could want. A name, plenty of money, beautiful clothes. We went to all the right parties, saw all the right people. You had it made. What was so wrong?"

She looked at him, realizing that he sincerely believed he had done nothing wrong. For all those years she had felt hate mingled with fear for this man, now she could only feel pity.

"Lloyd, if you don't know, I don't think I could explain it to you," she said quietly. "But clothes and parties aren't everything."

His features sharpened. "Didn't our marriage mean anything to you?"

She smiled sadly. "At one time it meant a great deal to me, but not any longer, because you killed those feelings. All you cared about was your precious money and social contacts. You never cared about me or Nikki. All you've ever cared about was yourself."

His eyes narrowed. "What you're saying is you'd prefer living with that backwoods sheriff than trying with me again."

Her laughter was bitter as all her anger spilled out. "Try with you again? Lloyd, I lived with fear and pain for most of my life. Since then I've learned not all men are like you. You lost the battle. Go on with the life you prefer, and let Nikki and me live in peace."

He shook his head. "You're a fool."

"If so, that's my problem."

Lloyd headed for the front door, but before he could place his hand on the knob, the door flew open and a dark-faced Travis rushed in.

"What the hell are you doing here?" he demanded.

Anne quickly crossed the room to stave off what she knew could turn into a physical battle. "He's just leaving, Travis." The hard look in her eyes as she gazed at Lloyd indicated that he was to do just that. "Goodbye, Lloyd."

The man looked at Travis with murder in his eyes, but did nothing except brush his way past.

Travis swung around, taking Anne into his arms. "Why did you let him in here?" he muttered, pressing her close.

"To release all the ghosts," she whispered, wrapping her arms around him and allowing his warmth to seep into her suddenly cold body. "Why did you come back so soon?"

He shook his head, holding her close, as if he would never let her go. "A feeling. I just knew I had to get back here in a hurry." He kissed the tip of her ear. "What happened?"

"He's convinced he's still the wronged party and that we could get back together again. He refuses to face the truth. I don't know, maybe he honestly believes he did nothing wrong during all those horrible years. I should still hate him, but I can't, Travis. He's a man to be pitied."

"I sure as hell don't feel sorry for him," he rumbled. "Not when I've gained all that he lost."

She wrapped her arms around his waist and laid her head against his chest. "It's still not all over, Travis."

He fell still. Was he losing her just when he'd found her? "What do you mean?"

"I want Nikki and myself to have some counseling, so we can settle all our past fears once and for all."

"Where would you get that help?" he asked cautiously.

"I'm sure Montana has excellent therapists to deal with this kind of problem." She tilted her head back to look up at him. "And I wouldn't mind a proper courtship into the bargain. You've been patient with me and I love you for it. I just hope you can hang on a little while longer." Her eyes pleaded with him to understand. "I want to be a whole woman for you."

A heavy sigh of relief rippled through Travis's body as he realized she wasn't going to leave him. "Lady, you're going to have the kind of courtship a woman dreams about. Fair enough?"

Anne flashed him the kind of smile that made his knees buckle. "More than fair."

Kamisha Hammill was sure that John Leopardo was more honest and desirable than any man she'd ever met in Aspen. Until someone tried to kill her. And John was the prime suspect....

SILVER LADY

Lynn Erickson

CHAPTER ONE

KAMISHA HAMMILL LOOKED the young man square in the eye. "So you're going to Hawaii, just like that." She snapped her fingers. "And I guess the commitment you made to the Ute City Club doesn't mean a thing to you. What about the party tonight? In a few hours this place is going to be packed with three hundred guests. You're my main bartender, Jeff. You can't just walk out on me like this."

"Look, Miss Hammill," he said, "I'm sorry. But this man I met offered me a ride in his Lear jet, and I can't just pass it up. He's going all the way to Maui."

Kamisha tried to keep the anger out of her voice. "Aspen is full of people with private jets. Get a ride next week. You *owe* the club, Jeff. Mr. Simons helped you with employee housing, your ski pass last winter, that bonus in April."

"But, Miss Hammill, I got this job offer in Maui."

In the end it was no use. Like so many of the youth who flocked to Aspen seeking the good life, Jeff could change jobs as often as his polo shirt—jobs, housing and girlfriends. Kamisha sighed, frustrated, and decided not to argue any longer. She'd had him in her employ at the Ute City Club for nine months, and Jeff had probably broken the club's length-of-employment record, anyway.

She stood gazing out onto the sun-splashed deck that overlooked the tennis courts and the crystal-clear Roaring Fork River below and figured that if worse came to worse, she'd tend bar herself. Maybe even Rick Simons, the club manager and her boss, could jump in if she got swamped. She guessed she'd better find him and tell him the score. He wasn't going to like it. Tonight was the midsummer charity fund-raiser, with over three hundred guests expected—tennis greats, movie stars, diplomats, politicians, business moguls and power brokers from all over the world. And now they'd be lucky to even get a glass of wine for their five-hundred-dollar donations! No, Rick wasn't going to be happy.

Kamisha informed some of the other employees about Jeff leaving and asked them the usual question: "If you know someone who could fill in tonight..." Then she headed into the sprawling depths of Aspen's largest tennis and sports fitness complex to find Rick.

She loved the club—the state-of-the-art exercise studios, the well-equipped weight rooms, the indoor-outdoor pools, Jacuzzis, pro shop, conference rooms, tennis courts, the brand-new sports medicine facility run by a National Football League orthopedic surgeon, the sedate rows of executive condos nestled in the aspen groves, the winding bicycle paths and summer gardens, the rugged mountains that jutted skyward directly behind the stone and wood and glass structures. She even liked its name—not something predictable such as "The Aspen Club," but "Ute City," Aspen's original name and the name of the Indian tribe who'd lived in the valley.

She loved Aspen, Colorado, too, her adopted home for the past eleven years, her refuge from a short marriage, her refuge from the media hype of her years as a ski racer on the Olympic team. They'd hung the Silver Medal for the downhill around her neck in 1980, and she figured it had been the highlight of her life. So much had been out of synch since then—her marriage to Josh Nichols, the Gold Medal winner in 1980, the divorce that had made headlines in every yellow press journal there was, her fight in divorce court to keep the little Aspen Victorian house they'd fixed up, her parents' comment: "Josh is such a nice boy."

For five years Kamisha had worked various jobs in Aspen—ski instructor, summer event coordinator for the prestigious Aspen Institute, the mountain retreat think tank for greats such as Henry Kissinger. But none of her jobs had been satisfying. She'd sensed her employers were using her as a figurehead and not giving her any real responsibility. Even as a ski instructor. She'd have gladly taken ordinary classes down the steep slopes of Aspen Mountain, but the ski school director of the Aspen Skiing Company had seen to it that she was assigned only private lessons for the celebrities that flocked to Aspen in the winter. They came for the fresh white powder snow, the azure-blue Colorado sky and the world-renowned nightlife.

But Rick Simons had given her a break. "Absolutely," he'd said when the club was still under construction, "you'll be running your own show as PR director. You'll put together all the events, all the exhibition tennis matches, hire your own staff, coordinate the food list with our chef, make up the guest lists. It'll be hard work, Miss...Kamisha, but there are a lot of perks in it, too."

"I'm not going to be a figurehead, Mr. Simons," she'd said. "I've been that route. I can handle any responsibility you give me."

"You have my word on it. And," he'd added, his white teeth sparkling in a narrow, darkly handsome face, "Mr. Leopardo, the owner, you understand, has given your employment his blessing. It's a go."

She'd worked hard. She'd worked her buns off to make sure the club ran smoothly. At thirty years old Kamisha felt she'd finally found her niche in life. Someday she'd find the right man, too, a man who'd understand her past, her insecurities, a man who'd father her children. And they'd raise them in Aspen, sharing the wonderfully satisfying life you could live here.

"Seen Mr. Simons?" she asked the tall blond woman at the front desk. Three hours...three hours till the guests arrived for the final evening of the charity event.

But the girl shook her head and resumed folding towels; they were shorthanded in the locker rooms, too.

"Say," Kamisha said, pausing, "have you got any friends who know how to tend bar? It's only for tonight. It pays sixty-five a shift and the tips are always great."

Nina Cassidy tilted her head. "Sixty-five *plus* tips?"

"Yep."

"I'm off at five. Would you give me a shot at it?"

"Ever slung gin before?"

"Once. I helped my boyfriend out at his bar."

"You're on. And, Nina, no shorts, no jeans. This is glitz city tonight. Look the part."

"I've got this shiny blue thing with straps..."

"Perfect. Be here at six-thirty to set up."

"You got it, Miss Hammill."

Well, saved in the nick of time, Kamisha thought. But she'd best let Rick know about Jeff just the same.

She headed down the carpeted corridor that led to the executive offices. She knew she looked disheveled, her long silver-blond hair falling out of its French braid, her white cotton slacks smudged from rummaging in the storeroom looking for a case of club matches. She stopped for a moment and tucked in the hot coral T-shirt she wore and tried to smooth her hair. It was rumored that the absentee owner of the club, the reclusive John Leopardo from New York City, was in town, and Rick might just be with him. It was odd, but she'd been working for Mr. Leopardo—albeit under Rick—for over four years now and had yet to lay eyes on the man. Of course, in Aspen, absentee ownership was hardly a rarity, but she'd have thought by now she would have met him at least once.

Indeed, Rick appeared to be in his office. At least the blinds were partially closed. And that meant he was busy and might not want to be disturbed.

Kamisha hesitated outside his door, her hand lingering uncertainly above the knob. He could very well be with Mr. Leopardo, and maybe she shouldn't interfere. On the other hand, she needed to tell Rick that she had to leave—to run some errands before the party—and, of course, she had to shower and change. She was curious, too, Kamisha admitted to herself. The rumor mill in Aspen had it that John Leopardo was connected to *the* Leopardos of New York. Bigtime Mafia. She'd never been able to help herself, but when she pictured the club's owner she imagined a Robert De Niro type, or Al Pacino from *The Godfather*. Dark hair. Olive skin. Expressionless black eyes. An aura of danger...

A silly decision, childish—knock or leave. She felt awkward standing there. Rick wouldn't mind if she interrupted for a moment and, besides, for all she knew he was alone.

Then she heard voices, two men, speaking quietly, intimately, and it just seemed wrong somehow to disturb them. Besides, if John Leopardo really were in there, then she'd meet him tonight. Sure.

Kamisha backed away from the door silently, her tennis shoes soundless on the plush green carpeting. She began to move past the window, heading toward the back door that led to the parking lot and her car, and as she did she glanced momentarily through the thin cracks in the blinds. She could make out the shadows of the two men inside the private office, standing, their dark heads bowed together over the desk. And then, for a fleeting moment, she was certain one of the men glanced up and saw her, or at least registered her silhouette poised in the hallway. A faint, unaccountable chill brushed her neck before she pushed open the back door and strode into the bright mountain sun.

CITY MARKET WAS jam-packed with summer tourists buying hamburger meat and buns and chips for their campsites. And all Kamisha needed was a few lemons and limes that the Denver food supplier had left out of the shipment. She stood in the long checkout line and glanced at her watch. She had to be showered and dressed and back at the club in forty-five minutes.

She knew people noticed her as she waited in the line. "That's...you know," she heard a man whisper behind her. "Ah... the downhill skier...ah...she married that blond guy...Hammill!"

"Shh!" came a harsh reprimand, probably the man's wife.

In the summer the tourists in the mountain hideaway were of a different breed than the winter ones. They were young families and older retirees on fixed incomes, people who often came in campers or brought tents and stayed in the many Forest Service campgrounds that dotted the mountains. Of course, there were people there for the Aspen Music Festival or the internationally famous Design Conference. But, for the most part, the winter tourists were wealthier—people who could afford the high-season prices. These wealthy visitors studiously ignored the famous. But in the summer...

All her life Kamisha had been told that not only was she a terrific athlete, but beautiful, as well. She did have a well-toned, lean body. She carried herself gracefully, and she had long pale blond hair that contrasted strikingly with her very blue eyes—her father's eyes. In the summer her skin tanned a nice, rich golden color and her features were good, well-delineated, close to the bone, her mouth a bit wide, her nose straight and smallish. She was five foot six inches tall but looked taller. It was her long arms and legs, her leanness, that lent the impression of height.

Yet, inside, she didn't feel particularly pretty. Her best friend, Brigitte Stratford, was always telling her that she had been an abused child. But no one, least of all her socialite mother or her busy oil executive father, had physically "abused" her. Rather, she realized, they had ignored her. Still did, in fact. Before boarding school in Taos, New Mexico, where she'd met Brigitte, Kamisha had been raised in Los Angeles, the "Hammills' darling little daughter." They'd dressed her adorably and shown her off to their friends; they'd exclaimed over how pretty and sweet she was; they'd flown off together to Houston and London and Mexico City and told her to be a good girl for Lucinda, the housekeeper. Heck, Kamisha often thought, Lucinda had been a better parent than her mother and father combined.

They hadn't been at the Olympics, either, when Kamisha had won the Silver Medal. They'd been in Japan at an oil conference. They'd sent flowers, though, dozens and dozens of roses. Josh Nichols had asked her to marry him on the plane home, and she'd thought about how lonely she was, and she'd said yes.

Then, for ten months, it had been Josh's turn to manipulate and use her....

"That'll be $3.58," the checkout girl said.

"Oh," Kamisha replied, digging into her purse.

"How are you today?" the girl asked.

"Oh, fine. Busy. The MS fund-raiser. You know."

"Yeah. Summer'll be over soon, though, and the town will be ours for the off-season."

That was Aspen. Small, intimate, the checkout girls at the store treated as equals to the wealthier residents. It wasn't odd to have your dinner served by a PhD from Harvard who was taking a season off from the "real world."

Kamisha drove home in her bright red Saab convertible along the back streets of Aspen. She *did* love the town. Winter or summer it was glamorous. Oh, maybe the silver miners of the 1880s were long gone, but the townfolk still reaped plenty from the "white gold" that covered the ski slopes in the winter and the elegant classical music that echoed in the valley in the summer. Kamisha could not recall a week in Aspen going by when there wasn't an art show or jewelry fair or charity event. There were horse shows, white river fishing, tennis matches, kayaking races. There was hunting and hiking and Jeeping. Bicycling. A car could barely make it up the steep inclines of Independence Pass east of town in the summer due to the joggers, walkers and bicyclers. It was crazy. Health-crazy. Sometimes she thought it was the dry, warm, scintillating air that brought people; other times she knew it had to be the charm of the quaint city streets. But when it came right down to it, she couldn't put her finger on what precisely made Aspen so unique, what lured people from everywhere, a special kind of independent person who had pride in his mind and body—a whole town full of Renaissance men and women.

She pulled up to the curb and smiled. Eleven years ago she and Josh had bought the Victorian on Bleeker Street at a bargain-basement price. Of course, it had been a miner's shack, really, and practically falling down. You could see the blue sky through the cracks in the walls. But they'd worked their knuckles raw, invested a few dollars and created the quaint, gingerbread-style Victorian, painting it gray with plum and aqua trim. There were only two bedrooms and one bath. A tiny kitchen. But the living room was adorable, centered around a turn-of-the-century potbelly stove. Lots of plants. Lots of wood furniture. And now, Kamisha knew, she could sell it for five times what she'd paid for it. Josh had gotten the bank account, Kamisha the house.

She opened the wrought-iron gate and hurried up the two front steps, remembering to turn the sprinkler on the garden out front. The dry mountain air felt great, but not to her grass and flowers.

Fifteen minutes later Kamisha was ready. She wore little makeup in the summer and had simply put two rhinestone clasps in her hair to hold it back. Matching the clasps was a wide glittering belt that she wore over an emerald-green silk jumpsuit that was both understated and elegant, draped in loose folds over her bosom, leaving one shoulder bare. She needed no other jewelry. The hair clasps and belt said it all. And, essentially, Kamisha was an athlete, not a glamour girl. Rick always complimented her taste, anyway. And she guessed that was what counted.

She found her clutch purse, slipped into comfortable silver opentoed sandals and headed back out. Fifteen minutes to spare. A miracle.

Naturally the phone rang just then.

"Kamisha," came the familiar dispirited voice of her best friend, her lifelong friend.

Kamisha sighed. "Hi, Brigitte, what's up?"

"I'm not coming tonight."

Kamisha knew her friend so well, knew exactly what was behind the insecurity and anxiety in those words. Brigitte was having one of her low spots. "Come on, Brigitte, everyone's expecting you. You promised."

"I can't. I'm miserable. I'd drag everyone down with me."

"You won't. It'll do you good to get out. Get your hair and nails done and get all dolled up."

"I don't know. I just..."

"Brigitte. You know you want to go. Wear your pink dress, the one with the fringe. You'll look gorgeous." They'd been through this before—Brigitte needing support, Kamisha providing it. Even before Brigitte's divorce and the move from Los Angeles to Aspen, she'd called Kamisha at least once a week for propping up.

"Do you think I can still get a hair appointment?" Brigitte was asking.

"Sure, call around." Kamisha glanced at her watch, tried to squelch impatience. Brigitte had been having a bad time lately, mostly because of her boyfriend Bullet Adams.

"I guess I'll try." Brigitte sighed. "Thanks, Kamisha."

"You'll be fine. Everyone will love you."

"You think the pink dress?" Brigitte's voice sounded brighter.

"It's perfect. I'll see you there, okay?" She glanced at her watch nervously. Ten minutes to spare now.

"Well, all right."

"Bye, I've gotta run."

The drive through the West End streets down to the river where the club was situated always calmed Kamisha and reminded her just how very much the town meant to her. Stately cottonwood trees planted by miners a century before lined the streets in front of the homes. She basked in the feel of the late-day sun that filtered through their slender leaves onto her shoulders. There were the cars parked in driveways, Jeeps covered in mud proudly sitting next to Grand Wagoneers and BMWs. A few kids on bikes, dogs chasing sticks. Cats sat in bay windows of the Victorian homes, framed by lace curtains and ferns. This was the quiet time of early evening when the downtown malls began to empty out for a few hours, the tables in the many outdoor cafés awaiting the night crowds that were certain to fill the streets and nightclubs and brick-paved malls. People watching mimes and jugglers, listening to the music students who had set up music stands right on the sidewalks, shopping, eating popcorn or ice-cream cones, sitting on benches in front of the splashing fountains.

It struck her then, out of the blue, as she drove. She wondered, for no reason whatsoever, if John Leopardo, the club's owner, had ever left the grounds of his club to see Aspen as it really was. She knew he stayed in the executive condo high above the river. She knew he had been seen by the grounds' keepers walking the river path early in the morning on his rare visits. But did this man really know the first thing about Aspen? How odd, she thought, a man who owned one of the most beautifully situated clubs on earth and who chose to live in the rush and clamor and pollution of New York City.

Kamisha arrived at the club to find Rick already in high gear. As always, he was rushing around the flagstone terrace, straightening chairs beneath the colorful umbrellas, pulling linen tablecloths an inch this way and that, replacing silverware on napkins, snapping his fingers at the waiters and busboys.

"Bobby," he called, "get four fresh wineglasses for this table. Now!"

She wished he would let her do her job—just once—without stepping in. But in truth, Kamisha knew, Rick really had kept his promise to let her take responsibility. It was just that he was so hyper. Handsome, hyper Rick Simons, a man who made it his business to know all the "right" people. Evidently he'd worked for Mr. Leopardo before in one of the man's other clubs—Miami, Kamisha recalled. And getting control of operations at the Ute City Club in Aspen had been a reward. Darn nice reward, too, she thought, watching him. And it occurred to her: if John Leopardo really was Mafia-connected, could Rick be, too?

Kamisha shook her head to clear her thoughts. There was so much left to do, and the guests would begin to dribble in before she knew it.

"Ah, there you are," Rick said. "Where's that kid, Jeff? He should be setting up the bar, checking the ice machine."

"He quit." Kamisha put her hands on her hips. "But don't worry. I've got it covered."

"Damn kids. Right in the middle of everything they walk out."

"Look," she said, "go on home and change. I've got everything lined up. We're in good shape."

Rick looked down at his white tennis gear. "Guess I better get ready. What do you think? My gray slacks with a pink shirt? The white ones?"

"White," she said. "Pink shirt and that sweater I love, the deep violet color."

"What would I do without you?"

"You'd manage."

For Kamisha, as hostess, it was a bit dressier. But, a former city boy, Rick adored the casual Aspen style. The joke around town was Aspen Black Tie: shirt, tie, sport coat, blue jeans and cowboy boots.

Three trips to the storeroom to help Nina get stocked and Kamisha was ready. She wouldn't dare venture into the kitchen, Chef LaForte's domain. Rumor had it that he'd worked on President Reagan's staff but was canned when he waved a French knife in the face of

the sous chef. Nevertheless, the man could cook up a storm, and
Kamisha had never known him to fail.

Although it was still daylight, she had the waiters light the torch-
lights that lined the perimeter around the sweeping flagstone patio.
The flowers still had drops of water clinging to their petals from the
gardener's careful hand, and the pine forests on the slopes behind the
club provided the scent for the final touch. Kamisha looked up. Not
a cloud in sight. She never knew if one of those frequent summer
cloudbursts would strike. But not tonight. It was glorious out. They'd
wine and dine outside and then, when it came time for Rick to present
the check to the Denver MS representative, they'd all move into the
inside tennis courts, now covered with a temporary floor, where there
was another bar and a band that was scheduled to play at ten.

The first guests began to arrive even before Rick was back, but
Kamisha enjoyed entertaining them and showing off the club. There
was the state representative from Glenwood Springs and his wife, a
stately white-haired woman who was dressed to the nines. And the
tennis celebrities, most of whom were actually movie stars who spent
the summer doing fund-raising events across the country. There was
Martina Navratilova, who lived in Aspen year-round, and Jimmy
Connors, her weekend houseguest. And then Kamisha noticed U.S.
Senator Luke Stern arrive. A popular man whom the *Washington Post*
had dubbed the Jewish Kennedy of the nineties. And as debonair as
they came, with his thick salt-and-pepper hair, a perpetual tan and a
physique that belonged on a thirty-year-old. He went straight to the
bar, ordered a double Scotch from Nina, flirted with her, then moved
off into the growing crowd of the rich and famous. At one point he
gave Kamisha a wink from across the patio, and she wondered if the
next President hadn't just flirted with her, too.

The patio filled up. Rick arrived and set about charming the throng.
And then Brigitte Stratford came breezing in, smiling, adorable, petite, teetering on spike heels, wearing the pink dress whose fringe
shimmered and swayed in the torchlight. Kamisha's heart sank. She
could tell, knowing Brigitte so well, that her friend had already been
drinking—to fortify herself. Oh, God.

Brigitte came over, trailing a few enthralled men and the scent of
expensive perfume. "Hi, Kamisha! Oh, wow, you look terrific,
honey! Listen, I'm so glad you made me come. I feel better already.
Is Bullet here yet?"

"No, not yet."

"Oh, well, I guess I'll just have to make do with this lonely guy," she said, flashing one of her admirers a smile. "Sweetie, could you get me a teensy-weensy drink?" And then she was gone, leading her captive away.

Nina ran out of glasses. Kamisha rushed to the basement. And then the ice ran out, too, and the machine hadn't recovered, so she sent a waiter scurrying downtown to the store, with *her* car. God, she hoped the kid could drive!

The last rays of sun struck the multimillion dollar homes on Red Mountain, reflecting off the picture windows and the copper roofs in dazzling bursts of burnished gold.

Torchlight flickered on the flowerpots and massed blooms. It grew cooler, but still warm enough to serve dinner outside. Some took tables. Some stood with plates of food in one hand, a drink in the other. Some just drank. But everyone was having a great time, rubbing shoulders with the celebrities who had come, talking tennis and golf, reminiscing about the great skiing they'd had in town last winter.

The cocktail napkins ran out. Kamisha quickly replenished them. And Rick took to mixing drinks with Nina, chatting all the while with the guests, a pro behind the bar. At forty-five he seemed to be experienced in almost everything, Kamisha noticed, thankful for his presence.

Senator Luke Stern buttonholed her once. "I'll never forget that downhill run of yours," he said, smiling, handsome, the consummate politician. "The Silver, wasn't it?"

"Yes. It seems another lifetime ago, though. Years and years."

"And here you are. In Aspen. You still ski much?"

"Not as much as I'd like. The club keeps me—"

"Kamisha!" It was Brigitte, now even drunker. "Where have you been all evening?"

"Working."

"And you're..." Luke Stern searched his mind. "I know. Brigitte Stratford. Soap operas. Let's see. *The Young and the...*"

"That *was* me," she slurred, "your former average all-American nice lady on TV. But you should get to know me better, Mr..."

"Brigitte," Kamisha said, "it's Senator. Senator Stern."

"No, no. I insist you call me Luke."

"Well, Luke," Brigitte began, and Kamisha ducked away unnoticed.

It was a crime, she thought while she ushered the busboys around, but Brigitte's drinking had only been getting worse since she'd moved to Aspen last year. Kamisha had hoped the beautiful clean mountain atmosphere would help. But obviously not. To make matters worse, her former boarding school roommate had taken up with Bullet Adams.

Bullet, Kamisha thought derisively. What a user. A former National Football League superstar quarterback who was now a sportscaster on cable TV, the thirty-seven-year-old stud continually rubbed Kamisha the wrong way. Currently he was living at Brigitte's Castle Creek home when not out on assignment. And Tracy, Brigitte's daughter, didn't like him any better than Kamisha did.

Casually Kamisha glanced around to see if Bullet had made his famous "late" arrival. She spotted him over near a group of attractive women, charming their panty hose off. He did have charisma—with men and women alike. He was outgoing, attractive in a rather rugged way—big, big-boned, with snub-nosed boyish features, curling sandy blond hair and a wide, mobile mouth. Some of the things that came out of that mouth, however, drove Kamisha to distraction. He wasn't exactly stupid, but uninformed about most everything except sports. In the six months that Brigitte had been seeing him, Kamisha had arrived at the conclusion that he was one of those super high school athletes who had gotten a college scholarship despite his poor grades. Oddly Rick, well-educated and worldly, had taken to Bullet, too. They played a lot of golf and tennis together, anyway.

Oh, yes, Bullet was in his element tonight, the usual "groupies" hanging around him, fawning over him, giggling. A legend in his own mind, Brigitte's daughter Tracy called him, and she was right.

If Brigitte didn't have so damn much money, Kamisha was sure Bullet would have dumped her long ago. Right now her friend was back at the bar, spilling her drink on her pink Dior dress, looking cross-eyed into the crowd, grinning vacantly.

Night settled over the valley, and the stars dotted the black velvet sky in mountain brilliance. A few of the movie stars who had played in the charity tennis matches gave speeches for the cause. Luke Stern took the microphone for a quick "hello" to the group, Bullet told a few bad jokes to the entourage, and even Rick managed a minute to step up and thank everyone for their generous support.

"In a few minutes," he said over the din, "we'll go inside and present the check to Aspen's favorite charity."

The check! Oh, my Lord! Kamisha rushed inside, flew past the front desk and down the corridor to Rick's office. Her fingers fumbled on the combination lock of the wall safe. She had to respin the dial. How could she have forgotten the check? But then there it was. A one-hundred-thousand-dollar cashier's check made out to the MS Foundation of Colorado. Phew, she thought, gripping it.

She turned to leave, reaching for the light switch, when abruptly she paused and stared at the desk, wondering. John Leopardo. Today he'd been here. But why wasn't he here tonight? Surely he hadn't flown back to—

"Christ, Kamisha," Rick's voice came from the door, startling her. "We're ready to present the—I see you've got it. I couldn't find you. I thought maybe you'd taken that drunken friend of yours home and forgotten the check."

Kamisha felt heat rise up her neck. "Is Brigitte—?"

"Hell, yes. You better call her a cab." He took the check out of her hand. "I don't get it," he said, "a great-looking chick like her. She'll kill herself like this."

"I know," Kamisha said softly. "I know."

They began walking down the hall together, Rick eyeing the check proudly. Kamisha cleared her throat. "You know," she began, "I understand Mr. Leopardo was here, and I was wondering—"

"How did you know that?" Rick stopped abruptly.

"Well, one of the maids mentioned that he was in the condo, and I—"

"Mr. Leopardo," he said carefully, "is a very private man. You tell that maid that if she wants to keep her job, she should keep her mouth shut."

Kamisha could only nod.

The check was presented right on schedule, and the band began to play. A moment later, as the rock music spilled out onto the patio, Brigitte Stratford, small and cuddly, with soft brown eyes and honey-brown hair, virginal and innocent-looking, slipped off the bar stool and sagged to the flagstones.

"Hell," Bullet said, slamming his glass down on the bar.

But Kamisha was there. "Never mind," she said to Bullet as she helped Brigitte to her feet. "I'll call her a cab."

"Yeah," he said, giving Brigitte one last look before disappearing inside, "you do that."

"Some friend you are," Kamisha muttered to his back.

Nina ended up calling the taxi, and Kamisha began to steer her friend toward the entrance and the long paved path that wound down, crossed the river on a narrow wooden bridge and led up to the parking lot. Brigitte was teetering precariously all the way. She reeked of gin.

"Where's Bullet?" she mumbled.

"I guess he's staying."

"Screw him."

"Brigitte."

"Ah, so what? I think I'll dump the creep." She rocked on her high heels, and Kamisha had to take her arm more firmly.

"Is Tracy home?" she asked.

"Don't know. Maybe she's spending the night at a friend's. I'm okay."

"You are *not* okay, Brigitte. You're drunk."

"Jus' tired."

"Sure. Tomorrow we'll have lunch and we're going to have a talk about this. You can't keep—"

Brigitte stopped, swayed and tried to focus on Kamisha's face. "Mind your own business."

"Come on," Kamisha said, "the taxi's waiting. You have any money?"

"I'm loaded, you know that."

"In more ways than one," Kamisha said under her breath.

Rick was waiting for her when Kamisha arrived back on the patio. "Where have you been?" he snapped.

"I was getting a taxi for—"

"That lush?"

"Look," Kamisha said, her hackles rising, "I can take a minute to—"

"Senator Stern wants to talk to you. And that waiter Bobby spilled a cup of coffee on Mona Claymore's dress. She's in the locker room now, and you better get in there and offer to have it dry-cleaned."

"All right, Rick," she said, "but getting ticked off at me isn't solving a thing."

"Yeah, well, then see if you can find Stern. Okay? He wants to talk skiing."

"Fine." Kamisha headed off to the locker room, smarting. She liked Rick usually; at least she respected his business acumen. But sometimes he treated her—and other women, as well—more like lackeys than people. He was one of those men who had never quite accepted the coming of age of women's rights.

The throng danced and drank till one when the band finally packed it in. Kamisha dutifully called taxis, chatted with tired but happy guests, as, one by one, they made their way down the lighted river path. The busboys finished clearing drink glasses and coffee cups and lights were turned off, the torches extinguished. In five hours, Kamisha knew, Nina was scheduled to open the front doors again and man the desk for the early-rising health buffs.

"Go on home," she told Nina. "I'll finish up. The cleaning crew will be here at seven, anyway. And thanks. You were a lifesaver."

"Miss Hammill," Nina said, putting on a sweater, "I'll do it anytime. I got rich tonight!"

Rick was nowhere to be seen. Kamisha assumed he'd headed on up to his condo. It was just as well, she thought as she turned off the last lights. He'd been curt with her for most of the evening. Heck, the event had been a smashing success. He was going to give himself a heart attack over nothing.

Wearily Kamisha walked down the hall past the offices and pushed open the back door. She remembered that kid using her car to go and get the ice earlier and wondered if her car was still in one piece out there. It'd better be. She fumbled in her purse for the keys, her footfalls sounding too loud on the pavement in the still night. It *was* late.

And then she heard it. As if someone were sobbing. She stopped short, cocking her head, the car keys dangling from her fingers. Odd. She listened, peering into the night shadows, into the stands of pine and aspen. Finally she shrugged and began to walk toward her car in the empty lot.

And it came again. Definitely a sob.

Kamisha strode purposefully toward the dimly lit edge of the parking lot. She could make out a figure then, leaning against a boulder, half hidden in the trees.

"Hello," she called, "is everything all right?" Her first assumption was that this woman—or rather girl, she saw as she approached—must have had too much to drink, or had had a spat with a boyfriend at the party. Whatever. But it was the middle of the night, and the club was really quite isolated. The girl belonged at home.

"Hello," Kamisha said again. "Are you okay?"

The girl turned her face up into the light. She was hugging herself, shivering. Her eyes were red-rimmed and swollen. Still, Kamisha recognized her immediately. It was Carin, the sixteen-year-old daughter of the Pitkin County sheriff, Ed McNaught. What was she doing here? Could she have been at the party? But she was much too young.

"Carin?" she began, then froze. On second glance it was clear the young woman's dress was torn at the shoulder, and there appeared to be blood dried on the corner of her mouth. Kamisha's heart swelled in her breast. Had the girl been raped? "Carin," she whispered, "what happened?"

It took a while. Carin McNaught sobbed and hiccuped and made little sense. Kamisha held her, stroking the girl's head on her shoulder, sitting on the boulder next to her. The girl was plainly terrified. But the story finally emerged, coming out in pieces in between the racking sobs.

"Senator Stern's party. He tried to...but I wouldn't! He...he hit me!"

"*Where* was this party?" Kamisha urged, her stomach knotted sickeningly.

Carin nodded upward toward the lofty row of condos. Of course, Kamisha realized, Stern was one of the club's guests. He was staying in the VIP condo, kept open for certain visitors, free of charge naturally.

"How did you end up at his party?"

Carin sniffed. "Sometimes I go to them," she said in a whisper.

"Go to them? There have been other parties like this?"

A nod.

Oh, Lord, Kamisha thought. "Tell me more about these parties. Carin, you must."

Slowly the truth began to emerge, and the picture the girl painted wasn't pretty. It seemed that every few months, always when VIPs were in town, Carin and a few other local girls—all shockingly young—were invited to attend private parties at the same condo. Invited. And then paid. There were out-of-town girls, too. From California, Carin thought. She didn't know. She did know, however, that they all received hundred-dollar bills for being nice to these "older guys." Booze usually flowed and other substances, too.

"Carin," Kamisha said, trying to control her voice, "*who* calls you?"

"I can't...I promised....."

"*Who?*"

A long moment of silence stretched between them. Finally the girl looked at Kamisha with glassy eyes. "Mr. Simons," she whispered. "Rick Simons."

A long moment of silence stretched between them. Then Kamisha rose in a single emphatic motion. "All right, Rick, I'll deal with it."

CHAPTER TWO

KAMISHA CLOSED the door of Rick Simon's office behind her. "Got a second, Rick?"

The club manager looked up at her, and she noticed he had circles under his eyes. As if he'd been up late...partying. "Sure, what's up?"

She sat down in the chair across from him, then wished she hadn't. This wasn't going to be easy, and she would prefer to be standing. At least it would have given her a slight advantage. She crossed one leg over the other and smoothed her linen slacks with a hand. "Well, I guess I better be frank. I was told last night that you're arranging private parties in the VIP condo."

Rick looked at her sharply and answered too quickly. "Yeah, so?"

"With underage girls, Rick."

"Who told you that?"

"One of the girls."

He pushed his chair away from the desk and tapped his fingers on the arm of his chair.

"It's against the law, Rick."

"Don't give me that baloney." He made a cutting gesture with one hand.

"Are you telling me the girls aren't underage, Rick?"

"I'm telling you, Kamisha, that it's none of your business."

She drew back. She'd expected glib explanations, denials, anything but stonewalling. "It *is* my business."

"Not unless you make it so."

She got angry then. "I'm supposed to ignore it? I'm supposed to carry on as public relations director, knowing that the club's manager is a pimp and he's selling women to the highest bidder?"

Rick straightened, his expression as sharp as a hatchet. "Watch your step, honey."

"*You* watch your step. You're breaking the law."

"What are you going to do about it?"

"Go to the police. I expect they'll call in the FBI from Denver."

Rick leaned back, a smug smile on his face. "You won't do that. It'd smear your precious club's reputation all over the scandal sheets."

"You'd be fired, Rick. Out of here."

But he only shrugged. "Don't be so sure of that."

All night. She'd been up all night planning this confrontation, framing her lines in her head over and over in the dark of her bedroom. But she hadn't expected this—Rick's complacency.

She felt cornered. Even knowing she was in the right, she felt trapped. She didn't mind taking physical risks, fighting the elements, but this verbal sparring made her heart pound sickeningly. It made her sweat. She uncrossed her legs, recrossed them the other way. "I'll go to Mr. Leopardo. I don't think he'll like it."

Rick made that slicing gesture again. "Don't bother. He's the one who sent down orders to arrange the parties. They're a great draw."

"You're lying."

"Am I? Fine. Go to him. But I'm only following orders, honey. And Mr. Leopardo will be really ticked off if you bug him. You don't want to tick off John Leopardo," Rick sneered. "You might end up in cement shoes at the bottom of the East River."

She thought furiously. Was he bluffing? My God, all those stories about the Leopardos. Were they true? Was the Ute City Club owned by a Mafia don, a criminal?

Rick was watching her appraisingly. Maybe he had more to lose than he let on. Or maybe he was only the middleman following orders. What should she do?

"Look, honey, don't worry your head about these parties," Rick said ingratiatingly. "A little harmless fun. The girls have a ball and make a few bucks. Nobody's hurt. This isn't your concern. You were hired to look pretty, not to think too hard. Relax."

Kamisha felt herself go cold all over. There it was again, that awful rut she could never escape. As if she were a mannequin to dress up, a perfect size six, with limbs that someone could arrange to suit his desires. There *was* no Kamisha at all, only the doll, and inside she was a void. She stood and held herself stiffly. She felt as if she'd break in a second, as if the facade would spill out in a black ooze.

"Go take a Jacuzzi," Rick was saying. He'd picked up a paperweight and was weighing it in his hand absently. "Play some tennis. Chrissy was in earlier looking for a partner."

"I don't think I'm in the mood for tennis, Rick," Kamisha said bleakly.

He shrugged, still hefting the paperweight, and smiled a tight little smile that split his narrow, tanned face like a cut. She turned and walked out and shut the door softly behind her.

"I CAN'T STAND IT!" Kamisha said, pacing. "It's disgusting. Perverted!"

"Take it easy, Kamisha," Brigitte replied, wincing. "You're making my headache worse."

"I've got to do something. I can't let this go on. The club stands for something fine and wholesome. It's one of the best clubs in the country. Simons is using it as...as a front."

"But you said this Leopardo is really the one—"

"Maybe Rick just said that to shut me up. Maybe I should see John Leopardo. For God's sake, why would he do such a thing?"

"For money, honey," Brigitte said wanly, "what do you think?"

"But Leopardo's filthy rich already."

"How do you think he got that way?"

Kamisha stopped pacing. "What if Rick's only following orders? My God, Brigitte, I can't work there. I can't. I'd have to quit. Do you realize the girls at those parties aren't much older than your daughter, than Tracy?"

Brigitte sipped at a warm soft drink and made a face.

"What should I do, Brigitte? What would you do?"

Brigitte ran a slender hand across her forehead. "I don't know. I can't think this morning. But knowing me, I'd ignore it and keep my job. You love that gig, Kamisha. Why would you give it up?"

"For my principles."

"Ha. You know how far principles get you in this life?"

"I think we've had this discussion before," Kamisha said dryly.

"About a zillion times, from ninth grade on. I say, 'lighten up and have some fun.' And you say, 'I gotta stick to my principles.'"

Kamisha sat on a stool at Brigitte's kitchen counter. She sighed and played with some crumbs on the tiles. "It hasn't gotten me anywhere, has it?"

"Well, going with the flow hasn't gotten me anywhere, either. And just maybe you like yourself better than I do," Brigitte said slowly. Then she asked, "Was I awful last night?"

Kamisha looked straight at her friend. They had never lied to each other. "Pretty bad."

Brigitte put her face in her hands. "It's that Bullet, that son of a... He never came home last night, Kamisha."

"You're better off without him, Brigitte."

"No," she said, her voice muffled, then she raised her head. "No, then I'd be alone. Completely alone."

"You have Tracy."

"It's not the same."

"*I* live alone. Heck, I haven't dated anyone seriously in years. I survive."

"I wouldn't, Kamisha. I'm too scared. You're brave. You're tough. I'm weak and lonely. I need him."

"Tough, ha!"

"You are."

"I don't feel it. God, Brigitte, you've seen me down, you've seen me at my worst. How can you say I'm brave?"

"You pick up the pieces and go on."

Kamisha put her hand on her friend's arm. "For God's sake, Brigitte, so do you."

IT RAINED that June afternoon, a typical mountain cloudburst that washed the dust from the air and fled across the Continental Divide as quickly as it had come. Kamisha ran to her car and slammed the door behind her. The rain beat on the fabric roof and sluiced down the windshield. She was leaving the club early; she couldn't stay another second, avoiding Rick, jumping at every interruption and phone call. She had to think things out.

She had a powerful urge to call John Leopardo despite Rick's warning. Of course, Rick had said that Leopardo knew about the parties. But if indeed Rick was throwing the parties on his own, the last thing in the world he wanted was for the owner to find out. On the other hand, if Leopardo was behind the parties, Kamisha would be putting herself in danger. At the very least, in danger of losing her job. At the worst, in danger of...losing her life?

She sat there in her car, hearing the rain drum over her head, and weighed her decision. You heard about Mafia killings, but how true was it? She was a nobody. She'd get fired, warned off, but she couldn't stay at the club, anyway, not if Leopardo let Simons run a whorehouse in the VIP condo.

Kill her? Ridiculous. Simons was just trying to scare her off.

Yes, she'd do it. She had nothing to lose, really. Maybe John Leopardo was a reasonable man.

Her pulse quickened. She thought of confronting this faceless man who held so much power over her life.

It was going to be interesting, all right. But then suddenly she frowned. She had no idea how she was going to get in touch with him. Private. Rick had told her how private he was. But surely Rick had his number in the index file on his desk. She could go into Rick's office, get the number.

No. That wasn't the way. Phoning the man wasn't going to cut it. It was darn near two thousand miles to New York, though. But by air only a few hours. She had her savings account: she could afford the luxury of this confrontation. It was going to be worth every penny. Face-to-face, Kamisha thought. It was going to be more than interesting.

She turned the keys in the ignition of her car, heard the throaty roar that never failed to lift her spirits. It was a powerful car, a turbo model, much too fast for the around-town driving she did most of the time. But it had fine engineering under its hood, and she loved speed and perfection in anything.

So her trip to New York could be dangerous. But no more so than flying down an icy mountainside at seventy miles an hour. Or hang gliding or lots of the things Kamisha had done in her life. She loved thrills. She loved physical danger. She adored putting herself at risk.

She drove out the winding driveway of the club, splashing through puddles, smiling at a bicyclist peddling miserably through the rain to get back to the club.

What made her seek danger? What switch in her brain didn't open and close quite right? Was it her way of assuring herself she existed? Or was it yet another way she lived with her insecurities rather than confronting them?

She knew that this peculiar facet of her personality verged on the self-destructive and didn't help her achieve happiness or fulfillment, but it had become a habit, an addiction of sorts. It was the way she achieved highs in her life—perhaps, she often suspected, because her emotional life was otherwise so very sterile.

Yes, she'd go to New York and see John Leopardo in person. The Ute City Club was her baby. Its reputation must remain intact. Leopardo didn't need the money. Surely he could be made to understand that he was only ruining a good thing.

KAMISHA LOVED TO DRIVE. In the summer she could drive to Denver's Stapleton Airport in three hours flat. Easier than flying, she always said, especially when Independence Pass, a steep and winding shortcut, was open.

She turned into the remote parking lot at Denver airport at 8:30 a.m. sharp, pulled her bag out of the trunk, locked her car and took the shuttle van to the terminal. It was already hot in the city, and the sky held a bronze tinge of pollution. She carried her white jacket over one arm and her carryon bag over the other. This was going to be a quick trip, a day or two perhaps, that was all.

She'd told Rick she had some business to do in Denver. No sense stirring him up. She'd know very quickly where Rick stood in this business—and where she stood. But she'd told Brigitte exactly where she was going.

"Oh, Lord, Kamisha," Brigitte had said. "Causing trouble again. Can't you just relax?"

"No."

"Well, good luck then. I think you're nuts. Did I tell you Bullet came back? He was so sweet."

"That's nice," Kamisha had said. "Now, listen, I'm staying at the Sheraton on Fifty-ninth Street. In case anyone wants me. But don't tell Rick."

"I won't."

New York was hot and humid. She always forgot how wet the air was back East. It hit her like a suffocating blanket when she walked out of the terminal toward the taxi stand.

"It's a heat wave," the cabbie told her proudly. "Gonna hit ninety-seven today."

She telephoned John Leopardo's office just before closing time. She'd been afraid his number would be unlisted—in fact, she'd concocted several contingency plans just in case—but to her surprise she found it immediately in the Manhattan directory. Leopardo, John, and the address. Nothing more. She wasn't even sure if the number were his home or office. She supposed it didn't matter.

The air conditioner in her hotel room whirred monotonously while she waited for someone to answer. She felt her heart beating heavily against her ribs—in anticipation and pleasantly stimulating nervousness.

"John Leopardo's office," answered a woman's voice, crisp, efficient.

"This is Kamisha Hammill from Mr. Leopardo's club in Aspen. I'm here in New York, and I'd like to see him about something very important."

Kamisha was put on hold for a minute. What if he said no? What if he was leaving town? Maybe he wasn't even there. She leaned back against the pillows and let out a long breath. *Be there, Mr. Leopardo.*

The woman came back on the line. "Tomorrow, Miss Hammill. Say about eleven in the morning?"

"That's fine. Thank you," she said, and hung up. It had been too easy, far too easy. Almost as if he'd been expecting her. Maybe he had been. Maybe Rick had telephoned him. *Darn.*

The next morning at eight o'clock the radio announcer said it was already eighty-eight degrees. Kamisha looked down from her window onto Fifty-ninth Street and watched the crowds surge across intersections, heard the muted, faraway honk of cars. She loved New York in small doses, but it could be darn uncomfortable in the summer.

She let the sheer drapery liner drop into place and padded across the room. Three hours to kill. Her breakfast tray sat on the table, a pile of empty plates and crumbs. Her white pants suit hung, freshly pressed overnight, in the closet. It was too hot to shop or stroll in Central Park, and she was too impatient to go to a museum.

John Leopardo. The name conjured up fantastic images in her mind, a leopard, sleek and powerful, a creature of quick kills and utter ruthlessness. She knew he had dark hair, from her glimpse into Simons's office in the club; the rest of his appearance was a cipher.

Was he a jolly plump grandfatherly Italian? A grim, whipcord-slim one?

She sat on her bed and stared into the middle distance. She was crazy to be doing this, out of her mind. She should have listened to Brigitte and left well enough alone.

John Leopardo. Perhaps he'd been born in Italy and spoke broken English. But he'd done well in the States; the address of his office was impressive, the very heart of the financial district. And his business—what was it? Did he just tell people he was in the "importing" business?

Did he even know who Kamisha Hammill was? Did he have any real interest in the Ute City Club?

She rose and walked across the room, her emerald-green silk pajamas clinging, and turned on the TV set. News, weather, a talk show. There would be something to keep her occupied.

While she watched Kamisha did her exercises, a daily routine, a calming routine. Fifty sit-ups, fifty push-ups, bending, stretching.

A shower, the spray sliding off her head. The water in the East always felt silky to Kamisha. In Aspen it was hard, reluctant to lather.

She wore a red silk tank top and the white suit. No jewelry. Her hair was caught back in a silver clasp. Very little makeup.

John Leopardo. She took a deep breath, let it out in a quavering sigh. She felt like an errant student called to the headmistress's office, yet *she* had been the one to initiate this meeting. She rehearsed what she would say to him, then gave up. She would just tell him, straightforward, frankly. He'd listen, believe her, understand what had to be done. And even if he were involved, as Rick had said, she'd try to convince him to be reasonable. The club made plenty of money without having to throw those parties on the side.

God, it was important to her! If he didn't listen, she'd have to resign. She couldn't stay at the club, not unless the parties stopped. Then what would she do? Where would she go? Aspen was small, its opportunities limited. He *had* to listen.

She could have killed time and walked to his office, but the heat enervated her, and she'd look bedraggled when she arrived. She took a cab, paid the driver and looked up at the office building. On brass plaques by the doors were the names of the tenants. Yes, there it was, tenth floor. John Leopardo. That was all. Not "company" or "enterprises" or anything. Just "John Leopardo," as if you were supposed to know what he did, who he was. Of course, maybe everyone in New York *did* know who he was.

His office door had the same understated brass plaque on it. His name, nothing more. She went in, noticing sweat on her palm as she turned the doorknob. The waiting room was carefully done in tones of gray, a cool room, meant to calm. Behind a semicircular metal desk sat a middle-aged woman with severely cut hair.

"May I help you?" the woman inquired.

"I'm Kamisha Hammill."

"Yes, have a seat, please. Mr. Leopardo is on a conference call at the moment. He'll be right with you."

She sat down and leafed through a magazine. Her hands were still damp, clinging to the glossy pages.

The door to his office was just behind the receptionist's desk. What was he doing in there? Talking to his Mafia partners, rigging an athletic event, arranging a drug deal, starting another club where the manager could throw "parties" with underage girls?

She tapped her fingers on the arm of the chair she sat in and stared, unfocused, at the pages of the magazine. John Leopardo. Tiny, nervous tremors shot through the tips of her fingers.

The woman was pushing a button, saying something into an intercom. She looked up, directly at Kamisha, and said, "You can go in now, Miss Hammill."

Kamisha stood, smoothed her slacks over her thighs with her hands and followed the woman, who held the door open for her. She stepped inside and was aware of the door closing with a quiet snick behind her.

The room was large, elegant and sparsely furnished, slightly dim. A spare contemporary couch in black leather sat against one wall, a heavy, bare glass coffee table in front of it. But her eyes were drawn to the desk across the room—chrome and steel. Very neat, very spare, very large.

A man sat behind the desk. He didn't move or speak. The window behind him cast his features in shadow, but she had the impression of broad shoulders in a dark suit, dark hair. A chill crawled up her limbs despite the heat outside. There was something about this man, something about the stillness of him and the pitch of his head.

She stepped forward. "Mr. Leopardo..."

"Miss Hammill." His voice was low, a rough voice held in check by a strong will.

She walked closer, aware of his steady gaze on her. He gestured to one of the chrome-and-black-leather chairs in front of his desk. "Please."

"Thank you." She sat, crossed her legs, smoothed her slacks again nervously. "I appreciate you seeing me so quickly."

"What brings you to New York, Miss Hammill?"

She could see his face now, and she studied him as she spoke. His eyes were dark, heavy-lidded and secretive, his nose a slab, his dark hair combed back. There was a Continental flair to him, something old world and solid. His suit was impeccably tailored, double-breasted. One button was fastened, and the coat hung open a bit, lying in elegant folds against his broad chest. European, Italian, yes, olive skin, a shadow of a heavy beard and a surprisingly sensitive mouth.

"Mr. Leopardo," she began, "there's a problem at the Ute City Club. I...I think you should know about it."

"I should imagine Mr. Simons would take care of any problems there." He spoke dispassionately, his voice neutral, his expression impersonal.

She looked down at her folded hands. "Rick Simons is part of the problem."

"I guess you'd better tell me then, Miss Hammill."

She told him, leaving out only Rick's assertion that Leopardo had ordered the parties. When she finished, he sat so silently for so long that she was ready to burst with anticipation.

"Well," he finally said, "this is all very interesting."

He kept his eyes on her, pinning her with his dark regard but not judging, not yet. A wild notion buffeted her: he might be sitting there, not three feet from her, planning her demise. *My God.* She looked up from her hands. His gaze was penetrating her, probing, silent and utterly unreadable. She had to swallow to continue. "I'm very upset about this whole thing, Mr. Leopardo. It's breaking the law. I'm not a goody-two-shoes, but these parties, the young girls... It's wrong. I was tempted to go to the police, but I decided to speak to you first. The publicity wouldn't be good for the club," Kamisha added.

A faint smile teased the corners of his mouth. She noticed that there was a mole near its corner. "No, it certainly wouldn't. And Aspen has had its share of bad press lately." He leaned his elbows on the desk. His hands, she noticed, were strong and square, capable hands. He wore no rings, and she could see the dark curling hairs that covered the backs of his hands and retreated up under the white starched cuffs of his shirt. "Does Rick Simons know you're here?"

"No."

He played with a letter opener, turning it over and over, slowly, deliberately. She stared at his hands. Did he kill people with those hands? Her eyes flew up to meet his. The notion was both frightening and exhilarating.

"Miss Hammill, I appreciate you coming to me with this problem." He set down the letter opener and steepled his fingertips, eyes still on her. "I want to assure you that I had no knowledge of these parties and nothing to do with them. You must have suspected that I knew, at the very least."

"Well, I..."

He spoke so calmly. They were speaking of his reputation, his honor, not to mention an employee who was deceiving him, yet he could have been passing the time of day. "I'm quite aware," he went on, "of the rumors surrounding a connection with my family. My father, to be precise. They are unfounded, I have never had any connection to the family business." The faint smile tugged at his lips again. "Rest easy. I'll make sure the sordid activities at the club end."

"I'm relieved, Mr. Leopardo. I really couldn't have gone on working there if you condoned such things."

"Certainly not. I understand completely. You're very courageous to come to me like this."

He was dismissing her. Her appointment was over. She felt confused, as if the meeting were an anticlimax. She wanted to believe him, but she had no way of knowing what he really felt. He could be lying.

She stood. "Well, thank you, Mr. Leopardo." Her words died away. It couldn't be this easy! He was playing with her, mocking her, lying so smoothly that she'd never know for sure... It crossed her mind swiftly that he might press a buzzer somewhere on his desk and two men, clad in black suits, would be waiting for her outside. They'd follow her, wait for the right moment...

"You're quite welcome, Miss Hammill." He rose then, picked something up that leaned against his chair and began to come around his desk. "And by the way," he was saying, "I was wondering..."

Kamisha had a moment of utter shock. He walked with a cane and had a limp. No one had told her. But he was talking, asking her something, and she had to wrench her gaze from his legs and look him in the eye and answer his question.

"...be pleased to take you to dinner tonight, if you'd so honor me. You've come such a long way. If you leave the name of your hotel with Martha, my driver will pick you up at eight. That is, of course, if you're not otherwise engaged."

Surprised, she hesitated just a heartbeat too long. Dinner? With John Leopardo? Then came the heavy, expectant pulse in her veins—the challenge, the risk. She smiled. "I'd be delighted to have dinner with you, Mr. Leopardo. What a lovely idea."

He took her hand for a moment. His other rested on the knobbed head of the cane. His fingers were warm and alive, strong.

Breathless, unnerved from bearing up under the aura of silent force surrounding the owner of the Ute City Club, Kamisha made a graceful escape.

CHAPTER THREE

JOHN SAT SILENTLY, utterly unmoving, and stared at the door where she had been only moments before. Never could he recall such exquisite poise in a woman. He let his mind dwell on the image of her cat-sleek body and those hypnotic, tilted eyes that had lured photographers since her early days as a ski racer. Surely every man who had ever been in her presence had been enthralled.

You're a damn fool, he thought, unaccustomed to the strong feelings he was battling. It had been ten years since he'd allowed himself such feelings, and then they had only caused him pain and rejection and failure. He knew he should call and cancel the dinner engagement. He also knew that, as surely as the sun would set, he wouldn't make that call.

A faint throb began in his leg. He stood, walked slowly to the window and tried to work out the annoying twinge that could too quickly become pain. As he stood at the immense plate glass window, his gaze fell to the street far below. He wondered if she was going to hail a taxi, or if she was walking along the street, the suffocating heat and humidity clinging to her, pressing on her. Perhaps he should have had Inky drive her to her hotel.

The buzzer on his phone sounded. Grimacing—the twinge was becoming an ache now—he moved back to his desk.

"Yes, Martha?"

"Mr. Leopardo, it's San José, Costa Rica. The contractor, on line two."

John frowned. He needed to talk to the man about cost overruns on the new health spa there, but he also needed a clear head. "Tell him I'll be back to him later today."

"Yes, Mr. Leopardo."

Kamisha Hammill, he thought, leaning back in his chair, propping up his leg, she'd taken him totally by surprise. And so had her accusations.

John slowly tapped a finger on the cool desktop. His eyes narrowed and a deep crease slashed his brow. Could Rick be involved in some illegal activities, using the club as a front? It was possible, of course. Booze, parties, young women—there was a lot of money to be made there. Rick was paid damn well. But his tastes were expensive. Or, at least, John had made mental note of that when Rick had still been at the Miami club.

He found his teeth clenching tightly in his jaw. The whole affair smacked of everything John deplored. By God, if Rick was truly involved in this business, there would be hell to pay.

On the other hand, he only had Kamisha Hammill's word to go by. And why should he trust her? For all John knew she might have some personal vendetta to settle. Rick might have come on to her. Maybe Rick had chewed her out, bruised her ego.

On the surface she appeared to be a cool customer. But John had reviewed her file when Rick first interviewed her five years ago for the PR position at the club, just as he reviewed every potential employee's file. It was another way of staying in control, of not leaving things to the vagaries of chance. Kamisha's file contained two photos: a picture from her ski racing days and a snapshot of her leaving the courthouse after her divorce that had made the front page of a yellow press newspaper. An unwelcome thought nudged him: none of the pictures had done Kamisha justice. In person she was even more spectacular.

He recalled, as well, mention of her family in Los Angeles. Her father was a CEO for an oil company. Kamisha's mother was a socialite who dabbled in art. An only child, Kamisha had been sent to boarding school where she'd taken up with Brigitte Stratford. John could only surmise that Kamisha's reputation as unattainable was a direct result of a sterile existence as a child, her barrier against an uncaring world. Idly John wondered if she allowed herself an occasional affair—Rick had commented in her file that around Aspen she was known as somewhat of a thrill junky, always seeking a challenge. Were men a challenge to her? Although, to give credit where it was due, Rick had since then updated her file to include such comments as: loyal, dependable, hardworking, private, capable.

A slight, ironic smile curved his lips for a moment. His mother would approve of this ''date'' tonight, though she'd ask if Kamisha were Catholic. His mother. He spoke to her on the phone on holidays and her birthday. She always cried. She begged him to make it up with his father, Mafia kingpin Gio Leopardo. But to do so would open a door that John preferred to keep closed. His father was always going to refuse to understand why John had left the secure, structured Mafia life that had awaited him when he returned from Vietnam.

Yes, John thought, he had made a decision to go it alone those many years ago, a tough, hard decision, and one that, to this day, he wasn't even certain he understood. It had come as a flashing insight, swift and sure. It had come in a moment when his life had become abruptly too short. On that battlefield, lying there, wondering if he were going to live. That had been in South Vietnam. Over twenty years ago. But suddenly it seemed like only yesterday....

He'd been in Nam for forty weeks and his tour would end soon. A couple of months, that was all, and he could go home.

It hadn't been John's idea to come to Vietnam, although many of his fellow soldiers in the Special Forces had put in for duty there. In fact, last year, at twenty years old and almost finished with his military hitch, John had been surprised when his orders had come in for the tour of Southeast Asia.

He'd been drafted; a single semester off from college and the military had nabbed him. But, unlike so many others, he hadn't tried to shirk his duty. Instead, he'd gone into the lower ranks willingly, patriotically, taken an interest in the intelligence schools offered by the Special Forces and, after a year in the war zone, achieved the rank of sergeant.

"The family is proud of you," Gio Leopardo, his father, had said on John's only stateside leave. "We know our duty and we do it. We're Americans."

His family was proud of him, true, but would they be so pleased when he returned to Brooklyn and told his father that he'd decided to pursue business interests outside the close-knit structure of the Leopardo empire?

John finished a short leave in Saigon on a stinking hot Sunday and returned to his outpost base near Chau Doc on the Cambodian frontier. He'd been on leave six days and, other than drinking and whoring and aimlessly roaming the French provincial streets of the city he hadn't done anything. He hadn't even bothered to call home. What was there to say? A distance had grown between John and his family, a need to put space between himself and the puppetlike strings with which his father manipulated everyone. The rift felt to him like a wound, deep and unhealed, and yet somehow inevitable.

Even after R and R John wasn't rested. No one in Vietnam ever rested. There was always that question hanging like a tarnished chain around a man's neck: would he make it out alive?

Now the steaming jungle rose around John's patrol and formed a lush canopy overhead. He checked the map and handed it back to Inky, his right-hand man, a black "lifer," huge and muscular with a shaven, bowling-ball head, who was both deadly and sharp in the field. If Special Forces offered a new school, Inky was the first in line. After eight years in the service, he knew his stuff.

The seven-man patrol moved west along the bank of the sluggish brown river. Their objective was clear-cut—intelligence gathering. There was to be no search and destroy.

A light rain began to fall, misting the jungle, silencing the invisible, exotic birds. John raised a fist, the sinews in his arm tightening, and the file of men behind him halted noiselessly.

He turned to Inky. "What do you think?"

"I can smell 'em."

John nodded. His patrol was six kilometers out from where the chopper had dropped them, close to Charlie. Aerial surveillance had indicated a VC buildup near a delta in the river. He checked the map once more.

"Half a klick," he told Inky quietly. "Pass it along."

Charlie was there, all right, erecting a veritable stronghold near the delta. Well camouflaged and well fortified. Crisp new tiger suits, the latest Russian weaponry. John and his men lay along the murky riverbank in a line, and he drew a detailed sketch of the camp. It would take more than a platoon and attack choppers to knock this one out effectively. An air strike would have to be called.

His mission complete, John signaled the men. On their bellies, ignoring a stinging cloud of mosquitos, they inched their way back into the thick undergrowth and moved away from the river.

So far so good.

"It's too friggin' quiet," the massive black man said. "Don't like it."

They spread out, crouching, silently forcing their way through the thick foliage, seemingly making little progress.

Wiping sweat from his eyes, John checked his watch. Three hours to go. The chopper would be in the clearing at 1600 hours, looking for the yellow smoke that would signal the pickup. They'd better get a move on.

The first sniper shot caught Inky in the flesh of his left forearm. The second drilled a neat hole in PFC Lemont's temple. Lemont was dead before he hit the soft jungle floor. John pulled his tags, and they were forced to leave him.

He signaled to his men, who had dropped for cover, and they crawled off into the bush again on their bellies.

"I can get 'em," Inky breathed fiercely.

"No." John shook his head. "Our orders are to get this intelligence to headquarters."

"Hell."

There was the distinctive odor of fear permeating the jungle now. It was seeping from John's men, oozing in oily droplets from their hardened bodies, soaking their camouflage shirts. But John wasn't afraid. There wasn't time for the luxury of listening to his heart. In the breast pocket of his shirt Lemont's tags rattled. John couldn't afford to listen to that, either.

Without drawing another shot they finally made it to the perimeter of the clearing. Twenty minutes early.

"How's the arm?" John turned to Inky from where they lay hidden together.

"Don't feel a thing." The black man's eyes bore into John's. "They're out there, Sarge, right behind us. Three, maybe four of the little—"

"I know."

"You want I should do a little circling?"

"No. Stay put."

"But, Sarge, we'll be sitting ducks when the chopper comes. I can knock 'em out!" He grinned and pulled out his knife. "Real silent like."

"No. We're not engaging. Orders. So forget it."

Inky bared his teeth in disappointment.

"Now pass it along, no talking. No anything. Got that?"

"Sure, Sarge. But they're gonna come in, anyway." He shrugged and moved off silently to tell the men.

Ten minutes jerked by. John lay on his back, his M-16 rifle cradled across his stomach, and looked up at the sky. The rain had stopped for the moment. There was a white haze filtering through the trees above, a patch of blue to the east. Reluctantly he saw Lemont's face, the hole in the boy's temple. He closed his eyes tightly to blot out the picture. Now he could see New York, Brooklyn. And his father's house was there. He imagined that it was winter. Winter in the city, cold and crisp. Patches of wet snow sat on the brown lawn and the maple tree's branches were bare and dark.

There was movement in the bush next to him. He opened his eyes and saw Inky, sweat streaming down the man's face. John killed a mosquito on his neck, rubbing it, red streaking his flesh.

"Gonna be more blood than that," Inky said, grinning dangerously.

Closing his eyes again, listening for the distinctive thump of the helicopter's rotors, John conjured up the house in Brooklyn once more. There was still snow, cool and inviting. Outside the front door of the solid, imitation-Tudor structure lounged two bodyguards in heavy black overcoats. The door opened and several laughing children raced out—his sister's children—dragging a brand-new American Flyer sled. Gio was standing on the threshold watching his grandchildren, smiling his big smile, chatting with his bodyguards as they lit cigarettes and rubbed their hands together.

"Handsome kids," one of the men said to Gio, his voice gravelly, rolling softly in the ancient accent of Sicily.

Behind Gio was the foyer. Dim and mahogany-paneled. Beyond that the hushed living room with its heavy dark furnishings and lace doilies. Farther on the warm kitchen. His mother. Substantial and womanly and gray-haired. Loving. There was no other security on earth like her embrace. No voice gentler, no hand more comforting.

And in that house John remembered a quiet strength. He drew on it as he lay on the murky ground, motionless and silent. His father, Gio, was the godlike source of that strength and the power, the restrained authority that ran the empire. There was often, when called for, ruthlessness, but Gio had a sense of right and wrong, as well. Simple lessons. God and mass on Sunday, a huge, animated family feast. On Monday Gio in his office behind closed doors and a ceaseless file of visitors. John's mother quieting the children.

"Damn chopper," Inky grumbled. "Where in hell—?" And as if to punctuate his complaint, the distant sound of thumping vibrated in the air.

"Thank God," came the voice of one of the men.

"Shut up," Inky whispered harshly. Then, his body growing rigid, he said, "Over there! In the bush!"

John snapped taut. Inky was right. There was movement in the bush. Charlie. They hadn't lost the enemy at all.

John looked to the east, over the treetops. *Thump, thump.* Yes! There is was, the chopper. If he could somehow get his men between the helicopter and the VC... Quickly he signaled for the yellow smoke canister to be blown.

A shot split the air. Another. Blind firing in their direction. Then, missing John's signal to stay under cover, two of his soldiers broke from the undergrowth and rushed, crouched in the swirling yellow smoke toward the open door of the hovering machine.

"Damn!" John shouted. "Get down!"

From the opening of the chopper a soldier was spreading a burst of machine gunfire toward the perimeter of the clearing. The two men made it on, a couple more broke for the helicopter, one went down heavily.

"No choice now, man!" Inky yelled to John, and the rest of them left the cover of the jungle and headed, firing rounds into the bush, toward the center of the clearing. One of the men stopped long enough to drag his fallen comrade toward the door, another crouched and tossed a grenade. Inky was ahead of John, firing also, cursing, yelping like an Indian. John scanned his surroundings, turned, fired a burst blindly behind him and ran in zigzags toward the chopper.

Twenty yards. Fifteen. His men, save for Inky, were aboard. Hope sprang in his chest. They were going to make it!

Suddenly pain exploded in his leg. He stumbled, tried to get up, stumbled again. There was a strange feeling of regret in him as he saw the VC breaking from the brush, their short forms crouched, swimming before his eyes.

Falling, staggering, falling again, John tried to wave the chopper off but, goddamn it, Inky was swinging out of the door! Never could follow orders!

Debris blown up by the rotors blinded him and sweat stung his eyes and the yellow air smelled of acrid gunpowder and torn flesh and gasoline.

He was really going down this time. Hell, his knee was half ripped off! He wasn't going to make it. His head thudded again with the pain, and everything was growing dark and, damn that fool Inky, he was crawling through the gunfire toward him, his teeth white in a grinning black face....

Again, the buzzer sounded. "I'm sorry, Mr. Leopardo, but it's San José again, your contractor. He insists—"

John frowned. "I'll take it, Martha."

The club, situated on the Pacific Coast on the Nicoya Peninsula of Costa Rica, was nearly completed now, but John had had a few reservations about his contractor and some of the cost overruns. They had to be dealt with, but he'd be damned if he was going to have checks cut until he reviewed every last invoice.

"Yes, Juan Luis, it's Mr. Leopardo here..."

CHAPTER FOUR

KAMISHA STEPPED out of the cab in front of the hotel. The heat smote her like a bludgeon, but she welcomed the physical discomfort. It was far easier to bear than the mental gyrations of her mind.

She felt confused and uncertain, unable to decide how she was going to deal with John Leopardo. All her life, well, since she'd been a teenager, men had always taken notice of her. She was used to their compliments and to their preening and posturing. And usually Kamisha performed for a man. She knew how to dazzle and tease and how to posture. It was a game. Man was attracted to woman. Woman made herself even more attractive, hard to get but alluring, desirable. And then, after all the courtship and circling, man took woman to his bed.

But with Kamisha the script ended differently. She knew just how to play the game, true enough, but when the time came for physical and emotional entanglement, she severed the relationship with the cool swiftness of a scalpel.

Brigitte, good old wise Brigitte, was forever telling her that it came from her upbringing, that Kamisha was afraid to risk her heart in case of disappointment. Her ex-husband, Josh...well, Kamisha had taken that risk with him and where had it gotten her? Josh had never been truly interested in what lay below the surface of her attractiveness and physical ability. And when the newness had worn off, and there was plain old Kamisha, insecure, desperately needing him, the winter of their marriage had begun.

They were all like that, Kamisha had come to believe. Not a single man in her experience gave a hoot who she really was deep down inside. She often wondered if she knew that answer herself.

But then there was John Leopardo. He hadn't even acknowledged her as a woman. She could have been anyone sitting in his office; it had been all business, an impersonal appointment. Of course, he'd asked her to dinner. That must have meant something. But what?

That she was an out-of-towner, an employee, alone? *Why* had he asked her out?

John. The man had such consummate self-control. She'd never in her life met a human being who exuded such power—power over himself and power over others. It was attractive, that authority, and frightening, too.

She went over every moment of their meeting, every word they'd spoken, every gesture and movement he'd made. She searched for nuances of meaning in the man's bearing, but he was a closed book, utterly unreadable.

Had he lied when he said he didn't know about the parties? She knew no more now than before she'd been ushered into his presence. Tonight. Perhaps tonight she'd discover more about John Leopardo. More about why he fascinated her so, why he'd set her mind to ask such difficult questions, why she cared so much to know if he'd really been telling the truth.

And his limp. She wanted to know why he limped. Had he been born that way? Had he been injured? She couldn't help imagining his leg under the perfectly creased trousers—twisted scar tissue, perhaps old surgical incisions. Somehow she knew that it wasn't a new injury that was healing, knew it from the way he'd held the cane, as if it were an intimate part of him.

Such a strong, virile-looking man, a man with no weakness, no vulnerability, a man in perfect control—except for one physical infirmity.

He'd touched her in some indefinable way. Touched the untouchable woman, and Kamisha had to respect that despite her misgivings.

So how to handle this enigmatic man? It was all very new to her, very disturbing. She walked into her hotel with a frown creasing her brow. If John was any other man on earth, she'd simply attempt to bewitch him. On the other hand, he *was* a man. Different. More tightly controlled. But a man nevertheless. Perhaps all this confusion was for nothing. What she should do, would do, was play the game, only with a little more caution.

That decided, Kamisha stood in the hotel lobby, surrounded by the eddying crowd, and wondered what to do with herself until eight o'clock. Eight hours. A lifetime. An entire long, hot summer day until she'd see John Leopardo again and begin the game.

Where would they go? Not someplace for the rich and famous. No, not John. His taste would be superb. He'd know of a small, intimate restaurant with discriminating service and a fabulous chef, and the maître d' would recognize him.

Kamisha wiped the tiny dots of perspiration off her upper lip with her forefinger and wondered suddenly what she would wear. She'd brought nothing for an evening out in New York, certainly nothing remotely acceptable for a dinner date with a man who presented the ultimate challenge.

She smiled at herself. Clothes. What else should a woman think of at a time like this?

There were several small, elegant boutiques along Fifty-ninth Street. Kamisha browsed, even going into a couple of art and antique shops, too, just out of curiosity. The saleswomen were cool, superior, Manhattan types, but they sized Kamisha up as a great advertisement for their wares.

"Madame would look fantastic in this," a saleswoman said, draping a sequined dress over her arm with a flourish.

"No, not a dress," Kamisha said. "Pants. A pantsuit, perhaps."

"I have just the thing. Size six, aren't you?"

But it wasn't "just the thing," and Kamisha went onward, out toward Fifth Avenue and the crowds and suffocating heat. She found it finally, a black knit jumpsuit, backless, with thin straps and a lovely way of draping off her shoulders. Very plain, very classic, very expensive. And shoes, naturally, silver sandals much like the ones sitting in her closet at home. How irritating. But tonight would be worth it, and John would notice. She was sure he'd notice every last detail about her.

At three she set her new purchases down on a chair in her blissfully cool room and ordered lunch from room service. She also made an appointment for a manicure and a pedicure in the beauty shop off the lobby. She would treat herself well today. Just this once.

John Leopardo. So very Italian in a way. Probably Catholic. With a big family, lots of brothers and sisters and a loving father and mother. A Mafia don father, but a loving one, nonetheless. Utterly unlike Kamisha's uncaring, law-abiding WASP parents.

She ate, then kept her appointment in the beauty shop. The manicurist was an eccentric-looking girl with a beehive of frizzy blond hair, an amusing conversationalist with magic hands.

"So you're from Aspen, huh? D'ja ever meet Donald Trump? I hear he hangs out there."

"I've seen him, but never met him personally."

The girl chewed gum energetically while she painted Kamisha's toes. "Is it true that people serve bowls of cocaine at parties out there?"

Kamisha laughed. "Not at any party I've ever been to. I think that's an exaggeration."

"I just heard it somewhere. Do you ski?"

"Sure, I ski." Kamisha smiled inwardly, both pleased and chagrined not to be recognized.

"Boy, it must be nice up there in the mountains. Not as hot as New York, huh?"

"No, not nearly as hot."

By seven-thirty she was ready. Her heart was beating too quickly, and even in the air-conditioned room she was afraid her makeup was going to run. A dozen times she told herself that this was merely an invitation to dinner, a kind gesture from her employer. Or perhaps his motives were deeper. He might be planning to offer her hush money, or to convince her to keep her mouth shut if she wished to keep her job. A part of Kamisha prayed it was going to be strictly business. Another part of her craved the challenge, the excitement, the magic, that small slice of time out of reality.

She paced, then lifted the drapes to look down at the street, as if she'd see John walking—limping, leaning on his cane—toward the door of the hotel. How silly.

She checked herself in the mirror for the tenth time, tugged at the bodice of her black jumpsuit, pulled at a wisp of hair so that it fell in front of her ear. Leaning close to the mirror, she rubbed at a smudge of lipstick at the corner of her mouth. She stopped in that position, held by the look in her own eyes—they were bright, expectant, filled with points of light, alive.

She walked to the window yet again and peered down into the street. She hated waiting. Ever since she'd been a small child, Kamisha hated waiting for anyone. She smiled ruefully. It was because of her parents, of course. Either she'd been waiting for them to return from Europe or the Far East, or just waiting for them to dress for a gala and come into her bedroom to say good-night.

Kamisha sat on the side of the bed, slipped off her shoes and wiggled her toes impatiently. There was one time in particular she'd waited on her parents—waited for the wonderful surprise they'd arranged. Oh, yes. She'd imagined a ski trip perhaps or a vacation with them in Europe.

"We'll tell you all about it at dinner tonight," her mother had said that July morning so many years ago. "Don't be impatient, dear." Grace Hammill's lips had brushed Kamisha's cheek, cool, impersonal lips, and Kamisha had left for her tennis lesson. How excited she'd been all day, excited and expectant. Her parents had planned something for her. Just for her.

Everything was splashed in Southern California sunlight when she got home just before noon. She found her mother by the pool, the telephone cord stretched across the neatly mowed lawn and through the rose garden. Kamisha tossed down her tennis racket and kicked off her shoes, stretched out on a cushioned lounge next to her mother's and listened impatiently to the phone conversation.

Grace's laughter tinkled. "Now, Larry," she was saying, "I know five thousand is a considerable donation, but think of the tax benefit." Grace laughed lightly again. "Oh, Larry, you are such a dear. I knew I could count on you. Now remember, the fund-raiser dinner is on the twenty-second."

When her mother was off the phone, Kamisha asked, "The art museum fund-raiser?"

"Yes, dear." Grace ran a slim brown finger down a typed list of names and numbers she had propped on her knees.

"Mom?"

"Yes, dear."

"Do you think we could have Ned drive us to Beverly Hills and have lunch together today?"

Grace began to dial the phone. "Lunch? Oh, Kamisha, darling, I simply can't."

Kamisha frowned and sighed. "Why not?"

Her mother cupped the receiver in her hand. "You can see I'm busy. Don't act spoiled, dear."

"I only thought..."

"Eileen? It's Grace Hammill," her mother was saying, "yes, sweetie. I know, it's been ages and ages." The bell-like laughter followed Kamisha inside and up to her room. Her mom *was* busy, and tonight she'd hear all about the surprise, anyway.

Dinner was served formally at the Hammill mansion. Not that the three family members ate together regularly. More often than not, Marcus was abroad on oil business, or Grace was entertaining or out to an event herself. In fact, Kamisha usually dined in the kitchen with the help. There she could laugh and joke and listen to Lucinda's stories about her family. Tonight, however, Marcus and Grace sat at opposite ends of the table, and Kamisha was in her place between them.

"Well, can you tell me now?" Kamisha asked.

Marcus exchanged a glance with Grace.

"Let me guess," Kamisha was saying, oblivious to her parents' unsmiling countenances, "I bet we're going on a ski trip to New Zealand. Of course, it could be Chile."

"Your soup is getting cold, dear," Grace said, eyeing Kamisha.

"Or maybe a trip to Europe." She looked at her father and cocked her head. "Last year you said we were all going on a bike trip some-day through France. Remember? I just bet—"

"Kamisha," Grace interrupted, "put your napkin in your lap. I can't imagine where you pick up such bad—"

"Grace." Marcus put up a hand. "I think it's time we tell her the good news. It's unfair to keep her guessing."

Kamisha would always recall that moment when excitement filled her, so much so that she failed to properly read the look of guilt in her father's eyes, or the cool, impassive expression on her mother's face.

Marcus cleared his throat and steepled his fingers. "We've enrolled you at the boarding school in Taos, Kamisha. You recall the place? We visited it three years ago when we were on that ski trip in New Mexico."

Kamisha furrowed her brow, uncomprehending. "What?"

"Boarding school," Grace said, smiling, sipping on her soup.

The enormity of what they were doing hit her then, and she couldn't get her breath for a minute. She looked from one to the other, her stomach knotting up, wanting to expel the food she'd so innocently put in it moments before. Boarding school. They were sending her away. They really were. They didn't love her, they never had, and now they were getting rid of her.

"You'll be able to ski there," Marcus was saying. "They have their own coach and ski team. They—"

"I don't want to go," Kamisha said through clenched teeth. She wanted to scream and cry, to pound the table and throw things, but she couldn't, she couldn't. Something deep inside her kept warning: *Be good and they'll love you.*

"Oh, sweetie, everyone says that," Grace replied lightly. "You'll love it once you're there."

"Please," Kamisha blurted out.

"It's all settled," Marcus said.

"But..."

Grace's face stiffened. She looked at her daughter sharply. "We thought this would delight you."

For a long moment Kamisha met her mother's hard gaze. Finally she said, "I'm not hungry. May I be excused?"

"Of course," Grace said, taking her spoon back up. "Oh, Marcus, did I tell you that Larry is going to donate..."

Kamisha left the room quietly, but when she reached the stairs she took them by twos, flinging open her bedroom door, unable to stop herself from slamming it so hard that the dishes in the kitchen rattled.

Not another word had been spoken about the subject.

Now Kamisha rose from the bed in the New York hotel room and padded to the window, pulling aside the heavy drape. Still waiting. He was five minutes late, too. Once more she smoothed her hair and checked her appearance in the mirror. She really hated waiting. If she was going to be disappointed, better sooner than later.

The phone rang finally. "Miss Hammill?" a strange male voice asked.

"Yes."

"I'm John Leopardo's driver. I'm waiting in the lobby."

"I'll be right down. How will I know you?"

She heard a low, throaty chuckle. "You can't miss me. I'm big and black and bald."

Well. Kamisha smiled. She was looking forward to meeting this man. Big and black and bald. At least the driver had a sense of humor.

He was there, close to the bank of elevators, when she stepped out. A big-barreled black man, his head shaved and shiny with dampness. He wore a well-cut pair of white slacks and a pale blue polo shirt. She walked right up to him and held out her hand.

"Hello," she said. "I'm Kamisha Hammill. And you're Mr. Leopardo's driver." She gave him a conspiratorial smile. "Or am I mistaken?"

"No, ma'am. You got the right man here. I'm Inky." He grinned at her, his teeth white in his dark face. "Ready? John's in the car."

The car was a black stretch limo, its windows smoky so that she couldn't see inside. Inky held the door open for her, and she ducked in, sliding onto the soft leather seat.

John Leopardo sat in the shadows, his cane resting against the back seat next to him. "Hello again, Miss Hammill," he said quietly.

She smiled and nodded. He looked very much at home in the big car, unselfconscious, relaxed. He wore a tropical-weight double-breasted gray suit with fine white stripes and a pale blue dress shirt with white collar and cuffs. His tie was a subdued navy and gray and burgundy stripe. He'd shaved. He must have to shave twice a day, a man with a dark beard like his. He smelled very, very faintly of a pleasant after-shave lotion.

The long car pulled out into the traffic. It was quiet and dim and cool inside. The heat and hot asphalt smell, the traffic noises, honking horns and screeching tires, all receded to a discreet distance.

Kamisha noticed that John hadn't acknowledged her appearance the way a man would on a date. A woman expected those things even if dealing with a customer as cool as Mr. John Leopardo. Inky had given her a second glance, though, back in the hotel lobby. Polite but approving. For the life of her she couldn't figure John out.

"I hope you had a nice day," John was saying.

"Oh, it was fine. I did some shopping," Kamisha replied casually. "It was too hot to do much else."

"It must be much more pleasant in Aspen."

"It is." She hesitated. "But then you were just there, weren't you?"

"I got back to the city two days ago." He nodded. His hands rested on his knees, those strong hands. They were very still, very quiet, as if he carefully kept them in check, not wanting to waste them on insignificant gestures.

"I saw you in Rick's office, but you were busy so I didn't stop in. Funny, I haven't met you before now." She gave him her brightest smile.

"I'm not in Aspen very often. A day here, a day there. I make it a point not to interfere in the club's management. Rick is very efficient."

"He certainly is," Kamisha remarked dryly.

He finally looked right at her. "Do you have any complaints about Rick's handling of the club, Miss Hammill?"

"I hadn't until I found out about these parties. Rick *is* efficient. Fair, smart. A tough manager but fair. I didn't come to New York to bitch about my boss, if that's what you mean."

"I like to clear the air about such things."

"So do I."

"I admire honesty."

What an odd thing to say, Kamisha thought, as if he was trying to convince me of it. She didn't quite know how to answer him. She judged that he didn't want the "proper" response, the glib reply. He wanted the truth. He was waiting for her next move.

"Too much honesty can be painful," she said carefully. "It's strong medicine."

He smiled. "Yes, but it cures many ills."

The car was stopping. Inky opened Kamisha's door and helped her out. John got out on his side. Coming around the front of the limo to join her, he walked slowly, a little stiffly on one side but steadily enough. She wondered if he really needed the cane or if it was a prop, a habit like smoking a cigarette or holding a glass in your hand at a cocktail party. She wondered too much about John Leopardo.

He took her arm and guided her under the red awning that led to the door of the restaurant. They were somewhere uptown on the West Side. Kamisha wasn't sure exactly where. She hadn't even seen the name of the place, but it exuded taste and style in a carefully unpretentious manner. The gleaming heavy glass door, the fern in a polished brass pot, the red carpet, the dark wainscoting and damask-covered chairs, all spoke of distinction.

"I hope you like Italian food," John said.

"I like almost anything," she replied, "if it's good."

"Oh, this is good."

The interior was small and hushed. Cool and intimate. The tables were filled, waiters in white jackets moved unobtrusively, and the place smelled tantalizingly of wine and garlic and the ever-so-faint aroma of the fresh roses that graced each table. It was definitely a big-city restaurant, different from the more casual ones in Aspen.

As she'd expected, the maître d' knew John. He even called him by his first name.

"Franco," John said, "meet Kamisha Hammill from my Aspen club."

Franco bent over her hand. "Absolutely charmed, Miss Hammill. Welcome to our humble establishment."

Their table was in a private corner. Their waiter was middle-aged and solemn, a professional. He also called John by his first name, and Kamisha wondered if they were all related to John somehow—

family. Yet they weren't too familiar; they treated John with utmost respect.

"This is a beautiful restaurant," she said. "Do you come here often?"

"Yes. My cousin owns it. But the reason I come here a lot is the food." He folded his hands on the white tablecloth. "Would you like a drink?"

"A glass of wine, that's all."

A bottle, frosted and perspiring, appeared on cue, a slightly effervescent white Italian wine.

The waiter poured their glasses full and stepped back. John raised his in a toast. "To the Ute City Club, Miss Hammill."

Her eyes had never left his during the ritual. She touched his glass with hers and sipped. "Will you please call me Kamisha? I'm not used to being so formal."

"All right, Kamisha. And you're to call me John."

They were supplied with menus. She read the delectable-sounding dishes but didn't register what she was reading. She kept glancing up surreptitiously, expecting to find his gaze on her. But he seemed truly engrossed in the menu. It irritated her. She was used to male attention. She knew it would sound disgustingly vain if she tried to explain it, but Brigitte understood why Kamisha craved attention. Too bad she wasn't there to explain.

Kamisha sighed inwardly. Why couldn't she get a handle on him? Finally she cocked her head and cleared her throat. She lowered the menu. "I'm curious," she began.

"About what?"

"I hope you don't think I'm being presumptuous, but I'm very curious about Inky, your driver. He isn't the usual sort..."

John gave a short laugh, the first time she'd seen him do more than smile faintly. "Inky. He's more than a driver, as you probably noticed. He's a friend. He also saved my life in the war. So he feels he's responsible for me for the rest of my life."

"The war?"

"Vietnam."

"Oh, you were in Vietnam. Somehow I didn't think—"

"I took a semester off college and got drafted. My timing was lousy."

Things began to fall into place in Kamisha's head. No wonder she got that feeling that there was something between the two men, some closeness that went far beyond employer-employee.

Their waiter hovered expectantly.

"I really can't decide. Please order something for me," Kamisha said. "Something with seafood and a big salad. I trust your judgment." He hadn't brought up the subject of the club or Rick, the subject that lay between them like a shared secret. She wouldn't, either; the ball was in John's court.

He ordered. Caesar salad, pasta with seafood sauce for her, some kind of veal for him.

She played with the stem of her glass, twirling it. "The war. I'm still curious."

"It was a long time ago."

"Your leg...?"

"Yes, in Nam. My knee got shot up pretty badly. But they patched me up."

"Um." He seemed completely unselfconscious about it. An interesting man. It occurred to Kamisha that she'd like to see him laugh, really laugh, in free, unconstrained mirth. She wondered if he ever did. She sipped her wine and studied his face, his strong neck, the way his hair was graying slightly at the temples.

She assessed him with the eye of a trained athlete. He was solid, his muscles well toned. You could always tell, even when a person was dressed. It was in the way he carried himself, in the way he moved. He must take care of his body. She wondered if he worked out at the Ute City Club when he was in Aspen. But she was sure she'd have seen him there if he did. She pictured him in shorts and a weight-lifting singlet, pumping iron, sweat-slicked, groaning with effort as the men did at the club. Yes, she could see him....

"Was your flight on time?" he was asking. "I know the Aspen airport gets backed up at times."

"Oh, I drove to Denver. I always do. I like driving, and in the summer it's almost as quick as flying. I have a car I really enjoy, too."

"A fast one?" he asked, smiling.

"Of course. A red Saab convertible. It's my one indulgence."

He watched her gravely for a moment, as if weighing her remark. "Your skiing," he said then. "I remember reading about you. The downhill, wasn't it?"

"Yes."

"Do you still ski?"

"Oh, yes, I love it. I think I enjoy it more now than when I was in training."

"I used to ski. A little. Before my leg."

She listened carefully. There wasn't one iota of self-pity or even wistfulness in his voice. He was merely stating a fact. She was determined to draw him out, to put him in a category with which she could deal. "Did you ever ski in Aspen?"

"No, here in the East. I wasn't very good." He looked at her. "I've seen downhillers on TV. You must like speed."

She grinned at him. "I'm crazy about speed. Cars, horses, skiing—whatever."

And then she waited for him to show curiosity about her remarks, the "whatever." Surely he got it, the mild reference to her fast approach to life, to relationships. But her meaning seemed lost on him.

"So," he was saying, "were you ever afraid when you were skiing?"

Kamisha felt a sigh of disappointment settle in her stomach. She shrugged. "Your body is ready when you're competing. You're nervous, but that's only the pressure of how well you'll do. You can't be afraid, not really, or you won't ski well enough."

"Did your parents like you racing? Weren't they worried about you?" he asked.

She shut down the quick, bitter remark that flew to her lips. "They were proud of me. I suppose they were worried," she said, lying and realizing that it was John who was drawing *her* out.

"How fortunate for you that they gave you the freedom to do what you wanted."

Freedom. That's the one thing the Hammills had given their daughter, but freedom without guidance or love became as much of a prison as overprotection. "Yes, I was lucky," she said.

"You must have worked at it."

"Oh, I worked, all right." She hesitated for a moment. "I deserved that Silver Medal, you know."

"I never had a moment's doubt about that." He regarded her for a moment, then asked, "I'm interested in your name. It's unusual."

She gave him a quick, wry smile. "Oh, it was one of my mother's fads—Indian art. She had the house full of it. One of her favorite potters was named Kamisha. So she named me after her."

"I see, Indian."

"Navaho, to be exact."

"It's a very lovely name."

"Thank you." If she were younger, less practiced, she'd be squirming in her seat, blushing. She wondered how he'd elicited such a girlish response in her. Odd. "John," she finally said, and realized it was the first time she'd said his name aloud. It rolled off her tongue with ease. "We're talking about me too much. Tell me about yourself. Are you from New York originally?"

"Brooklyn," he said shortly.

The food came. It was marvelous. She ate with relish. They talked, drank the alluring, effervescent wine of Italy. He smiled more often, and it changed his appearance so completely that she couldn't believe he was the same man. It was as if he wore the ancient Greek masks— first the mask of comedy, then switched to the mask of tragedy.

He'd been born in Brooklyn. His parents were still there. Yes, he had family in the area, one married sister, cousins, aunts, uncles. Whether or not he was single was never mentioned, but somehow she guessed he was. And still he never spoke of the club or Rick or why Kamisha was in New York.

"That was wonderful," Kamisha said, laying her fork down.

"Dessert?"

"God, no."

"Espresso?"

"I'd love some."

The meal was wending its way to a conclusion. He'd see her into his limo soon, drop her off at her hotel and that would be that. She'd fly to Colorado tomorrow and know little more than she'd known about John before coming to New York. She hadn't an inkling whether or not he'd lied to her about Rick. She hadn't any idea who he really was or what he was thinking. She felt awash with disappointment, left hanging in midair. She didn't even know what he thought about *her*.

There was the matter of her job, too. She needed that job. She loved her work. Her small trust fund from her grandparents certainly couldn't support her. What would she do if suddenly she was out on the street? He'd said he'd take care of things. But how? And when?

She'd ask him straight out. Not right now. Later, in the limo. She'd just ask him what he was going to do.

"I'll give you a choice," he said over the espresso. "I need to provide my leg with a little exercise after dinner. It gets stiff. I was going to go for a walk. It should be cooler out now. If you'd care to walk with me... Or I can drop you at your hotel.''

Her spirits seemed to lift miraculously. She wanted the evening to go on and on. She wanted to discover more about the mystery that was John Leopardo. She wanted to know why he drew her and challenged her. "I'd love to go for a walk.''

Inky followed them, above on the street, slowly inching the big car along as they walked a path down along the East River. It was a sultry evening, slightly overcast. Trees grew out of the concrete, and occasional birds chirped in the greenery. A few people jogged, slick with sweat, or walked their dogs along the pavement.

John moved slowly, stiffly at first. Then his leg must have loosened up, because his pace increased. Kamisha could feel the hot, damp air on her bare shoulders and the whisper of the fabric against her skin. Her hair clung damply to her neck, and she raised a hand to lift its heaviness for a moment.

The river moved slowly below them, brown and turgid, and lights reflected from it like thousands of eyes.

"Um, this feels good," she said.

"I come here often.''

"Do you walk a lot?'' she asked.

"It's good for me, the doctors say. One of the things I can do.''

"You know, we have the best sports medicine clinic in the country right in the Ute City Club,'' she began.

He cut her off. "You're a walking advertisement, Kamisha. Believe me, I've been there. I've been everywhere. What you see before you is the best you're going to see.''

"I didn't mean to—''

"You should get together with my mother. I'm sure the two of you could come up with a list of doctors for me to see,'' he said. But he wasn't angry, not at all. Obviously he found her suggestion, like his mother's, amusing, perhaps even a bit endearing.

He took off his suit coat then, shrugged out of it, and carried it over his shoulder, hooked on a finger. He loosened his collar button and tie. Dark curling hairs showed at the open V at his neck. Kamisha could see the tiny peaks of his nipples where the fine cotton of his blue shirt clung to his skin.

She felt utterly content walking with this man along the river in the heart of the hot, throbbing city. Utterly safe and at peace. Beside the very river that Rick had threatened John Leopardo would toss her into, attached to cement shoes. It was an ironic concept.

"Something funny?" he asked.

"Oh, no, just having a nice time," she replied.

Was John capable of killing her if she thwarted his plans? Was he showing her a preview of her own fate? She closed her eyes and let the warm, heavy air slide across her skin. She didn't care.

She was going to ask him what he planned on doing about Simons, but the time wasn't right. The spell was too powerful, too pleasant, to be broken.

He left her at the hotel late. Getting out of the long black car, he walked her to the lobby, stood in the too-bright light with her and touched her hand gently. "I enjoyed this evening, Kamisha. Very much."

"So did I. I'm glad you asked me."

He leaned on his cane, shifting his weight. "And don't worry about the club. I'll take care of it."

He'd brought it up himself, his timing perfect, relieving her of the responsibility. *I'll take care of it.* He would, too. She believed that. Just then she'd believe anything he told her.

"Thank you" was all she said.

"What time is your flight tomorrow?" he asked her then.

"Noon."

"Good. You have time for breakfast. Will you be my guest?"

"If I'm not interrupting your work."

"Not at all. I'll expect you at my apartment then. Eight o'clock. Is that all right?"

"Fine." At his apartment?

"Inky will pick you up. Say a quarter of eight."

It was happening too fast, and yet she knew she had to follow through on this new adventure, this new risk, this unique thrill. "I'm looking forward to it," she said.

"Good night."

"Good night, and thank you again."

It was as if neither of them wanted to end it, to finish the play. The curtain was about to fall, but the players were still on stage, following a script of their own.

"I'd better get this elevator," she said, gesturing.

"Yes. Sleep well."

She smiled as she stepped inside. The doors whispered shut on his face, and she thought it had looked a little sad, a little lonely.

But that, of course, was only her imagination.

CHAPTER FIVE

"MISS HAMMILL," the doorman said, "yes, you're expected."

For the first time that Kamisha could remember she felt out of her element. In Aspen everything was studiously casual. There were no doormen, few lobbies, fewer elevators. She absolutely never went to a man's home for breakfast. If she had an early appointment, they'd meet somewhere for breakfast—usually at the club. While she waited for the elevator doors to open, she glanced around the lobby, cool air from the central system washing over her.

There were two wingback chairs covered in gold lamé tapestry against a wall that was done in textured paper. Between them was a carved Chinese table and a large, ornate mirror. The floor was dark-veined marble, and a single potted plant stood beside one of the chairs. An old building, small and exclusive. She wondered if John Leopardo's apartment mirrored the lobby—impersonal, dim and hushed.

He opened the door himself. She hadn't quite known what to expect. A maid? A butler?

"Good morning," he said.

"Hello." Kamisha stepped inside past him. Her initial impression of John's apartment was one of spaciousness and light, with plenty of open floor space. Instantly she noted that there wasn't a plant to be seen or a thing out of place. Everything was lines and angles and spareness. The creature comforts were all present, but there was a distinct impersonal feel to the room.

Her discomfort increased. It was a mistake to have come here. Yet John seemed unaffected by her presence. Like the large area she stood in, the inanimate furnishings that greeted her eye, he gave off no feelings whatsoever. Unaccountably his self-control made Kamisha want to break his perfect shell to see what lay inside. And another thought made her heart knock against her ribs: she couldn't have been the first woman he'd invited there. John Leopardo surely had something in mind other than breakfast.

She put her purse on a chair, took a breath and felt as if she were in the starting gate, ready for a race, an important one. A sense of exhilaration filled her, quickly replacing her discomfort. Last night had been foreplay. This morning he'd proposition her. She wondered what he'd do when she turned him down cold.

"Orange juice, coffee?" he asked, nodding toward the kitchen.

"Juice, please." Idly she moved around the corner apartment. It was indeed sweeping, though that impression came more from the sparseness of furnishings rather than the square footage. The living room was ultramodern, a few pieces upholstered in shades of gray. There were carefully placed pillows on a steel-gray sectional. There was a cushioned chair on a stainless-steel frame, a pale blue-gray carpet on the floor. The walls were hung with architects' renderings of his holdings. She spotted the Ute City Club.

On the other side of the room was a long glass-topped table, four modern stainless-steel chairs around it—the dining area. But the table was covered with blueprints of some sort.

She wondered for a moment where they would eat, but then she noticed a patio beyond open sliding glass doors. There was a table set for two on it.

"They tell me it's freshly squeezed," John said, returning, "but I wonder."

"It looks fine, thank you."

He glanced at his watch, and she studied him over the rim of her glass. Yes, it was as if any emotion in John were like light from a black hole in space—it couldn't escape its source.

"The cook was due ten minutes ago," John stated with annoyance. "But I'm sure you have plenty of time to catch your flight."

"Lots of time." Kamisha followed him across the room toward the patio. He walked slowly—the cane. "You have a cook all the time?"

"No. She cleans twice a week and leaves a few things in the refrigerator. I'm a poor hand in the kitchen."

"Don't you eat out often?"

"I did last night."

"What about business luncheons and dinners?"

"I avoid them."

The patio, though narrow, ran the length of the apartment. From the rail Kamisha was afforded a spectacular view of both Central Park and the jumble of tall buildings that climbed skyward in Uptown Manhattan. Car horns blasting and an occasional siren could be heard below on the busy streets.

"Exciting," she said, aware of his nearness at her side. Maybe now he'd take the glass out of her hand, set it down and turn to her. She felt a tight knot form in her stomach. Perhaps she'd let his lips brush hers for a moment before she moved away. Perhaps...

"Ah," he was saying, "there's Gwen now. Would an omelet be all right? If you don't like eggs..."

"No. It sounds fine."

"I'll be back in a minute. Make yourself at home."

Kamisha smiled at the skyline. Yes, he'd have made his move if "Gwen" hadn't arrived. She was certain of it.

She turned and leaned her back against the rail. It was already warm out. Hot compared to the mountain climate she was used to. She could feel a thin layer of perspiration form on her upper lip, and her white linen suit felt damp and clinging next to her skin. John was standing inside, speaking to the maid—another woman pushing sixty, she noted. Kamisha watched him carefully, tilting her head slightly. He was wearing pearl-gray summer-weight slacks and a pink dress shirt rolled up once at the cuffs. His skin seemed pale next to the pink. City pale. His black hair, graying at the temples, was combed back, as if still damp from a shower. He smiled then, evidently at something Gwen had said, and Kamisha decided he was really quite handsome. A strong Mediterranean profile, strong jawline and teeth. Hooded black eyes. Eyes that told a person nothing.

She wondered again if he was really a member of the Mob. Oh, he denied it. But he would. She wondered if he was amused by her accusations or planning to have her silenced. Maybe he'd offer her hush money. Her thoughts were titillating, stirring her blood. She felt a single bead of perspiration roll down slowly between her breasts.

"I imagine," he said, stepping back outside, his cane in his right hand, "this is probably too hot out here for you. I could clear the table inside."

Kamisha smiled, pushing her hair behind her ears. "It *is* hot. And I'll help you with the table."

The blueprints spread out on the glass were of his latest venture. He began to roll them up. "Costa Rica," he told her. "The club is on the Pacific Coast. It opened a month ago, but the west wing still isn't completed.'' He was leaning over the table, reaching to point out the incomplete wing, his shoulders pressing against the pink fabric of his shirt. He had a good body, Kamisha thought once again, strong-looking despite the wounded leg. Her eyes traveled to his slacks, the nicely rounded buttocks, the firm thighs.

"It's one of the few peaceful countries in Central America," he was saying. "It's called little Switzerland. Has a neutral standing at the United Nations."

"I've never been there," Kamisha said, looking away, "but I hear it's lovely."

"You'd like it," he said as if he, alone, knew what she liked. "It's all mountains. Your kind of country."

"But no skiing."

"Definitely no skiing."

"Nice beaches?"

"Beautiful. Miles and miles of them in spectacular coves."

"Um, sounds lovely."

"It is."

Gwen served breakfast, then disappeared into the bedroom, probably changing sheets, gathering towels. Kamisha wondered if John had forgotten about the maid being there. She felt certain he'd invited her up for reasons other than breakfast. He must have. But why, then, hadn't he planned better?

He was nodding toward one of the preliminary sketches of a club on the wall behind them. "That one's in Amalfi, Italy."

"I've skied Italy, raced there. But I've never been to that coast."

"Ah, then you've missed a unique part of the country."

Kamisha put down her fork and dabbed at her mouth with the napkin. "You're very proud of your clubs."

"Yes, I am." His penetrating gaze held hers for a long moment over the rim of his coffee cup. The knot in her stomach grew to the size of a fist.

"How many clubs are there?" she asked, looking away, watching as the maid took a bundle of laundry and, keys in hand, left the apartment.

"Four," he replied. "The first one I built is in Miami. Coral Gables, actually. Then there's Amalfi and, of course, the club in Aspen."

"And now Costa Rica."

"Yes."

She wondered, while the conversation lingered on his accomplishments, if he was trying to convince her of his legitimacy despite his family's reputation. Perhaps. Or maybe he was simply making polite conversation. And she wondered, too, if he'd been married and divorced. Did he have children? There were no photographs anywhere that she could see. Perhaps by his bedside.

There was a lot about John, she realized, that stirred her curiosity. Too much.

"And you're from Los Angeles," he was saying, sitting back in his chair now, his fingers steepled beneath his chin as his eyes pinioned her.

"Yes. My parents still live there, in fact."

"You see much of them?"

Casually Kamisha shook her head. "We're all so busy. You know how it is."

"Um," he said.

She realized then that they'd been talking steadily since her arrival, but neither one of them had actually given a thing away. The conversation had stayed purposely on the surface of their lives. Remarkable. And she wondered just what had made John Leopardo as closed and wary as she was.

"Would you like more coffee?"

Kamisha shook her head again. He'd make his move now, she thought. The maid was off doing the laundry. Kamisha had to leave for the airport soon. He'd *have* to make his play now, or there would be no time. She felt smug with the knowledge.

She *wanted* him to lean across the table, to take her golden-brown hand in his strong, pale one. She wanted him to try to lead her through that half-closed bedroom door. This man might be the one she'd respond to. It was an intimidating realization.

"Are you sure you wouldn't like some more...?"

"No, no, I'm fine," Kamisha said, breathless. And abruptly she was on her feet. "It's hot, isn't it? Maybe some air."

"Of course."

But the air outside seemed too filled with smoke and car exhaust, too hot, too close. She took a white stretch band from her pocket and pulled her hair back, fastening it with the elastic. All the while she was acutely aware of John's eyes on her, black and expressionless. Her skin felt supersensitive, tingly, too warm.

"Do you like the city?" he was asking.

"Yes. It's exciting. The shopping, all the people, the theater."

"But you chose the mountains."

"Yes, or rather the mountains chose me. Actually, I was born in Texas, but my parents took me all over skiing. And then we moved to L.A."

"I know."

Kamisha raised a dark brow.

A thin smile split his lips for a moment. "All of my employees," he said, matter-of-factly, "have a file, Kamisha. I like to know who's working for me."

"And what's in *my* file, John?" she asked coolly, challenging him. He studied her for a time. "I'm afraid that's confidential."

"Oh, really?"

"Yes."

"I'd say it's more like secretive."

"What do you mean?"

"Like in the movies," she dared. "You know."

"No, I don't."

"The way big organizations...big *families* handle their affairs."

An ironic grin twisted his mouth. "I see," he said.

Casually her heart racing, she said, "Yes."

And abruptly the amusement left his face. "I told you, that's my father, Kamisha, not me."

"Then why the file?"

"I'm a careful man."

"Oh, really," she ventured. "How about Rick Simons, then?"

"I'm human. I'm capable of mistakes. It has yet to be proven, though."

"But I told you..."

"Yes, you did. I'm sure you believe that young girl, too."

"But you don't."

"Kamisha," he said, taking a step toward her, "I'll handle it. It's my affair."

"Of course." She could feel the rail against her back. There was nowhere to go.

"You'll have to trust me in this," he began, but then she could hear the front door open and close. Through the glass she could see Inky inside. An immense sigh of relief welled in her breast.

John, too, must have been aware of the interruption, but for an agonizingly long minute he stood his ground, too close, an emotion in his eyes now, but she couldn't read it. Finally he smiled and said, "Inky will drive you to the airport."

"I can get a cab."

"I insist." He reached out and took her elbow tentatively, as if he knew she was poised for flight. He steered her inside. "You're to mail me your tickets, too, and your hotel bill. This trip shouldn't have been at your expense."

"You don't have to..."

"But I do." And his tone left no room for argument.

Inky was checking his watch when Kamisha picked up her purse. "We better get rolling, Miss Hammill," he said. "Traffic's bad."

"Well," Kamisha said, turning to John and placing a smile on her lips, "I want to thank you for all the hospitality. You've been very kind."

"My pleasure," he said. He was standing in the center of the room, one hand in his trouser pocket, the other gripping his cane. She was struck by the aura of silent command in him, his strength and self-confidence. And then she saw Inky exchange a glance with him, a rather amused glance. She wondered about that as John opened the apartment door and they walked to the elevator. She wondered if Inky thought more had gone on back there than breakfast.

Kamisha was still tense, surrounded by two very compelling men. Men whose experiences together, whose obvious closeness, set her apart. There was too much understood between them, too much silence that seemed filled to bursting. She wasn't used to this, and she was wary of it.

John walked her to the car, giving the doorman a friendly nod. No, she wasn't used to any of this, to being acutely on guard, to being taken care of so lavishly. She wasn't certain she liked it.

John opened the car door for her and helped her in. "Have a safe trip. And, as I promised, don't worry about the club. I'll see to it."

"All right," Kamisha replied, wanting to believe him, needing to. "And thank you again."

The door closed with a solid chunk. She realized abruptly that she was feeling cut off, a tie was being severed. The notion left her at a loss and, as Inky pulled away from the curb, she automatically turned in her seat and watched John through the smoked glass. He was still standing there, favoring his leg, unmoving, his eyes following the limo until it rounded the corner and disappeared into the heavy flow of Manhattan traffic.

Kamisha sighed and turned back to face the front. What did John Leopardo really want from her? Why all the gentle treatment if he didn't expect something in return?

"Inky," she said, leaning forward, the leather cool beneath her, "you've known John for a long time, haven't you?"

"Yes, Miss Hammill, I sure have."

"Tell me, what's he really like? I mean, has he ever been married? Does he have children?"

But all she got in return was: "You better be asking him that yourself, ma'am." His coal-black eyes met hers in the mirror for a moment, then switched back to the street.

GETTING ON A PLANE for the return flight to Denver was like stepping out of Alice's Wonderland back into dreary reality. Colors faded, sounds became irritating, people were strident and ugly. Kamisha felt claustrophobic on the plane with its stale air and monotonous droning, closed in and unable to think.

Images kept flashing through her mind's eye: inescapable, pervasive thoughts chased one another through her head.

John, of course. Darkly handsome, a man of presence. There was a superb power to him, not to be denied or ignored, a carriage that defied any other authority. And yet he'd used her gently, with old-world courtesy, and not asked a thing of her.

What did he want? In Kamisha's experience people exploited her. Her parents had used her as an extension of their pride, a prop to their egos, another valuable belonging. Her ski coach had used her for his ego, too. Rick Simons used her, as he'd so bluntly pointed out, to look good and not think too much. Everyone had repeated this pattern all her life, taken advantage of her appearance, which was only an accident of genetics, and her athletic prowess, which was due also to her inheritance and her own hard work.

No one had ever looked beyond those attributes. Not her ex-husband Josh, not anybody, ever.

Except maybe John Leopardo. What did he want of her? She'd thought he was going to try to buy her off, but he hadn't even attempted to. She'd thought he was interested sexually. She hadn't been mistaken, either. Or had she? He'd made no move, spoken no word, ventured no suggestive touch. And yet...what other relationship could a woman have with a man? What did he want—mere friendship? Inconceivable.

The question puzzled her, bothered her, kept her restless and on edge. She couldn't read John, still didn't know if he was lying outright to her about the club. Maybe all his solemn courtesy was a sham, an act to put her off guard. Maybe he'd put out a contract on her as Rick had intimated. Cement shoes. How ludicrous. No doubt he'd just fire her, and that would be that.

She leaned back in her seat and closed her eyes. She could see John's face, the dark shadow of his beard, the mole near the corner of his mouth. She could see his strong neck and shoulders and hands—his hand on the cane. John used his cane as a courtesan used her fan, to beguile, to hide, to reveal. To warn. She had a sudden uncontrollable desire to see his bad knee, to touch the puckered scars, to knead it. A hot flush rose up her neck at the thought.

She wondered who had come off best in her meetings with John. Dinner last night—she'd say they'd been even. Breakfast. Well, perhaps she'd shown her hand a touch too much. Maybe he'd seen something she preferred to keep hidden.

No, no one except Brigitte really knew Kamisha. Others used her, and she'd learned to protect herself by using them back. Only Brigitte knew her down to her guts—and even Brigitte used her as a rudder, an anchor, a life preserver in the storm of existence. Kamisha loved her friend like a sister, but she recognized Brigitte's needs and knew she was one of them. And Brigitte was one of her needs, too, the only human being in the world with whom she never had to pretend.

She sat there in the droning airplane, thinking, remembering, recalling all those years ago when she first met Brigitte Stratford. They'd both been fourteen years old, freshmen at the exclusive Taos School in the mountains of New Mexico.

She'd begun high school with a chip on her shoulder. The girls came in from everywhere in the country, laughing, renewing friendships, moaning over Mommy's new husband or Daddy's chapter eleven, the drugs they'd tried, the beaches they'd been to, the boys they'd devastated. Kamisha had viewed them with disdain; their problems seemed utterly inconsequential, their experiences trite. She'd moved in a day early and waited for the other bed in her room to be taken. The headmistress's list said that her roommate was Brigitte Stratford, a new girl. Kamisha hoped Brigitte would be quiet and pimply and leave her alone.

Brigitte wasn't quiet or pimply.

She waltzed in a minute after curfew the night before classes started. A small, brown-haired, innocent-looking girl, slight and pretty, wearing a man's sweatshirt that read Harvard, jeans with holes in the knees and lugging an enormous suitcase.

"Goddamn!" she announced instantly, dragging her case in. "I had to hitch a ride. Missed the last bus." Then she grinned, and her face lit up with an inner glow of devilry and mischief and unholy glee. "But it was more fun that way." Then the girl held out her small hand, laughing, her head cocked prettily to one side like a bird. "I'm Brigitte and I'm going to be an actress. Who're you?"

Within three days they were inseparable. It was a revelation to Kamisha, who'd never had a really close friend. For the first time she felt accepted for herself. Brigitte was her alter ego, lonely too, abandoned by her rich society mother and her ambitious father in Hollywood, achingly insecure. Their dissimilarities were vast but unimportant. They were like differently shaped magnets with cores that cleaved one to the other.

One Saturday night in November Kamisha and Brigitte managed double dates. The four of them ate fiery Mexican food, drank a six-pack Brigitte's date Pete had stolen from home and got giggly together. At a quarter to eleven Kamisha reminded them all the curfew was in fifteen minutes.

Pete raised his head from the front seat where he was necking with Brigitte. "Bobby, take Kamisha back. Here are the keys. Brigitte and I are gonna sneak into my basement."

"God, Brigitte, are you nuts?" Kamisha asked.

"No, just in lust," came her friend's muffled voice from the front seat.

At four in the morning Kamisha was awakened by a windowpane smashing into the room. Groggily she got up to see Brigitte standing below the second-floor window, ready to throw another fist-size rock. "Oops," she giggled, weaving in the darkness. "I threw it too hard. Toss down a sheet or something, roomie."

"Shh!"

Brigitte snickered again, staggered and put her hand over her mouth. "Come on," she whispered loudly. "I gotta get in!"

Kamisha never understood how Brigitte managed to climb up the sheet. She was so drunk that she radiated waves of alcohol. She collapsed, panting and chortling, onto her bed. Then she sat up and tried to make her expression serious. "I have an announcement to make. I am no longer a virgin."

"Pete?" Kamisha gasped.

"I'm in love," Brigitte sighed dramatically, then sagged back and passed out.

Kamisha sank down onto the edge of her bed and put her head into her hands. Someone had to sign Brigitte in. *Everyone* had to sign in. It wasn't unheard of for an upperclassman to sneak in after curfew and sign herself in, but it was a risky undertaking.

Kamisha took a deep breath. She would have to do it. She put her bathrobe and slippers on and slipped out into the dark corridor. There was always the chance of the dorm mother prowling around at night, checking on the girls. What if she got caught? It meant grounding or expulsion or whatever the headmistress decided. Damn Brigitte!

Sneaking through the halls to the stairs, her heart pounding in her ears, stopping at every corner to listen. Silence. Blackness and silence.

The sign-in book was on a stand in the lobby. Quickly she scribbled Brigitte's name. If it didn't resemble her signature, Brigitte could say she was sick or something. Better sick than late.

So far so good. She glided away from the lobby. If she was caught now, it wasn't so bad. But what would she say? She was sleepwalking. That was it. She was a terrible sleepwalker. It happened, didn't it? She'd pretend to wake up and be confused.

Damn Brigitte!

Almost there. On her own corridor, passing the bathroom.

A flashlight beam caught her in midstride. "Miss Hammill? What's going on here?"

Uh-oh! It was Miss Donnelly, the dried-up old maid. "Oh, Miss Donnelly, I just had to go to the john."

"Very well, Miss Hammill. Next time please turn on the light."

"Yes, Miss Donnelly."

Brigitte finally appeared the next day at lunch, pale green and bleary-eyed. Kamisha was cold to her, torn between her anger and curiosity as to what it had been like for Brigitte to lose her virginity.

"Come on, roomie, what's the matter? I feel like a truck ran over me."

"Next time you pull that kind of stunt leave me out of it," Kamisha said. "I had to sign in for you."

Brigitte turned even paler. "Oh, God, oh, no! I'm sorry! I deserve it! You shouldn't have done it!"

"Well, I did it and saved your butt," Kamisha said, mollified.

"But don't ever put me in that position again. I mean it, Brigitte. I hate being used. I hate it."

"I *thought* I went down there and did it myself. Or was that a dream? I swear, I was lying there in bed thinking I had to get up and go down there... I must have dreamed it."

"Now tell me, what was Pete like?"

Brigitte put her head in her hands. "I can barely remember. Did we do anything?"

"I wasn't there," Kamisha said dryly, "but last night you said you lost your virginity."

"I did? Oh, wow, I guess I did."

"What was it *like?*"

"Damned if I can remember," Brigitte groaned, holding her head.

Kamisha hadn't changed much since those days, not really. Neither had Brigitte. Despite their marriages, Brigitte's daughter, their divorces, their careers and fame, despite it all, they were both the same insecure teenagers inside—alone, except for each other. Kamisha was still trying to save Brigitte from herself, and Brigitte was as reckless as ever. But Kamisha needed her friend, because Brigitte was the only haven Kamisha had where she could just be herself.

The plane circled and descended over Denver. The mountains lined the horizon, dark and jagged, beckoning. Kamisha stared out the window at the familiar peaks and thought over and over again: everyone of any consequence in her life had wanted something from her. So, then, what was it that John Leopardo was after?

CHAPTER SIX

KAMISHA TURNED the key and the Saab roared to life. Two rows over in the outlying parking of Denver's Stapleton Airport, a man was getting a jump start from a service station truck. Boy, the Saab had been a good investment; it had yet to fail her.

She drove with the top down, her hair in a ponytail, sunglasses in place. There weren't too many warm months in the Rocky Mountains, months in which she could feel the wind in her hair and, whenever possible, Kamisha took advantage of the ideal weather.

It was a glorious summer day. As soon as she cleared the city on Interstate 70, the sky opened up, a spectacular pellucid blue bowl overhead, and the foothills of the Rockies jutted up out of the plains before her. It had been a great snow year, too, and the fourteen-thousand-foot peaks that formed the Continental Divide to the west of Denver were still splashed in white. The day was so perfect, so cloudless, that the thin Colorado air caused an illusion of nearness and the sharp delineation of sky and towering rock and pine forest. Kamisha downshifted, breathing in the thinning air as she climbed, and the red Saab responded with the perfection of a finely crafted machine, leaping to life, pulling out ahead of the line of interstate traffic on her right.

Georgetown, Idaho Springs, the quaint Victorian mining towns of the last century, flew by as Kamisha ascended into the heart of the Rockies, up, up, passing the slower cars and trucks as they pulled up the steep hills, up toward the Divide, the ski area of Loveland that stayed open often until June, up to the Eisenhower Tunnel that bored through the solid rock of the Divide. The Saab whipped into the tunnel, and she slowed to fifty miles per hour. No point getting a ticket. As always, the exhaust trapped in the two-mile-long tunnel smote her, but she could see the pinhole of daylight ahead. She breathed shallowly.

When Kamisha drove or skied or bicycled, she thought of little else save perfection of movement. She was a good driver, although Brigitte always hated to get into the car with her. "Death Wish Three," Brigitte had dubbed Kamisha's driving. But what did Brigitte know, anyway? Kamisha smiled, her fingers light on the leather-covered steering wheel.

The sunlight on the western slope of the Divide struck her eyes, momentarily blinding Kamisha until she pulled her sunglasses back down. She passed two flatbed trucks crawling on her right, both hauling mammoth pipes—probably for snowmaking equipment at a ski area. All the trucks stopped at the far side of the tunnel because the downhill grade was one of the steepest in the country. There were two well-placed runaway ramps on the descent, and it wasn't unusual to smell hot rubber from the brakes of a descending behemoth or to see a truck sitting halfway up one of those ramps, askew in the deep, soft sand, brakes still smoking. It made a body shiver.

The trucks were one matter, cars another. Generally automobiles flew down the western slope, the driver unused to the steep grade, not realizing his speed. In front of Kamisha she could see a few cars in the outside lane, brake lights blinking on and off sporadically.

No, she usually never thought about much of anything except her driving, but that afternoon she found herself wondering if she was going to get back to Aspen and find herself without a job. It was possible. Especially if she'd misjudged John Leopardo. And even if she hadn't, Rick was eventually going to find out about her trip to New York, and if John didn't fire him, then working with Rick was going to be quite impossible. She guessed she couldn't complain too much around Brigitte, though, because Brigitte had warned her, hadn't she?

Darn that man ahead of her in the van! He wouldn't move out of the passing lane. Kamisha tapped her brakes while simultaneously touching the horn to let him know she wanted to get past.

She put her foot on the brake again, pumping it slightly, because the van hadn't gotten fully out of the way yet. She had to pump the brakes yet again, and she registered that they seemed low. She downshifted, wondering about that as she sped past the van and gave the driver a thank-you wave. She'd just had the car serviced, for Pete's sake, and in the Rockies you always had your brakes checked.

Two trucks on the right in a line, going as slow as snails in very low gear, but there was another car out in the left lane in Kamisha's path. Didn't he see her coming up fast?

She put on the brakes again. This time her foot was halfway to the floor before they held. A surge of adrenaline shot through her heart as she quickly downshifted and had to pump the brakes hard and fast.

The car ahead made it past the two trucks and, thank God, hurried into the right lane. By then Kamisha had put the Saab into third but was still flying. She tried the brakes and then swore. They were gone.

Oh, God. The last runaway ramp. Was it around this curve? Oh, God!

Kamisha's eyes flew to the dashboard. Sixty miles per hour. If she put the Saab in second gear, it would never hold at this speed. As if the brakes would magically work, she tried them again. Nothing. A loose pedal. Her eyes flew back to the road. Yes! There it was! The ramp! A cold sweat popped out on her back, and her hands gripped the steering wheel. Trucks and cars alike could easily flip when they hit that loose sand, especially at the speed she was going.

"Oh, God," Kamisha whispered, fighting for control. It was like seeing a new rut ahead on a downhilll race course and knowing you were just barely on the edge of control. Your blood pounded and you worked on adrenaline alone, that and every skill you could muster. But this...

The Saab had gained speed. Sixty-five, sixty-seven. She had only one shot at that steep ramp and it better be good! Kamisha lined the car up, thanking the Lord that no one was blocking her path in the right lane. Carefully, skillfully, she let her car ease across the center line until she was heading straight for the ramp on a perfect line— one tug of the wheel when she hit that deep sand would be the end of her. The front tires crossed the asphalt shoulder, the back tires. She was doing seventy-two miles per hour. And then suddenly the two front tires hit the sand. The car seemed to lurch forward sickeningly while sinking at the same time. It pulled abruptly to the left, settled back down, lurched again while still climbing the steep, sandy track. And then slowly, slowly, it stopped. For an instant all was utterly, deathly still. Then the car slipped backward, one foot, two, and finally came to a reluctant rest. It was a full minute before Kamisha let out the breath she was holding.

"WHAT DO YOU MEAN, *no* fluid?" she asked the man at the service station in the resort of Dillon. She peeked up underneath the Saab where it sat on the hydraulic lift. "I just had the fluid—"

"Well," the mechanic said, "I'm just telling you how it is, lady. Whoever serviced this car really loused you up."

Kamisha frowned. Gary had serviced it at Auto Trek. Gary had been working on her cars since she'd first come to Aspen. He was the best in town, absolutely reliable.

The mechanic was scratching his head, wiping his brow with a grimy bandanna. "I tell you, though," he said, "can't see how your line got cut. It's a puzzlement, all right, lady."

But Kamisha knew. The sudden insight was like a light bulb being switched on in her head. John Leopardo. She felt her heart thump heavily once, then settle back down. "How long will it take to fix my car?" she asked calmly.

"Tomorrow afternoon. Maybe late morning."

"Then where can I rent one?"

He gestured with the dirty bandanna still in his hand. "Two blocks down is a Holiday Inn. I think they got a National Car Rental there. Maybe it's Hertz."

"And where's the police station?"

THE CHEVY AUTOMATIC had as much pep as a tortoise, Kamisha thought as she floored it, trying to hit forty miles an hour climbing Independence Pass on the way home. She clenched her jaw.

Yep. John had wined and dined her—a Last Supper, she thought bitterly. She even remembered a casual question he'd asked: "Do you always drive to Denver?"

Of course, she'd boasted to him then about her car, given him the description—how eagerly she'd fallen into his trap.

And how many cars fitting the description of hers—with Aspen's famous ZG license plates—were parked at Stapleton?

"Ha!" she said aloud, pulling out around a camper on a steep, narrow curve near the twelve-thousand-foot-plus summit.

Oh, yes, John Leopardo had tried to have her killed. There was no other possible explanation except for a crazy series of coincidences that simply couldn't have occurred in a trillion years.

"Oh, man, are *you* stupid," she muttered. "And blind." God, how he must have been laughing. That was why she hadn't been able to get a handle on him. Of course! That was why he'd behaved so differently from other men. How many other men had she dated who'd been planning to kill her? What a stupid, blind, naive idiot she was!

She drove down the inclines of Independence Pass, pushing the six cylinders of the Chevy to the limit through the series of straight-aways and S curves that stretched along the lovely wide alpine meadows and the rushing Roaring Fork River. Then there was Aspen. It was late, but she headed directly to Brigitte's, bursting to tell her friend everything, to talk it all out. Despite Kamisha's self-reproach and anger, she knew she better come up with a plan—and quick. An SOB like Leopardo wasn't going to be stopped so easily.

"No, way" was Brigitte's initial reaction. "You've been watching too much TV."

Tiredly Kamisha propped her feet on the bar stool next to the one she was sitting on in Brigitte's kitchen. "I'm telling you what the mechanic said. And I saw it myself."

"God." Brigitte was wearing a bright red kimono, and she pulled the sash tighter around her small waist. She went to the fridge and began to poke around. "Want a white wine? I think I need one. Where's the darn bottle?"

"Are you listening to me?"

"Of course, I'm listening to you. I'd just like to talk this out over a drink, if that's okay with you."

It wasn't okay. But Kamisha knew Brigitte was going to search the refrigerator all night until she found the wine. "Listen," Kamisha said, rising, pulling the bottle of Chablis out from between a loaf of bread and a mayonnnaise jar, handing it to Brigitte, "I came over to sort this out in my head. But if you're going to get sloshed..."

"I am not going to get 'sloshed,' Kamisha. It's only a glass of wine, for God's sake. Cool it."

"Where's Tracy?" Kamisha asked, glancing into the darkened living room.

"Spent the night with a friend. They're going to a horse show early tomorrow, and you know how I hate all that banging around before noon."

"Still up at the crack of noon, are you?"

"You bet. Especially when Bullet's off on assignment. Here, you want a glass?"

"Okay, sure, why not?"

Finally Brigitte plumped herself down on a stool next to Kamisha. It was a huge two-story glass-and-stone house on Castle Creek, west of Aspen, but the gathering spot was still in the kitchen.

"You want my advice?" Brigitte asked, sipping, pushing her sleep-tousled brown hair behind an ear.

"That's why I'm here."

"Forget the whole thing. Tell Rick you made a mistake. Better yet, tell John Leopardo you were wrong. Apologize. That's what *I'd* do."

"Are you nuts?" Kamisha stared at her friend over the rim of her own glass.

"Look," Brigitte said, "you're the one who comes rushing in here at midnight to tell me someone tried to kill you. What do you want me to say? Tell you to confront this Leopardo again? You want I should hire you a bodyguard? You think I want to see you get yourself hurt?" Her voice had risen, growing shrill.

"Of course I don't. But when have I ever backed down from a challenge?"

"Oh, Lord."

"Come on, Brigitte, when?"

"Never, I guess."

"So forget the apologies. There must be a way to get that Mafia creep off my back."

"Sure," Brigitte sighed, draining her glass, pouring another as she dropped a new ice cube into the liquid, "I'm sure he'll back right down, shaking in his three-hundred-dollar shoes."

"I could go to the police."

Brigitte's eyes snapped up. "No," she said quickly. "God, he'll find out and really be after your hide. These kind of men aren't scared of the police. And what do you have on him, anyway?"

"Well...the parties, for one thing. I know I can't *prove* Leopardo had my brakes tampered with, but I could go after him through the parties, you know, get Carin McNaught to..."

"Forget it." Brigitte rose and paced the flagstone floor. Back and forth, one hand clutching her glass, the other on her hip. "No one's going to open up to the cops, Kamisha. No one. This is Mafia we're talking, kiddo, not a Sunday booster club gathering." She gestured in the air with her glass.

"You're some help."

"You bet I am! I'm telling you, apologize! Talk to them. Tell them you're sorry. I couldn't stand it if something happened to you." Her eyes, glassy now, bored into Kamisha's.

"Nothing's going to happen to me."

"Oh, right! You're tougher than the Sicilians. Great. Great thinking!"

"Will you settle down?"

"You've got me crazy, Kamisha. Isn't it enough that Bullet's gone half the time, and my daughter, God, my daughter's on my case about everything under the sun."

"What's wrong with Tracy?"

Brigitte put her hand on her forehead as if staving off a migraine. "Hormones."

"Is that all?"

"Of course it is."

"I think, maybe," Kamisha said tentatively, "she's worried about her mom."

Brigitte's reaction was to let out a string of oaths that would have impressed a sailor.

"Whoa," Kamisha said, shaking her head, "that was ladylike."

Another choice word from Brigitte. "Why am *I* always the problem around here?"

"You aren't," Kamisha said, walking on eggshells now. "It's just that we all love you so darn much and sometimes you—"

"Don't you start on me."

"Okay, I won't."

Finally Brigitte sagged against the counter across the room. "Hell. I need some sleep. I feel awful. But I won't sleep if I'm worried you're going to do something incredibly stupid."

"I'm not about to. The stupid thing was to trust that thug in New York."

Brigitte sighed. "That *was* odd of you."

"Yeah, well, I thought he was special. Different. He never even came on to me."

"That's a new twist."

"Isn't it? I was really on cloud nine there, too. He's something, all right."

"He's dangerous. You keep that in mind. Now let's hit the sack. You stay in the guest room, and in the morning—"

But Kamisha raised a hand. "No one's going to run my life for me, Brigitte. Especially not Mr. John Leopardo."

"Kami—"

"I mean it. I sleep in my own bed in my own home. Period."

"Swell."

"Yes, it is. I'll think of something. I'm tired now and not looking at this straight."

"Tired and mad."

"You bet I am."

"You won't go off half-cocked, will you? I mean, think about what I said, about talking to Rick and—"

"Okay, okay. I'll think it all out."

"Promise? And you won't let your temper make you do something dumb?"

"I promise. I'll cool off. I'll handle it."

"Good," Brigitte sighed, obviously relieved.

But it didn't quite work that way.

It was past one in the morning when Kamisha sat bolt upright in her bed and began to mumble to herself. "Oh, don't worry, Miss Hammill, I'll take care of everything. Right away." She frowned, punching a fist into her pillow. "Yeah, he took care of everything, didn't he? I wonder who he called in Denver to have my car worked on? I wonder how much it cost him? And some airport security! No wonder everyone complains!"

She tried a warm glass of milk, an aspirin. She tried watching an old Fred Astaire flick on a cable TV channel. But all she could do was pace and twist up her face and mutter to herself. What really rankled, too, was the fact that he'd totally taken her in. Oh, sure, she'd considered that he might have been lying to her in New York, but she really hadn't believed it.

What a slick character. Smooth as silk, so, so Continental, so suave, and that leg, the cane, the old war wound story! And what a prop Inky was! No wonder she'd let herself slip! He'd been too good to be true, hadn't he?

She dropped into the soft cushioned chair by her open bedroom window and rested her chin on her hands. A faint summer breeze stirred the lace curtains as she stared, unfocused, up at the night sky. A million brilliant pinpoints of light glittered above—a Rocky Mountain wonder. Tears of anger and frustration filled her eyes, blurring the spectacle. It wasn't fair. She didn't even care anymore that he'd tried to have her killed. Not really. It hurt too much to think that she'd actually liked him, been spellbound. If only she could break that hard, reserved shell of his and twist a knife into his guts just as he'd done to her.

Before Kamisha could rationalize her actions, she found herself reaching for the trimline phone by her bed. She dialed New York information. "Manhattan," she said, "Mr. John Leopardo on West Sixty-third Street."

Amazingly the operator had a listing. And then Kamisha sat there for a moment in the dark, the dial on the phone the only illumination in the room as she hesitated, holding the receiver in her hand. It was what time back East? Three-thirty in the morning? So what. He deserved everything she could throw at him. She began to dial: 1-212... Her fingers were shaky, her stomach knotted in anger.

The phone rang on the other end once, twice, three times. It occurred to Kamisha that she might be signing her death warrant, but her anger overcame all reason. She took a deep breath just as she would have in the starting gate at the beginning of a race. *Think.* If he answered, she'd better be darn clever.

"Hello?" Groggily, his voice deep and sleep-filled, hoarse. "Hello?"

Kamisha swallowed. She could see him lying in bed in her mind's eye—black silk pajama bottoms, no top—too hot. He'd be rubbing his eyes, his bristly jaw, coming to a sitting position...

"Mr. Leopardo," she said, careful not to use his given name, "this is Kamisha Hammill. Remember me?" It took all her effort to control her voice. It would never do to let the anger and the fear come through.

"Kamisha?"

"That's right. Are you surprised to hear from me?"

"Well, yes, to be honest. It's...ah, almost four in the morning here." His voice was losing its gravely pitch.

"That isn't what I meant," she said, then rose, pacing, the phone cord dragging behind her. "Didn't you think I was...dead?" Oh, God, she thought, what was she doing? Brigitte was right. She was playing a dangerous game with a lethal opponent.

"Kamisha," he said slowly, "I don't know what you're talking about."

"Oh, come on, John," she snapped, "we both know you tried to have me killed. I don't feel like playing this game with you."

There was a long pause on the line. "Let me get this straight. You think someone tried to kill you?"

Kamisha laughed bitterly. "I think *you* tried to have me killed."

He swore softly. She could almost hear his mattress creak as he came to his feet. She could see him switching on lights, rubbing that heavy growth on his jaw. "I want you to tell me what happened, *exactly*," he demanded.

"You already—"

"No. I don't. You've got to believe that. Now tell me."

She played along, amazed by his calm, by the fact that he thought her so gullible. "Now you tell *me*," she finished, "why I should think it was anyone *but* you."

"Damn," he said, temporarily losing that rigid control, "you should at least know that much about me, Kamisha. I'm not a killer. I'm not dishonest. But you, lady, are in serious trouble."

"No fooling."

"Listen, I'll try to forget this accusation. What I want you to do is this. I—"

"Come off it, John," she said, her anger welling up inside her again. "Brigitte knows what happened, and so does my lawyer," she said, lying. "If you pull another stunt like that, you'll never see the light of day again except through bars."

There was pulsing silence on the phone.

"You think I'm a dumb female, don't you? You're just like all the rest, *Mr.* Leopardo. But you've got my number all wrong. I know someone tampered with my brakes. It was no accident."

"Look," he said finally, his tone reasonable, though exasperation showed through, "I want you to go and stay with friends. You're not to be alone, Kamisha. I'm going to find out who's behind this. I swear it to you. But, meanwhile, don't do anything foolish."

"The foolish thing I did," she said, "was going to you in the first place."

"Kamisha, I—"

"Skip it, John. Just get off my back. I can play hardball, too."

Abruptly Kamisha slammed the receiver down. She dropped into the chair, let out a whistling breath between her teeth and then smiled shakily. Kamisha Hammill, a nobody, had just stuck it to Mafia king John Leopardo. An enormous feeling of satisfaction swept her. It was as if she'd just crossed the finish line a tenth of a second ahead of everyone.

CHAPTER SEVEN

KAMISHA ROLLED OVER, kicked the sheet off and promptly fell back into a deep sleep. And there it was again, the big, heavy black sedan, the kind you saw in thirties gangster movies. There was a faceless driver, and even as he steered with one hand, he leaned out the window and began blasting away at her with a Tommy gun. She was on foot. Running, running...

"Kamisha. Kamisha, wake up. You're having a bad dream."

Kamisha jerked awake, gasping, trying to run. But it was only Brigitte in her bedroom, shaking her. "My God," Brigitte was saying, "you're soaked with sweat. Are you okay?"

"Oh, Brigitte," Kamisha said, half gasping, "that dream. Oh, my Lord."

"Nightmare, huh?"

"Oh, a whopper. Oh, brother." She felt her head. It was drenched. And her pajamas, too. She looked down at herself as if someone else were in her body.

"I knocked and knocked," Brigitte was explaining, "so I used the spare key out front. God, I was worried."

"*You* were worried."

"Yeah, well, it isn't every day my friend tells me someone's trying to kill her." Brigitte got up off the side of the bed and straightened her skirt. "I'll go make some coffee and you get showered. We'll go to breakfast. Okay?"

"Yeah, sure, okay." She came to her feet a little unsteadily. "What time is it?"

"You'll kill me," Brigitte called over her shoulder, "but it's seven-thirty. I couldn't sleep so well after you left."

Kamisha sat back down. Brigitte, up at this hour? Something must really be bothering her. Then, as if to punctuate the early-morning hour, a persistent bird, a flicker, was calling from one of the tall cottonwood trees in the front yard, a raucous call, repeated over and over until, with a rustle of leaves and a flutter of feathers, it flew away.

It was Sunday. Sunday morning, Kamisha thought. A glorious-looking day. Cool out. Absolutely clear. She could smell newly mown grass somewhere, and more birds were calling from trees across the street. Well, she wasn't going to waste such a precious day worrying about John Leopardo and what he might or might not do. The summers were too short at eight thousand feet, rare and doubly priceless because of their brevity. Winter was brilliant and starkly beautiful, spring was a long time in making up its mind to behave decently, autumn was lovely and golden, but summer was perfection.

There were a dozen things she could do that day. She could play tennis or hike to Crater Lake. She could drive down the valley and ride a horse at a friend's ranch, or go to the music tent and listen to the Aspen Festival Orchestra dress rehearsal for its Sunday concert. Aspen was full of things to do.

But Kamisha lingered on the side of her bed, thinking. Maybe it wasn't such a great idea to go off by herself. Maybe John Leopardo had new plans for her now that the old ones had failed.

"Are you in the shower yet?"

Kamisha shook herself. "Just climbing in!" Yes, he might well be formulating something at this very minute. On the other hand, she thought as she slid out of her damp pajamas and tossed them into the wicker hamper, he might have been telling her the truth last night. She hadn't considered that. She'd been too strung out, too angry. But what if he hadn't been responsible for her accident? What if he was really checking into the incident, truly concerned about her? He'd sounded worried. Or had she just been hearing what she wanted to hear?

When she was dressed, Brigitte shoved a coffee mug into her hand. "You've got circles under your eyes, my dear."

"Yeah? So do you."

"Um."

"Where do you want to eat? I'm famished."

"Oh, I don't know. The Wienerstube or the Main Street Café or something." Brigitte draped herself on a kitchen chair. "Say, what were you dreaming about up there? You were a mess."

Kamisha took a swallow of her coffee. "A Mafia hit. On *me*."

Brigitte paled. "Don't say that. Seriously."

"And that's not all." Kamisha hesitated. But what the heck. She'd end up telling Brigitte eventually, anyway. "I called John in New York last night."

"No way...you didn't."

"I did. I had to. I couldn't help it, Brigitte." She began to pace back and forth in her small kitchen. "He had to know, darn it. I wasn't about to let him think he'd gotten away with trying to kill me!"

"Kamisha." Brigitte ran a hand over her face. She was really upset. "Do you realize what you're doing? You're flying off half-cocked, accusing a man of murder. This is serious. This is no game."

"I know that."

"Look, you don't even know for sure it wasn't an accident. You don't know who did it if it *was* deliberate. You're guessing. You haven't a thing to go on."

"It was no accident, Brigitte."

"You can't prove that. You can't even prove somebody meant to hurt you. Maybe they tampered with the wrong car. You don't *know* anything!"

Kamisha stopped and stared at her friend. "You sound like you're trying to defend Leopardo, for God's sake, Brigitte."

"I'm not!" she cried, agitated. "I've never laid eyes on the guy. I'm just trying to convince you how crazy you sound. You're paranoid!"

"Oh, no, I'm not. I upset the applecart, and somebody wants me out of the way. I told you what Simons said. Cement shoes in the East River!"

Brigitte put her head in her hands. "You're blowing this up into something it isn't. Leave it alone. If John Leopardo is involved in these parties, he'll fire you, that's all. Stop being so dramatic. God! You're addicted to trouble. You love it."

"*I* didn't hold those parties, Brigitte. *I* didn't start this whole mess," Kamisha said angrily.

"No, but you sure made it a lot worse."

"Was I just supposed to stand by and watch Rick Simons be a dirty old man and keep my mouth shut about it?"

"Yes, damn it. That would have been a whole lot better!"

"I don't believe it. I don't believe you said that. They could invite your daughter to one of those parties in a couple of years, and you think I should have let it drop?"

"What does Tracy have to do with it? You think these are the only parties with young girls in the world? Are you going to go around stopping all of them? My friend, the crusader!"

Kamisha couldn't believe Brigitte's attitude. Sure, her friend was a little lax at times, but this was too much. "You don't believe what you're saying. I know you don't."

"I believe it, Kamisha. I think you're a troublemaker."

"And I think you're totally unable to face reality because you and Bullet have been drinking together too much."

Frozen silence filled the room. Brigitte's face was pallid with anger. She took a deep breath and drew herself up to her full height. "And I think," Brigitte said quietly, venomously, "that you're jealous of me, and I think you're a workaholic so you don't ever have to face the fact that you don't have a man." Brigitte grabbed her purse and turned to leave. "And never mind breakfast. I'd rather eat alone," she said icily.

Kamisha stood in the still-paralyzing silence of her house after Brigitte left. She stayed there, unmoving, for a long time until she started trembling, and then she sank down into a chair and put her face in her hands.

"Oh, God," she whispered through her fingers. It was always the same, the wrenching sense of abandonment and betrayal. How could she surround herself with people who continually hurt her?

She sat there and cried and felt all that tearing emptiness again, and it occurred to her that maybe there was nothing wrong with the people around her. Maybe *she* was the one who was flawed. Maybe she brought out the worst in people. Maybe it was all her fault.

SHE WAS STILL UPSET on Monday, but she was awfully good at hiding her feelings. She'd had years of practice, and she knew no one at the club would come close to guessing what was going on inside her.

She avoided Rick like the plague. He was one person she wasn't up to dealing with today. She'd played tennis early that morning, her usual Monday morning mixed doubles match, with the usual club members. She'd had only one crisis, luckily—the aerobics instructor for the ten o'clock class had called in sick, and Kamisha had taken it over for twenty minutes until the replacement had arrived. The members enjoyed having Kamisha up there on the platform sweating along with them; they thought she was a good sport. Or so Rick Simons had told her. He'd said it was good for business. He'd even joked—in the past—that he'd take on an aerobics class once in a while if he looked better in tights. That had been when he and Kamisha had gotten along, back before she knew what kind of man Rick really was.

She stayed in open areas where there were people around constantly. Just as she'd done on Sunday. She wondered if she was going to have to spend the rest of her life in safe, crowded places. Maybe Brigitte was right, she thought once. Maybe she never should have opened her mouth in the first place. But then how could she have lived with herself?

Kamisha returned to her office to answer her mail, to set up a schedule for free visiting days for potential new members, to attend to a dozen other details.

Usually she spoke to Rick about now, just to check on everything, but she wouldn't today. She sat over her desk, still in a damp leotard, and leafed through the mail.

There were the usual brochures from other clubs across the country, trade magazines, invitations to club openings... A photograph on the front of one such invitation caught her eye. Yes, it was John's new club in Costa Rica, announcing its grand opening. There was mention of a Panamerican Trade Conference to be held there in honor of the new facility, and Kamisha frowned.

He hadn't mentioned the Panamerican Trade Conference. How nice for John and his new club. Did he have some kind of undue influence in Latin America, too? Did his underlings down there, drug lords and thugs, coerce men in high places to plan their meeting at John's club?

She tapped the pen she was holding against her chin. John. She had to admit the truth to herself—she'd wanted him to turn out differently from all the rest. When he didn't try to persuade her into his bedroom, she'd been at a loss, beside herself with a wild, crazy new sense of pleasure—happiness more pure than anything in her experience. No wonder she'd been confused.

But it had all been an illusion. A clever sleight of hand.

She glanced up to see Rick passing by her door. His eyes were straight ahead. Good, she thought. She didn't know how long she could continue this way, though, pretending around the guests and the other employees, smiling, acting as if everything was okay. She'd have to quit, Kamisha thought; they'd force her to—John and Rick. A formidable pair. And maybe it was for the best. She didn't know what she could do about the parties, but she'd figure something out. Whether she quit or stayed.

Suddenly she laughed. Maybe she'd go to the FBI, and they'd put her in the Witness Protection Program: a new identity, new home, sometimes a new face. Who would miss her, anyway?

Kamisha's grim amusement was interrupted by a call from Joel, the head maintenance man. "Miss Hammill, the showers in the men's locker room are leaking down into the conference room. You've got a luncheon set up there for the hospital staff. What do you want me to do?"

Oh, Lord. "Let me think. Darn it, Joel, I thought you had those pipes fixed."

"So did I, Miss Hammill."

"Well, have the crew move everything to the covered terrace in back. Just close the terrace off for lunch customers today. Put up a sign."

"Okay, Miss Hammill."

"And pray that it doesn't rain this afternoon."

Kamisha showered in the locker room and changed into tan slacks and a dark green camp shirt. She pulled her hair back into a big vertical clasp that kept it out of her way and put on lipstick.

She grabbed a sandwich at the coffee bar, then stopped in at the hospital staff luncheon. It was going well, the slightly dotty but lovable chief of staff telling his usual jokes. No one there had any idea their lunch had been scheduled for the conference room up until 11: 30 a.m. Another calamity averted.

All afternoon Kamisha sat at her desk clearing up details, working on the benefit for the substance abuse conference that was coming up in September. She was getting responses from some celebrities already. Substance abuse was a popular cause these days. Maybe she could even get Betty Ford to come; yes, the former First Lady did interviews. Mrs. Ford could dash over just for the evening from her place at Vail, only a hundred miles away. She'd write her a letter.

What Kamisha really wanted to do was to call Brigitte and apologize. This couldn't be the end of their friendship. It just couldn't. They'd weathered many storms together, bad ones, but they'd always held their friendship above their disagreements. Surely they could do that this time, too. She wished Brigitte would call her. Probably Brigitte felt equally as bad and was eyeing the phone just as she was. But Brigitte could be stubborn, and Kamisha, well, she wasn't sure what to say or how to say it this time. If Brigitte wasn't on her side in this mess, she didn't know what she was going to do.

The substance abuse benefit. She should get a big-name athlete—Michael Jordon of basketball or John Elway of the Denver Broncos football team, somebody like that. Most of them were willing to speak at benefits. She made a note to herself, then stared, unfocused, into the distance. Here she was planning a substance abuse benefit when the manager of the club was breaking the law using minors as prostitutes. Dear Lord. That was child abuse.

How could Rick do it? How could John do it? What did they see when they looked at themselves in their mirrors?

Maybe John didn't approve, though. Maybe it was Rick all alone who had had her brakes "adjusted." It was possible. He knew her car. He might have found out about her jaunt to New York. Sure. And maybe John was confronting Rick right now, calling from his New York office, from behind that stark, neat desk. Or he could be checking up on her story, phoning some of the guests who had attended Rick's parties, asking what really went on.

Perhaps Rick *was* throwing the parties all alone. It would be easy for him as manager of the club, really simple. No one would question his use of the VIP condo. Kamisha finding out was a problem, though. He'd tried to shut her up by threatening her with John, but when that didn't work, maybe he'd decided to get rid of her.

A shadow, a flitting movement outside Kamisha's window caught her eye. She held her breath. Dear God, she was alone in her office!

Kamisha could barely move. But there had been someone, something, lurking outside her window. She'd seen it.

Abruptly it reappeared. Her heart nearly burst out of her chest. But it was a kid, twelve, maybe thirteen years old. He saw her in the window and grinned, holding up a tennis ball to explain his presence behind the building.

Immediately Kamisha was on her feet, cranking open the glass. "Are you kids slamming balls over the roof again?" she demanded.

"Not us, Miss Hammill," he said with all the innocence of Jack the Ripper before he scooted off and disappeared.

Kamisha sank back into her chair. She was losing it. And just when she needed a buddy the most, Brigitte had gone all crazy on her, too. What the heck was happening?

It wasn't a minute later that the phone rang on her desk. She jumped a little, then pursed her lips. *Get a grip, woman.* She picked up the receiver.

"Miss Hammill, this is Jody at the front desk. There's someone here to see you."

"Okay, I'll be there in a minute. Hey, it's not the plumber, is it? He should see Joel."

"No, it's definitely not the plumber."

She walked down the corridor toward the lobby, covering a yawn with her hand; she hadn't been sleeping well, too many bad dreams. She'd like to go home and curl up with a good book. Or go to a nice, funny movie with Brigitte. No, not now, not with Brigitte. Oh, damn.

A man stood by the reception desk. She recognized him instantly and with utter shock.

"Hello, Miss Hammill," he said. "You're looking fine."

"Inky?"

"Yeah, it's me." He grinned at her.

She tried to fit her mind around the fact of his presence there. "What...?"

"John sent me. He wants to see you."

"In New York? But I..."

Inky chuckled. "Naw, he's here. We flew in this morning."

"John. *Here?*"

"Yeah. Seems there was a little problem he had to take care of."

Kamisha cleared her throat. "Where...ah...where is he?"

"In his condo, the VIP condo."

"Oh, right."

"So, Miss Hammill, can you come right now, or did I get you in the middle of something?"

"No, no, I mean, I'm not doing anything special. I can come now." But suddenly she paused. Was she truly nuts? Ambling along with Inky like a lamb to slaughter. She'd be alone with the two of them and—

But Inky seemed to be reading her mind. "It's okay, Miss Hammill," he said, nodding toward the door. "Mr. Leopardo told me to tell you that."

"Oh," she said, "he did, did he?"

"Yes, ma'am."

"So I can go along with you. Just like that?"

"Yes, ma'am," he repeated. Then, quietly, he said, "John's not what you think. You got my word on that."

"And I should trust you?"

He smiled. "Absolutely."

Kamisha cocked her head, studying this impressive man. She believed him. At least she believed that John Leopardo wasn't going to try anything on the club's premises. He was dangerous, true, but certainly not a fool.

She turned to the girl at the desk and said, very deliberately, "Jody, I'll be in Mr. Leopardo's condo if anyone wants me, okay? Let's go," she said to Inky decisively, feeling just that little spurt of familiar excitement, the kick.

They walked out of the lobby through the double front doors, down the steps to the winding path that led to the parking lot and the condominium buildings. Kamisha saw nothing—not the neatly white-clad tennis players or the girl weeding flower beds or the young man on crutches headed toward the therapy clinic. She was marveling at the thoughts that crowded her brain.

John, here. John wanted to see her. Why? What for? Was he truly worried about her, or was he planning a showdown with her—firing her? Had he come to charm her, to learn about her, to convince or to—

"You had a little trouble with your car, I hear," Inky said.

"Does he tell you everything?" she asked, striding alongside his big frame.

"Everything that matters," the man said. "He told me someone tampered with your brakes."

"Yes, someone did."

"Have you told the police?"

"Only the ones in Dillon, where it happened. I filled out a routine report."

"That'll do a lot of good."

"I know."

The sun filtered through the trees and dappled the walk. John, here. She'd see him in a few minutes. Would he act the same here? Would he still carry that aura of absolute control? Maybe he'd be diminished somehow here in Aspen, away from the accoutrements of his power. Maybe he'd look like a city slicker, too formal, ill at ease in the deliberate casualness of this resort town.

Maybe he was here to gauge her reactions, to figure out another way to get rid of her. Yes, he'd need to see her in person, to judge whether she would go running to the police, or if she already had. Sure, he'd told Inky to ask her that question. *Be careful,* she reminded herself. *John Leopardo is a dangerous man. You can't trust him.*

"Sure is nice and cool here after the city," Inky remarked.

"You still have that heat wave?" she asked, forcing the conversation.

"Yeah. Hot as Hades in New York."

The worst part was that she actually wanted to see John, ached to look into those black, hooded eyes, to discover what secrets they held. She wanted to watch him move with restrained dignity, using his cane. Why did he fascinate her so?

Be careful, she thought again.

Abruptly she recognized the way her heart beat too heavily, the way her mouth had dried up. She felt exactly the same as if she were racing down a ski run in a blizzard, half blind, exhilarated, tempting fate. She glanced upward to the condo. The sun had set behind the mountain, and the building looked dark and somehow sinister, its curtains drawn, its windows blank, unseeing eyes, its bulk suddenly, unnervingly, unfamiliar.

CHAPTER EIGHT

JOHN HADN'T REMEMBERED how intensely Kamisha struck him. It hit him again, as it had the first time he'd seen her, like a blow in the solar plexus. Her strength, her carriage, the brilliance of her coloring, the flash in her eye. There was so much more to her, he thought, so much to learn, to know, beyond what she allowed a person to see. Just like him. They were kindred spirits.

And she believed someone had tried to kill her.

"Kamisha, good to see you," he said, taking her hand.

"Is it, John?" She withdrew her hand a little too quickly. She gave nothing away, but he sensed she was nervous. Nervous and wary.

"Please, sit down. A drink?"

She shook her head and seated herself on a white couch. Yes, she was edgy, but then she thought he'd tried to have her killed. He turned away to give her a moment to gather herself, made his way to the bar and poured himself a fresh-squeezed orange juice.

"So, John, what brings you here so soon again?" she asked.

He turned slowly and looked at her. "Kamisha, I told you I admire honesty. Let's have no games between us. Your call brings me, what else?"

She sat with one knee up, her hands locked around it. She jiggled her foot and stared at him. "Sorry," she said. "I guess that was a dumb question."

His leg was stiff from the flight out to Aspen, and he was walking badly. He was acutely aware of her eyes on him as he limped toward her, then lowered himself into a chair, leaning his cane against the seat. "Okay, let's start over. Tell me how you are. No more accidents, I take it?"

"No. But maybe it's only lack of opportunity."

"You've been staying with friends, I hope? I should have thought to offer you this condo. The security is very good here."

She smiled. "Here? You must be kidding."

"Oh, I forgot. Naturally, if I'd tried to kill you, this would be the perfect place to try again," he said reasonably.

Studiously she refused him a reply.

"Where are you staying then?"

"At home."

"Alone?"

"Yes, I—"

"Kamisha, that's really not in your best interests, if you'll allow me to say so."

"You can say it." She shrugged. "But no one makes me leave my own house."

Oh, she was stubborn. Gloriously stubborn. There was that strength, that daring, the attribute that made her so very, very fine and special.

How to handle her? He sipped his juice and studied her and wondered. It occurred to him that he couldn't handle her. No one could. She couldn't be handled, only convinced by love and understanding and trust.

"You don't trust me," he said.

"I don't know you."

"You accused me of trying to murder you. You were pretty explicit about not trusting me."

She looked away. "I was upset."

"Understandably. I've been under fire myself. It makes you act rashly." He turned the glass in his fingers and stared at it, frowning. "Ever since you called I've been trying to figure out how to prove to you that I had nothing to do with your accident. It's a very awkward position to be in as your employer. I'm not enjoying it."

"I'm not enjoying myself much, either," she said coldly.

"I appreciate your frankness," he said with a tinge of irony in his voice. "Be that as it may, I've come up with an idea. It had to be done, anyway, and I thought it might clear the air. Help our little impasse."

"Oh?" She eyed him with suspicion, and he got the distinct impression that she was poised to flee, on guard, judging his every move.

"Kamisha," he said, leaning toward her, "you're safe here. I won't hurt you." He put a hand on her knee and felt her flinch. "I have never harmed a human being except in war, and then I viewed it as my sworn duty.'' He held her gaze for a long moment. ''Do you believe me?''

She returned his look, her dark brows drawn together. ''You want the truth?''

''Always.''

''I don't know. I'd like to believe you.''

''I'm guessing that my family is a problem. I can only tell you again that I have no contact with my father and nothing to do with his business.'' He wondered if he was wasting his breath; his past was so pervasive in his life that he had to fight it every day, every hour. He had to fight the battle for his beliefs and reputation again and again. And how many people really believed him? He clenched his teeth, feeling the familiar frustration wash through him. This time it mattered so very much that he convince her of the truth.

''I've asked Rick to join us,'' he said abruptly, tired of the struggle, tired of the way she was looking at him with accusation in those lovely eyes.

''Rick?''

''Why not? I'm going to ask him straight out about the parties. It's time to get to the bottom of this.''

She'd straightened, her expression puzzled. ''Do you want me to leave?''

''No. Why would I want you to leave? I think you should be here.'' He made his voice deliberately hard, testing her.

''Will you stand behind me on this?'' she asked. ''You believe me?''

''I'll stand behind the truth, yes.''

''He'll lie,'' she said.

''I'll judge that.''

''He'll fire me on the spot,'' she said. ''He'll have to. My job's on the line.''

John gave a short laugh. He got up, took his cane, walked across to the bar to set his glass down and turned to face her. ''In case you've forgotten, Kamisha, Rick Simons works for me. I own the Ute City Club. Either you want this matter brought out into the open and taken care of or you don't. Which is it?''

She eyed him steadily. ''Yes, I want it taken care of. It's just that your methods are a little...well, I guess unorthodox.''

''I abhor games. You came to New York to tell me about this

problem. I assumed you wanted me to do something about it. I told you I would. I keep my word.''

"It's a beautiful club," she said, "and I've worked very hard to make it successful. Nothing should spoil its reputation. I appreciate your concern." She spoke stiffly and fiddled with the collar of her blouse, a deep forest-green against her tanned neck. Her fingers were slim, with short nails and no polish. He wondered inadvertently how those fingers would feel on his skin. His gaze rose to her neck again, to the long silver-blond tendrils of hair that had escaped their clasp and curled, clinging to her skin. He felt suddenly tongue-tied. There were words churning around in his head, but he couldn't get hold of them. He was aware of Kamisha studying his face, and he wondered if his expression was as implacable as he hoped. He spoke often of the truth, to Kamisha he had, anyway. Perhaps he owed her yet another truth. Perhaps he should tell her of his innermost—

There was a knock on the door. Kamisha's head swiveled sharply. She looked at him. He nodded and went to the door and opened it.

"Mr. Leopardo, you wanted to see me?" Rick said. He had his normal breezy way about him—the easy smile, the casual clothes, the predator-sharp look in his eye.

He noticed Kamisha the minute he was inside the door. John saw him stiffen and saw the color drain from his skin, saw the rictus of muscles that turned instantly into a broad smile.

"Well, well, Kamisha. I didn't know you knew Mr. Leopardo," Rick said.

"We met very recently," John answered for her. "She visited me in New York."

Rick looked from one to the other, assessing, knowing, planning his escape like a wild creature caught in the fatal glare of a spotlight. John knew then. Rick was behind the parties, using the club as his private brothel, pocketing dirty money from the likes of Senator Stern and his cronies. Providing entertainment, young girls, the club's food and liquor in a classy, private, exclusive setting. Perfect. Lucrative. Discreet.

Rick was a pimp, pure and simple. John wasn't sure he could keep the man in his employ under any circumstances.

Rick put his hands in his pockets and stood in the center of the room, legs straddled. "Was there something you wanted?" he asked. "I'm pretty busy this afternoon."

"I'm sure you are, Rick, but this'll only take a minute." John shifted his cane to the other hand. "I've heard an unpleasant story about some parties you've had here in this condo, Rick. Parties with underage girls. Is this true?"

Rick blanched. "Who said that?" he blustered. "What son of a—"

"Kamisha told me," John said curtly. "She said she'd taken it up with you, and when you wouldn't listen, she came to New York to tell me. Are you denying her accusations?"

"Yes, of course I am. How dare she say that? What's she talking about?" Rick mouthed the words, but John suspected he was only saying what was expected.

"Another thing, Rick. She told me you said I was the one behind these parties, that I condoned them. I take real exception to that."

"She's lying," Rick muttered.

"I don't think so," John said quietly. "Why should she lie about it?"

"It's pretty obvious. She's a tough lady. She's ambitious. She wants my job, Mr. Leopardo. She's been scheming to get it from the minute I hired her. She's trying to get rid of me, the—"

"That's enough, Rick. Let's not have any name calling around here."

"You don't believe her, do you? God, she went behind my back and..." Rick was moving around in agitation, shooting scathing looks at Kamisha. But she only sat there, upright, lovely, her face washed clean of any feelings, her eyes taking everything in.

"I'm afraid I do believe her, Rick. She's given me the name of one of the local girls who was at the last party. I'll reserve final judgment until I consider all the facts, but I think, Rick, that I'm really going to have to reconsider your fitness for your position. I will not abide dishonesty in my management."

"You have no proof at all, not one bit. I didn't do it, Mr. Leopardo. You've got to believe me."

"I'll take it under consideration," John said.

"Mr. Leopardo, it isn't true. I wouldn't do a thing like that. You can't believe her."

"You know, Rick, I could go to the police with this. I have several reasons not to at this point. The reputation of the club, the lack of absolute proof. Let's leave it at that for now, why don't we."

"Kamisha." Rick turned to her, his hands out in a theatrical gesture. "Come on, enough of this. It's gone far enough. Tell him you made it up. For God's sake, Kamisha, I always treated you well, didn't I?''

"Yes, you did, Rick. But I told John the truth, and I can't change that. I'm sorry," she said.

Rick looked from one to the other, and his mouth twitched in a bitter smile. "Okay, I got the picture now. I can't fight what you've got going for you, Kamisha. Hey, I can't compete with that. Fine. You want your girlfriend in the top spot, Mr. Leopardo. I can't argue. Just don't make up stories about me to put her there.''

"You're disgusting, Rick," Kamisha said hotly, half rising.

He held a hand up. "Far be it from me to come between true love. I'll leave without a fuss."

"Don't push me, Rick," John said, his voice as cold as death. "I'm a fair man, but I will not be pushed."

"Nah, you don't need to do the pushing, do you? You got men you can call. Okay, I'm going. I'm going nice and quiet. But you're making a big mistake."

"Are you threatening me, Rick?" John asked quietly. He could feel his temper boiling, bubbling under his tightly controlled surface. The temper he'd fought so long to restrain. It was always references to his family that ignited it, his family and their Mob connections.

Rick took a step back. "No, Mr. Leopardo, hell, no."

"You can leave now," John said tightly, grasping the knob of his cane with both hands, holding on to it hard.

Rick was pale. He gave Kamisha a look, then John. He backed to the door, felt for the doorknob, turned it and let himself out. The door shut with finality behind him.

John let out a breath he'd been holding for too long and willed his fingers to relax their grip. He wanted to swear and throw his cane across the room. But, no, control, that was the only thing he had to hang on to. *Keep under control. Don't let anyone see that you're human, that you feel. Don't risk it.*

He turned to Kamisha. She was watching him speculatively, probably trying to figure out if he'd arranged this little farce to convince her of his innocence.

"I'm sorry you had to be part of that," he said to her. "Maybe you were right. I should have done it alone."

"His pride was hurt. I feel sorry for him," she said.

"Have you considered," John said slowly, "that Rick may have had your brakes tampered with?"

"Yes," she said. "I considered it. I suppose it's possible. He had the motivation. I'm not sure how he knew I was going to see you in New York, though."

"Did you tell anyone at the club?"

"No, only my friend Brigitte. And I told her not to let Rick know."

John paced, leaning on his cane. "I see. But it's possible he found out."

"I suppose so," she said doubtfully.

"I'd like to solve this problem. If Rick was responsible, you're still in danger. Even more danger."

"So are you," she said.

"I have Inky."

"Ah, yes, Inky."

John went to the bar again. He felt restless, not quite sure how to proceed from here. He should let Kamisha go, warn her about staying alone again, follow up on Rick to find out who had fixed the brakes on Kamisha's car. He should be thinking about who was going to manage the Ute City Club if he had to fire Rick. And there was the Montaña y Mar in Costa Rica. Business matters, vital concerns. There was no time in John's life for anything but business; he'd carefully structured it that way.

He found himself asking, "Would you like a drink now, Kamisha? I think I'll have one."

"Maybe a glass of wine."

They were being so careful with each other, both of them so terribly inhibited. Rick's insinuations had made them too aware of each other as male and female, too aware of what happened normally between men and women. If Rick only knew how very far he was from the truth.

He handed her the glass and wine and sat down, nursing his own drink. He wondered fleetingly if Kamisha believed him innocent, but then he couldn't know that, not yet. Her presence was enough, and he suspected that she'd stay if only because she was tempted by a challenge. "This isn't over yet," he finally said. "I have to find out more about the parties. Rick may not be working alone." He hesitated, swirling the ice in his drink. "You could leave, you know, take a vacation, get out of the way for a while."

"I don't run, John."

"It's a suggestion." He shrugged. He was pleased with her reaction, proud of her. Absurd of him. God, she upset his orderly life, made him feel things he didn't want to feel, had locked away for years. Youthful, futile dreams of a girlfriend, a wife, a family. But he'd decided long ago that he could never ask a wife and children to put up with his Mafia family, to put up with the bloodthirsty press that, to this day, found him guilty without a trial.

He held her eye. She was smiling slightly, covering up whatever uneasiness she felt. She was very cool, very poised, too damn beautiful.

"Come to dinner with me tonight," he said. "I don't know Aspen very well. You pick the place."

Their eyes met in acknowledgment of the challenge. She lifted the wineglass and sipped before she answered. "Are you sure it's advisable?" she finally asked.

"Yes, I'm sure."

She lifted her shoulders, then let them drop. As if it was unimportant to her, a thing of no consequence. Yet he didn't believe that for a moment. "All right, then. But I've got to change." She gestured at her casual attire.

"Inky will drive you home. Is that acceptable?"

"Sure, why not."

"May I ask where we're going?" he inquired.

"No," she said, giving him a smile, "I haven't decided yet."

When she was gone, John showered and changed. Aspen formal, they called it. Even an infrequent visitor like John knew enough not to wear a suit and tie out to dinner in Aspen. He wore white summer slacks, a white polo shirt and a beige slubbed-silk sport coat. He was ready too soon, far too soon. He wandered out onto the deck of the apartment, sat in a wrought-iron chair, leaned back and drank in the champagne-dry summer air, the warmth of the evening sun.

This woman excited him. He hadn't realized how isolated he'd become, how cut off from the reality of most human beings. Other men had wives or lovers. They fought and made love and nagged each other. It was messy, untidy, all uncontrolled feelings and emotional highs and lows. But it was life. What John was living was an artificial, insulated existence. Safe but empty. Now he'd met a woman he wanted, but he wasn't sure just what he wanted from her.

Did he want sex? Did he want companionship, friendship, love? Or was it merely a temporary flirtation, a passing lust?

He caressed the knob of his cane, felt its familiar smooth hardness and wondered whether he dared exchange its sterile support for that of a woman's warm, responsive flesh.

And yet... He felt instinctively that he could have something special with Kamisha. She needed someone to love and understand her, to calm her fears and earn her trust. Her vulnerability melted that frozen spot in him where his feelings lived. And like any frostbitten flesh, as it thawed out, it demonstrated that it was still alive by hurting like the very devil.

He hadn't learned to hurt yet when he was fourteen years old. He remembered those days with longing and guilt; longing for the security and happiness, guilt because John hadn't yet realized what business his father was in and still loved him unreservedly.

He gazed out at the mountainside, its lower part bathed in evening shadow, and let himself remember. It was the dinners, he guessed, that he recalled with such affection. His mother, Lucille, used any excuse for a feast. Birthdays, first communions, holidays—any celebration would do. It was one way of getting Gio to stop thinking about business and a way to lure his sister Camille and her family to the old house in Brooklyn. Camille was ten years older than John. She'd married Henry young and had twins already, spoiled little terrors, who called John "Unca Johnny."

Then there was Aunt Jessie, Lucille's spinster sister, who always came to any family gathering, a few assorted cousins, business pals of Gio, and—always—Mario. Glum-faced Mario with his Italian accent, heavy features and curly black hair. He was always there when Gio was home, and he went wherever Gio went. His chauffeur. In those days John had never thought to question Mario's presence or the omnipresent bulge beneath the breast of his dark suit. Back then the man was as familiar and comfortable as an old piece of furniture.

It must have been Thanksgiving, John thought, the one when the twins were three and Camille was pregnant again. He remembered that holiday in particular because everyone made fun of how his voice was changing.

"He's growing, so what can I say?" his father said proudly, the chewed cigar butt stuck firmly in his teeth. "He'll be tall, a real American, a regular John Wayne."

"Remember, Lucille," Aunt Jessie put in, "Uncle Louie was tall. That's where Johnny gets it from."

"Sure, I remember Uncle Louie. We thought he was a giant," John's mother replied.

"No, Lucille," Gio said, "you forget my grandfather from Palermo on my father's side. He was a big man. Johnny has his nose, too. No doubt about it."

Everyone had an opinion. Family or as close as family. They all talked about him while they ate the turkey, the pasta, the American pumpkin pie, the Italian gelati. And they *cared* about him. Every time anyone got up from the long table to walk by, he'd tousle John's hair, chuck the twins under their fat, dirty chins, clap an old friend on the shoulder, lean down to kiss a lady's cheek. There was always touching, kissing, embracing. Love. Love all around, fierce, protective love. Sometimes stifling but always there, unquestioning, utterly dependable.

Sure, he squirmed when they teased him about his voice and the fuzz on his upper lip, but he didn't mind, not really. It wasn't mean-spirited teasing.

His mother sat at one end of the table, beaming, the lady bountiful, the living cornucopia of all this largesse, the reason why all of them were together at this feast.

"Very good, Lucille," Gio would invariably say. "You outdid yourself."

"I'm bursting, Ma," Camille groaned. "There's no room inside me anymore."

"Eat, darling. It's good for the baby. Eat," Lucille said, beaming.

"How's football?" Henry always asked John. "You catching those passes?" Henry had played football in high school, but now he was getting chubby. John swore he'd never let himself get that way.

"Pretty good. I made a touchdown last game."

"Good boy," Henry said.

"He'll get hurt, Lucille," Jessie said, shaking her head. "Football."

"Ah, it's good for him," Gio replied proudly. "Toughen him up."

Lucille shared a look with her sister: *men, what can you do?*

They talked at one another, all at the same time, across one another, spilling the deep red wine on the white tablecloth, dribbling gravy and tomato sauce, arguing, gesturing widely in one another's faces, the women yak-yak-yakking, gossip, stories, children, sales in department stores. The men in a lower key—sports, cars, the new hippie generation. Everyone talking knowledgeably, self-importantly.

The twins got bored and slipped under the table to play among the heavy fluted table legs that were like standing elephants, crawling over everyone's feet, trying to tie shoelaces together.

John had done that when he was small, but now he was nearly grown, and the men included him in their conversation.

He could see them as if he were there, the big bellies of the men, their suspenders. He could smell the reeking cigar smoke and garlic and roast turkey, feel his full stomach and sense of belonging, of being beloved.

But that was a long time ago.

INKY RETURNED to fetch John at seven. "She's got this cute little house over in the West End, boss. Real cozy. It surprised me."

John sat in the back of the sedan and listened to Inky's opinions, something he did often. "Why were you surprised?" he asked.

"Well, she's so cool and sophisticated. I figured her for something more in character." Inky turned onto Main Street, heading west into the setting sun. "You know, more like your place."

Interesting. Kamisha chose to surround herself with cuteness and coziness. That said something about her.

"Right up here," Inky was saying, turning left off Main Street onto a side street that led toward the base of Aspen Mountain. "She's something, boss. If I wasn't married..." And Inky chuckled, putting John on the way he always did.

"Keep your nose out of my affairs," John said lightly. "This is a business date."

"Oh, sure." Inky rolled his eyes in the rearview mirror. "You shaved three times today for a business dinner. Right, boss."

"Goddamn it, Inky—"

"We're here, boss. You want to cuss me out in front of the lady, fine."

She was waiting before her house, dressed in a bright pink silk tunic and matching pants. The evening breeze tugged at the fabric, molding it against her breasts and thighs, then letting it drape into lines that touched shoulder, hip, knee. Inky opened the door for her, and she slid in, bringing with her the aroma of fresh air and shampoo and intoxicating femininity.

"Hello, Kamisha."

"Hello, John."

She sat near the door, as far from him as possible. She was still vigilant, alert for any move he might make. But she was there, with him, and he was confident that he could win her over and prove his innocence. "So, where are we going?" he asked.

"The Pine Creek Cookhouse," she replied. "It's up at Ashcroft, a ghost town about twenty miles away. I made a reservation. Do you mind the distance?"

"No, it gives me a chance to see more of this area. I've never been past the airport. Do you need directions, Inky?"

"Naw, I looked at a map. Ashcroft's on Castle Creek Road, right? Turn at the light out of town and past the hospital?"

"That's it."

Her hair was twisted up in a silver clasp, and tendrils lay on her neck. She wore no earrings, no jewelry of any sort.

"I hope you like this place. It's a bit different. It's an old log cabin, and the food and setting are very special. The ghost town is nearby. It used to be as big as Aspen."

"Sounds delightful."

She was relaxing a little, he thought. Enjoying herself. If she'd spend time with him, he was sure he could learn what made her tick, make her believe in him. But did he have that time?

They drove up a long, narrow valley. On the highest peaks snow still lingered. The mountainsides were deep, dark green, covered with spruce. Alpine meadows sloped up from the road. The sun had disappeared behind the mountains, but the sky overhead was deep and endless and blue shading to purple.

John saw it all with a sense of wonder, with new eyes. *To live surrounded by such beauty,* he thought.

"You're very fortunate," he said aloud. "Living here, surrounded by this."

"I know," she said softly.

"I can understand why people come here."

"They're really just visitors, though. They don't understand the real Aspen."

"It's a good thing. Picture this valley overrun with the crowds of Manhattan."

She laughed. "Sometimes us locals feel like they *are* here. But the Castle Creek valley is so peaceful, isn't it?"

The Pine Creek Cookhouse was a perverse blend of primitive log cabin and elegant dining. There was a large stone fireplace with a fire going; it was cool at this altitude on summer evenings. Casually well-dressed people filled the tables. Silver clinked and crystal gleamed. The conversation was muted and informed.

"Mr. Leopardo, two for dinner. Yes, right this way, sir," said one of the waiters, who was manning the door.

Kamisha followed the waiter, waved to an acquaintance across the room and stopped for a moment to smile and say hello to an older woman at a nearby table. John was unaccountably jealous that she lived here, fitted in perfectly, jealous of the Aspenites who saw her every day.

"Sorry," she said, "but Mrs. Wexner is a member of the club."

"No problem."

"You have to have the cold cherry soup," Kamisha said, not even looking at the menu. "It's their speciality."

The dishes were mostly vegetarian, with some fish, some chicken. Pilafs and vegetable soufflés and potato pancakes were featured.

John watched Kamisha study her menu. Her brow creased and she bit her lip. She was so beautiful. "You order for me," he said. "It's your turn."

"Oh, really, I'd rather not."

"Please. I'm not fussy. I'd love anything on this menu."

Their eyes met and locked and a jolt went through John. He wondered if she felt it, too. She must. And once again he had to ask himself: what did he want from her?

"Would you care to see the wine list?" their waiter was asking.

John took it, never removing his gaze from Kamisha's. She was flushing, a delicate pink staining her cheeks, her eyes bright and expectant. He put the wine list down and dared to take her fingertips in his. "I hope you're not afraid of me any longer," he said. "I want you to enjoy the evening."

She didn't pull her hand away, but she took her time answering. "I'm not afraid of you. I don't know. Maybe I should be. I told myself you were dangerous, but when I'm with you, I can't... I don't feel in danger."

"You're not, Kamisha, not from me."

"When you say that, I believe it, but when I'm alone, I think things. Does it bother you when I'm frank like this?"

He shook his head. "I want only the truth between us. On a business level and on a personal level."

She bent her head, and he had to strain to hear her. "But sometimes it's so hard to know what the truth is."

"Trust your instincts."

She looked up then and gave him a rueful smile. "My instincts are for self-preservation, for running away. Even from myself."

"You didn't run from me. You could have."

"Yes," she said slowly, "I could have."

He turned her hand over in his and ran his thumb across her palm. "You have calluses on your hand."

"Tennis," she replied. "First it's blisters, then calluses. Very unfeminine."

"Maybe to some."

He had a powerful urge to bring her hand up, to bury his face in her sweet-smelling skin, to rub her fingers over his lips. He let her hand go. He had to be careful with her, as careful as he was with himself.

"Wine?" he asked.

"Yes," she said, "a little."

They ate trout amandine, a grain pilaf, potato pancakes, perfectly cooked vegetables, sweet and crispy. Coffee and dessert. A pecan pie for him, raspberries over coffee ice cream for her. He watched her sip, watched her chew and swallow, watched her flick a bit of ice cream off her lip with her tongue.

She told him a lot about the silver mining history of Aspen, about the present-day problems—too many extravagant second homes, no affordable housing for employees, the narrow, dangerous highway that led down the valley to the bedroom communities where employees lived. The changing character of Aspen—from close-knit, free-living Shangri-la to ritzy jet-set resort whose inhabitants were all rich tourists and celebrities.

"I remember when they first paved Main Street," Kamisha said. "I was a kid, of course. Here with my folks. We stayed in the old Hotel Jerome. Now all the streets are paved, all the lawns sodded and all the houses protected by security systems. Well, the tourists' houses at least."

"Not yours?" he asked.

"No, there's not much to steal."

"Do you lock your door at night?" he asked.

"Lately I do," she replied soberly.

He considered asking her if she'd like Inky to stay with her, but decided not to. She'd object. But he might have Inky keep an eye on her without telling her. Yes, that wasn't a bad idea.

"Good," he said. "And my offer still stands. Use the VIP condo if you want."

"With you in it, John?" she asked softly.

He shrugged. "There's plenty of room."

She smiled secretly. "No, I don't think so."

"I can't force you."

"No, you can't."

The candlelight flickered on the ruby-red wine in Kamisha's glass, threw shadows on her bare neck, reflected points of light in her eyes. To sit across from this silver-haired woman he desired was so very unique; he would never have believed it if anyone had told him these passions would rise once more in him, a cornucopia of possibilities. Life was opening up before him, a cornucopia of possibilities.

"I'm afraid I'm going to have to get up. My knee is stiffening," he finally said.

"Oh, I'm sorry. You should have said so sooner, John."

"I'm fine. I just know by now when it's time." He raised himself and took his cane, studiously wiping any trace of a grimace from his face. He wouldn't be able to bear her pity, not Kamisha with her athlete's body and her skiing and her tennis.

A thought stirred in his head for an instant before retreating: perhaps Kamisha found him distasteful. His infirmity. A woman like her, so accustomed to living a life in which she could bike or jog or play nine holes of golf in the morning. In the afternoon it was tennis or an aerobics class. A swim, if she liked. She could hike the snow-capped mountains, ski...

"John," she was saying, "are we going?"

"Yes, yes, sorry, I was thinking."

She led, wending her way through the tables, a vision in shimmery silk, as bright as a flame. He could feast his eyes on her proud, straight back, on her slim neck, on the blond hair that was twisted on her head, on the hips that swayed ever so slightly under the loose tunic.

Inky drove them back down the valley toward town. The rented sedan was hushed, its ride smooth. They whispered past the ghost town, its gaunt gray skeleton buildings standing like sentinels in the dark valley, an echo of the past. A lopsided moon hung over a snow-silvered peak. Beauty walked in the night air.

"I had a very nice time," she said. "Thank you."

"I'm glad."

She sat closer to him than she had, he noticed.

"Are you leaving soon?" she asked. "I mean, to go back to New York?"

"Not immediately. But I do have a business engagement soon. I'd like to get this thing cleared up with Rick first. And you."

"I see," Kamisha replied. "So you'll be here for a day or two."

"I can stay."

"But you shouldn't."

"Kamisha," he said, "I believe this business in Aspen is more important than meetings elsewhere."

"Um," she murmured, and then looked at him, her features shadowed, then gilded by the lights of a passing car. "Listen," she began, "you really don't have to stay because of me, you know."

"It's my responsibility. It's my club."

"Well, I have to admit, I'm not looking forward to dealing with Rick." She made a face. "He's plenty miffed with me."

"I'll take care of Rick."

Inky pulled up at the curb in front of her house.

"Well, we're here," she said.

"I'll walk you to the door."

"That's really not..."

But Inky was opening her side and handing her out. John came around the car—too slowly, irritated with his stiff leg. He'd been sitting too much all day.

He took her arm, led her down the walk. "Did you lock up when you left?" he asked.

She nodded. "But, really..."

"Inky," he called, "take a look in Miss Hammill's house, will you?"

"John, honestly..."

"I'd feel better," he said. "Humor me."

She unlocked the door, and Inky went in. They stood there in the pool of light from a lamp. He could see that she was shivering a little.

"Nervous?"

"No." She gave a short laugh. "Chilly."

The lights went on in her house one by one. Inky came out. "All set, boss," he said, then retreated down the walk to the car.

"Thank you," she said, hugging herself.

"You can call me, you know. You have the number. Anytime day or night."

"I've already done that."

"If you hear anything. If you're afraid. Please call me."

She hugged herself and looked at him hard. He suspected she was getting ready to ask him in, to pursue what they'd been groping for all evening. To test her own courage. He sensed he was a challenge to her, a man and a challenge. The fact that he was impaired wouldn't matter to Kamisha at this point. He could acquiesce, enter her Victorian coziness and lose himself in it. For one night, one blessed night.

"John..." she started to say.

He took her hand and pulled it toward him, turned it palm up and bent his head to touch it with his lips. He heard her intake of breath.

"John..." she said again.

Yes, he could go inside with her, slip the shimmering silk from her shoulders, taste her. Still poised over her hand, he held her gaze for a pregnant moment. Her eyes were moist, her expression expectant. He knew that this was a game with Kamisha—a game she was accustomed to winning. Abruptly he didn't want to play.

He straightened and met her eyes again with his. "Good night, Kamisha," he said with more finality than he'd intended. He turned then, curtly, and limped down the shadowed walk to the waiting car.

CHAPTER NINE

THE ROSES WERE DELIVERED at ten o'clock, the scent of the two dozen red blooms filling Kamisha's office. She felt her cheeks grow as bright as the hue of the petals as she thanked the florist and watched him leave. On a clear plastic prong was a card. She closed her eyes for a moment, as if when she opened them she'd find the flowers gone, then took the envelope off the holder and stared at it.

What a mad, crazy charade they were playing, Kamisha thought as she pulled the card out. At the end of last night she'd have sworn he wasn't interested. For the life of her she couldn't figure him out. Still, for all her logic, her heart was beating wildly. She read the note again:

Inky will be at your house at one with a Jeep. I hope it won't inconvenience you to join me on a ride.

Yours, John

She smiled. He was asking her to take the afternoon off to be with him. And how could she refuse her boss?

All morning Kamisha rushed to get in a full day's work. She conned Rick's secretary into typing the letters to the celebrities she was asking to participate in the substance abuse event. She checked on the plumbing in the men's locker room and made calls to the Denver supply houses that provided soap and shampoo and razors for the locker rooms, placing next month's orders—she was a day late already. She checked with the Women's Forum president about next week's luncheon and arranged the menu with the chef. And still there were a couple of items left on her desk calender at noon. But what the heck, Kamisha thought, grabbing her zip-up sweatshirt and the flowers, the owner of the club had given her an order.

Leaving work, she felt carefree and young and deliciously guilty. Where would they go? The Maroon Bells Wilderness Area? To the top of Independence Pass? Maybe a walk along the Braille Trail. It was lovely and scented with pine, and you could hear the Roaring Fork River rushing, crashing down the steep ravines below. She wanted to show John everything. She wanted him to love her home.

In the rented car at the stop sign on Fifth and Bleeker Streets it occurred to her—how could she have forgotten?—that John was still the prime suspect in the murder attempt on her. What a perfect setup it would be to get her off into the wilderness alone. A convenient Jeep accident...

Yet her instincts told her he was a man of absolute integrity. She reached over to the passenger seat and brushed the tip of a ruby-red rose with her finger. A fleeting thought brushed her mind: the most perfect rose came with the sharpest thorn.

Kamisha pulled up in front of her house and spotted the bike leaning against the fence. Tracy's bike. And sitting on her front porch steps, the neighbor's cat in her lap, was Tracy. She looked absolutely miserable.

Concerned, Kamisha gathered up the flowers and her purse and stepped out of the car. "Hi," she called, "what a nice surprise."

"Hi." Sulkily.

"Cute cat. Isn't that Hogan from next door?"

"I guess."

Tracy looked enough like her mom to have been her sister, though she wore her honey-brown hair long and straight down her slender back. She was at an awkward age, too, thirteen and a little lanky, her front teeth still too big in her small mouth. There was a pimple on her forehead and one on her chin. Her eyes were swollen; she'd been crying.

Kamisha reached down and touched her shoulder lovingly. "Come on in. I've got to get these into fresh water. Come on."

"Can Hogan come?"

"Sure. But don't let him scratch my couch, button."

It was Kamisha who broached the subject finally. She was placing a rose in her crystal vase in the kitchen, Tracy sitting at the old oak table by the window, Hogan curled in her lap. "So, kiddo, what's new? You're looking mighty down in the mouth today."

Tracy sighed. "I hate Bullet."

"Oh. I see. Any particular reason?" Purposely Kamisha didn't look up, just went right on arranging the flowers.

"He's a jerk. He's always fighting with Mom and telling me to get lost."

"That's pretty nasty."

"I hate him."

"Did you tell your mom?"

"She doesn't care."

"Sure she does. She—"

"All they do is fight. And he makes my mom cry."

"Did this happen today?"

Tracy nodded. "Mom thinks he's got a girlfriend out in California."

"And I guess they must have fought about it, huh?"

"Yeah. And Mom was drinking, too, and Bullet broke her glass in the sink."

"This all happened this morning?"

"Yeah."

"I'm sorry, sweetie," Kamisha said, leaning against the counter, her arms folded over her sweatshirt.

Tracy looked up at her. "Can I stay with you? I don't want to go home."

Oh, boy, Kamisha thought. She took a minute to answer. When she did, she sat down at the table and put her hand on Tracy's knee. "I'd love to have you here," she began. "You know that. But we better reason this out, honey. It would only make things much worse. Your mom would be real hurt."

"I don't care."

"Right now I know you believe that. But in a day or two you'd start to feel awful and guilty, too. It would make it twice as hard to patch things up then."

Tracy hung her head.

"Honey, you'll have to trust my judgment on this one."

"What about Bullet? He doesn't want me there."

Kamisha sighed. "Listen," she said, "I don't think your mom and Bullet are going to be together that long. This is just between you and me. But I think that maybe if I have a heart-to-heart with Brigitte, she'll come around."

"You'll talk to her?"

Kamisha promised that she would, but just how she was going to accomplish it she wasn't sure. That fight they'd just had...

John arrived at one sharp, and Inky came to the door. "Jeep's all ready out front,'' he said, eyeing Tracy standing there in the living room. ''John would appreciate it if you could drive.''

''I understand,'' Kamisha said. She gave John a wave from the door. ''I'll be out in a minute.''

''I got lunch all packed for you,'' Inky called after her.

''Are you going Jeeping?'' Tracy asked, surprised.

Kamisha was gathering up her jacket, just in case of rain, taking up her purse. ''Yes, I'm going with a friend,'' she explained, ''but we'll drop you and your bike off at home first. Okay?''

''I guess so.''

She took Tracy's hand and led her out, locking up behind them. ''Your mom will be fine, sweetie,'' she said, collecting Tracy's bike. ''You'll see. I'll bet she misses you already.'' And then she added, ''Your mom loves you more than anything in the world.''

She loaded the bike into the back of the open Jeep and introduced John to Tracy, explaining they were going to drop her off.

''How do you do, Tracy?'' he asked, turning around in the front seat to shake her hand.

''Inky,'' Kamisha said, ''don't you want a ride back to the club?''

But it was John who answered. ''We've taken the liberty of checking on your car over in Dillon. Inky can return the rental and pick up your Saab at the same time, if that's all right with you.''

Kamisha looked at him for a moment. He certainly did take control. But it wasn't so bad. In fact, she realized, it was kind of nice to be taken care of for once. ''Sure,'' she said, then turned to Inky, giving him the keys to the rental, ''that would be great.''

''My pleasure.'' He gave her that big white smile.

While Kamisha drove toward Castle Creek Road, she took the opportunity to glance at John from time to time. He was dressed today in blue jeans and a short-sleeved polo shirt, a khaki color. As always, his hair had been combed neatly back, but the wind had loosened it so that a big comma fell against his sunglasses, and the hair around his ears and neck wanted to curl up. He looked younger, wind-tousled like that, she decided, and somehow the cane that rested by his leg seemed terribly out of place. She imagined him as a younger man, in his twenties perhaps, and tried to see him with a frequent smile and a relaxed carriage, but the image wouldn't stick. Maybe he had never been a carefree youth. Maybe his father's ''business'' and Vietnam had robbed him of those good years.

She listened while he talked to Tracy, turning around, one hand resting casually on the back of her own seat. "Do you like school here in Aspen?" he was asking her.

"It's not as big as L.A.," Tracy replied, still sullen, "but it's okay."

"You have a lot of girlfriends?"

"Some."

And then a corner of his mouth lifted teasingly. "You have a boyfriend, Tracy?"

"Gosh, Mr. Leopardo," Tracy said, surprised, "I'm too young for that."

"Maybe," he said, "but you're a very pretty young lady."

And Tracy got all embarrassed and giggly and hid her teeth behind a slim hand. Kamisha was surprised, too, but it was a new side to John that had her thinking. He'd obviously sensed Tracy's discomfort and found a way to alleviate it. Amazing. It suddenly seemed a crime that he had no children of his own. But, then, neither did she.

"Here we are," Kamisha said, turning onto Brigitte's road. She wondered if she should go inside, talk to Brigitte for a minute. But then Brigitte was coming out, her bathrobe still on. She looked agitated, pale, hung over. Darn.

They only spoke for a moment, Kamisha explaining that Tracy had stopped by to say hello. "And John and I are heading up the mountain, Jeeping, so I thought I'd give her a lift home from town."

"Thanks," Brigitte said, eyeing both Kamisha and her daughter suspiciously.

"Well," Kamisha said, turning to head back to the Jeep, wondering if she should introduce John. But, no, Brigitte wasn't in the mood. "Look," she said, "I'll call you. We'll talk, okay?"

"It's your dime," Brigitte snapped. "So that's John. John Leopardo, I take it."

"Yes, um, he just got here yesterday and—"

Brigitte glared at her. "Aren't you afraid that man will kill you up there alone? I mean, what is this, Kamisha, another one of your cheap thrills?"

Kamisha bit her tongue. "We'll talk, Brigitte, when you're feeling better." She began to turn and head to the Jeep, but not before she saw Bullet standing in the big plate glass window, staring at the two women. *Jerk,* Kamisha thought.

It was a six-mile drive back into Aspen and then across town to the Smuggler Mountain dirt road. But Kamisha had decided to show

John some of the old silver mines that riddled the steep face of Smuggler. Many of the century-old shafts dropped a thousand feet into the ground, then turned south and headed directly under the town of Aspen toward the big ski mountain. It was said that a few of the old-timers could still find their way through the maze of shafts, but the shafts were old and dangerous, and Kamisha had never ventured into one. She wasn't going to today, either.

She drove and felt a cloud shadowing her former good spirits. It was, of course, Brigitte. And she wondered, too, just why she was throwing caution to the wind by heading off into the wilderness with John. Brigitte had a point....

"You're awfully quiet," John observed over the drone of the Jeep's engine.

"Sorry." She slowed and steered cautiously around a boulder that forced the vehicle precariously close to the edge of the road. The drop on the driver's side was a good fifteen hundred feet.

"Nice road," he said, sitting up straight, looking over the edge.

"We'll be off this cliff in a few minutes. Then it's all woods and meadows. A few bad pitches, but we'll make it."

"And where are we headed?"

She glanced over and smiled. "The high country—God's country."

"Sounds interesting."

Kamisha wasn't sure just why John had arranged this get-together. She was accustomed to men being dazzled by her appearance, dazzled and distracted and held at arm's length. It was how she managed men, and it had always worked—until now. She stole a glance at John; he'd braced himself against the dashboard with one hand, a capable, square hand, a strong wrist that swelled into his muscular forearm.

The rutted road rose and fell into a valley and rose once more. They drove through deep stands of tall aspens and evergreens until they'd climbed above the altitude where aspens could grow. Then it was open meadows and thick evergreen forests, the road wending its way still upward.

Kamisha was glad for the solitude. She was sure John could sense her discomfort, though she wasn't quite certain whether it was due more to Brigitte or him. She knew one thing, however; she liked John's companionship a lot. Too much. She felt an odd sense of security despite the little warning signs that kept blinking in her head: *you can't trust him, not all the way.*

John was different from other men, fascinating but difficult for her to handle. He kept throwing her curves. Her usual techniques didn't seem to work with him. But she knew no other way of dealing with men. Weren't they all the same, really? Didn't they all want the same thing from a woman, from her? John must, too. He was just a little cleverer about it, a little more subtle.

Today she'd be able to manage him. She just needed time to figure out what he was looking for in her.

They were crossing a warm, sunny meadow when she felt his eyes resting on her. "Tracy seems like a nice child," he remarked.

Kamisha avoided a chipmunk that had the audacity to cross the road. "She's a good kid. I've known her since she was born."

"She was upset today."

"Yes. A spat with her mom."

"A spat?"

He was drawing her out. She knew it. And normally she'd have retreated, but with John it seemed okay to open up a bit. "More than a spat," Kamisha admit ted. "Tracy hates Bullet. He's that pro football star who—"

"I know who Bullet Adams is."

"Well, anyway, since Brigitte took up with him, Tracy's felt left out."

"I should imagine. And you, Kamisha, have you been left out, too?"

She glanced over. He was gazing at her solemnly, knowingly. "You could put it that way," she said. "But it's a lot more, too. Bullet brings out the worst in Brigitte. She doesn't need that...stuff in her life. She's always had a booze problem, and that guy only encourages her. He's a creep, if you must know. A real user."

"So I've heard."

"Anyway, Brigitte better get her head together, or Tracy's going to be permanently damaged."

"Are you two having a problem?" he asked, sincerely concerned.

"Yes. We had a fight. A real beaut."

There was a long, silent moment. "I don't suppose it had anything to do with me," he stated.

Kamisha raised an eyebrow. "As a matter of fact," she began, and then suddenly laughed. "Say, what's all this third degree, anyway?"

"Just trying to figure out who you really are."

She was suddenly, acutely uncomfortable. He was getting too personal. Her defenses rose automatically, and she raked a hand through her hair and tossed it back over her shoulder so that it rippled like a banner in the wind. She gave him a coy, sidelong glance and smiled. But John just continued to regard her soberly. Swiftly Kamisha switched her eyes back onto the road.

They stopped just below Warren Lake at the top of the mountain. There was a campsite nestled in the forest at the northern edge of an alpine meadow—a hunters' camp that wouldn't be used for a few months still. Kamisha got out the bag of food provided by Inky and spread it on an old telephone cable spool that was used by campers as a table.

"Um, chicken and potato salad. Want a soda pop?" She turned to find John standing some thirty yards away at the edge of the tree line where it met the sun-splashed meadow. He was as still as the granite rocks above, his weight supported on the cane, his head erect. Sunlight filtered through the pine branches and dappled his head and shoulders. The majesty of forest and meadow, the peaks beyond still capped with snow, John's stillness, struck her motionless. The grandeur of his surroundings diminished him, and he seemed so mortal standing there with his cane in hand, so insignificant.

We're both human, she thought, and a sense of surprising peace pushed aside her anxiety for a moment. Slowly she came up behind him. The summer wind soughed in the green branches above. A billowy white cloud cast the meadow in partial shade. She found herself whispering, "Lovely."

"Yes," he replied, unmoving, "it is lovely."

They ate their chicken and sipped the sodas, lazing back against a tree, knees up, hands behind heads. All the while Kamisha was so terribly aware of his constant, unwavering perusal. She knew her breasts pressed against her shirt when she put her arms behind her head. She knew her legs were there for him to see, long, slim, tanned, stretched out in front of her. But John didn't steal secret glances at her, not like an ordinary man would. Even though he studied her, he seemed oblivious to her physical charms, and it made her nervous. He wasn't following the rules.

Eventually he stretched out on the soft pine needle floor of the earth and sighed. "I like it here."

"Um, me, too," Kamisha said. She couldn't help looking at him.

His eyes were half-closed, one hand was behind his head, cradling it. He had a long body, she decided, lean and tapered in all the right places: belly, thighs, hips. A fly buzzed around his hand, and idly he shooed it away. How could she have ever thought that this man would harm her?

"You should spend more time in Aspen," she ventured. "Get rid of that city pallor."

"Would I look better with a tan?" he asked lightly, teasing.

"Everyone in Aspen has a tan. Year-round, in fact."

"Then my city white sets me apart." He turned his head toward her. "Is that so bad?"

"You like to be set apart, don't you." It wasn't a question. She tugged at an errant blade of dry grass, then plucked it, putting the sweet, reedy stem in her mouth. "Yes, John," she said, "I think you really like to be noticed, but in a low-key way. You're subtle but human."

"Oh, I'm human, Kamisha." He laughed lightly, mostly at himself. "In fact, I suspect I've got more than my fair share of frailties."

"You don't mean your leg."

"No, I don't. I mean problems, I suppose, personal problems."

"Care to share them?"

John shook his head slowly, still smiling. She found herself liking it when he smiled. "You can guess if you like," he said. "And you'll probably hit the nail on the head. I'm an open book, if you really want to know."

"So I'll guess. I'd say this rift with your family is one of your problems."

"A major one," he admitted, though there was a new edge to his voice.

"It's a shame."

"Isn't it."

"Seriously. My folks don't give two hoots about me. I know."

"That's not the way it is with me," he said. "It's quite the opposite."

"Do you care about them?"

"Very much."

"Can't your feelings, your problems, I mean, be mended?"

"No."

Kamisha leaned back against the tree and looked up at the sky that showed in patches through the branches of the evergreens. She chewed on the grass, thinking. Here they were—two mortals—darn close to bearing ugly truths to each other, so close that she began to quiver inside. It was rather like talking to a father confessor up here in the woods. In God's country, she'd said.

But that wasn't what she'd wanted at all. That wasn't what she'd meant to happen between them, and she wondered how he'd managed to turn the conversation to serious matters. Kamisha liked to keep it light, superficial, safe. With John she had to keep steering away from unpleasant subjects, and it kept her off balance.

She felt uneasy, not knowing whether to pursue the conversation or to let it drop. A part of her wanted to know all about John, to share his joy and hurt, to bare her own soul to him. But that wasn't *her*. It felt like a poorly fitted shoe.

She came to her feet and began to stroll around the campsite, kicking idly at pinecones. Here she was, up in the middle of nowhere, with an extremely attractive man, and all they were doing was talking.

She stopped and smiled. "Up over that ridge," she said, nodding, "used to be a real town."

"Up here?"

"Yep. On Saturday night the miners in Aspen used to hitch up the old wagons, climb on their horses, and hightail it up here for the good times." She found herself playing with her hair, tossing it, letting it drape over a shoulder loosely. She was aware that her movements became more provocative. It was a Kamisha she knew well and was more comfortable with than the one who talked about her parents and Brigitte to a stranger.

And John, seemingly, was playing along now. "And what did these miners find up here?"

True, she was comfortable with this side of herself, but she also hated it, the falseness, the sexual manipulation—and all because John had gotten a little too close. Tears pressed hotly behind her eyelids for an instant before she controlled them. She forced her smile; it was brittle and cold. "What did they do up here?" she said. "They came to enjoy themselves. You know, women, saloon women." The laugh she gave was short, nervous, too high-pitched.

But she couldn't stop herself. As if repeating lines from a long-ago failed play, Kamisha began to move toward John, tapping the blade of grass against her bottom lip. "Quite a trip just to let off a little steam, wasn't it?"

John had propped himself on an elbow. He was watching her acutely now, letting the drama unfold. His expression was impassive, but there was emotion in those secretive eyes and a watchfulness in the pitch of his head. She could see a muscle working in his jaw as she eased down onto the soft pine needles beside him. She was tired of talking, worn out. She had wondered before what it was that John truly wanted from her, and she was still wondering. It couldn't have been a nice afternoon chat. No. He'd arranged a Jeep trip to be alone with her, hadn't he? She wished he'd stop talking, stop requiring her to tell him things that were better kept quiet. She wished he'd make an advance—do something familiar, for God's sake, something she could deal with.

"Kamisha," he began, his tone odd, before she leaned closer, allowing the curtain of her hair to brush his cheek lightly before she, too, propped her head on her hand and faced him. She was so close to him that she could feel his warm breath on her neck. Yes, the talking was done. He'd pull her to him in a moment and she'd let him. She'd let him touch her and kiss her and press her against his hips until he couldn't think anymore. And then she'd be in control again.

"John," she said, a hoarse whisper, "I'm glad you came to Aspen."

"Don't."

"Don't?" Close, they were so close.

"This isn't what you really want."

"What do you mean?" She reached out with her free hand and ran a golden-brown finger along the inside of his arm. "You don't know what I want," she said softly. She knew she was lying because she'd never see it through. She never did. It was the old familiar game, an easy one, one she could win. John was just a man, after all, just another man. Maybe she hadn't quite figured him out yet, but she would. "John," she said, wetting her lips with her tongue, pouting a little, aware of the rise and fall of her breasts.

For a moment his dark eyes burned into hers, and then suddenly he was rising, reaching for his cane, coming to his feet. She felt utterly severed, out of control. What was he doing?

"John," she said, her breathing becoming uneven, a fear snaking around in her belly, "why are you...what's wrong?"

But all he said as he grabbed up their picnic litter was "Not this way, Kamisha, not this way." For an instant he stared at her and then strode away toward the Jeep.

CHAPTER TEN

KAMISHA COULD hardly wait to drop John off at his condo. She was barely able to meet his eye. He'd insulted her, humiliated her, rejected her. And in the back of her mind, somewhere in a deep, hidden place, she shivered with fear, because he'd seen through her act and recognized the falsehood of it.

She drove too fast down the bumpy, rutted road, but John didn't say a word about it. He sat beside her, quiet, unruffled, composed as ever.

Oh, God, she was so embarrassed. Why had she pulled that routine with John? She should have known better. He'd said over and over that he admired the truth, that he wanted only the truth between them. He'd been truthful with her. Yes, she was ready to believe that now.

She was through with his truth, though. It was too damn hard to live with. He was like someone from another century, some sort of knight errant with his outdated code of chivalry and honor.

"You don't have to try to kill us both," John said mildly after she skidded around a gravelly corner.

"I'm not," she said between clenched teeth, wrestling with the steering wheel, tasting dust in her mouth. "I just want to get home."

She pulled up in front of his condo building, stopping too short, lurching them both forward. John gave her a look but said nothing, only climbed out. "Why don't you take the Jeep home," he suggested, "until Inky gets back with your car."

"Fine." She wouldn't look at him.

But Inky, surprisingly, came out of the door of the condo just then. "Hey, boss," he said, his face grim.

"You can't have been to Dillon and back," John said, glancing at his watch. And Kamisha thought, Oh, great, now she'd be making the trip. Darn, why hadn't Inky gone?

She stared straight ahead, pretending not to listen.

Inky was saying, "Something came up, boss," and John was walking toward the black man. They spoke for a minute, heads together. Kamisha refused to look, tapping her fingers on the steering wheel in obvious impatience. She hoped he noticed.

But John seemed oblivious. She was aware that he was walking back toward her, of his cane rapping on the pavement. "Kamisha," he said, "something's happened."

She kept her gaze locked on the hood of the Jeep, tapping her fingers. She knew she was being childish, but she didn't care.

"Are you listening to me, Kamisha?" he demanded.

It was then that she finally turned and met his gaze and saw the bleakness of his expression. Her heart gave an unaccountable twang of fear. "I'm listening, John."

"Rick Simons is in the hospital. He's been badly beaten."

It took Kamisha a second to absorb the shock. Her eyes, wide with bewilderment, flew up to John's. There was no facade, no coolness or control or pretense. "Rick's been beaten up?" she whispered. "But who...why...?"

She was unaware of her hands gripping the steering wheel, her knuckles white. A quick, sickening image of Rick stabbed through her head: bruises, blood, swelling. Why in the name of God would someone—? It came to her in tiny jolts of realization, the flowers, the dinner, the Jeep trip, John's rejection just now. He hadn't asked her to show him the area to get her alone, to woo her, of course not. He'd been keeping her out of the way.

For a long moment she stared at him appraisingly, the disgust in her expression unconcealed. She knew he was reading her thoughts, too, and she didn't give a damn. When she mouthed the word, "You," it said it all to John. She didn't even need to finish. He'd used the Jeep trip as an alibi. He'd had Rick worked over because Rick had mishandled things.

She felt like laughing hysterically for an instant. She was the lucky one. John had spared her. But Rick's punishment would keep her silent, wouldn't it?

She stared into his eyes, tried to read what was there, but there was no expression in them, no message at all, neither sorrow nor anger nor surprise. He was absolutely closed to her.

Abruptly she gunned the accelerator, twisting the steering wheel, made a sharp turn in front of his condo and roared away, her heart pounding, her cheeks flaming.

She rushed up the walk to her house, grabbed the doorknob and twisted. Damn, it was locked. She'd forgotten. She'd only begun locking it recently. She had to fish the key out of her bag and struggle with the cranky old lock until it clicked open.

Oh, what a show! All that talk about the truth! And he'd been living a huge big whopper of a lie! And he'd used her to do it! John wouldn't dirty his hands. Of course not. He hired men, Mafia thugs. He probably didn't even let Inky dirty his hands, either. No, he just phoned his father and asked who was available, who could do a little job for him. Hit men. Contract killers. Oh, God.

And she'd believed him!

Kamisha sagged against the door, drained. She squeezed her eyes shut, but Rick was still there. Her imagination was running wild, tossing mental images helter-skelter into her head. Rick's jaw bruised. His eyes so purple and swollen they were closed.

She tried to take several deep breaths, to will the hideous pictures from her mind. But her breath caught in her lungs raggedly. And John. She could see him standing on the edge of the meadow, stock-still, contemplative. Oh, how she'd misread him. He'd been standing there, leaning on his cane, wondering if the job on Rick had been done yet.

She felt sweaty all over her body, hot and sticky. Burning. She pulled off her clothes and flung them onto the floor, stalking through her house. She got into the shower and turned it on hard, too hot, then too cold, then hot again. She washed herself all over, as if he'd touched her, as if he'd dirtied her. Her breath came too fast and her heart still thudded.

Then she put her face in her hands and stood there under the spray, sobbing, hurt and disappointed and ashamed to the depth of her being.

She sat in the dark later, not bothering to turn on the lights, unable to eat or sleep or read or call Brigitte to find out how Tracy was. The phone had rung several times, over and over monotonously, but she hadn't answered it. She sat there, hunched up, wearing an old red bathrobe that was faded, with a tear in her sleeve. She didn't care. All she could see in her mind's eye was Rick—handsome Rick Simons, his face a pulp. No matter what he'd done, how badly he'd messed up, he hadn't deserved this.

It occurred to her to get up and lock her door. She might be next. But a strange kind of perversity kept her huddled in her spot in the dark. She'd been so damn stupid, so blind that maybe she deserved the hospital bed next to Rick's.

John Leopardo. She'd thought him the most wonderful thing to have come along...

She'd get over him. She'd let John impress her just a little too much. She'd let him get inside her armor and cause a breach in her walls. But she'd plaster the cracks up and be as good as new. She'd make up with Brigitte. Sure, things would go back to normal.

Or would they?

Sometime later she was faintly aware of a car driving up and stopping in front of her house. She heard a heavy door open, then thud shut. So he'd sent someone. So they were coming. She sat up and pushed her hair back behind one ear. She wouldn't run. No, she'd face them. She took a deep breath. There was a knock at the door. She didn't move; she couldn't. Kamisha was paralyzed with a crazy, mute fascination, anticipating the worst. She actually wondered if she didn't deserve it for her stupidity. Another knock. Maybe she was mistaken. Maybe it was just an acquaintance, someone stopping by. They'd see the house was dark and leave. *Go on, leave!*

Another knock. Louder, more insistent. Then a voice, "Kamisha." *His* voice, muffled by the door. "Kamisha, it's John. Are you there?"

Maybe he'd leave if she just sat still in the darkness. She held her breath and hugged her knees to her chest.

She heard the doorknob being turned, heard him call to someone— Inky. "It's open. Wait a minute." She could hear his footsteps and the soft tap of his cane on the floor. A mumbled curse, then the click of the light switch and abrupt, blinding brightness.

For an endlessly long time John stared at her. There was absolutely no emotion on his face; it was purposely masked. But his eyes told a different story. She thought she could read in them a torrent of emotions: surprise, relief and something akin to fear.

Kamisha glared back at him over her knees. She felt drained, unable to deal with whatever new game he'd decided to play. When he took a step toward her, favoring his leg more than usual, she even flinched. She was at his mercy.

He finally sighed as his brow knitted. He swore softly. "Are you all right?"

Kamisha drew her tongue over her dry lips. "So far," she whispered, and felt the cool wall at her back as she pressed against it.

He seemed to want to reach out and touch her but then hesitated. "I tried calling you. I was concerned."

"I'll bet you were."

"Believe what you want. But I'd like you to listen to me for a minute. Will you give me that much, Kamisha?"

She only kept staring at him in complete distrust.

John sighed again. She could see him fight to control his anger. "Look," he began, "I didn't arrange to have Rick worked over."

Kamisha gave a short, bitter laugh.

John tried to ignore it, but she could see a muscle working furiously in his jaw. "For God's sake, use your head. Rick's up to his ears in something, but it doesn't involve me."

"Oh? Then who *does* it involve, John?"

"I wouldn't know. But I plan to find out. You can bet on that."

He was smooth; she'd give him that, all right. But she was learning, oh, how she was learning!

He was leaning on his cane with both hands now. She noticed inadvertently that his knuckles were white. "I spoke to the police, Kamisha. I made a full report. About the parties, about everything. The club's reputation isn't important enough to ignore this." He hesitated. "Do you think I could sit down?"

She made a distracted gesture with her hand, and he sank gratefully into a chair, rubbing a hand over his face. She got up finally, tired but restless, and pulled her robe tighter, yanking on the tie belt, walking on bare feet to the other side of the room.

"Kamisha," he said, "I'd like you to believe me."

"Of course you would."

"Look," he said after a moment, "it's been a long day. I—"

Kamisha spun around to face him. "A long day? Longer than Rick Simons's day?"

John made an obvious attempt to ignore her statement. "I saw Rick, as a matter of fact. He had surgery this afternoon. His jaw's broken, but he's going to be all right." When Kamisha made no reply, he went on. "I also arranged to have Joe Wilson fly on up and take over the club. He's a good man, my Florida operation."

"That's nice."

"Kamisha, listen, I'm going to do everything humanly possible to find out who did this to Rick."

"You mean you don't already have it figured out?"

"Not yet," he replied, a hint of anger and impatience in his tone. "If you'd have answered my calls... This isn't helping, Kamisha."

But she only shrugged, eloquently. "I haven't got anything to say to you."

"Then consider this. You could very well be in danger yourself. Whoever went after Rick is either desperate or totally ruthless."

"More *ruthless* than your family, John, the all-powerful Leopardo clan?" she said, facing him with narrowed eyes.

He was silent for a long time, his eyes shadowed, his expression unreadable, and Kamisha felt a spurt of unwanted guilt for her bitchiness.

"All right, Kamisha, you've said it. Do you feel better?"

She turned back to her window. She was aware that he was getting up from the chair, moving across the room. She refused to turn around, but her shoulders tensed in spite of herself.

"I would never harm you," came John's voice just behind her. "You're safe with me. I swear I had nothing to do with this business. How many times do I have to say it, Kamisha? What will make you believe me?"

She took a deep breath. "I don't know." The hairs on her neck prickled with his nearness. Her heart beat a wild staccato of fear and want. Then she heard his cane drop, and his hands came up to circle her neck, resting there lightly, ever so lightly, as if the wings of a bird touched her skin. Goose bumps broke out all over her body, and her breath stopped in her chest.

"I could, you know," he said softly into her ear, raising the hairs on her neck. "I could squeeze, just like this." His hands tightened imperceptibly. "You expect it. It would prove you were right."

She couldn't move. She felt the swift rushing of blood through her veins, the crazy juxtaposition of love and exciting fear, that sick self-destruct impulse. She just stood there, as still as a statue, waiting.

Then his hands were gone, and she sagged a little, released from tension.

"I had every opportunity to get rid of you, to shut you up, but I didn't. No one would have heard you or known." He put a hand on her arm and pulled her around slowly. "You made a mistake, Kamisha. You mistook who I really am."

He was so close, his face only inches away, his hand holding her arm hard, a kind of fierceness shining from him. "Do you believe me?" he asked.

"I...I don't know," she whispered.

"You flatter yourself. You're not so terribly clever. If I'd wanted to kill you, I could have, a dozen times between New York and here," he said angrily. "But I don't kill people. I'm not a Mafia hit man." He swung away from her and walked a few halting steps. "God, I'm tired of saying that. I'm so damn tired of having to say it."

Silence hung between them, filling the room. Her mind kept telling her to be afraid, to be cautious, but her heart felt pity and confusion. Her heart believed him.

A wrenching, unaccountable sadness gripped her. She saw his cane lying on the floor, and she knelt to pick it up, feeling the smooth burnished wood that his hand had caressed so often. She moved toward him and touched his arm from behind. He turned, tense, his eyes shadowed, his brows drawn.

"Here, John," she said softly, handing it to him.

He took it and searched her face for a time, an endless moment of recrimination and forgiveness and the faint stirrings of understanding. "Thank you," he said.

"Why did you come here?" she asked. "Why did you really come?"

He rubbed his hand over his face. "I don't know. I was worried about you, but I could have sent Inky. I guess I wanted to say what I just said." He looked at her. "Did it mean a damn thing?"

She nodded. A hint of self-consciousness came over her when she realized, for the first time, that she was clad in her old bathrobe with the ripped sleeve, her hair hanging uncombed, her feet bare. She pulled the robe around her protectively again.

"Look, Kamisha," John said then, quietly, with that gentle but unyielding authority restored to him. "I have to leave tomorrow. There's a Panamerican Trade Conference at my new hotel in Costa Rica. It's important. I should be there."

She felt disappointment wrap its tentacles around her. She tried to fight it off.

"I don't want to leave you here alone...for several reasons."

She remained silent.

He held her eyes steadily. "I want you to come with me."

"John, I couldn't," she said quickly.

"Forget your duties at the club for the time being. Joe's bringing a secretary with him from Florida. They'll handle everything. I want you out of harm's way.''

"You can't just order me around," she said, "and assume that my job isn't worth two cents.''

"I'm sorry. That was hardly my intention. I'm worried about your welfare. I don't want you to end up like Rick. As owner of the club, it's my responsibility to see you're safe.''

"Come on, John. Costa Rica?''

"Okay, I'll admit it's selfishness, too. I want to spend some time with you. Time away from here, away from everything. I want to prove my innocence to you once and for all.''

She studied his face. "Is it so important to you?''

"Yes.''

She looked down. "I don't know...''

"There'll be no strings attached. We'll have separate rooms. Do you understand? I'm not trying to seduce you.''

"You have a way of being as insulting as the devil, John.''

"I told you, I deal in truth. I mean that, Kamisha.'' He stepped close and tilted her chin up with one hand. "What do you say?''

She'd just been presented with the ultimate challenge—a man who stirred her blood, fascinated her, offered her danger and brand-new sensations, the lure of the unknown. Her curiosity was piqued beyond bearing. What did John really want from her? What was his "truth"?

"No strings," she said.

"That's right.''

"But why? Why Costa Rica...with you?''

He seemed to have to search himself for the answer, for his truth. "I think I want you to get to know me.''

She looked him square in the eye. Without hesitation she said, "Yes, I'll go with you.''

CHAPTER ELEVEN

IT WAS A MAD RUSH to get ready for the sudden trip. Kamisha barely allowed herself the luxury of thought. She put from her mind the club and Brigitte and Rick—Rick, who was lying in the hospital. And there wasn't time, either to consider the danger to herself or even question Inky's substantial presence on the street outside her house. It was all so abrupt. It was downright crazy. John had come into her life and turned it upside down.

She stopped packing once, sat on the edge of the bed, her hands automatically reaching up to touch her neck—to touch the places where John's hands had rested, to feel his nearness and to wonder once again: what did he really want from her?

The flight south into Central America kept Kamisha's rapt attention. Her entire adult life had been spent in the cooler climates: the Rocky Mountains, the Canadian Rockies, the Swiss and Italian Alps, northern Japan, Sweden. She'd never seen a jungle or active volcanoes. But, as the 727 streaked across the blue sky, she saw that the land below was green and lush, the valley walls rising to surprising heights, jutting upward to where the green canopy met solid volcanic rock. She could look right down inside the craters of the necklace of volcanoes that were strung in a line down the Pacific Coast of Central America. There were few roads, the Panamerican Highway being the only paved route south of Mexico. The land they flew over looked hostile, hot and steamy, uninviting to man.

"Different, isn't it?" John asked, closing the newspaper he'd been buried in.

Kamisha sat back in her seat and looked at him. "Sure I'm not going to die of the heat?"

"I hope not."

The flight path followed the Pacific Coast of El Salvador and Nicaragua, then headed inland, surprisingly low over the cloud-shrouded mountainsides of the Costa Rican interior. Then, up ahead, she could see a wide, lush valley and the spreading metropolis of San José, the capital city. The plane banked, easing its bulk carefully into the valley, in line with the small international airport.

"Is it a hassle at customs?" she asked.

He shook his head. "It can be, but my contractor is meeting us with a car. He'll have everything arranged."

She settled back, checked her seat belt; for all the hundreds of flights she'd been on, taking off and landing always made her a little nervous.

Flying could unsettle her, but strangely John no longer pushed those particular buttons. She was beginning to feel comfortable with him. She knew, too, that if she'd made love to John—if *he'd* allowed it—they would no longer have a relationship. It was an odd sort of foreplay, unlike anything in her previous experience, yet the sensation of his constant proximity held her as breathless as an intimate caress. She closed her eyes and took a deep breath. No man had ever stirred these feelings in her before.

"You aren't nervous, are you?" he asked, observing her, placing a hand gently on her arm.

"No," Kamisha said, turning to smile at him, praying he couldn't read her thoughts. "I'm fine."

It was hot and humid when they deplaned. Outside the airport, rumbling off the walls of the valley, was a thunderstorm. Rain pattered against the metal roof of the building, so noisy it was deafening. But, as promised, Juan Luis was there with a rental car for John, and they were miraculously whipped through customs and immigration while the tourists and businessmen waited in endless lines.

"That was convenient," Kamisha said, following the two men, glancing around. "Guess it pays to know the right people."

Her first impression of San José was how Mediterranean it appeared, not at all like Mexican cities she'd been to, but more Spanish, more European. They gave Juan Luis a lift into the center of town, and while the men talked about invoices and cost overruns and completion schedules, Kamisha sat happily in the back and took in the sights.

It was a cultured city, nestled in the cloud-covered mountains of Central America, sophisticated and clean. Theaters abounded, parks were crowded with exotic foliage. There were first-class hotels, exquisite restaurants and shops. The native Costa Ricans, or Ticos, as

John had told her they called themselves, were well dressed and walked with pride in their step.

Like San Francisco, the city was built on hills that climbed both sides of the valley to steep, lushly green mountainsides. Cars went flying past them down the hills and chugged up the next ones. The downtown streets were teeming with shoppers, hawkers, tourists—a wealthy city—and bright colors assailed her eyes everywhere.

John dropped Juan Luis off at the rental car agency where he had left his van.

"Do you want me to drive?" she asked when the contractor had gone.

"I'll drive for a while. I don't get to very often," John said. "And it's an automatic." Unabashedly he tapped his knee with his cane before climbing into the driver's seat. "You just take in the sights. Relax. You're on vacation, Kamisha, and in Costa Rica the pace is slower. They don't like to display stress here."

"How far is the Montaña y Mar Hotel?"

"It's on the northern coast of the Nicoya Peninsula. As the crow flies, a hundred or so miles. But driving, that's another story. This could take us five or six hours, depending on traffic."

It wasn't long before Kamisha saw what John was talking about. Shortly after leaving San José, the road narrowed and began to climb a precipitous mountainside. In the low-slung clouds myriad cars and trucks and buses crawled along, downshifting, spewing out exhaust.

Kamisha fastened her seat belt. "God, this is hairy."

"You get used to it."

John drove well, considering how seldom he chose to do so. And the car was peppy, a steel-gray Honda import, a model she'd never seen in the States.

The signs were in both Spanish and English, and when they stopped in a mountain village for lunch, she found that the menu was also bilingual.

"I thought I'd be floundering," Kamisha said, folding her arms on the wooden tabletop.

"The Costa Ricans are very well educated," he said. "They tell me there are twice as many teachers here as police. In fact, I don't know if I've ever seen a policeman."

"How often do you make this trip?"

"This is my eighth trip. But usually I fly up to the peninsula."

"You drove this time for me, then," she said, pleased that John had gone out of his way to show her the sights.

They both ordered fish. He told her that she should eat all the fish she could while there—it was some of the best in the world. Fresh, meaty, with names she'd never heard before. And each restaurant would cook it exactly the way she wanted. Over her cabbage and tomato salad she watched John in this setting that seemed to fit him so well. He could have been a Tico himself—dark-headed, olive-skinned, well-tailored in a lightweight khaki suit.

The fish was excellent, reminding her of bluefish. It was served with fried potatoes, hot and spicy, laced with peppers and onions.

They drove on, down out of the mountains to where the sun was shining brightly, and she could see the wide, deep blue waters of the Golfo Nicoya and the mountainous peninsula beyond. Then they turned north into the province of Guanacaste—cattle country, where the highway ran between two low mountain ranges and the valley was green and fertile, dotted with steers. It was a wealthy province. Sprawling haciendas graced the land, and Mercedes-Benzes, Audis and Volvos hogged the road. It could have been Texas—wide-open spaces with a bowl of lazy blue sky overhead.

Kamisha leaned back in her seat and let the balmy tropical air caress her face and bare arms. Languidly she asked, "Want me to drive?"

He shook his head and glanced over at her. He had one arm resting in the open window, the other draped casually over the steering wheel. "Maybe later."

"Leg not stiff?"

"Not bad."

They could have been husband and wife, Kamisha thought idly. A strange familiarity was growing between them. Yet behind the comfort was still that edge, that question: what, exactly, did John expect from her?

He drove, and she found herself watching him surreptitiously. Through half-closed eyes she took in the curve of his thigh muscles, his arms, the strength of his chin, the dignity of his carriage. He needed a shave. But she liked the dark shadow covering his cheeks and jaw and upper lip. She could imagine the burn it would leave on her own smooth face, that telltale red flush.

They turned westward now, leaving the main road. The country narrowed again, and the pavement gave way to a graded dirt road.

And the jungle. It seemed to spring up around them on all sides, thick and lush and wet. Cloying and hot.

"Want the air conditioner on?" he asked.

Kamisha was well aware of the perspiration on the back of her neck and in between her breasts. The waistband of her tan slacks was soaked. Still, there was a feel to the jungle, a scent, that she hated to spurn. "No," she said, "it would ruin it."

John finally pulled over in a small farming village several miles from the coast. "Do you mind?" he asked, climbing out of his seat stiffly. "I'm cramping up. And I don't know about you, but I'm dying of thirst."

"Whatever you're having, I'll take two."

They sat in the shade at a tiny restaurant that consisted of a tin roof, four supporting beams and a half dozen tables. There were no walls, only the roof.

A lady in a spiffy white cotton dress appeared from inside. Obviously her house was attached to the roadside café. She wiped her hands on her apron and spoke to John in Spanish.

"*Dos Coca-Colas con Limón, por favor,*" he said. Then, to Kamisha he said, "I'm afraid they don't have plain soda water here. Is Coke all right?"

"It's fine."

"You know, you can drink the water out of the tap anywhere in Costa Rica."

She looked at him doubtfully.

He laughed and made a cross over her heart.

"I won't get Montezuma's Revenge?"

"Not a bit of it. I promise."

The village was filled with sound, Kamisha noticed. Roosters crowed despite the afternoon hour, dogs barked, birds screeched and squawked from deep in the jungle. She asked John about the birds, pointing out a small green parrot with a crimson head that sat in a banyan tree across the road.

There were huge Wedgwood-blue birds scolding one another down the way. John pointed out a family of small brown monkeys resting in a tree. The jungle was lush and exotic and scented by a dozen odors, all unfamiliar. Kamisha could smell beans cooking in cumin and Tabasco from inside the woman's house. Flowers crowded the small, wooden-framed bungalows and grew in the jungle, up the sides of strange twisted trees, clinging to vines. Their colors were brilliant: red, white, purple, yellow, fuchsia.

"It's almost claustrophobic," she said, draining her Coke.

"But different." He turned on his hard wooden seat and stared into the jungle.

"Not much like New York," she said.

"No, it's not." He turned back and looked intently into her eyes. "I don't know if a man could get used to it."

"Could you?" she ventured.

Casually, too casually, he shrugged. His Coke bottle was half lifted to his mouth. "Too much like another jungle."

Vietnam, she thought, of course.

John stretched his legs for a few minutes, walking down the nearly deserted village road. He stopped once and spoke to an old man who was sitting on his porch steps. Kamisha saw him gesture with his cane toward the coast and the old man reply and nod.

"What were you talking about?" she asked when John came back and climbed into the passenger seat, his cane resting on the floorboards.

"I asked how far it was to Culebra. The hotel's near there."

Kamisha put it in drive. "So? How far?"

"Ten kilometers. An *hour*," he replied, and they both laughed.

The coastal mountains were filled with the ubiquitous jungle and wild fruit trees, as well. There were coconuts and mangoes and pineapples, the fruit ripe for the picking. Kamisha stopped several times to gather up fruit that lay on the side of the road. He laughed at her.

She did like being in his company. And she was immensely glad she'd come along, although she still wasn't exactly certain why she'd agreed. After all, she couldn't be absolutely positive that John wasn't involved in the whole mess with Rick and the club. Of course, if he wasn't, she might have been in greater danger staying in Aspen.

But there was another reason she had to consider, another reason why she was making this crazy trip. John fascinated her. His words stuck in her mind: *I want you to get to know me.* She wanted to know John better, yes. Much better. She wanted to drive on through the jungle, just the two of them alone—on and on and on.

She glanced over at his profile and toyed with a novel idea. It was possible that she was actually falling in love.

It was early evening when they arrived at the hotel. Kamisha pulled into the parking lot reserved for employees just as a Sasha Airline flight was coming in, landing on a narrow airstrip carved out of the jungle. How easily they could have taken the small commuter flight, she thought. But then every minute they'd had alone together had been precious. John had known that, hadn't he? He'd called Juan Luis from Aspen to have the rental car ready because he'd anticipated those moments. The notion gave her a warm, spreading feeling deep in her belly.

Kamisha's room was luxurious. It was a suite, actually, done in pale pastels with blue-striped cushions on the living room couch. The carpet was rose, the curtains a paler rose. There were pastel seascape watercolors on the walls that were painted with the slightest blush of pink. The bathroom was white marble. The dressing room had a dainty little stool in front of the mirror. Every imaginable toiletry had been provided in a wicker basket, right down to lemon-scented soap from France.

But the view from the balcony was best. Her suite faced the turquoise-blue waters of the Pacific, overlooking a wide cove. Mountains stood at the entrance, green sentinels guarding the tranquility of the bay. She opened the sliding glass door and stood on the balcony, her hands on the smooth rail, and breathed in the salty air. She'd expected adjoining rooms in the spanking new hotel. But John's room was down the hall and faced the verdant mountainside. With the Panamerican Trade Conference scheduled to begin tomorrow, she assumed he'd been hesitant to take up one of the better rooms. It was a typical gesture, Kamisha knew, for an owner.

Despite the fact that one of the four wings was still not ready for occupancy, it was a lovely hotel. Nestled on the side of the mountain, its whitewashed structures gleamed in the tropical sun. There were two swimming pools, covered cabanas, tennis courts, exercise rooms, outdoor restaurants and lush gardens everywhere. A set of stairs wended its way down through the jungle to the beaches below. For the less hardy an open Jeep made the trip down the dirt road every fifteen minutes.

She took in one last breath of balmy sea air, then went back inside. It was too late in the day for a swimsuit, so she changed into loose white cotton slacks that she rolled up to her knees and a bright red tank top and sandals. She put her hair back in a patterned red scarf, then sat on the edge of the bed and picked up the phone, dialing John's room.

"Would you like to go for a walk on the beach?" she asked. "It would be good for your leg."

"I wish I could," he said, "but I've got a dozen obligations right here in the hotel. But you go. I'll see you back here for dinner at, say, nine. Is that too late?"

"Nine it is. And, John," she said, toying with the phone cord, "thank you for bringing me. It's absolutely beautiful here."

"My pleasure."

It was nearly sunset by the time Kamisha began the descent to the beach. From the stairs she could see the small fishing village nearby, a quarter of a mile to the north. But there were no buildings on the beach anywhere, only rows of tall palm trees and a sandy parking area. The Costa Rican beaches belonged to the government and to the people. It was unfortunate, Kamisha thought, that so many of the U.S. beaches were plagued with high rises and overcrowding.

Though the sun was setting, the sand was still warm on her toes. She walked to the water's edge to try out the temperature of the Pacific. Warm, delightfully so. And then she began to stroll at a lazy pace toward the village, checking her watch. It was seven-thirty. Plenty of time before dinner.

The sun finally dipped into the Pacific, casting the beach and the face of the hotel in magenta and gold. Above the building clouds clung to the jungle-clad mountainside, clouds tinged a deep lavender from the last rays of light. She couldn't fathom her presence in this Eden. At home in Aspen it would be cool already, cool and dry and absolutely cloudless. Club members would be just leaving for their after-work exercise program. And Rick... But Rick was in the hospital.

She swept a loose tendril of pale hair from her damp cheek and marveled at how easily she'd left the stress behind. John had been responsible for that. And somehow the problems at the club and Brigitte with all her nuttiness and troubles seemed far, far removed from this hidden corner of the world.

Ahead, several fishing boats were just making shore. Her stomach began to growl just watching the men unload the day's catch. She ventured close, smiling when they looked up to see her there. The boats were low and squat, and she moved closer, curious.

"What kind of fish?" she asked one of the men.

He gave her a broad smile. "*Pescado*," he said, then shrugged. "Feesh."

"I know, but what kind?" she urged.

But he only smiled and pointed and said, "Feesh, *mucho* feesh *por la señorita.*"

Well, they looked marvelous, anyway. And she could hardly wait to join John. What would she wear? And what would he wear? She adored him in summer white. His skin pale, his dark hair combed back smoothly. Would they dine outside by candlelight, the warm, tropical breeze caressing them? And then later. What did the evening hold in store?

She began to head back along the darkening shoreline, her sandals dangling from her fingers. There were a few other strollers out now, too, probably guests newly arrived. The beach was irresistible. Ahead she could see the stairs that led up to the Montaña y Mar Hotel. Lights had come on, illuminating the luxuriant hillside, displaying the palms and flowers. A soft, sea-scented breeze touched her back, cooling her.

Yes, they'd eat and talk and probably walk the scented grounds. And then maybe a cocktail from the lounge. But she'd insist they sit outside, perhaps by the pool where the palm fronds would click above their heads. Perhaps John would sit near. He might take her warm hand in his, stroke her fingers. He might even press his lips gently to her bare shoulder. She could almost feel it, her skin tingling at his phantom touch.

God, but I want him, she thought, and the idea was both frightening and exhilarating. She wanted all of him. If he'd take her to his room, she'd play no more games. She'd let him make love to her.

But would he?

There was still that reserve in John despite his easy conversation. For all she knew he didn't even desire her, not in that way.

Sandals still dangling from her hand, Kamisha began to climb the stairs back toward the hotel. Perspiration broke out on her neck and brow and upper lip. But it wasn't the hot, wet night. It was John; it was wondering and agonizing and second-guessing. What did he really want from her? And if she knew the answer, could she even provide it?

CHAPTER TWELVE

HE PHONED HER ROOM at 8:30 to say he'd be a few minutes late. "I'm terribly sorry," he said, "but the meeting's run over."

"Don't worry, I'm fine."

"Hungry?"

"Starved," she replied with a laugh.

"Hang on. I'll be there as soon as I can."

She wore a turquoise silk suit with full harem pants. The neck of the jacket plunged into a deep V, and Kamisha knew the color made her eyes look very blue.

It was a familiar routine: hair, makeup, shoes, accessories. She questioned for the first time in her life why she automatically went through the motions. But from the beginning she'd been trained to look her best. Women were valued above all for their appearance, she'd been taught. But as she wandered out onto the balcony and breathed in the fragrant air, Kamisha questioned that ironclad rule. John had seen her at her worst, with a torn bathrobe and uncombed hair, yet it hadn't appeared to matter to him. And, if what she looked like didn't matter to him, then maybe it was Kamisha herself that mattered to him. He'd seen through every smoke screen she'd thrown up, every subterfuge she'd attempted, and he still wanted her for...something. Companionship? Friendship? What?

It was such an odd, discomfiting sensation, to know a man wanted her for what she truly was, not what she appeared to be. And yet it was a great relief not to have to pretend anymore. She'd have to tell Brigitte when she got back...if Brigitte would speak to her. She wanted her friend to know, to understand this new discovery she'd made. It was important. Oh, god, Brigitte would *have* to forgive her and be her friend. They'd only had each other all these years.

But now, maybe, Kamisha had John. She looked out into the black velvet night, drew in a heavy, tropical air and smiled to herself. Yes, maybe she'd found a man.

His knock sent a shiver of excitement through her. She opened the door, and he stood there, impeccably dressed in a white dinner jacket, black trousers, a cummerbund.

"John," she said breathlessly.

"Sorry I'm late."

"It's all right."

He gestured at his formal clothes. "I'm still working, unfortunately. There's a banquet going on downstairs, and I've got to make an appearance."

"Am I going to be in the way? I mean, if you..."

He smiled. "I'm sure they'd rather look at you than me. These Latin men appreciate a beautiful woman."

She stepped out into the hallway with him and closed her door behind her. "What about you, John? Do you appreciate beauty?"

He took her arm. "Of course. Are you fishing for a compliment?"

"I would be with another man, but with you... I think I really want to know."

"You're beautiful, Kamisha. But that's not why I asked you to make this trip with me." He met her gaze frankly. "In a painting or sculpture there is only beauty. In a woman there is also passion and intellect and tenderness and need."

"And in a man?"

He nodded. "Yes, the same."

She walked beside him, slowing her pace to his, and felt his hand on her arm, keeping her close. She was proud to walk beside this man, bursting with a newfound joy, full of insane ripples of happiness and hope and gratification.

The banquet was being held on a covered veranda overlooking one of the pools. A large banner announced the Panamerican Trade Conference in English and Spanish, and there must have been three hundred people seated, being served by legions of white-coated waiters.

John showed her to a table near the door that led back into the hotel. "The getaway table," he said. "This dinner will go on for hours. Speeches and toasts, the usual."

"You don't have to stay?" she asked.

"God forbid. I'll be introduced after the meal, I'll stand and bow and say a few words. That's all."

Good, she thought. Then she'd have him to herself for the rest of the night. She'd have him to talk to, to look at, to touch—perhaps to hold hands or kiss. He'd never caressed her.

Huge tropical blooms hung over the veranda in teeming fecundity, almost artificial in their size and brilliance. Somewhere in the underbrush surrounding them howler monkeys chattered and rustled. Flowers adorned the tables in gorgeous masses, pearled with moisture.

Shrimp cocktails appeared before them, and their glasses were filled. "I hope you don't mind," John said. "It's a set menu."

"I don't mind. Your hotel is beautiful, John, and I'm sure the food is just as good."

"Looking at it professionally?"

She smiled. "No, I'm on vacation, remember?"

"Yes, I remember." He toyed with his wineglass. "I phoned Aspen a little earlier. I thought you might want to know."

"Rick?"

"He's doing all right. He can't be visited yet. Apparently he's told the police nothing."

"Um."

He reached across the table and took her hand. "Now, shall we forget all that?"

"Yes, all of it," she said fervently. "You said you wanted me to get to know you. All right, I'm willing. What should I know?"

He kept her hand in both of his and searched her eyes. "You know most of it. I haven't hidden anything. My family, the war, my business. I'm a very simple man, Kamisha. There are no secrets in my life."

She shook her head. "No, you're not simple. You're complicated. I never know what you're going to do or say or what you think. John, I don't even know what you think about me." She took a deep breath. "I don't know what you want from me."

"I want from you nothing except what you want to give me of your own free will."

"What? What can I give you?"

"Your friendship, your caring, your needs," he said carefully.

"That's it?" She drew her hand from his and sipped her wine.

"Yes."

"Why, John? Why me?"

He looked away from her for a minute, then turned back. "Because I see something in you that is good and fine, Kamisha."

She started to say something, but he held his hand up to stop her.

"Not your body or your face, although they're lovely. I mean inside."

She drew in a quavering breath. This was difficult, wonderful, exciting, but so hard. "I'm a mess inside. Brigitte keeps telling me how I can't care for anyone because my parents didn't love me. I'm so afraid she's right, John."

He shook his head. "You're full of love, Kamisha."

"How do you know?"

"Trust me, I know."

Sudden tears burned in her eyes. She blinked, embarrassed, and felt one hot tear tremble on her lashes, then slide down her cheek. She raised a hand, but he stopped her and brushed it away with his own finger.

"See?"

Broiled fish arrived, with a béarnaise sauce, vegetables, rice. Kamisha ate a little, watching John all the time, noticing how he ate, seeing his hand on the fork, watching his lips, the muscles in his jaw when he chewed, his strong throat when he swallowed. The conversation rose and fell around them, the monkeys chattered, but she heard nothing, saw nothing but John's face and hands, the ruffled front of his shirt as it rose and fell with his breathing.

Her appetite faded. A feeling so powerful came over her that she could do nothing but give in to it. This was no game. This was love and trust. This was absolutely primitive—a man and a woman who wanted to be together, who needed each other, who fitted together like the two halves of a whole.

"Kamisha," he asked, "are you all right? You're not eating."

"I'm fine. I've never been better." She leaned across the table and took his hand boldly. "Don't worry about me."

It was late when the speeches started. A portly man at the head table stood and welcomed everyone in accented English. "We wish to thank our host, Señor Leopardo, for providing such a *marvilloso* hotel for our meeting. John? Where are you, John?" the man said, searching the crowd.

John stood up, raised a hand to attract attention, smiled at the gathering. "Thank you, Señor Umberto, it's my pleasure. Enjoy your visit here." Then he repeated his remarks in Spanish, and there was applause. Kamisha clapped, too. She was proud of John. Oh, yes, he was very special, a wonderful person, and he wanted her. He'd chosen *her*.

The heavyset man went on, introduced someone else who stood.

"Let's get out of here," John said quietly. "I retired as of this moment."

"Yes, let's," she whispered.

It was as if she walked on air, or floated. John's hand was at the small of her back, ushering her inside the hotel. Where were they going? she wondered. What would happen now?

A fine sheen of perspiration covered her as the humidity wrapped itself around her like a clinging veil. She felt the warmth of John's body next to her, and she knew she needed him beside her now, tonight, and tomorrow and always.

"Are you tired?" he asked.

"No."

He stopped, pulled her around to face him and held both her arms. "You owe me nothing, Kamisha. Do you understand? I will take nothing from you but what you want to give me freely."

She felt herself melt and sag inside. "I want you," she breathed. Then she just stood there, her eyes closed, waiting.

He drew her closer, touched his lips to hers. Exquisite bursts of pleasure exploded inside her.

"My God," he said against her lips. "Kamisha..."

A group of people, laughing, chatting, were approaching. John pulled away from her, touched her cheek and said, "Not here. It could be very embarrassing." He smiled down at her. "But if you insist..."

"No, no." She was hot all over, dizzy. Her skin tingled from head to toe and wild thoughts crowded her mind.

He took her hand and kissed her knuckles, then led her on, down corridors, around a corner. She was lost, had no idea where they were. She followed, sure of John, sure of herself, full to overflowing with her love.

Finally he stopped in front of a door. "This is your room."

"Yes, yes, I..."

"Your key." He held his hand out.

She found it, gave it to him, saw him open her door and hold his hand out to her.

"Come," he said quietly, and she went to him.

His lips were soft and hard all at once. She clung to him, opening like a flower under his touch. He was solid, hard-muscled all over, smelling of after-shave and wine. His arms were strong, holding her, his hands pressed her back, her buttocks.

She whimpered with her need and reached her hands under his jacket to get closer. His shirt was damp. She felt his fingers at her zipper. Then his hand was splayed on her bare back, his fingers kneading her flesh.

His tongue mingled with hers, and she could feel his heartbeat against her chest.

"Wait," he whispered. He pulled his coat off, loosened his tie, started taking the studs out of his shirtfront.

She helped him, fumbling at the studs. His skin glowed palely in the moonlight that came through the open balcony doors. Then her clothes dropped, sighing, to the floor, and they stood together, skin to skin, holding each other.

His beard was rough, as she'd imagined, but it felt good. His hands were gentle, knowing. They sat on the edge of her bed and kissed again, lingeringly, until he pushed her back and lay beside her.

He supported himself on one elbow and pushed her hair off her forehead with the other. "You aren't afraid anymore."

"No."

"I'm glad."

He leaned down to kiss her, drew his lips over her throat to find the spot where the pulse beat. Lower still his lips traced, finding a nipple, drawing it into his mouth until she moaned.

Outside the hot night wind rustled in the oversize fronds of the jungle, and a monkey scolded once, then was silent. Kamisha was in a foreign land, making love to a man who was a stranger to her. Yet his body was as familiar to her as her own. He fit against her and knew all her secret places, stroking, whispering, loving her. His fingers were light on her flesh, then demanding. He kneaded her hip and thigh as she lay next to him on her side. Feather-light, he ran a hand along the back of her knee until ripples of joy coursed upward, making her squirm and moan and twist her own fingers in his hair. He laughed gently, looked up into her eyes for a moment before his tongue again found a nipple. Kamisha arched her back and sighed in pure delight.

She had no shame, no self-consciousness. She loved John with her body, tasting, touching, wanting to give him as much pleasure as he gave her.

He entered her and filled her, rocking over her in a rhythm as old as time. Quicker, harder. She held on to him tightly and went with him, gasping, reaching…to the pinnacle, crying out her release, feeling him inside her, over her, all around her, loving him, adoring him.

Later she opened her eyes to find John propped on one arm again, watching her, smiling. His hair was mussed, and sweat gleamed on his skin.

"You were sleeping," he said.

"I wasn't."

"You were. Out cold." He drew his fingers through her hair that lay spread like a pale fan on the pillow.

She sighed happily. "I guess you must have tired me out."

"Go back to sleep," he murmured.

She nestled against him, drawing in his smell, feeling his damp skin, full of joy at his closeness. "Do you have to go back to your room?" she asked sleepily.

"No, not if you want me to stay."

"Stay," she whispered, closing her eyes again.

She woke to the sound of the shower on in her bathroom. The night came flooding back, and she lay there savoring the memory, utterly relaxed. John. The leopard. He'd attacked, caught his prey, devoured her. She was his now, part of him.

He came out of the bathroom, a towel around his waist, droplets of water on his skin. He looked young and happy, well rested.

"You're awake," he said. "Hungry?"

"Starved."

"You always say that."

She stretched, the sheet falling off. "I didn't eat much last night. I was otherwise employed."

He limped toward her, and she saw his knee for the first time. Yes, just as she'd imagined. A long, puckered ridge, shiny white scar tissue. Yet his calf below it was strong and curved, and above it his thigh swelled out against the white towel. His injury was part of him, just like his strong hands or the black hair on his chest or his thin, curved, sensitive mouth, and she accepted it, loved it just as she loved every inch of him.

He stopped, seeing her eyes on him, and looked down. "Pretty, isn't it?" he said.

"John. Come here." She held her hand out to him.

He moved toward her and stood looking down at her, his eyes shadowed.

"It's beautiful," she said, tracing the scar with her finger. "It's part of you, and I think it's a beautiful knee.'' She tugged at his hand, pulling him down next to her.

"Oh, God, Kamisha," he said, "where have you been all these years?"

"At your club in Aspen. Didn't you know?" she asked facetiously.

"I knew. I knew. But—"

"Shh.'' She ran a hand over his flat stomach and felt him tense up. "Are you ticklish?"

"I don't know. Try me."

She ran her fingers along his ribs. "Well?"

"A little. Maybe you should try lower."

"Naughty, naughty." She kissed him full on the lips, then drew her hand back. "Will anyone be looking for you? I mean, in your room. Do you have to go to work this morning?"

He glanced at the bedside clock. "Not for an hour."

"Oh, good."

She took his head in her hands and covered his face with kisses. He moved against her. "Ah, Kamisha," he said, "I wish..."

"What?" she whispered against his skin. "What do you wish, John?"

"For this, that's all, just for this."

She knelt over him, her hair hanging down like a curtain. His towel fell away, and she lowered herself onto him. He was ready. He filled her, grunting with pleasure. She rose over him and fell back, again and again, watching his face as the ripples of passion washed across it. She felt enormous power because she gave him that pleasure— her and no one else. She was full of strength and exultation and fertility, a primitive earth goddess.

It came on her suddenly, a wave of pleasure so intense that she nearly fainted. "Oh!" she cried out, surprised, lost. "Oh!"

Collapsing on him, she lay there, breathing hard, exhausted. She became aware of his hand stroking her back, up and down, up and down.

He loved her, too. He must. She had to be careful, though, not to assume too much, not to push him. John was a man who knew what he wanted, and he'd made it clear he wanted her. When he was ready to commit to something more, he'd tell her. There was time, lots of time. All she had to do was love him and wait.

"Do you have to go yet?" she asked, turning her head sideways on his sweat-slicked chest.

"Not yet," he said.

HE'D NEVER FELT this way in his life. He'd spoken to the chef and
the maître d'; he'd checked with the head housekeeper, and made a
call to Juan Luis in San José. He'd worked hard all day, doing his
job, making sure the hotel ran like clockwork, touring the unfinished
wing with the workers. But he was only going through the motions.
Inside he ached for Kamisha and thought about her every moment.

He'd only had time for a quick phone call after the formal luncheon.

"Hello," she'd answered breathlessly.

"It's me," he'd said.

"I know." She'd laughed. "Who else would call me here?"

"What are you doing? Bored?"

"No, I'm as happy as a clam. Reading, relaxing. I miss you."

"I miss you, too. Damn, I just can't get away until this afternoon."

"I know. Listen, I'll go down to the beach later. If I'm not in my
room, that's where I'll be. Come down and join me when you're
done."

"And get some sun on my city pallor?"

"Sure, risk it all."

"Kamisha..."

"Yes, John?"

"Nothing. I'll talk to you later. As soon as I can. Be good."

"Oh, John, I'm so glad you brought me here. I'm so happy."

"Look, I've got to go. Later, all right?"

"All right."

Impatience tore at him all afternoon, but things kept cropping up.
A shortage of a certain vintage of white wine, a problem with the
laundry, a new brochure to look over, an employee who was stealing.
A million small, nagging details that inundated him, drowning him
in aggravation.

At six he phoned her room. No answer. She was down at the beach
then. He hurried to his room, threw off his clothes and pulled on a
bathing suit. God, he hadn't been to a beach for years! Not since R
and R in Vietnam. No, he'd been too busy, too tied up, too damn
mature to put on a bathing suit and lie on a beach.

A shirt, open in front, sunglasses, his cane. Ridiculous, a bathing
suit and a cane. He didn't care. Kamisha was waiting, as impatient
as he was, her long, lean body awaiting him. Her love warming him,

resurrecting his dead heart. He felt young again, a boy who was going to meet his girl. This time it would be different; this time he wouldn't lose his woman to the voracious hunger of the press.

It had been ten years since he'd been crazy about a woman. Ten years since Jo, the girl he was going to marry. Oh, yes, it was going to work, he'd assured himself then. She'd been young and innocent and pretty, like a china figurine, but, oh, how she'd run when the TV cameras started following her and John around. She'd gotten hurt and frightened and left him cold.

Down the stairs to the beach. Damn his knee; it slowed him. Across the warm, giving sand. The sea sighed and splashed, blue, as blue as Kamisha's eyes.

Not many people were left on the beach; the sun was low. They were all resting in their rooms, showering, changing for dinner.

Where was she?

He walked with difficulty through the sand, his cane sinking into the softness, searching the beach, impatient.

"John," he heard. There, over there. She sat on a big red towel, her knees crossed Indian-fashion, wearing a black tank suit, her skin as smooth and tan as satin.

He waved and limped toward her.

"Hi," she said. "It's about time."

"Sorry, I got hung up."

"I know. I'm a workaholic, too. Only now I'm on vacation."

He sat on her towel and put down his cane. "What a day."

"Relax. Lie down. I'm so relaxed I think I'm going to melt." She laughed at herself. "Listen to me."

He leaned over and kissed her. "I'm glad you're enjoying yourself."

"I'd be enjoying myself even more if I had you to myself every second of the day."

"Selfish."

"Yes," she said. "Very."

"There's another dinner tonight."

"Oh."

"We don't have to go."

"Don't let me keep you from something important."

"I won't." He fingered a lock of her hair that lay on her shoulder. "I know my priorities."

"Work."

"I may rethink that priority."

She smiled and lay back on the towel, her eyes closed, her hand resting lightly on his knee. "I love it here," she said, sighing, and he recalled her sighs of pleasure the night before.

"Um." He sat there and looked at her, simply looked, drank his fill. He couldn't fit his mind around the reality of her there with him, giving him the precious gift of her body and her love.

He'd said he wanted only what she chose to give, and it was true. But what he'd received was so much more than he'd imagined. It was as if a dam, an emotional dam, had been broken in her, and the water was flooding over it, drowning everything in its path, a sea of passion drowning them both.

She tapped his knee. "Lie down, relax. Stop staring at me."

"How do you know I'm staring?"

"I can feel it."

"Your eyes are closed."

"It doesn't matter."

He stretched out next to her. The sea gurgled and whispered to itself, and the sun was still warm.

"I've been here for hours," she said lazily.

"What do you want to do tonight? Eat in the restaurant, walk to the village? There's a disco, too."

Her lips curved deliciously. "How about room service?"

"That can be arranged." He rolled over onto one elbow to see her better.

"Your room or mine?" she asked.

"Yours has a better view."

"What will the hotel staff say, John?"

"Nothing."

"But you're the owner. You're acting disgracefully." She was smiling, though, teasing.

He shrugged, but she couldn't see that; her eyes were still closed. "Does it bother you?" he asked, tracing a finger down her jaw, her throat, her chest.

"No."

"Me neither."

She sighed and rolled over onto her stomach. "Do you want to go swimming?"

"Is the water warm?"

"Chicken. Warm as soup. I bet you've never been in the water here, and you own the hotel."

"You're right. But I'm a good swimmer. It's part of my physical therapy program."

"Come on then." She sprang up and held her hand out to him. "Come on."

He took it. She braced herself and pulled him up, and they walked down to the water's edge, hand in hand. She let go then, ran in and flung herself into the waves, turned onto her back and paddled there, afloat.

John walked in, up to his knees, then his waist. He made a clean dive and felt the water surround him, support him. He surfaced and stroked out to where she floated on her back.

"Nice, huh?" she asked.

"Great. Now I know what to tell the guests." He floated, too, looking up at the sky.

"You can stand here. It's shallow," Kamisha said. She stood, sculling her arms to stay upright.

He jackknifed and dived underwater. Her arms and legs were greenish and wavering. He put his arms around her waist and pulled her under with him. She felt cool and slippery, and her arms came around him as they kicked to the surface together, bursting through to the air, laughing, gasping, splashing.

"No fair," she cried.

"Sure it is."

They clung together, sleek and wet. Her hair was plastered to her shoulders, her skin smooth and silky, warm above water, cool below. She entwined her legs around his, and he held her up like that, buoyed by the seawater. Bending his head, he kissed her, long and thoroughly. Her hands clasped his shoulders and her body pressed to his. She tasted of saltwater and sweetness. He tried not to think, tried to wipe his mind clean and take the pleasure as it came. Exquisite, blinding pleasure.

"Oh, God," she whispered, against his mouth. "You feel so good."

"I won't be able to get out of the water," he said lightly.

"No one will notice." She smiled impishly. "No one but me."

Eventually they returned to the beach. It was empty. The sun was setting over the ocean, washing the sky with tropical hues. They flung themselves down on the towel, dripping water, breathing hard.

"It'll be dark soon," he said idly. "And I bet you're starved."

"Salty and sandy and starved."

"We should go back," he said.

She rolled over on top of him, pinning his entire length to the towel. Her hair hung down, heavy and wet, tickling. She gazed into his eyes, leaned down and touched her lips to his. "You make me feel very special, John. I've never felt this way before. I'm afraid it's addictive."

He put his arms around her, loving the feel of her weight on him. "You are special."

"This isn't...I mean..." She looked away for a moment, serious suddenly. "This isn't a one-night stand for you, is it?"

"No, Kamisha."

"You're sure?"

There it was, that vulnerability again, the little girl lost. He hugged her tighter. "I'm sure."

"I won't let you go easily, John. I'm warning you."

"Be careful, lady. You're scaring me to death."

The sky was fading to purples and grays when they climbed the stairs to the hotel.

John felt as though his skin were sensitive—from the sun and sand, he supposed. But it could have been from Kamisha's nearness. He felt sensitive all over, inside, too, alive to all kinds of new possibilities.

Even Kamisha with her tan was a little red. He could see a line of white skin that followed the curve of her bathing suit straps and also along her thigh where her suit ended. Abruptly he wanted her, there and then, wanted to strip her suit off and see the white skin underneath.

He was out of control, spinning in the midst of new, remarkable sensations. But it was good, fantastic. It was life as it was meant to be lived.

There was the door to her room. She was opening it, turning to him. "Are you...?" she began.

He stepped in with her, set his cane against a chair and took her in his arms. Hot and sandy, gritty, salty, they stripped off their wet suits, let them drop to the floor, clung and caressed and whispered and loved each other.

CHAPTER THIRTEEN

JOHN WOKE AT DAWN to the cacophony of jungle noises outside the screened door and the swishing of the offshore breeze in the palm trees. He lay there for a time, savoring the moment—the feel of a woman next to him, the scent of her body, the soft soughing of her breathing. He couldn't remember the last time he'd awakened like this. Maybe he never had.

He felt happy, a singular and unfamiliar sensation that took him a minute to recognize and acknowledge. Not just physically sated but content inside. He lay there, his hands folded behind his head, and grinned up at the ceiling.

Eventually he rolled over and kissed her shoulder, breathing in the scent of her skin, feeling its softness. He was being selfish; he should let her sleep, but he couldn't wait another moment.

She stirred and murmured something, then her eyes opened sleepily.

"Wake up, Sleeping Beauty," he said.

She stretched, lithe and catlike, and turned onto her side to face him. "Hi," she whispered.

"I'm sorry I woke you. I couldn't help it," he said, smoothing her hair back. "I feel like we have so little time together."

"Do we have to go back soon?"

"No, well, not today, anyway."

"Good. Do you have to work today?"

"Not much. A couple of things." He kissed her nose.

"You need a little R and R. I can see that. Just lie around and relax. The beach maybe," she said lazily. "And room service."

"We never ate last night."

"I know." She laughed a little, her eyes sparkling. "My stomach's growling."

"Let me listen." He put his ear to her smooth, tanned stomach and listened, then turned his head to kiss her bare skin there.

"John," she whispered, and he felt her muscles tighten. "You better not do that."

"Why not?" he murmured against her belly.

"Um, you know."

He straightened and lay half on top of her, feeling her long, taut length against him. "I know, Kamisha, but what I'm not sure of is if you can perform on an empty stomach."

"I don't know," she answered, moving against him. "Should we find out?"

She entwined her legs around his and arched against him, her skin warm, soft satin sliding over muscle. He felt himself growing aroused, his breath quickening. His hands roamed her body. He kissed her everywhere, drawing response from her like a maestro on an instrument. And all the while he watched her, drank in her sleek beauty like a man too long denied water. Pale morning sun that filtered through the jungle mist fell in patches on her flesh, highlighting a hipbone, bringing forth a curving breast from the shadows. He touched the precious curves with his lips until her flesh quivered. Lightly, lightly, he drew his tongue across a nipple, pausing only momentarily at its crest before he moved lower to her belly.

He entered her finally, fighting for control, wanting to give her pleasure, to satisfy her as she'd never been satisfied before. He was poised over her, his breathing ragged, his eyes closed, and he felt her gather under him. She moaned and drew in her breath and cried out, and then he could release his own passion into her, his body hard and strong and absolutely fulfilled.

When she stirred under him, he sighed and rolled aside. He lay propped on an elbow and studied her face.

"Penny for your thoughts," she said.

"Not much going on in my head right now," he replied.

"Um. This is nice. Better than nice."

"Kamisha." He paused, unsure of what he wanted to say.

She touched his face with her fingers. "Ask me anything."

"Did you...I mean, have you...dated much?"

She smiled. "You want to know how many men I've slept with, don't you?"

"No, no, it's none of my business."

"It is. Everything about me is your business. John, I want you to know everything. I've never been honest with a man in my life, but I will be with you." She hesitated. "I was married for almost a year.

Josh and I were kids playing at house. I don't think he was a very passionate man. He was too selfish. I guess I wasn't very knowledgeable about men, so I didn't know any better. Now I know, though, and when I remember—''

"You don't have to tell me," he said.

"I do. I have to be honest with myself, too. I haven't had many men, John. Since Josh, very few. I flirt with men. I'm good at that. I control the relationship that way, but when it comes to sex, I back off. I guess...oh, I don't know... Maybe it's my way of getting back at men."

"You're so beautiful. How can you blame them?" he said, holding her hand, kissing her fingers one at a time. "You should pity them."

She shook her head. "All my pity was reserved for me. Men always looked at me, sure. But they never put any value on what was inside. A homely woman, she has a chance to be loved for what she really is, but not me. I suppose it's sort of like being rich. Then you're always on guard against men who will love your money and not you."

He thought for a minute, grateful that Kamisha could confide in him. Maybe all the pain he'd endured was worth something, after all; it had made him sensitive to her and able to recognize what lay under her brittle surface. Maybe everything in his life had prepared him for this time, this place, this woman.

"Am I making any sense?" she asked, searching his face.

He nodded.

"Okay, Dr. Freud," she said, nestling against him.

"What about your parents?" he asked. "Did you ever tell them this?"

"You're kidding." She ran her fingers through the fine hair on his chest. "I didn't even know myself, and they wouldn't have listened. They would have said what they always did, 'Kamisha, we did the best we could for you.' And it's true, you know. They did the best they were capable of. It just wasn't good enough. But, you know, I've come to terms with that."

"Do you see them much?"

She shrugged. "Not much. They drop by Aspen once a year to ski. Unless the snow's better in Europe. We speak on the phone. It's all very polite. Civilized. I might never have learned there was anything more to life."

He stroked the back of her head as it lay on his chest. "You knew."

"Maybe. I missed something. I didn't think it was a man, though."

"How wrong can a person be?"

"Very, very wrong," she said.

"Funny, my folks are just the opposite. Lots of wailing and fighting and loving. Typical Italian emotional outbursts. I loved my dad when I was a kid. He was a good father, and being the only son I was spoiled rotten, I guess. It was when I realized what he did, what he really did—I was in high school—that I turned away from him. It must have killed him, and my mother. I was very young and hard then, and you don't realize what pain you can inflict."

She lay there in his arms, quiescent, listening.

"When I look back, I think that's why I joined the army. I wanted to get farther away from him, as far as I could get." He paused, remembering. "I certainly succeeded."

"What was it like over there, John?"

"Hot, sweaty, smelly. Scary. You were scared all the time. You lived hard, played hard. Everyone had his own way of coping. It was a dirty war." He took a deep breath. "I made sergeant because I was the one with the most seniority, and our sergeant got blown up in front of me. There I was, a nineteen-year-old recruit, a college kid, in charge of a platoon of filthy, terrified men. You've got to wonder..."

"And Inky?" she said.

"He was in my outfit. My right-hand man. He knew more than anyone about war. Somehow you just knew Inky was a survivor. He was a lifer, but hadn't made sergeant yet. He kept getting busted. Fighting. Usually with his superiors."

"But not you?"

"Hell, no, *I* always listened to Inky."

"I wish I'd known you then," she murmured.

"No, you don't. I was a brash kid. You would have hated me. Besides, you were too young. You'd have been, let's see, eight years old."

"I would have adored you."

"You're prone to exaggeration, lady."

"And Inky, tell me how he ended up with you."

"Well, when the war was over, Inky decided the Special Forces were no fun anymore. That's the word he used—fun. He left the army, and we'd kept in touch, so he showed up one day. Just showed up. It was a time when I was low, feeling sorry for myself. My knee was giving me a lot of trouble. So Inky took over. He started me on a weight program. He...uh...he did me a lot of good."

"Friends are important," she mused, her fingers playing idly across his chest.

"Brigitte."

"Yes, good old Brigitte. I know how she looks to you, to the world. But she's the sweetest, most spontaneous person I've ever met. We were roommates in the Taos School. Both of us were outcasts, poor, lonely kids. Her parents sent her there because they couldn't handle her getting into trouble, and mine sent me to get rid of me. All in the name of doing what was best for their daughters. Maybe it was the best, because I met Brigitte. I couldn't have made it through without her. After my divorce, she took me in. Her marriage was pretty shaky at the time, but she took me in, sat up nights crying with me. And then when Freddy divorced her, she came to me. We've taken care of each other over the years."

"But you've taken care of her a little more," John suggested.

"I don't know. There are different ways of taking care of a person."

"Yes, there are."

"And I feel really bad about this fight we had. I can't understand why she got so upset at me telling you about the parties. It was almost as if she thought they weren't wrong, as if she were defending them. That's crazy, though. I know Brigitte, and if there were kids involved..."

"She'll come around."

"I hope so. Sometimes she gets so out of control that I get scared."

"Forget Brigitte for now," he said. "Remember, you're on vacation."

"Um, okay. I'll just lie here and listen to the birds like this all day."

"No beach? No room service?" he teased.

"Just you." She snuggled closer against him.

"Fine with me," he said into her hair.

She lay there, slender and warm in his embrace, and he thought that nothing had ever felt so good. He turned his head to say something to her and realized that she had dozed off. He smiled to himself and watched her for a while, drifting on a sea of pleasure, holding on to the perfection of the moment.

When he woke later, the sun was bright, the palms still, the morning offshore breeze at rest. He saw that Kamisha was awake, still buried in his arms, her mouth curved with a languid amusement as she watched him.

"Lazybones," she said.

"I'll show you who's lazy."

He found the tiny little spot on the column of her neck that held her pulse. He kissed it, then he drew his tongue downward, across her shoulder and collarbone, lower, to taste a breast again.

Kamisha sighed and squirmed gently as his hands moved beneath her and pressed her body to his. With infinite care John placed his lips between her breasts, kissing the hollow.

"Um," she said, "that feels so wonderful."

He smiled into her sleep-warmed flesh.

"Aren't you famished? We still haven't eaten since—"

"Hungry for you" was all he said, and it was true.

Kamisha turned his head up to her face and laughed. "I'm out of fuel, John, I'm going to have to eat something." She stirred, attempting to get up.

"All right," he said, propping his head on an elbow, "I suppose I shouldn't starve you."

"But you don't have to get up. I'll go fetch us some sweet rolls and juice and coffee."

"Call room service."

"I need to eat now. Not in twenty minutes. I'm faint."

"Are you always this famished?"

"'Fraid so. I'm such a pig."

"An active one."

He watched her pad across the room, the long thigh muscles in her legs curving femininely, her buttocks round and firm. She leaned to pick up her clothes, and her breasts hung deliciously. Naked, Kamisha was a centerfold, not as endowed as some, but beautiful to behold.

He hated to see her get dressed, and she teased him, tossing the smooth, silky curtain of her hair over a shoulder as she combed it out.

"Hurry back," John said. "I'm getting hungry, too." He smiled at her knowingly.

The room felt empty without her presence. Yet the aroma of their lovemaking lingered, a sweet male-female scent. He wanted her back. He wanted her soft warmth beneath him again. He was ready. And he was amazed at himself. Even as a young man he hadn't had this stamina. But then he hadn't known Kamisha, either.

It was a full ten minutes before he heard the key in the lock. He'd showered and shaved quickly and was standing in the steamy bathroom.

"John?" she called.

"In here. I'll just be a minute. Were they helpful in the dining room?"

"Oh...yes," she said, sounding strangely distracted.

"You brought coffee?"

"Ah, yes."

"Something wrong?"

There was no reply, and he wondered. When he came out of the bathroom, he saw her standing by the window, looking out. There was a tray of rolls and coffee and juice on the table, a folded newspaper. But Kamisha wasn't eating. She was frowning.

John's brow furrowed. "Thought you were starved."

"Oh," she said, turning to face him. "I am. I was."

He cocked his head, pulling on the white robe that the hotel supplied. "I get the feeling—" he began, but Kamisha interrupted.

"Oh, God, John," she said, her shoulders sagging, "I wasn't going to show you this. But you'd see it eventually." She reached down and picked up the newspaper, unfolding it. "Here," she said, walking to him, holding out the day's edition of the *Miami Herald* that was shipped abroad routinely the evening before.

"So?" he asked, taking it, looking at her.

"Read page two. Go on. Oh, John," she said, and there was a break in her voice.

John studied her strained face for a moment longer, then went over to the table, pouring himself a coffee, sitting down before he opened the paper. From the look on Kamisha's face he already knew he wasn't going to like this.

He turned to page two, shook the paper, folded it. The headline jumped up at him: "Aspen Love Nest, Mafia Involved. Mob running brothel in Aspen, claims Joanna Stern, wife of Senator Luke Stern of California."

John swore, then looked up at Kamisha. There were tears in her eyes. He tried to keep his cool.

"It gets worse," Kamisha whispered, and sank onto the bed. "Oh, John..."

With controlled effort he sipped on his coffee, then began to read the article. His fingers clenched the paper tightly:

At a Washington press conference today Mrs. Stern, 41, told reporters she was filing for divorce in California. Mrs. Stern claimed knowledge of "disgusting parties at Aspen's posh Ute City Club involving underage girls."

Mrs. Stern was quick to point out that the club's owner is none other than New York and Miami's John Leopardo, the son of famed Mafia kingpin Gio Leopardo. When asked if Senator Stern attended any of these parties, Mrs. Stern referred reporters to her lawyer.

John let out a deep, rasping breath. His rage made the print blur, but he forced himself to read on:

Mr. Leopardo could not be reached for comment today, nor was Senator Stern available. But this reporter learned that the manager of the swank Aspen club, Rick Simons, formerly of Miami, is currently in the hospital in Aspen.

Mr. Simons's doctor, John Freeman, told reporters that his patient received a bad beating at the hands of an unknown assailant. The assault raises several questions. Did Rick Simons threaten to go to the police with details of these parties? Has the self-proclaimed black sheep of the Leopardo family, John Leopardo, finally come back into the fold of brutality and vice?

For a long time John sat staring out the window, the paper drifting to the floor. It was happening again, all over again. The look on Kamisha's face—exactly the same. It was the nightmare that had come back to haunt him again and again over the years—the headlines, the filth in the papers, the tears and recriminations and, finally, the excuses, the severing and rejection.

He couldn't go through it again.

"John?" he heard her saying. "John, are you all right? John?"

He looked at her, and already the pain smote him like a bludgeon. "Yes," he forced himself to say, "I'm fine."

"How can they do this to you?" she asked, pacing the floor like a sleek, agitated panther. "It's so unfair."

He shrugged. "The press isn't in business to be fair."

"But you'll tell them the truth, won't you? Don't let them get away with this. If you tell them—"

"The truth," he mused, turning from her. Hadn't Jo said the same thing?

"It's horrible, horrible. Why are they doing this? Why can't they leave you alone?" Kamisha asked.

But he held up a silencing hand and then picked up the telephone. "Front desk," he said. He waited, his jaw clenched. "Have a bellman up to room 207 and room 220 in ten minutes. No, everything's fine, Alvarez. I've got an emergency at home. And arrange to have my rental car returned to San José. That's correct. When is the morning flight due in? All right, have them hold it. Thank you."

John replaced the receiver and put his hands on his hips, frowning.

"We're leaving?" Kamisha asked.

He had force himself to acknowledge her. "Yes. The commuter flight is due in twenty minutes. Can you be ready?"

"Well, yes, of course I—"

"All right. Twenty minutes, Kamisha. I don't want to miss this plane."

"We're going to Aspen today?"

"As fast as I can get there."

JOHN KNEW that from Kamisha's point of view he was being unreasonable. And cold. But he'd never been able to pretend. Anyway, he thought, she'd have to realize that they'd made a mistake in Costa Rica. Perhaps, though, it hadn't been a mistake. Rather, they both would do well to view it as an interlude, a brief affair. He'd been foolish to think otherwise even for a moment.

Now he was back to the real world.

They sat in a coffee shop in the New Orleans airport, waiting for the connecting flight to Denver. Kamisha sipped on a soda while John stared out the window at the tarmac. It was drizzling out, hot and steamy. Low, grainy clouds hung over the city. The weather suited his mood.

"John," he heard her ask, "can we at least talk about this?"

"There's really nothing to say, Kamisha."

"But there is. I'm a part of this, too."

He lifted a dark brow. "Are you?"

"Yes, I am."

"I don't think so. You have no idea what my life has been like."

"So am I supposed to pity you? Are you feeling sorry for yourself?"

"I was stating a fact."

"But you aren't your family. You aren't your father."

"Tell that to the press."

"What do you care *what* they think?"

"I don't care. Not for myself."

She was silent for a moment. "Is it...me, then, you're worried about?"

"Can we drop this subject?" he said, then turned away and looked back out the window.

The flight to Denver was no better. Kamisha kept trying to get him to open up, but John had closed her out, coldly, deliberately. His walls were back up, firmly in place. Kamisha Hammill barely existed to him. When they reached Aspen, he'd put Inky in charge of watching over her. She'd be safe until he got to the bottom of this. And then it was home to New York, home to try to repair the damage caused by Rick Simons and God knows who else.

Damn, John thought. All those years of distancing himself from his father, from his entire family. All the years of living a practically celibate life because, after Jo, he could never ask a decent woman to share his family's name. The dozens of times he'd dodged the press. The Internal Revenue Service audits every time his father had faced a Senate investigation. Oh, sure, he'd thought about changing his name. But a stubborn kind of pride had kept him from doing so. And besides, John knew, the press wouldn't have been fooled for more than a day.

Despite it all, however, he'd darn near succeeded in living a solitary life where the media couldn't really get to him. Four beautiful health spas, twenty years of hard work and careful planning. And now *this*. Again.

The long line of barrier mountains, the Rockies, rose to the left of the plane. It was evening, the sun just setting behind the great mountains that formed the backbone of North America. As the plane banked, turning two degrees west toward the city of Denver, John could see a blanket of twinkling lights glowing softly in the growing dusk.

He felt a heavy sadness. This morning he'd been near true happiness. It had been like entering a dream, living a fantasy. He supposed now that he'd known all along it couldn't last, but he'd let himself go for once, let himself drift right into the middle of that Shangri-la. The foolish thing was to have taken Kamisha with him.

John looked directly ahead, but he was still aware of her sitting, straight-backed, next to him, leafing through a magazine. He wondered if she could see the pages, or if she was accusing him in her thoughts, blaming him for dashing her dreams.

He could explain to her. He could tell her that life with him would be a living hell. Oh, maybe not at first. But eventually she'd tire of the press hounding her. She'd get fed up with the questions: what was it like marrying into a Mafia family? And children. A man owed a woman her own family. How could a child be expected to put up with the teasing and jeering, the humiliation, a lifelong trauma? He could tell her about Jo, lovely, warm, naive Jo, whose love had shriveled up and died under the spotlight of the press.

Sure. He could tell Kamisha what the future really held in store. But she wouldn't believe him. She hadn't already lived it as he had. It was best to let it drop. Let her think what she would. She'd get over it faster. And, maybe, so would he.

What had she said as they'd departed New Orleans? *John, talk to me. For God's sake, let me help.*

He'd answered her in steely silence.

The landing gear thumped down beneath their feet. The stewardess in first class was saying something. John glanced at the beautiful woman who sat next to him and felt regret stab him in the breast.

CHAPTER FOURTEEN

KAMISHA LIFTED her hair off her neck, feeling its dampness. Her nerves were scraping together. She glanced out the window of the commuter flight and saw the lights of Aspen twinkling at the end of the valley below. In a couple of minutes the plane would land. Inky would be waiting with the car. They'd drop Kamisha off at her house, and they'd pull away, severing the single, fragile thread that existed between her and John. She knew in her heart that this was the end of their relationship. She wanted to cry.

When they deplaned and walked in silence through the cool mountain air toward the terminal, Inky was indeed there. He was standing by the double glass doors, unmistakable in his loose khaki trousers, casual pink shirt and leather jacket. He wasn't smiling this evening, she noticed. Probably all of Aspen had either read about John Leopardo and the scandal at the club or they'd heard the gossip by now.

"Good flight, boss?" he asked.

"Uneventful," John replied.

"You want I should get your bags while you wait in the car?"

"Sure, that will be fine."

Then he turned to Kamisha and said, "By the way, Miss Hammill, I finally picked up your car for you."

"Thanks, Inky. I appreciate it," she said unenthusiastically. Her car. Once, she would have been overjoyed to have it back, but that was before. Before John, before something truly mattered in her life.

The interior of the limo seemed too big, too hushed, too hot with the engine running and the windows closed. Kamisha sat across from John, facing the rear. The panic twisting in her belly made her breathing shallow. She needed to talk to John, to get him to talk to her. There were only a few more minutes before Inky would be there with their luggage—a few minutes to tell John that she loved him and was going to move heaven and earth to get them through this ordeal.

If only he'd listen.

"John," she began, "can we look at this reasonably? Can we talk about it?"

He shifted his gaze to her for a moment. "There's nothing to be said."

"But there is. I want to help. I want to help find out who put Rick in the hospital. I want to go to the press, tell them who you really are."

He only made a distracted gesture with his hand.

"I have connections with the press," Kamisha said. "I can get them to listen."

"Don't be naive."

She sighed. "I don't think I am. John, I care about you. I care about *us*."

And then Inky was there, and the panic welled up inside again, coiling and writhing in her. John had become a stranger.

They dropped John off at his condo first, both men insistent that Kamisha not stay alone in her house.

"Inky can drive you to Brigitte's," John began. "I insist that you—"

"I'm not staying there," she said. "I'm going home."

"You can't stay alone, Kamisha. Not until I clear up this business with Rick."

Wearily she shrugged. She knew he could ask her to stay at the condo with him. She also knew he wouldn't. "I just want to go home," she stated, and once again felt herself biting back tears.

He hesitated, and through her misery she could see that he really was worried about her, that he was weighing possibilities, alternatives. Somehow the fact that he cared so much about her physical safety seemed unimportant, almost insulting. If he really cared about her, if he *loved* her, he'd talk to her. He'd stay with her. He'd care for her feelings, not the physical shell.

"Okay," John said, "but lock your doors and windows. I'll send Inky with you to check things out. Don't take any chances. Call me immediately if you—"

"Oh, for God's sake, John," she said wearily.

"All right, fine. You're tired. We're both tired. Just be careful," he said. "I mean that, Kamisha."

"Don't worry. You won't have me on your conscience," she said darkly, then watched his form as he walked, limping badly, toward the condo. She waited for him to glance back, to at least lift a hand—something. But he never did.

SHE TRIED TO SLEEP that night, wept a few hot, bitter tears into her pillow and got up to pace and sit by the bedroom window. And there, out on the street, a long, pale sedan cruised by once, then twice, then again. John's car. Inky.

Oh, God, she wished he cared as much for her soul.

Kamisha phoned John the next morning to let him know she was all right. She'd been tempted not to but decided to be mature about it.

Inky answered. "Glad to hear you're fine," he said. "John's in the shower right now, Miss Hammill."

"Can you have him call me back, please?"

"Well, we were going to the hospital to see Rick as soon as John's dressed," Inky said hesitantly.

John was avoiding her. Inky had been given directions. He was cutting her out of his life, like an irritating bill collector. She swallowed and took a deep breath, forcing the lump in her throat down. "I think that's a great idea. I'm coming, too. Pick me up, will you?"

"Well, Miss Hammill, I—"

"I'll be ready, Inky. Don't forget me." Then she hung up quickly.

The sedan pulled up at her curb precisely half an hour later. So he'd decided to give in on this matter. Perhaps in the name of fairness or out of some misguided desire to let Rick face his accuser. She didn't care. It was enough that he was there, in her reach, in her sight. Close to her.

"Did you sleep well?" he asked politely. Sunglasses hid his eyes. He looked pale. Perhaps it was true what they said, that one's tan faded on the airplane on the way home from a vacation. Her heart squeezed, remembering the sun of Costa Rica, the sand, the tropical air...and John.

"Yes, thank you," she lied. Her own sunglasses hid her expression from him. The two of them—back to square one. How pathetic.

She heard Inky swear softly as they started up the long drive leading to the hospital. "The press is here," he said harshly, putting on the brakes.

"Damn." John sat up straight, his body tensed.

Kamisha could see it then, a van with a satellite dish on top and

News Star 4 on the side. Word had certainly gotten out fast. Aspen was in the news again.

"Inky," he said, "turn left, yes, there. We'll go through the emergency room door."

The emergency room was empty. In the winter it would be full of skiers with injuries, but now the one nurse sat behind the counter reading the *Aspen Times*.

She looked up, took in the two of them, obviously uninjured, and eyed John with suspicion, then dawning recognition.

"Excuse me, but who are you looking for?" the nurse asked. "Visiting hours aren't until noon."

Kamisha's back bristled, and she was about to say something when she felt John's warning hand on her arm.

"I'm terribly sorry," John said smoothly, "but I'm trying to avoid the reporters in front of the hospital. I'm Rick Simons's employer, and I would very much like to see him."

His aura of gentle but absolute command worked like a charm. "Room 107," the nurse said promptly. "Just don't be too long."

They found Rick propped up on pillows in a bed near the window that overlooked Maroon Creek Valley and the glistening white peaks beyond. If one had to be in a hospital, this was the place. Still, he was far from comfortable, his eyes bruised and swollen, his jaw wired shut. A chocolate milk shake sat half-finished on the movable table. CNN News was on the TV.

"Hello, Rick," Kamisha said tentatively, approaching the bed. "How do you feel?"

He looked them both over, obviously ill at ease, then snorted. "Lousy," he said, the word a hiss coming through his clenched teeth.

"I'm sure you are," Kamisha said, then looked at John.

"Hello, Rick."

There was a mumble through the wires that held his jaw in place.

"Look," John said, "you can guess why we're here."

"I won't," Rick managed to say. "Won't tell you."

John studied him for a minute. "I understand. But do you want to live in fear for the rest of your life?"

"I want to *live*," he said. "Period."

And then Kamisha tried. "Rick," she began, "wouldn't it be smarter to tell us who did this to you? We can go to the police. If you don't, you'll always be looking over your shoulder."

But Rick shook his head adamantly. "Leave me alone," he muttered.

"Okay," John said, "we will." He grasped his cane and took a few steps toward the door. He stopped there, turned and assessed Rick one last time. "With or without you," he said, "I'm going to find out who's responsible for this. When it all comes out, Rick, it would go better if you cooperate. Think about it. You know how to reach me."

"He's frightened," Kamisha said as they closed his door.

"He should be" was all John muttered.

She supposed she should be afraid, too, but somehow the matter of the parties and Rick and even Senator Luke Stern's involvement paled in comparison to her inner pain. What she wouldn't have given to melt that frozen place in John's heart. If he'd just talk to her, listen for a minute.

They began to head back toward the emergency room where they could exit without running into the News Star 4 team, but it seemed luck was against them. Coming down the corridor was a reporter and his cameraman.

"Come on," Kamisha said, tugging on John's arm, "let's just go."

But by then the reporter was already hurrying toward them, his mike on. John had stopped abruptly and was shrugging off Kamisha's grasp. His brow was creased in anger.

"John," she began, but was interrupted by the newsman.

"Mr. Leopardo," he was saying, "Mr. John Leopardo, isn't it?" Then suddenly the cameraman was switching on the light on top of his handset and positioning himself alongside the reporter.

John's posture stiffened. "That's correct," he said. "I am John Leopardo."

"Would you comment on allegations being made as to your club's involvement in—"

"No comment."

"And what about Mr. Rick Simons, who is now lying in a hospital bed?"

"I had nothing to do with that," John stated.

"Your father is Gio Leopardo, isn't that true?"

"That is correct." John's entire body had grown rigid.

"And the lady with you here," the camera swung to Kamisha, the light hot and bright in her eyes. "You are Miss Kamisha Hammill?"

She nodded.

"And you work for Mr. Leopardo at the—"

"I really don't have anything to say to you," Kamisha interrupted, "except to inform you that you haven't done your homework. Mr. Leopardo—"

"Are you suggesting—?"

"This interview is over," John said abruptly, and he took Kamisha's arm, leading her down the corridor.

Behind them Kamisha could hear the reporter saying, "You heard it here first. Miss Kamisha Hammill has insinuated..."

"God, I hate those people," John said flatly.

"Maybe the way to handle them," she began carefully, "is to tell them everything."

"It never works that way."

"It could. I know. I was the object of their lust when I divorced Josh," she said, striding alongside him through the emergency room door.

"It's hardly the same thing."

She let it drop. He'd been hounded all his life, accused of crimes he'd never committed, stared at, discussed. It was an open wound inside John, a problem he had no control over and thus one he'd never come to terms with. She could tell him that, but he wouldn't listen.

John was silent on the ride back to Aspen. Kamisha tried her best to reach him, but she felt as if she were talking to herself.

"There's somebody nearby," she said. "That's why Rick is afraid to talk. Somebody who can get to him."

"Um."

"Well, that's good to know, isn't it?"

"Um."

She could barely remember what he'd looked like when he smiled, when he made love, when he told her she was beautiful. Or had she only imagined those things?

"John—?" she started to say.

"I want you to stay with someone," he interrupted. "Just to be safe. Can you stay at Brigitte's?"

She sighed and looked out the tinted window. "I suppose. Although I would hardly call Brigitte's safe. It's a madhouse."

"I want you away from this mess and away from reporters. You're on vacation until further notice,'' he said coldly. "Can you call Brigitte and make the arrangements?''

It was something Kamisha supposed she had to do, but she didn't relish the confrontation with her friend that was bound to come. For a moment she was about to tell John she could look after herself, but that would have been childish.

"Yes, all right,'' she finally said to John when they parked in front of her house. "I'll call her.''

"Inky can take you out there,'' he began, but Kamisha put her foot down.

"*I'll* drive myself, John. I can't go around afraid all the time. I *won't*. I'd rather end up like Rick.''

"No,'' he said quickly, "don't even think that. I'm going to get to the bottom of this, Kamisha. I promise you.''

She got Brigitte immediately when she called, but she wasn't quite ready to face her. Their fight had been the worst they'd ever had, and it had left scars.

"Oh,'' Kamisha said, switching the phone to her other ear, "it's you.''

"Who did you expect?'' Brigitte's tone was guarded.

"Tracy, I guess. How is she, anyway?'' Neutral ground, Kamisha thought. What a chicken she was.

"She's fine. She's off riding.''

"Is, ah, Bullet around?''

"He's been in L.A. for an overnight. He's due in on the six o'clock.''

"Oh.''

There was a long, uncomfortable minute of silence.

"Listen,'' Kamisha said, sighing finally, "I feel like hell.''

"Me too.''

"We were both being really childish. I miss you, Brigitte, and I apologize for the stuff I said.''

"Yeah, well, I guess I do, too.''

"Friends?''

"Friends.''

"Good, then I better tell you I need a big favor.''

"Shoot.''

"Can I stay with you for a while?''

"Of course you can. Kamisha, is everything all right? I mean...''

"Everything's fine. Well, not everything.''

"John Leopardo?"

"Yes," she admitted, "it's John."

"We need to have a talk, huh?"

"A nice long one."

They never quite got around to that talk, though.

By the time Kamisha arrived at Brigitte's, Tracy was there, the stereo was blaring, and Brigitte was already into a bottle of wine, wringing her hands over Bullet, as usual.

"Some goddamn bimbo called here at two," Brigitte said, pacing the living room. "It was long distance. I could tell. The little tramp said she was an old friend, but I knew."

"Maybe she..." Kamisha began, but Brigitte was working herself up, spilling her wine on the wet bar, tears beginning to squeeze out beneath her long lashes.

"When that louse gets home, I'm going to scratch his eyes out."

And then Tracy came out of her room, saw that her mom was getting drunk and slammed her bedroom door so hard that a china plate fell from the corner cupboard in the dining room and shattered.

"Damn it, Tracy! You get your butt out here!"

"I'll clean it up," Kamisha said, rising. "Tracy didn't mean to—"

"The hell she didn't!" And Brigitte collapsed into a sobbing heap on her beautiful white sofa.

It was Kamisha who cooked dinner. And while she and Tracy sat in the kitchen, choking down their food, Bullet arrived from the airport, swaggering, tie pulled loose, biceps and shoulders straining his shirt.

"Oh, God," Tracy remarked, rolling her eyes. "The legend is home." She got up from the table, went to her room and shut the door.

Kamisha didn't know whether to ignore him, try to be friendly or do the same thing Tracy had done—retire. The decision was taken out of her hands when Brigitte leaped off the couch and started in on him.

Kamisha couldn't escape the scene, as much as she wanted to; they were between her and the guest room. She heard Brigitte's accusations, every wounded, wailing, drunken one. She heard Bullet's nasty replies, heard the disgust in his voice.

"Shut up," he said, towering over Brigitte, his size dwarfing her. "You're drunk. Go sleep it off."

"I am not! You listen to me! One more of your *friends* calls here and we're through! Through! You're making me crazy, Bullet! You can't treat me like this!'' Brigitte wailed.

"Listen, sweets, I can treat you any way I want. For God's sake, pipe down. I'm hungry. Did you fix anything tonight?''

Finally Kamisha escaped outside to the deck. She could still hear them arguing, but at least it was muted.

She stood on the deck, leaning against the rail, hugging herself and watching the sun go down behind the mountains. She couldn't stay here in this house, she thought; she couldn't bear it. Brigitte's pain heaped on top of hers. Tracy's youthful anguish. Bullet's cruelty and selfishness. She stared out at the darkening mountains and thought of John—his calmness, his love—and ached for him. He was so close, a few miles, and as lonely as she was. The irony of it.

She stayed there on the deck until it was cold and dark, and she had to go back inside.

Bullet was in the kitchen, alone.

"Where's Brigitte?'' she asked, shivering a little.

"Ah, she went to bed.''

He'd fixed himself a sandwich and was perched on a stool, hunched over the counter. He was big, a broad, heavily muscled man. Some women, Kamisha supposed, would find his blunt features boyish and attractive. She didn't.

"You fix this tuna salad?'' he asked, smiling a mirthless smile, a bread crumb at the corner of his mouth.

"No. Brigitte must have made it.''

"Amazing.''

"Why is it amazing, Bullet?''

"Oh, you know, she can't do anything right lately.''

"She does okay,'' Kamisha said icily.

"Excuse me,'' he quipped. "I forgot what good buddies you two are.''

"That's right.'' Kamisha put her hands on her hips and faced him. "And you know what, Bullet? I think *you're* her problem.''

"That's really none of your—''

"It is my business. She's my friend.''

He grinned at her. "You've got a big mouth on you, Kamisha,'' he said. "If I were you, I'd quit poking around in other people's affairs.''

"You know,'' she said, her back stiff, "I don't like you, Bullet Adams.''

"Well, lady, I don't much like you, either."

She tried calling John. She wanted to hear his voice, to lose herself in his calm reassurance, but John was with Joe Wilson, Inky told her, and wouldn't be in till late.

"You'll tell him I called?"

"I sure will," Inky said, "and hang in there. Things will work out."

But she was beginning to doubt it.

She lay in the guest room bed that night and tried to still her ragged breathing. The turmoil around her had taken on the quality of a living entity. It seemed to beat and pulse in the night air. She felt helpless. John's anguish seemed so hopeless in the silence of the night. And Brigitte. How was she going to help her? She'd promised Tracy days ago to have a talk with her mom, but when? Brigitte wasn't going to listen. And Bullet. It was true. She thoroughly disliked him. He was using Brigitte, sponging off her to achieve a lavish life-style in Aspen that he couldn't really afford.

Kamisha closed her eyes and tried to will her limbs to relax. The day before yesterday, on that beach with John, she'd been in heaven. What had gone so wrong?

For the next few days it was impossible to reach John on the phone. Either his line at the condo was busy or she'd get Inky and he'd tell her that John was over at the club. She was going stir-crazy at Brigitte's. They'd finally had that talk—about John and Kamisha's feelings—but Brigitte had seemed distracted, worried about something, and she was unwilling to go into it when Kamisha began to pry.

Tracy buttonholed her several times, afraid that her mom was going to get sick. At Tracy's age she didn't truly comprehend a nervous breakdown, but Kamisha did. And Tracy was right: Brigitte was sick, getting worse by the day.

Bullet was a constant source of dissension in the house. Brigitte nagged and he made sarcastic remarks back. Tracy cried and Kamisha merely tried to stay out of the way. She couldn't go home, couldn't go to work full-time. She was bored, miserably disgusted with Bullet and her friend. She couldn't bear much more of that house. She'd give it, maybe, another day or two.

"I don't see what all the fuss was about," Bullet said at dinner that night. "Who cares if some prominent folks want to blow off steam?"

"God," Kamisha said, "don't you realize what was going on in that condo?"

"Good times." He shrugged, forking pasta into his mouth.

"There were young girls there," Brigitte put in. "That's not right."

"Probably of their own free will," he said, and grinned.

It rankled that officially Kamisha was on vacation. She made daily trips to the club, anyway, but it was as if Wilson's secretary needed her advice less and less. Invariably Inky would see Kamisha there and then follow her back to Brigitte's. But she never ran into John.

She took long hikes in the woods behind Brigitte's house. She went bicycling with Tracy—if Inky had seen that! She tried to keep fit and busy. But it was hard killing time, wondering, waiting, hoping.

Why hadn't he returned her calls?

She tried to put Costa Rica and the sweet interlude out of her thoughts. But inside a terrible fear and loneliness lurked, hiding in a shadowy corner of her soul, ready to spring into the light without warning.

John's rejection was killing her.

It came to her in the middle of the night. She awakened with a sudden knowledge, and she knew how she could help John.

Carin McNaught. The sheriff's daughter. The kid would never confide in her father. No. But if she could get the girl to talk to John, in confidence, of course, then maybe John could get a handle on some of the prominent men who regularly attended those parties. He could then get in touch with them, perhaps obtain more names. Eventually someone would talk. Whoever had beaten Rick Simons had surely been to at least one of the affairs. Someone would know. Someone would come clean. Maybe even Stern.

She lay in the dark and felt much better. In the morning she'd see John. She'd park her butt on his steps all day if necessary. Her idea had merit. He'd have to listen. And maybe they could talk about themselves.

INKY OPENED THE DOOR, a surprised look on his face. "Kamisha. Is something wrong? You okay?"

"I'm fine. Is John in?" She tried to peer past his great bulk into the hushed interior.

"He's...ah, here. But he's on the phone. Can I...?"

"I want to see him. Please, Inky."

His wooden countenance softened finally. "Come on in. Boss won't mind."

John was indeed preoccupied. He was talking on the telephone, pacing, the cord reaching its distance before he turned around. He looked tired and haggard. When he saw Kamisha, he seemed to pause, his dark eyes full of emotion until he quickly masked it. While he nodded for her to be seated, he spoke into the phone again. "All right, Ken, I understand," John was saying. "I know you've got a reputation to uphold. Yes, well, so do I. You think it over. Any help you can give me on this matter will be greatly appreciated. All right. Thanks." And he hung up.

"Ken?" Kamisha asked, curious.

"Kenneth Whelps," John replied, still distracted.

"Whelps Manufacturing? Isn't he a frequent guest at the club?"

"Yes, Kamisha, he is. He spends half the year in Columbus, Ohio, the other half here."

"You asked him if he'd ever been to one of Rick's parties?"

"Yes."

"And?"

"And nothing. This mess with Luke Stern's wife has everyone nervous."

"Um," she said.

John sat down and rubbed his jaw pensively. She could see tired circles under his eyes, circles made darker in contrast to his pale skin. He must have been on the telephone for days, using the master guest list from the club as his only source of information. Clearly no one was talking. It occurred to her that if John's father were doing the asking, maybe the results would be better. Who would have the guts to tell a Mafia don no? But then John wasn't his father; John would never push or threaten.

She crossed one leg over the other, absently smoothing her khaki pants, wiggling her toes in the open sandals. On the drive over she'd felt confident that John would welcome her suggestion about Carin McNaught. Now, looking at him, at his pale face and the drawn brow, she wasn't so certain.

"John," she said with care, "have you gotten anywhere?"

He let out a breath. "I've been told by a friend and associate in L.A. that there's some pretty big money involved. Big names and big money."

"And no one wants to rat."

"Exactly."

"What if you pushed a little harder?"

His gaze shot up to hers. "What are you suggesting?"

"I...never mind." She bit her lower lip. This wasn't going at all the way she'd imagined. He was so closed to her, a stranger. It was as if Costa Rica had never happened. She felt a stab of pain knife through her stomach. "Listen," she said, "I've got an idea. Will you hear me out, John? Will you try not to shut me up?"

He seemed not to notice her discomfort. "Sure," he said, "whatever."

"Remember in New York how I told you about this young local girl, Carin? She was the one who first put me onto Rick."

"I recall."

"Well, I was thinking. She's afraid to go the authorities. Her dad is sheriff of Pitkin County, in fact. But I bet I could convince her to talk to you. She could give you all sorts of names, and—"

But John had come to his feet and was shaking his head, holding up a hand. "Forget it."

"But—"

"I *said,* forget it."

Kamisha felt tears sting hotly behind her eyes. "Why?" she demanded.

He spun around to face her angrily. "She's a kid is why! Hasn't she been through enough?"

It was Kamisha's turn to get mad. "Come off your high horse, John," she said hotly. "Carin knew the score. She got paid plenty to attend those parties. It's time she faced up to what she did."

"She's an innocent victim."

"Girls her age aren't stupid, John. She's not a bad kid, don't get me wrong. But she still needs to learn that what she did is wrong. She could give you those names."

"I said no. The subject's closed."

"Everything's *closed* with you, isn't it?" she said before she could control her anger. "You won't listen. You won't let anyone help. John Leopardo against the cruel world! Well, I'm sick of it!"

For an instant he seemed about to respond, but just as quickly the expressionless mask covered his features again.

"John," she said, her voice cracking, "please. Please let me help."

"I'm sorry," he said, "but it's no good, Kamisha. I'm accomplishing nothing whatsoever here. I'm flying out this afternoon."

"You're...leaving?"

"Yes."

"But..."

"Inky's staying in 'Aspen. He'll watch over you."

"Damn it, John!" she said. "I don't need a bodyguard! I don't want one!"

"Your safety—"

"I'm going back to work, anyway. I'll stay at Brigitte's. But I need to be working."

"You'll be careful."

"Of course I'll be careful. It's all out in the open now, John. No one's going to bother with me."

"Still."

"John, please. I..."

But already he was ushering her toward the door, dismissing her. He was as cold as granite. "I am sorry," he said. But his voice was without emotion. "It's over, Kamisha. I made a mistake. A relationship can't survive the press. I've been through this before. Believe me, I—"

She stiffened. "What do you mean, John?"

He stared her right in the eye. "I was going to get married once. Be a normal guy. Unfortunately my father's activities hit the news just then. They came after me...and her."

"And she left you," Kamisha said, feeling the blood stop and freeze in her veins. "She couldn't take the heat and she left you."

"It was a long time ago. I don't blame her. But I won't do that to anyone else again. It's a promise I made to myself."

"But, John, I'm not her. I've been through this myself. I can take it. John..."

He was opening the front door, steering her gently but firmly. "If I caused you pain, I'm sorry. But my life doesn't have room for—"

"For what?" she demanded.

"For these kinds of interludes. Forgive me." And then he was closing the door, shutting her out.

She stiffened her arm for a moment and held the door open. "I don't forgive you, John. I'll never forgive you," she said, and then he was gone, the gleaming wooden door staring her in the face blankly.

For a long moment she stood there in disbelief. Her hands were fists at her sides, her chest was heaving. When she finally found her legs, she almost ran down the wooded path to where her car was parked. She left a patch of rubber on the drive and raced away, the wind tearing at her hair. She drove and drove, needing the fresh mountain air on her face and the hot sun on her shoulders. She didn't care where she drove or if anyone were following.

Silent and withdrawn, Kamisha finally made her way back to Brigitte's. She felt numb, in shock. If anyone said a word to her—Brigitte or Bullet—she'd burst into tears. All she wanted to do was be alone. She could let the tears come then, in privacy. Later, maybe later, she and Brigitte would talk.

She almost made it to her room.

"Oh, Kamisha," Brigitte said, coming out of the kitchen. "Oh, God, I'm so glad you're here. We have to talk."

Vaguely, through the haze of her anguish, Kamisha was aware of Brigitte's agitation. Her friend seemed sober, but she was wringing her hands, nevertheless. Her cheeks were pale and pinched-looking, and Kamisha made a fleeting assumption that this had to do with Bullet. Another spat.

"Kamisha, oh, Lord, *please*. I hope you'll forgive me."

For a moment Kamisha hesitated. "Not now, Brigitte. Not now," she managed to say, and then brushed past her and headed to the guest room. She was aware of Brigitte calling after her, of the urgency in her friend's voice. It didn't matter. Kamisha closed the bedroom door, locked it and sagged into a chair.

CHAPTER FIFTEEN

JOHN STOOD at the window in his office and looked out at the city. It was hot and hazy, not the awful heat of the month before, but pretty uncomfortable, nonetheless. The sky was white, not blue, and a brownish pall hung over Manhattan, as if the grime of the city rose from its streets and clung to the skyscrapers.

He stood there and stared, unfocused, battling his thoughts— thoughts about Aspen, about a magic little town nestled in the Rockies, thoughts about a woman. Unwelcome thoughts.

"Damn," he muttered, letting out a breath.

It would be cool in Aspen, with a clean snap to the summer air and a sky so blue that it was unbelievable. The mountains would, perhaps, have a dusting of early snow on their peaks, an army of white giants crowding the narrow green valley. The streets would be tidy and charming, the tourists strolling the downtown malls, stopping at outdoor cafés that were nestled in flower beds and groves of aspen trees.

He imagined the scene, down to the details of color and sound and smell, and then despite his better judgment he imagined Kamisha there. She'd moved back to her house, Joe Wilson had informed him, claiming that she was in no danger now that Senator Stern's wife had let the cat out of the bag. At any rate, no one was going to run Kamisha's life for her. He could see her as if he had mysteriously transported himself to be close to her. In her quaint living room, the sun filtering through the Victorian lace curtains, falling softly on her rich silver hair, warming it to his touch. Or at work, charming the club's guests, playing tennis, her long legs flashing in the brilliant mountain sun. She'd be busy, too, working on the upcoming substance abuse event, leaning over Joe's desk, her voice soft and just a touch husky, so close to Joe the man would notice her scent, would see the delicacy of her slim, sun-browned wrist.

Abruptly a stab of jealousy knifed through John. For an insane

moment he wanted to call Joe and tell him to get the hell back to
the Florida club—crazy, because Joe was still needed in Aspen. Rick,
whose fate John still hadn't decided, was in Florida now himself,
recuperating, on a paid vacation. John couldn't leave the club without
management.

But Joe Wilson. Single, forty-one years old. Handsome. A smooth
operator. Did Kamisha find him attractive? She'd come alive in Costa
Rica, a butterfly emerged from a cocoon of self-imposed hibernation.
Did Kamisha find Joe a new challenge?

Damn.

His dark musings were interrupted by Martha buzzing him. He
forced himself back to New York, to the heat and haze and wail of
sirens below on the street. "Yes, Martha," he said, pressing the button.

"Mr. Leopardo, I thought you might want to know. Miss Hammill
from Aspen called again. I told her you were in conference, as per
your instructions."

"Very good. Thank you, Martha."

He released the button and stood over the phone, staring at it as
if it would tell him something. Kamisha had tried to phone him several times over the past few weeks, but Martha had followed instructions. Though, for some perverse reason of her own, Martha insisted
on letting him know whenever Kamisha called. He smiled grimly.
He supposed it was his very efficient secretary's way of showing her
disapproval. She'd done the same thing years before when John's
father had tried to call him. But eventually Gio had given up. So
would Kamisha.

Sitting at his desk, John started going through reports from each
of his clubs. Figures, columns, numbers. The Amalfi club was a little
slow. He'd fly over and take a look, although he was sure his manager
there was quite competent. Nevertheless, it didn't hurt to have the
owner drop in. Yes, he'd do that. It would be good to get away.

The intercom buzzed again. "Mr. Leopardo, there's a man on the
phone from the *Boston Globe*. He'd like an interview."

"Tell him the usual, Martha," John said tiredly.

"Yes, Mr. Leopardo."

Good God, they'd never stop! There were still stories circulating
about the "love nest" in Aspen and Senator Stern, whose presidential
hopes appeared dashed, and the Ute City Club and the Leopardos.
The *Los Angeles Times* had even dug up an old photograph of John

when he was ten, holding his mother's hand in front of a New York courthouse, greeting Gio as his father emerged from one more trial or indictment or grand jury hearing.

He tried to study the weekly reports again, but his eyes wouldn't focus, his mind wouldn't concentrate. Kamisha. He'd had to leave her. She had her safe, protected life in the little town where no one paid the least bit of attention to celebrities. Where the media was tolerated but not admired and not necessarily believed. She'd moved there, she'd told him, partly to get away from the prying eyes of the world, as did so many other celebrities, and Aspen had accepted her without fanfare, judging her on her abilities, not her reputation. She had her life and her friends. She was surrounded by beauty. Her job satisfied her, and she was good at it. Yes, she had a fine life.

He'd known the moment he'd seen that paper in Costa Rica. The words had been so sickeningly familiar. Everything had come back to him, rushed in on him. He could never ask Kamisha to share the sordid life the press had created for him, to hide from cameras, interviewers, to hide from his own family, for God's sake. It was better he'd realized that in the beginning, before he'd made her any promises he couldn't keep.

He could live with his decision. He could live without love, without Kamisha, but it was hard. He could do it, though, because the alternative was worse. She'd despise him if he dragged her into his orbit. Sooner or later it would get to her, and she'd hate him. Only it would be messier, and it would take longer for her to get over it, and the press would have another weapon to attack with, to smear and twist the knife in the wound until he squirmed in shame and agony as Kamisha suffered with him. He could see it now, a media event as dreadful as Donald and Ivana Trump's breakup. No, he couldn't do that to Kamisha.

The buzzer sounded. "Mr. Leopardo, it's Harry in Coral Gables."

"Put him on, Martha."

"Hello, John. How's it up there?" Harry Kahn was the assistant manager of the Sea Star Club.

"Hot and dirty. How's it going, Harry?"

"Hotter but cleaner. I spoke to Joe just now, had a few questions. We're having some problems with the kitchen help, but it's slow down here now, so it's no big deal. I wanted to check with you on your policy of hiring Cubans, John. For the winter, you know."

"If they have papers, Harry. Real papers. We can't hire illegals. I'll stand firm on that."

"That's what Joe thought. Okay, but we may have some trouble filling all the spots."

"Joe always worries too much. You'll see that there'll be a seasonal influx of workers come fall. You have time. Besides, Joe will be back by then. It'll be his headache."

"He makes me do the hiring, John. My Spanish is better."

"Didn't I tell everyone to learn Spanish?"

"Joe hates languages. Says he failed Latin in school."

"I'll talk to him about it."

"Hey, don't tell him I told you. I gotta work for the guy." Harry paused. "Did I tell you I've been getting a lot of calls from the papers, John? They want to see the club, write us up."

John massaged his forehead. "Just tell them no, Harry."

"It's good publicity."

"Not the right kind."

"You sure? You know what they say, there's no publicity that's bad publicity."

"I'm sure, Harry. They're fishing. They want dirt."

"Okay, you're the boss." There was another moment's hesitation. It was obvious Harry had more on his mind than Cubans and the press. Harry was smart enough to handle those details without bothering John in New York.

"Look," John said, leaning back in his chair, "if there's something on your mind, I want to hear it."

Harry cleared his throat. "It's Rick Simons. He stopped by this morning."

"And he wants his job back, right?" John said. "So he figured you could put a word in for him."

Harry sighed. "We worked together, you know, for four years, Mr. Leopardo. You understand. And, well, I really think the guy learned his lesson."

"I'll be the judge of that," John snapped, irritated.

"Of course. I just thought..."

"It's all right, Harry. Enough said." John hung up shortly and steepled his fingers. He believed Rick had indeed learned a tough lesson, but the fact remained that Rick was still withholding the name of the man behind the parties, the man who had undoubtedly beaten him up. John didn't consider Rick a criminal. But Simons owed it to his position, to the club, to come clean. And until he did John had no intention of allowing him back to work.

It infuriated him. His temper flared every time he thought about the condo filled with big-name power brokers fondling young women—the booze and God knows what else flowing. But no one was talking. And until someone did talk John was going to be on the hot seat. Of course, Stern's wife was still talking. And every other word out of her mouth was Aspen. The Ute City Club. John Leopardo. Last week's scandal sheets had covered it all over again, the headlines changed, naturally, but the same muck: "Mafia Love Nest in the Rockies."

Goddamn it.

He wondered how Joe Wilson was handling it. His new manager there hadn't said. And John wondered, too, if the press was bothering Kamisha. There was certainly a human interest angle—the Silver Lady, they'd named her when she raced in the Olympics. He supposed it was too much to hope that they'd leave her alone. He could just imagine the questions they'd ask her. Were you aware, Miss Hammill, that the owner of the club you work for was connected to the Mafia? Do you know John Leopardo very well? What do you think of the parties that were held here, Miss Hammill? Did you ever attend one? Would you still vote for Senator Stern for President, Miss Hammill?

His intercom buzzed again. "Mr. Leopardo."

"Hey, boss, it's Inky. I got something for you."

"Send him in, Martha."

"Yes, Mr. Leopardo," she said very correctly, registering her disapproval of Inky's familiarity.

Inky sauntered in, holding a rolled-up copy of a newspaper. He shook it at John. "You might want to take a look-see, boss. Front page, bottom."

"What is it?"

"Today's *New York Times*," Inky handed him the paper and stood there, folding his huge arms.

John unrolled the paper and spread it out on his desk. His eyes traveled to the bottom of the page. "Leopardo Son Alienated from Mob Family," read the headline, "by the Associated Press. Don Gio Leopardo, longtime leader of one of the most powerful Mafia families on the East Coast, made an unprecedented statement to the press yesterday."

John gripped the paper, his mind whirling. Pop making a statement? He looked up at Inky, who stood there, smiling smugly, arms still crossed over his massive chest.

"Read on, boss," Inky said. He grinned more broadly.

"My son, John, is a law-abiding American. He fought for his country in Vietnam," the elder Leopardo said. "He won a Bronze Star and a Purple Heart. My son distanced himself from the family many years ago. He has nothing to do with the family's business concerns, and John Leopardo's health clubs are in no way connected to the family's business. In fact," Gio Leopardo said, "I have not heard from nor seen my only son in over eleven years. John is a Leopardo in name only." It is believed that the Don made this statement as a result of the allegations brought against his son's health club in Aspen, Colorado, where the manager was beaten in a bizarre string of events....

It went on, reiterating the whole ugly tale, but John stopped reading. He sat at his desk and stared at the print until it danced in front of his eyes. His father had gone to the press of his own free will! The man who hated reporters and publicity, who had more reason than most to shun it. The man who over the years had been indicted for dozens of crimes but never convicted, a Mafia boss, a criminal—he'd endangered his own position to go to the press and tell them that his son wasn't connected to his own illegitimate dealings.

"Unbelievable, huh, boss?" Inky said.

John leaned back and whistled through his teeth. "My God." He furrowed his brow. "Why?"

Inky moved to one of the black-and-chrome chairs in front of the desk and sat. "To help you."

"Pop?"

"Sure, he's trying to help you."

"But do you know what this does to him? He's practically admitting what he is."

Inky nodded.

John shook his head. "I can't get a handle on it. I can't figure it."

"Hey, boss, it's simple. He's your dad." The big man shrugged heavy shoulders. "He's taking care of his son."

John just stared at him, incredulous.

The phone rang all afternoon. Martha turned the calls away with a quote of "no comment," but even she began to get frazzled by five.

When he left the office, John had Inky take him to his health club for his routine workout. He was still dazed, thrown completely off balance, but he thought it would do him good to work up an honest sweat.

His father, going to the press of his own accord—to help his son. It boggled his mind. Gio put the organization first; he always had. He'd never endanger his operation, never be disloyal to the family. That was his first commandment. And yet he'd done this for his son. John could come up with no other conceivable reason for Gio making that statement.

John took a towel from the attendant. "Thanks," he said absent-mindedly, heading for his locker.

He swam a half mile. Every stroke reminded him of the beach in Costa Rica, the warm water, Kamisha, wet and sleek as a seal, the feel of her body, silky and slippery against him. Would he ever forget?

He pulled himself dripping from the pool and sat on the edge, chest heaving, remembering too much.

The weight room was busy these hours after the working day was over. It was, as usual, hot and damp and faintly smelly, despite the overlay of eucalyptus the attendants used to clean the place. All gyms smelled the same, he guessed, even the Ute City Club. He wondered if Kamisha worked out there. Yes, probably. He could see her in a leotard, tight-fitting as her tanned skin, all her muscles taut, sweat on her face, on her chest, between her breasts. He knew every muscle in her body, had stroked and kneaded every long, curved sinew. His hands itched with the feel of her, as if she were there and he could reach out and—

"Hey, John, how's it going?" A man he'd seen there for years was greeting him. He could have sworn the guy's tone was different, his eyes more assessing. Maybe he'd been following the stories in the paper.

"Okay," John replied. "And yourself?"

"Not bad, considering."

John did his curls, his bench presses, working hard at it. His arms and shoulders and chest were pretty good, but when it came to his legs—well, he was lopsided. He used machines to exercise his legs, but he always pressed more weight with his good leg than his bad one. Still, he kept at it, and his knee had become stronger over the years. It ached a lot, and it seized up at times, but at least it was still there. There had been a time when he thought they'd have to amputate his leg. There had been a raging infection....

Why in hell was he thinking about that now? He lay on his back on the leg press machine, pushing the plate, first the bad leg, then the good. Breathing hard, pushing. The muscles in his thighs bunched up, then relaxed, bunched up again. Sweat beaded on his forehead.

Why had Gio done it?

He'd said further on in the article that he was retired now, a law-abiding citizen like his son. Retired. Gio. It was probably a lie, but maybe Pop *was* retired. It could be. John didn't even know. He couldn't even remember exactly how old his father was. Seventy? Seventy-one?

He spoke to his mother a few times a year, but they never discussed Gio, not a word. They talked about his sister, about her three children, John's niece and nephews. But never a word about Gio.

My God, he *had* utterly alienated himself. He had no family, no friends but Inky. He'd gotten rid of the one woman he'd cared for, wounded her deeply.

For years his mother had begged him to talk to his father. *You're his only son, Johnny. Just call him once in a while. Please, Johnny.*

But he'd so detested the business his father was in that he'd refused. It was all mixed up with his brush with death and the war and youthful idealism. But he was older, and things that had mattered then didn't seem to matter as much now. He was so damn alone, so lonely.

Of course, it was Kamisha who'd made him reassess his situation. He'd just never noticed before how alone he was. He'd prided himself on being in control, but he'd so carefully isolated himself that he had no one to control, so it had been easy. Now it was hard. Now he knew what it felt like to be happy.

And the truth hurt.

He got his weekly massage from Thomas. The man had magic hands, and he spent a lot of time on John's bad leg, kneading and stroking, digging deeply to relax the stressed muscles and increase the blood supply. Usually Thomas's ministrations allowed John to empty his mind completely, then emerge fresh and ready to focus on problems.

Not tonight. He was impatient under Thomas's hands, tense, unable to escape the thoughts that plagued him.

"Hey, Mr. Leopardo, relax," Thomas said.

"Sorry, I'll try."

"You got business problems?" Thomas inquired. "Everyone does. Forget 'em for now."

Sure, he had business problems. But it was other kinds of problems that were torturing him. He felt the masseur's hands on his leg, pressing each muscle slowly, stretching each sinew. He closed his eyes and willed himself to relax, to forget. But his mind recalled Kamisha's hands touching him in the same places, touching the scar on his knee gently with one finger, looking up at him and smiling a lazy, sensual smile. Damn it all.

"Boy, are you tense today. Come on, Mr. Leopardo," Thomas said chidingly, still working on his leg. "I bet I know what's bugging you. I heard there was something in the paper, your father, something about him. I don't wanna be nosy, but how many guys get their dad mentioned in the *New York Times*? That's it, isn't it?"

Thomas had known him for years. There was no sense getting angry with him. "Might be," John allowed.

"Listen, take it from me. Parents, they can drive ya crazy, ya know? But they're your folks and they mean well. What are ya going to do? Ya forgive 'em. Ya live with 'em. They aren't going to be around forever, you know."

"I guess so."

"Nobody said it was easy."

Inky picked him up at seven outside the club. "So, boss you goin' home?"

"Yes, home."

Inky watched him in the rearview mirror for a time. Then, finally, he spoke. "What are you going to do about your dad?"

"*Do?* What can I do? I can't even figure out what he meant by it."

"Come on, boss, you aren't dumb."

"Stop mothering me," John snapped.

"Sometimes you need it," Inky shot back. "Don't be a damn fool, John. He's getting old. Says he's retired."

"Sure, retired."

"You gotta trust someone," Inky said darkly.

John ate alone. The cook had left something for him, but he

couldn't have said what it was a minute after he finished. He sat and chewed and looked out his window over the city that was just being touched by dusk.

After he ate, he pulled the *Times* out of his briefcase and read the article again. He was still too stunned by Gio's uncharacteristically selfless gesture even to begin to weigh its implications. All he knew was that he hurt inside. He was in pain, and his father and Kamisha were connected somehow in his mind. He couldn't figure out how or why, but he knew they were. What he didn't know was who in the hell he, John, was. He'd thought he knew, but the certainty was gone now. He was floundering, lost, unsure of everything. All the rules of the game were changed, and the players were acting illogically.

What are you going to do about your dad? Inky had asked. *Ya forgive 'em. Ya live with 'em,* Thomas had said. It was as if the world were pressing in on him from every direction, poking, prodding, turning him from the way he wanted to go, forcing him to rethink, reassess, walk a new path.

Gio had done something utterly unexpected. Unasked, he'd tried to help his son. It was more than John had done or was willing to do.

He stood and roamed around his living room, looked at the blueprints on his table, turned on a lamp, picked up a magazine, put it down. He limped, leaning on his cane, tired, drained of all his energy.

Suddenly, overwhelmingly, he wanted to pick up the phone and talk to his father. "Hey, Pop, thanks, that was a nice article, a nice thing to do. I appreciate it, Pop," he'd say.

"Well, son, it was the least I could do," Gio would say. No, a normal father would say that. He could no longer even guess what *his* father would say.

He limped to the window and looked out at the lights coming on all over the city. Lights in people's apartments. Kids turning on lights, mothers and uncles and aunts clicking them on. Lovers turning on lights, talking, touching each other.

Abruptly he threw his cane across the room. It hit a table with a sharp sound, bounced, lay on the carpet, a dead brown stick, a useless prop.

He was powerless. Powerless to deal with his father, powerless to treat the ills of his beautiful club in Aspen, to defend himself from the greedy press, to mend his relationship with his family or to accept Kamisha's love. Powerless.

John put his face in his hands, took a deep breath, then looked up. There was no deliberate decision, no thought, no rationalization. He headed straight for the door of his apartment, closed it behind him and took the elevator down to the lobby.

"You want I should call Inky?" the doorman asked.

"No, uh, no, he's off tonight. Just get me a taxi."

"Yes, sir, Mr. Leopardo."

It wasn't until the cab was halfway across the Brooklyn Bridge that he realized he'd forgotten his cane.

THE HOUSE LOOKED THE SAME, the shrubbery fuller, but otherwise the same. It was full dark now, and lights showed at the windows behind the draped lace curtains, old-fashioned curtains. It had been eleven years since he'd been there.

It was a mock-Tudor house, solid stone and stucco between dark beams, set on a street of similar enduring houses, each with a large, landscaped lawn. Well cared for and comfortable. Around the back, at the end of the curved gravel driveway, was a garage, and his father's Cadillac would be neatly parked inside.

John took a quavering breath. What was he doing?

"You gettin' out or what?" the cabbie asked.

"Ah, yeah, sure. How much do I owe you?"

The driver nodded. "It's on the meter."

The walk to the house was difficult. He told himself it was because he lacked the habitual support of his cane. He felt as if he was faltering. By the front door, in the shadows, was the ubiquitous guard. John had spotted him, or at least the glowing tip of his cigarette, immediately. The man moved into the light slowly as John approached. His back straightened, and John could see him flick the butt of the cigarette down the drive. Slowly his now-free hand moved up toward the breast of his dark jacket. It was all very familiar to John, though at one time the man would have greeted him and tousled his dark hair.

John neared. "It's Gio's son," he said, stopping for a moment. "Is that you, Mario?"

"John?"

"Yes, it's me."

"Well, I'll be damned."

He managed a smile for Mario, the man who had been his father's personal bodyguard for thirty years. He felt his hand clenching and unclenching at his side, automatically gripping a phantom cane. He reached out then and shook Mario's hand, noting the thick mop of gray hair on his head, the heavy jowls.

"It's nice to see you, John," Mario said.

"You, too." And then John stared at him hard. "Pop still needs a guard, huh?"

"A man can retire," Mario said, "but his enemies never do." He stepped back into the shadows and reached into his pocket for his pack of cigarettes.

John stood there for a moment and gazed at the door. He could feel his knee throb and his heart pound too heavily against his ribs. He wanted suddenly to turn and go. But he'd come too far.

His mother was inside that house, watching TV maybe or playing cards. Gio would be in the study or on the phone. Did he watch TV with Mom these days? Were they an ordinary aging couple?

The windows were open, and John could hear faint strains of music. Italian opera—*Rigoletto*. Familiar music that he'd heard his entire childhood.

Slowly he walked up the stone steps to the broad front door. Should he ring the bell or walk in?

Eleven years. He pressed the bell and heard it chime inside. A familiar sound. How many times...?

The front door opened. His mother. Older now. Gray-haired, plump, in an old-fashioned house dress. She looked at him, peered through her glasses, then turned pale and put her hand over her heart. "Johnny?" she gasped.

"Hello, Mama."

"Johnny. Oh, dear Lord, Johnny. What is it? Are you okay? Come in, come in."

He entered the house, the dark hallway exactly the same, the smell, the feel, the very air of his childhood exactly the same.

"I'm fine, Mama. I'm okay. I just thought..." God, his knee hurt.

"Let me look at you." She held his hands and cried and laughed, hugged him, wiped her tears. "Oh, Johnny, it's so good, so good."

A voice came from down the hall, a familiar, irascible voice. "What's going on? Such a noise. Lucille?"

A bent figure shuffled out into the hall, an old man, balding, white-haired, slight. But the voice was the same. "So, Lucille? What the—?"

The figure stopped, thrust his head forward and blinked. His mouth opened, then hung there.

John tried his voice. He wasn't sure what he said, something stupid. His throat constricted. In the shadows of his consciousness he was aware of his mother saying his name over and over, of her tears. And then his father, so old now, so very very old, was moving down the darkened hall toward him. An old, worn man.

CHAPTER SIXTEEN

KAMISHA SAID GOOD-NIGHT to Joe Wilson, checked in at the front desk to let them know she was leaving, then left through the back door to where her mountain bike was locked to a cottonwood tree.

She took a deep breath of the evening air. There was a snap to it already; autumn was setting in. Not even the second week of September and she could feel it—winter was just around the corner. On the noon news today the weatherman had said the East Coast was due for a September heat wave. It would be hot and grimy in New York. How could John bear it?

She pedaled the mile and a half to her house, trying to enjoy the ride and the fresh air, but inside her belly was a gnawing anger. It was that old biddy Martha.

I'm sorry, Miss Hammill, but Mr. Leopardo is tied up in a meeting. I'll give him your message.

How many times over the past weeks had Martha said those same words? Of course, John had given her instructions to put Kamisha off, so she shouldn't be angry with Martha. She knew that. But still...

She got off her bike in front of her house, walked it around back and locked it to the fence. She turned the sprinkler on the waning garden and realized that the flowers had lost their summer spark. But then so had she, Kamisha thought. She went in the back door, replacing the key over the ledge, and stood with her hands on her hips in her tidy kitchen. The house seemed empty, so picture-perfect and sterile. But that was how she'd wanted it, wasn't it? Since Josh had left those many years ago, she'd purposely lived that sterile existence—until John Leopardo.

What a fool she'd been. When she was young, she'd set goals and sometimes achieved them. But that was youth. A person could overcome an endless flow of troubles and keep going. She'd lost her energy now, though, and no longer had the strength to strive.

"Great," Kamisha said.

She pulled out the iced tea pitcher from her refrigerator and took a long drink. John had beaten her. Even Martha had her cowering. Once, she'd had the guts to fly down a steep ski slope with the icy wind in her face, and they'd hung a Silver Medal around her neck. The Silver Lady. Well, now the lady was tarnished.

THE SHRILL RINGING of her bedside phone startled her out of a deep sleep. It took a long moment to orient herself, to wake herself out of another lousy dream.

"Kamisha?" It was Brigitte. *What now?* Kamisha wondered, glancing at the clock—7:30 a.m.

"What's up? It's really early, Brigitte."

"Oh, I couldn't stay in bed. I've ah...I'm not drinking and... Well, I'm sort of nervous. Do you think we can go to lunch today? It's Saturday. You're off, aren't you?"

"Sure. Where? You want me to pick you up?"

"No, I'll, ah, drive."

"That's a novelty."

"The new me." But Brigitte sounded tense.

Kamisha arrived at the restaurant late. An unscheduled crisis at the club. There was always something, though, and a day off, a full day, was an impossibility. She spotted Brigitte sitting at a table near an open window in the dining room of the Hotel Jerome and gave her a quick wave.

"Sorry," Kamisha said, breathless, pulling out the chair across from her friend. "I had to run over to the club."

Brigitte smiled at her, a swift, forced twitch of her mouth. "That's okay."

She looked wan, scared, and the very pale freckles that usually didn't show were evident on her skin. She had no makeup on, and her soft, curling brown hair was simply pulled back in a ponytail. Kamisha noticed that instead of the usual glass of wine, a cup of coffee sat in front of Brigitte.

"What's up?" Kamisha asked, taking a menu from the waitress.

Brigitte shrugged, her eyes shifting away. "Everything's up, I guess. I'm trying to get my act together."

"The, ah, drinking?" Kamisha asked carefully.

"Yes. That and... Well, some other problems, too. You know."

"We all have them," Kamisha said. "Is it Tracy?"

"She's okay." Brigitte shrugged again.

"Bullet?"

"Oh, I don't know. Really I don't."

Kamisha studied her friend for a moment. "Do you want to talk about it?"

Brigitte's eyes switched to hers. "Do you want to talk about John Leopardo?" Her tone was defensive.

It was Kamisha's turn to shrug. "There's not much to talk about." Even the mention of his name was enough to prod the open wound, but Brigitte knew that. She had no secrets from Brigitte.

Her friend sat silently, assessing Kamisha. There was still that anxiety in her eyes, though, but Kamisha chalked it up to alcohol withdrawal. "So," Brigitte said, "has the lout answered your calls?"

"No." She tried to make light of the situation with little success.

"I feel so bad for you," Brigitte said, twisting a ring on her finger.

"I'll live." She could say the words, but she wondered if they were true. She didn't feel alive at all. Inside, she felt dull and dead.

"Oh, God, Kamisha, I know how it is. To love a man and have him shoot you down like that. Oh, I know how it hurts."

Kamisha bristled at her friend's automatic comparison of Bullet and John, as if they were equals, as if Bullet were fit to lick John's boots. But she held her tongue; Brigitte needed help now, not another quarrel. She reached a hand across the table and patted her arm. "Guess it's just you and me, pal, and to hell with men."

"Yeah, you and me. Like at school." Brigitte tried to smile, but her eyes were shiny with moisture. Quickly she looked down again until Kamisha could only see the top of her head.

"What is it, Brigitte?" Kamisha asked again, praying it wasn't another fight with Bullet, another infidelity or girl phoning long-distance or...

Brigitte looked at her then, her fingers twisting the ring, tendrils of her fine honey-brown hair lifting in the breeze from the lace-curtained window. "You'll hate me," she whispered. "You'll never speak to me again."

"Come on, what is this?"

"I'm sober, Kamisha. I want you to know that. I haven't had a drop all day, I swear." Brigitte's brown eyes were huge, her heart-shaped face pale and solemn.

"I believe you."

"I have to tell you something."

The waitress arrived to take their orders then, and Brigitte clammed up, but Kamisha could see her lips quivering. They ordered salads, and the waitress had to ask Brigitte twice, because she spoke so quietly that she couldn't be heard.

Kamisha studied the woman across from her, the woman who had been her friend for over half her lifetime. She *was* different today, scared and depressed, not drunk, and Kamisha was abruptly worried. Something was really wrong, something different. Maybe Tracy had been right. Maybe Brigitte was sick. Maybe she was going to have a breakdown.

"Tell me, Brigitte, what were you going to say?" Kamisha said carefully.

Brigitte bit her lip until it turned white, then she took a sip of coffee and set the cup down, spilling a little in the saucer. Her hands were shaking.

"Come on," Kamisha urged gently, "what are friends for?"

But Brigitte had turned inward, and it was no use. All through lunch, which neither of them finished, Kamisha had the feeling Brigitte was holding back on her. They talked about Tracy. They discussed Brigitte checking into the Betty Ford Clinic for a forty-five-day alcohol abuse program. They even discussed Bullet in a reasonable manner, and the fact that Brigitte knew in her heart that he'd been using her all along—her connections, her house, her money. But they never truly got to the heart of Brigitte's troubles, Kamisha suspected. And she wondered about that.

It happened when Kamisha got home. She should have known the attention of the press would turn to her eventually. But she hadn't expected the woman from the *Insider* to be parked on her doorstep.

"Excuse me," Kamisha said, "but this is my home. Call me for an appointment at the club."

"Just a few questions, Miss Hammill," the woman said, rising, ignoring Kamisha. She licked the end of her pen as if words were going to rush out magically onto the notepad. "Now rumor has it that you were in Costa Rica at—"

"I'm allowed a vacation, aren't I?"

"Then you aren't denying—?"

"Listen—" Kamisha began.

"And that while you were gone Senator Stern's wife walked in on her husband at a party where—"

"*That's* a lie."

"And furthermore," the woman went on, "you were the one to arrange these affairs and—"

"Oh, God, will you please listen?"

"You *are* PR director at the Ute City Club, Miss Hammill, and therefore responsible for—"

"*Lady*," Kamisha said in a quavering voice, "if you want the truth, then why don't you listen to it?"

But the woman never did stop firing inane questions in her face, and the only way Kamisha escaped was to go inside and lock her door.

Damn, she thought, throwing her purse onto the sofa and gritting her teeth. It had to stop! And just what was John doing about it? Hiding in New York? She couldn't believe that of him. He was a lot of things, but not a coward. Still, it was obvious no one was talking about the parties. Not Rick Simons, certainly not Senator Luke Stern or his cronies—no one. And neither the police nor the sheriff's deputies had gotten anywhere. She knew that because they'd called her and asked a lot of questions after Rick's beating. She'd told them everything she knew, which wasn't much, everything except the fact that the sheriff's daughter had been at some of the parties.

It occurred to her then: she couldn't go on working at the club under this cloud of suspicion. And another thought followed on the heels of the first. There was a way—Carin McNaught. She knew John had disapproved of using an underage girl to get their information, but it was starting to look as if Carin was their best bet.

It struck Kamisha that if John returned her calls, she'd run the idea past him one more time. Then just as quickly she realized there was little chance of that happening. Instead, she sat down and looked up the McNaughts' phone number. A few names, that was all she really needed from Carin, and no one ever had to know where the names came from.

But, by the next afternoon, Carin hadn't responded to the message Kamisha had left with her mother. She jumped every time the phone in her office at the club rang, positive one of the calls would be Carin or maybe, just maybe, John. She alternated between hope that Carin would help them clear the club's name and despair that John had so utterly rejected her. At one time she might have rejoiced in the challenge, but no longer. John had done that to her; his search for the almighty truth had made her see herself in a new light. No, she didn't need any more challenges. She didn't need to lay her life on the line for a cheap thrill, not anymore. Now she knew what made her happy, what fulfilled her, what gave her that emotional high. She knew what she needed. She needed John.

It wasn't until seven-thirty that evening that Carin finally called. "We've got to talk, Carin," Kamisha said.

"I can't. Really, my parents would kill me." The girl sounded scared, half crying.

"You have to, and they won't kill you. They'll understand once they know the truth. I'll be there with you. I'll explain everything. We need you, Carin."

"Miss Hammill, I don't dare!"

"Listen, I'll meet you somewhere private. Just hear me out. You'll be protected, Carin, because you're a minor. Just listen to me."

"Oh, I can't."

Kamisha pulled the last stop. "I'll have to go to your dad then, Carin. But wouldn't it be better if he heard it from you first?"

The next afternoon, on her lunch hour, Kamisha bicycled down the hill to the Roaring Fork River where the bicycle path began. She had her fingers crossed that Carin would show up, as she'd promised, that the girl wouldn't back out.

She stood, one foot on either side of the bike pedals, arms resting on the handlebars, waiting for Carin. John still hadn't called, she thought again. She'd been at work all morning and he hadn't called. She couldn't believe he was doing this to her—to himself. Why? What had wounded him so terribly that he had to defend himself even against her?

Carin pedaled up, only a few minutes late. She was a pretty girl, very fair, with strawberry-blond hair and a mature body for her age. She looked worried, though, and upset and awfully young to be mixed up in this messy affair.

"Hi," she said shyly.

"Thanks for coming, Carin. I mean that."

"Miss Hammill, will I have to tell how I got paid and went to the parties?"

Kamisha put a hand on the girl's arm. "Hey, it won't be so bad. No one's accusing *you* of anything. You're a witness, that's all. The police may need your testimony to put a very bad person behind bars, Carin."

"Who is it? You mean Mr. Simons? I mean, I know he got beat

up. God, the rag sheets at the grocery stores are still featuring all that stuff on the front pages.''

"Mr. Simons was involved, yes, but he had a partner, the man who put him in the hospital.''

"Oh, my gosh." Carin paled. "Who...who was it?''

"That's what we need you for, Carin," Kamisha said gently. "We've tried and tried to find out who was working with Mr. Simons, but everyone's afraid to talk.''

"But I don't know who.''

"I know you don't, honey, but you must remember a few of the names of the men who went to those parties.''

"I...''

"Carin, just a couple of names. No one will ever need to know you told.''

"I don't want to be a rat, Miss Hammill.''

Kamisha sighed. "In school maybe it's called that. But this is the real world. The man who put Rick Simons in the hospital is dangerous. He could have killed Rick, Carin.''

"But my dad, he'll be so mad at me.''

They walked their bicycles across the road and started pedaling slowly down the shaded bike path along the river. Kamisha kept silent, allowing the girl to think.

"Will I have to, you know, testify in court?" Carin finally asked.

"I don't think so. And besides, at your age it would all be private, anyway. What I'm hoping," she said, "is to find out who beat Mr. Simons, and then Mr. Simons won't be afraid to come forward with the truth.''

"Miss Hammill," Carin said, "is it really true?''

"Is what true?''

"The stories in the papers. You know, about the Mafia and all that stuff?''

"No, honey, it's a bunch of garbage.''

The girl finally came up with several names—names no one could fail to recognize. At the parties had been a basketball star known as P. T. Malloy, the all-time three-point king in the NBA. And there had been a well-known news anchorman, a Canadian, who worked for a national television station. But the most formidable figure Carin remembered had his face on the covers of at least three nationwide publications a week—Rory Dustin, a world power broker who owned hotels and casinos in thirteen countries and was estimated to be worth thirty-five billion dollars.

"He has a house on Red Mountain," Carin said, her head bowed. "He invited me and another girl, one of the ones from California, up one night after this party. But I didn't go, Miss Hammill. Honest."

"I'm glad you didn't. What a creep," she said under her breath, remembering a couple of tennis matches she'd played with him. She'd won, too, and now was damn glad she had. "You know," Kamisha said, shaking herself mentally, "we've got to tell your dad about these men."

"Oh, God."

"I know. It'll be hard. But I'll be right there beside you. And when it's over, Carin, you'll feel much better."

"He'll kill me."

"He'll *love* you for being truthful."

But the girl only hung her head.

CHAPTER SEVENTEEN

"MR. LEOPARDO," came Martha's voice over the intercom, "Mr. Rick Simons is on line two."

John's hand stopped short on its way to the phone. Rick. Well, well. How interesting. "Put him through, Martha. Thank you."

The line was obviously long-distance, with echoes and the sound of static.

"Mr. Leopardo?"

"Speaking."

"Uh, Rick Simons here."

"Yes, Rick, what can I do for you?"

"Look, I want to apologize for the way I acted in Aspen. I...I was upset and scared. I want you to know I appreciate you giving me a paid vacation like this."

John said nothing. He could almost hear Rick's quick, nervous breath, see his pale, sweat-slicked face.

"I...wondered if we could...talk."

"About what, Rick?" John kept his voice very even, but his hand tightened on the receiver.

"About those...the...uh...parties."

"The ones you had nothing to do with?"

"Well, Mr. Leopardo, that's not exactly the way it was."

Silence vibrated on the line between them.

"Go on, Rick," John said softly.

"Okay, I was wrong. I shouldn't have done it. But, you know, I figured it didn't hurt anyone. I swear I didn't know about the age of those girls, the kids."

"Why are you telling me this now?"

"I figure it's gonna come out. I mean that Stern woman, the senator's wife, well, she blabbed it all over. It's still in the papers. There's going to be a Senate investigation."

"I've heard," John said. "What exactly did you want to tell me, Rick? So far you've said nothing I don't already know."

"I think we can make a deal, Mr. Leopardo. I figure I'm pretty much finished with you, but I don't want to do time. If I talk, if I go to the police and clear your club, if I tell who was really behind the parties, I figure I can make a deal. And I'd like to know you won't bring charges against me in the middle of all this."

"It sounds reasonable, Rick. I can't speak for the authorities, of course, but if you cooperate fully with the investigation, I will allow you to resign."

"Sounds okay to me, then. I trust you, Mr. Leopardo. You've always been fair with me, and I'm sorry this all had to——"

"Fine, Rick, but I'd like to know who you were working with," John said in a curt voice.

There was a long, silent moment. "Bullet Adams."

The realization struck John cold. Bullet, Brigitte Stratford's boy-friend, the sports announcer, the one Kamisha didn't like at all. Hell, he'd just seen him announce a preseason NFL game on cable TV.

"Mr. Leopardo?"

"Okay, Rick. I appreciate this. I'll take care of everything from here on. Is Bullet the one who——?"

"Yeah, the son of a—— Yeah, he did it. He likes to hurt people. He's one dangerous dude. Too damn many steroids in his football days."

"You'll have to testify against him, depositions, probably at a trial, too."

"It'll be a pleasure," Rick said grimly.

"Where are you, Rick? The authorities will have to get in touch with you."

"I'm still in Miami. At my folks. Joe at the Ute City Club has my address."

"You'll stay available?"

"Yes, sir. There's nowhere I can run."

"All right, Rick. You'll be hearing from me. Thanks again. And I take it you're feeling better?"

"Yeah, it only hurts when I laugh," he said bitterly.

John put the receiver down very carefully. Bullet Adams. He conjured up a mental image of the man from the many times he'd seen him on television, and the brief glimpses he'd gotten of him at Brigitte's that day he'd gone Jeeping with Kamisha. Big. Not so tall, but broad and heavily muscled with the bull neck of a linebacker. Blond and good-looking in a blunt-featured way. John recalled that he'd been a favorite with the young groupies, teenagers really, in his football days. And hadn't there been some problem when he was in college? An assault charge or a rape or something? Yes, he thought, there had been.

Bullet had married some starlet, gotten a divorce, married another and gotten another divorce. An unsavory character, and Kamisha's instincts were right about him.

No doubt it had been a lucrative enterprise, arranging those parties. And Bullet must have been infuriated when Kamisha had caught on and cut off his supply of easy money. He'd evidently tried to get Rick to go on with them, Rick had declined, and Bullet had beaten him up. A violent man, shrewd but not too bright; his beating of Rick had been patently ill-advised.

Bullet Adams.

It occurred to him without a bridging thought. He had to let Kamisha know. My God, she'd been staying at Brigitte's house! Bullet could have done something whenever he'd wanted, gotten her alone. But now Kamisha was back at her own home, thank God. Maybe he should have left Inky there, after all, to watch over her. But after Joanne Stern had held that press conference, he'd believed she was safe. By then it had been too late for the instigator of all this trouble to save the situation.

Of course, there was always revenge. Would a man like Bullet resort to revenge, physical revenge, even if it gave him away? Was he capable of that?

John dialed Kamisha's number. It was midafternoon in Aspen, and he suspected she wouldn't be home, but he tried, anyway. He let it ring and ring. No answer. Damn! Why didn't she have an answering machine?

He tried the club then. "I'm sorry. Miss Hammill's line doesn't answer. Can I take a message?" the girl at the front desk asked.

"Do you know where she is?"

"No, I'm sorry. She's out of her office right now."

"Leave her a message, please. Tell her to call John in New York right away. It's important."

"Yes, sir, I've got that. Do you want to leave a number?"

"She knows it."

He stood and paced, thinking. Worry coiled within him, and he cursed the two thousand miles that lay between him and Kamisha. He was helpless and hated the feeling.

There was nothing he could do right now. The sheriff and the police in Aspen would have to be informed, of course, but he wanted to reach Kamisha first—warn her and get her out of danger. Then he'd call the authorities, or maybe she'd want to do that.

He could probably get her at home around five, Aspen time—in two hours. Damn.

The console buzzed.

"Yes, Martha?"

"Inky is here for you."

"I'll be right out."

He'd go to his health club, have a quick workout, then try her again. "Martha," he said when he reached her desk, "have the answering service pick everything up after you leave. I'm expecting an important call."

"Yes, Mr. Leopardo."

"All set, boss? The club?" Inky asked.

He told Inky about Rick Simons's call on the way to his club. The black man whistled. "So what now?"

"I've been trying to get hold of Kamisha, but she isn't available. I don't like the idea of that man on the loose around her."

"He'd be nuts to try anything, boss," Inky said.

"Yes, he would."

"But..."

"Yes, but."

From his club John checked with the answering service; he was standing in the steamy locker room, in sweat-soaked shorts, a towel around his neck.

"No calls, Mr. Leopardo."

"No calls," he repeated.

He dialed Kamisha's home number again. It rang and rang, echoing ominously in his ear. He pictured her lying there, like Rick Simons, her jaw broken, her lovely skin scraped and bruised. The image caused a hot wave of nausea to rise in his gut, even though he knew Adams had had plenty of opportunity to get to Kamisha already. Most likely she was safe, totally safe. But still...

At home he tried again, both the club and her house. She'd never picked up the message he'd left at the desk earlier. The new girl at the desk thought Kamisha had been in a tennis tournament at the Snowmass Club, and she'd probably gone straight home from there.

But where was she?

He felt a fist of fear tighten in his belly. He was turning a molehill into a mountain, he told himself again. Kamisha didn't have to go straight home from work. She didn't have to report in. She was a mature, single woman. She could be anywhere. *Relax,* he told himself.

By eight o'clock he gave up. He couldn't let this go on any longer. If he wasn't able to reach Kamisha, he'd have to contact someone in Aspen to do it for him.

Sheriff McNaught. He was going to have to call the man, anyway, about Bullet Adams. He'd wanted to tell Kamisha first, but he couldn't gamble, couldn't wait any longer.

He got the number from the operator. The Pitkin County Sheriff's Department. He dialed, tapping his fingers impatiently until there was an answer.

"Sheriff McNaught, please."

"He's gone home for the evening. Can I connect you to another deputy?"

Damn. "No, I need to talk to him. This is John Leopardo, owner of the Ute City Club. I have some information that he's been wanting."

"I'm sorry. Would you like to talk to—"

"It's an emergency. There's a possibility that someone's life may be in danger," John stated flatly.

Ed McNaught's wife answered the phone. She sounded irritated when she heard what John wanted, as if her husband was disturbed at home too often for her taste.

"Ed McNaught here."

"Sheriff, I'm calling from New York. I just found out something today that I think you'll want to know. It has to do with the assault on my club manager, Rick Simons."

"Well, I'll tell you, Mr. Leopardo, any help you can offer us in the case would sure be appreciated."

"I know who got to Simons. The same man who was throwing those parties at my club."

"The parties?" The sheriff's tone became wary, as if John had touched on a nerve.

"That's right," John said. "I intend to press charges against the man in Pitkin County, but I'm afraid you may come second to the Senate investigation that's due to start soon.''

"You mean Senator Stern's involvement?"

"Exactly."

"Well," McNaught said, "we'll see about that. This is my territory here, Leopardo.''

"That's your business," John said, a quick image of future headlines dashing through his head: Aspen Sheriff Battles Federal Government over Extradition...

"So who's this man?" McNaught was asking.

John tapped a pen slowly on his desktop. "Before I give you his name I want it understood that Simons came forward with this information. I won't press charges against him, Sheriff. He'll most likely be a friendly witness for the government at any rate.''

"*Who* beat up Simons?" the sheriff asked sharply.

"Bullet Adams."

"The sportscaster?" came McNaught's incredulous voice.

"That's your man. He also supplied the young girls."

"Bullet Adams," Ed McNaught was saying slowly, as if savoring the name.

"Yes," John said impatiently now. "He's the one." But then suddenly John knew why McNaught sounded so tense—the man already knew about his daughter's involvement. Somehow, either through Kamisha or his daughter, he knew. John wondered about that but kept silent. It wasn't his problem.

"Look," John said, "I'm concerned about Kamisha Hammill. She came to me in the first place about her suspicions and—"

"I know," the sheriff broke in. "I know all about that. *Now*."

"I see."

"Have you spoken to Miss Hammill?"

"I've been trying to reach her all afternoon."

"And?"

"No luck. I'm hoping you'll send a car out to her place. It's also possible that she may have gone to her friend's—"

"Brigitte Stratford."

"Correct, Sheriff. I don't think Adams is going to try anything at this stage, but—"

"I wouldn't put it past him," McNaught said darkly.

"You'll send a car then?"

"I'll go myself," the sheriff said, and John didn't like the sound of the man's voice. Not at all. The helplessness, the fear for Kamisha, began to twist in his gut like a knife.

KAMISHA DIDN'T ARRIVE home from the annual Snowmass Club tournament until after six. She threw her tennis bag onto a chair and then searched the refrigerator for something to drink. She was tired and thirsty and hungry, still in her sweaty tennis clothes. She was going to eat, then take a long, hot shower. Then bed, early.

Just as she was pouring herself a glass of grapefruit juice, the phone rang. Holding her glass, she answered it, tucking the receiver between her ear and her shoulder.

"Kamisha!" A man's voice, perturbed.

"Who is this?" she asked.

"Bullet. God, Brigitte's on the floor. I can't...I can't wake her up!"

"Bullet, wait a minute? What's going on?" She straightened, put the glass down, grabbed the phone.

"It's Brigitte! We had a fight. I left for a while. Just got back. She was on the floor, unconscious. A bottle of whisky, pills all over. I'm afraid—"

"Oh, no! Oh, dear Lord. Did you call the ambulance? The hospital? Oh, God, Bullet, is she...is she...?"

"I don't know! She's just lying here."

"Call for an ambulance! Right away. You hear me, Bullet? Nine-one-one. I'm hanging up. I'll be right over. You hear me?"

"Yes, okay, I'll call!"

She slammed down the receiver and grabbed her car keys, raced outside, started her car up, stomping too hard on the accelerator. Her heart was beating like a trip-hammer. Brigitte! Brigitte! Oh, no, it couldn't be!

Tears burned in her eyes, but she forced them back. No time. The hospital was close to Brigitte's house, though. They'd have her there in a flash. Oxygen, IVs. She'd be all right.

It only took her ten minutes to get to Brigitte's. She burst out of her car, leaving the door open. Her mind registered momentarily that there was no ambulance there yet. Oh, God, where was it? Soon. It'd be here soon. She'd be okay. Brigitte would make it.

She raced up the walk to the door, flung the door open, panting, her heart threatening to explode. "Bullet!" she cried out. "Where is she?"

"Here, Kamisha," came his voice.

The kitchen, he was in the kitchen.

"Bullet!" she gasped, running through the living room. "How is she? Did you—?"

She stopped short. Bullet was leaning back against the counter, a tall drink in his hand, a smug half smile on his face.

"Hello, Kamisha," he said coolly.

"Where's Brigitte? What...?" She felt as if something was wrong, as if she'd made some awful, irreversible mistake. Her eyes fixed on the glass casually held in his hand.

"Brigitte. Yes, well, she's gone with Tracy to a horse show."

"But you said...you called me..." Inadvertently she began backing away from him.

"Come in, relax, sit down."

"Where's Brigitte?" Kamisha asked, harshly now.

"I told you. She's at a horse show with Tracy. Newcastle, I think."

"Why did you call me then? Why did you...lie?"

"I wanted to talk to you," he said nonchalantly, upending his glass.

"You could have talked to me on the phone." Her heart was beating slowly and heavily now, a familiar rhythm, the one with which Kamisha met danger.

"I wanted to talk to you in person."

"About what?" She'd keep talking, keep her eye on an escape route—the kitchen door, the living room, the front door. If she showed fear, then like an predator, Bullet would strike.

"What do you want with me? Why did you get me over here?" she asked angrily. "You almost gave me a heart attack."

He smiled, his all-American, snub-nosed features turning malevolent. "You did me a bad turn, lady."

"What are you talking about?" Kamisha folded her arms and glared at him. In a minute she'd casually turn and leave, walk out the door, tell him she had to be somewhere.

"You and Rick Simons."

"*What?*" Knowledge was creeping upon her like a sickness.

"You stopped my lucrative gigs, Kamisha. You went running to the owner and got me into lots of trouble."

"*You?* You had the parties?" Her mind whirled dizzily, seeking support, and all the while she knew it made perfect sense—Bullet, the party boy, the jock who knew everybody, Rick's tennis partner.

Bullet straightened, placed his glass down carefully and took a step toward her. She moved backward, trying desperately to regain her wits, to think.

"Yeah," he said, "the parties were my idea. A great setup, good money. But you had to go and ruin it all."

Kamisha unfolded her arms and drew herself up. "You're damn right I did it. I'd do it again. You're a pimp, Bullet, a disgusting pimp."

"I told you once before about your big mouth, lady."

"All right, Bullet, you've had your say-so. I don't like your company very much, so I'm leaving. Save your stories for the police." Now was the time. She turned, watching him out of the corner of her eye, her muscles tensed, her pulse pounding that slow, deep cadence.

"Not so fast." His voice boomed at her, and she almost flinched, but she kept moving, steadily, toward the front door.

One step, two steps. Her breath rasped in her throat. She kept telling herself that he wouldn't dare touch her, wouldn't dare do anything. Three steps. The white living room carpet sank under her feet. Four steps, another.

A hand came down hard on her shoulder, and he thrust his face up close to hers. "I said not so fast," he rasped. He smelled of alcohol, and his eyes were bloodshot.

"Let me go," she said icily.

"Like hell I will."

She reacted instinctively, swinging her other arm, slapping him on the side of his face, yanking away at the same time. He grunted but kept his grip. Then his hand exploded against her face.

Shock, pain, fury crashed in her head. She must have cried out. He must have said something, too. But she didn't hear. She twisted, fighting him, clawing at his face, panting like a beast, but he held her at arm's length. He was grinning, his teeth showing. He hit her again, a glancing blow that made her sob with rage.

He was strong and quick, and he wasn't afraid of hurting her. She almost panicked, her breath coming fast, her face hot and pulsing with pain.

She doubled over, pretending to collapse. His grip loosened, and she lurched up, bringing her knee up to his groin, hard.

Suddenly she was free, gasping, heedless of the pain in her face, backing away, watching him on the floor as he writhed. *Good,* her mind told her. *Good.*

She ran then, across the white carpet, flung open the door and fled outside into the cool dusk.

But there was a car pulling into the driveway, a Pitkin County sheriff's car, and it was stopping, a man was getting out. She stood there, breathing hard, half dazed.

"Kamisha! Good God! What's going on?"

It was Ed McNaught. She took a step toward him, drew in a quavering breath. "Bullet," she tried to say, clearing her throat. "Bullet. He's in there."

"Are you all right?" The sheriff took her arm and looked at her closely.

"He hit me," she said.

"He's inside?"

"Yes, he's...in there."

"Okay, I'm calling for backup. You come here, sit in my car. Does he have a gun, a weapon?"

She shook her head.

The sheriff used his radio while Kamisha sat there, stunned. The fury had died, and in the aftermath she felt absolutely drained, shaky.

"Now you stay here. I'm going inside to talk to Adams. You okay?"

She nodded.

Within five minutes two more cars pulled up, their red lights rotating, sirens dying. They saw Kamisha, asked where Ed was. She told them, pointing, noticing that they unsnapped the flaps of their holsters as they went toward the house. She sat there, oddly incurious, and the revolving red lights of the deputies' cars pulsated in the autumn dusk.

She was still sitting like that when Brigitte drove up, just as the three men led Bullet out of the house. He was handcuffed, his shirt torn, a smudge of blood on his lip.

"Oh, God!" Brigitte screamed, bursting out of her car. "What happened? Bullet?"

But he never even looked at her, just ducked his head under the deputy's hand and got into one of the cars.

She saw Kamisha then, sitting silently in the sheriff's car. Running, she dragged the door open. "Kamisha, what's going on?"

"Miss Stratford," Ed McNaught said, "Mr. Adams assaulted Kamisha. He resisted arrest, too. I'm afraid he's going to be in some trouble here."

"Bullet?" Brigitte, eyes huge in her small, pallid face, looked from the sheriff to her friend, back and forth, searching for succor.

"Brigitte, he was the one running those parties," Kamisha said quietly.

"Oh, God" was all Brigitte said.

It struck Kamisha that her friend sounded more despairing than surprised. "You knew?" she whispered.

But Brigitte didn't answer at first. Her eyes welled over with tears, and she put a finger out to touch Kamisha's face where Bullet had hit her. "I'm sorry," she said in a broken voice. "Oh, I'm so sorry."

"You knew," Kamisha repeated.

Brigitte sobbed, put her face in her hands. Her shoulders shook. "I tried to tell you," she said, her voice muffled. "But you didn't listen. That night when you were upset about John and at lunch that day. I tried. Oh, Kamisha, I'm so sorry. I was afraid."

"You knew and you never told me. Oh, Brigitte, how could you?"

"He threatened me." She dropped her hands and looked at Kamisha. "I wanted to, oh, God, how I wanted to. I'm so sorry. I never thought...I never, never thought he'd hurt you."

"You knew he'd beaten Rick Simons?" Kamisha asked.

"I...I guessed."

"Oh, Brigitte."

"I know. Now I've really messed up. I was just so scared. Kamisha, I'll do anything I have to to make it up to you. Anything."

"We'll talk about it later," Kamisha said. "Okay? Later, Brigitte." She felt immeasurably sad.

"You won't hate me, will you? You'll forgive me? Please, Kamisha..."

"Don't worry, Brigitte. I'm just so tired now."

"Do you want me to drive you home, Kamisha?" Ed McNaught asked.

"Uh, no...I'm okay, really."

"I'd say it's a good thing Mr. Leopardo called me when he did. Can't tell what might have happened. Glad I drove right on out."

"John?" Kamisha's head snapped up. "*John* called you?"

"John Leopardo, yeah. Said he tried getting hold of you, but you weren't home. He got worried, so he called me."

Kamisha held her head with both hands. "John tried to call me?"

"Seems like. Anyway, it's a good thing he did. Guess he was right to be worried."

"John," she said, hugging herself around the middle, sitting in the sheriff's car while the red lights flickered over their faces eerily.

"You okay, Miss Stratford?" the sheriff was asking Brigitte then.

"No," Kamisha heard her say haltingly. "No, I'm not okay. I'm a mess."

"You want me to call someone?" he asked.

"No, no." Kamisha looked up and heard Brigitte say, "You don't need to call anyone. My best friend in the whole world is right here." And Kamisha felt a single, hot tear finally squeeze from her eye and slide down her cheek.

CHAPTER EIGHTEEN

KAMISHA CALLED late that night. John snatched up the phone on the first ring. His gut was churning, as it had been the whole evening since he'd spoken to McNaught, but hearing her voice now, knowing she was safe, he felt like an expectant father—out of his element, afraid, happy she was on the other end of the line and wary, too. Yes, he was still very much on guard with this woman.

They spoke in monosyllables. About Bullet, about Rick Simons, about the upcoming Senate investigation of Luke Stern and his trysts at the Ute City Club. The conversation was stilted, awkward, and John wished to God he could handle it better.

"Well," she was saying, "I know it's late in New York, but I haven't been able to get through to you at your office, and—"

"I'm glad you called," he said. "I was truly concerned about your safety."

"Well, thank you, but everything's all right now."

"Yes, finally."

"Well..."

"I'll be talking to you soon, I'm sure," John said, "and you take care."

"Oh, I will." There was a pause, then she said, "John, listen, I—"

"Please, Kamisha," he broke in, "we'll talk another time. It's late here. I have appointments in the morning."

"Oh, I'm sorry, well..."

"Good night, Kamisha," he said, and hung up abruptly. For a long, long time he sat in the dark in his room, his head bowed, his stomach knotted, his heart beating too fast. There was a moment when he nearly picked up the phone and called her back, but the instant passed, fleeing into the dark corners of the room.

Inky sauntered into his office the next day in the middle of the afternoon. "Thought you might want to go home early today. You know, after that mess last night," he said, perching one large thigh on the corner of John's desk.

"Doesn't Martha screen my visitors anymore?" John asked irritably.

"Not me. Besides, boss, she thinks you need some rest, too. Said you were hard to please all day."

"That's ridiculous."

"How well did you sleep last night? Come on, tell me."

"It's none of your goddamn business, Inky. Will you lay off?" Inky looked him square in the eye. "You been down, boss, since Aspen."

"I've been busy. Preoccupied."

Inky shook his head. "Man, I've never heard you lie to yourself."

"Knock it off, will you?"

"I'd like to, boss, honest I would," he said. "Just yesterday I promised myself I wasn't going to mention a thing, but—"

John held up a hand. "You're pushing, Inky."

"Yeah? And I'm gonna go right on, too."

For a long moment John eyed him furiously, his temper boiling.

"When you gonna admit you blew it, man?" Inky said, unperturbed.

"Blew *what?*" John whispered dangerously.

"Blew it with Kamisha."

"I won't discuss that with—"

"Yeah, man, I'd say you ruined the best shot you ever had at happiness."

That did it. John exploded. It was as if the past few weeks of tension and misery came spewing out in a gush. "You want me to go through that again? You think I should do that to Kamisha, too?"

"Geez, boss," Inky said, calm, "maybe you should've asked her."

"She doesn't know a damn thing about it, what it's like."

"Sure she does."

"Inky," John grated out, his face hot and flushed, "just go wash the damn car or whatever it is you do. Leave me the hell alone."

Inky did leave then, but he was grinning.

"Damn it!" John said to the echoing emptiness in his office. He was fed up with Inky's aggravating mothering, fed up with Martha and her silent disapproval, fed up with himself. He stood at the window and watched the frenetic movement on the streets of the city below and knew that his life would never be quite the same again.

It was as if he were a rock that had been shaken to its very core and cracked, irreparably cracked. He might live like this for his lifetime, weathering the storms, but he was changed forever.

He snatched up his cane and left the office, walking stiffly past a surprised Martha. "I'll be back in the morning," he said. That was all, no explanation.

He walked, bumping shoulders with hordes of shoppers and businessmen and street people for hours, it seemed. He found himself, finally, down by the East River, on the same path he'd taken with her. It was as if her shadow moved alongside him, a phantom in the bright September sun; he'd never be rid of that memory. He'd never be rid of that empty spot that she'd once filled. The yearning, the ache in his heart, was something entirely new for John. He felt like a man who'd been blind all his life, whose sight had been miraculously restored and then abruptly snatched away.

Inky found him on a bench. It was past 6:00 p.m.

"Goddamn, boss! I been looking for you for hours!"

"How did you find me?" John asked, only mildly curious.

"Well, hell, I looked every place else in this city, then I thought, Where would the boss go if he needed to think?"

"I feel like hell," John admitted, his knee throbbing to beat the band.

"I bet you do. Come on. I'll drive you home. Come on, John."

But he had to tell Inky. He was sick of the lie. "You were right," he said, looking up into the wide black face. "I did blow it."

"I know," Inky replied slowly. "I know, man. When you're lucky enough to have someone love you, you learn to live with whatever problems come up. Love's too special to dink with, boss."

"Is that so?" John asked, smiling tiredly.

"That's about it, I guess."

"Is that why I feel like hell? Is it love?"

"That, boss, and maybe there's this stranger inside you, too, this man that's afraid to come out 'cause it might hurt too much."

"Too risky, huh?"

"Yeah, I suppose."

"Have you been reading psychology books, Inky?"

"Naw. It's just common sense."

"Maybe for some," John said pensively. "Maybe for some."

The next day he flew to Aspen.

He waited in the Denver airport impatiently. He boarded the small jet that flew into Aspen impatiently. He was nervous, unused to this feeling of being unprotected, raw, his emotions so close to the skin that any small nick or bruise could make him bleed.

What if she had another man? What if she no longer wanted him? What if she laughed at him, scorned him, raged at him? She might have been hurt too much, wounded too deeply, to ever forgive him.

The plane banked, circling the green valley, and John could see the glint of the Roaring Fork River below, twisting along next to the ribbon of highway that connected Aspen to the outside world.

She didn't know he was coming. He hadn't had the courage to let her know. Or maybe he'd been afraid she'd have time to steel herself against him. No, it was better to just appear, to be there, to judge her reaction.

He wondered what she thought of him after that last awkward conversation two nights ago. She'd tried to break through his rejection, but she hadn't been able to. She'd tried before, but he hadn't listened to her then, either. She'd begged him to let her help him, but he'd turned from her with a hopelessness born of stubbornness and fear. He could hear her voice, taut with anxiety, asking him, *John, can we talk about it? I care about you. I care about us.*

And he'd turned away.

Aspen after Labor Day was a different creature: calm, sedate, quiet, a small town once again. The air was clear, the sky blue, the branches of the aspen trees hung with dancing golden coins. The driveway of the club was littered with fallen leaves, which a girl in cutoff jeans and a Ute City Club T-shirt raked into piles.

He had the taxi drop him at the door of his condo. It was getting late, nearly five, and he wanted to catch Kamisha at work, in a more neutral setting than her own house. Hurrying up, he left his bag in the middle of the floor and turned to leave again.

He hesitated. He could phone the front desk and ask her to meet him. But, no, he wouldn't; she could leave, refuse to see him. No, he had to walk in, no Martha or Inky to smooth things out and prepare the way. This he had to do himself.

He walked down the path toward the main building, concentrating on moving easily. A pair of tennis players passed him, laughing, red-cheeked with exertion. Two men jogged by, dressed in bright-colored shorts. A breeze rustled in the golden leaves and caressed John's skin, teasing, promising.

He limped across the narrow wooden bridge that spanned the river, which tumbled by, bright and clear, laughing at his slow progress.

The path rose slightly, making its way to the front door of the club; he felt his heartbeat respond to the altitude and his nervousness. His hand gripping the cane was slippery with moisture.

People were coming out of the club, carrying gym bags, their hair still damp from showers. Healthy, vibrant people. Kamisha's kind of people. She belonged here, he thought. But did he?

He saw her the instant he stepped inside the lobby. She was leaning over the counter of the front desk, conferring with one of the girls. She wore a jade-green leotard and matching headband, and tendrils of her hair were lying on her neck, damp with sweat. Her skin gleamed.

He watched her for a time, held motionless by uncertainty. He felt old and haggard and foolish standing there with his cane, dressed in a business suit. He could do nothing. He felt as if the situation was out of his control now, rushing to some kind of conclusion that fate had chosen for him—for them. And he'd relinquished control utterly. It was a frightening feeling but strangely one of relief, too. At last, finally, he'd given up and the burden was lifted from his shoulders.

He watched her until she sensed his presence and turned abruptly. It was then that he saw the bruise on her cheek, the dark smudge left there by a man's hand—Bullet's hand. His fingers clutched his cane, and he took a deep breath to control himself. He should have been there. He should have been with Kamisha.

Their eyes met. Hers widened, and he saw a flush rise on her skin. Her back grew rigid. It was as if the thin mountain air was suddenly sucked from that place, and he could barely breath.

She said something to the girl at the desk, straightened and came toward him. Her lips quivered into a half smile as she stood before him.

"John," she said, her eyes searching his.

"Hello, Kamisha."

"I didn't know you were coming."

"Neither did I."

They were being so careful with each other, as they had been at first, two people who were afraid to say what they really meant, two people with carefully constructed facades, unable to penetrate beyond the banality of their words. He ached to tell her how sorry he was that he hadn't been there to protect her from Bullet Adams. He wanted to tell her that she'd never be alone again, never.

"Well," Kamisha was saying, "you're here. I am glad, John. Did you get my message? There are going to be a lot of things for you to take care of. Bullet and a press release and—"

"We can discuss all that later," he said, cutting her off.

"All right." She stood there, waiting, slim and poised, waiting for him to say something, anything.

"I should have taken your calls," he said.

"Your Martha was just too efficient for me," Kamisha replied coolly.

"Martha," he said, "disapproves of how I've been acting lately."

"Oh?"

"She thought I should take your calls, too."

For a moment she looked surprised. Finally she nodded in comprehension. "Martha was right."

Silence hung between them awkwardly.

"John—" she began.

"Can we go somewhere and talk?" he asked quickly.

"Yes, of course. Just let me get something...." She gestured at her leotard.

She was back in a moment, a long shirt over her aerobics outfit. They went outside to the far corner of the deck and sat at a table under a big umbrella. He was so terribly aware of her proximity, the reality of her that had only been a dream for these past weeks. He wanted to say so many things, but the words never reached his lips.

"How is it in New York?" she asked.

"Muggy. Kamisha..." He hesitated, looked out over the tennis courts. "Look, I came here to...apologize, I guess."

She just looked at him for a heartbeat of time, then said, "I thought you came because of Bullet. I thought..."

"No, I came because of you, Kamisha."

A tremulous smile curved her lips. "John, you mean that, don't you?"

"I mean it."

She looked down. "You must have known how I felt about you. I didn't try to hide it. You hurt me, John."

"I know and I'm sorry. I'm not sure you can forgive me, but I guess I'm here to ask you to."

"Oh, John..." She reached out a hand and put it over his. "This role of penitent doesn't suit you very well. You're lousy at it."

"I don't have much practice," he said stiffly.

"And I'm not making it any easier, am I?" She smiled and then looked away. "I don't know. I'm just getting over the shock of you being here. Give me a little time." She gave a short laugh. "Let me figure out what I feel. I'm not even sure."

"Of course, that's fair." What had he expected, that she'd fly into his arms, swearing eternal devotion? He swallowed his disappointment and put a good face on it. He had time.

She leaned forward, elbows on the table. "Speaking of apologies," she said, "I owe you one myself for going to Carin McNaught when you were against it. John, I—"

"Kamisha, don't. You don't owe me an apology for that. I was being stubborn that day, so sure of my own power to solve every problem on earth. I was wrong."

She smiled and nodded. "As it turned out, Carin won't have to give a deposition or anything."

"That's good."

"Yes. It's enough she's working things out with her dad. And then just this morning— Oh, wow," Kamisha said. "I almost forgot to tell you, but Sheriff McNaught called and said the FBI searched Bullet's house in California and found not only all kinds of drugs and paraphernalia, but young girls living there—runaways, John, from all over the place. It looks like the government is going to have an ironclad case against him."

"I'm glad."

"So am I. He deserves it. You know, he was the one who arranged to have my brakes tampered with at the Denver airport."

John lifted a brow.

"Brigitte told him what I was doing. It wasn't her fault, though. She didn't realize—"

"Of course she didn't. Will Brigitte testify?" he asked.

"Yes, she already gave her statement to the FBI. She left this morning for the Betty Ford Clinic. She quit drinking."

"I'm glad to hear that. I hope she sticks to it."

"Oh, she will. This time she really will. I think she realized what she was becoming. It had to do with Bullet and the parties and Tracy. With all that."

John stood restlessly, aware of the other people sitting on the deck, tanned, fit people who were eyeing him with curiosity, the same bone-chilling curiosity that he'd tried to escape all his adult life. Would he always be so sensitive to strangers' scrutiny?

"Do you mind if we take a walk? I've been sitting too much today," he said, cognizant of Kamisha watching him, too, watching, weighing, wondering.

They made their way along the tree-shaded bike path, treading upon the crisp fallen leaves. He was aware of how effortlessly Kamisha matched her pace to his. Above their heads the leaves whispered, and at their feet the river rushed, dancing in the sun. But John still felt restless.

"I've talked to my father," he said, as if to himself.

Her step faltered for a split second. "Yes?"

"It was very strange after all this time."

"I can imagine. How is he, John?"

"He's an old man, Kamisha. That's what surprised me so. Old and defenseless."

"Was he...uh...glad to see you?"

He nodded. "Yes, grateful and glad."

"I envy you."

"My father has done terrible things in his time. I can't condone what he's done, but now, I think, I can overlook it. We're still family. I was wrong to deny that."

"It must have been hard," she said softly.

"Yes." He walked on for a time, comforted by her presence. "I learned from you, you know."

She regarded him in surprise.

"You taught me that love and loyalty must transcend a person's faults."

"I...um, don't really think..." Her voice died away. "I missed you, John."

"Yes, I missed you, too."

"I tried to call. Well, you know that."

"Yes, Martha made sure I knew every time."

"You never answered."

"I thought I was doing you a favor."

"Oh, God, John, how could you think that? I love you!" she said abruptly.

Pain gripped him. Pain and elation. His hand tightened on the cane until his knuckles turned white. Slowly he stopped and faced her.

"I've taken everything you could give me. I took your love and your trust, even your strength. It was because of you I spoke to my father. I don't know...I still don't understand the connection, but somehow, in my mind, I couldn't love one and spurn the other. I've used you and given you nothing back."

"John, you've given me everything."

He shook his head. "What about you? I love you, but I can't ask you to share a life with me. Do you want to be thought of as a Mafia wife? Do you want to be questioned, followed, hounded? I can't ask you to share that with me, Kamisha. I saw what it did to Jo."

"Was that her name?"

"Yes."

"I feel sorry for her."

"She couldn't take it, Kamisha. It hurt her, nearly destroyed her."

"Did you love her?"

He paused. "I loved the idea of her—squeaky-clean, innocent, pretty. We might have been happy."

"She was weak, though. She didn't love you enough."

"I suppose so."

"I'm not Jo. I'm tough, John." She looked at him, her eyes glistening with emotion. "Oh, John, why didn't you ask me before you put us both through this? I can stand it. I've stood it before. I've been through the worst they can throw at me. Don't you realize? You can't hide from the press. That just makes it worse. You've tried to hide all these years when you should have been open. If you talk, if you tell them everything, be absolutely frank, they'll get bored and leave you alone. I know. It happened when I divorced Josh. Once they have the facts, they're satisfied."

He stood there looking at her, torn between disbelief and hope.

"Oh, John," she whispered, "is *that* why...is that the only reason you left?"

Then she was in his arms, and he held her tightly, cradling her head against his chest. She turned her face up, and he saw that she was laughing and crying at the same time. He touched her cheek where the bruises marred it. "You got this because of me," he said sadly. "I should have been with you."

"Don't be silly."

"I'm not silly. But I could be wrong about a couple of things." He kissed her and drew back. "I just might be," he said, feeling foolish and happy and young.

She smiled through her tears and reached up a hand to caress his face. "Wouldn't that be nice for a change," she said softly, and it wasn't a question.

"I always thought a family, and love, couldn't withstand scrutiny," he said. "Do you think it can? Are you willing…?"

"Yes, John," she said firmly, looking into his eyes.

"Will you marry me?" he found himself asking, astonished at the certainty he felt.

"Yes, John."

He gathered her close and drew in the scent of her hair.

"We'll invite the press to the reception," she was saying. "Let the whole world know how much we love each other."

He laughed softly. The sun slipped behind the mountain, and a cool autumn breeze filtered through the golden leaves. Kamisha's hair was soft and fragrant, her body warm against his.

"There's magic here in Aspen," he said. "Everything is possible here."

"Yes, I feel it, too. You've given me the magic of trust, John. You make me feel worthy of love. I want to be with you forever. Wherever you are, as long as we're together."

"New York?" he asked. "The city?"

"If you're there."

"I've been thinking, you know, of having an office here. I can run my business from anywhere," he said.

"And how long have you been thinking that?" she asked, joy bubbling in her voice.

"Oh, about five minutes," he said.

"It's a nice place to raise children," she said shyly.

"A magic place," he repeated.

"Love is the magic, and it's our gift to each other, John."

Marcus James was solid as the Colorado Rockies. Since Lindsay Cornell's husband had died, they'd weathered a lot of storms. But now they faced the greatest challenge of all—denying the passionate love and romance they both wanted with each other....

TOUCH THE SKY

Debbi Bedford

CHAPTER ONE

EACH DAY LINDSAY CORNELL walked breathlessly into English literature class and took her seat looking as if she knew that something new and joyous was happening in the world. She was nineteen years old, a sophomore at Southern Methodist University in Dallas, and everything she loved, everything she treasured, was in order and stacked neatly against the walls of her life.

She was unaware of the eyes that followed her each time she entered the room that semester, of the girls who coolly assessed her shimmering taupe silk stockings and her classic designer outfits, of the men who studied her features, her endless legs, her tiny waist, with undisguised admiration. Lindsay was particularly unaware of Kendall Allen. Kendall sat in the third row from the door in the fourth seat back, the seat directly behind Lindsay. When she walked toward her seat and sat down so near to him, Kendall Allen could scarcely even breathe. She looked so dainty to him, like a piece of fragile china, terribly breakable. He had been hoping for a chance to say hello to her or to help her with a discussion question for weeks. He needed a friend so desperately just now, and he had become obsessed with Lindsay; by her gentle smile, by the way her rich, coffee-colored eyes danced. They had moving, burning flecks of gold and green in them and Kendall liked to think if he looked far enough into them, he would find eternity there.

He secretly called her "sunshine" because she looked like a mischievous fairy when she laughed, because all that he could see of her during class was her sunny hair. It was magic the way he was bewitched as soft cascades fell against her shoulders and then spilled off onto his desk. The long tresses were the color of Texas spun honey, and he longed to touch them, to play with them, to twist them or tug them. The warm silkiness of her hair all during the hour was almost more than he could bear.

Their chance to become friends finally arrived, and strangely enough, the opportunity came as a surprise to him and as an embarrassment to her. Dr. Bodkin was lecturing on *A Midsummer Night's Dream*. As the professor dove deeper and deeper into the Shakespearean comedy's plot, Lindsay became so entranced she forgot to take notes. This play was one of her favorites, and the professor was pulling out phrases and symbols with meanings Lindsay had never known were there. As she became engrossed in Dr. Bodkin's words, Lindsay absentmindedly clung to the basket that held her books beneath her chair. Kendall looked down at his feet with amusement. His favorite place to keep them during these long, boring lectures was propped in the basket of the desk in front of him. Lindsay had absolutely no idea she was clinging desperately to his feet.

Kendall was perplexed. For days he had been practicing. He knew just what he would say, how he planned to approach her smile, her eyes. "I think you are beautiful," he was going to tell her. "I would like to be your friend." He had the words ready, all drummed up and waiting to spill out of his mouth, when Lindsay leaned over to grab a notebook from beneath her desk. Instead, she saw her left hand still resting on his left Loafer.

"Oh, no." Her voice was a tiny chirp. "Oh, I'm sorry." Lindsay turned in her desk to face him. A flush was rising in her cheeks, and she smiled apologetically at him. Her eyes danced. The words he had been planning to say filtered away somewhere, and instead he muttered something totally inappropriate.

"I think you must like my feet," he said.

Her laughter rang out like a bell throughout the classroom. Lindsay leaned toward him and looked for a moment as if she was going to tell him the answer to some sad, forbidden secret. "I am not in the habit of playing with other people's feet," she whispered to him. "I apologize for the distress I may have caused your Loafers." Her eyes were burning, moving, shining like diamonds. She managed to somehow look playful and pensive all at the same time.

Kendall gave up all hope. He had had the perfect chance to impress her and make friends with her. Now she would leave class thinking that the guy who sat behind her with the Loafers was the campus crackpot.

The entire episode was a welcome amusement for Lindsay. During her first months at the university, she had studied faithfully to make the grades she needed on her examinations. She didn't have to study to make the "B"s everyone else seemed so proud of, but studying gave her something to hide behind. Lindsay had no desire to flock with her fellow students to the pizzeria for a pepperoni pizza and warm chatter. Chattering was something she was afraid of. Smiling and giggling and talking about nothing were foreign to her.

All her life, Lindsay had been taught to be a little adult. She knew exactly what to say to her professors, to professionals she met, to mentors from her father's circle of friends. When she had attended a party honoring the newest line of cotton fashions being introduced at the Dallas Apparel Mart or at a reception honoring the Governor of Texas, Lindsay had displayed all the graciousness, all the style and fortitude of a princess greeting her subjects. But Lindsay didn't know how to talk to real people her own age, the ones she met every day, the ones with problems and feelings and jokes to tell. When she met one of them, she would remember that she was just herself, not a princess, and she would lose her footing entirely. She couldn't dream and giggle with her classmates because she wasn't certain what her dreams were supposed to be. So she hid herself and watched through a veil of awkwardness as the university world moved by without taking much notice of her. Until the day she grabbed Kendall Allen's shoes.

Kendall was the first person she'd spoken to since she had enrolled in classes. She had been embarrassed, but he had been amused and friendly. She had been playing with his shoes. When she turned to apologize, he had asked her if she liked his feet. What a bizarre, wonderful thing to say. The memory of the scene made her giggle. How good it felt. The sun was sparkling against the horizon, and there seemed to be a hundred different things to see as she walked to the campus parking lot to find her car. She had a tingly, refreshed feeling inside now, all because of a sudden friendly smile and a funny pair of Loafers propped beneath her desk.

Two days later when English lit class met again, Lindsay made a point to smile at the guy with the feet and to tell him hello. He seemed almost bewildered by her smile and she was annoyed by his reaction. She had lectured herself long and hard the night before. She needed a friend, and the happy-go-lucky way he had about him made Lindsay think he might be an easy person to talk to. But maybe she had been mistaken. She decided when she saw the strange look on his face that she would make him her new challenge.

Kendall Allen was a nice-looking man, Lindsay decided. He had almond-shaped, smoldering charcoal eyes that looked almost sad every time she turned to him. Puppy eyes. Deep, demanding and desperate one minute and friendly the next. Lindsay supposed he could talk anybody into doing anything just by looking out at them through those smoky eyes. Kendall's lips were full and sensuous, and his hair was rich and wavy, a dark fudge-chocolate color of brown that shone almost auburn in the Texas sunlight that filtered in through the classroom window. When he smiled, an impish look came across his face, a look that was emphasized by a thick moustache that curved up on one end just a bit more than it did on the other. He was built like a tree trunk, Lindsay decided, sturdy, tall, stocky, like he could withstand a Gulf Coast hurricane or anything else life might toss in his path.

Lindsay was enthralled and frightened by Kendall all at the same time. After that first day of contact when she'd grabbed his shoes, he had been friendly to her, but not overly so. Something told her he was holding just as much back from her as she was from him. When he talked to her, he never said anything that mattered. He only told her simple jokes and laughed at the way she did things.

Kendall knew that Lindsay was amused by him. He could tell by the things that she said and the new sparkles in her eyes that she was enjoying and encouraging their friendship. Nearly every class now, Dr. Bodkin would have to glance at them and clear his throat before he could begin his lecture. Kendall and Lindsay always had their heads together giggling over something funny.

Kendall loved to tease her, to watch her little elfin nose and her primly-glossed full mouth turn thin and feisty as she rebuked his silly comments. "Why do your toes turn purple every time you wear those sandals?" he asked her in jest one day.

"My toes aren't purple." She looked horrified as she jerked her feet back beneath her desk. "Besides," she added, gaining her composure, "purple toes are the true sign of a real native Dallas girl. They prove that I've been wearing high-heeled shoes almost since the first day I could walk." She was being sarcastic and he loved it.

"If you are a true Dallas girl then you ought to be a fashion expert, too—" he thumbed through his notebook "—are you?"

"Of course." She nodded her head and this time she was deadly serious. "My mother and I spend long hours inspecting and critiquing the stores. Mom is a garment buyer for Neiman-Marcus. Let's see." She pointed to each of her fingers as she named the clothing stores off. "Marshall Field's is the place to find accessories, hats with tiny brims and shimmering veils, the shoes that can make even my feet look elegant and small." She lifted one of her long, slender feet from the floor and surveyed it before she continued. "Neiman's is where you find the classic things, the cardigan sweaters and the wool suits."

"That stuff sounds boring," Kendall interjected.

"Oh, but just wait," Lindsay said, laughing. "When you're in a daring mood, Sakowitz is the place to shop. You ought to be taking notes on this, Kendall Allen. Everything at Sakowitz is showier and more expensive. I tried on this one dress there that cost almost $5,000. It fell straight to the hips and then it frothed in tiers all the way to the floor. It was covered with thousands of tiny iridescent navy-blue beads and it glistened under the lights every time I even barely took a breath." She paused and Kendall studied the rapt expression on her face. "There are no words to describe what it feels like to wear a dress like that. It's incredible."

"Why do girls worry about clothes so much?" Kendall snickered. "You all look just as nice in a pair of $10 blue jeans as you do in a $5,000 dress."

"You're probably right," Lindsay agreed with him. "But I don't think it's really a matter of looks. I think it's how something like that can make you feel. A $5,000 dress can make me feel... well...perfect."

"There's no reason you should even want to feel perfect," Kendall said.

"Oh yes there is," Lindsay informed him. "In case you haven't noticed, we live in Dallas, Texas. The South. All the women here are still expected to be Southern belles. We're expected to keep a spotless house, have a magnificent career, two darling children, and to remain beautiful, bright and entertaining. And that, sir—" she paused for effect "—is a bit of a challenge these days."

"You know—" he propped his chin in the palm of his hand "—I begin to see your point."

"Good." She grinned and then she bent forward as if she had some shocking statement to share. "I do have a confession to make, though."

"What is that?"

"I, Lindsay Cornell, am not perfect," she whispered to him.

"Oh, I can't believe that," he said.

"I'm not a full-blooded Dallas girl any longer," she kept whispering. "I am a mountain woman as well."

"Maybe you had better tell me about these things," he suggested, giving her one of his best mischievous grins.

Lindsay's eyes darkened just a bit. "My dad died twelve years ago. He was a sportscaster and he had an automobile accident while he was in Houston covering a golf tournament. I was old enough to remember him, to remember the things he taught me and to remember how much he loved me. Anyway, there was a ranch that daddy always loved in Colorado way high up in the mountains. He took mom there for their honeymoon, and after I came along they took me, too. Daddy's aunt and uncle own it. It's in a little valley called Taylor Park and the Collegiate Peaks encircle the entire property. There's no way to describe that place to someone who hasn't seen it. Even photographs can't begin to define the grandeur that you feel there.

"A few years ago, dad's aunt, Margie Howard, called and asked if I'd like to come work for her and her husband, Dan, cleaning cabins for the summer. It worked out perfectly because mother had just gotten promoted to assistant buyer at Neiman's. She had several long buying trips and she was worried about leaving me alone. So I started spending summers at Howard's Guest Ranch. And that's how my two separate lives got started. I have a dressy, made-up city life and I also have a faded-blue-jeans life thirty miles away from the nearest paved road. That's the life where I learned how to fish and how to square dance and how to work miracles. And the way that makes me feel about myself...peaceful and reassured...well, it's better than any $5,000 dress."

Kendall didn't say anything. He just watched the expression on her face with a growing sense of amazement and wonder. When Lindsay talked about the valley, something akin to contentment and calm seemed to wash across her entire being. Her cheeks had taken on a new rosy glow, and she looked as if she might burst into song at any moment. Lindsay had always looked beautiful to him, but now, as she spoke of the mountains, her beauty took on an iridescence that simply took his breath away.

He found himself longing to tell Lindsay of his dreams of her, of his thoughts of her. But he didn't dare. Every time he considered it, he became cottonmouthed and foggy. He kept himself sane by telling her jokes he had heard on "The Tonight Show" the night before. He had so much to tell her about things that really mattered to him. His ground-school workbook. His church. His dreams of flying again. His dog named Buzzer. And even Sarah. For some reason he felt like he should talk to Lindsay about Sarah.

Ironically, it was Sarah who kept Kendall from telling Lindsay how much he was beginning to care for her. Sarah was still so real to him, and Lindsay was only a dream. Kendall was afraid to touch her with reality. She was like a butterfly whose wings would be broken if he tried to get too close. There were days, minutes, every moment, when he longed to reach out to her, to protect her, to love her and shelter her. Someday, he decided, soon...he would tell her about his airplane. He would tell her about how he was learning to fly again. Someday. As soon as he could get his courage up.

Lindsay was confused by the way Kendall looked at her now. There were times when he said something particularly funny with a faraway, wistful look in his eyes that made Lindsay almost want to weep. He looked sad and rumpled and rueful, like he was a little lost boy who needed someone to take care of him. He made her laugh so hard sometimes, but underneath his laughter was a bittersweet melancholy that Lindsay had just begun to see. She longed to decipher him. He had buried something deep down inside of himself, and Lindsay wanted to dig for it.

The digging sometimes took more energy than it was worth, though, Lindsay decided. And that realization annoyed her. Today in lit class, she needed Kendall to be a quiet friend. She didn't have any great catastrophe she needed advice on, just a series of little problems, an argument with her roommate, a headache, a low score on a test she had studied for. She needed a hug...and she already knew a hug was too much to ask of Kendall Allen. He never touched her with his arms or with his heart. He only tried to touch her tentatively with his jokes but his jokes never came close.

Kendall knew when Lindsay walked into the room that something was wrong, but it was impossible for him to try to find out what. He felt like it would take his entire personality out of the context of the affable friendship they'd established if he tried to comfort her. Especially since he still needed so much comforting himself. After class, the two of them walked out of the building together, he jabbering and she deep in thought. He was frantically talking to make her forget whatever was souring her mood this afternoon. And what she was thinking was souring her mood even further. Summer was coming and it would take wondering and worry on her part to keep this thing between them going. She decided at this instant that she wouldn't care about him. She didn't want to. She only had two more class periods before semester finals and then she would never have to see him again. Lindsay knew he would never call her or ask her out on a date. She had done something wrong with him and she didn't know exactly what. She only knew that something sad was making him hold an enormous part of himself back from her.

They walked along together until they reached the administration building. Lindsay paused in the threshold and waited for Kendall to hold the door open for her. He did so and then gestured for her to step in before him. As she passed him, she stumbled on one of the worn concrete steps, and as she pitched forward Kendall grabbed her elbow to steady her.

"Sorry I'm so uncoordinated," she said, smiling sadly up at him. "I've just had a rough day. Thanks."

Kendall gazed at his hand touching her arm for a moment and then, suddenly, he jerked it away. He reacted as if he had touched a hot stove. Lindsay walked on into the hallway trying to stay composed, trying to ignore the tingling near her elbow that his touch had caused. Something inside of her was stirring, something that was reaching up out of her and opening and stretching her all at the same time.

That night, Lindsay dreamed of him. The entire vision was poignant, as if it had been filmed in slow motion. She was sitting at her desk in English lit class when she felt Kendall's hand touching her on the shoulder. Again that electric feeling surged through her like a shock. Slowly, silently, she arched her neck and her back until her head lay on his desk, her hair fanned across his books and his note paper.

She looked at him and let the soft, smoldering feeling well up in her eyes. Then, slowly, almost agonizingly so, Kendall began to bend his face toward hers. She watched him as he moved closer, his eyes filled with a melancholy wonder and a very vital kind of love. His face moved closer, and after what seemed to be an eternity, his lips touched hers.

Lindsay woke with a start. For an instant, she had forgotten who she was and where she was and why she had been dreaming. Then she remembered. Her mind was playing a terrible trick on her. Her lips were burning where she had dreamed Kendall Allen had kissed her. Lindsay stared up at her ceiling in disbelief. Maybe she was going to have to work harder to forget Kendall than she had thought.

The feelings in her heart just now were both fabulous and frightening. She wondered if she even had the strength to give Kendall up. But she didn't know whether she had the courage to go where he might be taking her.

KENDALL LEANED HIS HEAD against the steering wheel of his gold Chevrolet Corvette and closed his eyes in a vain attempt to shut out the searing Texas noonday heat. Dallas was suffocatingly hot, even though it was already September.

It had been a relaxing summer, one he would remember for a long time to come, but now he was ready for the wind to blow in something that might even slightly resemble fall weather. The hot moist air had hit him just like a brick wall when he had walked out of the post office a few minutes before. Kendall wanted just to sit in the parking lot for a moment, to catch his breath, to imagine the feel of the ocean breeze he had just left behind at his sister's house in San Diego.

Nickie had been nice to invite him out to stay with her and Ron and the kids for the summer. He knew the invitation was more out of concern for him than anything else. Last summer had been a nightmare without Sarah. He was definitely too young to be a widower, and Nickie had tried to make him see that it had almost been a blessing Sarah had died so soon after their marriage. There had been no children, and Nickie told him over and over again that, even though a chapter of his life had come and gone, it was going to be easy for him to pick himself up and continue on.

The San Diego breeze had helped Kendall make a major decision about himself this summer. His classes at Southern Methodist last year had been a crutch, something to take his mind off himself and his skydiving. After Sarah died he had wanted to change his life. Totally. He didn't want any broken pieces of what they had had together sticking up and jabbing him with their rough places. But he had found out over the past eighteen months that many of the things he had shared with his wife were too important to him to be buried away. His dreams and his longings were all too strong. He had gone back to flying last year right after Christmas, right after he met and befriended Lindsay Cornell. And now, as he racked up the flying hours, he could feel a part of himself coming back, too.

There were times this summer when he felt like he had almost retrieved his soul again. He played football with the boys and bragged to Ron about the University of Alabama just like he used to. But something, some part of the hurt, was still inside of him tugging at his heart.

When he met Lindsay in Dr. Bodkin's English class last year, he had been so intrigued with her, so devastated by her beauty and her laughter that he had actually thought he might fall in love again. But he seemed to have a defense mechanism set against the idea. Every time he almost said something tender to Lindsay, every time he almost told her just how much he wanted to love her, something would grab at his guts, and there, dancing before his eyes, would be Sarah again. Her hand would touch his face, and her eyes would be smiling, and she would be telling him over and over again how much she loved him. Then, as suddenly as she appeared to him, she would be gone again, her lifeless body lying facedown in the crumpled folds of the rainbow-colored parachute. Kendall knew that he had killed her. She had begged him to teach her how to fly. She had talked about skydiving for weeks. At first he hadn't wanted to teach her, hadn't wanted to let her go, but finally she had talked him into it. He should have been strong enough to tell her no. Without him she never would have been quite brave enough to close her eyes and leap.

Kendall had jumped first. Sarah had been right behind him and, for minutes that clicked slowly by, they fell together while Kendall turned somersaults and showed off to his wife. The land was coming up to meet them and Kendall pulled his rip cord at one thousand six hundred feet. He watched, panic-stricken, as Sarah screamed and careered past him. Investigators had pored over her parachutes later. The number one chute had not been loaded properly and two of the nylon shrouds had become tangled. The chute had never started to catch the air.

When she came barreling past him, Kendall screamed at her to pull open the reserve chute. It took Sarah too many precious seconds to pull herself out of her shock and find the second cord. The reserve chute opened four hundred fifty feet above the ground but Kendall could already see that it was going to be too late. There was no air left to catch.

He squeezed his eyes shut in a vain attempt to block out the horrible memory. His lashes were laced with unshed tears.

After what seemed like an eternity, Kendall opened his eyes and turned his key in the Corvette ignition. As he did, the radio blared on.

"You're listening to Mike Seldon on KVIL," a jolly voice boomed over the airwaves. "It's a fabulous afternoon in Dallas, Texas. I don't know about you, but I get off the air in ten minutes...."

Kendall switched the machine off. He wasn't in the mood for light-hearted banter. He needed silence. He wanted to mourn alone.

He stretched his arms up over his head, flexed his neck and reached for the steering wheel. It was time to go. Then he caught a glimpse of her.

Kendall hadn't seen Lindsay since final-exam day in Bodkin's class and he was slightly surprised at her appearance. Her long hair was wound in one continuous French braid that looped down behind one ear and up in front of the other. Lindsay's hairdo made a soft, flowing, angel's halo around her face, and she had never looked so beautiful to him. Kendall was surprised at how very happy he was to see her.

She certainly did not look like a university student these days. She was dressed in a gray business suit, impeccably tailored of the finest, lightest wool. The pink silk blouse she wore was tied at the neck with a twisted scarf that became a rose-shaped knot in the hollow of her throat. She wore one strand of iridescent egg-shell pearls. Her pumps were gray and her silk stockings were the sheerest taupe. Kendall had to smile to himself. He had never seen anyone dress that way to run a marathon, and that's what it looked like Lindsay was doing. As she darted toward the door, she was yanking a handful of important-looking papers from her jacket breast pocket.

By the time Lindsay waited in line and rid herself of the important deadline story of the day, Kendall had composed himself and was waiting for her outside the door of his Corvette. He called gingerly to his friend as he watched her weave her way back through the parked cars.

"Kendall," she exclaimed. Lindsay was glad to see him, too. It had been a long time. "How are you?" She made a quick mental note of the faded jeans and the olive-green polo shirt he was wearing. The color was perfect for him. He looked like he had been somewhere in the sun all summer, and the shirt he wore only emphasized his rich, golden tan. She was aware, once again, that she was intensely attracted to this man. Just this chance meeting with him was sending chills up her spine.

"I'm okay," Kendall said, resisting the urge to hug her. "What are you doing? You look fabulous. Did you go to the mountains this summer?"

"No." She grinned matter-of-factly. "I worked here instead. After last semester at the university, I got a job as reporter for the *Dallas Times Herald*."

"I haven't seen your by-line." He smiled at her. He tried to keep the awe he was feeling out of his face.

"Look in the Lifestyle section on Sundays," she suggested. Her eyes held a glimmer of amusement. "You probably don't ever read that part. It's the women's section although they don't call it that anymore. They've revamped it."

"What kind of stories do you write?" he asked. He was honestly interested.

"I've got one coming out Sunday about the perils of working out in a health club. You should enjoy that one. I'm running all sorts of photos of women in leotards." She smiled radiantly at him, and he found his eyes riveted to her face. Everything he saw there was finely etched into a beautiful portrait. It was the face of a determined woman and an excited child all at the same time.

"You look wonderful." He whispered it. He almost hadn't gathered the courage to utter the compliment.

"Why thank you, Mr. Allen." Lindsay was teasing him with her Southern charm, but Kendall could tell she was pleased. "So do you. Nice tan. You must have spent your summer in some exotic spot."

"If you can call San Diego, California, an exotic spot. I spent time with my sister and her husband out there."

So that was it, Lindsay thought. Last spring she had decided she didn't want to see Kendall Allen again. But she kept having crazy daydreams about him. All during June she had secretly hoped he would call her. But when he didn't it only seemed simple and easy and right. Now she wasn't so certain. There was a special look in his eyes, that familiar wistfulness, that she almost couldn't bear. What were they doing to each other? Maybe if she stuck with him, worked on him a bit, she could make his eyes smile again. At least he was really talking to her now. He hadn't cracked one joke in the entire ten minutes they had been together.

As Lindsay stood there deep in thought, Kendall could not resist reaching out and touching her on the cheek. She looked so beautiful and so strong, yet so fragile in a soft, delicate way. Before, he had seen her as a cute college coed. Now he saw a different side of her, the colt wobbling, trying to stand on a brand new set of legs.

Lindsay reached up and touched her cheek where he had touched it. It was not a motion she would have consciously wanted him to see, but she was so lost in him just now that she didn't realize she was making the motion. Their eyes met. Both of them could read all the regret and the bewilderment there.

"Are you going back to the university this semester?" Kendall's question broke the poignant silence.

"I don't think so," Lindsay answered softly. "I like what I'm doing. I thought about changing my major to journalism and going back, but I can't see returning and spending the money to learn about what I'm already doing. Even my publisher said I would learn more in the working world. And the newspaper pays me. That fact swayed my decision a bit."

"I'm not going back, either," Kendall said, shaking his head. "Things just didn't work out for me there. I didn't find what I needed."

Again their eyes locked. The empty, aching chasm inside Lindsay's soul began to open again as she read something new in Kendall's eyes.

He reached for her shoulders and pulled her gently to him as Lindsay felt herself melting against his chest. This was better than any fantasy. Kendall cupped his huge hand around the back of her head and he pulled her face toward his. When their lips met, he could feel her trembling.

"Is this...all right?" he whispered into her hair as he pulled away. He didn't know if he was asking her the question or if he was asking himself.

"Oh, yes." She grinned playfully in response and then wrapped her arms around the back of his neck. He pulled her head up to his and they kissed again. At first carefully, almost painfully, and then with a growing passion, they probed each other's mouths and touched each other's souls. Lindsay prayed he would never stop kissing her here in this parking lot in front of the entire world. But finally it was she who had to back away and catch her breath. The sky was whirling, and the sun was spinning, and Lindsay realized that, before this day, she had never known what happiness was.

Kendall looked down at her with a thousand words suddenly in his eyes.

"Oh, sunshine." He smiled as his eyes searched her face. "I care so much about you...more than I ever intended to admit to myself. I missed you terribly during the summer."

"I missed you, too." She reached up and kissed him on the tip of his nose. "I missed everything about you, even all your dumb jokes." Light beamed from her face as he pulled her to him again.

Only this time, as he folded her into his arms and his lips met hers, the electricity of another time shattered the present. For a moment he forgot where he was. The woman he was holding was Sarah. It was Sarah's face he saw moving toward his. Through narrowed eyes he saw her eyes loom past him and she was falling... falling...and then there was no one. He never had a chance to catch her.

The memory hit Kendall like a fierce gigantic wave. His entire being went numb. He shoved Lindsay away from him so forcefully she almost stumbled backward onto the concrete.

"Kendall?" Lindsay sobbed out his name. "What did I do? I'm sorry. What is wrong?"

"Nothing you can change," he growled back at her. "Absolutely nothing. I have to go."

He jerked open the door to his Corvette, revved the engine and was gone before Lindsay had a chance to call out his name again.

CHAPTER TWO

LINDSAY WAS ANNOYED. She stared defiantly at the clock on the mantel. There were days when she became so used to hearing the continuous ticking of the antique timepiece she didn't notice it. But not tonight. The clock seemed to be groaning at her every time the massive brass pendulum swung to and fro.

Deadlines. Lindsay was beginning to hate them. Since she'd started working for the *Times Herald*, time had become crucial to her. The feature propped in her typewriter had to be written by eleven-thirty tomorrow morning. The story was about animals and the Dallas County Humane Society. This was the time of year when people who kept animals needed to protect them from the icy cold outside. Lindsay figured she would be writing this same article over and over again, each year at this same time, always looking for a new angle, a new lead, a new peg for the story.

She ran her fingers through her hair. There were still so many things she was unsure of. Her life here in Dallas, for instance. The lead sentence she had typed five times on a blank sheet of typing paper, for another. Deadlines like this one. And Kendall Allen.

It had been over two months since she'd seen him in the post-office parking lot. Two months since he kissed her so hungrily one moment and so angrily the next. Eight long, confusing weeks. During the first five or six nights after the encounter, Lindsay lay awake wondering, wishing and praying that she hadn't done anything wrong. She was almost certain she had.

Kendall had called her ''sunshine.'' He'd told her he cared more about her than he ever intended to admit to himself. Lindsay was befuddled. There was something else that made him push her away. Maybe someone else. But who?

She shook her head as if to clear her mind. She certainly didn't have time to worry about Kendall Allen tonight. He could have called weeks ago, but he hadn't. As she pounded on her Olivetti portable typewriter, she heard a sharp knock on her door.

"Come on in," she called without much enthusiasm.

"It's just me," her roommate, Rita, said as she pushed the door open and entered with a tray. "I knew nothing I did would get you away from the typewriter, so I decided to do some baking and bring the goodies to you."

Lindsay stuck the blue felt-tip editing pen behind her ear. "Okay smarty—" she grinned "—you know I'm trying to stay away from that stuff."

"How boring. I hate people who think they have to be on diets all the time. You certainly don't need to be. These will give you quick energy." Rita nodded her head in a motherly fashion. "Besides, one or two of these won't blow your figure." She waved one warm chocolate-chip cookie beneath Lindsay's nose.

"Sure." Lindsay shook her head sarcastically. "One won't do any harm at all. But how about five or six or seven?"

"Then we could have a problem," Rita admitted with a laugh.

As they spoke, the front doorbell rang.

"Who could that be?" Rita frowned. It was awfully late for anyone to be stopping by.

"No telling." Lindsay was pacing the room now and waving a chocolate-chip cookie in the air. She knew it was necessary to keep her blood circulating even when she was working against a deadline. Walking around the room helped her to think. "Don't go to the door unless it's someone important," she instructed Rita. "I've got to get this work done."

"And I don't want to listen to some insurance salesman by myself," Rita agreed.

"Maybe I can tell who it is," Lindsay said as she pulled back the sheer curtains and looked out into the street. She could barely distinguish the outline of a car parked at the end of the sidewalk. She squinted into the darkness. The car did look familiar. Suddenly, a memory came flooding back to her and she recognized the gold Corvette. She turned to Rita and gave a cry of excitement. She threw down the editing pen and ran to open the front door.

KENDALL, RITA AND LINDSAY sat around the fire in the den sipping decaffeinated coffee and munching warm cookies. "I think I timed this visit perfectly,'' Kendall announced, grinning at Lindsay as he popped another chocolate-chip cookie into his mouth.

Rita looked at Lindsay in bewilderment. Lindsay just shrugged her shoulders. Neither of them had any idea why Kendall had decided to drop over tonight. Rita was impressed, though. He was so good looking, he had a wonderful Alabama accent and he was definitely a gentleman. No wonder Lindsay had been so preoccupied lately.

When he'd arrived Kendall had stated in no uncertain terms that he had come to talk to Lindsay. Yet when Rita tried to leave the room, Lindsay grabbed her roommate's elbow and whispered ferociously in her ear that she didn't want to be left alone with him. So the three of them sat together for a long while, and Rita enjoyed listening to and laughing at all of Kendall's new jokes.

Lindsay was perplexed. Kendall was back to telling jokes again. And his eyes didn't tell her anything. It was as if a brick wall had been thrown up between them once again.

As the late-night news began on television, Rita stifled a yawn and smiled apologetically at her friend. ''I do have to get to bed sometime tonight. I've got three accelerated classes to teach tomorrow. I won't be able to keep up with my whiz kids if I don't have a proper night's sleep.'' Lindsay nodded her understanding and Kendall smiled his good-night, counseling Rita to ''sleep tight.''

When Rita left the room, Lindsay stood up, too. ''Kendall....'' She didn't know if her words were an explanation or an excuse. ''I hate to be inhospitable but I've got a story deadline in the morning.''

Kendall rose to his feet. His brain was churning. She was trying to get rid of him. He couldn't put this speech off any longer. He had been rehearsing what he had to say for two months now.

He wanted to tell Lindsay about Sarah. Lindsay would understand how he was still feeling. He could already sense that. He wanted her to know why he had to back away from her.

''We have to talk first.'' He took her hand. ''I have to apologize for myself. I...need to tell you...I will always need your friendship. I have to know how we will always be good friends.''

So that was it. It still didn't explain anything. ''Of course we're friends,'' Lindsay said, smiling at him.

''Thanks, Lin. I wanted you to know....'' Kendall's voice trailed off. He just couldn't do it. Not yet. To talk about Sarah to another woman was like giving a part of his love for her away. ''I just wanted to...to show you my new watch. What do you think?'' He playfully stuck his wrist under her nose. "Here. Turn me on. Push this button."

"Sure, anything you say." Lindsay laughed nervously as the watch faithfully began blinking the day and the date. "Okay—" she sighed "—forget the dumb deadline. Stay. It's good to see you." Her statement was true, no matter what he was hiding from her. And then, just because she was glad to see him, because she was mad at herself for putting a deadline before a friend, she grabbed a green velvet throw pillow from the sofa and slammed it against his stomach.

"I'm being attacked." Kendall chuckled as he doubled over in mock discomfort. His arm darted around behind her back and grabbed the other pillow that was adorning the sofa. "Bonzai, sunshine! You're going to pay dearly for this." He slammed the pillow down on top of her head.

The pillow fight kept up for almost twenty minutes and Lindsay and Kendall both exploded in fresh gales of laughter each time they twisted and cavorted and whopped each other.

"Truce! Truce!" Lindsay finally wailed. She was laughing so hard she couldn't inhale and Kendall was backing her into a corner again. "You've got to let me breathe or I'll die."

"Brilliant deduction." He grinned and then whacked her once more across her bottom for good measure. "I guess I can give you a break. I claim victory." He politely plopped the pillow onto his lap. "I know you can't handle tough competition."

"You'd be surprised what I can handle, Kendall Allen," Lindsay said, smiling at him sincerely. He *would* be surprised, she thought. The giggling, the screaming and the fighting had only served to make Lindsay more aware of her attraction to him. She had to be tough to handle the feelings welling up inside of her just now. An inner voice screamed out to her to take her eyes off him, but she couldn't.

Kendall was wearing a nubby gray turtleneck sweater, and its design only served to make him look more muscular, broader, stronger. *Damn, he looks good*, Lindsay thought.

As if sensing what was on her mind, Kendall's expression turned somber, and he stood up once again. "I've got to get out of here, Lin. I know you need to get back to your work." He didn't look at her as he reached for his leather jacket that was lying across the back of a rocking chair nearby.

"Whatever you say, Mr. Allen." She tried to sound lighthearted as she followed him to the door. He stood to one side as she reached for the doorknob and pulled the massive wooden door open for him.

He stepped outside and, as the cold December air wafted into the entry hall, he turned back and gazed at Lindsay a moment.

"Thanks," he stated.

"For what?" she asked.

"For being here when I need you. And for understanding what I cannot explain," he answered. With that, he bent slowly toward her and barely brushed Lindsay's right cheek with his lips. "Good night," he said, smiling down at her. "You go in there and get to work with that typewriter." Then he turned and walked slowly down the sidewalk without looking back.

LINDSAY THOUGHT SHE WAS going crazy. Bizarre thoughts kept flitting in and out of her mind, and she had absolutely no way to turn them off. The day Kendall called to her at the post office had haunted her for weeks. The entire meeting had bothered her, the way he talked, the way he looked at her, the way he held her. He had kissed her frantically that day and then he had pushed her away.

Now, something about this new kiss haunted her even more. It had been almost an hour since Kendall had driven away in his gold Corvette and the tingling in the spot where his lips had touched her cheek was still almost unbearable. Lindsay kept touching her cheek. She kept fighting to erase the memory of Kendall's face, how he had looked at her, how his lips had burned against her skin.

She stood up and began to pace. How could she start to work on the humane society article with Kendall on her mind? One thing was certain. Mr. Allen definitely did have rotten timing.

As if on cue, the telephone rang. Once again Lindsay was annoyed. It was after midnight. No one in his right mind would be calling now. Rita was already asleep.

Lindsay lifted the receiver. "Hello?"

"Sunshine?" Kendall's voice echoed across the phone lines, and Lindsay's heart almost stopped beating.

"It's me," she tried to sound nonchalant.

"I called to apologize," he almost whispered.

"For what?"

"For putting you on the spot like that."

"I don't know what you're talking about." Lindsay didn't understand.

"I kissed you. I came to tell you I wanted to be friends, and then I kissed you. I put you on the spot."

So it was true. The gesture had meant everything Lindsay had read into it earlier. "It's okay," she said. It was hard for her to keep her voice soft and innocent. She wanted to scream.

"Good," he answered simply.

There was a long, poignant silence between them. The sound of fat, Texas raindrops broke through the quiet as the rain outside started peppering against Lindsay's bedroom window.

"It's raining," Lindsay stated matter-of-factly.

"It is here, too," he answered.

There was another silence.

"Evil follows where Kendall Allen goes." This time it was he who broke the hush.

"I know."

Suddenly Kendall started laughing, and after a few moments, Lindsay joined in. "Well," Kendall said between chuckles. "I just wanted to make sure you weren't going to lose sleep over what happened tonight."

"I promise. I won't."

"Good then." He sighed. "If you aren't going to lose any sleep over this thing then I won't, either."

"I won't."

"Good night, then," he said.

"Good night."

The click on the other end of the line told Lindsay the connection between them had been broken. For a long time she stared down at the humane society notes on her desk. Then she made a note to herself to call Rex Martin, her managing editor, early in the morning. She would have to ask him to reschedule the article. There was no way she could concentrate on writing tonight.

Forty city blocks away, Kendall Allen lay in bed in his studio apartment trying to go to sleep. Even though both lamps were turned off, he could still see Sarah's eyes watching him. Those eyes. They were staring out from the portrait she had done for him two years ago. He still kept it on the top of his desk in the gilded frame she had picked out for it.

There were times when he thought he should put the portrait away, but the part of his heart that would always belong to her won the argument each time. Still, there were the nights like this one when her eyes seemed to bore right through him. He wondered if she could see him. The sky had cleared off, the rain passed quickly, and Kendall wondered if Sarah was up there among the stars, looking down, peeping into his life through the front picture window.

Noiselessly, he folded back the blankets and slipped out of bed. On bare feet, he walked across the room and lay Sarah's picture face down.

He climbed back into bed and snuggled in under the covers, but he could not relax. Every muscle in his body was tense. Her eyes were still there, all around him, floating aimlessly in the darkness.

Outside in the winter sky, thousands of sleepless stars flickered and danced in the heavens. Kendall squeezed his eyes shut trying to ignore the stars, Sarah's eyes, his thoughts. He knew that he would not sleep until the sun rose.

LINDSAY OFTEN PONDERED her bizarre friendship with Kendall Allen. Never before in her life had she had such a relationship with a man. Since that night six months ago when he'd kissed her on the cheek and called later to apologize, he had not physically touched her again.

He had touched her soul, though. Kendall had become a true friend, someone who was always there to listen when Lindsay had a rough day at the newspaper or when she had family problems. Kendall could always sense when something was hurting her, and he would work with her, coax her, make her trust him enough to let go of what she felt inside. She felt like she frequently cheated him, though. There were days when he was moody and melancholy, and she could not coax him to let go like he had done with her. She knew he needed to talk just as badly as she did, but he still hid himself behind a mask of jokes.

"How does Hitler tie his shoes?" he had asked her the last time he was in a sad mood, when she had tried to find out what was wrong.

"I don't know, Kendall," she had replied, sighing.

"In little Nazis."

He had laughed so hard at his own punch line that he had fallen out of his chair.

Despite her frustration, Lindsay was thankful for Kendall's friendship. Sometimes she would think of him and an intense feeling of gratitude would well up inside her. But other feelings would well up inside of her, too. She knew she was in love with Kendall. And the idea frightened her. She had so much to lose if they became lovers and then they lost that love. They would have gone too far. They would never be friends again, and all the peace and the strength that they had given each other would be gone.

Kendall couldn't remember when, if ever, he had felt so proud and so peaceful. Lindsay Cornell was slowly taking the pieces inside of him that had once been his life and was darning them back together again. She was always there for him now, and he had no idea how to tell her what being a part of her life meant to him.

She and Rita invited him over for supper often these days, and tonight he had asked Lindsay if he could bring Marcus, too. Marcus James was his best friend, had been since they were children and still was, now that they were men. Marcus had known Sarah and it was almost like anchoring down reality again to be able to introduce his friend to Lindsay. Marcus had been his stronghold right after the skydiving accident. He had offered Kendall the job as supervisor at the Love Field maintenance hangar last summer, and Kendall had been quick to accept. It was because of Marcus James that Kendall was flying again. Marcus James and Lindsay Cornell. His two strongholds against destruction. As he poured coffee in the kitchen and listened to their playful bantering around the table in the other room, he knew for certain he was feeling whole again. The pieces of his life were falling directly into place.

"It just looks funny." This man named Marcus James was snickering as he held up a section of soggy okra he had stabbed onto his fork.

"See if I let Kendall invite you over again," Lindsay joked. She wasn't quite certain how she should act around this new man. "That's my great-great-grandmother's secret recipe she brought with her across the ocean."

"Don't...don't..." Rita chimed in. "He's fixing to ask you if she brought it over from Transylvania or some place like that."

"You have ESP." Marcus turned to Rita. "That's exactly what I was going to ask. What a wonderful recipe. Okra Transylvania."

Rita was laughing so hard there were tears in her eyes. But Lindsay was panicking. There was something about the way Kendall's friend kept turning to her, something in the way his eyes flashed one moment and then closed over with darkness the next, that made her want to stay reserved around Marcus James. But some sort of an electricity between them wouldn't let her do that. It was as if he was drawing her out of herself with a rope.

Marcus turned to her just as she thought of him, and there was more in his eyes than she could read. Something deep there was flashing, straining to come out. But he wouldn't express it. "Really, Lindsay, I don't know why you don't just forget Kendall Allen and start hanging around with me," he joked casually.

"Actually—" Lindsay picked her words carefully "—I was considering it. But you're so uncomplimentary about my cooking, I think I've changed my mind."

"Sorry." The guarded look was still in his eyes. "I couldn't help but ask. Most girls think I'm very nice."

"Yes." Lindsay was flushed but composed. "Nice and lecherous."

She was relieved when Kendall came back into the room with the coffee. She felt safe again with him sitting there beside her. She liked Marcus. Matching wits with him was fine. But something else was happening, too, something that threatened her. And she didn't think she wanted to find out what it was.

Marcus James was different from Kendall in several subtle ways. He seemed to delve into life with just a bit less care than his best friend. He almost seemed more untouched, dreamier, yet surprisingly, more tenacious.

As Lindsay looked up to pass the cream pitcher around the table, she noticed a quick glance between Marcus and Kendall that horrified her. From Marcus, it was a look of gratification, of approval, and from Kendall it was almost a look of relief. Something cold seized Lindsay's heart. This couldn't be what Kendall wanted. The look she had seen was the look of a friend who was introducing a friend to a friend. Did Kendall sense all she was feeling for him now? There was something powerfully magnetic about Marcus that she had been trying to ignore. But maybe that's what Kendall wanted. Maybe this was an easy way out for Kendall to rid himself of the new things he must know were happening inside Lindsay. Introduce Lindsay Cornell to Marcus James and watch the problem resolve itself. Just like a soggy ending to a soggy novel.

Later, when Rita and Marcus left together to see a movie, Lindsay didn't know whether to shout at Kendall or to run away and weep. What do you want me to think of your best friend, Kendall? The question was on her tongue but she didn't dare ask it. Do you want me to fall for him? Will that set you free?

If Kendall could have read her thoughts just then, he would not have understood them. His own reflections were so far from hers. He was watching her standing over the kitchen sink, the steam from the hot water spiraling up to touch the silkiness of her skin. She had let her hair down out of the French braid that so often encircled her head and it fell in casual ripples down her back. Kendall swallowed the impulse to reach over and run his fingers through her satin mane. As she stood there, so solid and so strong beside him, it was all he could do to keep from reaching out and pulling her toward him. He never wanted to look back at his past, into his regrets or his remorse. How fine his life would be if he could only have Lindsay and needed nothing more.

She had shared so much of herself with him over the past several months. He had wanted desperately to know her, to be strong for her when she needed him. Now, too late, he realized that just knowing her would never be enough. He wanted to protect her, to possess her, and he could never do that without releasing Sarah.

At times Kendall wondered if he should quit seeing Lindsay. He thought it might be easier just to go through each day without stopping to call her or arranging to see her. But it wasn't. Some magnetic force would move throughout him, down his arm and into his fingers, and once again he would find himself dialing her telephone number. And it was always like magic when he suddenly heard her voice, sparkling with laughter, answer at the other end of the line. There was absolutely no way he could let go of her or of the comfortable friendship they had created. It had come to mean too much to both of them.

After the dinner dishes were spotlessly cleaned and lined along the drainboard to dry, Lindsay looked on as Kendall stuffed newspapers into the grate and started a roaring fire.

"All that work and look where it goes." Lindsay smiled dolefully as she watched several issues of the *Times Herald* curl and scorch in the fireplace.

"I should probably get out of here," Kendall thought aloud as he started to gather his things.

"You will do no such thing." She pouted playfully at him.

"You win." He reached over and flipped on the television and then plopped on the sofa beside her.

"That was easy." Lindsay smiled at him and he smiled back. He never wanted to leave, but he often tried to do so in hopes she would stop him. He knew Lindsay well enough to know she sometimes needed an extra hour in the evening to cushion herself against the challenges of her career.

"I've given that newspaper twelve hours today and I think that's plenty." She grinned. "Stay. I like the company." Ordinarily, she would have stopped him from leaving anyway. But tonight she was desperate to know what he was thinking. Why had he invited Marcus James to dinner? She turned to ask him, but when she saw what was in Kendall's eyes she couldn't say anything.

Kendall was watching her, not certain that he could bear her closeness. The firelight reflected off the roundness of her lips and the laciness of her lashes. The light from the fire made the tendrils of her hair glow. Looking at her now, it seemed as if the light was coming from inside of her, glowing, burning, flickering with every movement she made. She looked like a tiny, fragile angel, delicate and dainty, but an angel nonetheless, an angel strong enough to chase away all the hurt, all the hatred, all that was bad in the world.

Before Kendall's logic could argue against the gesture, he reached out one of his arms to her. With a gentle pressure on her shoulder, he pulled her close to him. Lindsay was lost in the peace of the evening and in the love and the trust she had in Kendall. She moved toward him gently, almost dreamily, and lay her head back against his shoulder. She had never guessed she could feel so protected in a place. It was as if she was surrounded by strength and sturdiness and warmth and, in the comfortable cocoon where she had been drawn, she knew she had the power to face all the sadness, all the work, all the tension that the world cast her way. She looked up at Kendall and smiled.

In that smile, Kendall saw everything he needed to see. His rational judgment, his fears, his past all dissipated when she turned her pixie face up to him and he saw what was in it. Slowly, with trembling fingers, he guided her chin up and over to him. She moved closer to him and their lips met, softly, gingerly at first, and then with more force and with more passion than Lindsay had ever known existed. Kendall cradled her neck in his huge palm and he pulled her to him time after time again, kissing her, probing into her soul, asking her questions with his touch he never dared to ask with his voice.

Lindsay was almost afraid to open her eyes and look up at the man who was holding her. These arms, this touch, had to be a vivid dream. She didn't fathom how it could be anything more. But as she molded her body to his and he moaned her name and called her "sunshine," Lindsay let the truth of the moment spill over inside her. Everything she had been hiding in her soul these last months tumbled out through her heart. She delicately backed away from him for a moment and reached up to touch his cheek.

"Don't torment me so, little sunshine." The love in his eyes gleamed down at her. "I've fought this so long." He took her hand in his and kissed each finger lightly. "You are a gift to me, you know. I have a special angel in heaven who has been looking for you all the while. What a lucky man I am."

Lindsay reached up to the soft wisps of hair that curled gently against his temples. She stroked his curls as she spoke. "You have given me faith in the world, Kendall. You've taught me so much about real people. About myself. It is you who gives gifts." Lindsay pulled his head down to hers. She kissed him with a wild abandon that both surprised and excited him. The soft silkiness of her skin was overpowering his other senses. As she pulled him toward her once more, she lay back against the velvet throw pillows on the sofa and he began to slowly unbutton the delicate pearl buttons that fastened the front of her mauve crêpe de chine blouse. The neckline opened to reveal the white satin of her skin and the delicious rose lace of her undergarments. As he ran his fingers beneath the lace, she lay her head back and moaned with all the love and all the desire that was pent up inside her heart.

Kendall bent to her and kissed her neck lightly, then he ran his fingers down to the silky hollow there and kissed her again.

"I love you, Kendall," she whispered to him and, as he held her, something deep inside of him stirred. He was happier than he ever dreamed he could be again. He tried to picture Sarah's face but he couldn't. The desire burning inside him for this woman in his arms crowded out every other thought. He bent again to taste Lindsay's skin, and this time there were no terrors, no tears, no taunts for him to forget.

Kendall and Lindsay did not make love during the night. Instead, they touched and kissed and explored each other in coves and nooks that neither of them had known existed before. There was so much of each of them that had been camouflaged for so many months that the joy in watching the walls come down was enough for both of them. They drank of each other for hours, until each had given everything there was to give, until both of them had scaled heights and climbed fences that would never need climbing again. Then, contented, they cuddled together on the floor beneath a nubby afghan Lindsay's grandmother had knitted for her the year before. They fell asleep in front of the still glowing embers in the fireplace.

Kendall could not bear to leave her until five-thirty the next morning when the first rays of sun peeked in through the kitchen window. He gathered his things and drove straight to the maintenance hangar at Love Field. It would do him good to get an early start on the day, he decided. Besides, when everyone was putting in bids on planes to fly this afternoon, he would be certain to get his first choice. He absolutely had to get up into the sky sometime today. Nothing was going to keep him on the ground. Even if they wouldn't give him a plane, he would just flap his wings and take off. She had given him back the sky.

"THROW THEM HERE or you die," Kendall hollered at Lindsay as she skittered around the front yard with his car keys. Even while he was doing his best to be disgusted with her teasing, he could not help loving her. She was so much a woman and still so much a little girl. As she bounded across the lawn just out of his reach, she looked every bit like a spring-born colt just learning to pick up speed and courage.

"I dare you," she challenged, giggling as she darted around the corner of the house.

The summer night hung heavily in the air, and Kendall could feel the Dallas humidity sapping his energy. "Get over here right now," he ordered as he plopped on the grass and pointed to the ground beside him.

She ran to him then and dropped beside him. As he reached for his car keys, she dropped them neatly inside her T-shirt.

"You want them?" she asked innocently. "Then you get them."

"Now, Lindsay—" he tried his best to sound persuasive "—how do you expect me to do that?" He rolled over on top of her and began tickling her in the ribs.

"Argggh." She let out a very unladylike wail. "Get off me, you big beast."

Kendall leaned over and grabbed her wrists while she thrashed around on the ground. "Hush, woman." Then, with a deep, passionate kiss, he silenced her.

Lindsay fought him off with flailing arms at first, but soon the enemy arms turned friendly, and she held him close. He kissed her again and again, and each time she had no idea what to expect. Kendall had an uncanny talent for giving a playful nip one moment and a soul-searching touch the next. Lindsay thought it was wonderful the way he kept her guessing.

Kendall pulled away gently after a bit and looked at her sadly. "I have to go, sunshine. I hate this moment more and more each time it has to happen."

Lindsay eyed him tenderly. He had so much work to do lately. The maintenance hangar was incredibly busy these days. The economy of Dallas was booming. Love Field was only a secondary airport to the city, but it was a convenient one, and more and more private pilots were using it as their home base.

Within the past four months, many people had been flying in from the West to attend buying sessions at Dallas Market Hall and Dallas Apparel Mart. The complex on the west side of the city was already threatening to become a little New York for the clothing industry. Lindsay loved the elegant fashions that were becoming easier to find in the stores at reasonable prices. Competition was wonderful for any market. But it wasn't good for giving her time to spend with her new love. The planes that flew in and out every day had to be kept in perfect condition, ready to take off at a moment's notice. Maintenance and adjustment time took its toll in dollars and cents. More of the maintenance work needed to be done at night now while the designers, the buyers and the wealthy Texas business entrepreneurs slept.

Lindsay placed a reassuring arm around Kendall's waist as they walked together toward the car. She looked up at him sadly. It was time to surrender the keys.

"Here you go." She pulled the keys from her cleavage and pitched them across the roof of the car to him. He caught them with one hand.

"Come here." He reached out once more and pulled her toward him. With two fingers under her chin, he gently tilted her head until her eyes reached up and met his. Her eyes searched Kendall's face for a number of seconds, but she never dared to guess what might be coming next. Each time they were together, each time their relationship grew stronger, was almost a surprise to both of them. It had all happened so carefully, so delicately, and there were times when Lindsay was afraid to even speak for fear she might shatter the reality of their happiness.

"I love you so, my little sunshine," he whispered against her forehead, and she wondered if he could feel her trembling.

"And I love you, too, Mr. Allen, so much that it hurts." She stood on tiptoe and planted a kiss on the very tip of the nose she had grown to cherish.

He looked down at her and there was something tentative in his eyes. She questioned what she saw there, and he answered slowly. "I really tried not to do this, sunshine. I honestly thought it would be easier just to stay the way we were, just to stay friends, just to be two people who needed to laugh with each other."

It was Lindsay's turn to look pensive. "It's all right," she answered. "It's worth the risk to me. I didn't know if it would be. But now I don't care what happens. The past few weeks have been worth everything that we might have to give up later." She was talking about their friendship. She knew in her heart that she was right.

"You've got to promise me something," he whispered down to her.

"What?" She was bewildered.

"Promise me that you'll always remember how very much I love you. No matter what happens, promise me that you'll always remember that."

Lindsay was concerned. She didn't like this conversation. At this moment it would have destroyed her to even think of ever being without Kendall. "I promise," she answered in a husky voice, "but you just make sure you're around to remind me of that every once in a while."

Kendall watched her for a moment, looking unhappy, and then as suddenly as the melancholy mood had come over him, he was jovial again. "I have to show you something." He grinned as he opened the car door and reached in to grab his wallet. "Here's a picture of my niece. Her name's April. She's my sister's little girl. I just got this in the mail today."

Lindsay took the wallet from him and gazed at the child in the portrait. The girl's head was surrounded by chestnut ringlets and her eyes shone a brilliant violet-blue. Her bow-shaped grin resembled Kendall's and there was a dark, gaping hole where her two front teeth once had been. The little girl was dressed in a red-and-white gingham checked pinafore.

As Lindsay looked over the mischievous little face, she felt a sudden, unexpected twinge of sadness and love…almost like homesickness. "She looks an awful lot like you, Uncle Kendall."

Kendall beamed with pride at the title. April did call him that. All Nickie's kids did. Uncle Kendall and Aunt Sarah. He and Sarah had loved those kids almost as much as they would have loved their own.

When April's picture had arrived from San Diego with her looking so grown up and so carefree and with those two front teeth missing, Kendall felt a fatherly urge to share this part of his family with Lindsay. His beautiful Lindsay. She stood there before him now, looking golden and bronzed from the Texas sun, studying the picture of his youngest niece. Lindsay wasn't missing anything, not the teeth, nor the eyes, nor the curls. He knew Lindsay was seeing everything that he wanted her to see.

His Lindsay. She was so intensely beautiful. Sometimes she was silly and sometimes she was somber, but always she was magnificent. He had seen her in a room of people often, and each time the phenomenon happened it happened the same way. Lindsay was so subtle and caring that she always floated into a room unobtrusively. But after only a few moments, her bright, tinkling laughter would waft out over the room and people would turn to see where the magical sound was coming from. They would pick out her smile, her incredible eyes, and after that every person in the room would be drawn to her for the rest of the evening.

"You're very lucky to have a niece, Uncle Kendall." She touched his arm, and once again his heart went out to her. "She's a very beautiful little girl."

"Someday you'll have a little girl like that—" he smiled down at her "—and you will think she is the most beautiful little girl in the world." He bent down and kissed her on the nose.

"You're probably right." Lindsay laughed at him. "I'll be so proud of my kid I won't be able to stand it."

"I am right." Kendall pulled her close to him for one last kiss before he had to leave her. "With a mother like you, a little girl couldn't help but be the most beautiful child in the world."

"Don't you think that it might have something to do with her father, too?" Lindsay questioned.

Kendall issued a deep, throaty chuckle, and before she could say more he was in his Corvette and driving away.

CHAPTER THREE

WHEN KENDALL CALLED LINDSAY at the *Times Herald* the next morning, there was a new tone of excitement in his voice. When he explained, Lindsay understood why. He had a plane. He wanted to take her up tonight.

Ever since they sat together in class, Lindsay had been enchanted with the way Kendall talked about the sky. While everyone else was reading *Macbeth*, Kendall was reading about air speed and altimeters. He painted such a magical picture of everything that surrounded flying; the blue sky above, the feeling of freedom, the feeling of taking off from earth and never having to come back down again. Ever since she'd known him, flying had been something Lindsay had longed to share with him.

Kendall had considered taking her up in a plane before, but he had so many questions. Would she love it the way he did? Would she be frightened? Would she trust him as her pilot? To his delight, Lindsay wasn't frightened at all. Other women he knew virtually panicked at the thought of him sitting beside them showing off and flying low and practicing touch-and-go landings. Most women he knew wanted to keep their feet planted firmly on the ground below them. But Lindsay wasn't like that. She was like Sarah. She loved to explore and to experience new things. She was strong and sensible, but she wasn't afraid to laugh or to take her feet off the ground.

Now, tonight, would be the time. He would be sharing something with her that meant more to him than anything else in the world. All day long he kept glancing over at the red-and-white Cessna 152 parked beside the runway. Its registration number was N482RJ, and the guys at the hangar called it the Romeo Juliet. That was fitting, Kendall decided. He knew why Marcus had made a point of assigning him the craft.

As the afternoon wore on, Kendall became more concerned about Lindsay. What if she didn't like flying? What if she fainted? At

3:30 P.M., he called her from the hangar and told her not to eat anything. "You might get sick," he warned her.

"Okay, Mr. Allen," she answered politely, but when he hung up, Lindsay had to stifle the urge to giggle. She knew she would be hungry before they took off, but Kendall was so cute today, calling her every hour to warn her of some new danger. She didn't have the heart to defy him even if it meant snacking on a bologna sandwich.

As it was, Lindsay wouldn't have had time to eat if she had planned on it. Kendall came an hour early to take her to the airport. She was still splashing languidly in the bathtub when she heard the doorbell ring. Rita knocked on the bathroom door only minutes later. "He's here, kid."

"Thanks, Rita," she called back. "You know, he sure is hyper about all this."

Lindsay freshened her makeup quickly and pulled her hair neatly back from her face with a thin gold bandeau. When she walked out to greet Kendall ten minutes later, she was wearing doe-colored gabardine slacks with a cotton sweater in shades of rust, navy-blue and vanilla.

"Looking good," Kendall pronounced, offering a long, low, appreciative whistle. "You look almost good enough to go somewhere and touch the sky."

"Thank you, Mr. Allen. Shall we go?" She offered him her elbow and they left the apartment.

"It's about time." He grinned mischievously. "I was ready hours ago."

"I'll bet you were." Lindsay shook her head in mock disgust. "You were probably ready to go when you got out of bed this morning. We're not supposed to leave for another thirty minutes, you know."

"I know," he said, grinning down at her. "I couldn't wait." He looked so much like a little boy just then. Her heart melted at his honesty.

"I love you," she whispered up to him. She did, she reminded herself, even though her stomach was growling.

All the way to Love Field, Kendall held her hand tightly next to his thigh on the car seat and told ridiculous joke after ridiculous joke. Every time she looked back on that night, she would remember him yelling "Why do people like bananas?" and then answering himself. "Because they have *appeal*."

When they arrived at Love Field, Kendall parked his car and led Lindsay to the hangar. He wanted to introduce her to everyone. And he was pleased to see all eyes riveted on her the minute they walked hand-in-hand into the room.

Marcus James met them in the front hallway and Lindsay grinned. Now that she was certain of Kendall's feelings for her, she regarded Marcus as a true, dear friend. The electricity between them had grown into an elastic playfulness, and Lindsay was always glad to be with him. "Had any Okra Transylvania lately?" she quipped.

Marcus made a rude noise with his nose. "Now Lindsay—" he patted her playfully on the shoulder "—you have taken my preoccupation for your okra all wrong. Let me say this. Before I met you, I never met an okra I didn't like."

"Very unoriginal, Marcus." She giggled at him. "Very unoriginal."

"Well, how can you expect me to be original while a woman like you is standing just three feet from me?" He winked at her then turned to Kendall. "What's the big idea of bringing her in here anyway? How can I expect my employees to turn out proper work with women like this one around?"

Kendall just laughed.

"Sorry...." Lindsay managed to look innocent and seductive all at the same time.

"I know." Marcus slapped Kendall on the back. "You thought you had to show her off. Well, I don't blame you. Now get this woman out of here before I decide to go flying with both of you."

"Go ahead," Kendall snorted. "Flirt with my woman all you want. You won't get anywhere. She's madly in love with my body."

"Your body and your mind," Lindsay said as she winked at both of them. "And his okra," she added as an aside to Marcus.

"Okay, okay." Marcus grinned back. "Here's your checklist." He handed Kendall a clipboard with a tablet and a pencil attached. Then he waved goodbye as the two of them disappeared out the door and into the night.

When they got to the red-and-white Cessna, Kendall proudly let Lindsay assist him in the important ten-point check. She held the clipboard while he flipped switches, checked lights and moved rudders. Lindsay watched him carefully as he went about his work. She was enchanted with the way he handled the machinery. She sat in the plane just watching him, loving him, delighting in the idea that he was sharing this with her.

Soon, he climbed into the craft, fastened the doors and placed a light peck on her cheek. "Are you ready for the sky, sunshine?"

She smiled impishly at him. "Only if you promise to put this thing on automatic pilot once we're up there. I've never kissed anyone at twelve thousand feet before."

"Sure thing." His eyes were mischievous, too. Then he turned his attention to the controls. Almost before Lindsay realized what was happening, the Cessna was picking up speed down the runway. With the pull of a lever and a slight twist of Lindsay's stomach, the plane was in the sky. She leaned over and watched as the lights of Love Field grew smaller below them. And as she watched, they flew over the skyscrapers of downtown Dallas, and she could see the flying red horse on the Mobil Oil Building and the Trinity River and Lake Dallas all below her in one spectacular panorama. She couldn't suppress a gasp of sheer amazement. She wanted to sing just from the pure delight of it all.

The entire night had a fairy-tale, magical quality about it. They flew over Greenville and Lewisville, over Fort Worth and Arlington where she could see Six Flags over Texas and Arlington Stadium where the Texas Rangers played baseball. They buzzed by her house in Richardson once and Lindsay wondered if Rita was clinging to the china cabinet when they passed. This was not the first time Kendall Allen had buzzed the house, and Rita was always ready to grab the glass buffet doors to keep them from rattling open. Lindsay grinned again at the thought.

"Are you ready for some expert flight instruction?" Kendall asked her. When she nodded, he showed her how to read the altimeter and the fuel gauge and the artificial horizon. He taught her how to pull back on the stick and make the plane climb higher into the sky, and he taught her how to work the rudders with her feet.

"There," he smiled at her proudly as she leveled out from a deep left bank. "You're flying the plane."

It was while they were getting ready to practice touch-and-go landings at Shiloh Airport in Plano that Kendall spoke into the microphone and Lindsay heard the name of the plane. "This is 482 Romeo Juliet," he spoke masterfully into the radio. "We need clearance for touch-and-gos."

"Roger," the answer came back. "You have clearance, Romeo Juliet."

Lindsay turned to him and smiled. "This plane is called Romeo Juliet?"

"Yep."

"I think you planned that."

"Maybe I did," he said as he put the plane down on the runway flawlessly and then pulled it back up again. "Or maybe Marcus did. He likes to rub it in, you know."

"I know." She nodded seriously. "What Marcus needs is a woman. Doesn't he ever go out with anyone?"

"He's too busy," Kendall answered. "He's married to two hundred airplanes."

"Oh," she answered. "Just like you."

"No." He shook his head. "Not just like me. I'm going to set her down this time, my dear, and let's take a walk around. I need to stretch my legs."

Lindsay nodded her agreement, and soon the Cessna was taxiing to a halt along the well-lit runway. After he parked the plane, Kendall took Lindsay's arm, helped her step down off the wing and, together, they strolled in among the private planes that were anchored to the ground with heavy metal chains. Kendall talked about each of them while Lindsay listened with amusement. He knew where each one was made, how well it flew and whom it belonged to. He *was* married to two hundred planes. Or he had two hundred children. Lindsay loved the absurdity of that idea. She wanted to take everything about tonight and wanted to drink it all in, to hold it inside forever. The darkness and the planes and the sound of the wind. She never wanted to let any of it go.

When Kendall saw the enchanted look on Lindsay's face, he came to her and kissed her gently. Together, their eyes traveled up toward the stars.

"How beautiful." Lindsay sighed.

"That's where we belong, you know," he said as he watched her intently. "Up there with the stars."

"It's such a delicate balance, isn't it?" Lindsay shook her head seriously. "Down here you can look up and see the stars. Up there you can look down and see the world. There's a small dark space up there where you can fly along and be a part of both."

"That's the sky," he explained with a faraway look in his eyes.

He looked down at her then and loved her with his eyes. The things she said were so endearing, so full of wisdom, so full of spirit. He had teased her once that she should write a book, a collection of all the wise things she had ever said. It was an absurd suggestion, but she liked it anyway, and the two of them now laughed merrily whenever she said anything he thought should be included in the text. She joked about it all the time but he was entirely serious. He wished there was some way to entrap and to save her every thought.

"Shall we go?" He reached out his arm to her, and she took it dejectedly. She wasn't ready to leave. They climbed back into the plane, and Kendall turned and kissed her full on the lips. With no further ado, he roared the little plane's engines, and they took off again.

The craft turned southwest toward Love Field, and Lindsay was afraid to speak for fear of shattering the night and the magic and the lights that hung above and below them in the same lacy pattern. She didn't notice Kendall turning to glance at her every few minutes. She didn't see the mischievous grin grow across his face. He had one more trick up his sleeve. He hadn't known if he should do this to Lindsay or not. Now, looking at her strapped tightly into their own little world, he knew she would love it. Kendall turned his head back to the instrument panel and checked his air speed, his altitude and his heading. Then slowly, secretly, he began to trim his air speed. He glanced at Lindsay once more and this time she caught his look.

"What are you doing, you show-off?"

As if in answer, the plane stalled and Lindsay's heart and stomach shot up into her throat in that queasy, wonderful way it does on a roller coaster. The plane fell into a nose dive as Kendall grabbed the stick, increased the speed and deftly pulled the plane back up. They were flying level again, only a few hundred feet below the plummet.

"That was wonderful!" Lindsay laughed, her eyes glittering with the joy of a child who has just discovered something new. "Do it again." She was drunk with excitement. Flying seemed like more of a miracle to her than anything else. She didn't care about aerodynamics or science. She just wanted to stay up here in the sky with Kendall for the rest of her life.

Kendall was pleased. He had just simulated crash conditions, and she had loved it. Most of the people he brought up were terrified of stalls. He smiled to himself. It was no wonder he was falling in love with her. If for a moment he forgot the degree of his involvement, something she said, some small gesture she made, some special look in her eyes would remind him all over again.

He stalled the plane two more times for her on the way back to Dallas, and each time she squealed with delight. He carefully explained the scientific forces behind the stalls. It was a training simulation for pilots, one that created the sensation of losing altitude at a high speed. He had been fascinated by the feeling, too, from the very beginning. Or maybe it was what that feeling represented: knowledgeably losing all control of something and then skillfully regaining mastery.

They both watched the runway lights turn from white to pink to red as Kendall landed the plane at Love Field. The wheels roared, and the wings shook and Lindsay felt sad and empty as every bump on the pavement jolted them. They were on the ground.

The lights on Lyndon B. Johnson Freeway looked eerie and plain as they drove home in Kendall's gold Corvette. Other cars sped past them in ripples of chrome, and somewhere outside a radio was playing a loud, wailing country-and-western song. Lindsay didn't want to see or hear any of it. She was still in another world, another silent place, way above all of this. She would never be contented with mundane everyday things again, she realized, smiling. She had flown into the sky with the man she loved. Her perception of the world, and of peace, would never be the same again.

THE LIGHTS GLARED in the kitchen as Lindsay happily munched a bacon, lettuce and tomato sandwich. Part of her wanted to tell Rita every glorious detail of the evening but another part of her wanted to hoard the experience away for herself. It was as if, by talking about the flight to anyone, she would let a part of it go, and Lindsay couldn't bear to do that. So she kept Rita satisfied with bits and pieces. They had flown over Greenville and Lewisville and Fort Worth. Yes, Rita had been watching "Magnum, P.I." on television when the plane had roared overhead. Yes, she had jumped up and grabbed the buffet and no, they hadn't lost any china. But Rita had missed three minutes of "Magnum" and she hoped Kendall Allen had enjoyed his escapade.

Rita stood up from the stool and rinsed the glasses that were soaking in the sink. "Well, Lin," she said, mentally preparing herself for the next set of her roommate's squeals. "I don't know how much good stuff you can take in one day, but I've got something else for you."

"What?" Lindsay turned and looked blankly at her friend.

"Gene Oliver called for you tonight. He wants to run your story. He needs to make some final scheduling decisions before Monday. You need to call him at his office first thing tomorrow." She pitched a notepad with a Los Angeles telephone number jotted on it across the room.

Lindsay caught the missile in midair. She stared at the name and number Rita had written down. Gene Oliver was the managing editor of *West Style* magazine. Ordinarily, a phone call like this one wouldn't have seemed so spectacular to her. She had had other articles published in national magazines. But this story was different. *West Style* would pay well, but she hadn't written this one for the money.

The whole story had bubbled up out of her one night when she had been homesick for the mountains and Taylor Park. It was written about the people she loved there, the square dances, the crisp cold, the late-night card games, the marshmallow roasts. It was the most beautiful piece Lindsay had ever written, but she didn't know it. Every time she had looked back over it to edit it, the words were so much a part of herself that she couldn't read it objectively.

Lindsay had been brought up to be a Southern belle. She knew how to be well-rounded...how to play the piano a bit, how to sing a bit, how to wear her makeup so she looked refined, how to select and wear the newest fashions. Throughout her life, the mountains had been her only grasp on another way of life. In junior high school when the other Dallas girls were learning how to teeter along on platform shoes, Lindsay was stomping down the halls in a pair of gray hiking boots with bright red laces. She would count the days until she would leave for her annual high-country trek. The mountains were her identity. So Lindsay had tried to explain in this one article just how much the mountains had given her.

The next morning, Lindsay dialed Gene Oliver's number. He came on the line at once. "Are you ready to get down to business?" he asked her after they chatted awhile. When she said yes, he began to tell her his plans for the Taylor Park story. He liked it. A lot. The article worked well and he expected it to receive critical acclaim. He wanted to use her article as the cover story. He needed a photograph for the cover of the magazine as well as several others to use inside in a layout.

By the end of the conversation, the urgency of the work at hand had soaked in. Lindsay had good photographs on file of Howard's Guest Ranch in Taylor Park, but nothing that was cover quality. She knew several photographers with the *Gunnison Country Times* in Colorado, but she didn't want to hire someone over the telephone. This story was too important. She wanted to look through the camera lens and see each photograph just the way it would appear in *West Style*. She wanted to supervise every angle and every color.

Lindsay counted the weeks on her desk calendar and then smiled smugly. She had a week of paid vacation still coming to her. She called Rex Martin at the *Times Herald* and asked if someone could cover for her the next few days. Then she called Tom Jorgenson in Abilene. He was the best freelance photographer in the business. He agreed to meet her in Denver. Finally, she called Frontier Airlines and booked a roundtrip flight from Dallas to Gunnison.

Lindsay was almost finished packing by the time Rita woke.

"What are you doing?" Rita leaned against the doorjamb and sipped a cup of steaming coffee.

"Da-dah!" Lindsay sang as she pulled blue thermal underwear from her dresser drawer. "Guess," she laughed.

"Don't tell me. The mountains. Talking about your article made you mountain sick. You have to go back right now or you will die."

"Close guess." Lindsay was tripping around her bedroom, and Rita wasn't certain if her feet were touching the ground. "They need a cover shot to go with the article. That means *front cover* glaring out at you from newsstands everywhere. I've got to run out there and get a few nice snapshots."

"Congratulations." Rita nodded her praise. "When do you leave?"

"At 4:05 this afternoon. I'll be back next Sunday. Everything's already taken care of."

Again Rita nodded her approval. Lindsay was always organized. She had four hours to get ready for a week's vacation and she was going to do it.

"Do you need a ride to the airport?" Rita asked.

"Thanks, roomie—" Lindsay grinned "—but I'll take the bus into town. I've only got one suitcase. I can manage. I was hoping Kendall could take me. He has the day off today but I can't get an answer at his apartment. Marcus must have called him in to work for a while this morning. If he isn't available, I guess I'll have to be independent and go for this thing myself.''

"Poor Kendall," Rita groaned. "You'd better get him. I don't know what he's going to do without you for a whole week."

"Yes, mother." Lindsay giggled as she pitched a slipper at Rita. Rita stepped out of the way to keep from spilling her coffee. "I think," Lindsay continued, "that you take better care of Kendall Allen than I do."

"Well, somebody has to take care of the poor guy while you're out gallivanting all over the country," Rita replied, laughing.

"I'll try him at home again," Lindsay decided aloud. She dialed Kendall's home number and when the line kept ringing, she frowned. This was the third time she had tried to call him this morning. Maybe she should try Love Field. When she did, Marcus's familiar voice answered on the second ring.

"Marcus? It's Lindsay. Do you live there or something? Every time I call these days I get you."

"Yes." He was clearly pleased to hear from her. "I have an automatic beeper that goes off each time it detects the sound of your voice." Lindsay was almost surprised by the warmth in his voice. "And thanks for worrying about me. Yes, I do live here. Airplanes never sleep."

"Neither do you," Lindsay teased. "I need to talk to Kendall. Is he around this morning?"

"Nope. He's not scheduled at all today. Did y'all have a nice flight last night?"

"Oh, we did." Lindsay's voice softened as she remembered the events of the night before.

"Do you want me to give Kendall a message? I did hear he might drop by around four this afternoon."

"No thanks," Lindsay said. "I'll keep trying him at home. If I can't get him, I may call you back."

Lindsay buzzed through her afternoon watering plants and tidying the house. She tried to call Kendall once more at 3:00 P.M. just before she left the house and again at 3:45 from the airport. She couldn't figure out why he wasn't answering his telephone. In desperation, she called Marcus again and left a message. She hoped Kendall would understand her leaving this way.

As the huge jet barreled down the runway and then nosed up into the sky, Lindsay closed her eyes and smiled to herself. She was secure in the fact that Kendall loved her. Rita promised to explain to him about the *West Style* article. She knew he would be just as excited about it as she was.

KENDALL KEPT WALKING. He had to. Nothing else would make the pain inside of him go away. He was dreaming again. He was hearing those horrible sickening shrieks as Sarah plunged through the sky. He'd lost count of how many times he had walked around White Rock Lake today. Perhaps it had been five times. If so, he was starting on the sixth time around. But that didn't matter. Only his pain mattered.

He'd thought he had vanquished this despair. He had taken Lindsay up yesterday and she'd loved it. He loved her so much. He knew that. But he couldn't love her the way he wanted to. It wasn't right yet. His dreams last night had proved that.

He was still a broken man and he knew it. He was trying hard to heal himself but it wasn't working. Those dreams killed him all over again.

This wasn't fair to any of them. Not to him. Not to Lindsay. Not to Sarah. Kendall still hadn't told Lindsay about his life with Sarah. Long ago, it would have been easier to tell Lindsay everything. She had tried so many times to find out what brought that horrible look into his eyes but he had fought off her attempts. Now, it was too late.

Last night while they were stalling the plane over the lights of North Dallas, Kendall knew Lindsay was strong enough to know. But today, he wondered if he was strong enough to tell her. If she looked at his face, he knew she would see everything. All the pain he had ever felt was bottled up into one hideous feeling. He was only half a man and Lindsay deserved so much more.

"Hey!" Marcus yelled at him an hour later as he walked toward the hangar. "You've got a message. Your woman has gone and left you, Allen. And you don't even know about it yet. Where have you been all day?"

"Nowhere in particular." Kendall gestured vaguely.

"Lindsay tried to get you," said Marcus, relaying the message. "She took off for Gunnison, Colorado, about fifteen minutes ago. She says it's good news and you're supposed to call Rita for more details."

"Hmmm." Kendall shook his head. He wasn't expecting this. But the more he thought about it, the more he liked what had happened. Lindsay's absence would give him time to get his thoughts straight. And maybe if he took a sleeping pill tonight, he could sleep without dreaming. He hadn't had to take any medication for months.

When Kendall arrived home, he put a frozen chicken pie in the toaster oven to cook, and then he pulled three huge boxes out of the spare closet. Here was Sarah's life, all twenty-four years of it, bundled up in bags and stuffed away. He knew by heart what was in each of them. Faded letters. Dried flowers. Crumpled pictures. Silly costume jewelry. He suppressed the urge to throw a burning match on the entire lot. He desperately wanted to rid himself of the burden of the past, but he didn't know how.

CHAPTER FOUR

WHEN LINDSAY BOUNDED OFF the plane in Gunnison, the cool July air was fragrant with pines and mosses and sage. She wasn't really in the high country, not quite yet, but she could already smell it.

· She looked over at Tom Jorgenson and swept her hand across the panorama of the quaint mountain village before them. "Look your last at society, my friend. You won't see another paved road for a week."

Lindsay rented a Ford Bronco for them at the only rent-a-car establishment in town, and then without the help of a map she guided the vehicle down the busy main street and up the highway toward the canyon. As they drove through Gunnison, Lindsay was animated. She pointed out Mario's Pizza on her right, the Cattleman Inn on her left and several of her other favorite places around town. But as the road grew narrower and began to climb higher, Lindsay turned pensive. As they wound higher up the two-lane road, the Gunnison River joined them and twisted and turned its way along every curve. The trees grew thicker and taller and the forests became so heavy that the duskiness of the evening could not penetrate to the pine-needle floor below. Every so often, as the drive wore on, a rock outcropping would break the serenity of the trees and Tom Jorgenson would catch a fleeting glimpse of the Collegiate Peaks. They loomed far above the horizon, their rugged outlines chiseled haphazardly against the sky. Tom felt a creeping sense of peace grow over him, and slowly he began to realize why this place meant so much to Lindsay. She was such an intense person, and on the plane from Denver she had talked of nothing but the sound of the river and the wind through the trees and the peacefulness of the area. He realized now what enormous strength she must draw from this place.

After Lindsay drove in through the front cattle guard and parked the Bronco outside the main lodge of Howard's Guest Ranch, she let out a sigh and then smiled at the photographer. In unison, they opened their car doors and walked toward the long covered porch. There was a dinner bell hanging on a wrought iron bracket near the door, and Lindsay reached up and thumped the iron clapper with her forefinger. The bell made a tinkling sound as Tom pried open the rickety screen door and held it open for her. From deep within the back room, Lindsay could hear the sounds of pots and pans banging. She was home.

"Lindsay Cornell.... I can't believe it." Margie Howard ran up the hallway toward her and then enveloped her in her arms. "You're really here." Margie was a tall, stately woman with intense blue eyes and hair the color of polished silver. "Just let me look at you." She pushed Lindsay away and eyed her appraisingly at arm's length.

"Do I pass inspection?" Lindsay grinned.

"Is that my girl?" Dan Howard banged into the front door and encircled Lindsay's shoulder with a giant hug. "I'm glad you could make it," he said as he chuckled. "The linoleum in the laundry room is cracking and we've got to redo it. The refrigerator in 7A needs to be flipped. It stopped circulating yesterday, and the lady who's staying there says her milk soured. Five A needs a new roof, and I thought I might let you tar it."

"Wait a minute!" Lindsay tried to look forlorn but she was too happy to do so. "I thought I was just here as a visitor this time. Or do you always boss everyone around this way?"

"You're the best help we've ever had around here." Dan laughed. "I can't let you just come here and sit."

Tom Jorgenson watched the three of them as they laughed and hugged and teased one another. He realized something he had never sensed before. Lindsay was nervous. Standing here in this huge lodge with the fire crackling, standing among these friendly country folks, Lindsay was as frightened as he had ever seen her. It was as if she desperately wanted to belong to these people, to slip into a comfortable place in their lives, but was uncertain if there was a place left for her. Tom couldn't figure it out, but here, in this place where she looked entirely at home—except for the white Bill Blass suit she was wearing—Lindsay was terribly afraid.

Lindsay felt Tom's eyes on her. She turned and held her arm out to the photographer. "Tom Jorgenson," she said. "Meet my adopted Colorado family. Dan and Margie Howard, this is Tom Jorgenson, one of the best photographers in the Southwest."

"Pleased to meet you." Tom moved forward politely and extended his hand to Dan.

"Tom's going to be following y'all around for the next few days, so I hope you'll like him."

"I'm certain we will." Margie winked at Tom as she took Lindsay by the elbow and marched her toward the kitchen. "I know this thing came up so fast you didn't have a chance to go grocery shopping. You never eat anyway...so I decided to feed you."

Dan watched as Lindsay gave Margie a glowing smile. "Y'all always know how to take good care of people here. Thanks." She waved a beckoning arm toward Tom. "Come on, photographer. You're about to have one of the best meals you will ever eat."

Lindsay wasn't exaggerating about Margie's cooking. The woman served chicken-fried steak with creamy gravy, baked potatoes with butter, fresh-snapped string beans from the garden, a Jello salad and homemade biscuits. For dessert, there was a caramel pie, an old-fashioned confection made from a recipe Margie's grandmother had concocted long ago in Oklahoma out of brown sugar, Mexican vanilla and butter. Tom thought he had never eaten a meal that was quite so simple, yet so exquisite. And Tom found himself enjoying the conversation just as much as he enjoyed the food.

Dan and the new cabin-cleaning girls kept the banter going back and forth all during the evening. Tom watched Lindsay closely. He was surprised she didn't join in the chatter. It was almost as if she was afraid to speak, almost as if she was afraid to acknowledge what this place, what these people, meant to her.

Each year of her life, usually during the middle two weeks of July, her parents had brought her here to this solitary group of cabins. And each year Lindsay had toddled on the brink of a new discovery. Catching rainbow trout when she was five. Square dancing. Laying linoleum, tarring roofs and defrosting antique Servel refrigerators. Lindsay had learned how to let go of the city, of the South, here. Anyone looking at her just then could read in her face an extreme devotion to this ranch, to these mountains, and to what they had given her. Mountain strength. It had been quite a gift. Every time she came to this park, the magnitude of such a boon hit her with so much force it almost knocked her breath away.

"But you don't know why Joe had to bring the boats back up." The tittering around the table centered everyone's attention back onto the meal at hand.

"Because Ron saw a bear down there running across the lake," one of the cabin-cleaning girls chimed in. "Joe was scared he would come up into the boat house."

Lindsay smiled. It was impossible not to get involved in this conversation. "Two years ago—" she put down her fork and leaned forward in her chair "—there was an old black bear that wandered up into Mabel Stoneman's cabin. He had a heyday in there, didn't he, Papaw?"

Dan was pleased to hear Lindsay calling him by his pet name. The girl was coming back. It always took him about three hours to pull her out of herself again. It was almost like she lived in two worlds, as if she had to go through a painful transition period to be comfortable in his.

"The bear went wild." He snorted with glee and winked at Lindsay. "He got into the shower and squeezed the shampoo all over his stomach and then he chewed up the soap. He was still there blowing bubbles when old Mabel got home."

By the time Lindsay and Dan finished telling the story, everyone at the table was rocking with laughter. Lindsay's eyes glistened. The laughter and the jokes and the snorting all seemed to be shouting "welcome home" to her. Suddenly, she missed Kendall terribly. All this was so much a part of her, and she wanted to share it with him. His presence and his laughter would have added so much to this gathering. Suddenly, it was his silly conversation she longed to hear.

Later that night, as Lindsay walked across the grass toward the cabin where she would be sleeping, she couldn't keep her eyes off the stars. Only last night she had been up there with Kendall. She was certain there were just this many stars over Texas, but something about the city lights seemed to dim their brilliance. Or maybe it was something in her soul. There must be a billion of them up there tonight. Bright ones and faint ones. Huge, beaming ones and tiny, delicate ones. Between every two of them was another and, for an instant, Lindsay understood infinity. Maybe tomorrow she would start counting them all. That should only take several hundred years, she smiled to herself. Several hundred years in this place sounded wonderful. Sometimes she felt like she had already lived it.

A faint stab of homesickness filtered into her heart. How she had missed this place. Odd, now, how she missed Dallas and Kendall. She wished there was some way to bring everyone, everything, every place that she loved together in one time and place. Her life would be perfect if she could only manage that. Suddenly, Lindsay realized that her homesickness frightened her. For a moment, she stopped to wonder why. And when she began wondering, she realized she was frightened because she didn't know what she was homesick for.

KENDALL HAD MADE his decision. It always took him three or four days to make one. People who made decisions on the spur of the moment found him agonizing to work with. But once Kendall Allen made a decision, he was certain it was the right one. He never changed his mind. It was a quality of which he was extremely proud.

The time without Lindsay made the decision much easier. When he got too close to her, his instincts became dulled. He had let that happen too often lately. On the Monday following Lindsay's departure, Kendall called Sarah's sister in Houston and asked her to take Sarah's three boxes of things. If he couldn't rid himself of the memories, at least he could share them with the other people who had loved her. He was working like a madman at the maintenance hangar, and the men he worked with assumed he was working fiercely because Lindsay was gone. Only Marcus was worried. He missed Kendall's constant jabbering and joking. He missed the fire in Kendall's eyes. All that was in his eyes now was the sickish, gray color of resignation. Marcus had seen that look on Kendall's face before but only in passing, a flash, a clouding, and then it was gone. Now, the sickness was hanging there, hurting there. Marcus was concerned. Something was terribly wrong in his friend's life.

"Hey." He poked Kendall in the ribs one afternoon when he thought he couldn't stand the cloudiness any longer.

Kendall gave him a long, vacant stare and then turned back to his work. "Keep out of this, bud." He whispered the comment only for Marcus's ears.

"I don't want to," Marcus answered. "I'm standing here watching you kill yourself, and I don't know why."

"Bull...."

There was a poignant silence.

"It's Lindsay, isn't it?" Marcus frowned.

Silence again.

"Just talk to me about it. I probably can't help...but I miss you." It took a lot for Marcus to say that but he meant it.

"Back off," Kendall growled.

"You don't know what you're doing if you're killing this thing off between you and Lindsay."

"I said back off," Kendall repeated.

Marcus gave up. He cared about his friend, but it wasn't worth creating a scene at the hangar. And it wasn't worth getting his head bitten off. He was almost certain that this had something to do with Lindsay. He could tell he had struck a nerve when he mentioned her name. Maybe Lindsay had decided she didn't want to see Kendall for a while. Maybe that's why she'd left town so quickly. Really, Marcus couldn't blame her. Kendall was a wonderful man, but he could be a real pain sometimes. And Lindsay was a beautiful girl. Marcus wondered sometimes if she knew how beautiful she was. She didn't act as if she did. She acted like somebody's miracle. Kendall's miracle. She had saved him. Sometimes Marcus thought he was in love with her, too, himself. He stopped for a moment to consider that and even then he wasn't certain. He knew his heart almost stopped every time Lindsay walked into the hangar. He knew he dreamed of her some and he thought that funny until he woke in the night longing to hold her. Marcus shook his head to clear his mind. It was absurd, no, preposterous, to think of loving his best friend's girl. He wouldn't allow himself to ever think of it again.

WHEN THE TELEPHONE RANG, Rita expected it to be Lindsay checking in. She was surprised to hear Kendall's voice on the other end of the line. Certainly, she told him, she'd meet him at Northpark for coffee. She flipped a pen in her hand. Where Lindsay was concerned, she could definitely give that man some very good advice. He probably was trying to figure out how to propose to her. He probably wanted Rita to find out her ring size. Those two were so in love, it was sickening to watch. It was uplifting, too. Rita knew that she had grown a bit just by being a part of their romance.

At 6:45 P.M., Rita grabbed her handbag and a blue angora sweater. She was meeting Kendall at Kip's Big Boy and, if the traffic wasn't heavy on Central Expressway, she would be there early. She was sitting at a booth by the window when Kendall walked into the restaurant. As she stood to hug him, she noticed a haunted, distant look on his face.

"I've already ordered coffee." She spoke cheerfully and tried to ignore her alarm. "I couldn't wait to indulge in my caffeine fix for the day. I hope you'll join me.'' She laughed nervously. Something wasn't right.

Kendall held up a forefinger to the waitress and asked her to bring him a coffee cup. Then he poured a cup of the steaming liquid from the insulated pitcher the waitress brought to the table.

"Kendall, tell me what it is you need.'' Rita was suddenly very uncomfortable with him.

"I will get right to the point, then.'' Kendall sipped once from his cup. "I need to get some information to Lindsay, information that is impossible for me to deliver in person.''

Rita was frowning. She could see his hand with the coffee cup shaking.

"Over the past year, we have all gotten to be very close...but there are things you do not know about me.'' He was picking each word delicately, carefully, as if he was sifting through a pile of something sharp and sad. "One of the things you do not know about is...about...Sarah.''

"Kendall—'' Rita gasped ''—what is it you are trying to tell me?''

"I am in love with someone else.'' Kendall's voice sounded cool but his heart was pounding so hard he was afraid Rita might hear it. He was on the verge of telling her the truth but he couldn't do that. It was too late. He would have to handle this another way. "I am going to get married next Friday.'' His soul crumpled up inside of him at his own words. "Tell Lindsay that I cannot see her again.''

That was it. He had done it. He had set Lindsay free. He had set Sarah free.

"You bastard.'' The word was barely audible but Rita spit it at him with a force that almost knocked him over. "I will not do your dirty work for you, Kendall Allen. If you've got the guts to get yourself into this mess, then you'll have to find the guts to get yourself out of it. I won't tell Lindsay anything.''

"Then she will never know the truth.'' The words twisted around inside his mouth and stung with their bitterness. "I will never contact her again.''

Rita jumped from the booth and ran to the door. She didn't look back. Let the jerk pay for her coffee. He had ruined Lindsay's life. He could afford it.

After Rita left, Kendall sat staring at the coffee in his cup. Rita said she wouldn't tell Lindsay, but she would. Not at first, though.

She would wait a day or two until she couldn't stand watching Lindsay slowly realize the truth by herself.

Kendall closed his eyes in a vain attempt to shut out reality. He knew he was a cowardly fool. But he couldn't face the truth just yet. He wanted to remain true to his wife. Things with Lindsay had gone too fast. He wasn't ready for her yet.

Now that it was over with, he remembered again what he had done, and a jagged, searing pain ripped through his entire being. He was alone now. He didn't have Lindsay anymore. He didn't have Sarah anymore. And suddenly he realized he didn't know if he even had himself anymore.

LINDSAY FLOPPED HER HEAD back against the seat and smiled tiredly as the flight attendant handed her a glass of tomato juice with a twist of lime. She was exhausted but she was content. She and Tom had managed to capture the essence of Taylor Park in six days of shooting. Mountain sunrises and sunsets. Stars. The ranch. The Tincup Town Hall. The old cemetery. Dan and Margie helping guests. It had been a fruitful week. It had been terribly hard to tell everyone goodbye at the end, though.

"Just don't go," Margie had said forlornly. "The girls are leaving for college Wednesday. We'll be needing someone to work here during hunting season."

"Yeah," Dan snorted as he poked her playfully in the ribs. "Twelve B needs another good coat of paint, and 2A needs a new roof. I'm certain I could find something to keep you out of trouble."

"Like wash and iron eighty sets of curtains or put a new floor in little 4? Sure, I know you'd keep me busy if I let you. But the typewriter calls." Lindsay playfully made little tapping movements with her fingers.

On the plane home, she kept reminding herself she was a professional journalist and she shouldn't be so tempted to remain in the mountains and scrub cabins. She should be thrilled she was winging her way back home to herself. And to Kendall. She smiled almost gleefully. Her life was so full of miraculous things.

"Rita. I'm home," she called as she stepped into the dark house a few hours later. *Oh well,* she thought, *Rita must be out.* Actually Lindsay was glad for the time alone. She would have a chance to unpack and to call Kendall. She plunked her suitcase on the floor in the dark bedroom, flipped on the light and headed straight for the phone. It rang on Kendall's end fifteen times before Lindsay gave up. Poor guy, Lindsay groaned to herself. They've got him working on Saturday night. She tried the number at the maintenance hangar. An unfamiliar voice answered. "Kendall Allen? No. He's gone for the week. He worked yesterday and then he took off. He'll be back next week."

Lindsay sighed. She should have called him from the ranch. She had thought about it many times, but there was only one party line into all six of the businesses in Taylor Valley. It served its purpose well in emergencies but it was impossible to try to enjoy a long, lingering phone call. There was always someone waiting, picking up the receiver and clicking the dials. It wasn't at all conducive to long-distance romance.

For an instant, Lindsay wondered if something was wrong, then she banished the thought from her mind. She would wait for Kendall to call tonight. She knew he would. She unpacked her suitcase and pitched several things into the dirty-clothes hamper. She decided not to get undressed just yet. She wanted to be ready to see Kendall when he called. She pulled her hair back from her face with a gold barrette and then lay on the sofa. She stared at the phone for a long, long time willing it to ring, but it never did. Finally, the phone faded into a mist of drowsiness and Lindsay fell asleep.

As THE DAYS PASSED and the telephone remained silent, Lindsay's fears began to multiply until they became gregarious monsters with nowhere to go. They snipped and snarled and tore down walls of faith in her love until Lindsay could scarcely bear the torment she felt. Rita moved around her in white-faced grimness. It seemed as though her roommate was always scuttling away somewhere else whenever Lindsay entered the room. But as the time went by and the hurt in Lindsay's eyes magnified, Rita knew she wouldn't be able to run away from divulging the hideous truth much longer.

One evening Rita grabbed Lindsay's arm and held it. "We have to talk."

"You mean you can tell me something?" Lindsay cried.

Rita's eyes were already telling a painful story. "I shouldn't be the one having to do this," she said sadly. But she was. Kendall had won after all. And Rita could see by the gray veil of hurt that covered Lindsay's face she should have given in to his wishes much sooner. She kept hoping the creep would call and take responsibility for himself, but he never did. The unhappy burden was falling on her shoulders.

"Rita, it's okay," Lindsay whispered to her. She sensed her friend needed help. "Go ahead."

"It's Kendall." Rita wanted to spit the name from her lips, and Lindsay flinched at her tone of voice. She hadn't heard his name spoken aloud for the last three days and she wasn't certain if she could face it now. But she had to. "Lindsay." Rita sucked in her breath and held it there. Here it came. "He's getting married."

"He's *what*?" Lindsay jumped up from the bar stool where she sat and upset a basket of fruit in the process. "It can't be. You can't be telling me the truth."

"That's all I know." Rita was crying. Lindsay's eyes were huge, like craters in her face. She had gone deathly pale and Rita found herself wishing she would scream or cry, but she didn't.

"No." Lindsay whispered the denial to no one. She looked around frantically. She felt like a caged animal.

"Oh, Lindsay." Rita was at her friend's side then, hugging her, and the two women held each other for a very long time. It didn't matter to Lindsay how Rita knew about Kendall's marriage. It only mattered that a love was gone. Lindsay's dreams were crushed, dead, lifeless on the ground, just as they had been starting to sprout up.

Lindsay cried for hours, but her tears didn't release the hurt that had jammed itself up in her throat. She had been such a fool! Her thoughts became an endless array of nightmares reeling in double and triple features through her head...the day she'd held on to Kendall's feet...the day he came an hour early to take her flying...the night he spoke to the airplanes as if they were his friends. Now, every place she would go, every road she would drive on, every morning she would wake would be a constant reminder of her life as it had been with him, her joys, her victories, her foolishness. Even getting dressed for each day would be torture. She would see other reminders of him hanging innocently in her closet, the sweaters she'd worn to go flying, the silk blouse with the pearl buttons Kendall had loved so much, the jeans with the grass stains on the knees from having played tackle football with him and Marcus at Heights Park.

She had to forget him. She had to get out of Dallas and she had to do it before Friday. Kendall's wedding day. If she was still here then, she would go insane. She had no choice.

At five-forty Wednesday evening, Lindsay slipped into Rex Martin's office for a private conference. She knew she was doing the right thing. For two days, she had banged away on her Olivetti typewriter with no results. The words weren't coming out. She knew what that meant. It had nothing to do with her heart. It had to do with her soul. She needed a fall cleaning. She needed to be pumping gas and tarring roofs and snowmobiling over Napolean Pass. She needed her mountains.

Lindsay called Margie early Thursday and asked for the cabin-cleaning job. Margie was ecstatic. They definitely could use her.

Lindsay promised Rita she would pay three months rent on the house unless her friend could sublet it sooner. Finding another tenant wouldn't be hard to do. Several of their girlfriends from Southern Methodist had volunteered to move in if space became available. It was a charming, cozy little home close to everything.

Victoriously, Lindsay stuffed several Villager suits, a St. Laurent dress and her newest Diane Von Furstenberg ensemble into a clothes bag. These were her best business clothes and she wouldn't need them in Taylor Park, Colorado. The beginning of the new Lindsay, she thought to herself as she zipped the bag shut. Or the beginning of the old Lindsay. Or the intertwining of them both. She wasn't certain which.

Lindsay was amazed at how easy it was to pick up every piece of her life and totally rearrange it. It was as if she was running down a checklist with a pen crossing off items at a grocery store. This was done. That was taken care of. And in the midst of all the organization, she did not allow herself to think about Kendall. She had a way of slipping her thoughts into overdrive whenever she began hurting. She could stay comfortably numb, comfortably organized, while some other part of herself bore the brunt of her pain.

Lindsay's flight landed in Gunnison at 5:45 P.M. Thursday. Margie had scheduled a grocery-shopping trip to City Market so she could be in town and give her new employee a ride to the ranch. The two women chattered all the way back up the canyon. Margie was curious about Lindsay's fast change of heart and her quick trip to Colorado. Lindsay explained as much as she thought was absolutely necessary. She didn't explain the wonderful things. Just the sad things. Just a few well-placed facts. She had fallen in love with a man who didn't love her. He was marrying someone else. Tomorrow. Lindsay flinched. She was trying to forget that part.

Margie seemed concerned about the situation, but not overly so.

She told Lindsay she felt a bit selfish for being so excited to have her again, no matter what the circumstances. Then she grinned. Several of the screens needed fixing, and all the windows needed to be washed. The girls hadn't gotten to either task before they'd left for school.

"Let's see." Lindsay figured in her head. "Twenty three cabins and two trailers with an average of five windows each. That's a hundred twenty-five windows to wash inside and out tomorrow."

Margie turned to her mournfully. "You're good with your math. That's exactly right."

Lindsay just grinned back at Margie's questioning face. Washing a hundred twenty-five windows. It sounded absolutely heavenly. With every window she'd wash, she would cleanse a part of herself as well.

All day Friday, Lindsay toted a tin bucket and washed windows. She slopped water all over herself and all over the ground and when she came in for dinner that night, her eyes shone almost as clear as her hundred and twenty-five windows did. She came in smelling of ammonia water, and Dan laughed at the newsprint ink all over her face. Instead of writing newspapers today, she had cleaned windows with them. She looked just like Cinderella. And it had all been a beautiful, ceremonious cleansing. Someone else was in Dallas today getting ulcers over whether the Lifestyle section would win any awards or not. Someone else had to wash the dinner dishes at home. Someone else was walking down the aisle with Kendall tonight.

Lindsay was so tired, she wanted to drop. All she wanted to do was snuggle down under three wool blankets and sleep forever. But that was not to be. Around midnight, a black bear came into camp and banged through the trash cans. The noise woke Lindsay with a start and it took her an hour to relax and drift off to sleep again. And when she did finally sink into unconsciousness, the dreams that greeted her there were terrifying.

She was in a fog, and people were turning in her direction as Lindsay floated down the aisle with a faceless man. A girl wearing a white suit and a white angora beret grabbed her arm and pulled her away, and she knew the girl was Sarah although she didn't know her name—and the faceless man was Kendall. Lindsay walked behind them, floating, drifting, her legs wouldn't take her but some invisible force did, toward a white altar covered with flowers. The faceless man turned to her and whispered, "You will be mine forever...and ever...and ever.'' The girl in the white suit screamed a desperate scream, and Kendall turned and ran out of the church, and everyone sitting in the pews heard the brakes screech outside in the street. Then Lindsay wasn't in the church at all, she was in the bathtub, and she could still hear brakes screeching outside. She grabbed a towel, wrapped it around herself and ran outside. Kendall was lying dead in the street. She ran toward him crying, but when she bent over him, he reached up to her and grabbed the towel away from her. He sat up in the street and sneered at her. He just sat there in the road while he laughed and his face turned into the devil's face, and Lindsay just stood there, naked, screaming in the street.

CHAPTER FIVE

MARCUS STARED AT HIS WATCH in disbelief. It was almost noon on Monday, and Kendall Allen hadn't bothered to come to work this morning. He was always in by eight, and Marcus was extremely concerned. If it had been another employee, Marcus would have fired the man on the spot. But Kendall was his best friend, too, and this kind of behavior wasn't like him.

During his lunch hour, Marcus drove to Richardson and did the only thing he knew to do. He parked directly in front of the Copperridge Apartments and took the steps two at a time until he reached the second floor. He banged on the door marked "209" but there was no answer. Marcus could hear a television blaring from somewhere deep inside. For the umpteenth time in the last two weeks, Marcus decided something was terribly wrong. Without hesitating, he turned his shoulder to the door and ran at it.

The hinges broke open with a splitting, splintering sound and there sat Kendall, on the sofa, glassy-eyed and looking wretched. From the look of the room, the television had been on for the entire week. Marcus was surprised it hadn't blown up by now. Kendall hadn't shaved for days, and Marcus didn't think he had slept, either.

"Hey, Ken," Marcus walked to the sofa and tried to sit down casually beside him. "You are killing yourself."

"I know." Kendall stared straight ahead, never moving his eyes from the television.

"We looked for you at the hangar this morning," Marcus interjected. "Your vacation's supposed to be over, you know?"

Kendall looked surprised. "Is it? What day is it?"

"Monday," Marcus answered.

Kendall shook his head. "Just leave me alone. Hire somebody else."

"I can't let you do this to yourself," Marcus persisted.

"Why not?" Kendall asked sarcastically. "I killed Sarah. Then I destroyed Lindsay. I deserve everything I get."

"Don't be a fool, Kendall," Marcus spit at him. "Nobody killed Sarah." There was a pause. "How long has it been since you've eaten?"

"I don't remember."

"Do you mind telling me what you are doing here?"

"I'm hiding from Lindsay. I have to hide from Lindsay."

"Why?"

"Because I love her." Kendall shook his head matter-of-factly.

"Don't do this to yourself." Marcus frowned. Now he understood. Kendall had ended the relationship, and Marcus supposed it was because he still thought he should be in love with his dead wife. He had known Kendall still felt responsible for Sarah's death, but he didn't know to what extent. Now, he did. This was frightening. Kendall was throwing so much away. He was screwing up his own life and Lindsay's in the process. Beautiful, delicate Lindsay. Marcus shook his head as if to banish that thought. He cared for her, too. In a way, he knew he loved them both.

"Look, Ken—" he knelt down right between Kendall and the television set "—you're making the wrong decision. This could be the worst thing you'll ever do your whole life. I am your friend and I am not going to let you screw this one up."

"Why do you care so much?" Kendall growled. "Is it me you're worried about, or is it Lindsay? Which one of us do you love the most, Marcus?"

"I love you." There were tears in Marcus's eyes now. Those three words weren't the easiest to tell your best buddy. "And I happen to know that Lindsay loves you, too. Do you have any idea how many times she called looking for you this past week?"

Kendall looked at him then. "I can guess. She called here, too, but I didn't answer."

"I'm surprised she isn't calling you right now," Marcus stated.

"No." Kendall shook his head calmly. "The phone calls stopped Tuesday night, didn't they?"

Marcus nodded.

"That's when she told her." Kendall's eyes were haunted again, and Marcus tried not to read what he saw there.

"Told her what?"

"About Sarah."

"Someone told her the truth?" Marcus was pleased.

Kendall was still shaking his head, though. "I told her roommate to tell her about Sarah...to tell her I am in love with someone else."

"But you didn't bother to tell her the woman you're still in love with is your wife who died almost three years ago?" Marcus roared. "What are you trying to prove to yourself, Kendall? How strong you are?"

"Yes." Kendall whispered the answer. He was embarrassed by it.

"You are weak, Kendall. A weak fool."

"What do you care?"

"I care about both of you. Maybe I care too much." Marcus was furious. He reached over and grabbed the telephone. "This is the most idiotic thing you have done in your entire life. Call her." He practically threw the apparatus into Kendall's lap. "Call her and tell her the truth. About Sarah. About you. About everything. Now. Before it's too late. Do it before this thing goes on any longer."

"It's already too late." Kendall looked like a little boy now, ready to collapse in tears.

"Let the circumstances be the judge of that." Marcus put an arm across Kendall's shoulders. He was pleased to see he was finally getting through to his friend.

For the first time in nine days, Kendall smiled. Maybe Marcus was right. The things he was saying kept making sense. Maybe some good could be found in all the lies, all the half-truths he had told. Maybe out of this agony, he and Lindsay could finally find happiness. Maybe he could be strong. Maybe he could face everything he had done wrong. He knew that he loved Lindsay enough to do that. He picked up the handset and dialed Lindsay's phone number.

"Oh." Rita almost dropped the receiver she was so shocked to hear his voice.

"I need to talk to Lindsay."

"Lindsay doesn't talk to married men." Rita's words were full of venom.

Kendall sighed. He was too worn out to explain. "Just let me talk to her, Rita."

"I can't." Her words were staccato, sharp, like little pins sticking into him. "She moved to Colorado. She's gone."

"Where in Colorado?" he asked. "I have to find her."

Rita paused for one brief moment. She wanted to shield Lindsay from any more hurt. "I don't know," she answered. "Colorado's a big state, isn't it? You could look for a long time and never find her.'' Rita slammed the receiver back down onto the cradle.

Kendall pulled the telephone away from his ear. Rita had hung up hard enough to hurt his eardrum. He turned and shrugged at Marcus. "That was Rita. She doesn't like me very much. Lin's in Colorado but I don't know where.''

"Do you have a way to find out?'' Marcus's eyes were dark.

"Believe it or not, I do.'' Kendall grinned.

They had all afternoon to spend in the library, Kendall reasoned. He didn't remember the name of the guest ranch but he would recognize it if he saw it. Lindsay had talked about it a lot. The ranch was a business, so it had to be listed in the yellow pages somewhere. He knew it started with an H, like Homo's or Holt's or Harmel's or something. And he knew it was near Gunnison. He would call all the guest ranches in the phone book if he had to. There couldn't be that many.

Four hours later, the librarian was flicking the lights on and off to let everyone know the building was closing. But Kendall had done it. It had been relatively easy to find the number for Howard's Guest Ranch. Lindsay had repeated the name to him at least a thousand times. This was the place she had written about in her article. He was certain of it.

"Howard's Guest Ranch,'' a cheery voice answered when he dialed the number a few minutes later.

"Yes....'' Kendall suddenly lost all of his self-assurance. His hands were shaking and he didn't know if he could even speak. "Lindsay Cornell.'' He said her name breathlessly. He didn't have to ask if she was there. He knew she was.

"May I say who is calling?''

"Kendall Allen. This is urgent. Tell her I must speak to her,'' he pleaded.

Margie hurried out to the metal trailer on Willow Creek. She found Lindsay flopped on the bed devouring a romance novel. "There is a Kendall Allen on the telephone for you.''

At the unexpected mention of Kendall's name, Lindsay's face went ashen. She could feel her soul turning inside out and ripping and tearing at all the tight places. Her eyes were as big as two moons when she turned them back to Margie. "I can't.'' The words were inaudible. Then, a bit louder, "Please tell him I cannot speak to him.''

When Kendall heard her response eight hundred miles away, he was undaunted. He had made a crummy decision. And, as far as he could remember, this was the first decision he had ever reneged on. He was surprised, but it felt good to change his mind.

When he'd decided to call Lindsay, a strange new peace had enveloped him. It was as if Sarah had reached down from the heavens and had willed him to be happy. An enormous weight was gone from his shoulders. He loved Lindsay. He loved Lindsay and he also loved Sarah, and therein lay his victory. He was free to do both.

Kendall pulled a suitcase out from under his bed and threw in one pair of jeans, some underwear, several flannel shirts, his razor and his toothbrush. He knew he would need more than that but if he was forgetting something important, he could borrow it from someone in Colorado. Colorado. He had never been to Colorado. A new state...a new airport...a new life...a new man.

By the time he drove to Love Field, Marcus had the Romeo Juliet ready to fly. After filing a flight plan and conducting a quick ten-point check, Kendall and the plane leaped into the sky and headed northwest across the Texas Panhandle. The Romeo Juliet landed in Gunnison at midnight local time. His only welcome was the lonely circle of the searchlight as it beckoned from an empty control tower. For an instant, Kendall faltered. What could he do now, he asked himself. But while he was securing his airplane, he caught a glimpse of a blinking motel sign in the distance. The place proved to be only two or three blocks away from the Gunnison airport, easily within walking distance. Kendall rented a single room for only a few hours where he bathed and slept fitfully. He was up by eight-thirty the next morning. He snatched a quick breakfast at the Redman Café across the street from the motel and rented a car. He was on the road up the canyon by nine.

Once he drove into Taylor Park, it was easy for Kendall to spot Howard's Guest Ranch. There wasn't much else in the valley and the cluster of red-roofed cabins beckoned warmly to travelers. Kendall could read the white letters on the monstrous red barn for almost five miles. Howard's Guest Ranch, the barn read and, all at once, Kendall felt the strange sensation of coming home to a place he had never been before. He drove in across the front cattle guard and looked around. Everything was just as Lindsay had described it to him. The old Conoco gas pump stood as a stately guard at the entrance. The circle of log cabins was small but friendly and, Kendall realized, very adequate for the life-style that people came here to experience. The lodge was long and low, and there was a wisp of smoke curling up out of a huge rock chimney. The center lawn was trimmed immaculately but the cracks and crevices where a lawn mower couldn't reach were bespeckled with glowing, dancing dandelion blooms and fragile, pink buttercup blossoms. The place looked just like Lindsay, Kendall thought. Practical but playful. Simple and old-fashioned in places yet complex and elegant in others.

All at once, as if her appearance had been timed with his thought and planned as a major production by a theater company, there she was. Lindsay stepped out from behind the bedsheets hanging on the clothesline just as if she had been stepping out on stage for a curtain call. Kendall froze when he saw her. It had been so long since he had held her that at times he thought his mind was beginning to play games with him. And now, as he watched her deftly taking sheets off the clothesline and folding them into a beat-up aluminum bucket, he knew all of his dreams of her were real.

She looked different to him somehow. Something had changed since he had seen her in Dallas. Kendall was dizzy just from the sensation of watching her. She looked happy and she moved like a young colt, graceful one moment and then springing into a disjointed motion the next. The mountains looked much better behind her than the Dallas skyline did. She moved with a self-assurance here that she did not display in the city. Even as she folded sheets, she radiated an eloquent beauty.

Lindsay felt anything but beautiful as she fought with the flapping sheets this morning. There were days when she enjoyed doing this task but today was not one of them. She hoped she wouldn't be too grouchy to everyone but it was going to be hard considering the amount of sleep she had lost last night.

Stupid Kendall, she growled to herself. She could remember when he called because he was worried she would lose sleep over one of his kisses. She should have taken that as a bad omen. She had lost plenty of sleep since then. Bizarre phone calls like the one she'd received last night certainly didn't help any. What had possessed Kendall Allen to call her? He was supposed to be on his honeymoon with somebody else.

After Lindsay folded the last sheet, she reached up to stifle a yawn. That's when she noticed a new car had pulled into the ranch. Someone new must be checking in, she thought, and she instantly became

worried. The cabins that were reserved for tonight had not been vacated yet. She picked up the bucket full of clothespins and sheets and
hurried toward the main lodge. As she pushed open the creaky screen
door, Lindsay frowned. Margie was signing the guest in on the registration book and his back was turned to her. But something was
oddly familiar about him, about the curve of his shoulders, the smell
of him, the style of his jacket. As Margie grinned at her and the guest
turned toward her, Lindsay let out a wounded gasp. It was him. Here.
In her special kingdom. Kendall Allen.

Lindsay didn't know whether to run into his arms or to turn and
run away. She stood her ground, bravely, defiantly. Kendall was
walking toward her, and she noticed something very strange and different in his eyes.

"Are you here for a cabin?" she heard her own voice squeaking.

He shook his head. "I'm here to see you. Can we talk?" He
grabbed her elbow as she grimaced up at him.

"What is there to talk about?"

"Everything." He looked down at her, and Lindsay felt her frozen
heart beginning to melt.

As they walked out of the lodge together, Lindsay glanced at the
automobile parked in front. There was no one with him on this trip.
What was he doing here? He had come to her, here, in Taylor Park,
this place that she loved above all others. Suddenly, as they walked
together, Lindsay saw everything through his eyes...the mountains...the old rundown trolley car in the back pasture...the familiar
line of Collegiate Peaks that surrounded the valley. And as she looked
at things through his eyes, she was just glad to be with him once
more. "Let's go to the back pasture." She touched his arm and
looked up at him. "We'll sit in the old trolley. No one will bother
us there." Her eyes were like two deep pools in her face and Kendall
felt himself slowly sinking into them.

Looking at her then, he felt a strange sense of awe and of fear.
During the past day, all of his energy had been spent getting to her.
Now that he had her walking beside him, he was almost in a state
of panic. What would he say to her? His mind was blank. He sensed
her distance but he sensed her wonder, too. She had no idea why he
had come. He felt like he knew her and he didn't know her. He had
no way to gauge how she would react to him, to his love, to his lies,
to the life he wanted to offer her.

"Up here." Lindsay turned to him and gestured toward the trolley.

She pulled herself up on one of the rusty metal handles and plopped onto a splintered seat. As she sat there above him, she almost grinned. She had practically grown up swinging around like a monkey on this old thing. It used to sit in the middle of the playground, but Dan had towed it off many years ago when it started falling apart in earnest.

"Will this thing hold me?" Kendall eyed the antiquated vehicle.

"Sure." She nodded down to him and then patted one of the worn seats with love. "This thing has held much heavier than the likes of you."

Kendall climbed up and sat down tentatively as if he expected the entire floorboard to give way beneath him. Then he looked at Lindsay in silence. He was still afraid.

But something calm and beautiful had happened to Lindsay. Kendall was sitting here in the old trolley car next to her and it seemed as if God had granted her a magical reprieve. She had one more chance to see him, to love him. She harbored no false pride. She didn't need it. Somewhere deep inside of her she felt her faith, her love, her hope being bound together into comforting strength.

"I have so much to say to you," Kendall finally whispered to her. As he spoke, the rain began to fall in tiny rivulets around them. "Should we run back to the barn?" He looked up at the sky.

"No." Lindsay shook her head. "We'll get wetter there than we will here." As she watched his face, she sensed he was going to need her help with what he was about to tell her. She had an uncanny way of intuiting his needs. "Okay, Kendall Allen." She put her hands on her hips. "These past few weeks, I've learned how to handle all sorts of wild information. I have this strange feeling I'm about to hear more of the same stuff."

He nodded. She knew his moods so well. He had lied to her for a year and still, sensing the truth and how hard it was for him, she was willing herself to listen.

Lindsay knew she would not be angry at him. Whatever he said, she would take his revelations at face value. She resisted the urge to hug him. He looked like an unhappy child who was trying to tell his mother he had broken the cookie jar or poured paint on the carpet. She loved him just as he was, wistful and proud. And brave. It struck her how brave he was to meet her like this, on her territory, on her battleground. His hair was wet now and it dripped in a mass of curls around his temples. She swallowed the temptation to reach out and rumple it.

Kendall took her elbow in his palm and pulled her toward him as he began to speak. He told her everything...everything that he was...everything he felt. Lindsay was shocked when he told her about Sarah. She found herself regretting she hadn't asked more questions a year ago. She had always wondered about his melancholy moods and the hard, sad looks she had seen on his face. Everything she knew about him now rapidly fell into place. She wished she could have soothed him during all his desperate times. He had not wanted her to invade his private places. But now he was inviting her in, and it made the act of understanding him all that much more precious to her.

Lindsay was sad, though. She couldn't help thinking of the things they could have had between them. Now he was married to someone else and they could never have those things.

Kendall saw the sadness on her face. He bent forward and kissed her on the nose with a question in his eyes. "Sunshine? Why so sad?"

"We missed our chance, didn't we?" She shook her head matter-of-factly. "I could have been a part of all that but you wouldn't let me. Now someone else is."

Kendall looked bewildered for a few seconds and then relief registered across his face. He had told her so much of what was important to him, but he had forgotten to tell her the end of the story. "Lindsay, look at me." He took her face in his hands. "I did not get married."

She gasped.

"It seemed easy to me," he explained painfully. "I love you. But I thought loving you was wrong. I still feel married to Sarah."

"No...no...." Lindsay was shaking her head and there were tears welling up in her eyes.

"Let me finish." He held up his hand. "This needs to be said. I don't feel like a whole person. I've been ripped apart, and all the pieces haven't been put back together yet. I don't think it's fair for you to have to put back the pieces for me. You're so beautiful, Lin, so bright and shiny. I don't have a right to take the joy you find in life away from you with my sadness."

Lindsay was laughing now, that same tinkling chime that made him want to laugh, too. But she was crying, as well, and her tears were mixing with the raindrops that kept sliding down her cheeks. "Oh, you crazy." She giggled at him lovingly as she took his head into her two hands and just held it there, looking at it for a long while. "You crazy, crazy, crazy."

He smiled at her.

"Don't you realize how much you've given me?" she questioned emphatically. "Do you think the dreams we've shared mean nothing?"

"I don't know," he answered honestly.

"If this is just a part of a man—" she jabbed one finger ruthlessly into his chest "—I shudder to think what would happen if all the parts were put together right. I love you, you crazy."

Crazy. Crazy. Crazy. Lindsay couldn't get that one word out of her head. That's what today had been. That's what her life had been.

Kendall put a finger under her chin and gingerly lifted her face until her eyes met his. "You're the crazy one, Lindsay Cornell. Why aren't you murdering me right now?"

"Nope." She grinned as she shook her head back and forth vehemently. "No murder at the end of this story."

Kendall heaved a sigh of relief. She wasn't furious. He would go on then. He hadn't flown eight hundred miles to the boondocks just to tell her the truth and beg for forgiveness. He had come to make her his. "I love you so, Lindsay." Kendall looked down at her longingly.

In one hour, everything that Lindsay had lost during the past weeks had been restored to her. She looked up at him, and all the passion and the fear that had been bottled up inside of her for the past days poured forth as he bent to kiss her. His lips crushed hers and she clung to him. There, in his arms, Lindsay could feel that everything they had searched for during the last year together had been found. Everything she ever needed was here locked deep inside his fierce embrace. When the kisses stopped, Lindsay was in a rosy, fragrant daze. She tried to smile with composure but the look would not come. She didn't really want to chase the wonderful, fuzzy, soft feeling away.

"I love you," Kendall whispered to her again.

She reached up and locked her hands around the back of his neck and pulled his face back down to hers. "I want to be the one who helps put all the pieces back together," she whispered into his lips.

"Do you, now?" He smiled playfully.

"Yes." She gave him a quick peck on the nose.

"Well—" his eyes brightened and a look of mischief brushed

across his face "—let's see you put your money where your mouth is."

"What do you mean by that?" Lindsay's eyes widened.

"Just what I said. Prove it to me."

"How?"

"Marry me," he stated lightly.

Lindsay stared at him.

"Well?"

"Me?" she asked.

Kendall looked around the back pasture playfully. "I don't see anybody else riding this silly piece of equipment."

"You want to marry me?" Tears were brimming in Lindsay's eyes once again.

Kendall stepped down off the trolley and reached his arms up to her. "Come here." He signaled with all ten of his fingers. Lindsay reached out to his shoulders and he circled his hands around her tiny waist. He lifted her down and she stood there, only a breath away, in front of him. "It's obvious that I'm going to have to convince you of this." Kendall wiped a wet wisp of hair off her forehead. "Yes, I want to marry you. And yes, that also means that I want you to marry me."

Lindsay just grinned up at him. "I think I'm in shock, Kendall Allen, and well I should be. Thirty minutes ago, I thought you were married to someone else." She looked so serious and so delicate standing there looking at him. There was a raindrop on the very tip of her nose and Kendall reached down and kissed it off. He began to be frightened again. She was questioning him. She was questioning what he told her and how he had treated her. He knew he deserved a firm "no" for an answer. But he wasn't going to accept that. He was hoping Lindsay would consider more than the facts. He knew she loved him, he hoped as strongly and as fiercely as he loved her. He prayed that she was willing to accept him just the way he was.

"I don't know." She turned from him and her mind was rushing in a thousand directions at once. However, above all the conflicting thoughts and doubts in her mind, one idea seemed to surge forward stronger than the others. She loved this man more than her own being. She knew she wanted to spend all of her life with him.

She turned to him slowly and smiled shyly.

Kendall was frozen to the ground where he stood. His mind was screaming out to her, begging her, but he could only stand there before her rigid with fear.

"I will," Lindsay whispered.

"You will?"

"You heard me." She started jumping up and down and squealing. "I will. Yes. Yes. Yes." Now that she had made the decision, she was jubilant. She kept bouncing around in a circle and pulling him with her.

"Calm down!" he shouted happily. Then, to silence her, he kissed her full on the mouth. He reached down, lifted her feet from the ground and swung her entire body up into his arms.

"Yes, sir." She saluted him teasingly and kissed him on the cheek.

Kendall reached up and placed her on the old trolley car once again. "I am so happy, my darling." There were tears in his eyes now, too.

"I've wanted so desperately to be your wife," she whispered to him. "I think today I am the happiest girl in these mountains." She swept one arm in the direction of the Collegiate Peaks behind her.

Kendall was too overcome with his feelings to speak then. He pulled her to him tenderly and kissed her forehead, her eyes, her nose where another raindrop stood. When his kisses reached her lips, she held him gently and returned them eagerly. And as Kendall loved her, Lindsay felt a fire slowly beginning to smolder and grow deep within her soul where nothing had ever burned before.

CHAPTER SIX

THE WEDDING WAS FOUR DAYS later. Once the decision had been made, Lindsay and Kendall could not wait to become husband and wife. Lindsay was obligated to stay in Taylor Park for another six weeks through elk hunting season and Kendall was beginning to feel tugs to get back to the maintenance hangar in Dallas. In six weeks, Lindsay would come home to his studio apartment. He would be a husband and soon, he hoped, a father. His every-day responsibilities suddenly became very important to him. He wanted to go back to Dallas and establish a beautiful life for his beautiful bride.

The wedding was in the main lodge at Howard's in front of the huge rock fireplace. Bob Richards, a retired Baptist minister from Denver, who was spending the autumn at his summer cabin in the tiny nearby town of Tincup, agreed to perform the ceremony. He had known Lindsay's parents since they had started coming to Taylor Park and he was honored to be included in the festivities.

On the morning of the wedding, Dan was up early finishing the daily chores around the cabins and Margie was merrily baking in the kitchen. Every day at Taylor Park, Lindsay felt like a princess. But on this day, her wedding day, she felt like she ruled the world. She looked back once again on the people here who gave her strength. The love they had given her had gently molded her life, had blossomed and grown into this wonderful magic feeling she would always feel for these mountains and this place.

Lindsay pulled her dress from the closet and eyed it thoughtfully after unwrapping it. She had absolutely no idea what had possessed her to bring this dress to the mountains. She had worn it once before in a beauty pageant she had won while she was in college. Being in a pageant was something Dallas girls were expected to do. When Lindsay was nominated and then quickly named a finalist, she had been overwhelmed and excited. During the weeks of preparation for the contest she had learned how to walk the right way, how to talk the right way and how to smile the right way. It had all seemed trivial and silly to her, and she wondered what her friends here would have said if they had seen her practicing on the brilliantly lit stage. No matter how silly the competition, the dress remained exquisite. It was designed of creamy cotton crocheted lace and lined with a rich dusty mauve satin. The lacy mandarin collar stood stiffly at her neck and emphasized her broad, square shoulders, her toned bustline, her graceful, slender arms. The dress closed with tiny pearl buttons down the front of the garment to the floor where it fell in lacy, thick folds that swayed with the rhythm of Lindsay's hips.

Exactly at the stroke of 3:00 P.M., Lindsay clutched Dan's elbow and moved toward the doorway. The delicate melody of a harp wafted through the lodge like a fragrance and Lindsay trembled as she heard the first familiar strains of Lohengrin's *Wedding March.*

The door swung open, and the appreciative gasp Lindsay heard circling the room echoed inside her own heart. The entire mantel was covered with evergreens, larkspur, wild strawberry blossoms and delicate mountain buttercups. Even the cash register and the hunting gear display was decorated with greenery and flowers. And there, standing in front of the blazing fireplace, was her groom, his arms outstretched to her for all the mountains to see. Oh, how she loved this man.

Kendall beamed at her as she walked slowly toward him to the lilt of the harp music. He looked like a god to her with his hair glowing cognac against the dancing firelight and the sunlight that was streaming in the front windows. Even in the navy-blue wool suit he had borrowed from Dan, who wasn't anywhere close to his size, Kendall's broad, sturdy shoulders, his muscular arms, his trim waist were all evident. They looked into each other's eyes and repeated the old, cherished words, and every word, every promise, every vow they made, they meant to the very depths of their souls.

The ceremony drifted by in a dream and was soon over, and Lindsay thought she had never seen so many jovial faces. Lindsay never guessed this many people lived within miles of Taylor Valley. She met the people who were living up in the Campbell Cabin and all the cowboys who worked at the cow camp over in Union Park. The girls from the Nugget Café were there, too, and Lindsay was thrilled to share her happiness with so many of these sturdy, country people. If she had taken six months to plan a wedding in the largest church in Dallas, the occasion couldn't have meant more to her than this did.

As Margie started serving cake and the delectable white mints she had made that morning, Lindsay found herself whisked into the arms of someone she wasn't expecting to see. "Marcus James!" she squealed as her husband's friend hugged her tight enough to take her breath away. "What are you doing here?"

"I couldn't have missed this major world event." He stepped back from her and bowed mockingly. "Your new husband made a few well-placed phone calls last night and I hopped a plane at Love Field this morning. I decided you two don't have enough excitement in your lives. I thought I'd just drop by and liven things up. Who are all these people, anyway?"

"Just friends." Lindsay shrugged innocently. "People just like you who thought they'd drop by and stir up some trouble."

"Thanks a lot." He stuck his tongue out at her.

"Don't take it personally," she said laughingly. "I thought nothing else could happen to make this day more wonderful. But now you're here and I know everything's complete. I am honored that you flew so far to be here."

"I have to be at work in—" he checked his watch "—another six hours. So I have to leave almost immediately. I just wanted to see you...both of you. I just wanted to give my regards to the most beautiful bride I will ever see."

"Marcus James." Lindsay said his name tenderly as she reached up and touched his shoulder. Somehow it was an intimate gesture but one she was comfortable with. "Someday you'll find your own bride and you'll regret ever saying that." A twinkle came into her eyes. "I'll be sure to remind you when the time comes."

"You won't have to remind me." Marcus looked down at her with something new in his eyes, something Lindsay didn't dare read. It was almost as if he was sad about something, desperate to be away from her, but Lindsay couldn't understand why. "Where's the groom?" he asked abruptly.

"Marcus." Kendall joined them then, and Lindsay noticed there were tears in her husband's eyes when he hugged his friend. "I should have known you would be here."

Marcus nodded. "You know me pretty well."

"You're responsible for all this, you know." Kendall swept his arm across the entire scene and made certain to include Lindsay in the gesture. "He talked me into finding you, sunshine. I didn't tell you that part. If it wasn't for Marcus, I couldn't have been brave enough to face you.''

"I should have known.'' Lindsay winked at her husband and then turned to hug Marcus. She was surprised when he stepped back to avoid her embrace. Instead, he turned to Kendall. "I do have to go now. It's a long flight back.''

"That's funny—'' Kendall shrugged his shoulders and grabbed Lindsay's arm "—we were just leaving, too. Let's make the grand exit together. Come on.''

Lindsay grinned and Marcus nodded and, together, the three of them ran out of the lodge, locked arm in arm, past the cheers of congratulations and through the whirl of rice that hung for an eternity in the air.

"COME HERE, MRS. ALLEN,'' Kendall reached out to Lindsay in the darkness. They stood on the front porch of the cabin they had rented for the night.

"I love you, husband,'' she whispered up to him. She loved being called Mrs. Allen. She loved calling him husband. She was trying on her new role already and she loved the way it fit.

"Shhh....'' He touched his finger to her lips. He reached inside the door with his free hand and flicked on the cabin light. "Now.'' He turned to her and swept her up into his arms.

"What are you doing?''

"Carrying my new wife over the threshold. Do you mind?''

Lindsay shook her head no, while he beamed at her.

"You know—'' Kendall smiled mischievously "—you certainly don't weigh much to be as feisty as you are.''

"Gee, thank you.'' Lindsay laughed.

"How much do you weigh, my darling?'' The teasing look did not leave his face. "About two hundred pounds?''

"Kendall!'' she shrieked.

"I'm just guessing, I'm just guessing,'' he said, trying to look innocent. "And that's a nice round figure.''

"That's a nice *round* figure all right!'' Lindsay giggled.

"You are a beautiful, beautiful bride, my love.'' The mischief in his eyes turned to longing.

"You sure are mushy—'' Lindsay kissed him on the cheek "—but I love it. Keep it up forever, okay?''

"I promise,'' he said, grinning.

"Now, will you please take me across the threshold or whatever? It's getting cold out here."

"Yes, ma'am." Kendall pushed open the screen door with his shoulder. "No wonder you like these cabins," he said, nodding toward the room. "Look at that bed." It was a monstrous thing, a bunk with a king-sized mattress on the top and the bottom. The posts on each corner were spruce tree trunks. "We should have invited more people. A whole army could sleep in that thing at once."

"Not on your life," Lindsay laughed. "That bed is just big enough for you and me."

"Tell you what—" there was a twinkle in his eye again "—I'll let you take the top bunk and I'll keep the bottom."

"Not on your life, Kendall Allen," Lindsay shrieked. Then she kissed him gingerly on the nose. "I think we're going to share either the top or the bottom. You get to choose. What's that?" There was something else in the cabin. Lindsay pointed to a round, steaming redwood tub at the foot of the massive bed.

"Just a little wedding present I dreamed up." Kendall set her down proudly, kissed her full on the mouth and then bowed deeply. "I know. Tell me. I think of everything."

"It's a hot tub." Lindsay was delighted.

"I thought you deserved to relax for one night."

At the mention of one night, Lindsay's face darkened. Tonight was going to be their only time together for a while. Tomorrow, Kendall had to fly the Romeo Juliet back to Dallas. It was horribly unfair to be married for only one night before having to say goodbye to each other, but Lindsay was content with the idea she would soon be with her husband in Dallas. Maybe she could even get her old job back at the *Times Herald*. And Kendall promised that, in time, the two of them would come back here, to this valley, and build a rustic cabin as a monument to their wedding day. Lindsay could picture their hideaway already; there would be an old wood-burning cookstove and a bouncy brass bed covered with a homemade quilt in bright sunny colors. Maybe she could find a trundle bed where she could stash two or three children. Children. That was an awesome thought. They would grow up running all over these mountains.

"What are you thinking about, sunshine?" Kendall asked her. Lindsay looked like she was in some distant place. He carefully pulled the pins from her hair and slowly began to unbraid it.

"That I can't wait to see you in that hot tub." She stood on tiptoes and kissed him on the nose. Then she pushed Dan's wool suitcoat off his shoulders, loosened his necktie and began to unbutton the front of his shirt.

"Hmmmm," Kendall sighed softly. "This could get very interesting."

"Let's see that it does," Lindsay whispered into his ear.

Slowly, he began to unwrap her, just as he would an exquisite package. He unbuttoned each pearl button on her dress meticulously, as if each was different, as if each needed special attention, until the creamy crocheted lace opened to reveal the silky underthings and her satin skin and her endless legs.

Lindsay reached up and finished unfastening her braided hair. As Kendall slipped the dress off her shoulders and then slowly began unclasping her lace undergarments, she let her hair cascade in wild froths down across her bare white shoulders.

Kendall moaned with unconcealed pleasure as she stood naked for him to see. Then gently, as if he was touching velvet, Kendall picked his bride up and placed her in the hot, bubbling tub. She watched as he deftly slid out of his clothes and then joined her in the water. Her eyes were huge, like a wild fawn frightened in the forest and, looking at her now, Kendall was overwhelmed by what she had entrusted to him.

Lindsay reached out to him, put her arms around his neck and pulled him toward her. He noticed a shy grin on her face and he looked at her questioningly. "What is that impish look on your face for?"

"I was just thinking." Her laughter was like bells echoing across the mountain countryside. "All this hot, bubbly water. Don't you feel like someone has got us cooking up in a big pot on a stove somewhere. Here we are." She raised her arms for effect. "Allen stew."

"Come here to me," he said with a chuckle.

She did, and he kissed her, and suddenly the warmth and the steam and her wet body pressing against him was more than he could endure. His hands began to caress every curve and every angle and every soft spot of her body under the water. She returned his passion, at first gently, and then with a growing eagerness.

Outside, the great horned owl of the mountains began to announce the arrival of the night. Inside, Kendall led his new bride to the monstrous bed, and there he loved her, tenderly and completely, while her body rose to his with an almost anguished need. Finally, after tasting the truth in each other's souls, they lay spent, content, secure in the knowledge that they were now totally husband and wife.

Lindsay was up early the next morning cooking scrambled eggs and pork sausage for her new husband. Kendall woke before she was aware of it. He watched her silently from the bed a moment, noting the curve of her back, the grace of her movements. "Good morning, wife," he said as he finally pulled himself out from under the covers. He wrapped his arms around Lindsay's stomach and squeezed her to him.

"Oh, darling." She wheeled around and threw her arms around his neck. "It is a good morning, isn't it?"

Kendall could see the pain in her eyes. He knew she was already hurting over the goodbyes they would share in hours. "It will be okay, sunshine." He lifted her chin with his finger. "I know this is hard, but it's also worth it, don't you think?"

"Of course." She squeezed him to her tightly. Of course this time together, however brief, was worth it. But it was also crazy. And it was sad. She looked up at him. "After we get through this separation, I don't ever want to live another day without you, is that understood?" She stomped her foot playfully, as if she was demanding obedience from a wayward child.

"Understood," he said as he nodded. Then, he kissed her. "Hmmm—" he grinned "—are you sure we have to get up so early? I was hoping to have breakfast in bed."

"Come here, then." She took a tray to the bedside table then plopped on the huge mattress once again. He went to her and for the rest of the morning they made love and ate breakfast and talked and touched. Lindsay drifted off to sleep after a while and Kendall slipped out from beneath the wool blankets and gathered his things. When he woke Lindsay, his face was the ash-gray color of sadness.

"I have to go now." He kissed her on the forehead. "Will you drive me in to Gunnison?"

She threw on some old clothes, splashed water on her face and brushed her hair until it shone like gold. Then she eyed the door and he nodded his head. Their time together was over.

As Lindsay drove to the airport, she was almost afraid to glance across the front seat at Kendall for fear he wouldn't really be there. When she did glance over at him, she was crying, and he was at a loss to comfort her. In desperation, he began to talk about everything he had seen the last few days, how much he had grown to love these mountains, how much he respected the people, how funny Dan Howard was when he snorted at the dinner table. Before long, Lindsay was laughing through her tears, and they were sharing stories. The drive blurred by as if it was a movie being played at an incredibly fast speed. And at the end of the drive was the airport and the Romeo Juliet.

As they stood by the plane, Lindsay and Kendall kissed each other goodbye over and over again. Neither could bear for each kiss to be the last. There always had to be one more, as if the kisses, like their lives together, would never stop. Kendall let Lindsay hold the clipboard while he conducted his check. Then he kissed her once more, fiercely this time, full on the mouth. As she stood there crying, he closed the cockpit door, waved his hand at her once, and the plane bounced away.

The Romeo Juliet doubled back on the runway and barreled past her as she stood there waving forlornly. As the craft lifted off the ground and shot up into the clouds, Lindsay was filled with longing. How she wanted to be up there among the clouds with him.

Lindsay couldn't stop the tears from streaming down her face. She could only whisper up at him. "Touch the sky for me, my darling. Touch the sky for me." And, as the little plane tipped its wings and disappeared into a cloud bank, she wondered if Kendall had somehow heard her.

As the Cessna lifted off the ground, Kendall experienced that same wonderful feeling of freedom he felt every time he became airborne. Suddenly, the world wasn't just flat with hills and valleys. The sky had new dimensions, new flavors. He could turn over and go home upside down at one hundred seventy-five miles per hour if he wanted to. Someday he might try that, he smiled proudly to himself.

He checked his altimeter and adjusted his heading. He was already above eight thousand two hundred feet and traveling south-southeast. Everything looked fine. He'd have to pull up higher to cross the Continental Divide at Monarch Pass, but he still had twenty-five minutes before he would reach the summit. That gave him time to steady his air speed.

Flying in the mountains had been a totally new experience, one he had wanted to try for a long time. There weren't many differences between flying over the mountains and flying over the Texas plains. You just had to watch your altitude closer here.

Kendall glanced down at the gold wedding band that now encircled his left ring finger. It looked perfect there. How he missed Lindsay already. He would have given anything if he could have brought her home with him now. Bachelorhood was nice, but for one night he had sampled something so much richer, and now it was going to be difficult to be by himself for another five weeks. Oh well, maybe the guys would give him some sort of party when he got home, and then maybe he wouldn't feel so lonely for her. The guys. A sly smile crossed Kendall's face. They would absolutely die. He was coming back to Texas a married man. He was sure all the employees at the hangar would make fun of him, but underneath they would be jealous. He had seen the way they looked at Lindsay. Even Marcus, when he thought Kendall wasn't looking. She was a woman to make any man proud. And now, she belonged to him.

A strange noise pulled his attention back to the instrument panel and the controls. He checked his air speed once again. It looked fine. From what he could tell from the weather reports he had looked over before leaving Gunnison, there could be some turbulence going over the top of this pass. The engine was droning differently, as if there had been a change in the air pressure outside. He decided to pull up another one thousand feet. That should do the trick.

As the Cessna climbed higher into the sky, a rush of adrenaline coursed through his body. New horizons. How he loved them.

As he sat reveling in the new heights he had reached, there was another change in the airplane's behavior. This time all of Kendall's senses jumped into alertness instantly. He felt the familiar sensation of his heart jamming up into his throat and, instinctively, he knew the plane was stalling.

He forced himself to remain calm. The plummet would increase his air speed and the plane would regain its lift. But precious seconds ticked by and he could still feel his stomach rising into his head. He had the air speed he needed now, but the Cessna's nose refused to level out. His trained fingers reached toward the throttle and he forced it wide open. Maximum RPM. The plane did not respond. Kendall's heart quit pumping. What was wrong? Not the engine. Somewhere, deep inside another dimension, he could hear it still throbbing.

It's the mountains, some distant voice screamed out to him. It has something to do with the mountains. Then he remembered something he had heard long ago during flight training. A wind sheer. A gust of high pressure air searing down from the mountains, particularly found in areas of extreme turbulence or near thunderstorm cells. The sheers had enough force to push a monstrous 747 passenger jet into the ground.

The plane was still not responding to his maneuvers, and Kendall began to lose hope. In one last futile attempt to save himself and the aircraft, he jerked the elevators to maximum climb position and then reached for the radio microphone. "Mayday, mayday," his voice boomed into the radio. "This is 482 Romeo Juliet flying south-southeast over Monarch Pass. I've got a problem up here. Losing altitude rapidly. Mayday. Mayday."

But by the time anyone at the Salida airport could respond to his call, it was already too late. Kendall was still trying to pull the plane up when the low altitude warning shrieked in his earphones. He tried once more and nothing happened. He was going down. His last thoughts were of the mountains and his Lindsay and the life together that lay before them. He didn't even feel it when the plane slammed into the ground and he was consumed by a wall of flame and darkness.

CHAPTER SEVEN

AS THE HOURS WORE ON, Marcus began to comprehend the intense horror Kendall must have felt when he had watched Sarah die. He must have felt so scared, so deserted, so responsible. Please, Marcus prayed, let them find something soon. But it was thirty-four hours after Kendall crashed when members of the Colorado Civil Air Patrol found the wreckage of his plane. The Romeo Juliet was registered to Marcus, so when the first hideous telephone call came, it came to him. The N482RJ Cessna 152 had been totally destroyed. The pilot had died on impact. The pilot of the craft was a man named Kendall Allen. Did he have permission to fly the aircraft? Did he have any next of kin who needed to be officially notified?

No one important, Marcus thought to himself bitterly. He had collapsed to his knees from the news. Just his mother in Dallas. A sister and her family in San Diego. Oh yes, and a brand new wife hidden somewhere close to Gunnison.

It was Marcus who volunteered to call Lindsay. The thought of an unfamiliar voice coldly informing her Kendall was dead made Marcus want to be sick. He would have to tell her. Somehow, he had to take partial responsibility for what had happened. In a way, he had done this to her.

When Marcus heard Lindsay's feeble voice on the other end of the telephone line, he wanted to weep. Why did she have to be so strong? He wished there was some way he could bear the pain, the loss, for her. But he couldn't. He could only tell her what they had found and wait for her reaction.

If Marcus could have seen her as he spoke to her, he would have seen her jaw clench and her facial features crumple until her face took on the hideous sharp angles of a gargoyle. She was gripping the receiver so tightly her knuckles seemed to throb and push right up out of her hands.

"Thank you for calling, Marcus." The words sounded gracious, well rehearsed, as if the Queen of England was saying them. It was as if Lindsay was standing on the other side of the room watching herself speak. This couldn't be real. Kendall couldn't be dead. Dead. The sky had killed him. For a long time, Lindsay stared at the poster of six dogs playing poker that was tacked up on the lodge wall. Then her mouth opened, and from some tormented cavern deep inside of her came a haunted, guttural moan.

The worst part of the trip back to Dallas for the funeral was climbing inside the Frontier passenger jet at the Gunnison airport. For two nights now, Lindsay had been tormented with dreams of airplanes crashing and flaming and flipping end over end toward the ground. She saw all of the aircraft in her mind, the huge passenger jets, the teeny private crafts, careering into the ground with explosions, expelling luggage and bodies as they went. They were all gruesome scenes, and Lindsay felt like she had lived them over and over again as she buckled her seat belt and made ready for the takeoff she knew would never come. There was absolutely no way an airplane could fly. She would not have to face the funeral because the plane would leap up into the air and then fall back to the ground again with a deafening roar. And Lindsay was glad. The burning inside of her, the loneliness, the longing, would be over. She closed her eyes and leaned back against the seat in preparation for the inevitable. But the inevitable never came. The Frontier jet taxied down the runway and lifted up into the sky perfectly. In two hours, the jet landed gracefully on the runway at Dallas-Fort Worth International Airport.

Because their loves had been so recently joined together, Lindsay had very little to do to store away Kendall's life. She moved through the days as if she was stumbling numbly along the ground, always stooped, never able to stand. Kendall's mother, Angela Allen, handled all the arrangements.

The service was held in the huge Methodist sanctuary on Belt Line Road near downtown Richardson. From all over the country came the people who had pieced together parts of Kendall's life. Nickie was there from San Diego with her husband, Ron, and Lindsay thought she might collapse when she saw the little girl she recognized as April marching up the aisle with her mother. Sarah's mother made a point to introduce herself to Lindsay, and later Lindsay would be pleased. But today, she could only stand frozen to one spot, nodding vaguely as if the world had ended. The men from the hangar straggled in, one by one, as if they were remnants from some distant, unnecessary battle. Lindsay made a point to speak to all of them, thanking them and touching them with her small white-gloved hand. *It would have meant so much to Kendall to have them here, she thought.*

It wasn't until Lindsay saw Marcus James that she almost lost her composure. The two men had been such close friends, and Lindsay hadn't realized until today how much their mannerisms, their movements, their words, favored each other. "Oh, Lin," he cried out to her as he pulled her to him and kissed her gently on the top of her head. He could read the devastated look on her face. Her eyes looked ravaged, and for a moment he wondered if this delicate beauty could live with all the cruelty the world had dealt her.

"Thank you for coming, Marcus." Her words were rehearsed and simple. Lindsay had already said them a hundred times or more in the past two hours. But, to him, they meant so much more. She spoke to him with her eyes, those smoky, burning pools that moved quietly as she whispered to no one except him, "You are the reason he came to me. Without you, I would not have been his wife. I owe you my thanks for that."

Wordlessly, Marcus folded her into his arms and the two of them stood together for a long time, he sobbing and she woodenly, with rigid, dry determination.

Lindsay had still not shed even one tear when she boarded the airplane to fly back to Gunnison. The sorrow she felt was buried so deeply within her now, she didn't think it could ever come up out of its searing, rotting hole. Kendall was dead. Dead. It was all so final, so ridiculous. They had shared one night together and then the world had ended. Again, desperately, Lindsay wished she had been in the Romeo Juliet with him. Her life would have been snuffed out just as quickly, just as painlessly, as his had been. Now, she had to live with it all...a lifetime of crying, of hurt, of anguish. If the tears started coming, Lindsay didn't think she would ever be able to stop them. She would mourn for her love silently, coldly, dryly. If she let her feelings bubble up too closely to the surface of her life, she would never be able to stuff them all back down inside herself again. It wasn't worth the risk.

For days, she moved around Howard's Guest Ranch in a haze of grief and determination. She attacked the daily cabin-cleaning duties with new vigor. Each cabin needed special attention now. Before the wedding, she had cleaned everything with a lick and a promise. She had known she could delve back into the work after Kendall was gone. Gone. She had planned things to do on the days after he had left her. But she had always thought he would come back. Gone. She hadn't dared to mean it in such a final sense of the word. Gone. Finished.

Two weeks after Lindsay arrived back in Gunnison, a package came in the mail for her. It was a Gunnison address and she didn't recognize it, so she ripped open the box, and the contents scattered out on the table. She sucked in a sharp breath of dismay. She had forgotten. A well-meaning friend of Dan's had brought his camera to their wedding ceremony. And now, there they lay before her, pictures of dashed dreams and devotion that should have lasted a lifetime. The photographer had captured everything. The groom and the bride exchanging wedding bands. Kendall and Lindsay exchanging the first kiss as husband and wife. It didn't seem real to her now. The bride was a stranger in a white dress.

There were other pictures, too, ones that were infinitely more painful. Pictures of Lindsay hugging Dan while Kendall looked on proudly. Lindsay snitching a mint while Kendall watched disdainfully from behind, his hands on his hips in mock disgust. There were expressions Lindsay had not noticed on their wedding day. She and her new husband should have been leafing through this packet together, giggling and pointing out funny things. She hadn't been aware he was watching her when she was snitching mints from the serving table. And now here he was with so many new expressions, new gestures, ones Lindsay hadn't even had the chance to learn to love yet.

Lindsay was overwhelmed suddenly with everything she had lost. Not only had she lost a new husband, a new love. She had lost a best friend, too. A new feeling welled up inside her, a feeling of intense sorrow for old people, people like her grandparents who had been married for sixty years. What must it be like to lose someone after living with him, loving with him, for so much of a lifetime? Every gesture, every breath, every thought of the other would be familiar. When someone left you, you wouldn't just be losing a great love. You would be peeling away a part of yourself.

For the first time in three weeks, Lindsay felt the tears welling up in her eyes and slipping velvetlike down her cheeks. She had lost so much less than an elderly spouse who had lived a lifetime but, in a way, she had lost much more. She would never have the chance to become a part of Kendall. She would never learn to love his silly gestures, his crazy antics, his bad jokes, his annoying habits. The tears were streaming down her face now, and Lindsay didn't try to stop them. Crying suddenly felt very good and very cleansing.

She stuffed the wedding pictures back into the box they had come in and hurried out into the back pasture to the old trolley car. There, she looked up at the sky and called his name once, softly, and then she covered her face with her hands and her entire body shook with her sobs.

LINDSAY SMILED GENTLY at Margie from across the kitchen table. "It's okay." She patted the older woman's hand with her own as the tears welled up into her eyes once more.

"I'm so sorry." Margie shook her head at the girl. She couldn't even remember what she had said now. Something about men. Something about Dan. Something that brought all the pain flooding back into Lindsay's face. She had to be so careful what she said these days. One twist of a sentence, one wrong word, and the torture came flooding back. The tears were slowly healing Lindsay, though. That first few weeks after the funeral had been terrifying to the people who had watched her. Her face had become the face of an old woman. The softness and the fullness there were transformed into stiff, gaunt angles. But the day that the wedding pictures came, the day Lindsay finally allowed herself to cry, had been the day her face became soft again. Now Lindsay cried at everything. Any word, any gesture, any movement that reminded her of Dallas or of her lost love would bring on a rush of tears.

But there were also the new moments of smiles. Dan, Margie and Lindsay had a wonderful laugh over the linoleum in the laundry room. Lindsay and Dan had worked all day to lay it. They had both been so proud of the job. But the next morning when Lindsay stumbled in before sunup to start the laundry, she had almost fallen over a huge hump in the middle of the floor. The linoleum must have stretched. No one could figure out exactly what had happened. But the hilarious lump now ran all the way across the room in front of all five washing machines. Lindsay had playfully dubbed it "The Continental Divide." The flooring had to be recut, remeasured and relaid, but Margie knew it was worth the work and the price of the new flooring just to see the glee on Lindsay's face once again.

There were other things Margie was concerned about, however. Lindsay's emotions were growing stronger each day but her body was growing weaker. Margie had watched her grow tired and dizzy by the end of every evening. She had seen Lindsay sit down quickly several times lately. She didn't seem to be eating well, either, and twice Margie had heard her being sick in the bathroom. This was a time when Lindsay's body needed to be well to fight off the mental demons that were still needling her soul. If Lindsay was falling ill, she might, indeed, lose her whole self.

"Here you go," Margie handed Lindsay another green floral-scented tissue from the box beside her. "Maybe I should order another carton of these next time I'm in town."

"Thanks, Margie," Lindsay's mouth wavered into a weak smile. She hadn't come across with a beaming grin yet, but she would soon. "I'm sorry I do this all the time. I just can't help it."

"It's good for you."

"Does it ever get so it doesn't hurt anymore?" Lindsay eyed her fork. She turned it carefully in her fingers as she observed it from all the angles. She had asked herself that question so many times. And she always got the same answer. No. It would never stop hurting. The pain would just remain like a dull weight on her soul until it would grow with time, until it would become more unbearable than it already was. She wanted to think about Kendall every day. She wanted to always remember how he'd looked at her. How he had touched her.

Margie smiled at her kindly. "Someday, Lin, you won't feel it anymore. He'll always be a part of you, but the hurting won't always be a part of him."

Lindsay's eyes bored into Margie's. "How do you know?"

"By the time you get to be my age, you lose a lot." The woman smiled at her tenderly. "Loss leaves a terrible void. But one day down the road, when there's no way to measure the time, you'll wake up and you'll do everything just the way you do it every morning, and you won't even realize that an edge off the pain is gone."

"Then does it just fade away?" Lindsay questioned.

"No," Margie answered truthfully. "There are days when a word, a smell, a song will bring it back with all its force. But those days grow fewer and farther between as time passes. Then one day, you won't even be aware of it the first time you do it, you will be thinking of someone with love and joy instead of sadness and despair. That's when you start to enjoy the memories."

"There is hope then." Lindsay sighed her relief as she took another sip of orange juice. "That's nice to know."

As the days wore on and the nights turned frigid, an aura of peace settled in around the old ranch. As each cabin was dusted out and boarded up for the winter, Lindsay felt a new sense of serenity. She would stay here in these mountains while everything froze and turned crisp around her. Her life in Dallas seemed so frivolous to her now. What did it matter which designer clothes she donned each morning or how scientifically she could apply her makeup? It was her face after all, and she wanted it to shine and glow because of something that had happened inside, not because of some substance she smudged across her cheeks. Here in the mountains, Lindsay knew she was keeping her priorities straight. She glanced out the window at the craggy row of purple peaks, and it dawned on her once more why she loved them so. They were still there...unchangeable...the same as they had been yesterday...the same as they had been when she first came to the park as a little girl. And she knew they had been the same when the first pioneers traveled across the Rockies and made their homes in this valley. They would look the same, with the same magnificent crevices and crests, when her descendants came to Taylor Park one hundred years from now. No matter who left her, who died, who moved away, these mountains would always be the same. Being surrounded by them made Lindsay feel strong and secure. She could not think of leaving them. Not now, anyway. They stood for too much in her life. Maybe they were a flight from reality, but Lindsay didn't think so. They were the only grasp on reality that she had.

Kendall was dead and she had come to accept the dull, grinding pain that still hung like a weight in the pit of her stomach. But all around her a new kind of life was blossoming. Winter in the high country. The ground was covered with crystal-white snow, and it was perfect weather for cross-country skiing. For several mornings now, she had ventured out on her skis, gliding silently among the ever-vigilant pines and the tender sleeping forest. Twice now, she had seen deer, a buck and a doe, feeding on the gray bark of the aspens. And once she had heard an elk bugling in the distance. The wild animals were coming closer to civilization now. It was as if the cold weather stunned the fear in the creatures. Both the hunters and the hunted gravitated toward each other in the winter. Each year, they celebrated a fraternal ceremony that observed survival. Together, man and beast would make it through one more bitter Taylor Park winter.

As each day became more brilliant, more treacherously beautiful, Lindsay longed to share her new discoveries with someone. And the more she thought about it, the more she knew who she wanted to share them with. She bundled up in her snow boots, a rose wool scarf Margie had lent her, and a fuzzy angora hat, and stomped her way through the deep snow toward the lodge and the telephone. Before Margie had a chance to ask her what she was doing, she had dialed the maintenance hangar at Dallas Love Field. The number came easily to her fingers and it didn't seem strange or unusual at all when she heard the oddly familiar voice answer on the other end. "Marcus?"

"Yes?" He was confused. There was something haunting about the way she said his name and it took a moment for him to figure out who was calling him.

"It's me."

"I know," he almost whispered. He was afraid he might shout he was so glad to hear from her.

There was a long silence on Lindsay's end of the line. "I don't really know why I called," she finally explained. "This morning was just so beautiful and I wanted to tell someone. I suddenly felt very far away."

"How are you?" His voice was louder now, more confident. "Since you called, I had better check up on you."

"I'm fine."

"I'm glad to know...you're still alive." The telephone line was crackling and hissing. It was hard to hear him.

"I am." Lindsay chuckled. "You should see it here. There is no way to describe what this place looks like after the first snow falls. The sun comes out and it looks like the entire world is covered with diamonds."

"You sound wonderful, Lindsay. Much better than you did the last time we talked."

Lindsay smiled. He hadn't heard a thing she had said about the diamonds all over the ground. He was still too worried about her. What a fatherly figure Marcus was turning out to be. He was so mindful of what he said, so careful to give her support when she needed it. For an instant, Lindsay was very sad again. The immensity of everything that had happened in the past few months rolled over her in one giant wave. "I'm doing better, Marcus. I really think I'm going to make it."

Marcus noticed the new sadness in her voice. "Are you coming home soon?" he questioned.

She answered him gently but firmly. "Marcus, this is my home."

"Oh."

"Don't worry." She smiled again and this time he could sense her expression from the tone of her voice. "This is a wonderful place. You'd love it here, too, if you ever stayed longer than two hours."

"I know Kendall loved it." Pain. Just hearing his name was like a knife stabbing her in the chest.

"It's not so bad," she whispered.

Marcus had to strain to hear her. The connection was terrible. "I'm just trying to save you from yourself, Lin," Marcus said. "I think it might be better if you came home and faced things."

"Yes, sir." She smiled for a third time. Marcus obviously thought she was turning into a hermit. "I *am* facing things. Right now I am facing the most glorious row of mountains you will ever see. You ought to stop by sometime and see them. You ought to drop by for dinner tonight," she teased. Drop by. From eight hundred miles away. The comment was in jest but she almost wished he would accept her invitation. It had been a long time since she had been party to anything wonderful and silly. It was a crazy idea, one that flustered her and delighted her all at once. "I'll even make okra gumbo for you if you come. My great-great-grandmother's recipe from across the ocean. Of course, you would have to bring the okra. They don't have any of that up here."

"A place without okra?" Marcus chuckled. "I think I'm on my way."

As Lindsay laughed on the other end of the telephone line, Marcus found his mind wandering in an insane direction. She had invited him to dinner tonight and he was going to accept. He wanted desperately to see her, to see for himself that the haunted, tormented look was disappearing from her face. It was the same sort of impulsive, spontaneous thing you read about in books or watched in the movies, and Marcus was going to do it. While Lindsay rattled on about the snow and the mountains Marcus was checking the weather report that had just come in over the wire. There was a high-pressure system lingering over the west, and the flight path from Dallas to Gunnison would be a clear one this evening.

"You sure are being quiet." Lindsay was laughing now. "I'm sorry if I interrupted your work. Maybe I had better let you go."

"No. Wait." Marcus almost shouted. "I have this idea. It's crazy but, did you mean it about the invitation to dinner tonight?"

"Only if you bring the okra," Lindsay said with a giggle. It hadn't yet dawned on her that he was actually considering the flight.

"Name the best place to eat dinner in Gunnison," he said solemnly.

"The Cattleman Inn," she answered quickly. "Why?"

"Because I want you to meet me there at five this evening. I have decided to accept your invitation. Only I'll buy the dinner. Be prepared for a steak. I think it's time someone decided to pamper you."

"Marcus James," Lindsay shrieked. "You can't come all this way just to have dinner with me. This is crazy."

"I know," he laughed. "But you invited me and I'm not going to turn an invitation from you down. Don't make suggestions to me unless you want me to take them."

"Marcus James...."

"Quit talking," he interrupted her. "I have work to do here. I have to take off in two hours."

"Oh." There was a sudden terror in Lindsay's voice. "You're flying."

"I wasn't planning on walking."

"Be careful," she said simply.

"I will be," he agreed. The words she hadn't spoken went without saying. Lindsay didn't need to lose him, too. "See you at five."

After he hung up, Marcus stared at the phone for a long while and then he grinned. What had possessed him? Why did he have to see her? Because, he reasoned, this was a wonderful new adventure for him. And because he was worried about her. And because he was suddenly very sad at the thought that she wouldn't be coming home to Dallas.

When Lindsay hung up the phone in Taylor Park, she was pleased and sad and confounded all at the same time. Marcus was acting so protective toward her. He was such a dear friend, but this quick flight to Colorado certainly surpassed any normal responsibilities he might feel he had. Lindsay thought she knew why he wanted to see her. He wanted to convince himself that she was doing okay. Marcus James was the one who asked Kendall to fly back to work the day after their wedding. It was his plane that crashed on the rugged terrain of the Colorado Eastern Slope. Marcus must be feeling very responsible for her life right now. And Lindsay didn't quite understand why, but she was suddenly very, very happy that he was feeling that way.

Three times that day, Lindsay almost picked up the telephone to call Marcus to tell him not to come. She was being selfish. He would be exhausted tomorrow. It wasn't fair for him to come all this way just to eat dinner with her, just to look in her eye to confirm that the mountains were slowly healing her. But the more Lindsay thought about it, the more she realized she wanted to see him, wanted to prove to him that she was growing strong again. So, in the end, she didn't call. Instead, she flitted around in the snow all day like a little bird and when the time came to drive to Gunnison to meet him, she warmed up the Buick Skyhawk and sped down the canyon. The hours today had seemed like years to her, and now she almost couldn't bear to wait another moment longer. And when he walked in the front door of the Cattleman Inn, she didn't know whether to laugh or cry. Just the sight of him walking across the room brought back every memory of Kendall and Dallas for her, each of them wondrous and tragic. She ran to him and hugged him and he held her for a long while before he would let her go. "You crazy, crazy man." She looked up and shook her head at him and when she saw the forlorn look in his sea-green eyes, she wanted to weep. She reached up and rumpled his sandy curls with her fingers and, when he bent to embrace her again, she knew that this moment was just as painful, just as poignant for him as it was for her.

"You're right, Lindsay," he whispered to her as the waitress led them to their table a few moments later. "I am crazy. But not too crazy to see that the mountains *are* the medicine you need. You look good."

"Thanks." She sat down and picked up the menu the waitress had left there for her. "You should stay awhile. This place has a magic all its own."

"Don't tempt me to stay," Marcus laughed. "You never know what I might take you up on."

"I know." She was giggling now. "I found that out."

Marcus watched her for a moment as she read the menu. He had thought he would always remember her with that tormented look he had seen in her eyes at the funeral. But she was so resilient, so strong, and he was amazed once again by the magnitude of her spirit. It was as if she was taking everything in her life that had been horrible and was molding it into something that was making her grow, something that was making her sturdy and vital. He was so proud of her.

He felt extremely responsible for everything she had been through, though. He considered her friendship an integral part of his life. Even before Kendall had died, he had talked to her often when she came to the hangar. Just knowing of her, of the things that were happening in her life, had almost been enough, then. He had watched her and Kendall strolling through the airplanes so many times, her hair dancing in the breeze, her laughter flitting through the air, and there were nights when he had driven home to an empty house and had sat there staring into the fire almost sick with jealousy toward his best friend.

When Kendall died, Marcus had not made any conscious decisions about Lindsay. There were some feelings deep inside of him now that he didn't have to keep as tight a grip on as he did at one time, but he still wanted to be careful. What he was feeling for her was silly, he lectured himself. But nonetheless the feelings were there. Something dramatic was growing out of the feeling of desperation that he had for an old friend and a kind of sad protectiveness he had for Lindsay. The desire to shelter her from life's hardships wasn't new. Marcus had felt that way long before Kendall had married Lindsay. It was one of the reasons Marcus had pleaded with Kendall to go to her. Marcus wasn't certain why he cared so much and he wasn't trying to interpret things just yet. Both he and Lindsay had undergone such turmoil in the last two months. All he knew was that he wanted to protect Lindsay from any more hurt. That was essential to him.

"I have a present for you." Marcus shook his head clear of his thoughts as he handed Lindsay a small white jewelry box. He had just bought it this afternoon. Marcus wasn't used to giving gifts on the spur of the moment, but this was something he had chosen in a moment of strange desperation. He knew himself. He knew how he was going to be feeling when he saw her and he had chosen this item to help himself laugh.

"Marcus James, you creep!" Lindsay winked at him as she pulled the delicate little charm from its box. It was a dainty silver okra, and as Lindsay held it up to inspect it, the first true broad grin since Kendall's death came to her face at last.

"Well—" Marcus tried to look innocent "—you told me to bring the okra."

"Your hate for this vegetable is now documented for posterity," Lindsay announced to him after leaning forward.

He had to fight back the urge to lean forward and kiss her. Instead, he turned the conversation to more practical things. ''Are you still working?''

''Not just now,'' Lindsay answered as she put the little charm back into its box. She would buy a chain for it tomorrow. ''The ranch is closed for the winter. I have a nice snug cabin near the lodge and I'm ready to start writing again. Maybe I'll do some freelance articles for travel magazines this winter.''

''I think you should work.'' Marcus leaned forward and widened his eyes, and for the fifth or sixth time today Marcus reminded Lindsay of her father. ''Something steady. Something that gives you a reason to get up in the morning.''

''These mountains are my reason to get up.'' She swept her arm across the panoramic view that was now hidden in darkness.

''I think you need more than that. I think you need a job.''

''So that's it.'' Lindsay laughed across the table at him. ''A woman's place is in the work force. Is that what you want?''

''Now, Lindsay,'' he groaned, but she didn't let him complete his sentence. She was already chattering on about something else altogether, and he suddenly didn't feel comfortable lecturing her.

''What's going on with you?'' Lindsay asked abruptly. Then her brows furrowed just a bit. ''What's happening in the airplane business?'' She was feeling particularly strong tonight or she never could have asked that question. But Marcus James was her friend and she wanted to hear about his life, too, even if his existence did revolve around the one thing that she feared and hated more than anything else in the world. She still had horrible airplane crash dreams every night. She didn't even like to look at aircraft sitting on the ground anymore. They were deadly machines. Lindsay promised herself that she would never set foot in one again.

Marcus respected her question about the airplane business. He knew how hard it still must be for her to ask. The fact that she was trying to conquer her feelings meant a lot to him. She wanted to know about him. When the sincerity of her question sunk in, Marcus James was very, very flattered. He told her a little bit about himself for the first time. He carefully avoided mentioning his work, but he did have some wonderful stories about growing up with two big sisters and how he'd tormented them by hiding all of their shoes before they left for school and telling them that a monster had eaten them for breakfast. He told her about the lime-green Mustang convertible he used to drive in high school, and how he'd pasted fake bullet holes on the front windshield, and how everyone had come to look at it, and how he had thought his car was the most wonderful vehicle on the road until the paint started coming off. It was painted pink underneath.

"I was driving around in this wonderful green car with pink polka dots." Marcus laughed and Lindsay did, too. "You know," Marcus said, chuckling, "Kendall used to think that car was the most hideous thing he had ever seen. Whenever it rained, my Mustang would catch water in the doors and Kendall would always get in the front seat, close the door and listen to it slosh, then he would say 'Marcus James, now I know how it feels to drive around in a slime-green fishbowl.'" Marcus didn't try to hide the faraway look in his eyes. "I had forgotten he used to say that."

"Marcus?" Lindsay asked. Her eyes were sad, too. "How did you meet Kendall?"

"You know," Marcus said again. "I honestly don't remember. We moved to Dallas when I was five, and I must have met him then. We lived on the same street for years. It's strange how when you look back, you can't remember all the important things, but instead you get these pictures in your head of times and days that didn't seem important then at all. We used to play softball in an open field behind his house all the time. I remember one year on Halloween when his mother blindfolded us all and made us touch all this weird stuff. She said they were eyes and then she unblindfolded us and they were just grapes."

"Just one of those indelible little things that you never forget," Lindsay commented.

"Kendall had airplane models hanging all over his room and we'd rearrange them every so often. He gave me three of his models one year for my birthday. I thought I was the luckiest kid alive."

Lindsay didn't say anything. She was learning new things about Kendall and she was learning new things about Marcus, too, and the bits and pieces of the two men's lives together were like patches on a quilt that Marcus was stitching together and laying before her.

"He used to spend the night with me when we were in junior high school. We had an old army tent that we would set up in the backyard and we'd sit up all night playing Risk and talking about airplanes."

"You guys and your airplanes." Lindsay fingered the intricate pattern on her crystal water glass.

"I know," Marcus nodded. "On Sunday afternoons, dad would drive us out to Love Field, and we'd sit and watch the planes take off and land. That's when Love Field was the main airport in Dallas...a long time ago. We used to look forward to it for days." Marcus stared off into space. "That was back in the days when airplanes were more important than women."

Lindsay's eyes widened mischievously. "I didn't know there ever was a time when airplanes had any competition from women at all."

"Maybe I shouldn't be telling you all this stuff." Marcus grinned. "In high school, we had this dance every year called Carousel. The girls always asked the guys. This girl named Julie asked Kendall to take her and he was too frightened to tell her no. So the day of the dance, he had me call Julie's mother and tell her I was his doctor and he couldn't go to the dance because he had some major disease." Marcus shook his head. "Poor Kendall. That lady saw right through the whole thing. She called his mother and made him take her daughter to Carousel. It was horrible."

"Marcus?" Lindsay asked softly. "What was Kendall like when he was with Sarah?"

"You know," he answered, "after he met Sarah, we didn't do much together. We lost touch for a while and I was really sad about it; a friendship like ours was, is such a treasure. We saw each other often at the airport when he would come in to rent a plane, but we never had time to just sit and talk." Marcus paused. "I was there the day Sarah died, though. The sky-diving team they went up with left from Love Field. I'll never forget his face that day, Lindsay, not for as long as I live. It was like stone, gray, gaunt, as if it was him who died instead of her. He just stood there in the corner of the room saying 'It should have been me...it should have been me' until I thought he had gone crazy."

"That's the way I felt, too." Lindsay sighed. "I kept wishing I had crashed with him. I kept thinking that it would have been so easy if I could have died, too. It's so hard for the people who have to go on living...." Her words faded into a silence.

Marcus took her hand. "I can't believe he's gone, Lindsay. I have these dreams. That he's still here. That it's all been such a terrible mistake, such a horrible joke. And then I wake up—" he sucked in his breath "—and realize it was all only a dream. That he's dead. Sometimes I'd give anything if I just didn't have to miss him so badly." Marcus started sobbing then, right there in the booth at the

Cattleman Inn, and Lindsay went around the table and encircled his heaving shoulders with her arms to comfort him. She knew she could have cried with him, but she didn't need to just then. She only wanted to hold Marcus and be strong for him. She was beginning to treasure her friendship with Marcus James more and more. A cloud of despair passed over her face once more. Maybe she was starting to treasure him too much. But, if Kendall could see her now, she didn't think he would mind. It just made Lindsay feel stronger to know that other people had to cry, too.

After Marcus dried his tears, the two of them spent the rest of the evening joking about okra and other assorted vegetables, and Lindsay spent a long time telling him about her hilarious antics learning to cross-country ski. Marcus was sad when he glanced at his watch and saw that it was long past time to leave her. "I have to go, Lin." He nodded at her, and for the first time in two hours she was silent.

"I know," she finally said to him. "I don't suppose I could talk you into coming up to the ranch and spending the night? You're bound to be tired."

"Thank you for the invitation," he said as he squeezed her hand and helped her up out of the booth. "I have to be at the hangar early in the morning. It's much easier for me to go now than it would be if I left later."

"I expected that response. I just hope you're not too tired to fly." Then, although she couldn't explain why, tears began to well up in her own eyes.

"Hey." He bent over and wiped two or three of them away. "What's this?"

"I don't know." Lindsay wanted to tell him she was terribly glad he had come to her. But she couldn't say the words just now. She knew she would choke on them. She hoped he already sensed how she felt. There was so much she was feeling that she couldn't share with anyone.

"Take care, Lin." His eyes searched hers for a moment and then Marcus pulled her to him for one last long hug.

"I will," she whispered into his shoulder. Then she reached up and touched his cheek. "Thank you for the dinner, Marcus. Goodbye."

He didn't say anything. He just turned away from her and started walking. If he looked at her just now, he knew that there was no way he could leave her. And he knew he had no choice but to go.

CHAPTER EIGHT

THE NEXT MORNING, Lindsay found an advertisement in the *Gunnison Country Times* that sparked her interest. She hadn't wanted to admit it to Marcus, but she agreed with him about getting a job. It would be good for her to have something to do every morning.

The paper's publisher wanted someone to edit the *Taylor Valley Review*, a weekly supplement to the *Country Times* that would circulate every Thursday in Taylor Valley.

"I don't believe this," she commented to herself in the mirror. "It's the perfect job." Lindsay always talked to herself in the mirror when she was considering something. It was as if, by examining her own reflection, she could determine her eligibility for the position. Instinctively, she started planning for the mandatory interview. Lindsay rummaged through several paper sacks in the bottom of her closet until she found a floppy, black portfolio filled with clippings of articles she had written for the *Times Herald*. Looking through them now, she gained a bit more confidence. Her work was good. She had quite an impressive display to hand this new publisher. She called the *Country Times* office and made an appointment for the first thing Monday morning.

When she walked in the front door, the publisher was already very impressed. One of his relatives from Nevada had just sent him the article she had written for *West Style* magazine. He hadn't had anyone particular in mind for the Taylor Park position, but he was expecting several of the local busybodies and maybe one of the retired school teachers to apply. He wanted someone who knew the lay of the land in Taylor Valley, someone who could write about the way of life there from firsthand experience. He hadn't realized there was a professional like Lindsay Cornell within miles of Taylor Park. To say he was overwhelmed by her application would have been an understatement. The clippings she showed him were extremely well done and the reference she had received from Rex Martin at the *Dallas*

Times Herald was equally pleasing. This woman was an impeccably trained journalist and an inspired writer. She also had good business sense, according to Rex Martin. She had rejuvenated his paper's Lifestyle section.

The publisher offered her the job on the spot. Out of all of Lindsay's credentials, he was most impressed by her enthusiasm and her obvious love for the territory she would be covering. She had long been an observer here. There were things she knew about the people and the place that would have taken months for a newcomer to learn.

When Lindsay arrived back up at the ranch, she was jubilant. She felt like a career woman again. She hadn't given up a career for the mountains. She had brought her talent with her, and now she could start piecing together a life for herself here.

Lindsay's work schedule fit her perfectly as the cold winter months rolled on. She worked all the time. Mornings. Afternoons. Nights. She kept each day full and fruitful. Each week when the newspaper was complete, she felt an almost overwhelming sense of pride and a little bit of anguish, too. These were her stories and her photographs, the darkness showing white on the huge opaqued negatives. She had accomplished it all one more time. And, in a few hours, the vicious week of reporting would begin again.

As soon as she finished delivering all two thousand five hundred copies of this edition to the post office and the newsstands in Taylor Park, there would be new phone calls to make, new interviews to conduct, new articles to write. Lindsay's life was now surging forward from deadline to deadline, and only when there was a lull in her pace did the deadlines frighten her. Living life week by week made everything seem so much easier. It didn't matter that she was tired all the time and that she was dizzy in the mornings. She didn't have time to think about Kendall. That was the important thing.

When Lindsay looked in the mirror now, she didn't see a face. She only saw two lifeless circles where her sparkling eyes once had been, hair that seemed to float around them like a cloud, and a formless nose and mouth that remained necessarily devoid of emotion. Oddly, it was easy to ignore the heavy feeling that kept tugging at her soul, at her hands, at her feet. Where once there was life, there was now only numbness.

It struck Lindsay as ironic that her periods had not come. Now, of all times, when her soul must remain fiercely strong, her body was finally giving way to stress. She had missed her cycle before and she had known it was because of the incredible things that were happening in her life then; her first senior prom, her only trip to Europe, her intense competition in the Miss Texas pageant. It seemed scary and sad to her that once her body had been affected by such wonderful emotions, and now it was responding in the same way to such a horrible loss. It almost seemed unfair, but Lindsay tried not to dwell on how unfair life seemed in general.

After Lindsay had been with the *Valley Review* for six weeks, the county was buzzing. No matter what she was feeling, the new section was good. Lindsay Cornell-Allen was a thorough investigative reporter. She was also a lovely woman. Several of the men whom she had interviewed called her and asked her to dinner, but she always had an excuse not to go. Men were something she did not have the courage to face just yet. Except for Marcus. He was more than just a man. He was a friend, too, and that made all the difference.

"Run that story three columns of page five with a double-deck headline," Lindsay instructed Chris Tee, her frantic layout artist. "I don't want to jump that feature if I don't have to. There's room for the whole thing there. I'll cut the last paragraph if I have to."

"Sure, Lin." Chris Tee's fingers were already deftly waxing the type galleys and placing them where Lindsay had pointed.

"Good. I like that." Lindsay was satisfied. She turned her attention to the old Royal typewriter in the corner. It was already almost midnight, and she still had cutlines to write. She ran her fingers through her tousled hair. A good story had broken late this afternoon, and she had totally rewritten the front page after supper tonight. It thrilled her that she would have such a timely story, but writing something on the spur of the moment always worried her. Under such circumstances, she was not able to give her work the attention and research it deserved. And this story was an important one.

Jack Jensen, one of the Gunnison County Commissioners, was suggesting that the county bring in several groups of high-density housing. Such a move was unpopular with his constituents, and Lindsay sensed that there was more to Jensen's suggestion than just "the economic growth of the county." That was the quote he had given her earlier in the evening on the telephone. Lindsay was hoping to do a thorough investigative piece on Jensen.

She never started out to find unflattering facts about anyone but she had a sixth sense about honesty that was uncanny. Something was going on behind the scenes with Jack Jensen, but she was going to have to wait to begin her investigation. Lindsay had several valuable sources at the county courthouse to whom she could turn for information about Jensen. They were all willing to talk to her during business hours, but Lindsay didn't think she should disturb them tonight. She didn't want to run the risk of alienating anyone by dragging him out of bed at this late hour. The in-depth article on Jensen would just have to wait.

Lindsay directed her thoughts back to the photographs on her desk, suddenly feeling incredibly tired. As she composed sentences on the rickety typewriter, the words on the paper began to waver and blur. She shook her head once to clear her vision, but the world was closing in on her like gray static on a television screen.

"Cory?" she called to her publisher. Lindsay stood up, then attempted to walk toward him. It was in her mind to ask him to help her, but there wasn't time. The walls turned black around her, and the corners twirled. She reached out to grab something to hold herself up with, but her fingers grasped empty air. She fell, unconscious, to the layout room floor.

LINDSAY OPENED HER EYES slowly. She could see Cory Smith's blurry figure leaning over her. Instantly, she knew what had happened. This was the third time she had fainted since Kendall died. Both of the other times had been at the cabin so no one knew how ill she had been. She had been meaning to see a doctor, but each time she considered it, she convinced herself there was nothing wrong. Her mind was doing this to her body. Kendall was dead, and she had been under lots of stress lately.

"I called a physician." Cory Smith's tone of voice was calm but he was more concerned than he let on.

"You didn't have to do that," she murmured apologetically in her soft Southern drawl.

"Somebody needs to look out after you." Cory patted her arm and then glanced at the rest of the staff.

Lindsay had never volunteered any information about her private life to her colleagues. Recently, Cory had told the staff a few things. He didn't mean to invade her privacy, but he thought Lindsay's closest co-workers ought to know. Cory had seen the pained, drawn look on her face when the artists and the photographers jabbered on about their husbands and simple, every-day domestic things. They took things like running home to fix dinner or putting in a load of laundry so much for granted, and it made Cory cringe when he realized what Lindsay must still be feeling inside. She hid her pain from everyone so well but occasionally a trace of it would surface in her writing. Her December column had been a beautiful piece that urged her readers to look at the true gifts of Christmas, the love in their lives, the hope that celebrating the birth of the Christ child should instill in everyone. There was a melancholy subtext to the piece that Cory knew was there because of how she had loved and lost; the precious gift she had been given, which had subsequently been torn away from her.

Lindsay still wore the dainty gold band on the ring finger of her left hand. She tried so hard to act brave and self-sufficient. She was one of the strongest women Cory had ever known, but he just didn't know if she was strong enough.

"Have you been feeling any different lately?" Dr. Carlton questioned Lindsay in the back room of the newspaper office.

"No, not really." Lindsay smiled at him apologetically. "Nothing's wrong. I'm just sorry they woke you up in the middle of the night. We have no decency around here, I'm afraid. In the newspaper business, you forget other people live normal lives."

"Not all normal people live normal lives, Lindsay." Dr. Carlton shook his head kindly at his new patient. "Least of all doctors. Now, suppose you think back over the past month or two and tell me of any symptoms you might have noticed."

"Well..." Lindsay thought back. "I've fainted once or twice before." She grinned at him and then her face grew pensive. "I think I'm more exhausted all the time, only it's hard to tell. I did start working an eighty-hour-a-week job six weeks ago, so that could have something to do with it. I don't know."

"You say you're tired now. Why?" the doctor asked.

"Because I love afternoons. I write better then. It's sunny and warm out despite the snow. I used to look forward to my writing spurts after lunch. But not anymore. About one-thirty every day, I get so tired that all I want to do is sleep for the rest of my life."

Dr. Carlton looked thoughtful. "Anything else you can tell me?"

"I had a touch of the flu a few weeks back. I was really sick to my stomach." She shrugged her shoulders. "Unfortunately, I don't seem to have that problem any more. Now I'm hungry for chocolate milk shakes all of the time. They give me quick energy while I am working. Unfortunately, they've also given me about ten extra pounds.'' Lindsay looked down at her waist and laughed. Then her eyes turned dark. ''Really,'' she added as if to convince herself. ''Nothing could be wrong. I've just been under a lot of stress lately. I...'' She stopped short. She had remembered something else. She supposed she should tell him about her missed periods, but she felt embarrassed about mentioning it to a relative stranger in the middle of the busy newspaper office. Maybe she should stop by Dr. Carlton's office in the morning and speak with one of his nurses, Lindsay thought.

Dr. Carlton made several notes on his pad and then turned back to Lindsay. ''I'd like to see you in my office tomorrow morning. Can you work that out?''

''I can run by at eight-thirty on the way to pick up the papers,'' Lindsay agreed. She was relieved. The decision had been made for her. Then, for the first time during the interview, a touch of concern slipped into her voice. ''Do you think something's wrong?''

''No,'' the doctor said. There was a glimmer of a smile in his eyes, and Lindsay wondered why. ''I do want to run a test or two in the lab. What I think your illness could be is not a major health problem.'' He watched Lindsay closely. He was certain she had no suspicion whatsoever. There was no need to shock her with the news until he was absolutely certain. ''It *is* something we should know about, though.'' He nodded his head. ''I'll see you in the morning. Meanwhile, finish this weekly edition quickly and get some sleep. If you start to feel faint again, sit down and rest your head between your knees. Stop pushing yourself so hard.''

''Thank you.'' Lindsay took his hand. ''I promise to obey your orders. And please tell my dear friends up front that I am not ready to kick the bucket yet.''

Dr. Carlton laughed. ''It's a deal.'' On his way out, the doctor stopped and told Cory that his employee was in excellent health.

''See.'' Lindsay smiled at her publisher as she hurried back to the lighted layout table. ''I'm perfectly fine.''

''POKE...JAB...URINE...BLOOD...up...down,'' Lindsay commented sarcastically to the nurse on her way out. ''Don't y'all ever get tired of sending people into the lab to get taken apart and then put back together again?''

''We never get tired of it,'' the nurse said, laughing. ''It's fun to see what they look like when they come out of there.'' She grinned at Lindsay. "Can you stop in at two for these results? Dr. Carlton will need to discuss them with you."

Lindsay frowned. This was typical doctor's office treatment. "He needs to see me three times in two days? This is getting weird. I can't be here at two. Is four-thirty too late? That's the best I can do today."

"That's fine." The nurse made a notation in her books. "See you this afternoon, Mrs. Allen."

Lindsay smiled to herself. She loved being called Mrs. Allen. Kendall's Mrs. Allen. Her byline was Lindsay Cornell-Allen, a name that symbolized the meshing of her new life with her old one.

Lindsay's day was hectic and she was huffing and puffing when she arrived at Dr. Carlton's office fifteen minutes late for her appointment. She had been running from newsstand to newsstand trying to get everything finished in time, but it had been impossible. She should have called and changed the appointment to another day, but Lindsay told herself it was going to be such a relief to hear everything was okay that she didn't want to put it off.

A different nurse came scurrying in from the back file room this time. "Please sit down, Mrs. Allen. Dr. Carlton will be with you shortly."

Shortly, Lindsay repeated wryly to herself. She had heard that term in doctor's offices before.

In truth, Tad Carlton was already in his office waiting for her. He was deciding exactly what it was that he should say to her. Considering everything Lindsay Cornell-Allen had already been through, this new piece of news was going to come as quite a shock.

When the nurse announced her arrival, he quickly made his final decisions and called Lindsay in. He watched her gravely as she entered the room.

"Yes, sir?" She smiled.

"Have a seat, Lindsay." He stood up and pulled a chair forward for her. Once again, she became concerned. She sat down gracefully in the brown leather chair that was now facing his desk.

"I have some information that is going to come as quite a shock to you," the doctor informed her. "Frankly, I don't know how it's going to hit you."

"Yes?"

"This could be good and it could be bad."

"I can handle it," Lindsay said, laughing nervously.

There was a poignant silence before he spoke.

"You're pregnant, Lindsay."

"I'm *what*?"

"You are going to have a baby, young lady."

"But that's impossible!" Lindsay gasped.

"Is it?"

"Yes, it is. I haven't...well...." She hesitated.

"Weren't you married briefly?"

"Yes, but...." Lindsay shook her head. "I was married for one day. My husband died in an airplane crash the day after our wedding."

"You did have one night together?" Dr. Carlton asked pointedly.

Lindsay felt like screaming. None of this made any sense. "Dr. Carlton," she said slowly, "my husband died four months ago."

"You are four months pregnant, Lindsay."

The reality of his statement started to sink in. "I don't know how...I just didn't know...I just never thought...Dr. Carlton, if I'm four months pregnant then I'm almost halfway through. Why didn't I know sooner?"

"Because you didn't ask." The physician was chuckling now. The hard part was over, and he liked what he was seeing in her eyes. "Because you were so busy hiding from all of your feelings. You were working so hard, you never had time to sit down and put two and two together. All the symptoms you described to me last night are things women know and watch for. You dismissed them as fatigue, the flu, about ten pounds of chocolate milk shakes and an extra dose of stress."

"Oh, no!" Lindsay's hand flew to her mouth in astonishment. Tears were streaming down her cheeks, and she was laughing at the same time. "You figured this out last night, didn't you?"

The doctor nodded. "I suspected as much."

"Oh, I love you." Lindsay impulsively jumped from her chair and hugged Tad Carlton. "You've given me the most wonderful news I could ever ask for."

"Good." The doctor was pleased. He gave her the name of an excellent obstetrician in Gunnison and instructed her to make an appointment with him soon.

"Yes, sir!" Lindsay saluted the doctor playfully. "I promise. Nothing but the best for this kid."

On the way out of the office, Lindsay hugged the nurse, greeted one woman she had interviewed for a newspaper article three weeks before, and knocked over a vase of fresh flowers in the waiting room. She was oblivious to it all. Everything inside her was overflowing. There was a baby growing inside of her. A baby that was part her and part Kendall. A part of the man she loved so much was still alive and growing within her. Lindsay had talked about miracles and magic many times during her life, but, for the first time, she truly comprehended what the word "miracle" meant. She was a woman. Everything inside of her was working just the way God had planned it to. And because of that, the man she loved had left her with the most precious gift he could ever have given her.

Lindsay felt different. There was another person growing inside of her. She could feel her child with her soul. She didn't even need to see the baby or hold him. She already knew what was in her child's heart. The feeling of love that was almost overwhelming her now told Lindsay everything she needed to know.

When she got home to her snug little cabin in the high country, she called everyone in Dallas that she knew. It felt so good to shriek and squeal with Rita again. Angela Allen was as shocked to learn she was going to be a grandmother as Lindsay had been to learn she was going to be a mother. Kendall's mother was jubilant once the truth sunk in. Lindsay made a point of inviting her up to visit once the baby was born.

Lindsay's mother was pleased but reserved at the news. "Can't you come home for a while so we can see you?" she asked.

"I can't." Lindsay's heart fell. She couldn't face Dallas yet. For several reasons. Despite the teeny little miracle that had entered her life that day. "I love you, mom."

"Why don't you just move home?" Lindsay's mother persisted. "You can live here at the house until the baby is born. And after that, you can get your old job back at the *Times Herald*."

"No, mom...."

"Besides," Lindsay's mother continued jokingly, "you want the baby born in Texas, don't you? We don't know if we can accept a grandchild that isn't a native Texan."

She meant the comment teasingly, but the immensity and the irony of the situation struck Lindsay full force. She was having a child in Colorado. She was alone. The only man she would ever love was gone. Dead. Never to return.

"No, mother...." Tears started streaming down Lindsay's face.

This baby would be the first in five generations to be born outside the state of Texas. If Kendall was alive, she would be home with him in Dallas now. Lindsay hoped her attempted laughter sounded genuine from eight hundred miles away. "I'm going to have a little rug rat that's going to run all over these mountains."

This was her life. She wanted to live in Taylor Park. She wanted her child to run free and play in the luscious, fragrant air of the high country. She wanted to see his rosy cheeks and bright eyes.

Marcus James was the last person on Lindsay's list to call. She wanted him to hear this news firsthand. When the telephone rang and Marcus heard Lindsay's voice, he almost jumped. It was just like "The Twilight Zone." He was holding the piece of paper with her telephone number on it in his left hand. He had tried to call her five minutes before, and her line was busy. He was just about to try again.

Something new was in her voice. Or maybe it wasn't new at all. Maybe it had just been so long since he had heard that much happiness in her voice, he had forgotten she could sound that way. When Lindsay told Marcus she was going to be a mother, he had to sit down. He was thrilled for her. She deserved this and much more. "Lindsay," he chuckled. "Kendall Allen always did know how to do things right."

"I noticed that," she laughed. She noticed something else, too. When Marcus mentioned Kendall's name, she didn't flinch. She hadn't felt that familiar stab of searing pain.

It was happening. She was healing, just the way Margie had said she would. Lindsay didn't know what she had done to deserve this, but God had seen fit to bless her with a cleansing gift. Because of this new life that was growing in her womb, it was happening even faster than she could have expected. Somewhere inside of her, an open, festering wound was slowly starting to close.

CHAPTER NINE

THE BABY WAS DUE ON JUNE 15. And on May 15, spring was just beginning to show itself in the high country. Taylor Reservoir was still frozen solid, but the last sticky, wet snowstorm of the season had spent itself almost three days earlier. Everywhere Lindsay went, she could hear the sound of the impending springtime. Everywhere there was dripping, gurgling, trickling, and Lindsay could feel the familiar renewal welling up in her soul just the way it did every year when the weather turned warm.

She laughed at herself all the time now. She had grown plump in all the special places mothers grow plump, and she figured that if anyone had watched her riding her snowmobile around the park during the last few months, they probably would have shot her. She looked like a space invader with one head, two arms, two legs, a roaring engine on skis and three stomachs. She knew she looked ridiculous delivering newspapers. That part of her work was getting a bit cumbersome. In March she had hired a young boy to make the rounds with her—to haul the heavy stacks of papers, to open the newsstands and to collect the quarters. She planned to quit work two weeks before the baby was due. She longed for time to make the baby's room ready. Last weekend, she had painted one wall of it a light sky blue. This weekend, she was hoping to add a cluster of wispy clouds. But she didn't know if she would find the time. She was still wrapped up in her work at the *Valley Review*. She had done several in-depth interviews with County Commissioner Jack Jensen about his high-density housing project and she still felt like she had only scratched the surface. Jensen was hiding something and she knew it.

During the past five months, Jack Jensen had argued and scrapped with the other county commissioners about bringing in the high-density condominium project. He had lost support over it, and Lindsay was certain he would lose more. It was doubtful Jensen would ever get reelected in Gunnison County. He had put his political career on the line for the project, and Lindsay knew there were hard-hitting motives behind his support.

Every day now, she was receiving letters thanking her for her research into the plan. She had written three columns about it and she was elated with the support she was drawing from the community. Her circulation figures were steadily rising, and Lindsay almost couldn't bear to think of quitting her job. The first of June came and went, and Lindsay still wasn't ready to quit writing. She decided to attend one last commissioner's meeting before she took her leave of absence. At that meeting, the development was approved by a two-to-one vote, and the opposing commissioner stomped out of the room infuriated. While the opposition was gone, Jensen moved the project be awarded to the Dexter Contracting Company, which operated out of Denver. Even though Lindsay was not pleased with the outcome, she was entranced with the drama. The story was definitely front page material.

Later that afternoon, Lindsay had a brainstorm. The article she was writing was the last Jensen piece she would run before her leave of absence and she wanted it to be a good one. A feature on the contracting company that would be building the project would be terrific. What style of building would they be bringing to the Western Slope? Would they do research to ensure that the buildings were aesthetically pleasing? And, most important, why had this company been selected so quickly? It was common county procedure to accept bids for a development of this magnitude.

Lindsay's first telephone call was to one of the secretaries at the county building. This woman answered directly to Jensen and she, too, was concerned about the county's welfare. The secretary proved to be an invaluable source. She knew she could trust Lindsay not to do anything unfair. And she knew Lindsay would never reveal where she got her information. She gave Lindsay the name of the man whom Jensen had been dealing with at Dexter, a Mr. Aaron Rogers, and a telephone number.

When Lindsay reached Rogers, she was taken aback by his attitude. After she told him she was with the Gunnison newspaper, he almost hung up on her. The warning bells in Lindsay's head tolled. Something was going on at the contracting company she wasn't supposed to find out about.

"Look, Rogers," she said, keeping a cool head. "I can always print the small but very damning fact that you refused to comment on any of this. My readers won't like that very much, you know."

"Ask me your questions then," his voice spit at her over the telephone line. Lindsay chuckled to herself. People were always so hateful when they suspected someone was on their tails. This was one interview she was glad she didn't have to do in person.

She was so nice to Rogers it was sickening, Lindsay thought later. She asked him all the easy questions first, questions about company history, employees, how many projects of this calibre the company had been contractors for before. She was particularly careful when she asked about the bidding process. How many projects like this did they bid on each year? Had they been asked to submit a bid on the Gunnison project?

As Lindsay's questions became more specific, Rogers became more vague. The last question she got in was: "Why was your company picked for this project when you weren't asked to submit a bid for it?"

"Honey," Rogers replied in a tone condescending enough to grate against Lindsay's nerves, "I'm sure you realize I am a busy man. I suggest you speak to someone in Gunnison about this. I have more to do today than talk to you."

He hung up on her. Lindsay shook her head in disgust. Talk about dry runs. There had to be another angle. She dialed the Dexter number again.

This time Lindsay asked to speak to someone in the landscaping department. She wanted to find out what sort of vegetation was planned for the new development. The receptionist quickly put Lindsay through.

"Landscaping," a friendly man's voice answered and Lindsay's spirits lifted. She began the quick introduction that had become such a habit during telephone interviews. "Hello, this is Lindsay Cornell-Allen with the *Taylor Valley Review*..."

"I know," the man answered candidly. "Jensen told you to call. I'd switch you over to his office but it wouldn't do any good. He isn't expected back for three days."

"Pardon me?" Lindsay was confused. "What did you say?"

"Jensen isn't in his office. He is still in Gunnison on business."

"Jensen has an office there?" Lindsay took notes furiously.

"Yes, he does." The man was apparently unaware that he was giving out forbidden information. He didn't usually answer the phones, but the secretaries in his building had taken a long lunch together and he would rather answer telephones than listen to shrill ringing during his break. He was a horticulture expert and he spent most of his time out in the field. He had been working on a project in Arvada the morning that Jack Jensen had called the emergency meeting and had instructed all the Dexter people with public contact not to give any information out over the telephones.

"Do you know Jensen?" Lindsay asked as the pieces of the puzzle began to fit together in her head.

"Know Jensen?" The man chuckled. "Sure I know Jensen. He signs my paycheck every week. He's my boss."

After a few more well-targeted questions, Lindsay slammed down the telephone gleefully. One quick call to the Colorado Secretary of State at the capitol building in Denver verified everything. Jack Jensen was listed as president of the Dexter Corporation's board of directors. He owned controlling interest in the corporation as well.

The company was introducing a line of high-density and, Lindsay suspected, high-profit-margin, condominium developments. If one community accepted the project, it would mean millions to the company's major stockholders. Jensen did not have Gunnison's best interest in mind. He had a horrible conflict of interest on his hands.

Lindsay knew she must reveal what she'd uncovered to her readers. She had proved every fact beyond a shadow of a doubt. She pounded the typewriter keys well into the night. Writing stories like this one was the hardest part of Lindsay's journalism career in the mountains. At the *Dallas Times Herald*, she had her friends, her family and her sources. Her professional life was cut and dried. The three groups never had a reason to become intertwined. But in Taylor Park, her friends, her business colleagues and her sources were all part of one group. When she wrote a damning story about someone, chances were that the someone would be a friend or a source. And, when that was the case, it was painful for everyone. During an interview or at the typewriter, Lindsay tried to be proud of the thick skin she was sprouting. But at home sitting at her kitchen table looking out at the row of snowy Collegiate Peaks, she realized she wasn't entirely proud of what she was doing in the line of duty. The mountains, Mount Harvard, Mount Yale, Mount Stanford, were all becoming special friends to her. They were incapable of betrayal. They stood there, straight, unbendable, majestic, when the sun came up every morning.

Lindsay wanted to be like them. She wanted to find that strength, that majesty, that fairness within herself.

Lindsay kept reminding herself of those qualities as she dialed Jack Jensen's telephone number at 9:30 that next morning. She felt an obligation to Jack Jensen. He had been a decent source of information and a friendly acquaintance ever since Lindsay had started working at the *Valley Review*. Several times when she had launched the supplement, when Lindsay was unfamiliar with strings of events or county policies that related to a story she needed to write, Jack Jensen had met her at the Redman Café and had filled her in on necessary facts over a steaming cup of hot chocolate. She knew he would explode when she told him she was running an article about his alleged underhanded business dealings, but she wanted to be fair to him. She wanted him to be prepared when the article hit the newsstands tomorrow.

When she called him, the county commissioner agreed to come to her office immediately. There was something that resembled trepidation in his voice, and Lindsay guessed that he already knew what it was she wanted to tell him. While Jensen was on his way, Lindsay reviewed the story with Cory Smith, and her publisher was pleased. Then she fed the edited copy to the typesetter and Xeroxed the story for Jensen. She would not make any changes for him. And if the article was already typeset and pasted down, it would be easier for him to accept. If he wanted to add comments, Lindsay could quote him and add an extra paragraph to the story after he left.

As it was, Jensen didn't want to add anything. Nothing he could say would change the facts.

"Jack?" she questioned, as she watched the blood drain from his face. He had only had time to read the first paragraph and he already knew the game was up. From the look on his face, Lindsay could tell she was right on target with her story.

Jensen did not answer her. He just held up his hand for silence. He wanted to concentrate on her every sentence, her every word, to see if he could catch her at anything. It would be nice if he could find something he could deny. That was unlikely, though. He had absolutely no idea where she had gotten her information, but her facts were impeccable, right down to the monetary figures and the profit margin.

"Any comment?" Lindsay questioned as he flipped over the last page and stared off into space.

"I suppose I could deny it all," the commissioner commented bitterly.

"You could," Lindsay said, nodding. "But do you want to?"

"No," he stated. "I don't."

"This is going to hurt your political career, Jack." She smiled up at him sadly.

"Hurt it?" he said matter-of-factly. "It's going to destroy it."

Lindsay grimaced. The tension of the interview was beginning to wear on her. Her stomach was tied in knots. She almost doubled over with the sudden pain. "I'm sorry. I'd feel better if you'd stomp around the office or rant and rave at me or something."

Jensen watched her carefully. He had seen her face go gray at his words and he was almost surprised. He thought she had more stamina than that. "I'm not going to rant and rave. I don't want you to feel better." His tone of voice became gentle. "When is this story going to break?"

"It hits the stands at ten tomorrow morning."

"I'll fly to Denver tonight," he said. "I want to be at Dexter when it comes out. I hope I can hold things together over there. I don't suppose you would tell me where you got your information?" he questioned.

"I can't and I won't," she answered.

"I suspected that," he said. "How can you prove it's all true?"

"The Colorado Secretary of State at the capitol will verify everything," she stated.

"You don't leave any stones unturned, do you?"

"No, I don't." Lindsay turned away from him. Her stomach was twisting and churning again. She felt as if she should lie down.

After the commissioner left, Lindsay crept out the back door into the bright spring sunshine. She felt better now. She was free. Her conversation with Jack Jensen had lifted an enormous weight off her shoulders. She knew the commissioner had not been pleased, but she knew she had earned his respect. As Lindsay walked down the alley behind the newspaper office, she slowly became afraid. Her back suddenly hurt so badly that she could barely stand. What if something was wrong with the baby? That thought absolutely terrified Lindsay. This miracle that had happened inside of her was Kendall's last chance at life. She almost wished she never had to deliver this baby into the world. The baby had grown to be so much a part of her that she wanted to keep it there inside of her, so close to her heart, so far from harm, forever. It was as if by bringing the child out into the world, by letting it breathe the air and see the sunshine, she was letting it go. It was as if she was jealous of the entire world. Only she wasn't jealous of the mountains. She wanted her child to see the mountains. And the sky. A shadow passed over Lindsay's eyes. She wondered if the baby would love the sky, would love to fly, the way Kendall had. It was a thought Lindsay had shied away from, and now she realized with an almost aching intensity that she hoped her new baby would love the sky as much as her dearest love had. She wanted the baby to be that much a part of him.

The baby. As she walked along the sidewalk among the Colorado tourists, something started to dawn on her. It was early for the baby to come, but not too early. As she wondered, she felt a pain that was longer and more intense than the last. Why did so much have to happen in one day? It was an absurd thought but an honest one, and before Lindsay realized consciously what she was doing, she had turned north and was walking toward Gunnison Memorial Hospital.

Dr. Carlton was on call and he examined her quickly. He winked at her once and then confirmed her suspicions. She was in labor. "Stay at the hospital," he told her kindly. "I want you to walk just a bit longer. Maybe ten minutes. Then meet me back here, okay?" He spoke to her now as he would speak to a very young child, and she shook her head feebly at him. She donned a thick, blue terry cloth robe over the examining gown she wore, let herself out of Dr. Carlton's office and strode quietly to the end of the hallway.

Lindsay spotted a pay telephone on the wall near the upstairs lobby, and she was instantly thankful. With everything that had been going on inside of her body, she had totally forgotten the day and her work and the deadlines. She had left the newspaper office with a flippant comment about getting fresh air, and she had never returned. It had been almost two hours. Lindsay put a coin in the telephone and dialed the *Country Times* number. Cory answered, and as it struck Lindsay later, it was the most hilarious phone call she had ever made in her life. "Cory?" She gulped as he answered the phone. She felt another contraction coming on. She had tried to time this phone call between pains but it hadn't worked.

"Lindsay?"

"It's me," she gasped. "Hang on for a minute."

"Sure."

She doubled over with the pain.

"Lindsay? Lindsay?" She heard him calling frantically from the receiver as it dangled from the wall.

"It's okay," she gasped into the mouthpiece. "I'm here."

"Where are you? What's happening? No. Wait." Cory interrupted himself. "I don't even want to know. Just come back here and get your car and take the rest of the day off. You've done enough work for five people these past two days."

"It's too late for that, sir." Lindsay giggled weakly. "I'm already at the hospital. I just called to see if I could have an hour or two off this afternoon. I think I've decided to have a baby."

Cory sat down in his chair. "You're having the kid *now*?"

Several of the women in the layout room squealed when they heard Cory's comment. In a matter of hours, the news would be all over town.

"Should we hold the Jack Jensen story and run a baby story on page one instead?" Cory teased.

"No!" Lindsay shrieked. "I want the Jensen story published yesterday. Leave me and my kid alone. You confounded newspaper reporters. You can't wait to stick your noses into other people's business, can you?"

Cory was chuckling heartily when he hung up the telephone. And Lindsay was standing in the hospital corridor pondering the ease with which she had spoken of her and her "kid." Everything that was happening was so good and so true and so natural. She was going to be a mom. A normal, everyday, laundry-washing, dish-cleaning, breast-feeding mom. To Lindsay, it seemed like the most glorious, glamorous thing she could ever wish to be.

Lindsay made three more quick calls, one to her mother, one to Angela Allen and one to Marcus James. Both of the women were so excited they could hardly talk. Lindsay doubled over in pain while she was talking to Angela and she had to cut the conversation short. "Call my mother," Lindsay whispered, and Angela could barely hear her from eight hundred miles away. "She'll tell you everything."

Lindsay didn't know exactly why she had to call Marcus. She knew that he would find out about the baby from Angela. But Marcus had been Kendall's best friend, and he suddenly seemed like the missing link between everything Lindsay used to be and everything that she was now. Some primary, desperate need tugged at her heart. She just wanted Marcus to know that Kendall's child, her new grasp on happiness, was coming into the world today.

CHAPTER TEN

MARCUS WAS JUBILANT as he walked through the front doors of Gunnison Memorial Hospital. The flight across the Rocky Mountains had been tremendous. And now he was here, only minutes away from her. Lindsay. Kendall's love. His friend. His.... He couldn't bring himself to complete the sentence. He didn't know what she was to him. He just knew that he wanted to be here for her...and for Kendall, he reminded himself.

Anyone watching Marcus right then would have thought he had a perfectly acceptable reason for being at the hospital. He looked like a nervous, proud father, himself. He felt like he had cheated fate and faith and half the grandmothers in Texas by sneaking out of Dallas the way he did. It wasn't his fault that the next available commercial flight didn't leave Dallas-Fort Worth International until 6:45 the next morning. He supposed he should have invited Angela and Mrs. Cornell to fly out with him, but he hadn't wanted to.

Marcus didn't know why he felt such a strong pull to be alone with Lindsay now. During their frequent telephone conversations and their one dinner together, Lindsay had often seemed like two people, melancholy one moment and mischievous the next. When she found out she was carrying Kendall's child, her voice had grown softer and the words she'd spoken had held more strength, more stability. Marcus was certain that the things he'd sensed from far away would be much more apparent when he saw her. What Marcus didn't realize was that he knew and understood Lindsay now more than anyone else ever had before. And that included his best friend Kendall Allen. Kendall had been desperately in love with Lindsay, but he had never seen her ripped to shreds the way Marcus had. Kendall's time with her had been a precious gem, one that had often glossed over reality with its shining facets. Kendall had never seen Lindsay when she was angry, or when she was hurting, or when she looked disheveled. Marcus was the one who really knew her now, and he was only oyous and thankful that he had been able to step in and become her friend.

When he asked for Lindsay's room number, the nurse didn't hesitate to give it to him. He was so intensely good-looking, so breathless, and his eyes were dancing so, she just assumed he belonged in the maternity ward with the rest of the expectant fathers.

Lindsay was too engulfed in her latest contraction to hear the door open. She had promised herself for the past five months that she wouldn't scream when she had this baby. She had planned, time after time again, to lay there in pink lace, her hair neatly brushed back and tied with a pink satin ribbon. She had expected to smile most of the time, maybe give way to a few motherly groans, and to be rosy-cheeked and radiant the first time her child turned its eyes to her.

But she realized now that such things were what fairy tales were made of. No wonder they called it labor. This was hard work. The yarn around her hair had come untied twice and the second time it happened, she had no more strength left to reach back and tie it again. Her hair lay in a tangled mess now, most of it mingled with sweat and clinging to her cheeks and her forehead.

Another woman who had shared Lindsay's room had already been wheeled into delivery. The nurses were preparing to bring someone else in. Lindsay didn't know there were this many pregnant women within miles of Gunnison. The woman who had just gone into delivery had had her husband with her the entire time. Lindsay had chuckled inwardly when the proud father-to-be had taken pictures of his wife in early stages of labor. But Lindsay's feelings had turned morose when the doting man never left his wife's side. He kept a cool cloth across her forehead and he mopped the sweat from her shoulders, and Lindsay realized then that the beautiful fantasy of lying in pink lace and moaning softly wasn't worth anything if there wasn't anyone there to see the show.

She missed Kendall more now than she had since right after his plane went down. Lying there, aching, she would gladly have given her left arm even to have him with her for just a few minutes. All she wanted was to kiss his nose and feel his arms around her, and she was certain some of the pain would go away.

As it was, the contractions were unbearable. The dull thud in her back had grown to sharp, cutting proportions. She felt like her back was slowly being pushed and twisted until her backbone was splintering apart. Dr. Carlton had quietly explained to her that she was

having back labor. He was a bit concerned, but there was no reaso
to be worried yet. The intensity and the position of the pain seeme
to indicate that the baby was in an unusual position. The birth shoul
still be relatively normal, Lindsay was told, but the pain might b
worse than either she or Dr. Carlton had anticipated.

"Good one, doctor," Lindsay had chirped weakly from the bed a
he had explained the situation. "Most people worry about babies tha
come out upside down or rightside up. And I have to worry abou
mine coming out backward altogether. Think I should take this as
bad omen?"

"Definitely not," Dr. Carlton had replied gently. But Lindsa
didn't see him look around worriedly a few moments later. He coul
tell already that this was going to be a long ordeal. He wished des
perately that she had someone here with her. But he didn't want t
frighten her by asking if anyone was coming.

When Lindsay had promised not to scream, she hadn't known wha
she was promising. She opened her mouth and let one escape. Long
Loud. Agonizing. It sounded hideous but it served its purpose. Sh
was letting off steam. Letting off pressure. She almost enjoye
screaming and then laughing at herself in the same breath. It kep
some sort of semblance of sanity in her mind.

It was during one of these long screaming and laughing period
that Marcus James crept into Lindsay's room. When he saw her ther
writhing and screaming, he thought she was dying, and tears welle
up in his eyes. But when he heard her begin to laugh, he realize
she was playing a game with herself, and tears started streamin
down his face in earnest. "Lindsay?" he whispered to her. At firs
she didn't hear him. "Lin?" he called to her louder.

When she recognized his voice and saw him coming toward he
Lindsay thought she was dreaming. She feebly reached her arm ou
to him, and he took her hand. Even her hand was swollen and sweaty
"Marc?" she whispered.

She had never called him Marc before and he didn't know whethe
the abbreviation had grown from their friendship or whether she ha
said it because she didn't have the strength to say his entire nam
Whatever it was, he liked it. "I'm here," he said softly. Lookin
down at her he fought back the urge to take her in his arms as he
face contorted with pain.

"I am so glad." Her eyes were sparkling and she smiled. Sh
didn't ask Marcus why he had come, and he was relieved. She ju

accepted his presence. His arrival was a special gift and she wasn't going to question it.

Looking into her eyes, he was suddenly flustered. All they had really ever talked about was Kendall and okra, and neither one of those subjects seemed terribly important just now. "I'm here to help you," he told her as his soul dove into the deep pools of her eyes. "I thought I could run in here and take care of you but I have to admit—" he stumbled over his words as he glanced helplessly around the room "—I don't know where to start."

"Oh, Marcus," Lindsay said with a sigh. "Thank you. You're helping me so much just by being here. I can't believe you are really in this room."

"Marcus James from Dallas, Texas, at your service, ma'am," he said, grinning at her. "And there must be something I can do besides just stand here."

A nurse entered in time to hear the second half of Marcus's speech. "Of course there is something you can do," the nurse interjected. She smiled to herself. She had seen this scene so many times before. The beautiful, young wife trying to be brave. The frightened, flustered husband longing to do anything, everything he could do to make the birth easier. The nurse handed Marcus a soft cloth and an ice bucket full of cool water. "Just keep her face and her shoulders cool with this," she instructed. "Hold her hand and let her cling to your arm when she needs to. And talk to her and smile at her all the time. That's the best advice I can give you."

Lindsay felt like a little girl as Marcus dampened the cloth and then pressed it against her forehead. Even though her entire body was still engulfed with contractions, she cuddled down under the blankets and a peaceful look settled in on her face. With Marcus James at her side, she felt like she belonged to someone again. Not that it was usually all that important to belong to someone. But this experience was different. As she smiled up at Marc, it occurred to her that she had never really looked at him before. His sandy-blond curls were tousled lazily upon his head and his green-gray eyes twinkled as they watched her. He was trying to act so fatherly. He was being so gentle, and when the corners of his mouth turned up in a smile to her, it looked almost as if he was holding something back from her.

Lindsay had noticed his friendly grin many times when she had visited Kendall at Love Field. His smile was wide and dramatic, and when it stretched to its widest expanse, there was the slightest hint of a dimple in each corner. Marcus's jaw was a finely chiseled square that eased itself into a jutting, jovial chin. His strong features made him look fearless, but the tiny dimples beneath each cheek made him look boyish and vulnerable at the same time.

As he mopped her forehead with the cloth, Lindsay fought back the urge to reach up and touch his cheek. It would be wrong to indulge the impulse, she lectured herself. She couldn't just reach up and touch this man she didn't really know. But his presence was so soothing to her. As she looked up at him, his face suddenly went hazy and she saw the face of an angel there. She closed her eyes to block out the vision, and when she opened them, she saw Kendall bending over her. She could resist the urge no longer. As she tenderly brushed her fingers across his cheek, the angel's face became Marc's again, and Lindsay started to cry.

"It's okay." Marcus stroked her hair and then dabbed the tears from her cheeks with his cloth. "Cry. I know this is hard. You are a strong, beautiful, special woman, and you deserve a good cry."

"Thanks." She sniffed and squeezed his hand. Somewhere deep in her mind, she remembered that if Kendall had been here this scene would have been played much differently. She would be at Parkland Hospital in Dallas surrounded by her family and all the doctors and comforts and devotion that money could buy. And as she thought about it, this quiet, simple birthing in the high-country hospital with Marcus James at her side took on a newer, more poignant meaning. She had pulled it off. She had changed her life. She had the things that really mattered to her now. They were simple things but they were real things. Things like the man bending over her now and the dilapidated calendar with the color sketches of Gunnison that was hanging on the wall, and the mountain sunset she could see coming on in a rainbow of colors outside her hospital room window.

For the first time in the last dozen hours, Lindsay became extremely aware of how she looked. She reached for her hair brush on the nightstand beside her bed. Marcus saw what she was reaching for, and he grabbed it first.

"Let me." He grinned at her as he helped her prop herself up higher on her pillows. He was trying not to laugh at the way she had to move. She looked like a plump, roly-poly turtle who had flipped over onto his shell.

"What are you grinning about?" she asked him.

He couldn't help but tell her. "The graceful way you move these days."

"Thanks." She stuck her tongue out at him weakly as he awkwardly untied the knot of yarn still tangled in the back of her hair.

"How do I do this?" He looked at her sheepishly. "I don't want to pull it out or anything."

"You won't," she laughed. "Just do it like you do your own hair."

"Yes, ma'am," he said, saluting her. As he stroked her hair, it began to shine and to circle her face like a gilded frame, and Marcus's heart was suddenly so full of her he thought it might burst open.

He stayed with Lindsay for most of the night. They talked about simple things like sunsets and colors and stars and mountains. She told him about the children that had vacationed at the ranch over the summer and what it felt like catching her first rainbow trout and how people laughed at her here when she said "y'all" or "I'm fixing to..." in her soft North Texas blacklands drawl.

Marcus told Lindsay how much he loved Dallas and how he snuck into the Dallas Cowboys' training camp when he was in junior high school. The guards had thrown him out, but not before he had finagled autographs from the quarterback and several other important team members. He told her how he'd felt when he was working on an airplane and how much he had wanted to fly when he was a little boy and Lindsay listened, her eyes bright with fascination and tears. She had heard this story in so many variations before, but never told with quite as much conviction and care.

As the hours wore on, Lindsay's contractions did not get closer together. Instead, they doubled and tripled in intensity. They came at her like a gigantic, blinding force, and as morning neared, she forgot trying to be composed for Marcus. She clung to his arm just as the nurse said she would, and there were times when she squeezed so hard he thought she was going to pull his arm off. He laughed at himself for even thinking such things. She was looking so brave and so beautiful right now, he gladly would have cut off his right arm and handed it to her on a silver platter.

It was almost dawn when the nurse gave Lindsay another thorough examination and decided it was time to wheel her into the delivery room.

"Thank you," Lindsay whispered up to Marcus as he turned to leave her bedside.

Marcus looked sadly at her as the group of nurses circled her bed and lifted her onto the gurney. For so long during the night, Lindsay had been the one who had desperately needed company. But now she was surrounded by nurses and interns. She would have the best professional care for the rest of this ordeal. Marcus realized that he was the one who was going to feel exhausted and terribly alone. He had felt so complete with her during the past few hours and now he wanted to scream at them that they couldn't take her away from him. He wished he could turn to Kendall Allen and quietly sob into his best friend's shoulder. He only knew that he was tired and frightened, and he felt like they were going to be ripping a part of himself away when they took Lindsay out of that room.

As they started to wheel Lindsay past him, Marcus called out to her. "Wait," he cried. And then he said the only thing that he had been able to think of all day and all night long. "Lindsay," he cried to her. "I love you."

Her eyes met his, and they widened as the full impact of his words hit her and sank in. She opened her mouth to say something and then she shut it again. Then she looked away from him as the group of interns wheeled her out of the room.

"MARCUS JAMES? What on earth are you doing here?" Angela Allen ran at him from across the waiting room and threw her arms around his shoulders.

Marcus almost jumped out of his skin. He had been asleep. He had been dreaming horrible things about Lindsay crying and a baby falling as airplane engines roared in the background. He looked sheepishly at the two women who had just entered the hospital lounge. "Did your plane just get in?" he questioned. He wanted to change the subject. He wasn't exactly certain what he was doing here, and he certainly didn't want to try to explain it to these two women.

"Yes." Angela eyed him suspiciously. "It was the first plane out since Lindsay called. I'd just like to know how and why—" she paused to light a cigarette "—you got here before we did." She watched Marcus closely as she took a puff. Then she started laughing. "Never mind," she commented with a sideways glance at the woman with her. "Don't answer any of my questions. I already know. I keep forgetting what it's like to have a pilot in the house." Her eyes darkened at the idea. "Always darting hither and yon without a hint of warning. Marcus James—'' she extended her hand to him ''—let me introduce you to Catherine Cornell. This is Lindsay's mother.''

"Pleased to meet you.'' Marcus took the woman's hand and squeezed it. Catherine Cornell was a lovely woman. Her hair was dark where Lindsay's was light, but she had the same deep eyes and the same elfin nose.

"Have you heard anything?'' Catherine was hungry for news of her daughter.

"She's in the delivery now,'' he answered. "I think she's having a rough time of it. I was with her until an hour and a half ago.''

Catherine looked grim. "I was so hoping this would be easy.''

"It's not.'' Marcus shook his head. "I don't know that much about having babies, but I do know everything's not going as well as it could be in there.''

Lindsay was pushing with all her might. She was trying desperately to love the child who was working so frantically to come out into the world, and she was almost ashamed of her thoughts. Everything had gone wrong. She wasn't dilating and her obstetrician had had to break her water himself. Lindsay's mind was alternately torn between frantic worry and hatred. Maybe the baby was dying. Maybe she was dying. Maybe she was never meant to have Kendall's baby. It would mean the death of everything that Lindsay loved and wanted. The nurses were kind and gentle around her, but Lindsay had no need for people who were gentle. She wanted someone who could help her. Someone who could take her far away from here. She heard herself calling out to Kendall, to Marc, to God, to her mother, to anyone she thought might be there listening.

"Push. Push. Push.'' Each of the nurses and the doctor urged her on. The only thing on Lindsay's mind was to get the baby out of her, away from her, so she could rest. Her body was entirely spent. This was unbearable. She wondered if anyone in Colorado or Texas would miss her if she died. That was a dumb thought, she laughed to herself. And then, she kept right on laughing. Somewhere deep inside of herself, somewhere buried beneath the pain, the spunk and the dry grit there made her understand that this was life in its rarest, most beautiful form. What she found deep in her soul gave her the strength to go on. And at 7:43 A.M., fifty-two minutes after the doctor had broken her water and she had begun pushing in earnest, Lindsay felt a sharp release of pressure, the nurses cheered, and she heard a gurgle and then the strong wail of a newborn child. One more push and she was free of it, she could breathe again, and the doctor was asking her if she wanted to hold her new son.

Lindsay had dreamed of this moment for ever so long. For weeks she'd wondered if she would look at her baby and see Kendall's eyes or her nose or his ears or her grandfather's hands. But all she really noticed about him now was that he was a miraculous, miniature person. He was tiny and pink and wiggly. He had wrinkled feet and his fingernails were perfect. She would remember his fingernails forever. That's all she could think of as the nurse took her son from her and she collapsed, exhausted, onto the pillow.

MARCUS FELT like a caged cat. He hadn't left the hospital for twenty-eight hours. It was useless getting a motel room because all he would do once he got there would be to pace the floor.

He didn't know what he had expected. Maybe he expected to be treated like a father. Or at least an uncle. He was feeling sorry for himself and he knew it. Lindsay had remained in the recovery room for twelve hours. She had hemorrhaged after the baby was born. Marcus didn't even know what that meant, and he didn't want to ask anybody. So he sat there silently beside Angela Allen pretending to understand everything that was happening. He felt helpless and very, very alone. The baby was still in the incubator but he looked fine. Even though he was born a full two weeks early, every part of him was perfectly developed, and he would be able to go home to the cabin in the mountains in a matter of days. Marcus stood there, his nose pressed against the glass, watching the baby boy for hours. The sign the nurses posted made him easy to find. "Allen. Male. Six pounds and four ounces."

"Ken, you didn't do too badly for yourself," Marcus whispered to the spirit of his dead friend as the child slept scrunched up inside the glass box.

Marcus could have gone into recovery to see Lindsay. Most of the nurses still thought he was Lindsay's husband. But Lindsay's mother was with her now, and Marcus didn't want to barge in on them. Lindsay had needed him last night, but things were better now, and Marc was toying with the idea of getting into his plane and flying back to Dallas without ever seeing her again. The commotion in his mind wasn't because he was trying to be noble. In truth, he was scared. He had lost all his composure and his reasoning last night. He had told her he loved her. Now that he had admitted that fact to himself and to her, he felt like he had loved her forever. She was such a part of him, such a part of his heart, of his life. It had been natural and good to come to her here.

The last look he had seen in her eyes as they'd wheeled her toward the delivery room would haunt him forever. Maybe it would be better if the long hours and the birth of the baby crowded the words from her mind. He prayed once that she would forget what he had said. He had shared so much of himself with her last night. Now, in the harsh light of the day and of reality, sharing so much suddenly seemed stupid.

Twenty minutes ago they had moved Lindsay into her regular room. Her blood count was back up, and her blood pressure had stabilized. They were letting everyone in to see her. Marcus was wired with adrenaline and caffeine. He'd lost count of how many cups of coffee he had poured down his throat during the past hours. Angela was with Lindsay now, giggling and carrying on and trying to figure out an appropriate name for the baby. As far as Marcus knew, Lindsay had not asked to see him. He knew he should leave but, before he did, he stopped in the hospital gift shop and ordered one long-stemmed red rose to be sent up to Lindsay's room. He pondered a long time over the card and, finally, he wrote: "To a precious mother and her new son. May you have many days filled with sunshine. Hugs, Uncle Marc." He read the message to himself once and was satisfied. It was definitely generic. It said everything and nothing at the same time.

Just as he was pulling a ten-dollar bill from his wallet to pay the cashier, Angela Allen tapped him on the shoulder. "You look like hell," she said, grinning at him. "How long has it been since you've shaved?"

"I don't remember," he replied honestly.

"Well, it doesn't matter now." Angela perused his face. "You had better get up to room 308. Lindsay had no idea that you were still waiting here. She wants to see you. Immediately."

Marcus grabbed the rose and his change and ran. He left the carefully composed card lying on the counter at the gift shop, but that didn't matter. He was delivering the rose and the message himself now. She wanted to see him. His heart was suddenly in his throat.

As Marcus turned the corner, he could hear her laughter tinkling all the way down the corridor. From the din he could hear coming from her room, Marcus decided the entire newspaper staff must be in there.

"You are never getting permission to go on a break again. Look what happens," a voice teased.

"Have you seen the baby yet?" This time it was Lindsay's voice and Marcus was dizzy from the sound of it.

"He's beautiful," someone commented.

"You have fan mail at the office," a man's voice said. "The entire Taylor Valley is crediting you with saving their property values."

"Jack Jensen resigned yesterday," another voice said. "He made it official just an hour after your story hit the streets."

"Enough. Enough." Lindsay was speaking again. "No more. I got pregnant so I could get a vacation away from all this. And here you all come traipsing into the hospital. Give me a break. I think I'm going to go crazy if you don't give me a week or two without newspaper talk."

People started filtering out of the room.

"Okay, okay," a man agreed. "We'll go. And you take that vacation. Take a trip around the world for all I care. But plan on coming back. I don't know what I'd do without you. You are one hell of a journalist."

"Thanks." Marcus heard Lindsay chuckle.

When he was certain all of her visitors had left the room, Marcus stuck his head in the door and grinned. "May I come in, ma'am?"

"Oh, Marcus." Lindsay held her arms out to him. "Do you have any idea how long I've waited for this hug? Get over here right now."

He set the rose down and went to her. He hugged her softly, gingerly, as if he was afraid he might break her in half.

"What can I say to you?" she questioned with tears in her eyes as he plopped down on the edge of the bed. He looked beautiful. Magnificent. Like a male guardian angel. He had come to her when she needed him the most, and she had just assumed he had flown back to Dallas the moment her mother had arrived. Lindsay's heart was a kaleidoscope mixture of wonder and confusion and happiness. She could scarcely remember the events that had occurred just a day ago. She only remembered Marc's face hovering over her in a haze, his gentle voice egging her on, telling her she could make it, telling her she was beautiful and that he loved her.

Lindsay knew she loved Marc, too, in a little-girl sort of way. She needed him to hold her hand. She needed him to cry over the telephone to. But she also knew she wasn't capable of loving him the way a woman should. He deserved so much, and she had very little left to give him.

Ever since the baby was born, Lindsay had been desperate to talk to Marc. When she closed her eyes in the recovery room, she saw his face. As she watched him in her mind, his image blurred around the edges and she had seen Kendall's face hovering there, disembodied. Three times, she had picked up the receiver to call him at Love Field. Three times, a nurse or a doctor or her mother had walked into the room and interrupted her. Lindsay did not want anyone to hear what she wanted to say to him. She wanted to give a part of herself away to him, a part of herself that had been entrenched in bitterness during the past months of hurt and anger.

Lindsay had never thought for one moment that Marc was waiting for her in Gunnison, sitting in the hospital waiting room three floors below, praying that she would ask for him. Lindsay had been so jubilant when she'd found out he was waiting for her, it had taken all of her reserve not to jump up and down on the hospital bed and not to scream at Angela Allen for not telling her sooner.

"Go get him," she had shrieked frantically. And, until the moment he had walked in the door, she had been unsure of what to say to him. But now, the words tumbled out over themselves in a mad rush.

"What have you been doing all this time?"

"Waiting around." He grinned. *Feeling happy. Feeling scared.* "I didn't know if you wanted to see me or not."

Lindsay didn't say anything for a moment. She just tilted her head and looked at him like a frightened little bird that might flutter away at his first movement.

"Yes?" His eyes widened.

She grinned then. "I have a small confession to make."

"Go ahead. Confess." He winked at her.

"Okay." She took a deep breath and then took his hand. "I still haven't told the nurses you are just a crazy visitor. They all seem to think we're related in some way." She cocked her head at him playfully. "And that means—" she paused dramatically "—that you may hold Matthew Lawrence Allen."

"Matthew Lawrence?"

"My son," she whispered. She quickly touched his lips with her finger as the door swung open and a nurse entered carrying a soft, blue bundle.

Marcus watched as Lindsay took the child in her arms and held him to her. He had always thought she was the most beautiful woman he had ever seen, but what he saw now virtually took his breath away. Lindsay was radiant. As she sat gazing into her son's eyes, Marcus could see that a huge chasm in her life had been filled. So many times when he was a little boy, his mother had told him the Christmas story, the story of the beautiful virgin mother who gave birth to the Christ child in a stable in Bethlehem. As he had grown, his understanding of the story had grown, but it had never been nearly as complete as it was to him now as he watched the joy, the wonder, on Lindsay's face. This one small life had removed so much pain from her life. This little boy had taken everything bad in Lindsay's life and transformed it to hope and faith. It was tremendous to see. The other night when Marcus had finally told Lindsay he loved her, his feelings had been spilling out of his heart like a waterfall, and he thought he could never love her any more than at that one moment. But he knew now, in a simple, gentle way, that he had been wrong. He felt a tragic longing for her somewhere deep down inside of himself. She looked so perfect, so delicate, so fragile. He was afraid to reach out and touch her.

"Matt. Matt. Matt," she clucked to the baby. "Look at him, Marc. Who do you think he looks like? Look at his eyes. Here." She held the bundle out to Marcus. "Hold him. Take a good look."

Marcus took Matt gingerly. He inspected the baby closely and then he laughed. "He doesn't look like anything spectacular to me. He just looks like a little kid. The kind you see on television. Cute. Cuddly. But he does have his father's eyes."

"Ah, Matt," Lindsay bent over and kissed her son. "Your Uncle Marc just gave you a wonderful compliment. You look like a television star and your father all rolled up into one. I think you passed inspection."

Marc grinned at her. And then he could hold back what he wanted to say no longer. As he handed the baby back to her, he gripped her arm. "Thank you." He didn't say the words aloud. He just mouthed them to her.

"For what?" she whispered.

"For not sending me away," he answered. "I've been crazy. I'm not certain I should even have come here."

"Kendall would have wanted you here," she said, her eyes blazing fiercely. "And I think I would have died if you hadn't come."

"I would have died, too." Marc grinned. "I'm just sorry that...."

"Don't." She touched his lips again. She knew what he was going to say.

"But I have to," he whispered his interruption. "I'm sorry. I can't just ignore what is happening to us...to me, at least. I told you that I love you. So now you know the truth. I'll always love you, Lindsay. I think now that I always have."

"Marc." This time it was Lindsay who gripped his arm. "I know we have to talk. You have to know what I'm feeling. It's fair." She paused for a moment then she continued. "I do love you, Marcus. But not in the way that people whisper over and dream about. I love you as a friend, as a brother. That's the only way I can give anything to you."

"Lin...." He tried to interrupt her, but she continued.

She gazed into her child's eyes as if the newborn babe could give her the answers to all the questions she was asking herself. "I can't, Marcus. I can't let Kendall go. And I can't love you the way you want me to, the way you deserve."

Marcus could sense his face going white. Lindsay certainly wasn't one to beat around the bush. She had obviously been thinking. He tried not to let his frustration show on his face. He had almost been certain that this was how it was going to end up. He had tried to prepare himself for her reaction to his confession of love, but he had known he was never going to be ready for it when it came.

"I need you desperately," Lindsay explained matter-of-factly. "I'm probably cheating you because I need you so. Because I can't give you anything in return. See this kid." She nodded down at Matthew Lawrence once more. "He's going to depend on me for everything. Not just love. Not just food. Everything. And there are parts of my life that are the same way, Marcus. I need you. But if I let you fall in love with me, I am sentencing you to a lifetime of giving and not taking. All I will do is take things from you."

"That's funny." Marcus knew what he had to say, even though it was cruel. "I remember somebody else telling me the same story."

Lindsay's face darkened. He was talking about Kendall. Kendall had felt the same way about Sarah. "Don't play dirty, Marcus." Her eyes flashed.

"I'm not playing dirty," Marcus answered. "I'm being honest.

You loved someone and you lost him and you feel like you can never give yourself to anyone again. Don't sentence yourself to that, Lin. It doesn't matter whether you fall in love with me or Robert Redford or King Kong, in the long run. Just don't drown yourself in guilt. It will kill you. It will kill the sparkle in your eyes and the energy in your soul."

"That isn't what killed Kendall," Lindsay said sharply. The nurse had entered the room and Lindsay handed Matt to her.

Marcus waited until the nurse left to continue. "Kendall would have kept running if you or I had let him. But we didn't. And look what came from it." He tilted his head in the direction of the nurse and the baby that had just left the room. "Maybe Kendall's happiness was brief. Maybe his life was unfair. But he lived for a while, Lindsay. What would have happened if he had waited? You think you have years in front of you, don't you? Well, so did your dead husband."

Lindsay flinched at his words. "Marcus. Don't."

"Maybe he didn't go about it the right way. But what would have happened if he had waited, Lindsay? Think about it."

"He might still be alive," Lindsay spat the bitter words from her mouth.

"Right," Marcus commented sharply. "Maybe he'd still be alive. Maybe he would be sitting in his apartment this very moment watching television like a zombie. Do you think he'd be feeling happy, Lindsay? Do you think he would be glad about the choices he'd made?"

Lindsay looked up at him now, her eyes full of tears and anguish. "Okay, so you win. I'm sorry. Maybe I'm just not as strong as he was."

"But you are, Lindsay." He wanted to shake her. He had to do something to make the truth sink in. But just this moment, he was at a terrible loss. "I want to take care of you, Lindsay. I want to give everything I have to you."

"I don't want you to." Lindsay tossed her hair back over her shoulder. "Please try to understand that."

"I do." Marcus straightened his shoulders, and his expression took on the unfocused edges of resignation. "I do."

Lindsay was trying to control the sobs that were shaking her, but she couldn't. It was just as well, though. She didn't want to hide anything from him.

"I had better go." Marcus looked away as he stood up. He couldn't bear to look at her face. She had hurt him, but he knew she was hurting, too. Someday, he was certain, she would realize the things he had told her were true. Someday she would find the strength within herself. She was stronger, braver, than anyone else Marcus knew. She was strong because she didn't believe in playing games, in hiding behind pretenses. He could have hit himself. Why did he insist on thinking good things about her, even when she cut him to the quick? He was going crazy.

He turned to her and shook his head. "You silly woman. Look what you're turning down." He held his arms out to her.

"Oh, Marcus," she laughed through her tears. "I'm not turning you down. I don't know what I'm doing. Maybe I'm just trying to be fair."

He didn't say anything. He just hugged her and then he winked at her. "Be strong. And take good care of that new little rug rat for me. I'll call you in a week or two, okay?"

He didn't wait for her answer. He didn't care what she had to say. But if he had turned around before he left the room, he would have seen Lindsay slowly nodding her head yes.

CHAPTER ELEVEN

LINDSAY LICKED the peanut butter off the knife before she pitched it into the sink. As she cut the sandwich into quarters with a sharper, serrated knife and poured a small plastic glass of milk, her mind went over the list of details one more time. Candles. Apple juice. Birthday napkins. And a Star Wars speeder bike. That should cover just about everything.

"Matthew," she called through the screen door. "Lunch is ready." She could see the child hesitating. Life was so wonderful outside. It was springtime again, and that was contagious. It was hard for Matthew to tear himself away from the sunshine and the warm air and the mushy snow.

Lindsay watched as her son looked mischievously at his two friends on the swing set and then back at the house. She held her breath as she watched him make his decision and turn toward the cabin. She smiled. She had been hoping he would obey. He didn't always do that anymore. He was reaching out in all directions now, growing and changing so fast that Lindsay thought if she turned away for a moment, she might miss something.

Tomorrow was his third birthday, and Lindsay thought she was more excited about it than he was. For three years now, Matt had been her entire life. Her soul, her love, had been wrapped around her son like a bandage.

She had given herself to Matthew in such a complete, devoted way. She loved her son with an intensity that was almost frightening to her. This intensity made her realize that the void within her caused by losing Kendall was still there. And that was frightening. The brief honeymoon she'd spent with her husband seemed like it had happened long ago in a fairy-tale world, and Lindsay thought it was crazy that one night with Kendall still threatened to haunt her for hundreds of nights to come. She would still wake in the darkness writhing, sweating, screaming, in the clutches of a dream about her dead husband and his airplanes.

Her only solace during those dark hours was the white cordless telephone that sat on the nightstand beside her bed and the kind voice that belonged to Marcus James, who always answered on the other end of the line. He was always there for her, no matter if she called at four in the afternoon or four in the morning. There were times she longed to see Marcus, times she needed him so desperately that she felt she might drown without him, but she didn't dare admit that fact to herself, much less tell him. She was afraid he would take her need for him the wrong way, afraid he might let himself think he still loved her, if she hinted at how vulnerable she still was to him.

How many times had she turned to him over the past thirty-six months? Hundreds? Thousands? She should have saved the phone bills and used them for a mental-health tax deduction, she thought to herself wryly. The calls, always the same yet always different, seemed to mesh in her mind now until they formed one long continuous plea for help.

"Marc?" she always questioned hesitantly when he answered the phone.

"I'm here. Lindsay, are you okay?" He would always ask, and it always amazed her that, no matter what time it was, he sounded awake, alert, just as if he had expected her to call.

"I don't know," she answered feebly. "I just couldn't sleep without dreaming again. I'm sorry I called." She heaved a little sigh. "I just saw the clock. It's still the middle of the night."

"It's okay." He chuckled. "It's an hour later here. So in Texas we're in the wee hours of the morning. That's a little better than the middle of the night."

"I'm sorry," she said again.

"Stop apologizing." He sounded both stern and playful. "So tell me about this. Are the dreams really getting terrible again?"

"I don't know what it is," Lindsay said slowly, softly, and he had to strain to hear her. "I've gotten myself trained lately. I see Kendall in all my dreams. I keep dreaming I'm back in Dallas and these planes are flipping end over end and then Kendall walks in. And when he walks in, every time I tell myself 'Lindsay, you know that this is only a dream.'" She paused for a moment and then gave a little sob. "But tonight I had this new dream. I dreamed he walked into the newspaper office here in Taylor Park and placed a classified ad for a missing person. He told the advertising director that he was the missing person, that he was looking for himself. Isn't that stupid? It sounds like some bizarre comedy you'd see at some off-the-wall theater somewhere.''

"If it didn't hurt so much, it would be funny, right?" Marc asked.

"Right." She nodded even though he couldn't see her. "But the bad thing was, I didn't know it was a dream. I woke up all jumpy and scared and ready to start my life all over. And then, I remembered that he wasn't here anymore. God, Marc, it's like he died all over again.''

"Lin?" he asked her as she sobbed into the phone. "Do you want to know what I think?"

"Yes, I do," she told him.

"I think it's a good sign." His voice was calm, soothing, terribly reassuring. Lindsay was already beginning to feel better.

"Why?" she asked. "Because I wake up every night and have to relive this thing all over again?" There was something that sounded almost angry in her voice now, but Marc knew that she was only angry at herself. "Am I just trying to prove how strong I am?"

"No, Lin," he told her. "But you're seeing him now in places that only belong to you. The newspaper office. The mountains. You two never really shared those things. You only shared Dallas."

"And flying," Lindsay corrected him. "We shared the sky."

"You're right," he agreed. "But you have your own life now. And your dreams show that you are placing more importance on your new existence. It's a sign that you really are letting go. I have faith in you, Lin. You, young lady, are going to make it."

"Marc, thanks." She closed her eyes, imagining his smile, and heaved a sigh of relief. "You know, I feel like such a little girl sometimes. Back when I was five or six, it used to scare me to death at night because I thought there was a hand that lived under my bed. I used to think that it was going to come up the foot of the bed one night while I was asleep and grab my ankles and pull me down. Every so often, daddy would hear me crying and he'd come in and take my hand and hold it until I built up enough courage to look under the bed. That was one of the most terrifying things I can remember. Bending down and looking under the bed."

"You're so brave," Marc said with a touch of laughter in his voice.

"Thanks, Marc," she told him. She was still deadly serious.

"Thanks for what?" He checked his laughter.

"For helping me look under the bed tonight."

"You're welcome, ma'am." He was honestly honored. "Tell Matt I send a big hug to him. You do still see the kid every once in a while, don't you?" he joked.

"Yes, Marc." She laughed at his absurd question. "I still see the kid all day long every day. In fact, I don't do much without him."

What she said about her son was true.

The only thing she did without Matt was work at the *Valley Review*. She had gone back to the editor's desk not long after he was born and hadn't missed a day at the paper since. She had hired a grandmotherly woman named Nina to care for her son on days she couldn't be home.

As Lindsay watched Matt munching his sandwich, she knew that it was going to be hard for her to leave him this afternoon. It would be so easy to skip work and play with the kids in the sandbox and the slush. But she couldn't miss the commissioners' hearing. Scheduled meetings seemed to rule her life these days. Some crazy California company wanted to build a major resort in Taylor Valley and the issue had been a bone of contention for weeks. Nobody wanted such drastic change in the community. Lindsay was finding it extremely hard to remain objective about this story. The entire resort idea was a joke.

Despite the opinion of the local people, the West Coast company was going ahead with the deal. The firm had purchased one thousand six hundred acres in the heart of the park. Plans included a golf course, tennis courts, an Olympic-sized swimming pool, three restaurants, a night club, a motel, a group of time-share condominiums and a one thousand-acre area that would be groomed and maintained for snowmobiling and cross-country skiing. The company executives were horrified with the roads, and they were willing to pump millions of dollars into the county's coffers to improve them. The commissioners were having a horrible time turning the deal down. It would mean so much to the county's economy. But Lindsay believed, as did others, that the venture was a mistake. The people who traveled to Taylor Park each year came to disappear from life, to catch a few trout, to hike through mountains that time had never touched. This valley did not attract the jet-setters who played tennis all day and partied all night. Whoever made the decision to spend the money here had made a horrible marketing blunder. Lindsay had already completed one column opposing the resort, and she was getting ready to run another one. Maybe the dialogue at this afternoon's meeting would give her ideas.

"I don't like tickles." Matt's small whine brought Lindsay back to their picnic in the cabin. He was holding up a bread-and-butter pickle Lindsay's grandmother had made and sent from Texas.

"Do you have a pickle on your plate?" Lindsay tried to look stern as she eyed her son. His wide brown eyes made her want to melt. Tickles. She should correct his pronunciation but she didn't have the heart to. The word he had said was perfect. That's exactly what Lindsay wanted her life to be full of. Tickles and other topsy-turvy wonderful things. Sometimes she wondered if she was losing her own identity while she was talking to teddy bears or racing around the floor on all fours playing space monster. But she didn't think so. She felt like she had found a part of herself she had never known before.

"I don't have a tickle here." Matt pointed to his side of the blanket on the cabin floor where they were eating.

"Then that means you do not have to eat any of them. You only have to eat what is on your plate," Lindsay explained.

"Why do you like tickles?"

"I like tickles because they taste good. And because I know how much love your great-grandmother put into the jar when she made them."

Matthew screwed up his mouth and looked suspiciously at the green things on his mother's plate. Her explanation didn't satisfy him one bit. How could something that tasted so bad be full of love?

Matt was still eyeing the pickles distastefully when Lindsay sighed and stood up from the floor. "I have to go now, Matt. I'm going to run and look Nina up. Eat up so I can tuck you in for your nap before I leave."

Matt looked up at his mother and again screwed up his mouth. How he wished she could stay with him this afternoon. They could both cuddle up together in the thick four-poster bed, and while the night was coming, they could have a fire, and she could tell him stories of the mountains, and he could tell her stories about Star Wars and space invaders. He wished his mother never had to go away. Even though he was almost three. Tomorrow he would be three years old! He kept forgetting that and then remembering it again. Everyone told him he was getting very big and old. And he already knew his mommy was very pretty and very perfect. She played so many special games with him when they were together.

Matt's other friends all had daddies, though, and he was sad he didn't have one. His mother was special and perfect and pretty, but he wanted a daddy. Not just any daddy. His daddy. His mommy was always telling him stories about airplanes and how they flew in the sky together before they had Matt, but one day the airplane fell down and daddy fell down, too, and he never came back again. It was all very hard to understand, and sometimes Matt did, and sometimes he forgot that his daddy wouldn't ever come back. He had fallen down lots of times, and he still came home. He kept thinking maybe his daddy would come back one day, and he told his mommy so because he thought she would be happy, but it only made her cry, and he was very sad. Then, mommy stood him in front of the mirror and pointed out his brown eyes and his soft stub of a nose and his little ears, and she said those things belonged to daddy and as long as Matt had them then daddy would always be there. And then she would be happy again and Matt would be glad that he belonged to her.

"Guess what tomorrow is...besides your birthday," Lindsay said as she kissed his ear. Matt lay tucked under the thick covers all by himself.

"I think I might know." His eyes widened and he nodded his head matter-of-factly.

"You do?" Lindsay was surprised at his knowledge.

"Nina told me this morning. Tomorrow is cartoon day. And that means you don't have to go to the newspaper."

Lindsay nodded. He was right. Tomorrow was Saturday. He was only three and he was already learning his days of the week by what came on television every morning. She tried to restrict his TV watching. However, that wasn't always easy. Lindsay wasn't a late sleeper, but she did like to stay in bed on Saturday mornings. It was such a luxurious, lazy feeling to wake up slowly to the sunshine, to stretch way down below the covers and to bury her head in the thick, down pillows.

Every Saturday morning, she could hear her son waking up beside her and she knew that, soon, when the sun started peeking over the Collegiates, Matt would tiptoe across the bedroom, his frayed, white baby blanket wrapped around him, with Rufus, his stuffed tiger, dangling precariously from the crook of his elbow. The cartoons came on every channel, and sometimes when he woke up too early, he would sit there and watch the test patterns and whisper stories to Rufus until the first show of the morning began. He kept the sound turned down low so she could sleep and usually the loudest noise in the house before 8 A.M. was his small, solitary whisper to Rufus. It seemed to Lindsay that his whispers were oftentimes louder than his regular voice. But later she figured she was just listening harder for his whispers. Sometimes, she thought that the things he whispered to Rufus were the most important things of all.

"Are you excited about your party tomorrow?" She stroked his honey-blond hair back away from his little forehead. She could tell he was already getting sleepy. "Would you like to help me make gingerbread men for all your guests after I get home tonight?"

"Can we put ears and buttons on them?" he asked plaintively.

"Sure." She was rubbing his back now. "I'll stop by the grocery store on my way home and pick up some red-hot candies and some confectioner's sugar."

"Can we make one and send it to Uncle Marc?" His words were slow and muffled by the pillow.

"Okay," Lindsay nodded. "I know he would like that. It will make him feel like he got to come to your birthday party." Lindsay bent over and kissed her son's ear. She could hear his soft rhythmic breathing and she realized he had already drifted off to sleep. She tiptoed out of the room and into the kitchen where she grabbed her briefcase and gave Nina a quick squeeze. "Y'all have a good afternoon," she whispered to her housekeeper.

Nina nodded in return. "We will."

The hearing that afternoon was long and tedious. Lindsay was impressed by the officials who stepped forward to present the project, and she was surprised by that. As the marketing staff from Walco Resorts, Inc., stated its case, she felt her heart sinking into her stomach. She didn't know why she was feeling so helpless just now. She didn't even totally understand why she opposed this resort so fiercely. The valley meant so much to her. It seemed to her that this was her last refuge from the rest of the world. If she let this project come into Taylor Park, she was certain that some of the things she was trying to stay away from would permeate this place, too.

At the beginning of the hearing, Lindsay hadn't decided whether she should testify or not. Now, after hearing the marketing experts speak, she knew she had no choice. And when she spoke, she knew she was hitting the mark. She didn't nix the idea of the resort altogether. She simply urged her county officials to approve one facet of the Walco Resort at a time. She knew that the project could bring changes to Taylor Valley. And she prayed that when the commissioners and the local people saw the changes coming, they would all run scared. She hoped desperately that her words, her ideas, were killing this crazy project. And when she saw the looks on the Walco officials' faces, she was almost certain her words had done just that.

"You're quite a scrapper," one of the marketing representatives commented to her after the meeting was adjourned. "They tell me you're the newspaper editor here."

Lindsay nodded. For a moment, she was afraid. They were a big-city operation. What if they put bombs in her office in order to change her mind? "I am."

"Give us a chance," he requested as he held the door open respectfully for her.

WAVE AFTER WAVE OF RELIEF flooded over Lindsay as she lay in the darkness. It had only been a dream. It had been technicolor and terrifying, but it had only been a dream. About airplanes.

Lindsay buried her head in her pillows. She glanced across the bed to make certain her gyrations hadn't bothered her son. She was relieved to see Matt still sleeping peacefully.

Her airplane dreams had been haunting her less and less lately, but this one had unleashed itself in full fury. It hadn't been a dream of flames or impacts or explosions. It was at the terrifying time when she felt the plane stall and her stomach jam into her heart and the woman sitting next to her screamed "Oh my God, we're going down."

Tonight had been one of the worst dreams she had ever had. The plane was going down. Two minutes until impact. Kendall was sitting next to her holding Matthew in his lap, and Lindsay was laughing because everyone told her Kendall was dead but he couldn't be because he was sitting there right next to her. Suddenly, she wasn't on the plane anymore. She was standing in Taylor Park watching a monstrous 747 skid down the street on its belly toward her. The wings of the giant craft were knocking over trees and cabins and children and mountains and everything else that got in the way. Then, the telephone rang and it was the county commissioners calling to tell her to write a story because the Walco Resort had opened for business. And then all she could see were the wings of the plane whizzing past her and she heard people screaming inside, and one of the voices belonged to Marcus James. He kept screaming "I want to take care of you, I want to take care of you," until the plane was out of sight.

The telephone kept ringing. Lindsay tried to shut the sound out by burrowing under the covers but it didn't help. She hoped whoever it was would hang up eventually. What time was it, anyway, she asked herself. It couldn't be later than six-thirty on Saturday morning. She hadn't slept until almost three. Once again, she remembered the horrible dream.

She glanced across the bed and discovered that Matt was already up. She felt for the cordless telephone on her nightstand and then plopped back on the pillows before she could manage an almost undistinguishable, garbled hello.

"Lin?" It was a man's voice. Who was this? She was always so disoriented when she had to pull herself out of a dead sleep.

"I'm sorry it's so early and I can tell you're still asleep, but I just called to tell you you're crazy."

"Oh, yeah?"

"If you could see Texas in all her glory today, you would be extremely sorry you'd left."

"Marcus?" Lindsay propped herself up on one elbow. "Is that you?"

"The one and only Marcus James at your service, ma'am," he joked.

"The only service you are is a wake-up service—" she tried to sound stern but he could hear the laughter in her voice along with her grogginess "—but I guess I can forgive you for that. I think you owe me a wake-up call or two."

"So maybe I forgot there's an hour's difference." He laughed, and Lindsay could picture the mischief in his eyes. "It's seven-thirty here. The sun is fabulous. A bunch of us guys from the hangar are taking off to Lake Dallas for the weekend. The bluebonnets and the Indian paintbrush are incredible. I guess the sunshine and the flowers make me think of you."

"How mushy, Marc," Lindsay groaned. She loved to tease him these days. She was secretly pleased with his compliment. "I know you're just calling to check up on me. Go ahead. Admit it."

"I admit it. I'd call and check up on you every day if I thought you wouldn't hang up on me," he said.

"Sure. You're right." Lindsay chuckled. It had been almost two weeks since she had called him last. "If you want to know what I eat for breakfast every morning, I could send you a menu."

"Okay," he teased. "I know you, Lindsay. I realize you're doing wonderfully. I really just called to talk to the kid. Isn't today that national holiday known as Matthew Lawrence Allen's third birthday?"

Lindsay was silent for a moment. She was thinking back to the day three years ago when Marc had come to her and stayed with her while she was in labor. She had needed him desperately then. She needed him much more now. But she wondered if she was being fair if she told him that. She had sent him away three years ago without much hope and it seemed wrong to tell him how she was feeling now. No, she wouldn't do that. Not until she was certain of what she truly felt. She couldn't use Marcus. She cared too much for him.

"Lin? Are you there? Let me talk to the kid. Is he awake yet?"

"I believe I do hear Bugs Bunny on the television in the other room. He'd be up if you called any time after five on Saturday mornings. He doesn't sleep much after the television stations have signed on."

Marc chuckled. "A man after my own heart. Face it, Lin. The kid has good taste. It's so good to know someone else who recognizes the cultural merits of Sylvester the Cat and Tweety Bird."

"Of course—" Lindsay giggled "—I knew there was something about you two that was strangely similar. Your highbrow tastes. How could I have missed that?" Lindsay was enjoying this conversation immensely. This morning she felt like she was in her own nest surrounded by all the people who loved her. "Let me get Matt. A commercial just started. I should be able to pry him away for at least sixty seconds. That is, if it isn't a Star Wars vitamin commercial. He really likes to watch those."

Again, Lindsay was teasing Marcus. Nothing could have held Matt back from talking when he found out Marc was on the telephone. The two of them had developed a wonderful friendship over the past year. Marcus was becoming almost a stand-in father for him.

"Uncle Marc!" Matt exclaimed in his whimsical three-year-old fashion.

There was a pause.

"Road Runner." Great. Marcus was extolling the virtues of Saturday morning cartoons. Just what Bugs Bunny needed. More positive reinforcement.

"I'm having a birthday party today," Matt told Marc. Lindsay decided she had better get up. Twelve three-year-olds were coming over this afternoon to eat lunch and play and open presents.

"I'm big now—" Matt kept jabbering "—I'm this tall." He put a hand on top of his head and Lindsay had to hold a hand over her mouth to keep from laughing at him. He was exactly right. He was that tall. She was already learning to love his analytical mind.

"We're having pasgetti," Matt chattered on. "I'll give Thomas a meatball right on his head. He took my truck away yesterday."

"Matt." Lindsay shook her head disapprovingly at him. It certainly was not polite to invite someone to your birthday party just so you could plaster him on the head with a meatball. She would have to keep a close eye on that situation.

"We made gingerbread men last night for everybody and we made...."

"Don't tell him that," Lindsay interrupted him. "That's supposed to be a surprise."

"I can't tell you because it's a surprise," Matt was whispering into the phone. When Lindsay turned away she heard him say conspiratorially, "We made one for you and it looks just like you. Mommy says it's very handsome."

Lindsay sighed as she shrugged into her fleece robe. When those two put their heads together, she couldn't help but feel ganged on. But she wasn't complaining. She almost enjoyed it.

"I love you, too, Uncle Marc." Matt handed the receiver back to Lindsay. "Here, mom."

"So you made a handsome gingerbread man that looks like me?" he queried. "That sounds fascinating."

"Give me a break." Lindsay propped the receiver against her neck while she pulled her hair back with a barrette. "All of the gingerbread men look the same. Except yours has a few extra red hots on its face. Matt thought you might want those."

Marc chuckled. "It sounds like you're going to have a wild party there today," he said, laughing.

"I'm afraid so," Lindsay agreed. "Want to come?"

"I wish." Marcus was pensive. "Listen," he began then paused. He was uncertain how to bring this next subject up. "That is sort of what I wanted to talk to you about."

"I'm all ears." She took the receiver in her hand and straightened her neck.

"I called to invite Matt to come to Dallas for a visit. We all want to see him. And since his mother won't come and bring him herself, I am having to take drastic measures."

"When?" Lindsay sat down. She didn't know what to think. She tried not to let the idea of Matt leaving terrify her. Her mother had been inviting Matt to come to Dallas for almost a year now, and Lindsay had been hoping something would work out. Matt needed to spend time with Angela, too. But Lindsay had not been able to tear herself away from the *Valley Review* long enough to put her and her son on an airplane and make the trip. Maybe it wasn't so much an issue of time as it was an issue of means. She didn't know if she could bear to let Matt fly. She thought she might go crazy watching him careering down the runway making ready to jump into the sky. She could see the headlines now. Insane mother chases Frontier Flight 187 down Gunnison runway. It would be like letting her son go and never knowing if he was going to return to her. The entire idea was painful.

But Marcus was still explaining everything to her. He was actually being calm. He had tickets to the Texas Rangers-Baltimore Orioles game on June fifth at Arlington Stadium and he wanted to take Matt to Wet 'n Wild, the new water park, and Six Flags over Texas amusement park. Lindsay's mother wanted Matt to spend the nights with her, and Angela Allen wanted a day to take him to the zoo. Marcus knew he was too young to fly alone on a commercial aircraft, but he had managed to get a plane a week from Saturday and he would be willing to be-bop by Gunnison, have a sandwich and a Coke with Lindsay and then fly the kid back down to Texas where he belonged.

Lindsay was almost angry. It sounded like they had all gotten together over dinner one night and made major plans for her and her son without once consulting the child's own mother. Never mind that Marcus was calling now to ask her permission. It was already too late. She already felt left out.

"Let him come," Marcus pleaded. "He needs it. You need it."

A bright thought entered Lindsay's mind and swept away a piece of her despair. Marcus was coming to Gunnison again. "I can't believe you want to come and pick him up."

"Why don't you let me pick you up, too?" Marcus suggested. Something in her voice sounded wistful and sad, he reflected.

"I can't come, Marc," she answered weakly.

Marcus sighed. He had tried. She was just too obstinate to accept his invitation. In a way, he felt guilty. He felt like he was trying to pry her son away from her. Maybe the whole idea of the visit wasn't fair.

"If I let him go, do I get a special hug from the pilot?" she asked timidly.

Marcus's heart jumped. The idea of seeing her again made him want to screech with joy. Since he had gotten this newest plan, he hadn't slept at all. It had been three days now. "You will receive up to ten special hugs from this very pilot if you agree to the deal." He laughed hesitantly. "In fact, you might even have to hold the pilot back. He might go for fifteen or sixteen special hugs. Now, what do you say? Do I come to Gunnison or not?"

"That's bribery, you know." She giggled nervously. "Let me think." The phone line was silent for several moments. She was staring at the back of her son's head as he sat enthralled in Road Runner cartoons. She had to admit he was growing up faster than she had ever imagined. The time with Marc would be so special and good for Matt. The poor kid didn't even know what a baseball game was. And it was very fair and important for her son to spend time with his grandparents. She was certain he would return to Colorado with a wonderful drawl and a new respect for the state of Texas. That wouldn't be so terrible, Lindsay admitted to herself. Matt would absolutely adore Six Flags and the plane ride with his Uncle Marc. And, if everything went well, he could take a commercial flight home. It suddenly didn't seem right to say no to either of them.

"Okay." She said it so quietly Marcus had to strain to hear her. "I'll call mom tonight and finalize these plans with her. I'll die without him for a week, you know?"

"I know."

"I'll let you tell him about this." Lindsay sighed, and again, Marcus prayed he was doing the right thing. "There is another commercial on right now."

For the rest of the day, the Cornell-Allen household was bedlam. Matt was so excited, he couldn't eat breakfast. He was antsy about opening all his presents this afternoon, but now he knew the best present of all was coming in two weeks. He was flying in an airplane with Uncle Marc. To Texas. Where all the cowboys lived. Where all his grandparents lived. He was going without his mother. That thought made him sad but it made him happy, too. He was getting big now, bigger than he had ever been before.

Lindsay couldn't have handled his excitement if she hadn't been feeling just a bit excited, too. The spaghetti sauce was simmering in the cast-iron pot on the stove and Lindsay stirred it, focusing vacantly, caught up in everything that was happening around her. She wouldn't think of the day Matt was leaving her. She would only think of Marcus. Her peaceful, quiet existence was suddenly a topsy-turvy jumble of new ideas and new challenges. It was fabulous. In two weeks, Marc would be in Gunnison. He would probably stay for two hours. That would be fine. It was long enough to see him and touch him and realize he was real again. Hugging Marcus and seeing him again was going to be like touching solid earth after a trans-Atlantic flight, or as if she had spent three years on a tossing boat and was just about to step down the gangplank and onto the soil. Maybe that's why the Pope always kissed the soil of his homeland. The best part of it wasn't actually bending over and putting lips to the ground. The best part was anticipating the glory and the symbolism of it all.

Nina offered to stay into the afternoon to help wrangle Matt and his dozen friends at the birthday party, and Lindsay was extremely grateful. Matt was the king of the day. He did try, once, to put a meatball on Thomas's head, but Nina saw him in time, and the fierce look she darted across the table at him could have halted an entire army.

The kids feasted on buttered spaghetti with meat sauce, cream corn—Matt's two favorite things—and homemade garlic bread. Dessert was a double fudge cake with peppermint ice cream. The ice cream was by far the hit of the party. It had green and red peppermint candies in each serving, and the guests dove into the drippy scoops like pirates digging for buried treasure. Most of the ice cream melted while the children counted and compared their candies. On any ordinary day, Lindsay would have chastised Matt for digging in his dessert, but today she ignored it. Besides, there were twelve of his friends doing it, as well as Nina. Lindsay couldn't very well scold an entire valleyfull of children and her housekeeper, too.

Matt was overjoyed by the gifts he received. Thomas gave him a bank with a rocket on it headed toward a planet, and when you put the coin on the nose of the rocket and pulled a lever, the coin shot up inside the planet. He got a plastic army boat from one of his friends and a pair of Superman pajamas from one set of grandparents. He especially loved the Star Wars speeder bike his mommy gave him and the baseball cap and bat that Uncle Marc had sent.

The last present of the party was from Nina. The grandmotherly woman winked at Lindsay as she marched into the room with a small shoe box. Matt wondered why this box had holes stuck in it and he wondered why it wasn't wrapped in birthday paper. Something about this present was different from all the others. It was moving. Something was scratching in the box. Something wanted out.

Matt ripped off the lid and squealed when a teensy black and white head looked out and started purring. Matt yelped and Lindsay winked at Nina. She had given her approval for this gift days ago after a mouse ran across the kitchen floor. This kitten was the teeniest, fattest little cat Lindsay had ever seen, and it sat on the kitchen table primly cleaning its left front paw looking like nothing but a wad of fur with two eyes.

After most of the guests left and Matt was outside playing with the kitten, Lindsay had the chance to give Nina a sisterly squeeze of thanks and to tell her the details of Matt's trip to Dallas.

"I know it's hard for you to let him go," Nina nodded sympathetically. "But you're doing the right thing."

"I know, I know," Lindsay moaned. "But keep reminding me anyway. I seem to keep forgetting that one detail."

Nina pitched the last three dirty paper plates in the fireplace and watched them while they burned. "Your son will come back a fuller person. He'll grow while he's gone. I bet he'll come back a whole five inches taller."

CHAPTER TWELVE

LINDSAY READ THE NOTE she found on her desk once and then she read it again. The public relations director from Walco Resorts, Inc., had called from Los Angeles. He and his staff members had arranged a meeting for all Gunnison government officials. The county commissioners and Lindsay Cornell-Allen were requested to attend. The meeting was scheduled for two weeks from Monday and would run for three days.

This sounds like a normal county commissioner meeting, Lindsay groaned to herself. Even the hearing to decide whether or not to rezone Joe Vader's six hundred acres north of town took three days. But as Lindsay read on down the list of details, her eyes widened. The meeting was going to be in Los Angeles at Walco International headquarters. There was a plane ticket waiting for her at New Horizon's Travel just up the block. Already bought and paid for.

"I can't do this," she said aloud to herself as she plopped a pile of notes on her desk. She was working on a feature about the spring cattle roundup. "I can't leave the office. I can't fly in a plane. I can't leave Matt that long."

But Matt was leaving her. The dates quickly clicked. He was leaving Saturday with Marcus. And she would need to be in Los Angeles by ten Monday morning. The Matt excuse wouldn't work. But the newspaper excuse would. There was absolutely no way she could miss five days of writing. There was no one to cover for her. And if there wasn't a new issue on the newsstands by eleven Thursday morning, she knew several hundred townspeople who would have her hide. They had come to depend on her weekly information. She sat back in her chair and sighed. What a relief.

But the relief didn't last long.

"I hear you're going on a trip," Cory said when he stopped by her office a few minutes later and handed her a mug of steaming coffee. He always brought her coffee when he wanted to sit and discuss something with her.

"Nope." Lindsay held her hand up and shook her head. "I can't get away, Cory." She didn't like the look she saw in his eyes. "Don't you agree?"

"No, I don't agree." He set his coffee cup down on her desk, and his eyes met hers. "Walco is footing the bill for you to write the feature of a lifetime. I'm not letting you turn this one down. I'm sending you out there on assignment."

"Great." Lindsay smirked at him. "Just what I wanted to hear. You know the only stuff they're going to give me will be their puffy, polished PR stuff," Lindsay reminded him.

"Since when are you satisfied with the information people give you? You know how to ask pertinent questions. You're a professional journalist, Lindsay. You know how to sort the wheat from the chaff." Cory shook his head.

"I could set up interviews with the president and several other staff members." Lindsay was nodding her head now. "I can go over that company and observe every angle...under the pretext of enjoying their hospitality."

"You're beginning to get the right idea," Cory agreed.

Lindsay stopped by New Horizon's Travel to pick up her plane ticket, and as she eyed the brightly printed envelope with the boarding pass inside, it struck her as ironic how much this ticket really signified to her. She was flying again. Maybe this was all she had needed all along to come back to herself. This and a nice long shopping trip at Neiman-Marcus.

The thought of shopping made Lindsay think of Rita. It had been so long since she had seen her old roommate. The two of them used to go on fabulous shopping sprees together. Sakowitz. Neiman's. Marshall Field's. The idea of it all almost made Lindsay dizzy.

Rita would definitely love shopping in Los Angeles. When Lindsay thought of that, her mouth dropped open. Why hadn't she considered the idea before? Of course. Rita wasn't teaching classes this summer. Maybe the two of them could meet on the West Coast.

When Lindsay called her old friend a few hours later, Rita was overjoyed. The trip was a new idea to her, but it was a good one. She had been considering an exotic vacation somewhere, but she didn't have any close friends in Dallas that she felt comfortable traveling with. This trip would be more than perfect. It had been so long since she had seen Lindsay. Her old roommate had buried herself away so far from Dallas and the way of life there that Rita had almost forgotten to worry about her. After Kendall had died, it was as if Lindsay had died, too. This phone call, this suggestion of a trip, was like someone, some part of Rita's life that had been missing, suddenly being restored to her. By the end of the conversation, the two women had made plans to shop every day, to visit a movie studio, to spend a day at Disneyland and to spend lots of sun time on Malibu Beach.

When Lindsay hung up the telephone, she didn't feel much better about telling her son goodbye. But now she knew she would have a friend waiting on the other end of that long flight to California. And that suddenly made all the difference in the world.

MARC'S PLANE APPEARED high in the sky at the appointed hour Saturday morning. Mother and son were sitting in the parked car just off the runway. They had been searching the sky for almost thirty minutes. Lindsay's blue Buick Skyhawk was packed full of suitcases, bags and boxes.

Somewhere in the pile was a gathering of stuffed animals. Mr. Jinx had come and so had Rufus and Garfield. Matt decided he would be horribly lonely if he went on his first wild adventure without Mr. Jinx. Then he decided that Rufus would get his feelings hurt if Mr. Jinx got to go and he didn't. Garfield would have been upset, too. And so would about ten other stuffed bears and tigers and dogs if Lindsay hadn't drawn the line somewhere. She made her son pick out the three top finalists to take to Uncle Marc's house. The rest would have to remain at home in a melancholy little zoo all lined up against the wall in Matt's room.

When Marc's plane appeared overhead, the shock that this was actually happening rocked Lindsay. Somehow, she was going to handle her son's departure. She had been secretly hoping the plane would never appear and that she would never have to face all this Matt growing-up business. But when she saw the landing lights flashing on the little craft, she knew she was thrilled. It was Marcus...swooping down into Gunnison from twenty thousand feet.

When Matt saw the plane, he started bouncing up and down and cheering. Lindsay watched him and laughed. This was not going to be your typical, everyday, normal family reunion. This was going to be something special.

The little Piper landed into the wind, and at the sight of the plane bouncing toward her, Lindsay's heart skipped a beat. She had been here before. A long time before.

The Piper sped toward them with its wings jostling to the rhythm of the droning engine. Lindsay and Matt were out of the car now, waving, and she toyed with the thought of running toward him. But the headline she had imagined earlier came to mind, "Crazy Woman Runs Down Runway," and she decided she had better wait. Forget the rough Colorado girl who longs to run up runways. Remember the Dallas girl. Remember sophistication. Remember the Alamo. It was a cry to change all history.

When Marcus stepped out of the plane, Lindsay couldn't believe how good he looked.

"Matthew Lawrence, is that you?" He flung out his arms to Matt and winked at Lindsay all in the same fluid motion. His sandy curls were tousled by the Colorado wind and his green-gray eyes seemed to sear into her very soul. When he smiled down at her son, his cheeks molded themselves into two precious dimples, and for the first time in a long while, Lindsay realized how much she had physically missed him.

"Marcus James," she whispered almost in disbelief.

"Here I am, the one and only." He grinned down at her and then, after a second of silence, he folded her into his arms.

"Is this hug number one?" She laughed up at him.

"Of course," he laughed. "I can see you plan on keeping count."

"I don't want to miss a single one of those fifteen or sixteen that you promised me," she said seriously.

He felt so good to her. His jacket was a new leather one, and it was cold from the air-circulating system in the plane. He smelled like spices and new leather and Dallas. What was that fragrance? Lindsay wasn't certain. But she was feeling the same heady sensation as a wife who welcomes her husband home after a long trip. It was magic to see him again. To rediscover him.

"I can't believe him," Marcus commented into Lindsay's ear while he nodded toward Matt. "Last time I saw him, he was a little squealing pink thing with a pug nose." Looking at the child, he grinned and said, "You've grown into a regular person, kid."

Matt was frozen where he stood. He had guessed that Uncle Marc was going to be very tall and very strong. And he looked just like the person in the pictures mommy had shown him. So Marc looked familiar and sounded right. But he was so much more than Matt expected. The total person was much more than the sum of his parts. Matt was pleased. He knew he loved Uncle Marc so much just now that he wanted to cry, and he didn't really know why. Matt knew that the three of them, in some strange way, made up some sort of family.

Anyone watching the group from the airport terminal would have wondered what was happening. They greeted each other like a normal family would have. But then they all three stood there and looked at each other for a long while. There was so much for each of them to see, to learn, to discover. And as Marcus stood there watching Lindsay and her son together, he felt a tug in his heart. The two of them so obviously belonged to each other. And Marcus wanted to belong to each of them, too. Right here, at that moment, he would have given anything to fulfil his wish.

"I can't send my guys off without feeding them," Lindsay announced as she skipped toward the car. She pulled Marcus with her. Matt was running along on Marc's other side. "Let's run over to A&W for a hamburger. My treat."

"I might just take you up on that, pretty lady," Marcus said as he grinned. "Eight-hundred miles is a long way to travel in one morning."

"I want a corny dog," Matt said as he smiled conspiratorially at his mother. A&W was a special treat for him. He had only gotten to go there once or twice before. And he could tell that his mother was in a very good mood. Maybe she would let him order onion rings, too. Onion rings and a plane ride to Dallas all in one day. If Matt Allen had understood fully what heaven was, he would have believed he was in it.

Before long, the trio was merrily chatting over juicy hamburgers and one greasy corny dog. Matt told Marc all about Felicia the Feline, his new kitten, and Mr. Jinx and how he was taller than he sounded on the telephone. And when Lindsay joined in, she talked about things she hadn't been able to talk about for a very long time. She told Marc about the joy she experienced watching Kendall's son grow. She told him how lonely she sometimes was and how she treasured his telephone calls. She told him how she'd found Nina and what good friends they had become. And she told him how excited and frightened she was about her trip to Los Angeles and her plans to meet Rita.

Marc watched the child soak up his mother's every word, and he decided, as he sat at the orange Formica table munching on a Teen-burger with bacon, that he had discovered life at its fullest. "Are you ready for a great baseball game on Monday night?" he asked Matt.

The baseball game. Matt felt another surge of excitement. He put the half-eaten corny dog on his plate and sighed. There was no way he could eat all of it. He wasn't hungry anymore.

"Too many onion rings." His mother shook her head at him and clucked her tongue. "I'll wrap this corny dog up in a napkin so you can take it with you on the plane. You might get hungry before you get to Dallas."

"Can I take the onion rings, too?"

Lindsay nodded. "The onion rings, too. Now, go to the restroom and wash those greasy hands." Lindsay looked up at Marcus and spied a mischievous look on his face. What was he thinking? Instinctively, Lindsay knew. She had been caught acting like a mother. Wrap up your corny dog...take your onion rings, too...I'm sure there are starving children in China. Marcus was very observant.

"Thanks," she said, giggling at him. They were alone for one blessed moment. She could really talk to him.

"For what?"

"For putting up with an obnoxious old mother," she answered.

He took her hand. "I am more than putting up with you. I am saving you. I'm taking the kid away so you can have an entire week of rest and relaxation, aren't I?"

"Yes—" she nodded "—you are." Marcus could see her eyes starting to fill with tears again, and he decided he had better change the subject.

"You look beautiful."

"So do you." She grinned at him through watery eyes. "I keep forgetting."

"Forgetting? About my charm? About my warm vivacity? How could you?"

"I don't know." She was smiling wholeheartedly now. "Maybe I want to. Maybe I have to. Maybe none of this is fair to either of us."

"We can make it fair, Lindsay." His eyes searched her face.

"I'm not ready to work that hard yet, Marcus."

He knew what she meant. Back off, Marcus. Maybe I'll be ready to love you in three more years, Marcus. Or maybe in six more years. Or maybe never. She looked so fragile sitting across the table from him, and he found himself longing to take her into his arms and to protect her from all the bad things in the world. But that wasn't possible. She wouldn't let him. She was infuriating him in a prim, delicate manner, and he couldn't do anything except curl up and hurt inside.

Marcus didn't even consider that Lindsay might be falling in love with him. He only knew she had already accepted some of what he had to give her and had grown strong because of it. But what was going to happen when he started adding conditions? He knew that sooner or later he was going to have to. He couldn't hang on to her forever. He needed her desperately still, and if she had known that, she would have been surprised. He needed her to hold him. He needed her to love him. He needed her to fix him pork sausages every morning along with two pieces of melty, floppy cinnamon toast and two eggs fried sunny-side up. He needed to know that she was there to care about all the little things for him.

"That was neat soap in there, mommy." Matt was back at the table. "It was green and it had little shiny things in it."

"I'm glad to hear you paid so much attention to the soap." Lindsay winked at Marcus. "I hope that means you did a very good job of washing your hands."

"I did." Matt shook his head seriously. "See." He held them out for both his mother and Uncle Marc to inspect. They were cold and still dripping. He hadn't been able to reach the hot water or the paper towels.

Lindsay saw Marc checking his watch. "Think y'all had better take off?" She frowned. She hadn't been prepared for this afternoon to go so quickly. She found herself wishing it could last forever.

"Yup." Marcus nodded slowly, sadly. The time had gone quickly for him, too. "We should be getting back. I filed a flight plan at Love Field this morning and I want to stick pretty close to it."

Once they were back in the car heading toward the airport, Marcus noted the massive assortment of suitcases stuffed into the hatchback. "Do you think the kid is going to have enough to wear, Lindsay?" he questioned sarcastically. "After all, he's going to be there an entire week."

"Most of it's for me," Lindsay explained lightly. "I'm flying out to meet Rita this afternoon. I think you can reach me at the Downtown Sheraton. That's where the meetings are. But if I'm not there, I'm on the beach. Or out to dinner. Or prancing through Disneyland." Suddenly, her plans sounded frivolous to her. She didn't want any of them. She just wanted to stay here clinging desperately to Matt and Marc. The two men who meant more to her than anything else in the world were sitting in the car with her right now expertly re-wrapping a corny dog in a paper napkin. And the onion rings, too. Matt had wrapped each onion ring separately. There was a growing pile of them in each of Marc's jacket pockets. Lindsay caught Marc's eye and winked at him once again. She hoped he could tolerate all the new, special things he was going to learn during a week with her son. She had faith that he would.

At the airport the wind had picked up, and it whipped Lindsay's hair as she helped Marc and Matt load the airplane. Matt had two suitcases for himself and a cardboard box for his Grandma Cornell and one for his Grandma Allen. Marcus carefully loaded the brown paper bag that was full of stuffed animals. Matt spied a familiar arm poking out of the sack, and he grabbed it. Mr. Jinx happily popped out of the bag. "Is it okay if he rides with me?" Matt questioned the tall pilot.

"Certainly." Marcus nodded, and Lindsay could almost swear she saw the clown's embroidered smile grow an inch or two. He had beaten Rufus and Garfield in the popularity poll and had earned the place of honor right up in the cockpit buckled between Matt and Uncle Marcus. As Lindsay's thoughts encircled the skinny, floppy clown, she was almost jealous. Mr. Jinx was brave enough to fly to Dallas and she wasn't.

When the time came to lock the doors and taxi up the runway, it was almost more than Lindsay could bear. She gave her son a long, hard squeeze and a watery kiss on the forehead. Marcus received a quick kiss full on the lips and a long, lingering look. "Take good care of my kid," she whispered to him.

"I will, Lin."

As the two of them turned away and started walking toward the plane, Lindsay was surprised to find that Marc was the one she couldn't stand to let go. "Marcus?" she called out to him once more.

"Yes?" He turned to her.

When she saw his face again, she knew she couldn't bear it, just letting him fly away like this without telling him everything she was feeling inside. Everything about him today seemed so familiar yet so new, so wonderful. It was almost as if she was seeing him for the first time, seeing his broad chest, his heaving shoulders, his eyes, his hands. She ran to him then and clung to him.

"Lin." He cradled her head in his hands as she reached up and pulled him to her.

"Marc?" This time his name was a question on her lips. "Oh, Marc, I need you so."

That was all she could say. The feelings welling up inside her now denied words. She needed him in a primitive way, a way that would fulfill the longings that had only begun to grow within her on her wedding night, longings that would have long since died away if not for this one man who knew how to touch her so expertly now.

Lindsay was vaguely aware of her son watching them from the runway. She wanted Marcus so desperately just then that everything else around her faded away and lost its meaning. She reached up and kissed his ear once and she felt him tremble.

"Lindsay." He pulled her to him and kissed her with a slow, tantalizing tongue that made feelings rise in her that she had long since forgotten. And as she stood there before him, breathless from joy, she felt him gently push her away. "We have to go now." He sounded almost as breathless as she did.

Lindsay just looked at him and swallowed hard and nodded. She couldn't speak. She waved and blew kisses to both of them as the airplane's engine revved and it turned to bounce toward a takeoff. She waved for as long as she thought Matt could see her. She blew one more kiss as the Piper roared past her and then shot up into the sky. But the kiss was a futile gesture, and Lindsay knew it. The craft had shot by her so fast that neither of the men inside could possibly have seen her long, fluid motion. She decided she didn't like blowing kisses anymore. They were empty. Like sucking on a straw and getting an airy gurgle in your mouth instead of a liquid.

As the plane grew smaller and smaller against the Colorado sky, Lindsay thought she saw Marcus tip his wings once in a gallant goodbye. "Auf Wiedersehen," Lindsay whispered to the sky. Until I see you again.... Her rendition of the German was straight from Frau Wilkersen's tenth-grade class at J.J. Pearce High School in Dallas. Lindsay hadn't thought of German class for a long time, and it surprised her that the foreign word came out of her mind. She was interested to note she was still pronouncing the words with a thick Texas accent. A Texan German. Nice. But she was glad she had the expression to call on. It fit just now. She was standing here beside the runway holding her heart in her hands. And she was surprised to find that she didn't need to cry.

Lindsay's flight to Los Angeles didn't leave for another three hours. That was a long time to wait, but it satisfied her. She wanted to remember everything about the time she had spent with Marcus. She didn't want to worry about dashing home to load the car again. The canyon road was disastrous when you were in a hurry. It seemed to Lindsay that every time she was on deadline, she wound up behind a line of travel trailers from Nebraska or a herd of cows.

Not many people were boarding the commercial flight in Gunnison so Lindsay had her pick of seats. She was proud of herself. She had actually walked up the rickety aluminum steps and had boarded this thing. For an instant, a topsy-turvy sense of reality hit her, and she wondered how a huge metal contraption like this one could be lifted by air. Never mind the aerodynamics she had learned in science class. Flying was a miracle. Lindsay whispered a quiet prayer as she buckled herself into the window seat she had chosen. "Our Father in heaven—" she had her nose pressed up against the window so no one would hear her "—please pick this thing up in your arms and set it down safely in California. Amen." It was a simple prayer, but a beautiful one. A plaintive cry of help from someone who was trying to trust God but trying not to let go of her own life at the same time. Lindsay's blood was pumping slower now. It wasn't her problem anymore. If this thing got off the ground, it would be God's doing, not hers.

She smiled at that thought later, after the plane had taken off, landed in Denver to take on twice as many passengers and taken off again. God was doing a wonderful job. Lindsay was beginning to gain faith in the pilots as well. That was a good thing considering her son was gallivanting across the Southwest with one of their profession now, she reminded herself.

The evening was clear, and Lindsay guessed she could see three hundred miles from horizon to horizon. The plane was flying due west, directly into the sunset, and, as the colors of the sky faded into darkness, Lindsay could see hundreds of miniature diamonds begin to sparkle and dance around her. There was a pleasant, comfortable familiarity to the sky. How long had it been since she had hung suspended like this, somewhere lost between the earth and the rest of the universe, measuring the value of it all by the sparkling facets that twinkled in carats around her? She had been flying over Dallas, Fort Worth, Greenville and Richardson. Touch-and-go landings at Shiloh Airport. Flying in the Romeo Juliet with Kendall.

The feeling she held in her heart at just that moment surprised her. "Kendall." She whispered his name aloud. She thought about him again, hard. Just to try the new feeling on for size. Or maybe she should have thought about what she felt as an antifeeling. Because that's what it was. There was nothing; no hurt, no guilt, no remorse…just nostalgia.

Lindsay had thought this day would never come. It had taken her four years to accept Kendall's death. But here, balanced between the lights of the nameless cities below and the faceless stars above, here where lights blazed and the guy next to her was listening to blaring punk music on the complimentary earphones, and the stewardess was passing out fizzy Coca-Colas in plastic glasses, Lindsay felt normal once again. Their love affair had all started here in the sky, and suddenly it seemed right and fair that it should end here, too. Kendall. She had loved him well, and he had given her so much. Smiles and springtime in February and her son. But she didn't need him anymore. Something locked deep inside of her soul had finally been set free.

CHAPTER THIRTEEN

LINDSAY'S TRIP to Los Angeles was a beautiful mixture of fantasy and frolic. She experienced a wonderful sense of renewal and rejuvenation hopping off the plane and seeing Rita again. Her friend looked fabulous standing there in a patchwork suede skirt and a silk cream-and-brown-striped blouse. She was tan, her chestnut hair was cropped into short curls, and she looked so svelte and sophisticated that Lindsay felt like an awkward country bumpkin walking along beside her at the bustling airport. Within minutes, the two were babbling on about all the old wonderful comfortable things, like Rita's latest shade of lipstick and Lindsay's latest favorite Danielle Steel novel. It was marvelous to talk about life again, life as it really was, trivial and tangible.

They spent their first entire day together at Disneyland, and the time there was joyous. Lindsay and Rita had been to amusement parks before, but never to one like this. The joy of each ride was not in the thrill or the speed, but rather in the sheer artistry of it all. Everything was so authentic, so genuine. The fantasy was real. Lindsay wished for Matt a thousand times during the day. She made a mental note to bring him here as soon as possible.

The Walco meetings were grueling. A series of important sessions were scheduled back to back, and neither Lindsay nor the commissioners had more than ten minutes in the middle of the day to grab a quick sandwich. Lindsay's schedule was even worse. She had set up interviews with everyone she could think of, including the president of the company, but she knew that if she went crazy this week trying to get everything done, it would all be for a fairly good cause.

Lindsay's interviews went almost too well, though. Every question she asked was designed to be a seduction, to lead the interviewee onto ground he might be trying to protect. But Lindsay got the impression almost immediately that Walco was a well-respected above-board company. From the quotes she received, it sounded as though the Taylor Valley project was the first to meet any opposition at all. The company had built elegant, spacious businesses in all corners of the world, including one luxurious hotel in Dallas that Lindsay had admired ever since it had been built. Everyone she talked to was eager to disclose all the information she needed, and as a journalist she was impressed. Either the staff members had nothing to hide or they had all been primed and polished by Walco's public relations department. It was a PR director's dream and an investigative reporter's nightmare.

In the end, Lindsay decided to give up on this angle of the story, and the county commissioners voted to take one more extension. They would hold off making the final Walco decision until mid-August. Lindsay knew that the Walco management was not pleased. They wanted to get the final word in before the vote. But the Gunnison County Commissioners were too conscientious for a quick decision. They cared about Taylor Park. They cared about the project. And, most of all, they cared about getting reelected.

When Lindsay got to her room at the Sheraton, she rang for a soft drink and some ice and started playing with the lead for her story. Rita was out at the pool. They could spend the whole day on Malibu Beach tomorrow if Lindsay finished writing this story today. It was going to be tough. It was going to be a story that made Walco Resorts look good, and, unfortunately, that sort of story was as boring to write as it was to read. Lindsay decided she wasn't in the mood to write this afternoon. Despite the bright sun streaming in the window, she felt melancholy. She missed Matt desperately. Matt. She gasped audibly when she thought of him. She had been so wrapped up in her Walco research and her time with Rita, she hadn't thought to take the time to call him. He was already halfway through his visit, and Lindsay felt guilty. Very guilty. And sad. What if Matt thought she didn't love him?

Lindsay dialed the operator frantically. The call went through quickly. "Hello?" A woman's voice answered.

Lindsay was taken aback. Who was this woman answering Marc's telephone?

"I'm sorry," she apologized. "I must have dialed the wrong number." Dumb operator. Her finger must have slipped.

"What number are you trying to reach?"

"Is this the Marcus James residence?" Lindsay asked politely. She thought the lady on the other end might be able to help.

"Just what I thought," the strange voice said. "You have the correct number."

"I do?" Lindsay was baffled. "I mean...I'm sorry...this is Lindsay Cornell and I just thought...." She was so flustered, she forgot to use Kendall's last name.

"You must be Matthew's mother." The sentence was a statement, not a question.

"Who is this?" Lindsay wanted to know who was hanging around with her kid.

"Clarissa."

"Oh," Lindsay said. Just Clarissa. That explained everything. Who on earth was Clarissa?

"Matt's a great boy," Clarissa stated.

"Is he there?" Lindsay asked.

"No, I'm sorry. He and Marcus ran to the store to get some lettuce and some cheese. I'm making the guys tacos for dinner."

"That's nice," Lindsay said. "Is he spending time with his grandparents?"

"Every night," the woman named Clarissa answered. "And he's spending the day at Angela's tomorrow."

This woman knew more about her son's life than she did. The thought struck Lindsay as funny at first, and then it seared through her like lightning. "I just wanted to make sure everybody was doing okay down there," Lindsay said. "Will you tell them both that I called?"

"Sure," Clarissa answered. "Any message?"

"No, not really." Lindsay tried to remain calm. "Just tell Matt I love him. And they don't need to call me back. I was just in my hotel room and I thought I would touch base with y'all. Goodbye."

Y'all. The all-encompassing Texas term of endearment for a group of people. It had stretched even further this time to include the omniscient Clarissa. Who was Clarissa? Marcus had never mentioned anyone else in his life to her. She had felt safe on a hill in her golden castle. An unfamiliar pang of jealousy scraped through Lindsay. She knew it wasn't fair to feel that way. She had never given Marcus anything in return for what he had given her. But now she saw doors slamming in her face that she didn't want closed yet. Lindsay tried to start back to work on the Walco story, but her mind kept wandering. She kept seeing Marc and Clarissa and Matt all gathered around a table in a warmly lit kitchen. All three of them were happily munching on tacos. Lindsay was very uncomfortable with the scene she saw in her mind. Tacos for dinner with a man and a woman and one little boy sounded much too perfect. They looked too much like a family. Lindsay almost cried she felt so lonesome for Matt and Marc all of a sudden.

MATT FELT LIKE HE WAS the guest of honor at three separate madhouses. He was glad his grandparents wanted to see him, but he was tired of eating. "I saved the big meal for supper since you were going to be here, Matthew." His grandmother said that every day. Then she would serve all sorts of things he had never seen before, like okra gumbo and blackeyed peas and yellow squash. His granddaddy even put pepper sauce in the pea juice and ate it up and said it was the best pot liquor he had ever tasted. All Matt really wanted was a pile of Tater Tots and one of his mother's super-deluxe, extra drippy, peanut butter-and-honey sandwiches. He was getting homesick. He wanted to hug his mommy and he wanted to take Mr. Jinx down to the fishing hole by the waterwheel and teach him how to catch rainbow trout. He wanted all those things so badly that sometimes he felt like sitting on his bed and crying all day long.

The only person who didn't make him feel like crying was Uncle Marc. Uncle Marc made him laugh all the time. Matt wanted to hug him and forget all the other things he was sad about. They had done all sorts of wonderful boy things together. Uncle Marc took him down to the creek behind his apartment and taught him how to catch crawdads with a string tied to a piece of bacon. Uncle Marc taught him how to do a magic trick and take a whole egg out of his ear without anybody ever knowing where it came from.

The best day of all was the baseball game day. There were skydivers that came down in the middle of the stadium, and Uncle Marc bought a bag of peanuts and showed him how to crack them open, and there was a man named Fergie who threw the ball and made everybody scream.

Going to Six Flags over Texas amusement park was a fun day, too. In fact, it would have been the funnest day of all if Aunt Cissa hadn't decided she wanted to come, too. Aunt Cissa was this lady and she was nice, but she came over all the time even when Uncle Marc didn't invite her. And Uncle Marc told him that's why he should always ask before just going over to somebody's house and starting to play. Aunt Cissa cooked good things when she came, like tacos and fried chicken, but she always just sat around and talked to Uncle Marc about things that weren't interesting at all. On the day they went to Six Flags, they were doing okay together until they went into the petting zoo and this brown-and-white nanny goat took a big bite out of Aunt Cissa's leather purse. She screamed real loud, and the man that worked there had to take the goat away, and Matt felt sorry for the goat. He also felt sorry for himself and for Uncle Marc. But he didn't feel sorry for Aunt Cissa.

After the goat bit her purse, Aunt Cissa went to ride on dumb things like the merry-go-round and she went to watch a puppet show and then to hear some lady sing, so he and Uncle Marc got to ride some of the good things by themselves. They rode the Egg Scrambler and the Texas Chute-Out and the Log Flume and the Runaway Mini-Mine Train.

And then, all of a sudden, he had that sad feeling inside again and he started to cry. His mommy loved to do boy things, and he wished she was here, too. Uncle Marc didn't understand what was wrong, and when he bent down to find out if he could help, Matt just hugged him tight around the neck and cried "My mommy likes goats." And that's all he needed to say. He could tell that Uncle Marc understood exactly what he meant.

LINDSAY WAS COUNTING the days until Matt came home. Only three more to go. Two days after tomorrow. Her life would be on the right track again. She could settle down to the important things once more; working hard and spoiling her kid. She grinned at no one. She couldn't wait.

She knew now that the trip to Los Angeles had been a victory for her. The Walco story would run next Wednesday, and even though it didn't disclose anything spectacular, it was a complete story, one that the citizens of Taylor Valley deserved to read. A week of giggling and sharing secrets with Rita had worked wonders. Lindsay didn't even feel guilty about the plastic bag full of new designer suits she had brought back with her.

She had found a lovely cranberry Diane von Furstenberg and a teal-blue Oscar de la Renta. Both of them were sinfully expensive, but she had no reason to say no to them. It was almost absurd to think of wearing such things in Taylor Park, Colorado. But Rita had been relentless. "You are going to be the hottest little number beside the trout ponds." Rita had giggled, and Lindsay had finally purchased both the outfits just to prove to Rita that she would have the guts to wear them when she got home. And she was glad she had. When she got off the plane in Gunnison wearing the teal-blue suit and her California suntan, she felt like the sunshine she had absorbed on the beach was radiating up out of her very soul.

One of the most precious gifts of the week was Lindsay's renewed friendship with Rita. From the moment they had hugged each other and then woven their way through the intense Los Angeles traffic toward downtown, it was as if the four years that had crept between them had magically disappeared. Like teenaged girls, they lay awake all night long talking about choir trips from long ago and how many rolls of toilet paper it once took to wrap Rita's old boyfriend's house. In a fit of giggles one afternoon, Lindsay remembered the time Rita's big sister took them cruising on Forest Lane in Dallas and boys kept ignoring them because they looked so young, so Rita's sister smeared makeup on them and made them sit on phone books in the back seat.

"We went through so much torment for guys back then," Rita said as she hid her face in her hands.

"Back then?" Lindsay laughed. "Speak for yourself. Some of us are still going through the torment."

Rita looked at her, and Lindsay was silent.

"I'm sorry," Rita apologized. "I forgot—"

"Don't worry," Lindsay interrupted. "I guess torment was the wrong choice of words."

"I'm not so sure it was." Rita screwed up her mouth in an expression that reminded Lindsay of Matt's favorite look whenever he was eyeing a jar of pickles. "You know, I never forgave Kendall."

"Rita—" Lindsay gave her a sisterly pat on the shoulder "—you don't have to say anything. I know."

"I don't want to be disrespectful," Rita continued. "I know you loved the guy. I know he's the father of your kid. But he killed you, Lindsay. He didn't kill you because he died. He killed you because he was never honest. You never really knew where you stood. Face it, Lin. The guy was not a strong person. I often wonder if he was worth everything that you have been through." Rita looked at Lindsay. She expected to see tears streaming down her friend's face and was surprised when she didn't.

"I've thought that, too." Lindsay was nodding. "When I loved him, I think I was loving a fairy tale. And now, I think I'm afraid of doing the same thing again."

"What are you trying to tell me?" Rita asked.

"I'm trying to tell you about Marcus James." Lindsay grinned. "I think it's happening again." For the next three hours, as they lay on the beach, Lindsay chattered on about Colorado's powerful summits, her son named Matthew, the cat named Felicia the Feline and the man named Marcus.

"Didn't I meet him once?" Rita asked during the course of the conversation.

"Yeah." Lindsay stopped to think a minute. "Yeah, you did. Kendall brought him over for dinner once. Y'all left and went to a movie later."

"I remember," Rita said, giggling. "Really nice build, nice smile and very polite. He tried to pretend he wanted to be with me at that movie, but he was wishing he could have stayed there with you. I think he fell in love with you that night, Lindsay. As I remember, he really adored okra gumbo, too."

The two of them giggled in the sand some more, and then Lindsay lay back against her beach towel and closed her eyes. "This is going to sound corny, but I feel like I lost you and then found you again. Don't go home tomorrow. Fly to Colorado with me. Spend a few days there and see why it means so much to me. We can even wear our designer suits out to the trout ponds and impress everybody."

"Hey—" Rita rolled over and grabbed the suntan oil "—I'd like that. A real wonderful, spontaneous adventure. Sure. I'll come. I don't have to be home until Saturday night."

"Good." Lindsay flopped back on the grass and grinned. She was satisfied. Then her grin grew broader. "Now, tell me what you think."

"About what?"

"About Marcus." Lindsay was suddenly embarrassed. She felt like a sixteen-year-old giggling over a member of the football team.

"What do you want me to think?" Rita asked.

"I don't know—" Lindsay shook her head "—I just...wonder about him sometimes. I feel like I'm getting stronger, like I'm not as desperate for help any longer. And then I realize that I don't know if I can let him go or not...that I still want him, not just to be there, but to hold me."

Rita just stared at her friend for a moment. Then she grinned. "Lindsay," she asked, "do you ever think about what it would be like to make love with him?"

Lindsay looked at her friend, gave a shy little giggle and then hid her face in her hands. "To put it bluntly," she whispered through her fingers, "yes. All the time. Particularly after he flew to Gunnison to pick up Matt. I kept seeing things about him that I hadn't noticed before. Like his hands. I kept seeing his hands and wanting him to touch me. Isn't it crazy? It was never this way with Kendall. I don't totally understand what's happening."

"Making love isn't something to be frightened or embarrassed by, Lin," Rita answered slowly as she gazed out over the water. "It is beautiful, a priceless gift that two people in love long to give each other. I don't think there's anything wrong with what you're feeling. There's nothing crazy about it at all. In fact, it's much better than crazy. It's wonderful. Because you're finally thinking of trying again." She rolled over again and looked at Lindsay. Then she started laughing. "I think you should go for it."

"Just 'Go for it'? Is that all you're going to say? That all seems too simple." Lindsay rested her chin in the palm of her hand.

"Life—" Rita smiled at her seriously "—is oftentimes very simple."

Lindsay called Marcus the night before she left Los Angeles. She finally got the chance to tell Matt how much she loved and missed him. Marc said they were both doing fine except—he whispered this part so Matt couldn't hear—for several strong bouts of homesickness. Lindsay was almost relieved to hear the news. She was afraid Matt might have such a good time he might never want to come home. She thanked Marcus for taking such good care of her son, and Marc was surprised at the coolness in her voice. He suspected her reaction was due to her conversation with Clarissa. That idea left him feeling more than a bit encouraged.

His heart had leaped into his throat when he and Matt got home from the Tom Thumb Market and Clarissa said Matt's mother had called. Clarissa had been none too pleased by the event. But the fact didn't daunt Marcus. Before he'd started dating Clarissa, he'd told her about Lindsay, about how badly she needed him, how much he loved her. Clarissa agreed to go out with him anyway, and now Marcus was concerned the girl might be falling in love with him. She had certainly worked hard to stake out her territory now that Matt was here. It was she who insisted Matt call her "Aunt Cissa." But Marc knew he had been extremely fair with her. She had known the score before she'd even started playing the game.

Marcus had felt no need to tell Lindsay about Clarissa. The woman was not important to him. But, in a childish way, he was pleased Lindsay had talked to her. Marcus was getting impatient, not with her but with himself. He wondered if Clarissa's voice might fill Lindsay with a new sense of urgency. But then, he didn't know if he wanted to take Lindsay on those terms. She was growing strong enough now to accept other things.

Lindsay knew she was growing stronger. But she knew she wasn't home free yet. Home. She glanced out the side window toward her favorite view of the Collegiates. They stood there frozen in time. This scenery was certainly different from the skyscrapers in Los Angeles. Here was her serenity. Her knees felt wobbly, and she plopped on the bed. Sometimes, even she couldn't drink in the majesty of it all. The telephone rang just then and Lindsay answered it. "Hello?"

It was Margie Howard on the line, sounding just as bright and cheery as the sunny morning. She had a favor to ask Lindsay. She knew her old employee was busy running the newspaper, but a call had come in from Bob Beatty, a retired minister from Ohio, and Margie needed help. The cowboys who were going to be wrangling the horses in Tincup this summer had asked permission to live in Beatty's old lodge. The place hadn't been dusted out all winter and Beatty was anxious to know everything was well-maintained during the summer. The Howards' cabin-cleaning girls could handle the routine maintenance, but Margie wanted to do the first cleaning herself. She wondered if Lindsay would help.

Lindsay knew the lodge well. It was an incredible two-story pine structure with a balcony running along the top floor. The main room was cavernous with a massive rock fireplace on one wall and a player piano on the other. Handwoven Navaho rugs and an assortment of hand-hewn tables and chairs lined the room. The kitchen was almost as large. There was a formidable iron wood-burning stove standing right in the middle of it.

"I don't know if the arrangement is going to work out or not," Margie explained. "I can't pay you much, but I need you desperately. Will you come?"

Lindsay was already grinning. Margie was working so hard to talk her into it, and she wouldn't stop explaining long enough for Lindsay to tell her the answer. It sounded glorious. Scrubbing. Hard work. Just what she needed. Just the sort of thing she wanted to share with Rita to help her friend understand the strength and the magic of this valley and her people. "I'll be there. And I'll bring my best friend. She's visiting for a day or two."

Margie was ecstatic. She promised to stop by in the jeep and pick Rita and Lindsay up shortly after seven the next morning.

Margie drove up the next day in the familiar army-green jeep loaded with mops, frayed rags, the vacuum cleaner named "Dingie," scrub brushes, pine cleanser, abrasive scrubbing powder and a dented, tin bucket. Lindsay had dressed in her cabin-cleaning best this morning—a blue-green-plaid flannel workshirt, faded jeans and her crumpled blue bandana. Her hair was tied back at her neck, so she didn't mind the wind racing through her long mane as the three of them and their cleaning cargo bounced along in the topless jeep toward Tincup.

When they arrived, Lindsay was appalled. The place was filthy. If they were lucky, it would take three days to clean. No wonder Margie wanted extra help, she thought.

"Where do we start?" Rita's eyes were wide.

"Don't ask me," Margie replied. Even she looked defeated.

"Why not here?" Lindsay flicked her cloth at a dirty spot on the wall. "Oh, no." Now there was a clean slash where her rag had touched in the middle of an entirely dirty wall. "Does this mean I have to wash the whole wall?"

"Yep." Rita popped her on the bottom with a cleaning rag. "That's exactly what it means. You'd better get moving," she teased.

Margie took charge. She was on a tight schedule and the three of them were going to have to work hard and fast to meet it. She assigned Rita the kitchen. Lindsay agreed to wash the walls and polish the main room. Margie volunteered to scrub the bathroom and to dust out the bedrooms upstairs. Before long, all three of them could see progress. Lindsay was wiping down the second wall when she heard Rita laughing in the kitchen.

"What is it?" Lindsay called.

"I have an interesting fact to share with you." Rita kept laughing. "I've made a terribly important discovery."

"What?"

"This stove is blue."

"That black stove?"

"Underneath all the years of soot, this thing is a gorgeous color of baby blue," Rita said, chuckling.

"Great," Margie called from upstairs. "Who got us into this, any-way?"

"I think you did," Lindsay called up to her. She was enjoying the playful banter. It brought back many happy memories. She was wiping over the fireplace now and the dirt was coming off in clouds. There was a clock to be dusted on the mantel and two brass candle-sticks to be polished. And what were these strange objects she now held in her hands? She certainly wasn't going to polish them. "Rita?" Lindsay called into the kitchen once more. "I need advice."

"What about?"

"These." Lindsay walked into the kitchen carrying two bent, rusty tin cans. Both had been shot through with holes. "Should I polish these?" she asked, joking. Then her face turned serious. "I hate to just leave them sitting around. Everything else is going to look so nice. These things are horrible."

"They look like they've been here forever," Rita agreed. "They can't belong to anybody. Why don't you throw them out?"

"Just what I was going to suggest," Lindsay said, nodding. She aimed carefully and then tossed both the rusty cans into the kitchen trash can.

Three hours later, the kitchen glistened and the main room was spotless. Lindsay and Rita were pounding up the pine stairs to help Margie finish the bedrooms when the heavy door below banged open.

"Holy Moly," a man's voice boomed. "I could have a party in here."

Rita and Lindsay exchanged a glance and then grinned. The cow-boys were home. Margie joined them on the stairs and the three of them trampled back down.

"Hello," Margie smiled.

"We're the cabin cleaners," Rita explained.

"We figured that much." The largest cowboy nodded. "It sure does look nice in here. I'm Jake Nelson." The man introduced him-self, extending his hand to Margie. She took it and shook it vigor-ously. "And this is my head wrangler, Justin Tredway." The second man nodded.

"It's nice to meet ya'll." Lindsay smiled up at the cowboys. She liked both of them. When the two men had walked into the lodge, everything suddenly seemed just a bit more in order, a little more cushiony and comfortable.

"You didn't get that accent around here." The man named Justin

epped forward. Lindsay knew he was referring to her "y'all." That
ne word was always a dead giveaway.

"I'm originally from Dallas," Lindsay explained quietly. She liked
e way he was looking at her. His eyes were wide and warm and
entle, and Lindsay thought she might sink into them.

"Wait until you see your stove," Rita teased. She was comfortable
ith these newcomers, too. "It's blue. Always has been. A really
ice shade. I'll bet you didn't know that."

"Holy Moly," Jake Nelson's voice boomed again. "I better take
look at that, now. I might never see it like that again in my life-
me." He followed Rita and Margie into the kitchen.

"I think we're just about finished." Lindsay nodded shyly at Jus-
n.

"Gee, that's too bad," he said, grinning. He wished he could think
f something to make her stay. "There's bound to be more work to
o around here somewhere." He glanced around the room once. Then
e eyed the mantel with something akin to disappointment and worry.
Something's missing here."

"What?" Lindsay was horrified.

Jake, Rita and Margie had joined them by then.

"I don't see anything," Jake said. But then, Justin tapped the man-
l with a forefinger, and realization spread across Jake's face. "Our
ophies are missing," he stated.

Relief flooded Lindsay's body. She had seen no trophies. Surely
iis was a joke. It had to be.

"There were two of them here," Justin explained with genuine
oncern in his voice. "They were about this tall—" he showed them
ith his hands "—and about this big around."

"They were sitting right here when we left this morning," Jake
ointed to an empty space on the mantel beside the clock. A sick
ort of recognition began to filter through Lindsay.

"I think I might know what you're talking about," she whispered.
his was crazy. If the trophies weren't what she thought they were,
er companions would think she had gone cuckoo. "Were they
ound?"

"Yes," the men answered in unison.

"And...rusty?"

"Yes," Justin said as he nodded. Relief was flooding into his eyes.
indsay wanted to scream.

"With holes all shot through them?" Rita interjected.

"We're great shots, aren't we?" Justin grinned to reveal a row of perfect teeth. They were so luminously white they practically glowed against his tanned face.

"Are they...cans?" Lindsay questioned.

"Of course," the cowboys shouted and Lindsay turned to Rita and covered her face with her hands.

"I threw them away," she mumbled meekly.

"You did what?" Jake bellowed.

"I threw them away," Lindsay took her hands down and scrunched up her face.

"*No.*" Justin's eyes were playful once more. "You have no idea how long I had to practice to be able to shoot up a can like that. I can't believe you threw away our trophies."

"They're over here." Rita led them into the kitchen and retrieved the precious trophies from the trash can. Justin proudly polished the cans with his shirt sleeve and then set them back in their place of honor atop the mantel.

"We have to go." Lindsay glanced at her watch. "I've got to pick Matt up at the airport in two hours." She was obviously gleeful about that prospect.

"Who's Matt?" Justin asked. He was trying not to sound too interested.

"My kid," Lindsay explained. "I'm really excited. I haven't seen him in a week. I've really missed him."

"I'll bet," Justin said as he nodded. "Little guys are funny sometimes. You can't wait to get them out of your hair. But once you do there's this big empty space you keep tripping over."

"You're right," Lindsay agreed. She liked what he'd said. He obviously loved "little guys," as he called them.

Who is this person? Justin watched Lindsay intently for a moment. He knew he had seen her somewhere. She looked familiar. And when she started talking about Matt, Justin tried to place her with one of the ranchers he knew. But that wasn't right. Then, as she and Margie mentioned a cabin at Howard's Guest Ranch, something clicked. He had only been to Howard's once...to a wedding...and...then he knew Lindsay had been the bride that day. She married some guy from Texas. She wasn't wearing a wedding ring now. Justin bet there was an interesting story behind this one. But he didn't dare ask. He would just observe. And be her friend. And hope her ex-husband was out of the picture.

"Why don't you girls plan on coming up to go riding," Justin added on the spur of the moment. "We'll be bringing the horses up from Gunnison in another three days. It's okay if they come up, isn't it, Jake?" He looked at Lindsay.

"Sure," the big cowboy agreed.

"Thanks...we will," Margie and Lindsay chorused in unison. Rita was shaking her head sorrowfully.

"I have to fly back to Texas this afternoon. I wish I could."

"See," Lindsay poked her in the ribs. "I told you that you would love this place."

"You were right," Rita said, smiling.

They were out the door and climbing into the jeep before Justin remembered the other question he was going to ask. He was out the door and running after them as the jeep started down the hill. "Are you coming to the square dance Friday night?"

"Yes," Margie called back. "We go every week."

"How about you?" Justin pointed at Lindsay as he ran along behind them.

"I...don't know." Lindsay shook her head.

"You know you're invited," he called. "Even though you threw away our trophies. We'll go out of our way to be cordial on this one."

Lindsay threw back her head and laughed. It had been years since she had gone to one of those dances. She had loved them so while she was growing up and working at Howard's. But once Kendall had died, she hadn't felt much like whirling around the room in a breakneck polka. That had been a carefree part of her a long, long time ago. She didn't know if that part of her was worth pulling out of mothballs and dusting off or not. Maybe it would be. This cowboy seemed to think so. For an instant, she marveled at the excellent physical shape this man was in. He had been chasing the jeep and screaming at her for almost a half mile.

"Try to come," he called once more as he slowed to a halt. "I want to see all of you there." *Especially you*, he thought to himself as he watched the woman with the deep, pure eyes and the golden hair ride away.

CHAPTER FOURTEEN

THE IDEA OF THE square dance haunted Lindsay from the very mo ment Justin Tredway suggested it. The dances were the social even of the Taylor Park summers. Long, long ago, she had dragged he mother and father to them. They all sat there on the hand-hewn bench looking just like every other tourist Texan in the place. Lindsay had longed to learn the dance steps and to tromp to the fiddle tunes. When she was eight or nine, she had finally grown big enough to pull he daddy out onto the dance floor and to try to imitate the steps of the accomplished dancers.

During the years Lindsay was a cabin-cleaning girl at Howard's she had practiced the dances until she knew every step and every turn. She and her friends had initiated themselves that summer, danc ing with each other if they had to, or grabbing the boys who worked down at the boat house or some unsuspecting man who was staying at Howard's. It was those good old dances, musical chairs, the hokey pokey, the bunny hop, that Lindsay was thinking of now. Matt was old enough to learn to love those dances, too, and she was strongly considering taking him up to the Tincup Town Hall to tangle with the tourists next Friday night.

The melancholy of telling Rita goodbye was balanced by the joy of seeing Matt again at the airport. Her son looked as though he had grown a foot when he jumped off the airplane and into her arms that Saturday afternoon. He was talking in a precious Southern drawl now he even said "y'all" every once in a while, and Lindsay was so proud and excited each time she heard that word, she thought her heart might burst. Matt had come bounding off the Frontier turbo prop that day dragging poor Mr. Jinx along the ground by one arm and he couldn't wait to show her the set of pilot's wings the stew ardess had pinned on him. Mr. Jinx had a set of pilot's wings, too Matt looked so strong and so big and he babbled on for hours about Uncle Marc's magic egg trick and the skydivers that came down in the middle of the baseball field and how granddaddy ate pot liquor right out of the serving bowl.

The only thing he said about Aunt Cissa was that a nanny goat bit her good leather purse, and she screamed, and the goat had to go away, and it was very sad. But Lindsay just smiled and said that it wasn't sad at all, it was really very funny, and Aunt Cissa ought not to go around carrying such delicious purses.

"I WANT TO TEACH YOU something new. What do you think?" Lindsay suggested to her son as she popped a cold Tater Tot into her mouth.

"What?"

"It's a dance. It's called the hokey pokey. I think it's time you learned it."

"Why?" Matt wasn't certain about dancing.

"Because I'm thinking of taking you someplace special on Friday night."

"A baseball game?"

Lindsay's heart sank. She had known it would be difficult to compete with the entertainment Marc offered in Dallas. "No," she explained. "It's a square dance. It's fun. Everybody dances and claps and stomps and yells. And you can do all those things, too."

Matt thought clapping and stomping and yelling sounded wonderful. He liked to stomp and yell but he usually got in trouble for it. "Can Felicia come, too?" Matt picked the kitten up and stroked her fur.

Lindsay laughed. "I don't think Felicia would be happy at a square dance. She might get stomped on."

Matt decided that she was right. He was certainly planning on stomping around and he wouldn't want to stomp on the cat. But just the same, he decided to teach Felicia how to dance, too. So Lindsay cleared the table and put on a cassette tape, and the three of them danced well into the night, Lindsay singing, Felicia squawling and Matthew just jumping around.

LINDSAY STOOD on the front porch of the old town hall for a long time. The light streaming from the windows and the cracking paint and the ruckus going on inside all seemed to mesmerize her. They were stomping around in there like they had always stomped, like they would always do, and Lindsay felt a strange urge to turn around and run. She hadn't stood on this step for so many years, and she felt like a ten-year-old who had run away from home and was now returning, forty-five minutes later, tired and hungry. She felt like she had forsaken this part of her life. Or had it forsaken her? The only thing that kept her rooted to the spot now was the timid little boy who stood bravely next to her trying to pretend that he wasn't clinging to her arm. All was brightness and madness inside that huge, wooden door. And standing out here in the dark, it took a great deal of courage to walk through. In the end, it was Matthew who finally succumbed to the enchantment and the music inside.

"Come on, mom." He pulled her arm so hard she thought he was going to pull it off. Lindsay smiled as she stepped under the glaring lights. Now she knew how her father had felt all those years ago when she'd almost tugged his arm out of its socket so he would dance with her. The next dance started just then and Matt bopped her on the knee. "I know this one," he shrieked, and Lindsay saw herself in him as she watched the child jumping up and down with glee. Sure enough, it was the hokey pokey and, before Lindsay knew what was happening, Matt had dragged her out onto the dance floor, and she was waving her hands in the air and clapping and twirling.

"You put your right hip in, you put your right hip out..." the voice on the record instructed. As Lindsay giggled and acted silly there in the middle of the dance floor, she felt a huge spring of happiness welling up inside of her, and if she hadn't been dancing, she probably would have had to squeal just to release a bit of it. Then, just as suddenly as she grew happy, she grew pensive again. How she wished she could share this part of her life with Marcus James. Maybe someday she would be able to. Lindsay wondered what Marcus would think if he could see her throwing her hips in and out of the hokey pokey ring and hurtling across the hardwood dance floor with her son. He would definitely approve of all this stomping and all this joy. She tried to picture Marc there with her and for a moment she did. In her mind's eye, she watched him scoop Matthew up in his arms and take her by the crook of the elbow, and together the three of them pranced through the town hall to the tune of "The Cotton-Eyed Joe." It was a Cinderella scene to her and Lindsay smiled in spite of herself. Marc would look magnificent here. It struck her as strange that she hadn't realized it sooner. His face was such a fine face. The sun and his habitual expressions had etched something deep, something determined there, and his eyes were a portrait drawn with wisdom and faith rather than inks or oils. Every girl in Tincup Town Hall would die of envy if Lindsay walked in that huge wooden door with Marcus James by her side. It would be wonderful.

But it also would be terribly unfair to Marcus, Lindsay realized. In dreaming of him this way, she was idealizing him. Marc would certainly fit in fine during the summer tourist season, she thought, but when the days turned cold and the campers returned to their three-piece suits and their bi-level homes in the city, things would be different. Dallas was Marc's home just as it had once been Lindsay's, and she had no right to assume he would ever leave it. Airplanes, flying high in the sky, were his inspiration just as the mountains were hers. In one fleeting desperate moment, Lindsay wondered if there was any hope for the two of them at all.

"I want to do another dance," Matt bellowed, interrupting Lindsay's train of thought. The hokey pokey was long since over. The little boy was jumping and stomping without any music as he pulled his mother toward the bench. Out of the corner of her eye, Lindsay could see Justin weaving his way through the dancers toward her and her son.

"Hi," the cowboy said, grinning as he plopped down beside her on the splintered bench. "What's happening?"

"Nothing yet." Lindsay's eyes met his, and she wanted to shrink away. She hadn't meant to sound so forward.

"Well," he said, laughing back at her. "Things are going to get moving now."

Great, Lindsay thought sarcastically. Justin certainly did have confidence in himself.

"Who are you?" Matt questioned.

"I'm the local cowboy," Justin's voice boomed over the music. "And you must be the kid."

"Yep." Matt liked the way this man talked to him. "I'm the kid."

"You like horses?"

Matt's eyes widened, and he was nodding his head when the next song started. The familiar strain of the fiddle made Lindsay jump up off the bench. She had forgotten about the Salty Dog Rag. She just stood there giggling. She felt nine years old.

"Do you want to...." Justin was just about to ask her to dance, but it was too late. Someone else grabbed her by the arms and whirled her away. As Lindsay gaped up into the face of Jake Nelson, he bellowed down at her. "A pretty little thing like you ought to be up dancing instead of sitting around talking to a no-good cowboy like Justin Tredway."

"Thanks for the advice, Jake," she said as she winked up at him. That's all the conversation they had. The words to the song started and they each paid close attention to the dance steps. The Salty Dog Rag was a particularly furious dance.

"You're a great dancer." Justin was at her side as soon as the music stopped. "You dance like you were born here."

"Well, I wasn't," Lindsay answered slowly. She was breathless. Jake nodded his thanks for the dance and walked away. "But Matt was." She cocked her head toward her son, who was riding in Justin's arms. "Someday he'll be dancing circles around all of us."

"That's going to be hard—" Justin's eyes were appreciative. "—considering the obvious talent of his mother. You're the best. How do you know these things so well? I've never seen you at a dance before."

"I'm what you call a native tourist," Lindsay said, laughing. "We've been coming here every summer for as long as I can remember. I grew up someplace different, but there's always been a part of my spirit that stayed here in this valley."

Justin just looked at her for a moment and soaked up her words. She looked as strong and as sturdy as these mountains she loved. The things she said about this place were simple and they made sense. He was still watching her when the music started again. "Run along, kid." He set Matt on the floor and pinched his bottom. "I'm going to dance with your mama." Justin was feeling wonderful just now. He and Matt had just completed an interesting chat. Matt had told him all about his daddy and how the plane fell down.

Lindsay looked up at her partner hesitantly as soon as she recognized the music. It was a polka...a very fast one.

"You can handle it." He nodded his head encouragingly at her. "Just close your eyes and watch my feet and make sure I don't step on you, and you'll feel like you're dancing on a cloud."

"How can I watch your feet and keep my eyes closed at the same time?" Lindsay roared at him over the music.

Justin reached down and kissed her lightly on the nose. "Like I said, you can handle it."

"Great," Lindsay screamed up at him, but as Justin took her into his arms and started spinning her around, she threw her head back and her hair was flopping, and she couldn't figure out if she was dizzy from the centrifugal force or the sheer ecstasy of the experience.

Justin only tromped on her feet three times. She felt a wrenching, throbbing pain, and Lindsay wondered if she might have lost a toenail but didn't have the heart to tell him. He looked so happy, and the world was sliding by them in a prism of color and faces. Once, they tore right through an unsuspecting crowd of tourists and into a bench. There was nowhere to go except up and across the bench so they did, and the tourists jumped around and moved every way they could to avoid getting trampled. The record skipped because Justin was stomping so hard, and even though the record changed time on them, everybody kept right on spinning anyway. Lindsay felt like a wildcat present-day Cinderella flying around. At just this moment, she knew she could clobber anything that tried to beat her. But what she didn't know was that there were several women in the room who gladly would have tried to. They had come to dance with Justin Tredway tonight. But it was obvious that Justin Tredway had only one female on his mind—the delicate little woman with the impish grin who was dancing the polka like wildfire.

"OKAY, MARC," Lindsay snorted. "So what if the Dallas Cowboys are predicted to win the Superbowl again this year. One week in spring training doesn't mean anything. I'm still holding out for the Denver Broncos."

There was a pause then he spoke.

"Sure," Marcus said. "I don't care what Clarissa does. She can sneak into Danny White's football dressing room anytime she wants. She sounds like the typical Dallas woman to me."

Lindsay giggled like a teenager.

She had finally asked Marcus about the infamous "Aunt Cissa," and Marcus was doing his best to be mysterious. He wanted to keep Lindsay's interest piqued. He had to do something to save his self-esteem. He loved Lindsay so desperately. He had known her—her joys, her victories, her sorrows, her defeats—for so many years now. He had been with her when Matt was born. He had held her after Kendall died. He had loved her almost unbearably then. But now she was blossoming into a new sort of flower. She had taken on new dimensions each time she dared herself to stretch. She had become his dearest friend and his closest confidant as well as the woman he loved, and he knew someday he would tell her that. He hadn't told her anything about his feelings for her since the day Matt was born. He wanted to tell her that she seemed real to him now, not like a princess or an angel, but a real woman whom he needed. She was so far away from him, and it frightened him that he could not hold her. In all her growing and changing, she had kept her delicate fragility. She was constantly swinging from being a helpless girl to a noble woman, and there were times when Marc didn't know whether to buy her an ice cream cone or to stand up and salute.

"I hear Clarissa carries nice edible purses," Lindsay said then giggled. She hadn't confessed to Marcus that she knew about the "goat incident."

"What has your son been telling you?" Marcus tried to sound aggravated, but he couldn't.

"He tells me that you and your friends are awfully hard on goats."

"You tell Matt," Marcus said, chuckling, "that I went by to see that damn goat yesterday. She tried to eat my suit coat. She's doing fine."

"I'll tell him." Lindsay snickered. It was just like Marcus to drive back to an amusement park to check on the welfare of a goat. She could hear him now carrying on the conversation with the zoo keeper. "How is Miss Nanny today?" If Marcus could have seen Lindsay at that moment, he would have seen a duskiness creep into her eyes. He had taken care of that silly goat exactly the same way he had taken care of her. He had a loving heart that just kept giving and giving and giving.

Lindsay had realized so much about her feelings for Marcus after she returned from her trip to California. It was as if she had awoken to the brilliant, sparkling row of Collegiates on her first morning home and had grasped every piece of her life firmly in her hands. She knew how desperately she needed Marcus. She had needed him before, to comfort her, to guide her, to take a part of Kendall's place. But she needed more of him now; his hugs, his laughter, his dreams, maybe even his love. Nevertheless, she was still waiting, even though she wasn't exactly certain what for. Above all, she knew she wanted to be sure her new longings weren't being brought on by the interesting appearance of "Aunt Cissa." It wouldn't be fair to either her or Marc if her current feelings turned out to be only jealousy.

"Have you taken that new Cessna up?" Lindsay questioned. As she spoke, there was a knock on her front door. Lindsay didn't hear it. Matt ran to open the door with Nina close behind him and, when the door swung open, there stood Justin Tredway.

"It's the cowboy! Come on in," Matt squealed. Felicia was already purring and rubbing against Justin's legs and Nina was stumbling over all of them trying to take his coat away.

"It's nice to be wanted." Justin chuckled as he stepped into the front room. "Where's your mom?" He looked disappointed that Lindsay hadn't come to greet him.

"She's in there on the phone talking to Uncle Marc," Matt explained matter-of-factly.

"Who's Uncle Marc?" Justin asked. He didn't mean to pry. He was just curious about everything in this little boy's life. And in the boy's mother's life.

"He's my really good friend," Matt explained. "And he's mommy's good friend, too. He used to know my dad—" Matt looked pensive for a moment "—and he flies an airplane and he came here one time to pick me up."

"That's nice of him." Justin enjoyed conversations with youngsters. That's one reason he enjoyed taking children on trail rides. They were his joy.

"He says he loves us very, very much." Matt nodded up at Justin. Justin was surprised by the manly look on the child's face. "I think he wants to adopt us."

Justin smiled. He had gotten what he asked for. An honest answer. And in the childlike simplicity of the words, Justin had learned much, much more.

Felicia jumped into his lap and started purring happily, and Nina brought him a glass of 7-Up. Matt and Justin sat there together on the sofa waiting for Lindsay. Matt's short, plump legs were swinging ten inches off the floor to the rhythm of Justin's tapping boots.

When at last Lindsay stepped through the door, she was vibrant. Justin thought he might drown in the smiles and the sunshine that entered the room with her.

"I'm so glad you're here," she said as she bent down and took Felicia from Justin's lap. "I was listening for you, but I guess I didn't listen hard enough."

"That's okay." Justin winked at Matt. "The kid told me you were right in the middle of an important long-distance phone call."

"I was," she smiled. She cast a knowing look at her son.

"I don't want to rush you," Justin added, "but it's going to take a while to drive to town. The movie starts soon."

"That's fine." Lindsay laughed and her laughter sounded like a summer breeze. "Will you kids be okay here for tonight?" She looked at Nina when she asked the question, and the old woman smiled.

"Bye kid," Justin said to Matt and waved. Then they were off, bumping and bouncing along the dirt road in Justin's dusty green Ford pickup truck with the broken broom handle sticking out of the tail gate.

They had driven about three miles before Justin looked over at her and grinned sheepishly. "Thanks for agreeing to go into town with me tonight. I was going to call this morning and ask you what you were going to wear."

"You were?"

"Yeah," he said, nodding at her across the cab. She was wearing a yellow linen dress that went perfectly with the look in her eyes and the sky outside. "I was worried you would dress up or something. I don't have any suits."

"Justin Tredway," Lindsay laughed. "I think you look wonderful." His jeans were worn and faded, but they were clean, and he wore a camel flannel shirt and a hand-tooled Western belt. He had chosen to leave his Stetson off this evening, and Jake had practically snarled at him when he left the lodge. "You look like a real city dude, Tredway. What's gotten into you that you think you have to dress so continental around that woman?"

Justin didn't look "continental" to Lindsay at all. He looked outdoorsy and rugged and strong, and Lindsay wondered if any room in any building could contain him. He still smelled of leather and tobacco and pine. Lindsay had been dreaming of someone like him ever since she had been coming to Taylor Park. She had ridden on several of the Timberline Trail rides when she was growing up, and she had fallen in love with several of the wranglers when she was eleven. Justin was a little-girl dream come true for her, but she didn't know exactly how to tell him that.

"Oh...." Justin remembered something just then. "I brought you these."

"Thank you." Lindsay took the little box from his hand. She opened the box carefully and exclaimed when she saw what was in it. "Oh." It was a set of mushrooms. There was one large one and one small one meticulously hand-carved out of aspen. He had made them for her. What a treasure they were.

"Look at the bottom of the little one," Justin ordered.

Lindsay turned the wood sculpture over and read the base. "To Lindsay, Love, Justin," the carving read.

"Just a little something to remember me by." He laughed as she turned to him, her eyes gleaming. "Check the bottom of the other one."

"Ba...Ba...." Lindsay struggled. "I can't read this word," Lindsay admitted.

"Basidiomycete," Justin helped her. "It's the biological term for 'mushroom.' I decided you needed a lesson on biological terms this evening."

Lindsay looked at Justin in amazement. "How do you know that?"

"Because in the winters when I'm not playing cowboy, I'm a biology teacher at the high school in Fort Collins," he confessed.

"You sneak," Lindsay said, crossing her arms in mock disgust. "I thought you were a real American cowboy. The last of a dying breed. And here I find out you earn most of your living teaching high-school students. Boy, did you have me fooled." But Lindsay was secretly pleased. She had guessed that there was more to Justin than met the eye. He was a biology teacher, probably with a master's degree in amphibians or something else challenging and unique. Interesting.

Their evening together was simple and special. The academy-award-winning movie they had planned to see at the Flicka had already been sent to another small town somewhere, and the only thing playing was a B movie called *The Terror Comes After You Die*. Justin was about to suggest they try a different form of entertainment when he noticed Lindsay pouting. "Do you know how long it's been since I've seen a movie?" she asked. "I think it's been five years. I don't care if the movie's lousy. I just want to sit in there and eat popcorn."

"Sure thing." Justin held the door of the truck open for her. "We'll stay. But I think this movie will take *lots* of popcorn."

The movie was horrible. In fact, it was so horrible it was wonderful. Lindsay and Justin sat on the third row from the screen, giggling and throwing popcorn at each other. Halfway through the movie, Justin put his arm around her and hugged her to him, and Lindsay felt like she was on her first date all over again. There was a bewitching, magical quality about everything they were doing, and

Lindsay wished they could sit there howling at the movie all night long.

After the show was over, Justin insisted on taking her to eat at Mario's. Lindsay was so stuffed with hot buttered popcorn that the idea of eating more almost turned her stomach. But Justin wanted to show her his favorite pizza place, and Lindsay didn't have the heart to turn him down. So they ate at Mario's Pizza on Main Street in a secret cubbyhole in the back of the room. Justin ate an entire pepperoni pizza, and Lindsay ate half of her Canadian bacon sandwich, and they both laughed and snitched each other's potato chips, and Justin demonstrated his talent for juggling wadded napkins. He tried to teach Lindsay the trick, too. They sat there for two hours trying, and by the time they'd finished there were napkins all over the restaurant.

"This is so I can come back here and juggle anytime I want to." Justin winked at the waitress as he dropped several coins on the table. "Actually, these people here should be paying me to come and perform for them. A good juggling act could attract quite a bit of pizza business, don't you think?"

Lindsay just looked up at him and grinned. Then she gave him a hug for his talents as they strolled out into the cool high-country air arm in arm.

As Justin walked along beside Lindsay, he was almost surprised by how pleased, how relaxed, he felt. There was something refreshing about this woman, about the way she presented herself to him. She didn't walk or hold her head at the jaunty angle that indicated she expected others to notice her beauty. She only tripped along as if her feet never touched the ground, as if she was an angel who could observe the rest of the glamour, the electricity of the world without anyone observing her. She seemed to flutter along beside him as if she was a teeny, feathered bird. Her very movements, even her casual motions, made her seem almost unfocused to him, as if he was looking at her face through a thin veil of gossamer silk.

He stopped short for a moment and just looked at her. Then he turned to her and pulled her toward him. He kissed her once full on the mouth and was surprised when Lindsay neither returned the kiss nor pulled away from him. She only stood there before him as if what she was doing now was simply a duty that had to be performed, and Justin was almost angry. Why had she reacted that way? He was instantly on his guard.

Lindsay just looked at him sadly, her eyes full of remorse, and Justin knew then that it had not been the right time to touch her. Something in her face told him that it might never be the right time. He wondered if she had ever really recovered from the death of her husband. And then he wondered if she might be in love with someone else. Justin had seen Lindsay whirling across the dance floor at Tincup Town Hall. He had seen her reach out to people, to her son, to Nina, and give them everything she had inside of herself to give. And that is how he knew that, now, something was terribly different about her. It was as if, when he had kissed her, she had thrown a brick wall up between them.

"Lindsay. I'm sorry," he told her quietly. "Perhaps I should have waited, should have asked...." His voice faded out. He had almost expected her to stop him, but she hadn't.

"It's okay." Her eyes were round and bright with unshed tears as she lifted them up to him. "It's my fault, too. Maybe I shouldn't have agreed to come with you. But I wanted to so badly. And I've had such a nice time. I'm just not very...kissable...these days. I don't know what else to say."

"You could start by telling me why." He could not hide the trace of disappointment that crept into his face.

She shook her head. "I don't exactly know why. I thought that maybe—"

"Lindsay," he held up a hand to stop her from saying more and then he grasped her by the shoulders. "Don't worry. I only assumed some things about you. I assumed that you were available. I assumed that you wanted me to kiss you."

"You had a right to assume those things, Justin," she said, nodding.

"No—" he shook his head "—I didn't." He laughed. "I suppose that I flatter myself with such thoughts much too often."

"No." This time she laughed, too, and he was relieved. "I'm flattered that you want to be with me. I've tried to make myself available...to anyone...." She picked her words carefully. "But I can't."

"Forgive me, okay?" Justin swept his arms out dramatically and gave her an awkward little bow that started her laughing again. "I would do anything. I'm willing to undergo all sorts of terrible things. Starvation. Banishment," he joked. "You only have to name my torture."

"Hmmm." She held her hand to her chin in a mock gesture of thought. She was beginning to enjoy this evening again. She was surprised at Justin's sensitivity, surprised that he had even noticed she was holding herself back from him when he kissed her. "Let me see what I can think of. Something horrible. Oh, I know...." She paused for effect. "You can take me back to that movie. We can sit there and eat more popcorn and watch *The Terror Comes After You Die* again. What do you think?"

"No! No!" He held his stomach and flashed her a look of half terror, half glee. "Anything but that."

"Well, I don't know." She took his arm and began skipping down the sidewalk beside him. "I might let you off," she admitted, then raised her eyebrows at him. "Maybe just this once."

"Thanks," he looked down at her and then couldn't resist giving her a quick brotherly peck on the cheek. "You know, Lindsay Cornell-Allen, you are a real doll."

Knowing Justin added much laughter and frolic to Lindsay's life. She seemed to sparkle since she'd met him. Everyone noticed. Her staff at the newspaper. Nina. Even Marcus. Every sentence she said was punctuated with a new lightness, and Marc took to calling her more and more to hear the new brilliance in her voice. He wondered what wonderful things were happening to her. He was almost certain she was seeing someone. And his thoughts were confirmed while he was talking to Matt one afternoon before Lindsay got home from the newspaper.

"We get to go riding horses today," Matt informed him gleefully. The little boy was so excited he was exploding with the information. His mother hadn't told him until this morning because she was afraid he wouldn't have slept at all the night before.

"I wish I could be there," Marc said, laughing.

"So do I," Matt exclaimed. "I know Mr. Justin would let you go on a horse, too."

"Mr. Justin, huh?" Marcus smiled in Dallas. "Who's he?"

"A *real* cowboy," Matt shrieked. The way the child said the word "real" made it sound like it had four or five syllables. "He's nice."

"Where did you meet him?"

"He's mommy's friend. And he knows how to rope and how to herd cows. And he likes goats, too."

The guy must be pretty special, Marcus thought. Especially if he likes goats. That was Marc's and Matt's secret signal ever since Aunt issa got her purse nibbled on. Anyone who liked goats was nice. Anybody who didn't like goats wasn't worth worrying about.

Later that day, Matt, Lindsay and Justin headed their horses toward Napolean Pass. The evening spread before them like a gem, and as they trotted toward the bald peaks before them, the sunset reached across the sky in hundreds of magnificent tendrils. Lindsay was once more overwhelmed by the grandeur of this place. But Matt was more interested in the mountain creatures that were skipping across the horse's path. There were chipmunks and field mice and pine martens and marmots. Justin pointed out a lone elk that was grazing along Willow Creek, and Matt found fresh deer tracks in the mud. It was too late in the season for most of the wild flowers, but columbine and larkspur still dotted the countryside with color.

Every creature in the forest around them seemed to be skittering and fluttering in preparation for the nightfall. Two beavers flopped merrily across a pond, and Lindsay eyed them silently. Beavers were terrible for trout fishermen. She remembered seven years ago when Dan Howard had dynamited several of their lodges so the water and the fish could flow freely onto ranch property. It seemed like such a horrible waste of nature's energy, such a cruel joke to play on the hapless creatures, and Lindsay had lain awake all that night feeling sad. Now, looking at the wet animals skimming across the quiet pool, Lindsay felt the same sense of loss washing over her. Life could be so frighteningly cruel or so painfully honest. It could also be terribly joyous, she thought to herself as she glanced back at Justin and Matthew. Terribly, terribly joyous.

"Shhh," Justin put a finger to his lips and motioned to Matthew. "Here's another family you need to see."

As the horses slowed, Justin pointed to a small pond to the left of the bridle path. The water was dancing and rippling in the remaining sunlight. On the pond swam a mother duck followed by her nine downy ducklings. "They hatched a little over three weeks ago," Justin whispered. "I've watched her teach them to swim. Look how good they are. They don't fly yet—" the cowboy smiled "—but they'll be doing that soon, too."

"Will she teach them how?" Matt's eyes were huge as Justin nodded.

Lindsay watched Justin's face with a sense of awe. He knew so much about growing up and growing away. And he accepted it all

for the miracle of life that it really was. The way he loved the famil
of ducklings made her want to cry.

Darkness was approaching now, and Justin grinned as he turne
to Lindsay and reached into his left saddle bag. "I brought you
surprise." He rummaged around until he found what he wanted. "
thought you might be hungry after all this rough riding—" he winke
at both of them "—so I brought along some supper." He pulled
package of wieners out and waved them in the air victoriously. "Any
body for a cookout?"

"Do you know how wonderful you are?" Lindsay grinned up a
him after she jumped off her horse and tethered the animal to a tree
Her stomach had been rumbling for miles.

In no time, the fire was crackling, and Matt was digging in th
saddle bags to see what other delicacies he could find. There wer
hot-dog buns, cans of Sunkist orange soda, graham crackers, marsh
mallows and Hershey's chocolate bars. It was a feast that tasted fiv
times better than it should have because all three of them were rav
enous.

Matt was busy roasting his fifteenth marshmallow over the coals
and Lindsay was munching another charred wiener without a bu
when Justin moved closer to her and draped his arm across her shoul
ders. Lindsay wanted to move closer to him, to lay her head agains
his chest and know that she belonged there, but she couldn't do that
Something deep inside kept tugging at her. The thought of the duck
lings and the beavers and the serenity of the campfire were all s
wonderful she only wanted to share everything with Marcus. Whe
she glanced at Justin, she felt guilty and sad all at the same time
She didn't understand why she couldn't release all her old memories
her old hopes, and plunge into this new relationship. She loved th
things that Justin was teaching her. But Lindsay realized that she wa
inexplicably bound to Marc's memory.

Justin saw a dark look cross her face, and he was afraid to interpre
it. He gave her a questioning glance, and she answered it by suddenl
teasing him. "I know you, Justin Tredway." She playfully jabbe
her elbow into his ribs. "I've heard all the rumors. You've probabl
gone out with every single woman at that square dance."

"Who? Me?" He tried to look innocent, but the look on his fac
was devilish.

"Go ahead," Lindsay teased. "Admit it."

"Okay." His eyes turned toward her again and this time he wa erious. "I admit it. I've never dated one girl longer than one month in my entire life. Until you. That's why everyone in this valley is so amazed by us. Nothing like this has ever happened to me before."

Justin watched her eyes to see how she would react to his words. He couldn't read anything there except surprise. He had tried to tell her so much in that one sentence. Something about Lindsay, something about her strength and her vulnerability and how she balanced the two made him admire her more than any other woman he had ever known. He was feeling something for Lindsay that he had never felt for any woman before. He wasn't certain that he recognized what his new feeling was. Gratitude. Amazement. Protectiveness. Awe. Perhaps love. It was all mixed up in his heart in a healthy jumble and he was aware of it every time he looked at her. It's just a summer romance, he kept reminding himself. An easy trap to fall into. But some inner voice told him that this was turning out to be much more.

"Thanks." Lindsay was smiling at him now, her face etched like a pastel portrait in the firelight. "You pay nice compliments."

"It's nothing," he said as he tossed his arms nonchalantly into the air. "You deserve to be praised." Then, in an attempt to lighten the mood, he darted a teasing glance at her. "I don't know why you're worrying. A girl like you probably has guys in every city in the world. I know what girls like you are like."

"Justin Tredway," she laughed, but then she remembered Marc, and her face darkened. "No, I do not have men in every city...."

Something in the way her sentence trailed off at the end made him turn and look at her. He knew what he had to say now. His heart dropped to his toes. "Lindsay," his eyes caressed her face. "I have to ask you something."

Lindsay turned to him to finish her jestful sentence, but what she saw on his face sobered her. She remained silent.

"I want you to tell me about Marc, Lindsay." Justin's eyes were full of something soft and sad and smoldering.

Lindsay gasped. Why would he make a request like that? And then she followed his gaze toward her son who was sitting meekly by the campfire with melted marshmallow and ashes spread from one ear to the other.

"You have a nice kid with a big mouth," Justin said, reading her mind. "Besides, Matt loves this guy a lot."

Lindsay pulled in a deep breath and then sighed. It had been a

long time since she had even tried to put into words what Marcus
James really meant to her.

"I don't know for certain...." She turned to Justin and her eyes
were huge and round and sad. "He was Kendall's best friend a long
time ago...my husband." She stopped to see if Justin understood and
he did. "He flew here to be with me when Matt was born.... He's
like Matt's father, I think.... He's just...always been there for us."

"Do you love him?" It was a blunt way to ask the question but
Justin had to know. Her answer meant everything to him just now.
He had to know before he let himself go further.

"I don't know." Lindsay was crying now. "I don't know, Justin."
She hid her face in her hands. But before she hid her eyes, Justin
saw everything there that he needed to see. The raw pain he read
there told him the entire story. But it told him something else, too.
She was telling him the truth. She really didn't know. Something in
her life had totally blinded her to the feelings deep within her heart.
Lindsay was desperately in love with this Uncle Marc character. And
the sad thing was, she had absolutely no idea.

CHAPTER FIFTEEN

THE COUNTY COMMISSIONERS filed into the hearing room. It was 3 P.M. Wednesday, August twenty-seventh. The time for the final Taylor Park resort project vote had arrived.

The Walco staff was ecstatic on its side of the hearing room. On the other side of the room sat the ranchers, the business owners, the workers of Gunnison. Most of them opposed the project. Some of them didn't. But they all sat together, en masse, as if to signify they would rally around each other no matter what the decision.

Lindsay Cornell-Allen sat alone at the press table on the platform just below the commissioners' benches. She was doing her best to look professional, reserved and confident. She knew the valley was going to survive. She knew the project would be overturned. No amount of professional marketing presentations or monetary offers could sway these commissioners. They knew what their constituents wanted. Lindsay had faith in the public system. Big money wouldn't win. The people would.

"The matter before the county this afternoon is the decision on Proposal Twenty-eight A," the clerk announced into a microphone at the speaker's podium. "This is concerning the Walco Resort Project on one thousand six hundred acres in Taylor Park."

One by one, the county commissioners stood and cast their votes. One by one, the three men gave their opinion and their decision. Lindsay did not listen to the words they spoke. It was too late for words, for opinions, for justification. What mattered now were the numbers.

When the final tally was announced, the Walco men clapped each other on the back. Congratulations were certainly in order. One man handed his boss a prepared list of construction dates. The contracting company had already been hired. Groundbreaking would be two weeks from today. Construction could start in as early as three weeks.

Lindsay's entire body crumpled when she heard the results of the final vote. She struggled to keep back the tears. But then she decided

it wasn't worth the trouble. Why not cry openly? Why not let thes
business executives see what they had done to this valley, to thes
people? By a two to one vote, she and Gunnison County had lost th
magic, the mastery of this valley. The changes would come now
There was no way to stop them. And Lindsay couldn't help won
dering if, by losing this valley, she had lost a big part of herself a
well.

MARCUS JAMES HATED business dinners. It wasn't because he fel
out of place. He could wear a tuxedo and chat about yearly earning
along with the best of them. The aircraft company's board of director
was visiting from Detroit, and as aircraft maintenance director, Mar
cus was required to put in a token appearance.

Most of the men had brought their wives with them this evening
and Marcus had considered bringing Clarissa along, but he'd decide
against it. He had quit asking her out three months ago. He didn'
think it was fair to give her encouragement, because he still fel
absolutely nothing for her. Not that she needed encouragement, any
way. She still appeared on his doorstep to fix him meals and talk t
him, but he could tell by the resolve he saw in her face that she ha
finally accepted the truth. She knew he was in love with Lindsay.

Lindsay. Marcus glanced around the room at the panorama befor
him, the frowning waiters in their starched red jackets, the liltin
music, the fairy-tale dresses that swooshed along the floor and glis
tened in the candlelight. *Lindsay would be the most beautiful on
here if she was at this party*, he thought. He had promised himsel
so many times that he would stop trying to see things through he
eyes and quit trying to think like her. He tried to stop loving her
too, not altogether, just a bit, just enough to take an edge off wha
he was feeling. He wished that his thoughts of her would waft gentl
in and out of his days instead of pouncing on him first thing in th
morning before he even brushed his teeth.

Marcus looked around the room once more. He was at Kirklan
House, the most prestigious restaurant in Dallas. It sat thirty-tw
stories up on a spire beside Kirkland Inn, one of the most luxuriou
hotels in Texas. The best thing about the restaurant was that it re
volved. As you ate your extravagantly expensive meal and visite
with some of your extravagantly boring business associates, a three
hundred-sixty-degree view of downtown Dallas spun by once a
hour. The view from Kirkland House was incredibly beautiful. Bu

not nearly as breathtaking as Dallas could look from up in an airplane.

Marcus smiled to himself. He was thinking like a pilot again. He and his colleagues were the only kind of people who thought nothing in life was more spectacular than it was from twenty thousand feet above. For an instant he thought of Lindsay again. Maybe that's why he loved her so. She was just as spectacular up close as she was when he tried to look at her from different angles. She didn't need the extra height, the extra lights or the new dimensions to be resplendent.

Idly, he fingered the matchbook that was propped open attractively in the ashtray beside him. How he missed Lindsay tonight. How he wished he could have whisked her into this elegant place on his arm. Maybe he should do something sentimental like save this matchbook cover and send it to her. If he ever got brave enough again, he could tell her how badly he had needed her here with him tonight. He picked up the matches once again. He was planning to drop them into his pocket, but something about the printing there was familiar and he stopped. "Kirkland House," the cover read in a lovely metallic silver script. Then, in smaller letters along the bottom, it read "A Walco Resort Accomplishment."

Marcus wanted to leave. It was either that or smash his lovely crystal goblet up against the wall, and he didn't think that was appropriate. Lindsay had called him two nights ago in tears because a project of this magnitude, designed by the same company, had been approved for Taylor Park. Lindsay had been devastated, and Marcus hadn't really understood why. Looking around him now at the beautiful women in all their finery, wearing their porcelain-perfect foundation and blusher and their frosted shades of eyeshadow, Marcus finally understood everything. Lindsay would have been the most beautiful woman here tonight. In fact, she would have risen far above the rest of them. But the thing was, she was too much a real person now to even care.

Marcus started laughing. There were waves of relief flooding his entire being. He still had a chance. Because he had found something incredible here in this room tonight. He had figured out exactly what Lindsay Cornell-Allen was hiding from.

"I REFUSE TO ACCEPT THIS, Justin," Lindsay said, frowning at the cowboy beside her. When he didn't acknowledge her comment, she bent her neck back and glared at the clear sky through the ceiling of pine trees that rose above her. "Maybe I can't let myself accept all the things I'm supposed to accept. About people growing. About places changing. Why is it so wrong for me to want this valley to stay the same forever? Everybody likes it the way it is. So why can't it just stay that way? Why does some businessman from California barge in and get to make all the decisions for us?"

"I don't know, Lindsay," Justin almost whispered his reply to her. "I don't know." He had opposed the Walco project, too. They had all fought a fair fight together. But now, there was nothing to do except sit back and allow the changes to happen. Justin was willing to do that, but Lindsay wasn't. She seemed to have a personal vendetta against the Walco Resort. For some reason, she couldn't let go.

"Maybe I'm wrong, Justin. Do you think—" She cut herself off, was silent for a moment, and then smiled sadly at Justin. "Why don't you just shoot me and put me out of my misery? Isn't that what they do for horses? I'm certain you're sick of all my whining."

"Yes," he admitted, then smiled back at her, and he looked sad, too. "I'm sick to death of hearing about that resort. But I'm not tired of listening to you. Things always seem to make more sense when you say them."

"Thanks." She touched his cheek. "You're a wonderful friend to put up with me."

"Anytime." He winked at her. "Anytime." Justin's eyes lingered on Lindsay. He was leaving Taylor Park in two days to go back to his teaching position in Fort Collins. And he wasn't certain if he could ever come back to this place again. This summer had been phenomenal for him. The time he had spent with Lindsay Cornell-Allen had been priceless. He would never forget the chattering and the bantering back and forth between them as they had trotted on horseback through the trees and across the streams. He would never forget the tromping and the twirling at the dances. He and Lindsay had captured a magical time, a time he knew could never be repeated and would never return. He knew that someday he would find a love of his own. But he also knew that, from now on, in every woman he met and loved, he would always be looking for parts, for pieces of this one celestial woman he was leaving behind. He watched her as she stood slowly and ran a hand across the horse's withers. He wanted to drink in her every movement, every intonation of her voice, every expression in her eyes.

"Think he's ready to go?" Lindsay asked him as she cocked her head at a mischievous angle. She had been challenging him to a race all afternoon.

"Sure." Justin nodded at her. "We've got time to go farther." He watched her as she mounted her horse, Grande, and then he did the same. As they rode west toward the summit of Napolean Pass, Justin studied the sky closely. The sun was already behind the tallest peaks. It must be about six-thirty. They would have to ride hard on the way back. Justin spurred his horse on, and as he caught up with Lindsay he leaned across her horse and kissed her lightly on the cheek.

"Hey, watch out for Grande," she scolded playfully. "You need to learn to be nicer to these animals."

"Oh, Lindsay—" he stuck out his tongue at her "—all you ever think about is horses."

"No," she laughed. "You're wrong. All I ever think about is horsing around." Then she threw her head back into the wind and laughed at the sky. Her laughter came sparkling up out of her like water gurgles up out of a fountain. It was the first time she had laughed with such abandon since the Walco hearing. Justin loved to see her finally relaxing.

"Yah," he cried as he spurred his horse past her and then called back over his shoulder, "Want to race?"

"Not fair, Justin Tredway." He could hear her horse's hooves thundering behind him. "You gave yourself a head start."

"I deserve a head start, woman," he called back to her. "Grande runs faster than Gray Lady. Meet you at the fence," he challenged, nodding his head toward the end of the meadow.

"Yaah!" Lindsay commanded and Justin knew she had decided to race him. Together they flung themselves, pushing, fighting, urging their horses on, and as Lindsay's horse edged past Justin and Gray Lady, she felt like she was flying. For one moment of racing across the meadow below the mountains, she forgot the problems, the demons, the cares that were holding her back. As she reined Grande in and then turned the animal to face Justin still barreling toward the fence, she felt strong. She felt powerful and she felt free. She threw her head back and laughed another splashing-water laugh that cascaded and tinkled its way toward Justin, and he wanted to shout for the sheer joy of the sound.

"Oh, Justin," she called and he turned and followed the gaze of her eyes. The happiness in her voice had been replaced with a whisper of melancholy, a dash of regret, and when he saw where she was looking, he understood why. She was looking at the duckling pond. Today there was no young family learning to flop and swim and flap and quack. There were no playful swirls etching themselves across the pond. There was nothing. Each of the ducklings had flown away one by one, and the mother duck had flown away, too, and now, the only sound that rose above the water was the rustling of the wind as it moved through the tall native grasses.

Lindsay turned to Justin with a half smile. She did not try to hide the tears streaming down her face. "I'm sorry," she apologized, then laughed gently at herself. "You probably think I'm an incurably mushy person. But I feel so much like those dumb ducks. So much is over for me. The smart thing to do would be to fly away and leave the pond behind. But look at how silent this meadow is. Just like them, what will I leave behind me? How will I know where I've gone?"

Justin dismounted and held his arms up to Lindsay. She let him help her off Grande and then she just stood there, secure in his embrace.

"Look up there, Lindsay," Justin put a finger beneath her chin and pushed her head back until her eyes met the sky. All she could see was an infinite place above her growing darker and colder as the sun sank lower behind the Rockies. "That's where you'll be," Justin whispered to her and, for the first time, she heard the love in his voice. "That's where they are. Flying somewhere that they couldn't begin to understand before. Do you think they ever fathomed how big the sky is, Lindsay? They did it and so can you. You know what's up there. That's why it's going to take more courage for you to flap your wings the first time and start rising off that pond."

He stopped and looked at her for a moment and he saw a look on her face that had never been there before. A smoldering realization of her own strength that was preparing to burst into a flame. And he loved her all the more for what he saw there. "You can do it, Lindsay. You can let go. But you can't do it alone. You have to take faith with you. Plenty of it. Use what you believe, to give you wings."

"I don't know." She hid her face in her hands. "There is so much involved now. It isn't as simple as it used to be. I'm trying to be fair to everybody."

"Lindsay." He pulled her hands from her face and he just stood there before her for a moment. "Quit trying to make everything fair. It's time that you realized that life just isn't fair. And now it's time for something else. It's time for you to go to him."

Her eyes opened wide. "Do you mean Marcus?"

"You are very smart, young lady." He took her shoulders in his hands. "Yes," he said, gripping her tightly. "You and the man you love have an incredible life ahead of both of you."

Lindsay hugged Justin close to her for a long time as she laughed,

and the two of them cried together. "You're so good for me, Justin."
She sniffed up at him. "What am I ever going to do without you?"

"You'd better miss me, ma'am," he said softly. Then he bent
down and kissed her tenderly before he playfully slapped her on the
bottom. "Get your horse. We've got to get back to the stables."

"Yes, sir," Lindsay answered him, and as she untethered Grande
she glanced around the meadow, searching for one last time, wishing
she could touch the almost palpable coziness and the serenity there.
She was still taking in the panorama of the meadow when she saw
an eerie glow rising above the trees to the east. She watched for a
moment, thinking the glow would disappear as soon as the sun fell
behind the trees. But a cold stab of realization assaulted her. The sun
had been gone for almost twenty minutes. This glow was the harbin-
ger of something altogether different. Something dangerous.

"Justin." Her voice was shrill, and he came to join her quickly.
"Look. What is that?"

His eyes followed her pointed finger. "Oh no." His next breath
was a painful one. He sniffed the air. There was a faint odor of wood
smoke in the air. The full impact of terror hit Justin. "Let's get over
there," he instructed Lindsay.

Before he mounted Gray Lady, Justin stooped to the ground and
pulled up a handful of brittle grass. It was bone dry. That's the way
the forest was now. In the middle of July the daily afternoon mountain rainstorms had stopped coming. And the snow wouldn't start
flying until mid-September. The United States Forest Service con-
sequently ran ad after ad begging campers to be careful with their
fires. This was a time in the high country when a cigarette butt could
burn thousands of trees and living mountain things. In August, all of
Colorado was brittle and parched. One stray spark could ignite an
inferno.

"Is it a fire, Justin?" Lindsay was trembling. The glow was coming from one of the more populated areas of the valley.

"I think so," he called back. "Hurry."

Together they raced across the meadow and back into the trees.
Surely someone else had seen the fire by now. The forest rangers
kept one pumper truck at the base of the reservoir dam. If the fire
was any bigger than one truck could control, and Justin suspected it
would be, the rest of the equipment would have to come up from
Gunnison. And the canyon road was a tedious drive for emergency
vehicles. There was no way to guess what the loss of forest—or of
life—might be.

"Justin," Lindsay screamed as her horse ran beside him through the trees. Her voice was sharp. It seemed to shatter the forest around them. "Do you see where we're headed?"

Justin had lost his bearings racing in and out among the trees. But Lindsay hadn't. This nightmare was becoming more and more sickening as they rode forward.

"It's the Walco land," Lindsay cried. Justin almost fell off his horse when the force of her words hit him. The fire made sense now. The glow did not look like a small blaze that was started by an unwise camper. Someone had deliberately torched the Walco property. Someone who had wanted to save the serenity of this valley so desperately, he had to destroy it to do so. Arson. Sick, ugly, unnecessary destruction. Justin wanted to cry.

As they neared the blaze, both Lindsay and Justin's worst fears were realized. The Walco land was ablaze, and the fire was roaring out of control. The U.S. Forest Service pumper truck was already at the site along with several auxiliary pickup trucks and jeeps. They could hear the shouts of the firefighters from almost two miles away. It was hard to see against the dancing flames and the darkness, but Lindsay could distinguish faces and figures in the distance. The thirty or so men had formed a human assembly line with one another, passing buckets, pouring water, stomping out small grass fires, digging trenches, cutting through underbrush. Jake Nelson was there and so was Dan Howard. Lindsay also recognized Randy Carver from the Nugget Café, Joe Sherman from the boat dock and Bergie Jackson from the general store.

Lindsay's horse began moving closer to the men, while Justin's mount reared back. "Should we try to take them on in?" She turned to him anxiously.

"You can take Grande closer," Justin said, nodding his head, "but I can't do much with Gray Lady. Jake's used Grande to fight some grass fires on his ranch near Alamosa. But this old girl—" he patted Gray Lady's withers and talked softly to calm the animal "—has never seen anything like this before."

Lindsay didn't hear the last of his sentence. She was awestruck, mesmerized, by the sheer force of the flames that were rising before her. The fire seemed to be alive. It jumped from treetop to treetop. It was as if the flames were jeering at the people who were working a distance away, doing everything possible, but still not doing enough. It was sickening.

Joe Sherman spotted Lindsay and Justin on their horses, and he ran stumbling back across a muddy trench toward Justin. "How fast can you get down to the lake on one of your horses?'' He screamed the question over the deadly crackling sound behind him.

"I can make it in ten minutes," Justin yelled.

"The radio's gone out on the truck, and we've got to bring in more help." Sherman was screaming louder. "This whole valley could go up. We need everything they've got in Gunnison and more. Tell them to bring in the helicopters and do some water drops. I don't know if they'll be able to get that big tanker truck up here or not."

"Sure," Justin yelled. "Is your place the closest base station?"

"Yeah," the man answered. "Tell Rosemary who you are and what you need. She'll set the radio up for you."

"You stay here," Justin screamed at Lindsay. "I can go faster alone. Grande works well around fire and they may need you. They can't chance getting a gasoline-powered vehicle too close to that heat." He kissed her once and then galloped off.

The fire was spreading rapidly. It had almost reached the banks of Willow Creek on the west. More local men were flocking in to help, but their equipment wasn't adequate. Justin had been gone for three or four minutes now. He must be almost halfway to the lake and the radio by now, Lindsay thought as she wiped the perspiration off her forehead with her shirt sleeve. She wished she had her camera with her. These men and this disaster would certainly be her lead story for this week's *Valley Review*. She hated looking at disasters like this one and thinking of them in terms of "news." It was times like this when she felt like an outsider. She was always present to take pictures and cover a story, but she was never involved. Since she couldn't take pictures or jot down notes now, she swept the grisly scene with her eyes. She took mental pictures of the sweat there, mentally wrote images of the pain, the guts, the tears. She shifted gears into her professional mode, and for a moment what she was watching wasn't real. It was a picture, a painting, moving across a stage in meticulous slow motion. And as she observed the scenario with every one of her senses, she heard something no one else did. It was a low, wailing, guttural cry that was almost lost in the clatter and the crackling and the clanging of the trucks and the buckets.

At first, Lindsay thought she'd imagined the sound, but then it came again and she was certain she heard it. No one else turned to acknowledge the noise. She spurred Grande, and the animal moved cautiously toward the danger across the river. It was difficult to distinguish shapes and movements across the water against the background of dancing shadows and roaring flames. Lindsay had to search the far river bank three times before she found what she was looking for.

There was a woman huddled against the rocky riverbank, and she was clutching a young child. The sound of her voice had been virtually swallowed up by the roaring fire that was consuming the forest behind her.

"Are you hurt?" Lindsay shouted as she egged the horse on farther toward the fire. Grande was beginning to balk.

"I'm not hurt, but my daughter is," the huddled woman screamed back, but Lindsay couldn't hear her.

Lindsay knew she was going to have to cross the river. The current was too strong for anyone to try to walk or swim, particularly an exhausted woman carrying a child. But Grande's strong legs could carry them all. Lindsay lifted a swift, silent prayer to the stars. "Joe. Dan," she screamed to the two men who were working nearest her. "There's someone over there. I'm going across. Keep a watch over here in case there should be trouble."

Lindsay saw Dan Howard raise an arm in response. And she heard Jake Nelson's voice bellowing above everything, even the cacophony of the fire. "Holy Moly, Lindsay! Good girl. Keep a firm, tight rein on that animal. He'll get you across."

She raised an arm in acknowledgement and then urged Grande on. The horse knew her well after four months of racing and climbing and herding cattle, and Lindsay knew he trusted her. The rocks in the river were treacherous for him, and he poked and pushed with his hooves before he switched his weight for each step. As Lindsay drew closer to the woman, she could see her better. She wasn't much older than Lindsay and she was covered with scratches. Her hair was a filthy mop around her head, and she looked like she had been walking a long way. Her face was black with soot, but there were flesh-colored streaks where her tears had marked a course down her cheeks.

"Are you hurt?" Lindsay called again.

"No, I'm not," the woman answered, "but I think my daughter is. She can't walk. I think her leg is broken. She fell and I've had to carry her a long way."

Lindsay was on the east side of Willow Creek now. She dismounted Grande so she could bend close to the woman and kept a firm grip on Grande's reins. The heat around them was intense, and she was afraid the horse would spook. "How far have you come?"

"I don't know, but the fire has followed us all the way. We were camping up there." The woman nodded eastward with her head. "I was cooking dinner, and my husband saw the fire coming. We dropped everything and ran.''

"Where is your husband?" Lindsay questioned her. She glanced up and down the river. Maybe the man could help get them across.

"We got separated." The woman shook her head. "I know he's okay. He knows these woods better than I do."

"Okay." Lindsay raised up and surveyed the situation. "We've got to get both of you across the water. These trees around you are getting hot enough to go up any minute." Lindsay eyed the young girl. She was seven or eight and could probably ride with her on Grande without trouble, despite the broken leg. Her mother could help Lindsay lift the girl into the saddle.

Lindsay was terribly worried about the woman. She was in shock, and there was no telling how long she had been pushing herself to carry this girl. But the three of them were too much for Grande to carry across at one time. Lindsay would have to take the girl and then come back. She would have to do it calmly and she would have to do it fast. The wind was coming up, and the fire was moving rapidly toward them. Just then, Lindsay remembered the saddle bags. She prayed that Justin had put his regular supplies in them before their ride this evening. She held onto the reins with one hand and practically ripped open the left saddle bag with the other. For the second time in the past ten minutes, she breathed a prayer, this one of thanks. There were two handwoven Navaho blankets rolled up inside the bag. She took one of the wool blankets and dipped it into the river. She placed the dripping blanket around the woman's shoulders.

"This will keep you safe for just a while longer," Lindsay said, then smiled gently at her. She took the second blanket, sopped it in the water and wrapped it around the child. She didn't want to take any chances.

Justin was back from the boat house now, and he called encouragement to her from across the river. The woman struggled to help Lindsay lift the child onto Grande's back, but Lindsay bore the brunt of the child's weight. After what seemed like an eternity, the girl was securely tied onto Grande and Lindsay mounted the saddle behind her. "Move it, boy." She clucked to Grande, and the giant horse understood only the urgency in her voice.

Justin and Dan Howard were waiting for Lindsay when she reached the other side. Other men had offered to help, but Dan had waved them back. They needed the manpower fighting the fire, not swimming in the creek. The fire had already jumped the water in two places and was threatening to do so in a third.

Dan untied the girl, and Justin cradled the sobbing child in his arms. "Jake's got his truck up the road," Justin informed Lindsay. "All the emergency vehicles from Gunnison will be here in half an hour." He had already spotted one helicopter circling above. If they had medical emergencies now, they could send the copter back to town. But this young lady looked like all she needed was a calm drive to Gunnison in a pickup truck and a good doctor to set the broken leg.

Linday looked back over her shoulder. The flames were moving closer and closer to the child's mother. She was crouched at the water's edge, her eyes glazed like those of a frightened animal.

"I have to go back."

"I know." Justin shook his head and then reached up and brushed his lips across her hand. "Take good care."

"I will," she smiled. "Come on, Grande." She talked to the animal like she was taking him out on an outing on a beautiful spring morning. If she was scared, her voice did not betray her. Justin watched her as the horse faithfully followed her instructions and swam out into the river the second time.

Lindsay and Grande were halfway across the river when the flaming tree fell. The woman on the opposite bank let out a blood-curdling scream. The tree was a charred lodgepole pine, one of the monster trees that grows in the forest for decades, swaying, wielding independence, until at last a younger tree overtakes it and its roots begin to weaken. The flames had swirled around the tree for twenty minutes or more, nibbling at its needles at the top, bleeding out its sap at the bottom.

"Lindsay." Justin's heart crammed itself into his throat when he saw the massive pine hurtling toward her. It took precious seconds for the horror of it all to register in his brain, and by then it was too late.

Lindsay had seen the tree coming, but she could not dart out of the way. Grande was already moving as fast as he could across the rocky river bottom. As the animal saw what was falling toward him, he reared and shrilled a warning, but as he backed he stumbled and fell. And as the tree plummeted down beside him and landed in a thwack that echoed across the valley for miles, the horse realized that his rider was no longer with him.

Justin was panic-stricken. He didn't think the tree had hit Lindsay directly, but he had seen Grande throw her. Now she was lying face down in the water. He had seen nightmares like this one before. Cowboys moving their herd across shallow creek beds. The horse stumbles and rears. The cowboy cracks his head on a rock and is gone.

There was a long, low whistling sound beside him, and Justin felt a strong arm grip his shoulder. Jake Nelson was calling his horse. Grande moved toward the shore.

"Get Lindsay out of the water," Dan Howard bellowed. She looked like a rag doll, crushed, floppy, floating downstream on the swift current.

Dan Howard jumped into the water, and Jake was not far behind. He was swimming in with Grande. The huge animal was trembling. But even in Grande's fright, he would be a great help to the people in the river.

Justin was already gone. He was streaking through the trees on Gray Lady toward the boat house and the radio again. This time, the call he made was even more critical than his last. They had to land that helicopter immediately and get paramedics for Lindsay. It had to happen immediately if they wanted to save her life.

When Jake and Dan reached Lindsay in the river, they could not detect any breathing or find a pulse rate. Dan swam on across the water and rescued the shocked woman who was waiting on the opposite side of Willow Creek. Jake floated Lindsay on her back toward the shore on the other side.

It was one of the Walco men who met them at the bank. He had just completed a six-week lifesaving class at the company. He used his knowledge of cardio-pulmonary resuscitation and breathed into Lindsay's motionless body. Just when he was beginning to lose hope, she caught her own first, timid breath, and Jake shouted that he could detect a faint pulse. She wasn't dead. But she was close to it.

CHAPTER SIXTEEN

THE HOSPITAL was a cold, sad, detached place that seemed to be sterilized from the rest of the world. The only problem was, the rest of the world kept plowing in, strong, tragic, day after day after day. The doctors and the nurses did everything they could to stave off the cruelty of illness and death, but their efforts were often futile.

Lindsay had been placed in intensive care and the staff kept telling Justin they couldn't let him see her. It had been only twenty-four hours since the paramedics had brought her in from the wilderness, and she still hadn't opened her eyes and acknowledged anyone. Tad Carlton was becoming concerned. The longer she failed to respond to the lights and sounds around her, the worse her problems could become. Maybe he could allow this man Justin to talk to her. The familiar voice of someone who loved her might be the catalyst she needed to come out of this nebulous unconscious state before she sunk down into a full coma. He gave his approval for the visits, but he wanted them kept short. Justin Tredway could have ten minutes with Lindsay every hour.

Justin was supposed to leave for Fort Collins today, but nothing was going to drag him away from this hospital. He called his principal and explained that someone very dear to him lay injured, almost dead, so the man agreed to bring in a substitute teacher for three days. If it was going to be longer than that, the school board would have to hire someone to replace him.

Justin knew that three days would have to do. At least that would give Lindsay time to get some of her strength back. At least he would have the chance to tell a real woman goodbye instead of a sleeping, sick, silent head on a pillow.

It was Nina and Justin who sat together with Matthew and told him his mother was very sick. Matt cried long into the night that first night. They wouldn't let him go see her and she wasn't there with him. He tried to imagine her laughing at Felicia poking her paws into a paper bag or hugging him and telling him her favorite story, called "Where the Wild Things Are." But pretending didn't do any good.

The little boy talked to Justin on the phone over and over again. He kept asking Mr. Justin to hug his mommy for him and to make her get well. Justin could tell Lindsay everything he knew, but he had no way to tell if she heard him. So he waited patiently for his ten-minute visits with her, and he held her hand and he whispered things to her that he hoped she had the will and the strength to understand.

The nurses took pity on him. He looked exhausted and bedraggled and he didn't even notice the soot he left on the yellow plastic bench every time he sat there. The nurses brought him coffee and one snuck him a pile of Oreo cookies from the staff lounge. There was nothing any of them could do to convince him to leave the bench by the intensive care entrance. He only left it to visit Lindsay or to make his hourly telephone call to Matt and Nina.

Lindsay made the front page of her own newspaper that week. Cory wrote the story about the fire on the Walco forest land, about the stranded campers from Oklahoma, about Lindsay's rescue attempt and the tragedy that almost killed her. According to eyewitnesses, Cory's story said, the fact that the horse reared and threw Lindsay probably saved her life. Justin knew Lindsay would think that the front-page billing was hilarious...if she ever got to read it.

He had lost count of how many times he had taken off his Stetson and quietly slipped in to see her now. Maybe this was his twenty-fifth visit in the last day. He was here with her the way her husband should have been. Supporting her. Fighting for her. Egging her on. But all she had was a filthy cowboy who smelled like horses and soot and sweat. Essence of Corral Number Five, Justin thought disgustedly. It suddenly struck him how very sad it was that Lindsay had run from the people in Dallas who loved her. She had run away from a life she didn't feel comfortable with. She had run away from the ideals she couldn't handle. But Justin suspected the strength she needed to support her own ideals had grown inside of her long ago. She just needed to reach inside herself now and be surprised to find it all growing there.

There was a movement at the bed, and Justin inched closer. He held his breath and took her hand. It was the first time he had seen Lindsay move since Grande had thrown her into the river.

She was beginning to murmur, and Justin knew he should call Dr. Carlton, but he couldn't bring himself to do that. He wanted to be here with her, to hear what she had to say, who she needed, how she felt.

"It's okay, Lindsay—" he stroked her arm "—it's okay. I'm here. Careful, Lin."

She was still muttering something unintelligible, and her eyes had not opened. Justin wondered if she was dreaming. That was okay. That was much more acceptable than reality just now.

"What is it?" Justin cooed to her. "What is it you want?"

It was on her lips to say "Kendall," but some strong part of reality stuffed that thought back down inside of herself. "I want..." she whispered, "I want...to fly."

Justin knew now she was dreaming.

"It's okay, Lindsay." He played with the strands of hair that were lying close to him on the pillow. "It's okay." And then he stopped. He watched her in horror as all the pain she felt and all the losses she had experienced twisted their way out of her heart and across her face. Her features became those of the tormented gargoyle once more, and her head went back, and all Justin could make out of her shrieking as he slammed out the door and ran to find the nurse was the name she was calling over and over again. Marcus.

Her shrieks reverberated up the corridor until an intern and her doctor rushed in and sedated her. But the name bounced away inside Justin's brain for a lot longer than that. Marcus James. Uncle Marc. The Dallas man who loved Lindsay. "I think he wants to adopt us," Justin remembered Matt telling him. Justin also remembered the raw pain in Lindsay's eyes when he had asked her about the man. For some reason, she had convinced herself she could not have the one man she truly wanted. Justin just sat there in the hallway for a moment. And then he grinned. It was such a simple answer to so many complex questions. The solution had been invisible to him until Lindsay had screamed Marcus's name to him.

Justin dropped a coin into the pay telephone and dialed Lindsay's home number. Nina answered it on the first ring. "How is she, Justin?"

"I don't know. She's dreaming. Muttering things. And the doctor seems to think that is a good sign. Let me talk to Matt."

"He's right here."

"Matt," Justin announced when the child took the receiver. He didn't plan to mince words. "I'm going to call your Uncle Marc and tell him about your mother. Do you think that would be a good idea?"

"Yes," Matt practically shouted, and Justin had to pull the earpiece away from his head. He valued his hearing. And he also valued Matt's opinion. "I know that will make her feel better," the child added matter-of-factly.

"Okay," Justin consented. "Do you have his phone number?"

Matt knew his mother kept the number written down somewhere. He didn't know exactly where and Nina helped him, and at last he found a wrinkled corner of paper with the number written on it. It had been folded and carefully tucked away in Lindsay's nightstand.

For a few moments, Justin stood there staring down at the number he had jotted on the inside of the tattered phone book that hung on a chain beside the pay phone. Justin couldn't believe he was going to do this. He was going to give her away. But he had already made his decision several weeks before after he'd seen the look in her eyes when she'd spoken of Marcus. Justin had known he would have to let go—not give her away—because she didn't love him. No matter what he had to offer her, this faceless, ageless Uncle Marc could offer more. And Justin instinctively knew why. Marcus James was a part of Lindsay's whole self. He had been there holding the parts of her life together for her. Marcus James took her soul and tied it all together. And Justin loved her enough to want her to have Marcus's love. He dialed the number.

When the phone rang, Marcus was up to his elbows in his salt-water aquarium. "The Tonight Show" had been amusing as usual. There was an interview with the winner of a national whistling contest, a chat with a young starlet who couldn't do anything except knit her heavy eyebrows furiously and giggle, and a discussion with a comedian who was opening next week for his third appearance at Caesar's Palace in Las Vegas. Marcus liked "The Tonight Show," but he wasn't in the mood to watch comedians on television tonight. He wasn't in the mood to laugh.

Clarissa had come over earlier to bake paprika chicken, and she tried to interest him in going to a movie, but he wouldn't hear of it. He sent her home and she pouted all the way out the door. Having Clarissa around didn't begin to assuage Marc's loneliness anymore. Every time she walked in his front door, his heart filled with longing for his Lindsay, and that was almost too painful to bear. He supposed he was feeling sorry for himself, but his feelings had taken a terribly painful turn during the last three months. He was beginning to realize that he might lose Lindsay for good if he didn't do something fast. But he had already done everything he knew how to do. He tried not to think of her, tried not to care for her. But every time he would almost push her out of his mind a silly joke would come on television or he'd hear some piece of interesting news, and he'd find himself hurrying home so he could call her and tell it to her. He had even put an ugly note to himself on the telephone...he had drawn a stick figure with frizzy hair and incredible fangs on the receiver, but even that didn't stop him from wanting to share with her, to give his life to her. He knew he still had everything to give to her. He just kept looking at that funny little figure there on his phone and reminding himself that she would not accept the things he was capable of giving.

Just now, he was trying to take his mind off all that. His humbug damselfish was learning to eat frozen brine shrimp off his giant forefinger. When the phone rang, Marcus jumped and the humbug damselfish swam to hide behind some plastic sea grass. It was going to be a long time before he could coax the fish to come that close again. But Marcus didn't care. His mind and his heart were thudding together inside his chest. This was her. It had to be. She was the only person who called him this late. The two of them had spent so many midnights giggling together. Already, Marc anticipated the melody of her hello wafting across the western states toward him. But the sound Marcus heard when he answered the telephone was not Lindsay's musical voice. It was a stranger calling from far, far away.

"Marcus James?"

For a moment, Marcus had the silly urge to say "No, he isn't in. This is his butler speaking." It sounded like someone calling to sell him aluminum siding for a house he didn't have. Finally, he acknowledged the voice. "This is he."

"You don't know me, Marcus...." The voice on the other end of the line sighed deeply, and Marcus was instantly on his guard. Something was wrong. He sensed it. "My name is Justin Tredway. I'm calling from Gun...."

Marcus cut him off. "What's wrong?"

"It's Lindsay. She had an accident."

"Oh, God."

"She's okay, Marcus." Justin could feel a knot growing in his stomach, heavy and hard, like a fishing weight, a tight tangle of sadness. "She's been calling for you. She didn't say anything before tonight. She needs you now, and I don't think she even consciously realizes that. I've given her everything I can, but it's not enough."

Marcus was silent. It was a deep, poignant silence, one that told Justin everything he needed to know.

"When can you be here?" Justin asked.

Marcus checked his watch. It was midnight now. It would take him at least an hour to throw some clothes into a bag and check out e plane from Love Field. If he could get the flight plan he wanted, e could be on the ground in Gunnison by six in the morning. "I'll meet you at six," he told Justin. "I've been to the hospital. I'll just nd you there."

"You can't get in to see her that early," Justin answered. "They might not let you in to see her at all. You might as well get a few xtra hours of sleep."

"I couldn't sleep now," Marcus answered. "I'll meet you there. Ve need to talk before I go in to see her. And they'll let me in. Last me I was there, those crazy people almost let me go into the delivery oom with her. I'll tell them I'm her brother or something. If they on't let me in, I'll just bash down walls until they do."

Across the miles, Justin smiled. He liked this guy. He should have nown he would. Lindsay had great taste in men. "See you at six."

"Hey..." Marcus called over the phone, and for a split second, he ouldn't remember the man's name who had called him. And then, came back. How many times had Matt told him about the special orseback rides he had gone on with Mr. Justin? "Justin." There as another poignant silence. "Thanks."

ARC'S PIPER touched down on the Gunnison runway at 5:00 A.M. unnison time. He considered checking into a motel and washing p, but no motel manager in his right mind would be renting rooms is early. He would go directly to the hospital. He could tell them e was Lindsay's brother. Then he could get in to see her as soon as ossible. He wouldn't be all that much too early for his meeting with r. Justin the cowboy.

When the elevator opened and Marcus stepped out onto the inten-ve-care floor, he realized he couldn't have arrived early for this eeting with Justin. The bedraggled man with the soot on his jeans d two days of stubble on his chin was already there waiting for m. He had obviously been there all night.

"I'm early," he called down the hallway and as Justin turned and eir eyes met, each of them sized the other up. Marcus saw the aramel-colored hair, the dark, deep eyes full of caring, the stocky ild, and again it almost bowled him over when he thought of how uch this man was doing for him. Justin saw the dimples, the laugh-r, and the love in Marcus's eyes, and he knew then he had done e right thing. This man loved Lindsay just as much as she loved m.

"You're not too early," Justin grinned. "Let's go down to the

cafeteria and grab a cup of coffee.'' He wearily clapped Marcus o
the back.

The conversation between the two men was comfortable and easy
They sat by a window, and their knowledge of each other, their re
spect, came just as simply and naturally as the morning sun that rolle
up over the Black Mesa. The delicate glow of dawn grew into th
cheerful sunshine of morning and, before the metamorphosis wa
complete, Marcus James and Justin Tredway had become friends. S
much was exchanged between them, about the woman they loved
about their lives and their needs and their values, that Marcus felt a
if he was full of grace, full of a new type of bravery, of gallantry
Marcus understood without words how deeply Justin was in love wit
Lindsay, and it didn't strike him as sad or unusual. Other wome
collected demitasse teacups or silver spoons from places they ha
traveled, but Lindsay collected people who loved her. She gave he
grace and her sunshine to men, women and children alike, and, t
both the men sitting there sipping coffee, it all seemed good and righ
and true.

Marcus and Justin agreed about what had to be done for her, bu
it was up to Lindsay to accept it. She would have to make the fina
decision. And she couldn't do that until she was coherent and stron
again.

After breakfast, Marcus made a quick call to Nina and Matt, an
Nina promised to bring Matt to the hospital to see him as soon a
they could eat some cereal and pile Felicia and Mr. Jinx into the ca

Justin insisted Marc visit Lindsay alone this morning. From nov
on, they would be sharing the ten minute visiting period and Justi
thought it fair for Marcus to have the first one. Marcus was about t
accept Justin's offer but, as he pushed open the door, he though
better of it. They both needed to be with Lindsay now. They neede
her in different ways, but they both needed her just the same. S
together they marched into the room and stood before her, like tw
lost princes watching over Sleeping Beauty. And that is how it hap
pened that, just like the fairy tale, Lindsay awoke that morning ou
of what seemed like a very deep, long sleep and saw both of then
there leaning over her, their voices hushed, their heads together. Sh
reached out a hand to each of them, and they all three sat there, secur
in the love and the caring and the hope that filled the room.

Justin rang for the nurse eventually, and within seconds there wer
nurses of all shapes and sizes invading the room and shooing the tw
men out.

"But our time isn't up," Justin teased one of them, and another rather portly nurse chased them out anyway.

"If I see things correctly," the portly nurse told them in an argumentative tone of voice, "they'll have her moved into her own room by noon. You can see her all you want during regular visiting hours then if you want."

"Don't give me that," Justin growled. His forty-eight hours without sleep were beginning to take a toll on him.

"Come on." Marcus put his hand on Justin's arm. "Let it go for while. It will be good for you."

The rest of the morning was spent watching doctors running in and out of intensive care to test Lindsay. Finally, Justin did give up. Marcus had long since slipped away to spend time with Nina and Matt. Justin made himself comfortable on one of the long, low orange couches in the waiting room. He decided to lie down and rest for five minutes. Two hours later a nurse was shaking him. Lindsay had been moved into a private room, and she was begging to see him.

"Justin Tredway," Lindsay shrieked at him through a jungle of daisies and chrysanthemums as he stepped into the room. "Are you the one who called him?"

"Yes." He nodded as he neared her bed. Again, he realized he had made the right choice. Lindsay was pale, and there were dark circles beneath her eyes, but she was beaming.

"Why did you call him?"

"Would you believe Matt told me to?" Justin teased her.

"No," she laughed. "I wouldn't believe that. The kid's smart but he's not brilliant. And lucky for me, he can't seem to read his mother's mind the way you do."

"You know you made the front page of the *Valley Review*, don't you?" Justin struggled to change the subject. He did not want to talk about Marcus with her. He was aware of what he had done. He hadn't done it to be fair or to be unselfish. He had done it because he loved her.

"Yep." Lindsay waved the newest edition of the newspaper in his face. "I read these things, you know."

"Then you know that Grande is getting all the credit." Justin grinned across the bed at her. "They're saying that horse saved your life when he threw you."

"Well," Lindsay was serious now. "They can say anything they want. But they're wrong. If anyone has saved my life during this entire ordeal, it's been you."

"No, Lindsay." Justin was embarrassed. He thought she was teasing him.

"Justin." Lindsay spoke his name softly and she was shaking her head. "I am not kidding. So maybe you didn't physically save my life. But you've saved so much else of me. You've saved my laughter and you've saved my soul. You've taught me how to fly on a horse and you've taught me the power behind growing up and growing away. You've salvaged so much of me for the life I have left." She was crying now and so was he. "I care about you so much, Justin Tredway. I think I'll always care about you." She reached out to him, and he cradled her in his arms for a long time, just hugging her and holding her and feeling all the sadness that he dare feel for the love that he had just given away.

"Mommy. I love you," Matthew exclaimed as he pounded into the room and threw his arms around Lindsay's neck. Justin took advantage of the moment to slip away. He passed Marcus and Nina in the hallway and he winked at both of them. Then he was out the door and into his dusty green pickup truck before anyone missed him. He could stand a good night's sleep and a close shave and after that maybe a long solitary ride through the meadow on Gray Lady. He still wanted to work on the barbed-wire fence around the east pasture before it was time to head to Fort Collins and the classroom. Maybe the long ride would make him forget the throbbing in his heart. He knew that in time his pain would go away. But he knew it wouldn't go as soon as he hoped it would. Or maybe it would go too soon. Maybe he always wanted to feel this way about her. Maybe there was enough poignancy in this hurting to keep him feeling like he was close to her for the many long years to come.

CHAPTER SEVENTEEN

LINDSAY SAT PROPPED UP against the pillows. Her head still ached from the blow she'd received, and the doctors were watching her for signs of complications, but there had been none so far and everything looked good. All that was left for her to do now was to lie in bed smiling prettily at the doctors and surrender to the ruthless pampering of the nurses.

It was as if she was surrounded by everyone she cared for in the world just now. Marcus bought Matt an electric train set at City Drug, and the two of them had played for hours setting up curves beneath the curtains and tunnels beneath the bed. As Lindsay closed her eyes and lay back against the pillows, she heard the shrill little whistle of the train and Matt's ceaseless giggling, and she thought she had never been in such a wonderful place in all of her life. The idea that it was her special place absolutely enchanted her.

All Lindsay could see of her son right then were two chubby legs poking out from under the foot of the bed. Marc's voice was muffled and distant, like he was calling out for help from some faraway, dusty place. "Help me, Matt. Push that section of track over this way."

"But it hits the wall."

"It won't, though," Marc's muffled voice explained patiently. "It will go just like this."

There was another explosive gale of giggles.

Lindsay smiled at Nina who was sleepily knitting in the corner. She thought about yesterday when Nina had sneaked Felicia in for a short visit. Lindsay had been horrified that the hospital board might kick all four of them out of the room and out of town. But it was impossible for the dainty cat to do much harm. She'd strolled around the room and lazily explored all the nooks and crannies until there was not much left for her to see. She'd curled up in a sunny patch on the floor and slept until the nurse came in with Lindsay's lunch. Then Felicia, having prowled under the bed, eagerly pounced on the ankles that extended up from the white leather shoes. She'd nipped at them with all the tenderness of a mountain wildcat.

The nurse's face had gone white, she'd stammered something unintelligible and left, lunch tray still in hand.

"Great cat," Lindsay had snorted. "There went my lunch."

"Oh, you're not missing much," Marcus had teased. But he decided that the cat's excursion had lasted long enough. He tucked Felicia into his overcoat and delivered her safely back to the cabin.

Ten minutes later, another nurse had entered the room with another lunch for Lindsay and had looked around warily as she came in. "Is there an *animal* in here?" the woman barked.

"No, ma'am," Lindsay answered sweetly. Her best Southern manners had taken over. And she wasn't lying. The *animal* was gone.

Today, Marc and Matt were hoping for the same barking nurse. Lindsay felt a bit guilty. Nurses worked so hard all day to care for sick people, but she figured they deserved some fun, too. And Lindsay was happy to share her family with them.

As it was, the nurse who came to serve Lindsay her lunch was a portly, jolly person, a sort of female Santa Claus who had been elected by the nursing staff for this job because she had a wonderful sense of humor when it came to patients. She stepped into the room and sized them all up in a glance. She noticed the miniature twist of railroad track that stuck ominously out from under the bed. She made a point to step into just the right place so when the train chugged out at her, it would encircle her ankles. She screamed appropriately when the train did so, and after she screamed she laughed and served Lindsay her lunch as if nothing had happened.

Marc and Matt and Nina laughed, too, and the nurse was glad she had been picked for this assignment. What a sunny, laughable, wonderful place to be. She felt sorry she couldn't stay in Lindsay's room all day.

"You've got a special family here, girl," she told Lindsay. "I'd hold on to every single one of them if I were you."

"I plan on that," Lindsay said as she winked back at the nurse.

"I do think you need a rest, though," the nurse admonished both the little boy and the big boy with one shake of her index finger. "I think you two ought to have your fun somewhere else for a while."

"Yes, ma'am." Marcus nodded his head in rugged compliance. Then he scooped Matt up in his arms and took Nina by the elbow. "Come on, kids. Let's let old grandma over there have her afternoon nap."

Lindsay waved sleepily from her side of the room. She had to dmit it was going to be nice to doze off. There were rumors around he hospital that her doctor might release her the day after tomorrow. n a way, she was excited about that, but in another way she was isappointed. The days after the accident had been exquisite, and she idn't know if she could let Marcus go. When he left for Dallas this me, it was going to be very final, very sad, as if she was peeling a art of herself away. Like peeling a navel orange. Except Lindsay lready knew what was going to be inside when she pulled away the kin. She had done it already too many times before. There was othing left except...nothing. An endless chasm of emptiness. The nd. Lindsay wasn't certain she could face that again. Before, she ad been so strong. Maybe she wasn't strong enough anymore. But he truth was, it wasn't a matter of strength at all. It was a matter of omething much, much different.

Just as she was on the dark fuzzy edge between wakefulness and leep, there came a soft knock at her door. It took Lindsay a full ten econds before she was awake enough to speak. "Who is it?"

"Me. Marcus."

"Come in."

"I know we're supposed to leave you alone, but I never can get ou by myself anymore." He smiled ruefully. "I left Nina and Matt t the soda fountain down the street. I brought you a present." He anded her a crumpled brown paper sack and smiled a contented, zy smile.

"Thanks." She ripped open the bag and squealed in delight. "Oh, Iarcus James...you creep. How did you know these were my favorite ings in the whole world?" She pulled out a package of peanut utter cups and opened them hungrily.

"Would you believe Felicia the Feline told me?"

"No." She beamed. "But I would believe the story about a little oy who wanted you to buy them for his mother because they just appen to be his favorite things, too. I love you, sir." She winked at m playfully.

Marc's face was suddenly serious. She didn't realize what she had ist said to him. How long had he waited for her? How long had he reamed of her saying those words to him? "Do you?" He snatched e chocolate from her hands. "You can't have this back until you ll me the truth."

"I...."

"And remember, everything you say will incriminate you even irther." Marcus was smiling stiffly at her and teasing her at the me time. Every fiber in his body was tense enough to snap. Here it came. The talk. The final verdict. The beginning of the end that had started in this same hospital the day after Matt was born. Marc didn't know if he could bear it.

"Marc," Lindsay whispered his name as she tilted her head toward him. Everything she felt, everything she was, everything she needed, was apparent in the searching look she gave him.

"What is it, Lindsay?" He was almost afraid to touch her, but as he saw the look in her eyes, he reached out to her with trembling hands and swept her long hair back from both of her temples. "Lindsay. Look at me." He held her face for a moment as he tried desperately to read what he saw written there.

"You're crazy for coming all this way to be with me. You know that, don't you?" she asked him.

"No, Lindsay." He shook his head at her. "I wish you would quit telling me I'm crazy. Because I'm not. I had to come. Because I love you. Because I know you need me."

Lindsay smiled impishly. She wasn't quite certain whether she should tease him now or be totally honest. "Who told you that?"

"Justin Tredway."

Lindsay smiled wistfully. "That's what I thought. Justin is very perceptive. And now the two of you are ganging up on me, right?"

"He's in love with you, Lindsay." Marc's face was expressionless

She looked sad for a moment. "Did he tell you that?"

"He never would have called me if he wasn't. He called me because he thought it was the right thing to do for you, Lindsay. Was he right?"

Lindsay was silent for a moment, and Marc was afraid she would hear his heart pounding up out of his chest. After a poignant silence Lindsay reached up and kissed Marc on the tip of the nose. "Yes. He did the right thing."

"Do you really think so?" Marc's eyes were huge, but as he watched Lindsay, they narrowed and a hint of laughter sparkled in them. "You always did have a way of attracting wonderful people How on earth do you survive all the kindness people give you?"

Lindsay giggled as she gingerly grasped his elbow. "You're right," she said, beaming. "I do attract wonderful people. Like you I used to feel guilty about it. Like I was taking something that didn't belong to me. But I don't feel that way anymore. I have things to give in return. I am a wonderful person, too."

"I'm glad to see you have so much confidence in yourself." He smiled proudly down at her. "I've wanted you to feel that way about yourself for a long time."

A fleeting sadness traced its way across her face once more. "Sometimes I think I've done it, Marc. But then other times, I'm not so sure. Like with the Walco resort... I fought against that thing so. And then their land burns, and I'm almost happy about it.... I'm really ashamed of myself." She closed her eyes and leaned back against the pillow. "And the dumb thing is, I don't really understand why I was fighting so hard."

Marc stood up from her bed and walked to the window. He gazed for a long while at the row of Collegiate Peaks where Lindsay had made her home. Then he turned and spoke gently to her. "I know why, Lindsay Cornell-Allen."

She turned to him and gave him a forlorn little grin. "Okay, why?"

"Look at these mountains, Lindsay." He swept his arm across the panorama outside, and her eyes followed his direction. "This place is a sanctuary to you, Lin. It has hidden you from everything in Dallas you are frightened of; the clothes and the makeup and the perfect 'Dallas girl' image; the feelings you had for Kendall; the dreams you had for yourself. This place is solid, stable—and therein lies the strength you draw from it. But I have to tell you." He turned to her now. "You don't need this place anymore."

She sat up quickly with a shocked look on her face. Then she reached out to him with both arms. As he came to her, she bit the side of her tongue in thought, and then she smiled with honest glee. "It's in me, isn't it? And I don't have to be in the mountains to have it, do I? I have the strength of these mountains inside of me now, don't I, Marcus?" Lindsay was so happy suddenly that she wanted to sing.

All the victory Marc was feeling in his heart poured forth in the look he gave her. She had finally discovered what Marc knew had been growing up inside her for a very long time. He cradled her in his arms like he would a very small child. "That's why you were so afraid of Walco, Lin. Because every change that comes to this valley is a change that also comes to you. And that doesn't always have to be frightening. The changes that come mean you're growing."

"I know that." There were tears slipping down Lindsay's cheeks now. She just looked at Marc for a long, long while. He was so good to her, so strong and solid, so familiar to her. Lindsay knew she didn't have to act like a princess or remember to say the right things to Marcus. He loved her no matter who she was. It didn't matter whether she said silly things or if she cried until her nose turned purple or whether she won the Miss America pageant. Marc had loved her in

Dallas and he loved her now, and that very thought, in all its simplicity, made the difference to her.

Lindsay looked up at Marc and took in every detail, every facet
of his breathtaking good looks. He looked like a mischievous child
and a beautiful man all at the same time, and Lindsay realized suddenly what a treasure it would be to wake up next to him each morning, to have him touch her while her hair lay tangled and the sleep
was still in her eyes.

"Come here, Marc," she called to him and as he moved toward
her, she almost shouted from the sheer wonder of what she was feeling. "I love you, Marcus James."

He just stared at her for a moment. He was certain he had heard
her wrong. But she reached up to him and touched his cheek with
two fingers and then found his neck with her lips, and he knew that
all his dreams of her were real at last.

"Hold me, Marc," she whispered into his curls.

He wanted to crush her to him, but he remembered just in time
that she was in the hospital, that her body was slowly repairing itself,
so he gingerly took her shoulders and pulled her to him.

"Here," Marcus stuck the candy bar back under her nose after he
kissed her. "You earned this. You can eat this now. Just eat this and
be happy and listen to my plan."

"Yummmm," Lindsay said as she took a nibble of the peanut
butter cup and then tipped her head toward Marcus like a little girl
about to share in a wonderful secret. "What's the plan?"

"How do you feel about airplanes?"

"I don't know." Lindsay thought for a moment. It had been a long
time since she had dreamed of them and had awakened screaming
and sweating on the verge of a crash. Maybe, somewhere deep in her
being, she had finally let that go, too. But it was an odd question for
Marcus to ask. Lindsay watched him for a moment before answering.
Beautiful, solid, strong Marcus. He had always been there for her,
holding her up for all the world to see. For a moment, she wanted
to take everything about him, his fuzzy hair, his burning eyes, his
playful dimples, his dreams, his determination, and cradle it all in
her arms. He had given so much to her just by being who he was, and
now she understood how he'd found the strength to give so much
over the years. She wanted to pour herself out to him.

"I am so in love with you," she whispered once again, and Marcus
had to bend closer to the pillow where she lay to hear her. When he
did, he wanted to screech for joy. He wanted to swing her around
the room with her legs and her spun-honey hair flying every which

way. All of his life had globbed itself into this one moment. All leading to a common end. This lady. This love.

Instead of twirling her around, he had to settle for jumping up and down in the middle of the hospital room while he sang seven measures of Handel's *Hallelujah Chorus*. Lindsay lay on the bed giggling so hard she thought her heart might burst. She had been so frightened he would tell her it was too late for him to love her.

"Lindsay," he said as he danced toward her and then landed with a thud on both his knees beside the bed. "Here is the plan. I don't know what you'll think. I want you to come home to Dallas with me."

"For how long?" Lindsay's eyes were great pools of questions now. Marcus loved to see them that way. Because there was something new floating on the surface that he had never seen there before. Trust. Faith. Marcus wanted to sing.

"For how ever long you'd like," he answered joyfully. "For a week. For a month. Forever."

Lindsay was quiet. This was something she had never let herself consider before. There was too much at stake.

"I wonder what Matt would think," she mused aloud.

"I could make a great Texas Ranger fan out of him. Give me a chance, Lindsay." It was a plea, not a statement.

"But the cat...."

Marcus threw back his head and guffawed. After a week of attacking nurses, running away from an electric train and exploring a hospital, the cat could handle anything. "Honestly," Marcus leaned over again and confided to Lindsay in mock concern. "The poor cat's bored to death. She told me just this morning that she was looking for a new adventure."

"Oh, you...." Lindsay bopped Marc on the head with a pillow. And then she started chuckling, and the chuckling expanded into laughter, and Marcus and Lindsay just sat there laughing about the cat until finally Lindsay looked at Marcus and grinned. "Guess what."

"What?"

"I'm going."

"Going...where?" Marcus was still laughing so hard about the cat, he couldn't remember what they had been talking about.

"Home. To Dallas. With you. And Matt and the cat."

Marcus froze. Surely he was dreaming. He had thought it would take her hours to decide she wouldn't go with him. In an instant, this new commitment that she felt for him grew a thousandfold in his eyes. He knew now that his life was changing because of her. "Oh, Lindsay." He reached out to her and swept her into his arms and cradled her head in the crook of his elbow. "I don't know if I'll ever have the chance to prove everything I feel for you."

"You already have." Lindsay reached up and stroked his cheek with her fingers. "You've proved it over and over again during these past years. You've never ever let me down. I've needed you so badly, and each time you've been there for me. Now, it's my turn to prove things."

"We'll prove them together, my darling." There was a soft, warm glow in his eyes as he bent to taste her lips with his. "I love you, Lindsay. I can't believe you love me, too."

He kissed her gently again and again as she lay there. Finally, he pulled away and just watched her for a moment. He felt like a child who had just caught his first glimpse of the Christmas tree on Christmas morning. Miracles. Magic. Sparkling lights and impossible gifts. All that had come to him now. Slowly, surely, this miraculous, magic Lindsay was spinning a web of joy throughout his entire life.

LINDSAY LOOKED around the cabin once more. It looked so empty, so forlorn now. She didn't want to remember it this way. She wanted to treasure it as it had been, a warm loving home for her and her son.

Marcus was outside loading things into the car, and Matt was spending the afternoon at Nina's. The grandmotherly woman had given him a surprise going-away party this morning, and then he had begged to stay and eat lunch one last time with her. Lindsay was glad for the time alone. Things had happened so fast during the past few days, and it was nice to relax for a moment and reflect on the changes that were coming into their lives. Lindsay wandered around the empty house for a few minutes as if she was wandering through a forest that she had never seen before. Then she shook her head clear and went into the bedroom.

She couldn't believe that the packing had gone so quickly. All the rooms were clear except for this one. She opened her top dresser drawer and began pitching lingerie into the suitcase. Once she'd finished clearing out the dresser and her vanity, all she had left to do was box up the linens in the front closet and fold up the blankets that still lay on the bed. Then Marc could dismantle the furniture and deliver it to the shipping company that would truck it into Dallas.

And she could do all the last-minute things like paying the final electric bill and having the mail forwarded.

When she finished emptying her dresser drawers, she sighed once then turned to gaze out the window toward the west. She didn't mean to look sad. She was glad to be going. In fact, it was she who had been hurrying Matthew and Marcus along these past few days. Oh, but how she was going to miss the scene from this window. The Collegiate Peaks sprawled across the sky before her. They stood rugged, solid, against the azure morning sky. The rocks that jutted above timberline at their summits were glowing a soft tone of apricot in the September sun. Lindsay stared at them for a long time. Then she turned away from the window and closed her eyes. She could see them again, indelibly etched in her memory forever. She really was taking the mountains home to Dallas with her. They would always be there inside her soul giving her strength and solitude.

Marcus stomped in the front door and found her like that, standing in the empty room with her eyes clenched shut. When he saw her there, he thought she must be crying and he didn't know exactly what to say. His mother had cried every time they'd moved somewhere, and Marc had always teased her. But he didn't feel right teasing Lindsay the same way. Just now, while he was outside arranging boxes in the car, it had struck him once more how many things she was leaving behind so she could fly home to Dallas with him. He'd felt so blessed by her, so honored that he could make her happy, and he didn't feel comfortable kidding her about things that meant this much to her.

"Marc," she said softly as she turned to him with a gentle smile. He was surprised to see that her eyes were bright and clear. She hadn't been crying at all.

"What were you doing just now?" he asked her.

"Probably being silly." Her smile widened into a grin. "I was just saying goodbye to the mountains." She cast one more lingering look out the window. "They are so beautiful. I'll always remember them. But I don't think I'll be back here for a very long time."

"Are you terribly sad about that, Lindsay?" He walked to her and held her for a moment.

"No." She shook her head into his chest and then she backed away from him so she could see his face. "I'm not. I'm very content."

He gazed down at her and studied the warm glow in her eyes. "I'm glad, Lin."

"Should we get back to work?" she asked him before he had a chance to say anything more.

"You're a slave driver, you know that, Lindsay?" he laughed.

"I can't help it." She gave him a little pout that looked impish and innocent all at the same time. "I'm ready to go home."

"Okay." He clapped his hands. "Tell me what else needs to be done."

"Just this room." She led him into her bedroom. "I finished clearing out the drawers. I can put the things in the front closet in a box while you finish in here. Oh, I just remembered, I have another cabinet to do in the kitchen."

"We're almost finished." Marcus nodded his head.

"It's amazing how much work it is to pick up an entire family and move it from one place to another," Lindsay commented.

Marc didn't agree with her. He just stood there in the bedroom with a sad look on his face.

"Marc?" She turned to him. "What's wrong?"

He hesitated for a moment before he said anything and then he shook his head. "I was just thinking. And wondering. Are we a family?"

Lindsay just sat down on the bed and looked up at him. "I don't know, Marcus James. Do you want us to be?"

"Yes." He shook his head and then his eyes met hers. The sad look on his face had been replaced by a mixture of expectancy and fright. "I do. I want the kid and I want you and I want a little house close to Love Field."

"What are you saying, Marc?" Her voice was soft.

He sat down beside her on the bed and gripped her shoulders once more. "I am telling you that I want you to be my wife, Lindsay."

Lindsay hid her face in her hands for a moment, then she took her hands down and just looked at Marcus for a long while. "Oh." She sighed, and for one horrible moment, he thought she was going to tell him no. "I love you so much, Marcus. And the idea of going back to Dallas is so exciting now. I keep thinking of new things I'll get to do, good friends I'll get to see. Like Rita. She's my best friend. She gives me good advice about everything. During our trip to Los Angeles, she gave me some wonderful advice about you."

"And what advice was that?" he asked tentatively.

"She said—" Lindsay looked away from him and then started slowly tracing the floral pattern on the sheet with her fingernail "—that if I ever got the chance to belong to you...."

"Yes?" He didn't mean to interrupt her. She was just being infuriatingly slow about giving him an answer.

"Rita said...that I should go for it." Lindsay shook her head. "And I am inclined to agree with her."

Marcus visibly jumped, and then he started laughing. "My wife. My family. I can't believe this. I love you. You've made all my dreams come true in the last weeks. You know that, don't you?" He kissed her on the forehead.

"What would you have done if I had told you no?" Lindsay asked.

"I would have called my lawyer and started legal proceedings to adopt both your son and you immediately."

"Ah...." Lindsay wound one of his curls around her index finger. "So I didn't actually have any choice at all."

"No, you didn't." He lifted her chin until her eyes met his. "I just wanted to see what you would say."

"You are mean to me." She laughed and tried to give him a playful swat, but he caught her hand in his before she could do so. Then he forcefully pulled her to him, and she cradled her head against his shoulder.

"I've wanted to love you, to make you mine, for so long now," he whispered.

She looked up at him. "I've wanted a great many things for us, too, Marcus." Lindsay reached up to him and then gently pulled him down with her as she lay back on the mattress. Then, slowly, she kissed his face, his ears, his neck. She was almost surprised by the intense passion that was welling up inside of her. It took her breath away. She swallowed the insane urge to shout. Where had this wonderful feeling been all her life?

"Lindsay?" Marc sighed her name, and his eyes, his face, his voice all asked the same question.

"I want you, darling." She mouthed the words with her lips and only a whisper of the sound came through. "Like I've never wanted anything else before."

Marcus reached down and began to slowly untie the pink satin bows that held the silk blouse she was wearing around her. He had never touched her this way before and he was dizzy with the smell of her and the softness of her skin. As he slowly undressed her, she bit her upper lip and gave him a shy little grin. She tried to look like she wasn't so eager, like she didn't want him as desperately as she did. She considered running away and hiding beneath the blanket she had just folded, but the exquisite velvet sensation that kept rising higher and higher within her kept her waiting anxiously before him.

When he reached out to her and bundled her in his arms, she rose to meet him. Marcus was entranced by the things he knew she was able to give him now. He almost wanted to weep when he saw her there ready to give him her love and her life. "Oh, my love." He bent to kiss the dainty silver okra that still hung from the chain around her neck. "Oh, my Lindsay."

"Don't ever leave me, Marc," she whispered up to him as she lifted his head with her two hands and searched his face. "Sometimes it frightens me when I realize how much you've come to mean to me."

"I am yours," he said, smiling. His words caressed her just as his hands were caressing the skin beneath the layers of silk and of lace. "I promise to be yours forever. Just as I will want you forever, Lin." And with those words, he bent to kiss her with a wild abandon that blocked out the rest of the world and left in its place only peace and warmth and passion.

As Marcus made love to her, he touched her with such tenderness, with such compassion that Lindsay felt herself sinking into him. This was the first time she had made love to a man since the one night with Kendall, and she felt today like she had discovered an entirely new portion of herself. Everything about loving Marcus was different from loving Kendall. She wasn't frightened now, she only wanted to show him the things that were welling up and pouring out of her heart. Even her body was different. She had given birth to a child. Her breasts were larger and lower. Her hips were wider. And the glorious thing about those changes was that they signified a change in her, too. She was making love to Marcus James as a woman in every sense of the word. She would never lose her carefree laughter or her *joie de vivre*. But somewhere between the time she first told Marcus James that she needed his friendship and the present, she had left the little girl part of herself behind.

This was a moment of total commitment for Lindsay. She had belonged to Marc in every other way for so long, that the things she had to give him now were strong and good and glorious. She touched him with a fervor, with a passion that surprised them both. It was as if she was taking everything she had felt in her heart and was handing it to him with her two hands. She loved Marc gently but she loved him well, and when they both lay spent, Lindsay had released every pain, every defeat she had experienced. When she finally gave herself to Marcus, it was as though all the bad things she had ever known had freed themselves from her and flown out the windows of her soul like little fluttering birds.

LINDSAY DIDN'T WANT to let go of the heaving shoulders that encircled her. Goodbyes. She hated them. Here they all were, all the people she loved in these mountains, standing before her like sparkling jewels. They would be treasured, each and every one of them, and Lindsay promised herself that none of these friendships would become tarnished with age or from lack of attention. It was terribly hard to tell Dan and Margie goodbye. They had both been such a family to her, and she kept hugging Margie because neither woman could bear for their last hug to be the final one. Dan was dry eyed but he looked forlorn, and he didn't even give her one last teasing word to remember him by.

Lindsay knew that telling Nina goodbye was going to be the hardest of all, but her housekeeper had promised to come visit them all in Dallas soon. Matt wanted to take her to Six Flags Over Texas amusement park to see the goat, and Lindsay promised to take her shopping at The Galleria. What fun it would be to see this beautiful grandmother waltzing around the dressing room at Saks wearing a $4,500 dress. Such were the things that home was made of. Sakowitz. Neiman-Marcus. Visiting garage sales with her mother. Texas Aggie football games. The Cotton Bowl parade on a frosty New Year's morning. Lindsay had the feeling that all of life was beginning again. For everybody. This moment. She had a second chance. And she was going to take it.

"Take good care," she ordered as she pecked Margie on the cheek for the third time and tried desperately to ignore the tears in the woman's eyes.

"Come on, Lindsay," Marcus called from the plane. He had already finished the flight checklist. Matt was already seatbelted inside the aircraft with Felicia in her cage. Felicia was meowing loudly, and Matt was trying to keep her calm by telling her how she could catch crawdads in the creek when they got to Texas.

"Okay, Marc." Lindsay waved goodbye to the group huddled together at the terminal once more and then headed for the plane. She had taken maybe ten steps when she heard someone calling her name.

"Lindsay. Wait!" Justin Tredway had been running for three blocks now and he thought he might never catch her. He had driven almost five hours this morning and he was beginning to lose heart. This reminded him of every time he had seen her. The chase after the jeep to invite her to the square dance. The chase after the car to invite her to dinner and that horrible movie. Now there was a chase after the airplane to tell her goodbye.

When he saw her, she was dressed in a white wool suit and a sky-

blue silk blouse. He had never seen her wearing things like that before. He stopped and just stared at her for a moment as she turned
to him. Lindsay was different somehow. More confident. Comfortable. She wore the suit as if it was a pair of faded denim jeans.
Sometime during the past two weeks, Lindsay had discovered everything Justin had sensed was changing about her. There was a new
dimension to her face and in her manner. She looked fantastic.

"Justin." She threw her arms around him and he kissed her.

"I had to come, Lindsay. I had to tell you goodbye." He was
breathless from the chase. "And I wanted to give you this." He
handed her a medium-sized box wrapped in silver-foil paper and tied
with a blue ribbon. "It's nothing fancy. Don't get too excited." He
heaved a sigh of relief. He had made it to Gunnison with Lindsay's
going-away present. A kiss plus the little item in that box Lindsay
was holding. She had to have it.

Lindsay was starting to untie the bow when Marcus called to her
again. "I'm sorry, Lin. I can't shut this motor down to give you more
time."

"I know, Marc." She turned back to Justin.

"Goodbye again." He grinned. "You can open that on the plane.
I know you'll like it. And think of me the next time you go juggling
napkins at Mario's."

Tears welled up in Lindsay's eyes. "I don't think I'll ever juggle
napkins without you, Justin."

"Don't kid yourself." He pulled her toward him for one last genuine Colorado cowboy bear hug. "I know you. You'll juggle napkins
again."

And then he turned back toward the terminal and was gone.

Lindsay ran to the plane and Marc helped strap the seat belt around
her properly. Then he climbed in beside her.

"Are you ready for this?" His eyes asked a thousand questions of
her as he secured the door.

"Yes," she nodded.

And then, with a revving of the engine and a handshake from the
pilot to the three-year-old co-pilot in the back seat, the craft bounced
down the runway, gathered speed and spit itself into the sky.

They were soaring. Déjà vu, Lindsay thought. And yet not déjà
vu. This part of her life had never happened before. This takeoff was
a brand new beginning.

She sat there silently with her tiny hand in Marc's large one. And
as she watched the mountains growing smaller beneath her, she remembered Justin's gift in her lap. Slowly, Lindsay untied the bow

and untaped the folded paper. Underneath all the fancy wrappings was a dilapidated cardboard box. Lindsay lifted the lid of the box and looked in.

"Oh no," she shrieked, and she didn't know whether to laugh or cry. So she did a lot of the first and a bit of the second at the same time.

She pulled it out of the box and held it up so Marc could see it.

"What is *that*?" Marc scowled.

It was the mangled, rusty can all shot up with holes. It had been sitting on the mantel at the lodge in Tincup for months now. Justin's trophy. Lindsay had thrown it away once because she thought it was dirty and disgusting. And now he had sent it to her as a going-away present. And the wonderful thing about it was that Lindsay knew exactly what Justin was trying to tell her.

"Looks like a rusty old tin can to me," Marc laughed. "The guy's got class, Lin. Lots of class."

"You're not looking at it right, Marc." She held the can up to the sunlight and grinned through her tears. "Look at this thing again and tell me what you see."

"An ugly, mangled can."

"You know what you're supposed to see when you see this?" Lindsay questioned. "You're supposed to see the holes."

"What's so great about the holes?" Marc laughed.

"Someone had to practice for weeks, maybe months, to be able to shoot up this can like this. It's a trophy. It's a dream come true. It proves something if you look at it right."

Marcus glanced across the cockpit at Lindsay. Every time he looked at her, the love inside of him welled up and spilled out of his soul like it would from a sparkling fountain. As he looked at her now, he didn't know whether his heart could contain everything that he was feeling inside for his beautiful, new love. And his entire being filled with joy at the simple, wise things she said. He felt honored that she had shared the secret of the trophy with him. Because now, as they flew along fifteen thousand feet above the ground, their life together had become a trophy of sorts, too. What they had was a dream that had never been possible before. He had always had so much confidence in the woman who now sat beside him. And he knew that, together, they had proved everything they needed to about growing strong—and about loving.

HARLEQUIN SUPERROMANCE®

...there's more to the story!

Superromance. A *big* satisfying read about unforgettable characters. Each month we offer *four* very different stories that range from family drama to adventure and mystery, from highly emotional stories to romantic comedies—and much more! Stories about people you'll believe in and care about. Stories too compelling to put down....

Our authors are among today's *best* romance writers. You'll find familiar names and talented newcomers. Many of them are award winners—and you'll see why!

If you want the biggest and best in romance fiction, you'll get it from Superromance!

Available wherever Harlequin books are sold.

HARLEQUIN  PRESENTS®

HARLEQUIN PRESENTS
men you won't be able to resist
falling in love with...

HARLEQUIN PRESENTS
women who have feelings
just like your own...

HARLEQUIN PRESENTS
powerful passion in
exotic international settings...

HARLEQUIN PRESENTS
intense, dramatic stories that will keep you
turning to the very last page...

HARLEQUIN PRESENTS
The world's bestselling romance series!

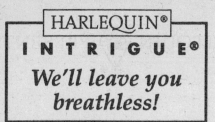

LOOK FOR OUR FOUR FABULOUS MEN!

Each month some of today's bestselling authors bring
four new fabulous men to Harlequin American Romance.
Whether they're rebel ranchers, millionaire power brokers
or sexy single dads, they're all gallant princes—and
they're all ready to sweep you into lighthearted fantasies
and contemporary fairy tales where anything is possible
and where all your dreams come true!

You don't even have to make a wish…
Harlequin American Romance will grant your every desire!

Look for Harlequin American Romance
wherever Harlequin books are sold!

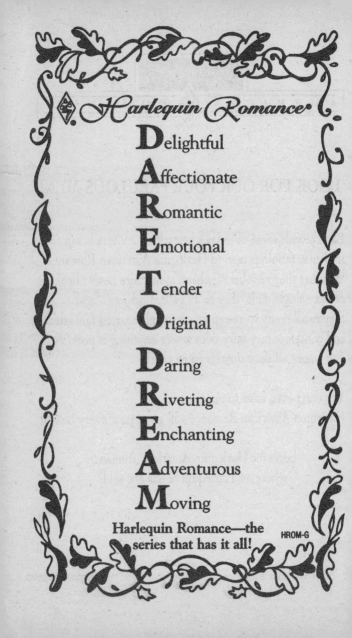

Harlequin Romance

Delightful

Affectionate

Romantic

Emotional

Tender

Original

Daring

Riveting

Enchanting

Adventurous

Moving

Harlequin Romance—the
series that has it all!

HROM-G